Omnibus 1

THE BABYLON 5 NOVELS

BABYLON 5™

Omnibus 1

Book 1: Voices
by John Vornholt

Book 2: Accusations
by Lois Tilton

Book 3: Blood Oath
by John Vornholt

Based on the series by
J. Michael Straczynski

BOXTREE

Voices, *Accusations* and *Blood Oath* first published by Del Rey®,
a division of The Ballantine Publishing Group, New York

Voices, *Accusations* and *Blood Oath* first published in the UK 1995
by Boxtree

This omnibus edition published 1999 by Boxtree
an imprint of Macmillan Publishers Ltd
25 Eccleston Place London SW1W 9NF
Basingstoke and Oxford

www.macmillan.co.uk

Associated companies throughout the world

ISBN 0 7522 1778 X

9 8 7 6 5 4 3 2 1

A CIP catalogue record for this book is available from
the British Library.

Printed by Mackays of Chatham, PLC

Book 1
Voices
by John Vornholt

Historian's note: The events of this novel take place shortly after the events depicted in the second-year episode, 'Points of Departure', and prior to the events in 'A Race Through Dark Places'.

CHAPTER 1

"WELCOME to Mars," said the sultry, automated voice. "The time is 24:13 Martian Central, and the temperature is currently 201 degress Celsius. Tomorrow's high temperature is expected to be 274, with light winds and dust. Please watch your step as you disembark, as Martian gravity is thirty-eight percent that of Earth. Have a pleasant stay."

Yes, thought Harriman Gray, his step did indeed feel springier as he negotiated the moving walkway. A shy, reserved person, Gray did not usually have a bounce in his step, nor did he whistle while he worked. His job as a telepath for Earthforce required a demeanor slightly less serious than that of an undertaker.

But he couldn't help feeling rather chipper tonight, as he was about to embark on a new assignment—liaison to Mr. Bester. Bester was the top Psi Cop, the one who got the tough cases chasing down rogue telepaths. But he was much more than a Psi Cop, as Gray well knew. Bester was one of the most powerful figures in Psi Corps, the closely guarded organization charged with training and regulating both military and civilian telepaths. Although Bester's name did not appear on any list of prominent citizens, a more powerful man in the Earth Alliance would be hard to find.

Gray was distracted by some children bounding several strides ahead of their parents in the light gravity. He was glad that he didn't have any of *those* to worry about, although, lately, he had been feeling unaccountably paternal. It was Susan, he thought, Susan Ivanova from Babylon 5. She had brought out these strange feelings in him, and what had he brought out in her? Loathing and disgust. He was afraid to give himself encouragement when it came to Susan, but toward the end of his eventful visit to Babylon 5, there had been a twinge of sympathy, a smidgen of understanding in her response to him. Or so he imagined.

After all, nobody *chose* to be telepathic. Better than anyone, Susan Ivanova should know that. She could have unlimited sympathy for her mother, a rogue telepath, so why
couldn't she have some for him? Was he any different, just
because he had chosen to accept his gift and allow the Corps
to train him and place restrictions on his behavior? Was he
any different than a soldier, trained to kill one moment and
keep the peace the next? They lived in a society that had
rules, and the rules were for the good of everyone.

Okay, Mr. Gray had to admit, the rules worked better for
some people than for others. But nobody wanted anarchy,
such as the revolt on Mars a few weeks earlier. The fighting
was over, he reminded himself, and most of the real damage
had occurred on another part of Mars, not this region. Stopping the dissension on Mars would be easier than winning
Susan's heart. If only he could return to B5 and have another
chance to talk to her, to convince her that he wasn't a monster.

A moment later, another female intruded into his mind. It
was the security guard at the end of the walkway, and Gray
separated her voice from the innumerable voices which bab-
bled inside his head whenever he was in a crowded place.
They weren't real voices—they were thoughts—but his mind
translated the thoughts into an interior monologue. If he concentrated, he could pick out the voice he wanted, amplify it,
and even look behind it at the emotions and motives which
informed it.

He produced his identicard a moment before she asked for
it. Then he felt a jab of fear from her in response to the card
and his Psi Corps insignia, although her smiling face said,
"Have a pleasant stay on Mars, Mr. Gray."

Many telepaths loved that instantaneous fear they inspired
in total strangers. They got off on it and were disappointed if
a person's psyche didn't cower before them. Gray only found
it depressing.

With his guard down, he was struck by a mind-scan so
severe that it staggered him. If it hadn't been for the Martian

gravity, which bounced him harmlessly off a wall, he would've fallen to the floor.

"Are you all right?" asked the guard as she grabbed Gray's elbow and steadied him.

"Yes, yes," he rasped, trying to clear his head. Who the hell had done *that* to him?

A small, middle-aged man in a black uniform stepped from behind a pillar. He smiled, trying to look friendly, but he only succeeded in looking heartless.

"Your friend will look after you," said the guard cheerfully, literally pushing Gray into the man's gloved hands.

"So pleased to meet you," said Mr. Bester without speaking a word.

Gray blinked in amazement and answered telepathically, "I didn't expect you to meet me personally, Mr. Bester."

"You'll find," said the Psi Cop in spoken words, "that I believe in the axiom 'If you want something done right, do it yourself.' "

Gray almost protested over the way he had been scanned without permission, or warning for that matter. But he knew it wouldn't do any good. Bester was above the law, if anyone was, although he preferred to work from behind pillars and politicians, not in front of them. In a privileged class, Bester was the most privileged.

Harriman Gray was a slight man, and he took some comfort in the fact that Mr. Bester was no taller than he. In fact, without the considerable amount of hair that Bester possessed, he might have been even shorter.

The Psi Cop frowned. "Yes, but I'm a P12, and you're only a P10."

"I didn't mean anything by that," said Gray apologetically.

Bester smiled and started down the corridor. "Of course not. Do you know, there have been studies showing that shorter men are actually more predisposed toward telepathy. Do you suppose that could be evolution making up for a height disadvantage?"

"I read the Berenger Study, too," answered Gray, "but I

didn't think that he proved his hypothesis. For example, the same study showed that taller women were predisposed toward telepathy. It looks to me like a statistical aberration."

"That's why I wanted to pick you up myself," said Bester with satisfaction. "To have some time to talk with you. You know, this assignment won't last very long, just until we iron out the details of the conference and get the weekend started. However, I am looking for a new assistant."

Gray was caught off-guard by Bester dangling a ripe promotion in front of his nose, but he blocked his reactions as best he could. He could feel the Psi Cop probing his mind for a reaction, but he thought he had a very effective way to shut the probing down.

"Yes, I heard about poor Ms. Kelsey," said Gray, shaking his head. "Terrible tragedy."

Bester shrugged and stopped his scan. "She knew the risks. We got our man, that was the important part. Of course, when *you* went to Babylon 5, you also came back minus one."

Touché, thought Gray. "Yes, that was also a tragedy," he said with all sincerity.

"Nonsense," snapped Bester. "Ben Zayn was a weakling, a war burnout. Just like Sinclair."

The man in the black uniform swept down another corridor, and Gray hurried after him. Except for the ease of moving in the light gravity, there was no indication that they were on Mars. The docking area looked like any other space facility designed for oxygen-breathers; there were the usual crowded corridors, gift shops, florists, newsstands, restaurants, and credit machines. One had to go to an observatory dome to see anything of the red planet.

Bester went on with his diatribe about Babylon 5. "Neither Sinclair nor Ben Zayn was right for that post on B5. Now we've got another war hero there—John Sheridan. That's the trouble with the Senate and the President, always appointing war heroes to positions of command, just because they're popular."

"You don't think much of Captain Sheridan?" asked Gray with surprise. "Everyone at Earthforce think it's finally the right move."

"At least Sheridan is by the book," conceded the Psi Cop. "An honest plodder. But he may find that Babylon 5 is not covered in the book. I'll reserve judgment until I see how he handles the pressure."

"You would rather have someone from the Corps running B5?"

"No," answered Bester. "We work better behind the scenes. But it would be nice to have a *friend* in that post."

Gray cleared his throat and thought that he had better turn the conversation back to the promotion. "If you get a new assistant, doesn't he or she have to be a Psi Cop?"

"That has always been the conventional thinking—Psi Cops sticking with other Psi Cops. But it's not official policy. In some respects, it would be better to separate my assistant from my backup person. I can always find new cops to go after the rogues, but an able assistant is a bit harder to replace."

After negotiating another corner, Bester continued, "My assistant has to be a member of the Corps and be willing to undergo a deep scan. That goes without saying. Otherwise, it could be anybody."

The older telepath turned abruptly, stepped in front of Gray, and looked him squarely in the eyes. "I've done a lot of research on you, Mr. Gray. I especially like the way you manage to come out on the winning side of every skirmish. That quality, plus your military background, is very appealing to me."

Gray waited for the blast of a deep scan, but it never happened. Bester just looked at him, a satisfied smile on his surprisingly youthful face. It was as if he was saying he could jump his mind anytime he wanted to, but he wasn't going to, for now. So the liaison official took the offer at face value—he was on a trial period to be Mr. Bester's full-time assistant.

However, Gray couldn't forget the fact that he had a job to do, and that was to promote the military's needs in the up-coming conference of high-level telepaths. Press releases claimed the focus was on commercial applications for telepaths—and there would be representatives from the com-mercial firms—but everyone knew who really controlled the Corps these days. Military and corporate telepaths were fighting for crumbs of power compared to what Bester al-ready had. They controlled their own domains, but Bester and the Psi Cops controlled them.

"The monorail is this way," said Bester. "We have a pri-vate car."

"My luggage," said the young telepath.

Bester smiled. "It's being delivered to your suite. I think you will find that the Royal Tharsis Lodge is being quite accommodating."

Once inside the security of the sealed monorail car, Harri-man Gray finally relaxed and took in the sights, such as they were on a dark Martian night. The angry red planet didn't look so angry when it was crisscrossed with monorail tubes, prefabricated dwellings, and shielded domes. It looked like a giant gerbil habitat on a dusty parking lot.

A canyon yawned beneath the monorail tube, lit up by a science station perched on the rim. The canyon was, Gray estimated, about six kilometers deep, or about three times the depth of the Grand Canyon. The canyon faded into the dis-tance before Gray could get a very good look. With a mini-mum of gravity and friction, the monorail was breezing above the surface of Mars at a speed of four hundred kilome-ters per hour.

Gray shifted his gaze toward the distance and their destina-tion, the famed Tharsis Rise—a jutting plateau of volcanic ridges that was five kilometers high. It was lit up like the Pyramids, but the lights failed to convey even one-tenth of its size. By daylight, it was a monstrous thing that seemed to go on forever, but Gray knew it was only about three thousand kilometers across.

Tharsis Rise was a bona fide tourist attraction, no one could deny that. And the Royal Tharsis was a posh resort, so posh that both the manager and the chef were Centauri. Fine, thought Gray, but once you got past a few Centauri luxuries, there wasn't anything out here to see but a big flat rock. He would have preferred an Earth setting for the conference—with greenery and water—not hot, dusty rocks.

Bester was quiet and thoughtful as he gazed out the convex window. "You don't see anything of interest out there, do you," he remarked.

"I'm afraid I don't," answered Gray. "I've always found the mystique of Mars to be sadly lacking. Behind all these sleek tubes, there's a lot of poverty, dissension, and . . . nothing. People came here looking for something, and only a few found anything of value. Now they want to blame the planet they came from for all their problems."

"Yes," said Bester, staring at the vast, rose-hued horizon. "But if you find something of value here on Mars, it may be priceless."

Even though the two men were totally alone in the private car, Gray leaned forward conspiratorially and whispered, "There are rumors about what's going on at our facility in Syria Planum. If I may ask, Mr. Bester, what's going on out there?"

The little man bristled. "That information is on a need-to-know basis, and you don't need to know."

"Sorry, sir," said Gray, straightening in his seat.

Actually, the military had a good idea what was going on at the Psi Corps training center, and Gray had been secretly briefed about it. But this was not the time or place to pursue the matter.

Bester relaxed a bit, but he still looked preoccupied. "Don't you see," he explained, "we can't tell anyone about Syria Planum, because *we're* the only ones who can keep a secret."

"Yes," admitted the young telepath, nodding his head

sagely.* It was their burden, in a way, that all the mundanes, the nontelepaths, were doomed to become a second class under the telepaths. He didn't really like it, but he understood it as a sort of natural evolution of society. Who could stand in their way?

"It's late," said Bester, "but I can arrange a tour of the hotel for you right away, if you like."

"I've been here before," answered Gray, "although I was only here for the day. It's a beautiful facility."

"Secure, too," said the man in the black uniform. "The monorail is the only way in or out. Except for overland, which would be insane. During the weekend of the conference, we can make sure that only the Corps and our handful of invited guests even get off the rail."

Gray shook his head apologetically. "I've been traveling around so much, I haven't kept up. Are we still worried about the separatists?"

"Bloody idiots," muttered Bester. "They haven't got a chance. We're not going to give up Mars to a bunch of illiterate miners, I can tell you that."

Gray cleared his throat. "Of course, the military would have preferred to go to Earth for the conference. West Point or Sparta, some place like that."

Bester smiled. "Have you ever played Martian basketball?"

Now Gray sat forward eagerly. "No, but I've heard about it."

"It's just like Earth basketball," said Bester, "only with the low gravity, *everybody* gets to dunk it. They have some lovely courts here, and perhaps you and I can take some time for a match in the morning. We don't have to sign the contracts with the hotel until tomorrow afternoon."

"I'd like that," answered Gray, beaming.

---

* For six generations since telepathy had been scientifically proven, Psi Corps had been testing and monitoring telepaths. It had grown from a minor subdepartment into the most feared organization in the Alliance, and most telepaths considered themselves genetically superior.

The young man was feeling more relaxed already. Certainly all those terrible stories about Mr. Bester were simply not true. He could see the hotel very clearly now, an art-deco monstrosity that looked nothing like a lodge, as he thought of a lodge. Only the jutting ridge of Tharsis gave the complex any perspective whatsoever.

An explosion suddenly lit up the jagged rock face, and a flaming section of the hotel spewed outward, along with tables, chairs, and other objects that were sucked into the thin atmosphere.

The flames went out immediately, but debris continued to fly out. The shock wave jarred the monorail and would have knocked them out of their seats, if not for their restraints. Lights flickered in the car, and the monorail screeched to a bumpy halt.

The oxygen wasn't gone yet, but Gray was already panting for breath.

"Stay calm," ordered Bester. "Whatever you do, don't take your restraints off. What's the matter with this thing?"

He pounded on the panel over his head, and a dozen oxygen masks fell out, hanging from the ceiling like the tentacles of some bloated jellyfish. Swift changes in air pressure made papers and cups fly around the room.

"Put a mask on," ordered Bester, although Gray already had four of them in his hands.

They secured their oxygen masks and waited in the flickering lights. Gray felt a tug at his clothing, and the hair on his arms and neck seemed to rise with the drying of the air. They were going to be in oxygenless, 200-degree heat in a few minutes, he thought in a panic! He glanced at the gaping hole in the Royal Tharsis Lodge, and he saw things still flying out of it—things that might be human bodies! Or Centauri bodies. The voices started to bombard his head, and Gray closed his eyes and concentrated on breathing.

Bester ripped his mask off and sniffed the air. "Stay in your seat," he barked. "That is an order. I am going to loosen my restraints and try to get this thing into reverse."

Gray lifted the lip of his mask. "No, Mr. Bester! If the air gets sucked out, you might, too!"

"Do you think I want to sit here and bake to death?" asked Bester, unsnapping his restraints. He sprang to his feet and ripped out an entire bank of panels over his head. "Although," he remarked, "dying of dehydration is supposed to be one of the more pleasant forms of death."

"I wouldn't know!" shrieked Gray. He gulped and drew the oxygen mask back over his face.

Bester was like a man possessed, ripping out panels in the ceiling, on the floor, in the storage bins, and the bathroom. He occasionally had to grab a mask for a hit of oxygen, but he never faltered from his task. Finally, in the panel above the water dispenser, he found what looked like a pair of old-fashioned levers.

"Manual override," he panted. "Undocumented feature. It's amazing what you learn when you read people's minds all day."

Bester took one more breath of oxygen from a nearby mask and reached over the water cooler to grab the levers. His normally coiffed hair was plastered across his forehead in dripping ringlets, and the sweat drooled off his chin. The Psi Cop braced himself to give the levers a forceful jerk.

He needn't have tried so hard, because the levers moved easily in his grasp. There was a comforting clunk, and the car shuddered on its overhead track. One second later, the car flew into reverse so quickly that Bester was dumped on his backside. Gray considered himself fortunate that he was still strapped in.

Bester sat up groggily and staggered like a drunk into a seat, any seat. He strapped himself down, reached for a gas mask, and gratefully sucked oxygen.

Gray suddenly realized that he was a quivering rag of sweat, too. He tried to remain composed, but it was difficult with the dark hotel and its gaping wound in his direct line of vision. That was when the voices, the screams, and the agony grew louder! Gray put his hands over his ears and shrunk down into his seat.

"Don't give in to them!" growled Bester. "Block it. You can't help them now."

The assured words helped to calm Gray and give him some control, which he used to push the voices into the background while he tried to concentrate on his home in Berlin. His home was a grim little apartment, on the second floor, with stark furnishings and one window with a flower box that looked down upon a koi pond. He loved it. Gray had just gotten the apartment a few months ago, and he was very proud of it, even though he had only spent a handful of nights there between assignments.

He wanted to bring somebody to his apartment for dinner. Somebody like Susan. He tried to concentrate on Susan Ivanova until the terrified voices faded from his mind.

Bester coughed and cleared his throat. "Well, the Royal Tharsis Lodge is off the list. Where do you think we can hold this conference on short notice? No, do not suggest Earth or the training center at Syria Planum."

"If not Earth," said Harriman Gray, "I was going to suggest Babylon 5."

Bester took out a handkerchief and wiped his face. "Hmmm. You want to go to B5, eh?"

"Yes," said Gray, straightening up in his seat. "We'd both like to see how Sheridan is getting along there. The station is self-contained and relatively secure. I know Mr. Garibaldi has an attitude problem, but he gets the job done and has a good staff. We have a resident telepath there, Talia Winters, who can act as our coordinator."

"Let me get this straight," said Bester. "You'd like to invade B5, on a few days' notice, with the four hundred highest-ranking telepaths in Psi Corps?"

"Yes, sir."

Bester tapped his finger to his lips and smiled. "Even though we can't play Martian basketball there, that does sound like fun. You approach Ms. Winters, and I'll work through my channels. We want her to ask Captain Sheridan for permission, but we want to make sure he won't say no."

Gray swallowed and started to say, "Commander Ivanova . . ."

"Will be difficult as always." Bester clicked his tongue with disapproval. "A spotless record, except for her strange aversion to Psi Corps. You would think her mother was the only telepath who had ever been put to sleep."

Gray shook his head and decided not to mention Susan again. Bester didn't have to know about his personal life, although he might have already found out about his crush on Susan during that unexpected mind-scan. Well, thought Gray, he was on a new assignment and headed back to B5, and that was all that was important.

The young man chanced another look out the window. Half of the hotel on the great ridge was illuminated again, which was encouraging. The emergency systems and airlocks must have kicked in. Best of all, thought Gray, the voices had died to a whimper.

"Do you think the Mars separatists did that?" he asked softly.

"Who else?"

"I wonder how many people died in that explosion?" Gray mused.

Bester closed his eyes. "I counted twenty-six."

CHAPTER 2

"27 PERISH IN MARS HOTEL BOMBING!" exclaimed the banner headline in the *Universe Today* newspaper.

Talia Winters paused in her stroll down the mall to stare at the newspaper displayed on the newsstand of a small gift shop. The statuesque blonde only had to glance at the first few paragraphs to know that her all-expenses-paid trip to Mars was in serious jeopardy.

The report began:

> "The Royal Tharsis Lodge in Central Mars was the target of a terrorist bombing early this morning, in which 27 people, mostly hotel employees, died. Authorities have yet to make an arrest, but a previously unknown terrorist organization has claimed responsibility.
>
> "The organization, calling themselves Free Phobos, issued a communiqué saying that the purpose of the bombing was to prevent a scheduled conference of Psi Corps officials at the hotel. A Psi Corps spokesperson said the hotel was only one of several facilities under consideration.
>
> "Authorities believe the attack was made overland, because suspicious tracks were found on Tharsis Rise."

Talia Winters looked away, wondering if the problems on Mars would ever end. She had an appointment, so she couldn't dwell on her own little problems. With a sigh, she continued her stroll down the main corridor.

As usual, heads turned to watch Talia, but she paid them no attention. She was a beautiful woman, with sleek blond hair, an intelligent face, and a long-legged body wrapped in a tailored gray suit. Her P5 psi-level was only average, but her classy presence at a meeting or negotiation was as much in demand as her telepathic abilities. Even when both sides were friendly and had no intention of lying to one another, Talia brought an aura of professionalism and importance to the meeting. And she knew it.

However, her confidence was at a low ebb this particular day. Not only was she upset about the conference on Mars having to be postponed, in all likelihood, but she was mystified by the client she was going to see.

Talia was accustomed to not understanding the intricacies of every business deal—that was normal. In those cases, she would merely concentrate on trying to decide if the opposing party was sincere and truthful. Did they want to make a deal for mutual gain, or were they running a scam for their own personal gain? On most occasions, she didn't need to know the difference between a Brussard hydrogen scoop and an ice cream scoop.

This client was different. Not only didn't she understand Ambassador Kosh or his negotiating partners, but she often didn't understand the purpose of their meetings. For a telepath, being in the dark was the most irritating sensation in the universe. She had hoped to ask for opinions about Kosh from her colleagues at the conference, but now that was off. No conference, she thought glumly, and nothing to look forward to but a mind-bending encounter with Ambassador Kosh.

The attractive telepath finally reached the small cafe on Red-3. It was a local place, frequented by residents of the Red Sector looking for refreshments that were simple and quick. Why Kosh liked it so much, she didn't know; his ambassadorial quarters in the Alien Sector were on the other side of the station.

But she had a theory as to why he called the time they often met the Hour of Scampering. Briefly, between shifts, the cafe on Red-3 did turn into a pick-up bar, especially for the people who lived there and were headed home. Even Earthforce personnel felt comfortable on Red-3 during the Hour of Scampering.

Talia sauntered in and stopped. Kosh always stood out like a statue in the park, covered with a tarp to keep the birds off.

He was right there at his usual chest-high counter. Rather his ornate, bulky encounter suit was there—no one on the station had any idea what he looked like under it. Talia envisioned Kosh to be *big,* because a weakling could never carry that enormous suit around. She had no proof that he was big, but that was her theory.

The suit had a collar, carved from a gorgeous marblelike stone, and the collar was bigger than most of the tables in the restaurant. A mountain of rich fabrics cascaded off this neck-wear, including a breastplate festooned with lights. The breastplate looked like an affectation, until one witnessed a precision instrument issue from it to perform some intricate operation. The breastplate also housed Kosh's communicator, which translated his musical squiggles of a voice into standard Interlac.

She took a deep breath and strode up to his table. "Pleasant Hour of Scampering, Ambassador Kosh."

"To you, Ms. Winters." The enormous head-gear nodded. It looked like an artistic rendering of a viper's head, without eyes or orifices. All the orifices were on his collar, and they were constantly revolving, sucking, expelling.

"Has your guest been detained?" asked Talia, looking around for the other half of this meeting.

The notes twinkled, and the lights flashed. "She is here," answered the communications device. The immense head-gear nodded toward the other corner of the counter.

"She is?" asked Talia, shaking her blond hair. Then she winced and put her hand to her head. "Don't tell me, your friend is invisible?"

Kosh nodded.

Talia tried to smile, but her fingernails drummed the countertop. "Isn't that special, an invisible friend. Look, Ambassador, I'm a licensed commercial psychic, not an escort service. If you want to ask me for a date, I may not even charge you. You don't have to pay my top rate just to get me out for a drink. Especially during the Hour of Scampering."

Kosh nodded insistently toward the empty space at the counter. "Her name is Isabel," said the synthesized voice.

"Invisible Isabel," Talia muttered. "Okay, Ambassador Kosh, that's it. I don't need any more commissions from you. You've jerked my chain for the last time."

The encounter suit seemed to rise up a few centimeters and pause in the air, commanding her attention. "Scan her," ordered the voice.

Talia swallowed. It would only take a second, she thought, and then she could leave and collect her paycheck. Scanning an imaginary person wasn't as bad as talking to one, she supposed. Could there really be someone there?

She had heard of cloaking suits, but she had also heard that they weren't very effective at close quarters. Thus far, Talia hadn't heard any other voices in this quiet corner of the room, and she was certain that Invisible Isabel was nonexistent. But she took a deep breath and tried to concentrate on the blank space at the end of the counter. Kosh would know if she faked it, even for a pointless purpose. Many of the other scans she had performed at his request had been pointless, although perhaps not as pointless as this.

Scanning something nonexistent proved to be more difficult than anticipated, and Talia had to concentrate to shut out the other voices in the room. If Isabel were invisible, she reasoned, then her psychic voice would be the only thing there was to pick up of her. Eliminating every voice in the room would prove that she was correct, and that Ambassador Kosh was crazy. At least that was Talia's rationale as she began her scan.

One by one, Talia isolated each voice in the room, determined who possessed the voice, and eliminated it. It took a lot of concentration, and she found herself shifting her eyes from one person to another. That Narn gone, that Antarean, that Centauri, those tourists, the two security officers, the waiter, the bartender—one by one she knocked them all out of her mind—until there was just her, the massive suit that was Kosh, and one other.

There *was* one other voice in the room.

As soon as Talia isolated the voice, it was gone. She

looked back at Kosh, startled. "What happened to her? Where did she go?"

The Vorlon shook his head-gear. "Gone."

That was not what Talia wanted to hear, and she was shaken. Had there been someone, or hadn't there? She had done a fifteen-minute scan that had given her a tremendous headache, but it was inconclusive.

She pointed a manicured finger at Kosh. "I'm thinking about raising my rates on you."

"Your rates are not the problem," remarked the Vorlon.

No, she thought, that was the truth. Playfully she said, "I would like to meet Invisible Isabel again."

"When the time is right," answered Kosh. "You will be very busy."

Talia sighed and put her elbows on the bar. "No, I don't think so. I cleared my schedule for a conference on Mars, but now it's not going to happen. *C'est la vie.*"

"*Tous les jours,*" answered Kosh.

The young woman gave the Vorlon ambassador a friendly smile. "Today was better than most of the scans I do for you, although I couldn't say why. What happened?"

The twinkling notes sounded, and the Vorlon bowed his bulky suit. "Our business is concluded."

Without another word, the mountain of armor and fabric glided out of the room.

A tall, balding man in an Earthforce uniform strolled jauntily down the corridor toward the briefing room. He began to whistle. The worst thing he could imagine happening had happened, and he had lived through it! His best friend, the man who had gone out on a limb to make him the security chief of Babylon 5, was gone. But Michael Garibaldi still had a job.

The security chief couldn't believe it, but it was finally sinking in. Jeff Sinclair was gone, but he was still here. If anyone had told him a month ago that Jeff would be leaving and he would be staying, he would've laughed in his face. Jeff was the war hero, the handpicked savior of the Babylon project, and Garibaldi was a broken-down drunk, bouncing from job to job, coasting into the sewer. It was all thanks to Jeff that he'd gotten the job in the first place, and he was certain that if Jeff ever left, he would be handcuffed to his trunk. Would a new commander, a complete stranger, want to keep him on as chief of security? Not bloody likely.

Yet here he was! Sinclair had wanted him to stay on B5, and, miracle of miracles, so had Captain Sheridan. The captain had reviewed his reports and found his conduct and actions to be acceptable. Not great, mind you, but acceptable. According to Captain Sheridan, there was always room for improvement.

The captain had made it clear that Garibaldi served at his pleasure, to be replaced at a moment's notice. But Garibaldi had been replaced so many times in his career, he figured he was on probation for the rest of his life, anyway. Having it official didn't matter.

Hell, thought Garibaldi, *I'm still here!* Wasn't there a song with that title? He tried to remember the words.

"Mr. Garibaldi," said a no-nonsense female voice.

He turned to see an attractive brunette woman in an Earthforce uniform striding to catch up with him. He stopped and waited.

"Hi, Susan."

"Please," she whispered, "we're on our way to a briefing. Let's try to show some decorum. Call me Commander." She raised an eyebrow. Ivanova's eyebrows were famous for what they could do to people.

Garibaldi smiled and leaned down. "Tell me, Commander, how come when I had a friend running the station, I was relaxed about it. Now that you've got a friend running the station, you're all uptight."

"He's not my friend," she whispered, "just my former CO. And I'm worried about *you,* not me."

"Well, don't be," said Garibaldi with confidence. "What could Captain Sheridan possibly tell us that would spoil this beautiful day? I mean, the worst thing that can happen has already happened, right? Jeff is gone, but I'm still here, and you're still here. The station is still here. No ka-boom.''

"Yet," added Ivanova grimly.

Garibaldi grinned. "And Captain Sheridan has had a salutary effect on the other races. I love the way he's not trying to make friends with them, or coddle them. They hate his guts, but they think you and I are great!''

Ivanova cleared her throat, put her hands behind her back, and strode toward the briefing room. She waited for the door to open, then charged in, followed by a grinning Garibaldi.

The captain was already there, leaning over a computer screen. He looked as handsome and distinguished as always, thought the security chief. Garibaldi was about the same age as Sheridan, around forty, but he didn't think he would ever be able to look as distingished as that, even if he had all his hair. The junior officers saluted, and Sheridan snapped off a salute of his own.

"Commander, Chief, have a seat."

"Are we expecting anyone else?" asked Ivanova, slipping into a chair at the conference table.

Sheridan smiled. "I believe we will have one more before too long, but essentially it's the two of you I want to see. I brought you down here because we have several consoles at our disposal; and I think we may be looking up schedules and personnel files long into the night.''

Garibaldi started to say something sarcastic, like "Great!" Then he remembered that this wasn't Jeff Sinclair. He folded his hands and waited patiently.

"I've just been talking with Senator Hidoshi," the captain began. "And a most interesting opportunity has come our way. You must have heard about the hotel bombing on Mars?''

"That made no sense," muttered Garibaldi. "Who are these Free Phobos people? I never heard of them. Almost everyone they killed in that blast was just a working stiff, most of them *from* Mars!''

Ivanova shot him a glare at his outburst, and Sheridan

stiffened his back and cleared his throat. "Mr. Garibaldi, you have served on Mars, I take it?"

The chief lowered his head and scratched behind his ear. "Yeah, for about a year."

"Then you know," said Sheridan, "the problems of Mars are very complex. Ivanova and I served together on Io, far removed from most of the difficulties, and that was bad enough. The thing is, the infrastructure of Mars is so fragile that we can't really wage war there. We can't wipe out the terrorists, so they have all the advantages. They can destroy targets—and the Royal Tharsis was a very astute target—but if we destroy anything, we'll kill thousands and create a mess that will never be cleaned up."

"In other words," said Garibaldi, "we could win it, but there wouldn't be anything left to take home."

"Precisely," agreed Sheridan. "So let's not get too riled up about Mars, because the Senate will just have to suck it up and find a political solution. In one small way, though, we can help."

"What is that, sir?" Ivanova asked brightly.

The captain wiped a speck of lint off the table. "Did you know that Psi Corps was planning to hold a conference at the Royal Tharsis? And now they can't."

"Yes?" answered Ivanova, suddenly very grim.

Gabibaldi wasn't about to say what he thought of that. It was hard to hate someone who made Psi Corps squirm.

"Anyway," said Sheridan cheerfully, "we have a chance to thumb our noses at the terrorists. We can make sure that Psi Corps has their conference—right here on B5!"

Ivanova squirmed in her seat. "How many telepaths are we talking about, sir?"

"Only about four hundred."

Garibaldi's elbow dropped off the table, and he very nearly hit his jaw on it. "But, sir, in a few days—four hundred guests. I'm not sure the station can accommodate . . ."

"Housekeeping informs me there's no problem," said Sheridan. "We've been remodeling Blue-16, and we simply step it up in the next forty-eight hours and get those rooms ready.''

Ivanova looked truly stricken now. ''Are we talking about Psi Cops, like Bester? Or commercial telepaths, like Ms. Winters?''

Sheridan crossed his arms and stared at his subordinates in amazement. ''Who do you think we're talking about? The four hundred highest-ranking telepaths in Psi Corps, that's who! No, they're not Snow White and the Seven Dwarves, but they're a damned important bunch of people.''

''But why do they want to come here?'' asked Garibaldi suspiciously.

The captain shook his head puzzledly. ''I thought you would welcome this as a golden opportunity, which it is. It's a chance for us to show everyone that B5 is past her growing pains, that we're a suitable place for a high-level conference. You know, everybody thinks we're a jinx! Psi Corps is doing *us* a favor by coming here.''

Garibaldi glanced at Ivanova, but the commander's lips were clamped tight. He knew that she had decided to withhold comment about Psi Corps for the moment.

He gingerly held up his finger. ''Sir, it's just that, in the short time we've been open, Psi Corps has shown unusual interest in us.''

''Nonsense,'' snapped Sheridan. ''Psi Corps shows unusual interest in *everybody*. But what are we going to do about it? Make them mad, so they show even more interest? The next time the Senate considers our appropriations, it would be very nice to have Psi Corps in our corner. Besides, all telepaths are not cut from the same cloth as Bester. Our own Ms. Winters is highly respected, and so are hundreds of other private telepaths. And, Chief, unless you lied in your report, Harriman Gray saved your life.''

''Yes, he did,'' admitted Garibaldi. He appealed to Ivanova. ''Are you going to say anything here, or do you want Bester and four hundred of his friends to show up tomorrow?''

The second-in-command sat up in her chair. "Captain," she began, "if I may speak freely."

Sheridan sighed. "Mr. Garibaldi has no problem speaking freely, so why should you?"

"I have a revulsion to Psi Corps," she declared. "It's personal. I have never let this interfere with my duty, except for the fact that I will not submit to a scan, for any reason. I'm sure this will hamper my career advancement at some point, but I will not let it interfere with my duty."

Ivanova took a deep breath and concluded, "I will get all of their ships in safely and assist in the Psi Corps conference however I can. I will do my best to put the station in a good light. However, if one of those buggers tries to scan me, I will rip his lungs out."

Garibaldi nodded in agreement. "Yeah, and it'll take five guys to pull her off. And another five guys to arrest her, then all those doctors in medlab. Do we really want to risk it, sir?"

Sheridan rubbed his eyes. "I have sympathy for your feelings, but they can't stand in the way of this opportunity. Therefore, Commander, you will be restricted to quarters during the duration of the conference, except for your normal hours of duty. In fact, Commander, you are under orders not to talk to the attendees. If they don't like that, you can talk to them just long enough to tell them to come see me."

"Uh, sir," asked Garibaldi hopefully, "could we arrange it so that *I* don't have to talk to them either?"

"I'm afraid not, Chief. They're going to be paranoid about security, especially after this Mars thing. To put it bluntly, it's going to be a nightmare for you. I could requisition some outside security to help you, but I don't want to risk it. We don't know who they might send."

"No, that's okay," said Garibaldi, his shoulders drooping. "Hundreds of paranoid Psi Cops, just what I always wanted. I don't suppose there's any way you could be talked out of hosting this shindig?"

"Well," said the captain, "if you had offered reasoned arguments against it, I might have listened. If your only objection is that you hate Psi Corps, that's not unusual enough.''

Sheridan tapped the link on the table console. ''Captain Sheridan to Ms. Talia Winters.''

''Captain!'' said her startled voice a moment later. ''I was just about to call you! Did you hear about the conference? Isn't it wonderful!''

The captain surveyed the long faces of Ivanova and Garibaldi. ''Oh, yes, we're jumping up and down here. You are supposed to make an official request, I believe, on behalf of Psi Corps.''

''Oh, I'm so relieved to hear you say you will accept! I had the silly notion there might be some problem.''

''Of course not,'' said Sheridan magnanimously. ''We're down in the briefing room now, and perhaps you'd like to join us and get the ball rolling. Oh, Mr. Garibaldi wonders how many of the attendees will be actual Psi Cops, like Mr. Bester.''

''About a hundred or so.''

Garibaldi buried his head in his hands.

''The theme is commercial applications,'' Talia added. ''I'll be right down to tell you all about it!''

''I look forward to it,'' answered Sheridan. ''Out.''

The captain looked grim as his gaze traveled from Ivanova to Garibaldi. ''An advance team from Psi Corps is already on its way to help coordinate, and the rest will follow in the next day or two. Listen, people, for the next six days, you *love* Psi Corps. And your mission in life is to make sure they have the best conference they ever had. Do you understand?''

Garibaldi and Ivanova just looked at each other and sighed. ''Yes, sir,'' they muttered.

CHAPTER 3

"WELL," said Garibaldi, leaning over a stack of diagrams, "we've got the Blue recreation room. You can have that. Unless our work crews fall asleep, a couple of Blue meeting rooms will be ready. The cafe in Blue Sector is under private contract, but the proprietor says he'll have it open in time for the reception."

"We'll want to run a security check on the proprietor," said Talia Winters. "And we'll need more than a couple of meeting rooms. The idea of this conference is to break off into smaller discussion groups. Intimate gatherings."

Garibaldi cocked an eyebrow. "I'll bet."

Talia pursed her lips, but she let it pass. "What about the meeting rooms on Red and Yellow?"

The security chief scowled. "I'm trying to keep all of your people in the Blue Sector, and pretty much seal it off. For their own safety."

Talia smiled even while she shook her head. "No way, Mr. Garibaldi. These people don't like to be told that certain places are off limits. No place is off limits for them."

"Wait a minute," he protested, "I can't give them complete run of the station! You don't want them Down Below, do you? With that element. Or in the Alien Sector. What if they meet up with the carrion-eaters? I can't protect them on every square centimeter of every cargo bay of B5."

"I think you will find, Mr. Garibaldi, that most telepaths are capable of taking care of themselves. Besides, most of them have never been to Babylon 5. They'll be disappointed if they don't receive the full experience."

"Is that so," grumbled Garibaldi. "You know, Ms. Winters, we've had our share of murders and disappearances here, and a couple of the other Babylon stations were blown to bits. The *full* B5 experience is not what I really want them to have. I want them to have a safe, boring experience. I want them to go back to their slimepits and say, 'Gosh, that B5 was the most boring place I've ever been. There is certainly no reason to go back *there* again.' "

Talia's icy-blue eyes burned into him. "This is only our first day of planning, Mr. Garibaldi, and I will not allow you to start insulting the Corps. If we have a problem we can't resolve, I suggest we get Captain Sheridan to arbitrate it."

"I'm doing exactly what the captain wants," the chief countered. "He wants us to look like grown-ups, no more Wild Frontier stuff. He wants B5 to look like a proper place to hold a high-level tête-à-tête, and I don't blame him. The more money we can bring in by ourselves means the less we have to rely on our allies and the Senate."

Now Garibaldi looked into Talia's eyes, something he did not mind doing whatsoever. "Look, Talia, B5 is not a swank resort, and that was their first choice. Security is going to be stretched like we've never been stretched before, just dealing with the arrivals. We haven't had time to get the word out, so all of our regular traffic will be piling up at the docks. I'm not saying we can't do it, but have a heart!"

"All right," conceded Talia, "we will label certain areas, such as Down Below, cargo bays, and the Alien Sector as 'Travel at Your Own Risk.' In the handouts, we'll advise the attendees not to go there. Satisfied?"

"Not exactly," muttered Garibaldi. As Talia was not going to back away from him, and her closeness was making him nervous, he found a chair and began to go over the diagrams again.

"Okay," he told her, "Green Sector has a business park that hasn't been opened yet. It has a lot of standard offices and meeting rooms, even a few larger rooms for light manufacturing. Hey, that's nice—a few of these offices have dual-atmosphere. Anyway, I guess your folks could take over the whole business park. So you'll sleep in Blue-16 and party, or whatever you do, on Green-12."

Talia sat on the desk and crossed her legs, and the tight gray skirt rode up to midcalf. "Panels mostly. I'm moderating a panel on currency exchange, and I'm going to attend

two seminars on mining law. You know, everybody thinks
when telepaths get together, they study telepathy. Hell, we
already know about that. We have to bone up on the other
stuff, that everybody else knows."

"Okay," said Garibaldi, "so maybe this won't be so bad.
And if it gets too boring, we can always send for some Martian terrorists to liven things up."

The telepath sat forward, looking grim. "You won't let
that happen, will you?"

Garibaldi lowered his lofty forehead at her. "Let us say
that nobody will get into Blue-16 or Green-12 except your
people and my people. But you had better give the attendees
an advisory about the rest of the station."

He frowned. "And I'll give the rest of the station an advisory about them."

"We do want to be able to use one more room," said
Talia. "The casino."

"Whoa, wait a minute. Telepaths aren't allowed to gamble. Why would they want to go there?"

Talia insisted, "Just to have someplace fun and cheerful to
go. Would you like to be cooped up in a bunch of boring
offices and crew quarters? You said it before, this isn't a
luxury hotel, but we should go the extra centimeter to make
it pleasant. The casino would simply give them someplace to
go, to mingle with the populace. As for the gambling, shut
down the games."

"Shut down the games?"

"Out of consideration." Talia tossed her sleek blond hair
and leveled him with her firmest gaze. "Look, Garibaldi,
I've given in on everything. You are getting it as easy as I can
make it. Don't you think you can give me one thing—a place
to party, as you call it. I will go to the captain with this, if
you insist on fighting me."

"No, no, leave the captain alone," said Garibaldi. "He's
up to his eyeballs in VIPs, and they're not VIPs I want to
see."

"Yes, I know," replied Talia, pulling up the flap on her

leather glove to check her timepiece. "I really should be going to meet them."

Garibaldi pushed the link on the back of his hand. "Link, take a memo. For the benefit of our conference guests, the station is assigning extra security to Blue-16, Green-12, the docking area, connecting corridors, and connecting tubes. Oh, and the casino. The attendees will be told that all other areas are to be entered at their own risk. They are not protected in the other areas."

He lowered his hand and smiled at Talia. "I believe in getting things in writing."

"So do I," agreed Talia. "Make sure you mention that gambling in the casino will be prohibited all weekend."

"Yeah, yeah," muttered Garibaldi. He spoke into the back of his hand. "Gambling will cease in the casino in exactly twelve hours, not to be resumed except by my authority. End memo. Priority distribution."

Talia grabbed the diagram of the business park in Green Sector and studied it. "Are these spaces expensive? Maybe I'll lease one, when this is all over."

"Lady," said Garibaldi, "you get me through this, and I'll make sure you get the nicest one—for free."

Talia gave him her professional smile, the one that dazzled the opposition and made them realize they had been beaten. Garibaldi was suitably dazzled.

"Thank you, Michael," she replied. "It's been a pleasure doing business with you." Talia sauntered to the door and tossed over her shoulder, "I'll get you a schedule of the panels."

"Thanks!" he said, as if he really wanted one.

When the door finally shut, Garibaldi rolled his eyes toward the heavens. As miserable as this black cloud was, even it had a strand of silver lining. No matter what else happened in the next six days, he was going to be spending a lot of time with Talia Winters.

"Be still, my heart," he told himself with a chuckle.

* * *

Talia Winters was a bit surprised to find no one waiting at the docking bay except for Captain Sheridan and half a dozen extra security officers. She didn't expect a brass band exactly, but a small show of ambassadors or dignitaries would have been in order.

"Captain," she said. "Are more people coming?"

"Hello, Ms. Winters," he said, not dispensing with the niceties simply because she had. "We've got everyone working double shifts down in Blue Sector just to get it ready. Mr. Bester will have to be content with you and me."

"What about Ambassador Mollari?" she asked. "Or Ambassador G'Kar?"

"What about them?"

Talia started to say that Commander Sinclair would have gotten the ambassadors to come, but she squelched that thought before it left her lips. Odd, she mused, how you didn't notice certain qualities in people until they were gone. On the face of it, Captain Sheridan was a cultured, charming man; but underneath he was intractable, like a sword in a supple leather scabbard. Commander Sinclair had been intractable on the surface, but underneath he was open-minded, ready to sympathize and take risks. Perhaps too ready.

The captain gave her a pleasant smile. "Are you scanning me?"

"No," she said defensively. "But I was comparing you to Commander Sinclair. I'm sorry."

Sheridan nodded. "That's understandable. When I came here, I was surprised to learn how popular my predecessor was. On Earth, they said he was crazy, a loose cannon, but here people thought he was a saint. Now compare that with the way General George Armstrong Custer was perceived during the conquest of North America. His commanders in Washington thought he was brilliant, but in the field, everybody knew he was crazy."

"Perceptions are not what they seem," remarked Talia. "That's why we need telepaths."

"You've never regretted joining Psi Corps?"

"No," she answered, taken aback by the very idea. "Do

you regret the training you had? Does a musical prodigy regret his musical training? We are seeing the emergence of a new talent in thousands of people, and it must be nurtured and regulated. Psi Corps is everything anyone could hope it would be.''

"But Psi Corps has become an issue," the captain declared. "People fear it, people discuss it. People try to stop it. My predecessor at this station became an issue, and that's what ultimately hurt him. That's where I'm different—I want my presence here to be neutral, just enough to make the station run efficiently. So don't expect me to go overboard, on anything.''

"Understood," said Talia. "I sincerely appreciate your cooperation on this conference. However, Captain, I don't think that Psi Corps can take a backseat any longer. We have a certain destiny to fill, and we need to be up-front about it.''

Sheridan nodded thoughtfully. "I would suggest you remember one thing, Ms. Winters—when you're up-front, they'll shoot at you first.''

Talia nodded curtly and stared down the walkway at the closed air-lock. On the eve of this important conference, she didn't need to hear ominous warnings from her station commander. On the other hand, it was evident that they wouldn't be here if terrorists hadn't bombed that Martian hotel. Was Sheridan trying to tell her the same thing Garibaldi had been trying to tell her? Keep it safe. Keep it low-key.

Talia had been thinking just the opposite. She wanted to show the world that Psi Corps was more than a few failed cases of telepaths gone rogue, or sleepers getting depressed. Psi Corps meant commerce, diplomacy, military preparedness, and, yes, a more efficient government. Telepaths had their place everywhere, in every endeavor. That was the message she wanted the conference to spread.

But maybe Sheridan was right. Talia often ignored the backlash against Psi Corps as being mere jealousy from the mundanes. Perhaps it was more ingrained than that—perhaps people really did want to stop them. Although she didn't agree with Captain Sheridan, she would heed his warning.

The affair would be low-key, manageable, without controversy. Maybe it would even be slightly boring.

Sheridan's link chimed, and he lifted his hand to answer it. "Yes?"

"Captain," said Ivanova, "transport *Freya* has just docked. Your party should be disembarking any moment."

"Thank you, Commander. Any word from the ambassadors about our invitation?"

"No, sir."

"Sheridan out." He lowered his hand, looked at Talia, and shrugged. "I did invite the ambassadors to attend the reception tomorrow night. But I never know what they'll do. If you would like to talk to them . . ."

Talia shook her head and smiled. "No, Captain, let's keep it low-key, shall we?"

He nodded. "I agree."

The air-lock opened, and a man in a black uniform strode off the dock and down the walkway. He was followed by a slight man, who looked expectantly around the docking area, as if he was looking for someone. A handful of other passengers followed, and a few of them were also wearing Psi Corps insignia. None but Mr. Bester wore the black uniform of the Psi Police.

"Captain Sheridan," said Bester as he produced his identicard. "Congratulations on your new command."

"Thank you, Mr. Bester."

The security guard nervously finished with Mr. Bester and sent him on his way. "Ms. Winters," said the Psi Cop with a nod.

She smiled. "Mr. Bester."

Talia was waiting for Bester to scan somebody, anybody, because he hardly needed any preparation. He did it with as much effort as it took to brush the lint off one's sleeve. Plus, he had the authority to cut corners, which usually meant that he took what information he needed, from wherever it was in people's minds. But the famed Psi Cop was on his best behavior; he waited patiently for the other members of his party to be checked through.

"Mr. Gray, how are you?" Captain Sheridan called to the young man in a chummy tone.

The military liaison stopped looking around long enough to smile. "I'm fine, Captain, thank you. Let me also congratulate you on your new post. Everyone at headquarters is pulling for you."

Bester looked at the telepath with amusement on his ageless face. "Come now, Gray, not everyone. You were thinking about a certain general, for instance."

Gray bristled. "I don't believe I was. Excuse me, Captain, but where is Commander Ivanova?"

"Busy," snapped Sheridan. "You won't be seeing much of her, I'm afraid."

Talia looked away from the flustered Mr. Gray to see who else from Psi Corps had arrived on the *Freya*. There was a small, dark-skinned woman, who fumbled with her identi-card. Instead of her making the guard nervous, the guard was apparently making her nervous. Behind her, waiting patiently, stood a tall man with a professorial air to him, no doubt helped by his graying goatee. He looked older than the last photograph she had seen of him, but there was no mistaking the profound intelligence in his sad, dark eyes.

"Mr. Malten?" she asked.

He smiled apologetically but boyishly. "Pardon me, but I'm terrible with names. Isn't that an awful thing for a telepath to admit?"

"Not at all," she said, extending a gloved hand, "because we've never met. I'm Talia Winters, resident telepath on B5."

The guard motioned Malten through as quickly as he could, so that he could complete their handshake. The distinguished telepath was beaming. "I was hoping I would run into you right away, Ms. Winters! May I present my associate, Emily Crane. She'll be assisting you this week."

The small, dark-skinned woman held out her gloved hand, and Talia took it. "Very p-pleased to meet you," stammered Emily.

Talia smiled. "Likewise." If it hadn't been for the Psi

Corps insignia on Emily Crane's collar, Talia would never have guessed she was a telepath. She barely seemed the type who could tie her own shoelaces.

"Yes," said Malten, "I'm turning Emily over to you. You'll find her quite a whiz with newsletters, press releases, and such. I always find that a conference goes better when there are plenty of newsletters to keep everyone abreast of changes. Don't you?"

"Oh, yes," agreed Talia.

Malten smiled proudly at the tiny woman. "Emily's real job is chief copywriter for our firm."

Our firm, Talia repeated to herself. It was amazing how blithely Malten could refer to Earth's biggest and most prestigious conglomerate of commercial telepaths. The Mix, as it was known across the galaxy, had offices in virtually every corner of the Alliance, and on some nonaligned worlds.

Talia turned to Emily. "I've been reading about telepathic copywriting. How does that work?"

"Well," said Emily, "say the client has an advertising campaign in mind, but they c-can't express it in words. Or it's only half-formed in their minds. We d-do a scan. We learn what they really want, even when they don't know what they really want." She grinned, happy to have gotten that speech out.

"Yes," said Malten, "we started out thinking we could do the finished ads in-house, but it turned out to be more cost-effective to contract our services directly to the ad agencies. By the end of the year, we'll have seven branch offices doing nothing but this."

"You'll have to c-come to my panel," Emily added. "We'll d-do a demonstration."

Malten gave both women a gentle push down the corridor. "Looks like they're leaving us behind."

Talia turned around to see Captain Sheridan, Mr. Bester, and Mr. Gray walking briskly down the corridor about fifty meters ahead of them. All of a sudden, none of those three men seemed very important to Talia, not when the man beside her was pioneering the invasion of telepathy into everyday life and business.

"They're just going to look at security grids and the like," said Talia. "But I know a great place where we can get a Jovian Sunspot."

Arthur Malten laughed. "I presume we can pick up our luggage from customs later tonight. Lead on!"

Needing the computer consoles, Garibaldi turned the briefing room into his temporary headquarters. For the umpteenth time, he rubbed his eyes and squinted at his screen. "Come on, Baker, are you going to tell me that you need four guys around the clock on one lousy access port?"

"That's the primary access port for Green-12," answered Baker. "If we're going to seal it off, but let the VIPs through, we've got to have lots of eyes."

"I'll give you two guys," growled Garibaldi, "and that's only because one of them might have to go to the bathroom."

Seeing the young woman's crestfallen face, the chief added, "After we get most of these jokers through their arrival and customs, we can free up some people. I'll give you backup as soon as possible."

Baker smiled. "Thanks, Chief."

"One more thing," said Garibaldi, "that *is* a crucial spot, and your people can't leave it for anything. I don't care if they have pee running down their legs, or bug-eyed monsters are eating everyone in sight, they cannot leave that post."

Baker swallowed nervously. "Is it true they can make us see things that aren't there? Put suggestions in our heads?"

Garibaldi nodded glumly. "I imagine they can. We won't have much control over the people at this party—all we can do is keep other people from crashing it. I mean, if somebody from Psi Corps flips out and decides to blow up his buddies, we're in a world of trouble."

That thought was sobering enough to put an end to all conversation in the briefing room. After a moment, Garibaldi waved wearily to the half-dozen subordinates who were still with him. "Go to bed. That's an order."

"Good night, Chief. 'Night," they muttered as they quickly filed out.

The security chief might have sat frozen in the position he was in all night long, just worrying, too tired to move. But the lack of oxygen and sleep made him yawn. That yawn was enough to make him stand up, stretch his arms, and reach for his jacket.

Just when he was about to escape to his own quarters, his link buzzed. "Security," he muttered into the back of his hand.

"Mr. Garibaldi," said a voice. "It's me, Talia."

Oh, Lord, thought the chief, the ice queen. "What can I do you for, Ms. Winters?"

"I'm down in Red-3, with a couple of friends. I was wondering if you could take us on a little tour of the Alien Sector. Maybe Down Below."

"What?" snarled Garibaldi. "Didn't we just agree today that your friends were not supposed to go down there?"

"Aw, come on," said Talia. "The conference hasn't even started yet, and these are real VIPs."

No kidding. VIPs. Garibaldi knew he was going to get tired of hearing that real fast. On the other hand, it was Talia Winters. Late at night, in a party mood. Maybe he would get lucky.

"Red-3, you say?" He yawned and checked the PPG weapon hanging on his belt. "Order me a cup of coffee—I'll be right there."

And so it begins, thought Garibaldi, as he buttoned his collar and slouched out the door.

CHAPTER 4

"THAT'S it for me," said Ivanova with a sigh. "The station is yours, Major Atambe."

Her replacement nodded and assumed the command post in front of the main viewing port of C-and-C. The docking bays were quiet—only two ships were preparing to depart for the jump gate, and the station was secure. Ivanova paused at the doorway and looked back.

"When is the next transport from Earth due in?"

Major Atambe punched up the shipping register. "Oh seven hundred," he replied.

She nodded. "I'll be back then. Wouldn't want to lose any of our VIPs, would we?"

Ivanova strode through the doorway and toward the lift that would take her to her humble quarters. She was thinking about her bed, her most prized possession in the universe. It wasn't a remarkable bed—just a standard-issue single bed, extra firm—but it represented her sanctuary, her escape. No matter what madness was swirling all around her, she could always collapse into that bed and find peace in immediate slumber.

Ivanova began thinking about a remarkable vacation she had planned, if only she could get away with it. In this dream vacation, she would lie in bed as much as she wanted. The link, the alarm clock, the computer, anything that might wake her up would be banished deep into her sock drawer. Perhaps a waiter would come, at her bidding, to bring her bonbons and other snacks, but otherwise she would do nothing but sleep. If she woke up, she would look around to content herself that she was still safely in bed, then she would roll over and go back to sleep.

She chuckled to herself. What had her grandfather always said? "You can get a Jewish woman to do anything in bed but wake up." Her grandmother, she recalled, had never learned to make matzo ball soup in sixty-three years of married life.

Well, thought Ivanova, she had never learned how to make matzo ball soup either. Unfortunately, there was no one around to make it for her.

"Susan," said a voice.

She stopped dead in the deserted corridor, as a feeling of dread crept up her backbone. A figure stepped out of the shadows but made no movement to come closer.

"Hello, Susan," said Mr. Gray, a smile tugging at his thin lips.

"Gray," she snapped. She strode past him.

He ran after her. "Susan, please, I just want to talk to you!"

"I'm not allowed to talk to you. Captain's orders." She pushed the button and waited for the lift.

Gray waved his hands desperately. "Susan, I don't want anything from you, really."

"Then go away." Where was that stupid lift?

The door opened, and she stepped in. To her disgust, Gray followed. Now they were alone in the narrow confines of an elevator car.

"Deck eight," said Ivanova, then she lifted the link to her mouth. "If you persist in harassing me, I will call security."

"Harassing you?" muttered Gray. "All I said was hello!" He stared straight ahead at the door, as if he didn't care to speak to her again either.

"Hello," she said disgruntledly.

"I just wanted to tell you about my new apartment," said Gray. "In Berlin."

Ivanova looked at him. "Berlin. I'm impressed. I didn't pick you as being the avant-garde type."

"You don't know me very well, do you?" asked Gray. "Did you think all telepaths lived in some medieval dungeon somewhere?"

"Yes."

Gray chuckled. "Oh, some of them do. Most of us live out of a suitcase, in army barracks, or metal boxes like this one."

The lift door opened, and Gray waited expectantly. Ivanova stepped out, stopped, and lifted her shoulders in a tremendous sigh.

"Please, Susan," Gray pleaded, "stop thinking of me as the enemy. You know I didn't choose this path—I wanted to be a soldier. I've got a career, and I'm trying to get somewhere in the channels that are open to me, just like you. I'm all alone, just like you."

The young telepath lowered his head. "Maybe it was a mistake trying to see you. I'm sorry I bothered you."

He turned to go, and Ivanova reached out her hand. But she couldn't bring herself to touch him. "Your place in Berlin," she asked, "is it anywhere near the Free University?"

He turned excitedly. "Yes, it is! It's about ten blocks away, and I can take the U-Bahn, or walk. I love walking around Berlin. I know many people find it depressing, because the whole city is like a museum to the destructive power of war. But what can I say, I'm a war buff."

Ivanova shrugged. "Whatever turns you on. I went there on a summer study program to research the dadaists." She headed down the corridor, and Gray scurried along beside her.

"That's a fascinating period," he admitted, "although the dadaists are a bit extreme for my tastes. There are some interesting comparisons between the dadaists and the performance artists of the late twentieth century. Wouldn't you say?"

Ivanova frowned in thought. "I'm not sure. In both cases, their aim was to shock the bourgeoisie and the accepted art establishment. But the dada movement was more of a collective effort, and performance art was very individualistic. I read about one woman who would take a Zima bottle and put it . . ."

Gray suddenly grimaced and put his hands to his head.

"What is it?"

He slumped against the wall and motioned for her to look behind them. Ivanova turned to see a small man in a black

uniform standing at the end of the corridor. He smiled and
strode toward them.

"I knew I would find you here, Mr. Gray," said Bester.
"With the Lieutenant Commander."

"Stop that scan on him!" commanded Ivanova.

But Gray was already regaining his composure. "It's all
right," he said hoarsely.

"It's *not* all right," snapped Ivanova. The fiery officer
glared at Mr. Bester. "None of what you do is all right. You
act like telepathy is some giant leap in evolution, but the way
you use it is just the same old crap. Control! That's what it's
all about.

"Where I come from, we've seen the czars, the Bol-
sheviks, the secret police, and we know all about you. You
just want to tell people what to do with their lives, and to hell
with them if they have other ideas!"

Bester took a deep breath and squinted at her. Ivanova
braced herself for perhaps a scan, but Harriman Gray stepped
between them.

"That's enough, Mr. Bester," said Gray, trembling but
jutting his jaw. "As of now, you can forget about me ever
being your assistant. I don't like the way you operate. Unan-
nounced scans were not part of the job description."

"My boy," said Bester like a favorite uncle, "don't take it
personally. It's just a way we have of shortcut communications. Instead of you briefing me about your whereabouts, I
just take a quick peek. I hadn't realized telepaths in the military were so sensitive to these shortcuts."

The Psi Cop looked at Ivanova and smiled like a cobra.
"Besides, I see you are attending to personal business. As
for that other matter, there's plenty of time to make a decision. I hope you both have a pleasant conference. Good
night."

Bester swiveled on his heel and walked briskly down the
corridor.

"Some shortcut," sneered Ivanova. "All one-way."

Gray whirled around and stared at her. He was clearly

shaken, but he managed to say, "You were quite magnificent."

Ivanova was too drained to take in any more. "I'm sorry, Mr. Gray, but I've got to get some sleep. And I think the three minutes I promised you are up."

"Please," he begged, "a large favor. Would you call me Harriman and let me call you Susan?"

She stared at him with amazement, then softened and nodded. "All right, but only when we're alone. Around other people, let's be formal."

Gray beamed with pleasure. "Does that mean we're friends?"

"Don't count your luck," she said. Ivanova turned to go, but she halted after one step. "I'm glad to hear you won't be that schmuck's assistant. Good night."

"Good night, Susan," he said softly.

"For humans," said Garibaldi, handing out the breathing masks, "the Alien Sector is always something of a disappointment. You can't see a damn thing, and if you could see, you wouldn't want to. We keep trying to improve it, and the one thing we want to avoid is making it look like a zoo. So, if a bunch of closed doors in murky, unbreathable air is your idea of a good time, let's go."

"Surely, it's got to be more interesting than that," said the tall one, Mr. Malten.

Garibaldi shook his head. "Not really. Most of the folks down here have special food, drink, and atmosphere requirements, so they don't go out much. Ms. Winters can tell you. She's got a regular client in here."

"Yes," said Talia rather proudly. "Ambassador Kosh of the Vorlons. We invited him to the reception tomorrow night, and I hope he'll attend."

Garibaldi added, "But all we ever see of him is his encounter suit. It's up to you if you want to stroll through the sector, but you won't see anything unless we bang on people's doors."

"I hadn't thought of that," said Talia. "I only come down here when I have an appointment."

The small telepath, Emily Crane, looked up at the storklike Mr. Malten. "I don't want to d-disturb the residents."

"Neither do I," answered Malten, placing the breathing mask back on the shelf. "But I don't expect to be short-changed out of our tour of Down Below."

"Of course not," said Garibaldi. "What do you want to see? There's smuggling, stolen gear getting stripped down, a bunch of derelicts nodding out. You name it, we've got it."

"All of it." Arthur Malten smiled.

Talia winced and Emily screwed her eyes shut as a hairless behemoth belted some scaled creature and sent him flying over shipping crates and crashing into broken shelves, long since looted. As the grubby crowd of derelicts screamed their approval, the hairless thing went slobbering after its prey and commenced the beating anew. The babble of the bettors was insane, sounding like quadraphonic bedlam inside Talia's mind, and she would have left if the men hadn't been enjoying it so much.

"What do they bet?" asked Malten.

"Just about anything," shouted Garibaldi over the din, "credits, goats, dust, passage out of here! Passage out of here will settle almost any debt."

"I c-can't stand this," muttered Emily into Talia's shoulder. "It's barbaric."

"I agree!" Talia replied. "We must leave this terrible place at once."

Suddenly, there was a disgusting cracking sound, followed by howls of rage and joy, in equal measures. Talia averted her eyes from the sights on the other side of the room and found herself looking at Garibaldi. Even he was preferable. To her, Garibaldi looked more like a criminal than most of the criminals—crude, shifty, wolfish, a man who prowled instead of walked. On occasion he said something funny, but those occasions were not as numerous as he believed. She would have to be out of her mind to get too friendly with him, yet he obviously liked her. It was hard to hate a guy who drooled whenever he saw you.

The bedlam had died down to a roar, and she was able to hear him say, "This is not a terrible place for Down Below. This is a *nice* place. You see a fight, and they serve you some flavored antifreeze and take your money. What more do you want?"

Then he smiled and rubbed his chin. "Oh, I forgot, you folks can't gamble."

"Isn't that a silly regulation?" asked Malten. "I don't see any way we could determine the outcome of this primitive sport, so what would be the harm in betting on it?"

"It would be wrong," said Emily simply.

Malten smiled. "Yes, I suppose so. But we don't know anything about some of these species, do we? They could be far more telepathic than us, yet no one tells *them* they can't gamble. I think it's a ridiculous rule. Everybody knows who we are, and they can let us play at their own risk."

Garibaldi frowned. "Can't you be horsewhipped by Mr. Bester for saying stuff like that?"

The private telepath snorted a laugh. "I've been saying stuff like that for a long time, only nobody listens. I've worked for thirty years to have telepaths accepted as just another professional class, no different than doctors or pilots. Do you think I like to see Bester and his crowd ruining all my work?"

Talia shifted uncomfortably on the crate where she was sitting. She tried to change the subject. "These fistfights—they can't possibly be legal."

"No," admitted Garibaldi. "We could shut this place down, but the fights would just spring up ten minutes later in a manufacturing bay, or a cargo bay. We haven't got the manpower to patrol all of the station. Down Below was used a lot during the construction of the station. Then funds ran out, and it was left unfinished. People get stranded on B5, or kicked off the crew of their ship, or just dumped here, and there's nowhere else for them to go."

He shook his head in amazement. "I don't understand this

place either, but we've had social engineers through the station who say that Down Below is normal. If it hadn't grown organically from poor planning, we would've had to invent it. If you have order, they say, you also have to have chaos."

The chief looked meaningfully at Talia. "Does that make sense to you?"

"I think chaos can be avoided," she replied.

"It makes sense to me," said Malten. "I want to see more."

Garibaldi led them into a grungy corridor and sniffed the air. "If I'm not mistaken, down this way we have people sifting through garbage. I don't know how they reroute it down here, but they do."

Emily crinkled her nose. "P-people steal garbage?"

"Yes," said Garibaldi with a reassuring smile. "But they don't keep all of it, just the good stuff."

"I think we can pass on that," said Mr. Malten. "What's down this corridor?"

"A shanty camp. Do you want to see it?"

"Yes," answered Malten forcefully.

Talia hung back, but she couldn't hang back too far as Garibaldi led them briskly through a scene of both despair and amazement. Aliens of every description—with jutting jaws, fins, segmented limbs, hairy pelts, or compound eyes—commingled with humans. Adults, children, old people, the dying—they all had a haunted look on their faces as they stared at the visitors. The shanties had been cobbled together from old crates, stolen panels, sheet metal, shelves, and whatever else might stand up.

"We give them fresh oxygen," said Garibaldi. "That's about all they get from us, although the Minbari run a soup kitchen. We can go there next."

Talia couldn't decide which was worse, the sense of despair or the smell of the place. To her surprise, the voices she heard in her head were not demanding, begging, or insistent. Some were resigned and helpless, others were angry at their plight and their well-dressed visitors, and a few were clearly insane. It was a mixture, like any bunch of people, and she knew that some of these unfortunates would scrape their way out of here. Others would sink even deeper until there wasn't a trace of them left.

A thuglike woman stepped in front of Mr. Malten and glared at the telepath. "Hey, buddy, got some chewing gum?"

"No," said Malten, taken aback.

She sneered, "You want to buy some?"

"Beat it, Martha," growled Garibaldi. "You know that chewing gum is illegal on the station."

He hurried his party along.

"Top quality!" the woman called after them. "Real sugar!"

"I doubt that," said Talia.

Emily Crane shuffled along beside her, holding a handkerchief over her nose. "I'd like to leave now," she sniffed.

"So would I," agreed Talia. "We're not going to let the attendees run loose down here, that's for sure."

"All the more reason to see as much as we can," said Malten. "One or two more stops, please."

"It's your play," said Garibaldi. He halted in front of a long tunnel that was rather badly lit. "This way is a shortcut to that Minbari soup kitchen."

Talia looked doubtfully at him. "A dark, deserted tunnel?"

"It's not deserted," said Garibaldi. "I see someone moving around down there. And I can't help it if people keep stealing the light fixtures."

Talia peered into the gloom. There did seem to be vague shapes moving through the passageway. She wished she hadn't asked Garibaldi for this VIP tour, but now she had to trust his instincts.

"Come on," said Malten, stepping into the entrance. "There are four of us, Mr. Garibaldi is armed, and we can always protect ourselves telepathically."

"Only against humans," Talia added.

The foursome started moving down the tunnel, and Garibaldi and Malten had to stoop where smaller ducts crossed overhead. The ducts were seeping a foul-smelling liquid, and Talia dashed under each one. She stumbled, and her hands brushed against the sticky walls. For once she was glad to be wearing gloves for a reason other than to avoid skin contact. When Talia found herself shoving Emily Crane in the back to hurry her along, she told herself to calm down. They were still on Babylon 5, her home base, just in an unfamiliar part of it.

However, Garibaldi's talk about chaos had made her nervous. She didn't like the idea of chaos, and she suspected Mr. Malten wouldn't like it either, if he were actually confronted by it. This was precisely why the control offered by Psi Corps was so important. It could make order out of chaos. She hoped.

Talia noticed that the vague figures at the other end of the tunnel were not at the other end anymore. And they weren't vague anymore. They were three large, hooded figures, and they were rapidly walking toward the party of genteel telepaths and one security officer. There would be a confrontation, Talia could feel it. For one thing, they barely had room to squeeze past each other in the confines of the tunnel.

She didn't want to pry into their minds, but she had to know what the three strangers were thinking as they strode briskly toward them. She could see them clearly now, even in the dim light, and she tried to hear their voices.

Talia gasped. Their minds were cold and alien! They were not human!

"I know," said Malten, hearing the alarm that was sounding in Talia's head.

"Just pay them no mind," Garibaldi suggested, although he didn't sound like his usual, cocky self. Talia noticed that his hand was resting on his PPG weapon.

The security chief quickened his step to get out in front of the others. He waved jauntily as the first hooded figure drew abreast of him. "Top of the mornin'!" he called.

The alien never stopped moving as he slammed his shoulder into Garibaldi and crushed him into the bulkhead. A huge knife flashed under the dark robes, and Emily screamed.

The other hooded thugs rushed toward the telepaths, knives gleaming in their gloved hands!

CHAPTER 5

"UNHAND him!" cried Malten. With a grunt, a hooded alien gave the telepath a right cross to the jaw, and Malten dropped to the grimy floor of the tunnel. Emily threw her body over him, screaming.

Talia did as she had been trained in self-defense classes, which was to attack the vulnerable spots, and she lashed out with a kick to the shin of the nearest attacker. She hit hard armor and nearly broke her toe.

But Garibaldi was fighting back. At least he had grabbed the knife-hand of his attacker and was holding him at bay. "Access tube!" he yelled. "About ten meters down! It'll take you *up!*"

The thug pressed his knife to Garibaldi's throat, but the chief shoved him back with a loud groan and staggered to his feet. The two of them traded blows, and Garibaldi caught one in the stomach. She saw him drop to his knees.

The telepath was still on her feet, so she was the first one to be moving toward the hatchway ten meters away. It was right where Garibaldi said it was, near the floor, and she grabbed the wheel and twisted. Maybe it was her adrenaline, but the hatch sprang open at her touch, and the crawl space beckoned.

"Come on!" she yelled.

The attackers were menacing Malten and Emily with their knives, but the telepaths managed to scramble to their feet and stagger down the corridor. Talia shoved them into the tube, and they scurried like groundhogs into the darkness. She took one glance back at Garibaldi.

A hooded alien had him by the throat and was shaking him like a dog shakes a toy. The other two advanced on him with their knives.

"I'll handle them!" croaked Garibaldi. He was reaching for his PPG.

Talia shook her head and fled in desperation. The hatch clanged shut behind her, and one of the aliens rushed to bolt it behind the fleeing telepaths. The alien holding Garibaldi dropped him and roared a hearty female laugh. She pushed back her hood to reveal her spotted cranium, jutting jaw, and the thick ridge of muscles around her neck.

Na'Toth laughed. "These are the ones who have all of you shaking?"

Garibaldi stood up with a groan and rubbed his jaw. "Hey, Na'Toth, that's not the way it was supposed to work! After you scared the hell out of us, Talia was supposed to rush to my arms, trembling, and I blast my way out of here. You weren't supposed to beat the crap out of me!"

Na'Toth couldn't stop laughing, and her two fellow Narns joined her in the merriment. "I'm sorry," she apologized, trying to restrain herself. "You see, I take favors such as this very seriously. Excellent sport, Garibaldi, thank you for contacting me."

"I do owe you one," the chief admitted. He dabbed his sleeve at his bloody lip. "Do you think that will keep those jokers out of here?"

"Yes," answered the Narn. "They have no stomach for stronger foes. Oh, Ambassador G'Kar and I will be attending the reception. Please inform the captain."

"I will," muttered Garibaldi. "Well, I'd better go after them and at least *describe* how I blasted my way out of here."

"She is attractive," Na'Toth conceded, with a hint of womanly envy.

"Oh, Talia?" Garibaldi shrugged. "She's crazy about me."

"I can see that," the Narn answered drolly.

Garibaldi rubbed his lower back. "I think I'll avoid that rabbit hole and go back the way I came. Maybe I can catch another fight."

"That was a good place to pass signals," Na'Toth remarked. "I will see you in several hours."

Garibaldi limped down the tunnel and waved. "Thanks."

By the time the weary security chief reached the main corridor, stooping under the slimy ducts, he didn't feel like going anywhere but to bed.

He tapped his link. "This is Garibaldi to all on-duty personnel. If anyone reports me as being missing or in trouble, please tell them I am *out* of trouble. I am still Down Below, but the situation is under control. Garibaldi over."

The security chief was strolling back toward the makeshift fight arena, still probing his swollen lips, when a furtive figure bumped into him. The bump caught him in a tender rib, and he groaned and grabbed the little man.

"Ratso, what's the matter with you?"

The grubby derelict glanced around and winced. "Let go of me, Chief! I'm in a hurry!"

Garibaldi tightened his grip on the man's raggedy collar. "If you're in a hurry, then somebody's about to be ripped off or mugged. What's the hurry, Ratso?"

The little man sulked. "I'm not gonna tell you."

"Listen, buddy, don't mess with me. I'm in a real lousy mood. Who's in trouble?"

The little man whispered, "It's me who's in trouble. Deuce is back on the station."

"Deuce?" muttered Garibaldi. That was not good, and the timing was even worse, with Psi Corps squirming all over the place. "Are you sure?"

"Does a packrat have puppies? Of course, I'm sure."

"Why now?" asked Garibaldi. "Doesn't he know we have a warrant out for him? Why would he risk it?"

Ratso winked, or maybe he twitched, it was hard to tell. "We've got 'em all here, don't we? Like, this is the center of the universe. If you were one of those crazy Martians . . ."

Garibaldi nearly lifted the man off his feet. "Deuce is helping the terrorists?"

"Sshhh, sshhh!" cautioned the derelict, pressing his fingers to his lips. "I've told you too much already. I gotta protect myself! Deuce might be settling some old debts while he's here."

"How did he get in? A forged identicard, what?"

But the raggedy man slipped out of his grasp and scurried down the corridor, tossing furtive glances over his shoulder.

Garibaldi scowled. With the attendees due to start arriving in only a few hours, the bulk of his staff were getting their last chunk of sleep before the crush. He had no idea who he could order down here to look for Deuce. Garibaldi would normally do a job like that himself, but he couldn't even assign himself to it. Martian terrorists and the crime king of Down Below—that was a bad combo.

He tried to imagine why the terrorists would need Deuce. Deuce was an expert at smuggling stuff into the station and out again, often in a different form. His loansharking had won him an army of desperate couriers who would do almost anything for a meal and a few credits off their debt. Why did the terrorists want Deuce? What could Deuce get into the station that they couldn't?

A bomb.

But not the kind of bomb that had wiped out earlier Babylon stations, thought the chief, not the big ka-boom that Ivanova joked about so fatalistically. Deuce wouldn't want to blow up his playground and ruin everything. The terrorists would probably settle for some kind of bombing that would be more a symbol than an absolute disaster. But with four hundred psi freaks running around, it wouldn't take much to turn the conference into an absolute disaster.

In fact, thought Garibaldi, if the terrorists had Deuce and his underground network, they wouldn't even need to show up! They could press the button from afar, so to speak. Security would have to look at every single person on the station, not just telepaths and new arrivals, but even the everyday scum.

The security chief looked up from his thoughts and noticed several of the denizens of Down Below watching him. They turned away quickly when he saw them, but that didn't make their scrutiny any less troubling. They knew. Like everyone else in the Alliance, this rowdy crowd of malcontents and misfits had no love lost for Psi Corps. Hell, for all he knew, some of them could be rogue telepaths hiding out down here. His current orders were to protect Psi Corps, and that pretty much pitted him against everyone else in the universe.

Well, so much for the idea of getting any sleep tonight. The captain had been right about one thing—this was your basic nightmare.

"Come in," said Captain Sheridan, wiping the crumbs off his lip with his linen napkin.

The door of his quarters opened, and a crumpled Garibaldi slouched inside. "Good morning, sir."

"Good morning, Mr. Garibaldi. Breakfast?"

"No, thank you, sir. I don't believe in eating breakfast unless I've actually slept." He looked at the captain's sumptuous tray. "Well, maybe a piece of toast."

Sheridan stood and buttoned his jacket. "Feel free to finish it, Mr. Garibaldi. The melon is quite good. I had an urgent message from Ms. Winters last night, and she said that you were in some terrible danger Down Below. Yet when I checked, there was no report of an incident, just a cryptic note from you. I didn't see any report in my download this morning either."

Garibaldi chuckled. "Well, sir, when people ask for a guided tour, you want to liven it up for them. You know, like when you go on a Wild West stagecoach ride, and a couple of bandits rob the stagecoach."

Sheridan frowned. "I didn't know we offered that service, Mr. Garibaldi. Nor was I aware that you were the recreation director of this station. If you would like that job, perhaps it can be arranged."

Garibaldi stuffed a strawberry into his mouth and considered the offer for a moment. "Don't tempt me, sir."

The captain shook his head. "I know this conference presents many problems for you, but we have to go by the regulations whenever possible. I'm pretty sure there's a regulation against mugging visiting dignitaries."

Garibaldi wiped his mouth on the captain's napkin. "Captain, did you happen to see the download of the first issue of the conference newsletter?"

Sheridan rolled his eyes. "Yes, I did."

"That Emily Crane wrote a great editorial, didn't she? In strong language, she warned her friends against going anywhere near Down Below or the Alien Sector. Said their telepathic abilities would be useless if they got into any trouble down there. It even scared me."

"Granted," said Sheridan, "your little stunt worked to our advantage, but no more of that. We'll be under close scrutiny for the way we handle this, and I want it by the book. Is that understood?"

Garibaldi stood to attention. "Yes, sir, understood. I just wanted to show Psi Corps that there are parts of this station beyond their control. The fact is, we do have a major problem Down Below."

"What's that?"

"You've seen a fellow named Deuce mentioned in a number of reports."

"Yes, of course," said Sheridan. "I've read the ombud's list of charges against him. Murder, extortion, smuggling, endangering the station—a nasty character. And a fugitive."

"And he's back. That's not what I'm worried about, because Deuce was bound to come back sometime to check his enterprises. But why now? Could it be because of this conference? Believe me, Deuce wouldn't be against taking money from terrorists."

Sheridan asked, "You're sure he's back?"

"I've got a passenger from a tramp freighter who just sort of disappeared after he came aboard yesterday."

"Can't we find him?" asked the captain.

"With what resources? I've got everyone on my staff committed to the conference. And Deuce is The Man down there. Even if we didn't have this conference to worry about, we might not find him." Garibaldi sighed and rubbed his eyes. "At this point, I don't think I could find anything but a bed."

The captain's link sounded, and he lifted his hand. "This is Captain Sheridan."

"Ivanova here," came the familiar voice. "The *Glenn* is docking in bay six. The manifest says they have fifty-three Psi Corps members aboard, and Mr. Bester has requested that you greet them personally. He also wants Garibaldi to be present to answer questions about security."

Garibaldi winced and grabbed the last piece of toast.

"I'll tell Mr. Garibaldi," said the captain. "We're on our way."

"Oh," said Ivanova, "another transport arrives with twenty-seven VIPs at 8:40, another one with thirty-eight at 9:21. A heavy cruiser with nineteen military telepaths arrives at 10:58, and two transports . . ."

"I will stay in the docking area," Sheridan assured her. "Have the work crews vacated Blue-16?"

"Yes, sir. Although they say the paint is still wet."

Sheridan nodded somberly. "We can take them to the casino for a couple of hours, give them lunch." He looked at Garibaldi and smiled encouragingly. "Very wise to have halted gambling there. We'll get through this, people. Remember, you *love* Psi Corps!"

"We love Psi Corps," Garibaldi muttered with disbelief.

Talia Winters sat down to breakfast in the newly opened cafe on Blue-16, and Arthur Malten sat across from her, looking dapper in a checked suit with patches on the elbow. Befitting its location, the decor was mostly blue, with a bit of burnt orange. It wasn't so bad, thought Talia, except for the faint smell of paint.

"I feel so guilty," said Talia, "leaving Emily with all that work. Are you sure we shouldn't be greeting people as they arrive?"

"And deprive Mr. Bester of all his fun?" Malten smiled and poured some coffee for them. "Don't worry, Talia, we'll have plenty of time to hobnob at the reception, and all weekend.

"Besides," he said cheerfully, "this may be my only opportunity to get to know you, before I get dragged off to breakfast meetings and high-level discussions."

"As for me," said Talia, stirring her coffee, "I'll have plenty of panels to attend, but no high-level discussions."

"That's a pity," answered Malten. He stroked his graying goatee. "Babylon 5 is a backwater, you know. I realized that last night, after that ugly incident. You could do much better than this."

Talia sighed. "Mr. Malten . . ."

"Please call me Arthur."

"Arthur, you should know that I'm only a P5. I'm lucky to have this assignment."

"Nonsense," said Malten angrily. "Your success on B5 has shown that psi ratings are worthless when it comes to judging aptitude for a given job."

He lowered his voice. "That's why I'm against giving so much power to a class of telepaths who have nothing going for them—except that they're P12s and P11s. Being P12 doesn't mean you're well adjusted, have common sense, or good communication skills. In most cases, it means you're neurotic as hell."

Talia shifted in her seat, once again nervous with this sort of talk. All of this was easy for Mr. Malten to say. He was a P10 himself and the founder of the biggest conglomerate of private telepaths in the Earth Alliance. Although the Mix was created under the internal security act of 2156, which meant the corps had technical jurisdiction over it, the Mix was relatively independent; he didn't have to kiss up to Psi Corps for choice assignments.

Malten smiled apologetically. "I know what you're thinking. It's true, I've carved out my own niche. But in the commercial world, we're not so wrapped up in who's got the biggest number. We look at long-term results. Talia, you've got proven interspecies skills which we could use in the Mix."

The young woman blinked at him in amazement. She didn't even see it coming! After all, B5 already was her dream job—to get a chance to leap up another rung so soon was beyond her expectations. And what a rung this was—the top! It seemed too good to be true. There had to be a catch.

"I—I don't know what to say," she answered honestly. "I don't know what Psi Corps will say."

The scholarly telepath patted her hand. It was leather on leather, but his touch tingled her skin for a moment. "Let me worry about Psi Corps," he assured her. "We have a great opportunity ahead of us. We're going to take telepathy into every corner of this universe, not as an object of fear and control, but as a valuable service. We'll say, 'Let telepathy be on *your* side, not just the other guy's.' "

"It sounds wonderful," Talia said truthfully. But she felt a pang of regret over the idea of leaving B5 so soon. It had barely been a year, and she was finally building up her practice. Despite her loyalty to Psi Corps, she was used to being her own boss, a lone operator. Sort of like Garibaldi. She couldn't imagine what it would be like to be one of thousands of telepaths in a gigantic firm with hundreds of branch offices.

"In the meantime," said Malten, reaching into his pocket, "I would appreciate your attendance at one of those high-level discussions I was talking about. It's a secret budget meeting."

He set a data crystal on the table. "Ms. Crane put some information together about the budget. I rely on her, but she's essentially a writer and researcher. She's not at her best when there's a debate, and this could become a fiery one. You and I will have to defend the needs of the civilian sector against Mr. Bester and the military. Will you come?"

Now Talia was afraid her jaw was hanging open. If a job offer had been a shock, the invitation to a high-level budget meeting was a two-by-four to the head. "Why me?" she asked. "I can't argue these points like you can. In fact, I'm not even sure I agree with you."

Malten smiled. "Do you want an honest answer?"

She nodded.

"Because you're beautiful, and you'll be a distraction." He pointed to the crystal. "And I expect you to read what's on there and remember the statistics better than I do. Besides, you're practical proof of what I'm talking about. If you can be a success in this depot for aliens, it just proves that commercial applications can succeed anywhere!''

Talia took a deep breath and pushed a streak of blond hair off her cheek. It still felt as if she had been bludgeoned by a two-by-four, but she picked up the data crystal and put it in her handbag.

''I'll be there,'' she promised.

At that same moment, a hand encased in a grimy glove with the fingers cut off at the knuckles placed a similar data crystal on top of a dented filing cabinet. A cat jumped out of one of the drawers, rocking the cabinet and nearly knocking the crystal to the floor.

Careful! whispered a voice in his head. *If we lose that, we lose all.*

''We're not going to lose it,'' purred Deuce in a jaded Southern twang. ''I just wanted to show it to you, because a deal's a deal.''

It looks like any crystal, the voice said.

Deuce lifted the data crystal to eye level and studied it. ''That's the beauty of it, ain't it? One of a kind. Speaking of crystals, you got the diamonds?''

The voice answered, *Yes,* and Deuce was told to look down at the floor. He saw a black briefcase in the dim light of the storage room and smiled. As soon as he set the crystal back on the beat-up cabinet, a gloved hand snatched it away.

''You'll need this, too,'' said Deuce, pulling a remote control device out of his coat pocket. ''You know how to operate this?''

Yes.

CHAPTER 6

GARIBALDI still hadn't managed to escape from the docking area. He was assaulted from all sides. "Excuse me, Mr. Garibaldi," sneered a cadaverous-looking woman in a black uniform. "These arrangements are simply not acceptable. I can't possibly share a bathroom with somebody!"

"The person in the next room is another woman," explained Garibaldi, checking the manifest and room assignments on a handheld computer. "You see, Blue-16 is crew quarters, and we haven't got unlimited water or space. The only doors that open to the bathroom are from your two rooms. You just lock the other door when you're using it and leave it neat, and . . ." He waved his hands. "Pretend you're at summer camp."

The older Psi Cop batted her eyelashes at him. "It's my security I'm thinking about. I don't know if you know this, young man, but I'm a VIP on the Mars Colony. The terrorists would like my head."

A dozen snappy comebacks competed for attention in Garibaldi's mind, but he didn't use any of them. "Lady," he said slowly, "everybody here is a VIP. A VIP and half a credit will get you a cup of coffee. We threw this shindig together for Psi Corps in two days, and we're not the Ritz-Carlton on our better days—the least you could do is be gracious about it and sleep where we tell you."

The lady Psi Cop snapped to attention. "I see that your overriding concern is for our safety, and that's enough for me. Who is my bathroommate, if I may ask?"

Garibaldi checked his miniature screen. "That would be Ms. Trixie Lee." He blinked at the name in remembrance. "Didn't she used to be a stripper?"

"Yes, she was. It will be good to see her again." The woman smiled slyly. "I was a stripper, too, at one time. It's good training for a Psi Cop. Their minds are rather blank when you're right in front of them, and you can . . ."

Garibaldi laughed nervously. "Yes, well, enjoy your stay. We are serving refreshments in the casino. Just follow the signs."

"Casino?" said the woman, impressed. "Surely, we wouldn't break the taboo on gambling?"

"Surely not," answered Garibaldi. "The games are shut down."

The woman lifted a heavily mascaraed eyebrow. "Mr. Garibaldi, do you consider strip poker to be gambling?"

"Yes," he answered, pushing her along. "Next?"

Before he could prepare himself, Mr. Bester was in his face, oozing niceness. "Mr. Garibaldi, this is my colleague, Mr. Becvar. He has a security matter he needs to discuss with you, and I would appreciate it if you could accommodate him."

Garibaldi smiled obsequiously. "We aim to please."

With that, Bester left him with a handsome, dark-haired man who spoke with a Spanish accent. "Mr. Garibaldi," he said, lowering his voice, "have you heard of the Shedraks?"

"Shedraks?" repeated Garibaldi, shaking his head. "Sorry, that's a new one on me."

Mr. Becvar pointed to an air shaft. "They come in through the air ducts, and they strangle a person in his sleep. I insulted them when I was on Tyrol III, and they have been following me ever since, waiting to get me alone."

He grabbed Garibaldi by the collar. "I am not making this up!"

"No, of course not," said the security chief, calmly removing Becvar's gloved hands. "How do we stop these . . . these Shedraks?"

"The air vents," the man answered. "You must plug them up, do you understand?"

The chief consulted his handheld device. "Let me see what room you're in, Mr. Becvar." He paused a moment. "Oh, that's excellent! You have room 319, which is one of the quarters equipped with special baffles on the air vents. We can close those from central command!"

Mr. Becvar groaned with relief. "Oh, I am so glad."

"And I'll have my people keep an eye out for Shedraks here at the dock," Garibaldi assured him. "Are you okay with sharing a bathroom?"

The man shrugged. "As long as there are no air vents."

"We'll close them up, too." Garibaldi pretended to make a note. "Just follow the signs to the casino, and have a good time, Mr. Becvar."

The handsome man nodded and shuffled off, glancing worriedly at the air vents over his head.

Bester sidled up to Garibaldi. "Thank you, Mr. Garibaldi. Mr. Becvar had an unfortunate assignment several years ago, and he suffers some aftereffects. If you can believe it, he is a brilliant instructor on blocking techniques. He works at our center at Syria Planum. I understand you know about that facility?"

"Doesn't everybody?" asked Garibaldi cheerfully.

Bester's face darkened. "No, they do not. I would advise you to keep that information to yourself."

"I don't know why a training facility on Mars should be such a big deal."

Bester scowled. "Everything about Mars is a big deal. I need your assurance on this matter."

"Okay," said Garibaldi, "I won't mention it again."

Bester nodded curtly. "That is wise. Oh, hello, Mr. Pekoe, welcome to the conference!"

Garibaldi breathed a sigh of relief as Bester moved off to greet an Asian contingent of telepaths. Captain Sheridan stepped next to him and smiled.

"How is it going, Chief?"

"I *love* Psi Corps."

"Have they asked you to do anything you can't handle yet?"

Garibaldi considered the question for a moment. "Actually, they have, but I'm not going to give them the satisfaction of knowing it."

Sheridan patted him on the back. "You're doing a fine job, Garibaldi. Opening the casino to them was a stroke of genius. I think that's the key to our success, to keep them busy."

"The casino was Ms. Winter's idea," admitted Garibaldi. "I wonder where she is?"

"I hope she's enjoying herself," answered Sheridan. "She's an attendee at this conference, remember that. We're the hired help."

As Talia Winters and Arthur Malten dallied outside Emily Crane's quarters, Talia lifted her mouth to meet his. She worked around his goatee and mustache to give him a kiss that she hoped showed interest, but not too much interest. Malten was divorced, she knew, and he could do more for her career than anyone she had ever met. Nevertheless, she had to go slowly.

Talia decided to detach her mouth before their thoughts started intermingling, and she pushed him away gently. She was blocking for all she was worth, and so was he. That was good. It showed a healthy amount of distrust on both their parts. She wasn't sure she could handle another full-blown relationship with a fellow telepath. The last one had nearly torn her apart.

"I have to get to work," she said. "Don't you have some sort of high-level discussion to go to?"

He smiled boyishly. "I suppose I should go to the casino and see some old friends. Will you be there later?"

"That's my plan," she answered, "after I check out the arrangements on Green-12. If I don't make it, I'll see you at the reception."

"Fine." Malten bent to kiss her again, and the door slid open. Emily Crane peered out, not hiding her shock and disapproval.

"Excuse me," she said, starting to close the door. Her hand fumbled around on the unfamiliar wall panel, trying to find the right button.

"It's all right," Talia assured the woman. "I was just coming to help you. Sorry breakfast dragged on."

"Terrible service," Malten added. "I will have to speak to the captain about it. I'll see you both later."

The dapper telepath started down the corridor, then he turned abruptly. "Oh, Ms. Crane, I won't be needing you to come to the budget meeting with me tomorrow. Ms. Winters will be coming with me. So you can concentrate on scheduling, the newsletter, and such. Thank you."

He walked away with a jaunt to his step, and Talia could feel Emily's eyes drilling into her.

"That was f-fast," said the small woman.

Talia slipped into Emily's guest quarters, where the smell of paint was still strong, and she shut the door behind her. "Hey," she began, "if there's something going on between you and Arthur, just tell me. In fact, I'll listen to anything you want to tell me about him."

Emily Crane went back to her bed, upon which were spread reams of transparencies. She was stacking them together into different combinations of names, panels, and meeting rooms, preparing to run off corrected transparencies.

She swallowed and waved helplessly at one of the piles. "The moderator of the sleep deprivation seminar has c-canceled," she said. "He says that his equipment was lost. Can you think of anyone?"

Talia folded her arms. "Is that all you want to talk about?"

Emily lowered her head and screwed her face into a bitter frown. "I love Arthur. He doesn't think of me . . . in that way. When I heard that the two of us would be c-coming here alone, I hoped, being away from the office, we could . . ." She swallowed and couldn't finish her thought.

Talia felt like putting her arm around the young woman, but she didn't really know her very well. Besides, the answer was—no, they weren't an item. And one awkward, unexpected relationship at a time was more than enough.

"Come on," said Talia, picking up a stack of transparencies. "We've got a show to put on. This kind of confer-

ence isn't only about tax laws and penal code—there's a
sexual undertow that's difficult to avoid."

Talia gazed at herself in the small mirror over the vanity,
and she saw an attractive woman, flushed by the power she
was having over people. Yes, she was only a P5 among P10s
and P12s, but let's face it, she was better adjusted and better
looking than most of them.

"It's about control," said Talia, fluffing her blond hair.
"And what's better for control than sex? You planned to use
it, didn't you? I like Arthur, but I would have to think twice
about getting involved with another telepath."

"I'm already involved," said Emily.

"I would forget about him, in that way," Talia advised.
"Unless I'm totally wrong about him, I would guess he plays
the field."

"Will you be going to the budget meeting with him?"

"Yes. I may never get another chance to meet these people. Arthur calls B5 a backwater, and maybe he's right when
it comes to these kind of high-level contacts. So I should
meet as many of them as I can, before they go away."

The small woman gave her a knowing smile. "Watch
yourself."

"These Minbari," said a portly telepath from the military,
"we've got to get all of them off the station. Immediately!"
He looked around at the bustling dock area and lowered his
voice. "They could be spies."

Garibaldi also looked around and lowered his voice. "I'm
pretty sure some of them are."

"Then why don't you get them off?" the telepath demanded.

The chief shrugged. "We aren't at war with them, for one
thing."

"That's temporary," scoffed the military telepath. "With
the Wind Swords and the Sky Riders and their other warrior
castes getting the upper hand, it's only a matter of time. I'm
an expert in Minbari intelligence, and I tell you we have to

get them out of here. They're vicious! They could try to kill us!"

Garibaldi looked at the portly man and sure hoped that he didn't look like that in his similar uniform. "This is your basic free port," he explained. "Our charter is that we're diplomatic—we like everyone. Even Psi Corps. The Minbari helped to finance B5, and this is their most important diplomatic mission with the EA. We can't just throw them off B5."

The telepath muttered, "What a stupid place to hold this conference."

"I'll drink to that," said Garibaldi. "So is there anything else I can do for you?"

The military liaison bumped the security chief with his stomach and glared at him with piggy eyes in a florid face. "I'm serious, Mr. Garibaldi. I won't stay on a station with Minbari present. My life would be worth nothing!"

Garibaldi looked around in desperation and spied a savior. "Lennier! Lennier!" he called.

The friendly Minbari strolled over in his rustling satin robes. He crossed his arms and smiled angelically, the shell-like crowns on his head looking like a halo.

"Lennier, do you want to kill Mr. . . . What's your name?"

"Barker," said the man in shock.

"Why, of course not," answered Lennier. "I don't even know Mr. Barker, and I'm sure if I did know him, I would lay down my life for him."

"I wouldn't doubt it," answered Garibaldi. "Mr. Barker, meet Mr. Lennier, who is the aide to Ambassador Delenn and a member of a religious caste, not a warrior caste."

Lennier smiled beatifically. "Quite pleased to meet you."

The portly telepath glowered at the Minbari. "I was just telling Mr. Garibaldi that I wanted your people cleared off the station."

"What a novel idea," answered Lennier thoughtfully. "If this would be in the manner of a paid vacation, as you call it, I'm sure we could negotiate it. Would you like to go to the casino and discuss the arrangements? Where would you be willing to send us? Acapulco? Io?''

Mr. Barker looked helplessly at Garibaldi as Lennier led him down the corridor. The security chief gave him a shrug and added, "He does it with kindness."

The chief stifled a yawn and tried to unglue his eyes. If he didn't get some sleep soon he would probably say or do something that would start a war.

He handed his computer terminal to a subordinate and told him, "Just agree to whatever they want, and contact me in an hour to explain it. If it's not too unreasonable, we'll give them whatever we can. But don't contact me before an hour unless it's an emergency."

"Yes, sir," answered the officer.

Garibaldi looked around briefly for Captain Sheridan. Not seeing him in the crush of dignitaries, quadrupled security, and regular traffic, he gave up and wandered off. The simple act of rounding a corner and walking away from those oppressive black uniforms and that holier-than-thou attitude made him feel ten times better.

Just to relax for a few moments, to watch a few old cartoons, and forget all about Psi Corps—it probably wasn't possible, but it would be nice to try. He had done all he could, put all the people he had right where they ought to be, alerted them to all the possibilities. Sure, something could go wrong—it wouldn't be B5 if it didn't—but a major breakdown in security wasn't likely. With a little cooperation and a lot of luck they could get through this. Then Sheridan would owe him one. Big time. There was still an awkwardness between them, born of unfamiliarity. This would go a long way toward easing that.

Garibaldi was feeling pretty good about himself as he got out of the transport tube and headed into the homestretch of the corridor outside his quarters. He didn't even hear the footsteps pounding up behind him until it was too late.

A bearlike body whirled him around and shook him by the shoulders. In his blurred vision it looked like a scarlet monster, seven feet tall! Garibaldi tried a karate chop, but a brocaded forearm knocked his hand away and gripped his arms.

The alien sputtered as he talked. "How on Centauri Prime could you close down the gambling! What's the matter with you? You call yourself a *host?*"

Garibaldi focused on the big spiked hair, the throbbing dome of a forehead, and the jagged teeth, bared in a snarl. "Londo," he muttered, "if you knew what kind of day I've had, you'd have some pity on me."

"And what kind of day do you think I've had?" countered Ambassador Mollari in his peculiar accent. "First, I come within a hair of breaking the dice table, but my, er, escort was getting sleepy and I had to tuck her into bed. Then I go back to the casino, thinking I will double my jackpot, and what do I find? Gaming tables shut down, by order of Mr. Big Shot Garibaldi!"

The Centauri poked Garibaldi in the chest with a stubby finger. "They cannot even give me my winnings until you—you personally—open up the tables again! So what is this, huh? A conspiracy? Did G'Kar put you up to this?"

"Please," Garibaldi begged, "just give us a few days without gambling. We've got all these Psi Corps telepaths on board, and they can't gamble."

"Well," scoffed Londo, "they don't have to gamble if they don't want to! Let them play fish, or old maid, or whatever they do in Psi Corps. In case you hadn't noticed it, Garibaldi, I am not in Psi Corps. I do not wear those drab, funereal outfits. I wish to frolic. I wish to gamble. I wish to do whatever I was doing before they got here!"

"Amen to that," said the chief. "But it's only four days. I'll tell them to release your winnings to you, and maybe we can open up the tables for a few hours while they're in their seminars."

Londo grinned and narrowed his eyes slyly. "You know, Garibaldi, if these Psi Corps are not allowed to gamble—and they are in charge of everything else—then gambling is the one activity they are dying to do. Why don't you arrange it, and get some compromising visuals on them. Excellent opportunity here, Garibaldi, for what you might call a little office politics.''

''I'm too tired to blackmail anybody today,'' yawned Garibaldi, backing to his door. ''But thanks for the idea.''

''I could do it for you,'' offered Londo. ''Might be a bit of fun.''

''Don't mess with these people,'' Garibaldi warned. ''Take that as an order, and a good piece of advice. Humans who are full of themselves—you want to stay away from.''

The Centauri frowned. ''What does that mean? 'Full of themselves'?''

Garibaldi took out his identicard. ''Well, they're people who are pompous, who think the universe revolves around them, who think they're better than everybody, and deserve special treatment.'' He pushed his card into the slot, and the door opened. ''Like nobody you would know.''

''I should hope not,'' said Londo with mock horror.

Before Garibaldi could seek refuge in his dark cave, his link rang. He rolled his eyes, debating what he would do, although he knew he would answer it. ''Garibaldi here.''

''Chief, I'm sorry to bother you, but there's a major incident in the casino.''

''Who? What?'' he snapped.

''It's G'Kar. He's beating the crap out of one of the telepaths. Captain Sheridan just waded in to break it up.''

Londo shouldered past him on his way to the lift. ''Tell the telepath I am on my way to help him!''

CHAPTER 7

THE muscle-bound Narn lifted a squirming, black-suited Psi Cop over his head and bounced him off the bar. He rolled into a glass shelf and brought a row of bottles crashing down all around him.

"That is enough!" barked John Sheridan, stepping in front of G'Kar and pushing him back.

"Unhand me, Captain," snarled the alien, his spotted head pulsating with agitated veins.

"No!" said Sheridan. "This is a public place, and we have guests aboard the station. If you want to fight someone, then how about you and I step outside?"

"Wait, sir!" called Garibaldi, charging into the hushed casino. He pushed his way through the crowd that was pressing around the action.

"G'Kar, what's the matter with you?" he demanded.

Londo peered over the bar at the bloodied Psi Cop and pointed back at G'Kar. "I will help you press charges against this ruffian, if you like."

The Narn shook his head and got flustered. "Well, it . . . it was an overpowering feeling I got from him that he wanted to *kill* me."

"All you got was a thought?" asked Sheridan.

"It was a very clear threat," answered G'Kar.

The security chief snapped his fingers and pointed at his staff. "Get a medteam on that man."

"Already called," the officer replied.

Garibaldi glared around at the blank-faced telepaths surrounding him. "Were any of you with the wounded man before the fight started?"

A young female Psi Cop stepped forward, the black looking good on her. "Hoffman offered to bet us that he could plant a thought in the Narn's mind, as a sort of experiment. I don't know what he mistakenly put there, but the Narn jumped out of his seat and commenced to pulverize him."

The medteam, led by Dr. Stephen Franklin, rushed into the casino, and this distraction killed the possibility of further interrogation. Captain Sheridan leaned over the bar and noticed that the Psi Cop was bloodied but moving about, even fighting the medics who were waving smelling salts under his nose.

The captain narrowed his eyes at Ambassador G'Kar and was still angry at the Narn for starting this battle. Or did he start it?

"Listen, you hotshots!" called Garibaldi, demanding the attention back. "Even counting all of you, humans are the minority on this station. We also had an incident last night, so be careful!"

"Rest assured, that man will be punished!" crowed a voice from the back. Heads turned as Mr. Bester shouldered his way through the crowd. He peered over the bar at the wounded man with a smile of satisfaction. "He will be stripped of all his rights and duties." Bester smiled. "After a proper hearing, of course."

The Psi Cop turned magnanimously to G'Kar. "My dear Ambassador, please don't allow this incident to spoil your evening. Even telepaths sometimes forget that every gift has a price. Their price is responsibility and discipline. Gambling, abuse of power—these are things we do not tolerate."

Bester bowed and clicked his heels. "Please accept my sincerest apologies, Ambassador G'Kar."

Londo leaned against the bar and muttered, "Oh, brother."

But G'Kar smiled and bowed, looking like he was imitating Bester. "Apologies accepted. Communications are our greatest difficulty, I have always said."

"I hope you're going to attend the reception tonight," said Bester.

"Why, yes, I am."

Dr. Franklin poked his head above the bar and told Sheridan, "He's sedated. He has a broken wrist and a lot of cuts, but his injuries don't appear to be serious."

"Throw him in the brig," suggested Bester.

Franklin frowned. "I think medlab would be better."

"Medlab it is," ordered Sheridan. "With restraints and a guard."

The doctor nodded, and they lifted the unconscious Psi Cop onto a stretcher and took him out. This gave Captain Sheridan a chance to look around at the strange gathering. Garibaldi looked exasperated and exhausted; Londo was eagerly absorbing a description of the fight from the bartender; and Bester and G'Kar acted like old college chums. Strangest of all, thought the captain, he was surrounded by a roomful of humans who seemed more alien and unpredictable than the aliens on the station.

Sheridan realized he had been quite mad to allow this conference on B5. The longer it went on, the more likely something dreadful would happen. There was just too much tinder, too many matches lying around. He heard a voice in his mind, that same little voice that alerts the captain just before his ship hits an iceberg or an asteroid. The danger, said the voice, was just under the surface, waiting for the right moment to rip them apart.

Garibaldi and Ivanova had tried to warn him, thought the captain, but that didn't do them much good now. He had pigheadedly plunged ahead and let Psi Corps bring their conference, and all their baggage, right to his doorstep. Their first site had been bombed, as if that shouldn't be hint enough! Despite all their hard work and dedication, B5 was by design a sieve, a zoo without cages. Whatever was he thinking about?

Well, it was time to make amends and stop depending on his staff to get him out of this mess. "Garibaldi!" he called.

"Yes, sir?" The security chief didn't bother to salute.

"Go back to your quarters and sleep until you have to get dressed for the reception. I figure that will give you almost three hours."

"But, sir," said Garibaldi, "there's so much going on here . . ."

Sheridan lifted his hand. "Link, have all calls for Mr. Garibaldi routed to Officer Lou Welch until twenty-hundred hours. He will assume Garibaldi's duties. Captain Sheridan out." He looked sternly at Garibaldi. "Before you go, is everything all right for the reception on Blue-16?"

"We're shutting down the cafe in about an hour, and we'll reopen with full security."

"Good," answered Sheridan. "Tomorrow I want everyone searched who is going in and out of the conference rooms."

Garibaldi looked thoughtful. "We were going to do a hand-scan on anyone who entered Green-12. Plus, we were going to eyeball for Psi Corps insignias. Did you have something more elaborate in mind?"

"I don't want a strip search," said Sheridan, "but look inside handbags, briefcases, backpacks, handheld stuff. Pat them down, if need be."

"That's fine with me," agreed Garibaldi. "I was going to suggest it, but I didn't think they would let us get away with it."

"As long as it's by the book," said Sheridan, "let's use whatever means are at our disposal. This may discourage them from going in and out of Green-12 too much."

"What are we looking for, sir?"

The captain smiled wistfully. "Some peace of mind. But I don't think we'll find it until they leave."

He hated prowling the corridor waiting for her, but he didn't know how else to approach Susan, without making it look something like a coincidence. Fortunately, Harriman Gray was one of those people who blended in. He didn't blend in very well when he was playing the odious role of the hard-boiled telepath, ready to leaf through a person's mind like a nosy visitor snoops through a person's medicine cabinet; but he could blend in well enough when there were crowds and a swirl of people.

The longer he was around them, the more Gray liked the

alien rhythms and voices of Babylon 5. It made him feel
more normal to know that he couldn't read the minds of most
of the people here. To them, he was just another alien.

So he circled the corridors where she had to cross, hoping
he wouldn't miss her when his back was turned. Perhaps she
would get a bite at her favorite restaurant between shifts. She
was working a double shift, he was certain, until all the conference attendees were safely aboard the station, where they
became somebody else's problem. That was the way Susan
worked, making sure there were no lapses on her watch. She
hated all of them with a passion, but she would guide their
ships to safety as if they were carrying her own mother.

The thought of Susan's mother brought Gray up short.
That was the root of her hatred for Psi Corps, and was there
anything he could do about it? Would it do any good to
apologize? Or to tell Susan how lousy it made him feel to be
tarred with the same feather as the Psi Police? Was there
anything at all he could say that would erase her years of pain
and hatred? No. Not as long as he wore the Psi Corps insignia on his lapel.

What was he doing this for? Why couldn't he come to his
senses and forget about Susan? There were plenty of women
who would welcome a man with his prestige and career potential, women who would consider him a catch. Well,
maybe.

The problem was, Harriman Gray had always wanted the
wrong thing, the thing he couldn't have. He had wanted to be
a soldier, before his psi abilities had manifested themselves.
After that path had been taken away from him, he had wanted
to serve the military in a liaison capacity, going home every
night to his tidy apartment. Instead, he was shunted from one
high-level assignment to another, each one more surreal than
the one before it. Now he loved a woman who hated him.
Sheesh, thought Gray, maybe he was more neurotic than
Bester.

While he considered giving up and joining his colleagues
at the casino, he caught a glimpse of a gray uniform dashing

into the sweets shop. His heart leaped as quickly as his feet, as he hurried into the shop after her.

"I'll take one of those," said Ivanova, pointing to a dark confection.

"Susan," he said.

Her back stiffened, and she refused to turn around. "Are you following me?"

"Yes," he admitted. "I don't suppose you're going to the reception later on?"

"No."

"That's why I had to follow you."

Susan sighed and finally turned around to look at him. He was reminded of the way his big sister used to look whenever she was annoyed with him.

"You know, Harriman, by the captain's orders, I'm not supposed to be talking to you. Or any of your friends."

"I know," Gray admitted. "I've read all the travel advisories. 'Do not visit Down Below or the Alien Sector. Do not travel alone. And do not speak to Commander Ivanova.' "

She smiled in spite of her herself. "I hope there's a suitable punishment for doing so."

"Speaking of punishment," said Gray excitedly, "did you hear that Ambassador G'Kar beat the stuffing out of a reprehensible Psi Cop named Hoffman? In front of everybody!"

Ivanova smiled. "No, I didn't hear that. We're all doing our part to make this an enjoyable conference."

She grabbed her pastry and waited for Gray to get out of her way. "Excuse me, I've only got about five minutes before the next transport is due."

"Please eat," insisted Gray. He rushed to pull out a chair at an empty table. "It's all right, I'll do all the talking."

Ivanova shrugged resignedly and set her snack on the table. "I can push my own chair in."

"Of course," said Gray, sitting across from her. "I just wanted to tell you—I'm thinking of quitting my job as a military liaison and going into commercial practice."

"That's nice," replied Ivanova with her mouth full of cake.

"Yes, maybe I can even get assigned to Babylon 5."

The officer looked puzzledly at him and swallowed. "We already have a resident telepath."

"Ah," said Gray, "Ms. Winters may be leaving."

Ivanova frowned. "Really? I was just getting to know her. Why would she leave?"

"Better offer."

"How do you know this?" she asked suspiciously.

Gray smiled. "Let's say, a gathering of telepaths is not the best place to keep a secret."

Ivanova set her fork on her plate and just stared at him. "Harriman, if you're trying to get an assignment on B5 just to be close to me, you're wasting your time. Having a strained conversation like this, every now and then, is the best you could ever hope for."

He looked down, deeply wounded. "That's rather cold, isn't it?"

"Yes, it is," she admitted, standing up. "I'm sorry, but I don't want to lead you on."

Gray countered, "There's something else. I *like* being here on Babylon 5! I feel comfortable in this place, like a regular person, not a freak or a snoop."

Susan opened her mouth, as if she were about to say something, but she finally just shook her head and walked off. When she was gone, Gray slammed his fist on the table.

Despite the cruelty and finality of her words, a voice in his head told him that she was still the one for him. Who should he listen to, if not his own heart? If not his own voice?

"Susan," he muttered to himself, "if a strained conversation is all I'll ever get, then I'll take it."

Talia Winters slumped away from the viewer and rubbed her eyes. She had looked at everything on the data crystal ten times, and it still didn't make much sense. It was a lot of bogus figures that didn't add up correctly, a lot of statistics on job creation for telepaths that definitely favored the commercial sector, some pie charts that attacked military spending, and the request for a new research and development center. She didn't know how any of this would coalesce into a convincing argument for the needs of commercial telepathy.

Of course, she told herself, this was just raw data. You had to have it, because sometimes logic alone wouldn't work—there had to be numbers to plug in, charts to pull up. When it came down to it, she felt the strongest argument was that commercial telepaths were the only segment of Psi Corps who managed to pay for themselves. Bester and all his top-secret budgets were a total drain, and so was all the psychic-weapon research the military did. However, she doubted whether either one of them liked to be reminded of this.

And none of these charts or statistics addressed the real problem—that Mr. Bester and his ilk decided who got what in Psi Corps. What kind of argument could overcome that reality?

A knock sounded on her door, and Talia looked up with a start. As she pressed the button to open it, she called out, "Come in."

Emily Crane stumbled into the room. She was wearing high-heeled shoes and a peach evening gown with a single strap. It didn't look half-bad on her, thought Talia. If she could get accustomed to asserting herself, she had promise.

"What are you d-doing?" Emily asked accusingly. "You should be getting ready for the reception."

"Oh, sorry," said Talia, glancing at the clock over her screen. "I've been studying this data crystal you put together about the budget. Now I sort of wish you were going, because I don't think I'll be familiar with this by tomorrow morning."

"Do you think I am?" asked Emily. "You know the things to say. We can back it up later in a memo."

"All right," sighed Talia. "I don't think I can read any more of this crystal tonight, anyway."

"Then g-give it to me," said Emily, stepping carefully toward the viewer. "I have some updates for a few of those charts. I don't think you'll need to show them anything, but I'll give it back to you before the meeting, just in c-case."

She drew the crystal out of its slot and tucked it down her bra. "What we want is the research center. The rest is all smoke and m-mirrors."

"Thanks," said Talia. "I guess I had better get dressed now."

Emily nodded and hobbled out the door. After it shut, Talia thoughtfully pulled off her gloves. It felt good to have her fingers free, and she used them to unzip her skirt and let it fall to the floor. She stretched her fingers and pushed back her hair as she moved languidly toward the shower.

Garibaldi was having a wonderful dream. He was in the shower, with the water cascading all over him. This obviously was not on Babylon 5, he decided, because the water on B5 mostly dribbled. Anyway, he was in the shower, cleansing himself, and he knew that when he stepped out, the four hundred telepaths from Psi Corps would all be gone. It would be just the usual two hundred and fifty thousand dregs of humanity and aliens. He could hardly wait!

He turned off the shower and jumped out, already dry. He liked this shower. And he strode through a dreamworld of laughing, cheerful people, raising glasses and toasting him for ending the horror of the Psi Corps conference. There was Londo, grinning in his snaggletoothed way.

"I got the tape on them!" claimed the Centauri, lifting his glass.

"Excellent," replied Garibaldi with a big grin.

"Well done, Mr. Garibaldi," said Captain Sheridan, patting him on the back. "You're an asset to this station."

"Asset," muttered Garibaldi, thinking he had been insulted.

Then he saw Talia, who was dressed exactly as he was, which was not at all. "I'm taking a shower," she remarked, but her naked body floated past.

He wanted to follow her, but more people were pulling him along, raising their glasses to him. Without warning, the security chief bumped into someone he wanted to see in real life, but not someone he wanted to see in a dream. It was Deuce, the grubby kingpin of Down Below.

"Aw, Garibaldi," drawled Deuce, "you didn't have to get rid of them. I would've done it for you." He laughed and stepped back into the shadows.

Then it was Lennier, underfoot as usual. The peaceful Minbari held up a wad of cash. "We came to an understanding," he explained.

Ivanova walked somberly beside him, deep in thought. "Could you love a telepath?" she asked. "Could you really love one of *them?*"

"I love Psi Corps!" he replied, which seemed to be the right answer. Everybody smiled at him.

And the last being at the end of the line was Kosh, the Vorlon ambassador. The mountain of marble and fabric moved directly into his path and cut off his escape.

"Where have all the Martians gone?" asked the Vorlon in his strange combination of musical notes and synthesized voice. Kosh peered at Garibaldi with a tubelike telescope that issued from his stomach, and added, "Long time passing."

"They are all gone!" cried Captain Sheridan, raising his glass. "Here is to Mr. Garibaldi and his remarkable solution to the problem of Psi Corps."

Since everyone else stopped to look at him and lift their glasses, Garibaldi did likewise. Only he wasn't holding a glass—he was holding a block of wires with globs of dirty plastique. The denotator ticked menacingly!

Garibaldi gasped and tried to throw the bomb away. As it left his hands, it turned into a seering blast of white light and a monstrous *KA-BOOM!*

The last thing Garibaldi saw was Bester howling with laughter—then he mercifully woke up, clutching his blanket in his sweaty hands. Garibaldi's link was blaring, and his personal computer seemed to be shrieking at him, too.

"Okay, okay!" he growled. "I'm up."

"Twenty-hundred hours," said the computer.

He tapped his link, and the captain's voice sounded, "Garibaldi, this is Sheridan. Everything is under control, but I just wanted to make sure you didn't oversleep."

"No danger of that," croaked Garibaldi, smacking his lips to get the weird taste out of his mouth.

Sheridan answered, "Glad to hear it. I'm at Blue-16 now, and it's already filling up. We've had some would-be gate-crashers, but the only outsiders we've invited are the ambassadors and their aides. So access has been fairly easy to control."

Garibaldi didn't like hearing the captain sound so nervous, especially after the dream he had just had. "Fifteen minutes," he promised. "Thank you for the rest, Captain, I'm a new man."

"We could use some new men," said Sheridan glumly. "Excuse me, Mr. Bester has arrived."

Talia Winters took a drink of her Centauri wine and smiled at Ambassador Delenn. The Minbari female looked as small and fragile as a porcelain doll, but Talia knew there was a tough, hard-nosed politician under that demure exterior. A member of the Grey Council and an early backer of Babylon 5, Delenn understood the importance of the station as few others did.

"My aide and Mr. Barker seem to have hit it off," remarked Delenn, looking with satisfaction at Lennier and a stout military man. They were leaning into each other, involved in an animated conversation that excluded all others.

"Well, they should," remarked Talia, "they both hate your warrior castes."

Delenn's smile faded only a little as she looked up at the taller women. "You don't seem yourself tonight, Ms. Winters. Is there something on your mind?"

Talia pushed back a strand of yellow hair, which perfectly accented her black evening dress. Her white shoulders gleamed like a spotlight above the black décolletage.

"You're right," she admitted. "I'm agonizing over a decision. In fact, it's a whole bundle of decisions all wrapped up in one knot."

Delenn cocked her head. "One should never make a decision hastily. Or alone. I am not much for mingling at parties, and I would be happy to give you my full attention."

Talia swallowed. "All right, I've been offered a new assignment, probably on Earth, with a very big firm. They say they want me for my interspecies experience, but I got that experience working here. In other words, I'd like to take this opportunity, but I don't want to leave B5. Does that make sense?"

"Perfect sense," answered Delenn, taking a demure sip of her tea. "If this firm is who I think it is, there may be a solution. Why don't you open up a branch office for them on B5? Then you can fall under their umbrella while staying with us."

Talia chuckled, then grew somber. "I thought of that. Unfortunately, my physical presence is required for some aspects of this deal."

Delenn smiled knowingly. "Ah, that is often the case. Although you are the one who has to make the decision, my opinion is that B5 will remain a most advantageous base for your career."

Talia looked down at her drink. The greenish liquid seemed to mimic her murky thoughts, and she wanted to throw it out and get something clean.

But a thought touched her mind, a sweet one, and she looked up to see Arthur Malten, now dressed in a very conservative dark-blue suit. Even his eyes were smiling.

"You look lovely tonight, Talia," he said. He turned to Delenn and bowed. "Do I have the pleasure of addressing Ambassador Delenn?"

"You do," she replied.

"Arthur Malten," he announced. "Of the Mix. I have spoken to many of your colleagues."

"Yes," said Delenn, "and we must talk about the proposed branch office you wish to open on Minbar." She smiled at Talia. "But not tonight."

"Yes," said Malten, grabbing Talia's hands through her black velvet gloves. "I'm afraid I must take Ms. Winters away for a moment. Mr. Bester is here, and he's in a very good mood, granting favors left and right."

"Right this moment?" asked Talia hesitantly.

"No time like the present," Malten replied. "At least that's what I've always heard."

"Haste makes waste," countered Delenn. "Isn't that also one of your proverbs?"

Malten glanced at the Minbari. "I'm very decisive," he told the ambassador. "When I see what I want, I go after it. I'm patient, too, if need be."

"An admirable trait," said Delenn. "It is easy to be decisive, difficult to be patient."

But Malten was already whisking Talia Winters away.

CHAPTER 8

TALIA stiffened her back as she strolled across the Blue-16 cafe. Part of it was the touch of Arthur Malten's bare hand on her wrist. Why wasn't he wearing gloves? she wondered. Probably just another example of his well-known penchant for rebellious behavior.

She wanted to tell Arthur that she hadn't made her decision yet—but then she was dazzled by the sights, sounds, and voices of a roomful of influential telepaths. Many of them turned to look at her and Malten, and the attention was alluring in its own right.

Did she really want to bury herself on a station full of alien life-forms and alien concerns? Or was this where she belonged—with her peers, in the midst of important decisions that affected the entire Earth Alliance? These were the people who made the Senate and Earthforce jump, the ones chosen by natural selection to lead.

She put on her most placid smile as Arthur steered her toward Mr. Bester. He was surrounded by his usual black-suited band of sycophants, with a handful of military and commercial telepaths in attendance as well.

When Bester saw Talia and Malten approach, he smiled expectantly, the scorpion waiting for the beetle to come closer.

"Good evening, Mr. Bester," said Talia.

"Good evening, Ms. Winters, you look lovely." He glanced with disinterest at her escort. "Hello, Malten."

"Hello, Mr. Bester," said the tall man. He gestured around at the gayly decorated cafe, jammed with people. "Don't we owe Ms. Winters a debt of gratitude for pulling all of this together so quickly?"

"Yes, we do," agreed Bester.

Talia shook her head politely. "Captain Sheridan, Mr.

Garibaldi, and the entire staff of B5 are the ones who really did it. I merely asked them.''

Bester smiled. ''Don't underestimate your powers of persuasion, Ms. Winters.'' He glanced at Malten. ''I've seen them at work.''

Malten bristled slightly but kept a polite smile on his face. ''I think we all realize how valuable Ms. Winters is. Although Babylon 5 is an important post, it's rather removed from the action. There are many of us who feel that Ms. Winters is being wasted here and could better serve Psi Corps in another capacity. Closer to Earth.''

Bester shrugged. ''She would make a wonderful rogue-hunter, but with a P5 level, what can we do?'' Several of the Psi Cops chuckled.

''We could use her in the Mix,'' said Malten.

Bester continued to smile, but he looked more threatening than friendly as he fixed his dark eyes on the entrepreneur. ''One would almost think, Mr. Malten, that you were trying to get a monopoly on all the talented commercial telepaths.'' His eyes narrowed. ''Getting greedy is not a good idea.''

Well, thought Talia, this conversation was certainly going downhill. ''I see Ambassador G'Kar,'' she said, ''and I wish to hear his side of the incident, which I missed. If you'll both excuse me.''

Walking off, she heard Malten hiss to Bester, ''That was uncalled for!''

Talia took a deep breath and decided not to bother G'Kar after all. He could be a bombastic sort, and she didn't really want to hear a blow-by-blow account of some bar fight. Despite the cheerful dance music that was playing, Mr. Gray looked lonely, standing by himself at the bar. So she headed his way.

''Hello, Mr. Gray,'' she said, grabbing a seat at the counter. As an afterthought, she added, ''Do you mind if I sit here?''

He blinked at her from his dazed reverie. ''Not at all, please have a seat. Are you having a good time?''

Distastefully, she set her glass of wine on the counter. "It'll be better after I get a new drink."

Gray twisted his hands nervously. "Ms. Winters, you've spent more time among aliens and even regular humans than I have. Can I ask you something?"

She smiled at him. "Certainly."

"Can a telepath and a nontelepath love each other?"

Talia smiled, thinking about Garibaldi. "I'm sure it happens all the time, on a superficial level. Whether a telepath and a mundane could stay together for sixty years and watch their grandchildren grow up, I don't know. I would think the odds are against it. On the other hand, I haven't seen many nontelepathic couples stay together for a long time either."

She motioned around the room. "Don't you find it amazing that so many of our kind are either single or divorced? We're all lone wolves."

"Yes," said Gray worriedly. He took a seat beside her and lowered his voice. "When I signed up for Psi Corps, I didn't know it would preclude living a normal life. They told me they would bring out my abilities, not kill everything else." His shoulders slumped. "I suppose, as long as one party is telepathic, there will always be distrust."

"And when both are telepathic," Talia added, "it's too intense to last long."

"So all we have is each other," said Gray, "and we can take very little solace in that."

"None," answered Talia.

She looked up and saw Arthur Malten headed their way, a peeved look on his face. She grabbed Gray's gloved hand. "Would you like to dance?"

He beamed with surprise. "Thank you, I would."

They escaped to the dance floor moments before Malten caught up with them. Talia could see him by the bar, sulking. She guessed that Mr. Bester had turned down his request to have her reassigned. Drawing on her usual optimism, Talia wondered if this wasn't for the best. The conference had barely started, and people were fighting over her. She supposed that was good, although it felt rather vulgar to be fought over like a head of cattle.

Mr. Gray was actually an accomplished dancer; he didn't step on her toes, and he kept a respectful distance. Talia used the roving platform of the dance floor to survey the other attendees at the reception.

Garibaldi and Sheridan, both of whom looked like they were at a wake, gave in to moments of polite laughter followed by long periods of somber realization. Of the ambassadors, G'Kar had the biggest following, and most of them were military telepaths. Apparently, bashing a Psi Cop could make you very popular with the military. Londo had brought an attractive Centauri woman with him, and they had quite a retinue of telepaths following them from one hors d'oeuvre table to another. The Psi Cops gravitated around Bester, and the commercial telepaths had broken up into small groups and couples. Hmmm, thought Talia, if she could find Emily Crane, perhaps she could introduce her to Mr. Gray. But the small woman in the peach dress was not in her line of sight.

On her second pass around the dance floor, Talia was glad to find Arthur Malten talking to Ambassador Delenn. The Minbari would be a good distraction for him, keeping his mind off matters that were up in the air. Up in the air was right where she wanted to leave those matters.

"Thank you for coming," said Captain Sheridan. "It was a pleasure. We are pleased to have you here. Think of us during the appropriations. Have a good conference."

To his credit, thought Talia, he managed to say the same thing a hundred times without sounding like a broken soundchip. She was reduced to a simple smile as the conference attendees filed out of the reception on Blue-16. They'd closed the place down, at the preset hour of 23:00. Almost no one had left early, save for Ambassador Delenn, and the proprietor of the cafe was tallying up the bar tab with a smile on his face.

"Detail two," said Garibaldi, "escort as many of these

folks as you can to their quarters. We don't want them wandering off to other parts of the station."

"Technically, they could go to the casino," said Talia.

Garibaldi scowled. "Do everything but read them bedtime stories," he told his people, "I want them in bed. I'll go with you."

The security chief and his officers took off after a knot of attendees who had halted in the corridor to study their door keycards. Soon those who needed help were taken underwing, and no one was left in the cafe except the workers, tidying up. Talia yawned, and Captain Sheridan looked at her sympathetically.

"I feel the same way," he admitted. "The conference business is not for me—too much conversation. But I think it's been successful, so far."

Talia nodded. "Captain, they are having a grand time. For this group, they were doing handstands they were so happy. Some of these people never feel welcomed anywhere, and you put them at ease. After a few rough spots, the ambassadors fit in very well, too. Although I was disappointed that Ambassador Kosh didn't come."

The captain shrugged. "Well, you know Kosh."

Talia shook her head and laughed, because both of them knew that was a very dumb remark.

"I've got to get to bed," said Sheridan. "My mind is a jumble. I suppose a few hundred telepaths will do that to you. Good night."

"Good night, Captain."

Talia watched the captain go, feeling good about shutting the place down, being the one to turn out the lights. Despite a few personality conflicts, this *was* a successful conference so far. Of course, she reminded herself, this was only the first official function out of two hundred and sixteen panels, seminars, luncheons, and meetings. So there was plenty of time for something to go wrong. But each day without incident was a feather in her cap. Now Psi Corps knew who she was and what kind of territory she had, and B5 was more than an acronym to them.

She stepped down to the corridor level and took a slow stroll toward the exit. All things considered, it was good to know that there was an upward path for her in the commercial sector. But what price did those paths have? It wasn't just the obvious pitfalls that had her worried, but the hidden ones, the ones worked out between Malten and Bester while her back was turned.

And what exactly did they want with her interspecies experience? While it had commercial applications galore, it also had military applications. She didn't want to become an experiment gone awry, like the only man she had ever loved. Nor did she want to become a spy against alien races, such as the Minbari. She had to tread very carefully, eyeball everything, and get it all in writing.

Talia wasn't particularly surprised when she felt his presence waiting for her around a bend in the corridor. He was being sweet again, trying to be apologetic. He would make it up to her, he promised, for those several awkward moments. All his fault, he assured her. Talia smiled and was about to tell him to buzz off for the night, because she really was tired.

"Arthur," she began, rounding the corner. But it wasn't Mr. Malten.

It was Mr. Bester. She glared at him, and he smiled at her.

"That is anatomically impossible," he said. "But a popular sentiment."

Talia sputtered, "You . . . you pretended to be . . ."

"Yes, I know," Bester conceded. "It is very difficult to work around a corner, and the signal is weak—but I can do it, if I know the person. The advantage, as you saw, is that you can pretend to be someone else."

"I don't appreciate that," said Talia.

Bester's smile faded. "Now you sound like your boyfriend, always whining. This is the big leagues the two of you want to play in, so you had better come ready to play ball." He smiled at her. "Do I make myself clear?"

Talia swallowed. "Okay, what do you want to approve my reassignment to the Mix? If that's what I decide to do."

Bester licked his lips. "We shouldn't talk about this out here in the corridor. My room is right down there."

Talia smiled. "I know exactly where your room is, and there's a recreation room even closer. It's perfect for talking. Or a quick game of Ping-Pong."

"Of course," said Bester with a disgruntled expression. "Lead on. I could use some recreation."

The room was empty, and Talia had to wipe her gloved hand over the wall panel to activate the lights. As she had specified, the Ping-Pong table had four new paddles and a package of balls; there was a chess set on one of the card tables, and decks of cards on the other two. In the corner was a compact weight-lifting machine with a video screen for instruction.

"How are you at Ping-Pong?" she asked.

"I react very quickly," answered Bester. "I used to be quite good. But that wasn't the game I had in mind."

Talia sat at one of the card tables and opened up a deck. "Isn't it odd, but everywhere you look there are invitations to gamble. You would think members of Psi Corps would be above temptation, but it comes after us just as much as anyone."

"It is the resistance that makes us strong," answered Bester, making a fist to dramatize his point. He took a seat opposite her and smiled. "Again, that is not the game I had in mind."

"How much will it cost me to work for the Mix?" asked Talia point-blank. "And leave Mr. Malten out of the equation."

"That is wise to leave Mr. Malten out," said Bester with approval. "He started the Mix, but now it has outgrown him. It could perform as well without him as with him."

Talia stared evenly at the Psi Cop. "So it has to be something I can pay for, on my own. How much?"

Bester leaned forward and asked hoarsely, "How badly do you want to go?"

Talia smiled. "Not that badly." She leaned back in her chair. "Is there an economy rate?"

Bester laughed. "You still haven't found the game I want to play yet. I want to play show-and-tell."

"How do you play that?" asked Talia suspiciously.

"It's very simple," said Bester, reaching into his jacket pocket. "I show you a picture of your Uncle Ted—that would be Theodore Hamilton—and you tell me where he is."

Bester tossed a photo of a rakish man with long blond hair onto the table, and Talia was stunned by the juxtaposition of her Uncle Ted and Mr. Bester. One was a ne'er-do-well lady-killer, and the other was, well, Mr. Bester. She laughed with both relief and amazement.

"I can get into the Mix by telling you about my Uncle Ted?" she asked puzzledly.

"You don't have to tell us anything about him, except where he is."

Talia looked helplessly at the Psi Cop. "I think, when I last saw him, I was about fourteen years old. He was just headed for Mars." She peered at Bester. "Oh, I see—this has something to do with Mars."

"You really don't know what he's been doing for the last two years?" asked Bester incredulously.

She shook her head. "I haven't had much contact with Mars." Talia wanted to say that her uncle would never become a Martian revolutionary, but that wasn't true. It probably was something the old romantic would do, especially if there were women involved.

"I would guess that he's been blowing things up on Mars," she said.

"Worse than that, Ms. Winters. Your Uncle Ted has been explaining the separatist position in a very clear way, and people are starting to listen to him. He's popular, and the colonists are hiding him. We've been trying to find him for two years."

Bester leaned urgently across the table. "We want him."

"I haven't a clue where he is," she answered, shaking her head. "And why would *you* want him, Mr. Bester? He's not a telepath, rogue or otherwise."

Bester smiled and answered, "That is on a need-to-know basis, and you don't need to know. But now you know the cost to get into the Mix—on your own terms, without Malten's help. Once you're in there, you can use him or not, as you wish. I believe this is a price you can meet, Ms. Winters, and it won't compromise your high ideals."

"Mr. Bester," she protested, "I haven't seen my Uncle Ted in something like fifteen years. How can I help you?"

"Come now, you're family. You can go to Mars or Earth, ask around, show some concern. Say you only want to say hello to your beloved Uncle Ted before the bad guys get him. Give him a hug for old times' sake."

Bester winked. "Surely, you learned a long time ago to read your mother's mind, without her knowing it. This is her brother we're talking about. Find out where he is."

Talia tried not to throw up, but she did start to gag on the idea of scanning family members without them knowing it. She stood weakly from the table and swallowed down the bile. "I'm not feeling very well, Mr. Bester. I really don't think I can be any help finding Ted Hamilton. Good night."

"The offer won't be on the table forever," warned Bester. "Good night."

Talia Winters slammed the door behind her and leaned against the wall for support. How could it be that talking to Mr. Bester always made her feel dirty? She couldn't avoid him—she would see him at the budget meeting in just ten hours—but she should refuse to discuss anything of a personal nature with him.

Then again, she had asked for it. With ambition and desire came the price. Even in the workaday world of the mundanes, it was no different. Talia had let herself be lured into this insane game, and she shouldn't panic just because the stakes got high. She could always drop out.

And she would. Tomorrow, right after the budget meeting. She'd go back to being the only resident telepath of Babylon 5 so far, and be thrilled with it.

Talia headed for the main checkpoint, and she felt relieved

to see Garibaldi and two of his officers, hanging out, looking edgy but better than they had earlier.

"Good evening," she said.

"Hello, Ms. Winters," the younger one said.

Garibaldi smiled at her. "We took a vote—we all like your outfit. I wouldn't want you to think it was just me."

"Thank you," she said wearily. "I haven't got any witty repartee left. Good night."

"I could walk you home," offered Garibaldi.

"Nope," she said, heading away from Blue-16. Then she stopped. "How did you get away from those aliens last night?"

"Oh, that," answered Garibaldi with a shrug. "I shot one in the foot, and I slugged another one. Then I ran like hell."

"There were three of them," said Talia.

Garibaldi rubbed his nose in thought. "Well, the third one came after you, but I guess you moved pretty fast."

"Yeah," the telepath agreed. "I'm moving fast these days. Good night."

"Good night."

Garibaldi lay in his bed, still thinking about his disturbing dream from earlier that day. His sense of duty kept prodding him to go Down Below and turn over every mattress and garbage can until he found Deuce. But he would have to get really lucky, or Deuce would have to want to be found, for that to work. With four hundred telepaths on the station, Garibaldi didn't feel really lucky, and he didn't think Deuce wanted to be found.

For one thing, Deuce was keeping very quiet. There had been no reports of beatings or murders, no jump in robberies or threats. Nobody had been caught transporting unusual contraband or stolen goods. And Deuce had not been spotted in any of his usual haunts, by any of several informers that Garibaldi had hired. Whatever Deuce's business on B5 was, he was keeping it low-key, just like they were trying to keep the conference low-key. Unfortunately, Deuce was doing a better job of it.

He rolled over in his bed and tried to get comfortable. It was no good. There were too many things around here that should not mix—Deuce, Bester, Martian terrorists, aliens who didn't give a hoot about Psi Corps, telepaths who didn't give a hoot about aliens. Even Captain Sheridan and Talia Winters had looked bagged by the stress, and if it could get to them, it could get to anyone. Come to think of it, neither Bester nor Gray looked too good either, Garibaldi decided. A feeling of paranoia was eating at all of them.

Worst of all, the conference proper didn't really start until tomorrow! He pulled the pillow over his head and tried to go to sleep.

CHAPTER 9

"Yes, ma'am," said Garibaldi pleasantly, "we've got to open up your briefcase and look inside."

"I d-don't know why you should," muttered the short, dark-skinned woman. But she started to unlatch her case, anyway.

Garibaldi calmly took the case and set it on the table. As most of the contents were folders of transparencies, brochures, and business cards, he didn't empty it onto one of the bins set aside for that purpose. But he did feel around on the bottom to come up with four smaller objects: her identicard, a creditchit, a dictaphone, and a data crystal.

He held the data crystal out. "What is this?"

The woman put her hands on her hips and gave him a quizzical stare. "Are you saying you don't know what it is?"

"No," said Garibaldi, dropping the crystal and the other objects back into the case. "Just wanted to make sure it was yours. Officer Baker will search your person."

Huffily, the woman stomped on, and a female officer took charge of her.

Garibaldi sighed and looked up to find the cadaverous female Psi Cop.

"Uh, good morning," he said warily. "Did you have a pleasant evening?"

She grinned evilly. "Yes. Trixie and I stayed up all night, talking about the good old days. I never laughed so hard in my life." She winked at him. "We were experimenting a lot in those days."

"I'll bet," admitted Garibaldi. He pointed to her bag. "Can you open it, please?"

"Gladly." Without hesitation, the black-uniformed cop opened her handbag. "You are doing a fine job, Mr. Garibaldi. If anything happens, I know it won't have been your fault."

As he checked her bag, he whispered, "What do you think is going to happen?"

She held her regal chin up and sniffed. "It's just something in their air, isn't it?"

"No, that's fresh paint," said Garibaldi. "Thank you."

"You will pat me down personally, won't you?"

He winked at her. "Maybe the last day."

With a deep-throated laugh, the woman moved on. Garibaldi went through the same routine with dozens of telepaths, all of whom offered various levels of resistance. However, many of them seemed to feign their anger; they secretly welcomed the overt demonstration of security, even if it did suggest that Psi Corps didn't entirely trust its own members.

Garibaldi was just getting into a good rhythm, working the attendees through the main entrance to Green-12. That's when he looked up to see Mr. Bester.

The Psi Cop smiled and held up his hands. "No briefcase or bag." He tapped his head. "I keep everything I need up here."

"That's convenient," said Garibaldi. "I'm going to wave you through. No pat-down."

"How disappointing," said Bester, glancing at Officer Baker. "Is conference room number nine secured?"

"We've swept it twice," answered the Security Chief. "The lock will only open for the attendees on my list." He showed him a transparency of the invited guests for the ten o'clock budget meeting.

"Hmmm," said Bester with interest. "Ms. Winters is coming, too. What a pleasant surprise."

Garibaldi screwed his mouth shut and nodded. "I've got people piling up here, excuse me."

"Go on, go on," said Bester with a wave. He strolled through into the Green Sector, greeting people standing among the potted plants, refreshment tables, and beckoning doorways.

Garibaldi sighed and went back to the next glowering telepath. "Excuse me, sir, you'll have to open up your briefcase."

"By whose authority?" grumbled a black-suited Psi Cop.

The chief smiled. "Security Regulation 13, section 4, sub-paragraph B, Special Circumstance 2."

Talia lifted her arms and let the pat-down conclude as quickly as possible. It was embarrassing. Was Garibaldi doing this just to prove he was in charge? Oh, well, she had too much else on her mind to worry about the games he might be playing. She had come down through a lift entrance from another Green deck, thinking that she might avoid a security check. Fat chance.

"Sorry, Ms. Winters," said a young female security officer, handing her portfolio back. "Just following orders."

She nodded and tried to smile. "How are the attendees taking it?"

"Okay, mostly." The lift opened again, and the officer was distracted. "Excuse me, sir, I'll have to look inside that."

Talia shook her head and moved on. The overzealous searches were a statement, but maybe they were the right statement. Despite the success of the reception the night before, there was a pall hanging over the conference. Of course, that was due mostly to the bombing of the original site, which was symptomatic of the ongoing problems of Mars. Everybody was thinking about Mars, but nobody wanted to talk about it. Mr. Bester had called down early that morning to abruptly cancel two seminars on Mars.

Oh, well, there was still plenty going on. Too much, in fact. She checked her watch to make sure she wasn't running late to what was shaping up to be her most important appointment of the conference.

"There you are," said a warm voice, and Arthur Malten was upon her. He was dressed in a very conservative gray suit this morning. It was almost an Earthforce uniform, except for the fact that it only had one insignia, Psi Corps, the only one that mattered.

"Arthur," she said noncommittally, barely brushing his outstretched hand with hers.

He lowered his voice. "I'm sorry we never got back together last night. You knew, I struck out with Bester."

"That's fine," she said cheerfully. "There was nothing left to talk about. In fact, I'd rather not talk about it this morning."

She started to move away from him, but Malten doggedly followed. "Now don't be discouraged. That was just the opening salvo. I thought we could slip it past him, so to speak, but he understands your worth. He'll want to take something out of my hide for hiring you, I can see that now. But there are other approaches. We'll find the right one."

Talia wondered if she should tell Arthur right this minute that she wasn't interested in leaving B5. No, she decided, this wasn't the time or place to muddy the waters. Concentrate on the job at hand, her inner voice told her.

Malten rubbed his hands together. "At any rate, now we know he's interested in you and your career. This is something good to find out." He quickly added, "For you."

"Of course," she agreed, thinking of her disturbing conversation with Bester last night. Right now, she just wanted to get this budget meeting finished, then move on to the more pleasant aspects of the conference.

"How should we proceed?" she asked.

"Don't attack Bester or the Psi Cops directly," answered Malten. "But it's okay to rake the military over the coals. I believe in being positive, expressing all the good things we're doing."

He guided her down the corridor, which was flowing in both directions with conference attendees trying to find the right room, or the right person, or the right intimate group. Garibaldi's security people were on hand to provide directions and give everyone another dose of suspicious scrutiny. The ebb and flow calmed her nerves for a moment and made her realize that she, Bester, and Malten weren't the only ones in this place. As much as they thought the universe revolved around them, it didn't.

In three short days, Bester, Malten, and all these self-important people would be leaving. Back to their slimepits, as Garibaldi so succinctly put it. And she would be going back to her peaceful life as the resident telepath on B5, none the worse for wear. What was she so nervous about?

Emily Crane nearly bumped into her. "Oh, excuse me," the researcher said sheepishly.

"Hi," said Talia. She looked over her shoulder, but Malten had been waylaid by a band of commercial telepaths who were giving him last-second instructions.

"How's it going this morning?" asked Talia.

Emily made a face and shrugged. "I'm afraid m-most of the panels and seminars will be free-for-all messes. But what can I do about it?"

"Exactly," said the tall, blond telepath. "That's going to be my attitude from now on. What can I do about it?"

"Oh," said Emily, fishing in her briefcase, "here's that d-data crystal. Nobody takes time to look at figures, but you can say we have them."

"Thanks," said Talia. She slipped the crystal into her slim portfolio and sighed. She had to tell somebody. "Emily, I don't think I'll be joining the Mix anytime in the near future."

The small woman smiled. "Well, it's not for everyone."

"But," said Talia, "I would like to talk to someone about opening a branch office someday. Here on B5."

Emily fished in her briefcase for a program. "There's a seminar on that very subject, t-tomorrow at noon. Terrible time, isn't it?"

"I'll be there," Talia promised. "Thanks for everything."

"You've been a help, too," Emily assured her. "Mr. Malten would never ask this, but you might want to sit close to Mr. Bester."

"I will," said Talia. "Since I don't feel comfortable with this material, I'll be as distracting as possible."

"Good-bye," said Emily. She touched her watch. "I've got a d-demonstration to prepare."

"See you later."

The small woman scurried off down the hall and dashed around the corner. Everybody was in a hurry but Talia; she felt as if her feet were in molasses, and her head wasn't much better. This decision not to press Bester, not to push for promotion, had made her calmer, but it had also left her feeling drained. The adrenaline and emotions that had pumped all day yesterday were gone, without much left to replace them. It was just as well she wasn't doing any demonstrations, because she didn't feel as if she would be able to do an accurate scan on a two-year-old.

Suddenly, Talia had a strange image of Ambassador Kosh in her head. It was a flashback to that silly scan of "Invisible Isabel" three days earlier. She could see the Vorlon's mysterious bulk looming over her, the questioning tilt of his massive head-gear, his tubes and orifices probing the air.

The voice which was not there . . .

A little explosion went off in her head, and she staggered for a moment. She caught herself on the wall before falling down completely. Malten rushed over to catch her.

"Are you all right?" he asked with concern.

"Oh, sure," she lied. "Just lost my balance. How much time do we have?"

Malten checked his timepiece. "About ten minutes, although I suppose you could go in and sit down now." He looked worried. "You aren't scared of Bester, are you?"

"No," she continued to lie. "The only control he has over me is what I choose to give him."

"That's a healthy attitude," agreed Malten with a smile. "The commercial sector had such a banner year last year that he has to give us something. Let's just be polite, and keep hammering away."

"Hammering away," Talia repeated, holding her head. She looked around. "I think I will go in and sit down. Number nine, isn't it?"

"Yes," said Malten, glancing over his shoulder. "I'll see you in a few minutes. I have some hand-wringers out here who need to be reassured."

Talia managed a smile. "Go ahead. I can take care of myself."

She walked to the door of conference room nine, expecting

it to open at her touch. But it didn't open. Then she remembered and pulled out her identicard. When she pushed it into the slot, the door slid open, to her relief. Talia slouched into the well-appointed conference room, expecting to find no one there. But she was wrong.

A chair swiveled around at the head of the amber table. Mr. Bester smiled at her and formed his gloved hands into a triangle.

Talia tried not to look surprised. She almost set her portfolio down at the opposite end of the table, but then she remembered what Emily Crane had suggested. So Talia walked slowly to the head of the table and took the seat to the immediate right of Bester, setting her bag on the floor.

The Psi Cop nodded approvingly. "I figured you to be a punctual person, Ms. Winters."

"I try," she remarked.

"You know," said Bester, "before telepaths came along, people used to do studies on body language and spatial relationships—to find out what people were thinking. For example, there were many studies devoted to the way in which people would arrange themselves in a room, when given free choice in seating."

He smiled. "It tells me something that you would take the seat beside me when there are all these empty seats."

"What does it tell you? Besides the fact that I don't want to shout across the room."

"It tells me," said Bester, "that you wish to be close to the seat of power. We need to see if your colleague, Mr. Malten, will take a seat at the foot of the table, thus showing how much he opposes me. That would also demonstrate how much he wishes to keep his distance."

The Psi Cop motioned to the closest seats. "The military will gang up and surround me. They would have taken your seat, so I thank you for taking it first. My own people will sit to my right, and there'll be two people from Corps Administration. You and Malten alone will represent the profiteering side of things. Do you know, Malten could bring more people to this meeting, but he prefers to do everything on his own. To be honest, Ms. Winters, your presence is just a sub-terfuge.''

If that wasn't a kick in the teeth, thought Talia, she had never had one. So she asked him point-blank, ''Do you know how this meeting is going to turn out? I mean, do you have an open mind, or is this all a facade?''

Bester narrowed his eyes at her. ''I don't know what will happen any more than you do. I'm always prepared for the unexpected.''

The door opened, and three military telepaths entered, looking very important, grim, and ready for battle. One sat beside Talia, and the other two sat across from her, taking the three seats closest to Bester.

The Psi Cop looked at her and smiled.

Mr. Malten, however, did not sit at the foot of the table. He sat to the left of Bester, about four seats away, and nobody sat directly opposite Mr. Bester. Despite his nonthreatening seat, Malten was doing most of the talking in the early part of the meeting.

''You want long-term?'' he asked. ''Look at what we've done. We have managed to infiltrate more cities and planets than you and the military could ever dream about. Bester, while you try with pathetic results to keep what you're doing on Mars a secret, I have a dozen offices there. I have nearly as many people as you have. Because we can work openly, we will always have the advantage.''

Malten leaned forward. ''Commercial telepaths work among the people, and they're not afraid of us. When they receive their first scan in a nonthreatening commercial situation—and it doesn't hurt—then they're more receptive for a security scan later on. We do a lot of good for Psi Corps. We want to keep a bigger percentage of what we make, that's all. We're pulling the load, but we're not getting paid for it.''

One of the military liaison officers began to sputter, but Bester held up his hand. The Psi Cop wasn't angry, thought Talia; he seemed to be enjoying the banter with Malten.

''Granted,'' he said, ''our services are not as popular as

yours. But which are more necessary to the safety and security of the alliance? When telepaths go rogue, nobody but us can bring them down. What should we do afterward—stand on streetcorners and pass the hat?''

The other Psi Cops at the table laughed, but Talia felt another white flash in her brain! She screwed her eyes shut to fight the headache and the dizzy sensation. Luckily, no one was paying the slightest attention to her, because Bester was still speaking:

''When you work in secret, Mr. Malten, as we do, you cannot expect support from the public. You and I are like two different fortune-tellers. One of us gives the customer good news, and the other one gives them bad news. You will be paid well, while we work in ignominy. Don't begrudge us a little handout.''

''I'm crying for you,'' Malten scoffed. ''If your budget is too tight, at least look at some of that huge research and development slush fund in the military.''

''One moment!'' blustered a military liaison. ''We must always be ready in the event of war, not to mention the Martian separatists, and one or two new threats. If any of these cold wars become hot, psi weapons may turn the trick. All of our enemies are using them.''

Talia sat up in her chair and blinked to stop the pain. Blast it, she didn't know what was happening to her, but it felt as if her head was becoming unhinged! She kept thinking of Ambassador Kosh and the strange scans she had been performing for him.

''Gone, like the pickled herring,'' came Kosh's words.

Malten had turned his attack on the military. ''While you go out of your way to antagonize other races, including the Minbari, I'm opening up an office on Minbar. Who is in a better position to do intelligence, you or me?''

Bester rapped his fingers on the table and asked, ''You would perform intelligence tasks with your people?''

Malten smiled enigmatically. ''Let's see what we get out of this budget. If you will stop and look, I think you will find that the commercial sector is poised to be very useful. We have the grass-roots organization which both of you lack. We're everywhere, even Babylon 5. If we had the right facilities and support, all of you could be in commercial jobs, purely as cover, and still be doing exactly what you're doing now."

While Bester and the military liaisons digested that one, Talia Winters bolted to her feet. It was overwhelmingly oppressive in the conference room, and she had to get out!

She thought she was quite calm as she said, "Excuse me, I have to go to the bathroom."

Bester looked at her thoughtfully. "Yes," he agreed, "you had better take something for that headache."

"Thank you," she muttered, but Bester had already turned his attention back to Malten.

"I've heard this before," said the Psi Cop, "vague promises that your people would start doing intelligence work for us. But when it comes time to implement it, they're too busy with their regular jobs! Well, let me tell you . . ."

Talia staggered to the door and pressed the panel that opened it. She couldn't get out quickly enough, and she beat on the door to make it open faster. Then she squeezed out before the door had even opened all the way.

Although it was exactly the same remanufactured air in the corridor, it smelled so much better than the air inside the room that she almost skipped with joy. Maybe she was having a reaction to the fresh paint, she thought with a burst of realization. That was probably it. A thing like that might curtail her conference activities.

Just as she was about to stop and catch her breath, a monstrous explosion ripped through the doorway of the conference room, and the concussion hurled her off her feet! The corridor filled with acrid smoke, and alarms and people started shrieking at the same time. It was bedlam in the corridor, and she was nearly trampled by people rushing to see what had happened.

It was finally a security officer who dragged her out of the way and propped her against the wall. "Medical emergency!" he shouted into his link. "Explosion on Green-12, conference room nine! Injuries and possible dead! We need medteams! Bomb squad!''

"The hull is secure!'' somebody was yelling. "Everyone just stay calm. This was a localized explosion!''

People ran through the corridor with fire extinguishers, and they shot streams of foam into the smoldering remains of conference room nine. Talia looked down at her sleeve and could see drops of blood, although she wasn't bleeding. It was somebody else's blood! The stench invaded her nostrils, and the sirens and voices of the dead and dying split her senses.

Talia covered her ears and screamed! But that scream was more than her mind could accept, and it shut down. The voices stopped, and she toppled over into oblivion.

CHAPTER 10

TALIA Winters awoke in her own quarters, lying in her own bed. She was even wearing the thick flannel nightgown that she liked to wear when she was feeling cold or ill. With tremendous relief, she realized that the horrible explosion had been a dream. Conference room nine wasn't really in flames, and people weren't dying.

It had been a weird dream, she thought, having Kosh in it, hooded aliens, and a bunch of people she didn't know. But how much was dream, and how much wasn't? Was Babylon 5 crawling with telepaths, or was she the only one? What time was it? Where was she supposed to be? As Talia began looking around her tidy quarters, she began to get a sinking feeling, as if she were slipping back into her nightmare.

For one thing, hanging on the closet door was the dress she had worn to the reception the night before. And if that had been real, maybe the budget meeting on Green-12 was real. And if that had really happened . . . well, it couldn't have, it was too terrible to contemplate! It was just the sort of thing that her fevered imagination would concoct before a stressful day. She was probably late to her own panels.

Talia started to get out of bed; but something else caught her eye, and she gasped!

Standing perfectly still by the door was Commander Ivanova.

"I can't believe it," whispered Ivanova. "I was just about to leave." She lifted her link to her mouth.

"Wait!" demanded Talia. She sat up in bed and wiped errant strands of blond hair off her face. "What's happening? Why are you in my room?"

Ivanova took several strides across the small room and sat on the bed beside her to whisper, "Keep your voice down. You've got two Psi Cops outside your door, and I think they would as soon kill you as look at you. But there are two of

Garibaldi's people to keep an eye on them. Of course, all four of them are out there to make sure you don't go anywhere."

Talia rubbed her eyes and tried to figure out what was happening. She decided to repeat the question until she got an answer. "Ivanova," she said through gritted teeth, "why are you in my room?"

Ivanova cocked her head. "I volunteered to watch you. I had to see the woman who reportedly killed four Psi Cops and a military liaison."

Now Talia buried her face in her hands and cried. She tried desperately to wake up again, to leave this nightmare for anything, anywhere else! But she couldn't conjure up any other visions or memories that would drag her away from this tawdry scene. She was stuck here, and she couldn't change it.

The commander activated her link. "Ivanova to medlab. Ms. Winters is awake now."

"Thank you," said Dr. Franklin. "I'll be right there."

"I didn't kill anyone!" insisted Talia.

"Careful what you say," warned the officer. "You might want to talk to a counsel before you talk to me. I'll have to report anything you say to Garibaldi."

"But I didn't kill anyone!" Talia wailed.

There was immediate pounding on the door, followed by a booming voice, demanding, "We want to see the prisoner!"

Ivanova shook her head glumly. "You're in a load of trouble, Talia."

The telepath slammed her fist into the bed and muttered, "I didn't kill anyone, I didn't." She looked up bleary-eyed. "The people who died . . . was Malten one of them?"

Ivanova shook her head. "Malten came through scot-free. Bombs are weird like that. Everybody who was sitting to the right of Mr. Bester got it. You would've gotten it, too, if you hadn't left the room."

"That's crazy!" moaned Talia. "I didn't take a bomb into that room!"

There was more irate pounding on the door, but Ivanova ignored it. "Actually, the evidence is clear that you *did* take the bomb into the room. It was hidden in that slim handbag of yours."

"No!" screamed Talia.

The door banged open, and it was Dr. Franklin fighting his way past two black-suited Psi Cops. "Stay back!" he ordered them. "She's under my care!"

But one of the black-suited cops burst into the room with the doctor before the door shut. He was a muscular lad, still young, with pimples on his face and a scowl of hatred. "Why did you kill them? Why?"

"Get out of here at once!" snapped the doctor.

The Psi Cop pointed a black-clad finger at Talia. "We'll do a deep scan on you. We'll find out why. You know what we do to rogues!"

"Now!" ordered Franklin, balling his hands into a fist.

The young Psi Cop banged the panel to open the door, then he stepped out into a din of angry voices. Talia held her hands over her ears and tried to shut them out, but the voices wouldn't go away until the door finally shut.

Dr. Franklin knelt in front of the frightened woman and looked into her eyes with a small beam of light. She twisted away, still disoriented and hysterical. Finally Talia took a deep breath and told herself that she had to stay calm and face this. She gripped the sleeve of the doctor's smock, holding it steady so that he could complete his examination.

"I didn't set off a bomb," she told the doctor.

"Guess what?" he replied. "It's not my job to figure what you did or didn't do. It's my job to get you well. You were in shock after the bombing, so we sedated you. But physically you appear to be fine. Tell me immediately if you feel any pains anywhere. Otherwise, just get lots of rest. Or as much as they let you."

Franklin stood up and shrugged helplessly. "Medlab is sort of crazy at the moment, so I had them bring you here. You could go to medlab if you wanted, but you might be more comfortable staying here."

Talia wrung her hands and looked from Ivanova to the doctor. "Am I under arrest?"

Franklin looked back at the door and frowned. "I wouldn't expect to be going anywhere real soon."

He turned back to Talia and said sympathetically, "You rest, get something to eat, and we'll give you a thorough exam later. I'll do my best to see that you aren't disturbed too much. I might be able to keep the newspeople out, but I don't know about the rest of them."

Franklin grabbed his bag. "I've got to get back to my prize patient."

"Who is that?" asked Talia.

"Mr. Bester. It's definite—he will live. Whether any of us in medlab will, with him as a patient, I don't know."

Franklin started to the door and turned. "Good luck to you, Ms. Winters. It's been hell for all of us, but that will be over in a few days. Your hell is just starting, I'm afraid."

The angry voices rose a pitch as he opened the door and ducked out, and Talia fought back the temptation to answer them all with a primal scream.

"Wrong," she muttered. "They're wrong."

Ivanova sat on the bed beside her and shook her head in amazement. "I don't know you all that well, Talia, but I never figured you to be a Martian terrorist."

Talia half-laughed and half-cried at the absurdity of it. "Is that what they're saying? I've never even liked Mars—a dusty old place with rabbit warrens for cities. All blue-collar, no decent restaurants."

The telepath suddenly grew very somber. "Listen, I need to talk to the captain or Garibaldi and tell them I'm innocent. I need to clear this up."

"You need to talk to legal counsel," said Ivanova somberly. "You need someone to argue for you, and advise you. You're looking at charges of mass murder, terrorism, and treason. On top of that, the Psi Cops might decide you're a rogue. If they get custody of you . . ." She shuddered and couldn't finish her thought.

Talia started to reach for Ivanova's hands, but she stopped when she realized that neither one of them were wearing gloves. "Help me," she begged. "You be my counsel. Command officers can, in an emergency."

Ivanova leaped to her feet. "I don't think I can. I wish you well, but I don't think I can spend weeks on end talking to *them*. Besides, with charges this serious, defending you could become a career."

"Please," begged Talia. "Just until we see what's going to happen."

"Why me?" asked Ivanova.

"I need somebody who won't be afraid of them."

A firm knock sounded on the door, and the women looked up with a start. "It's Captain Sheridan," called a familiar voice. "And Mr. Garibaldi."

Talia rubbed her eyes and pointed to her closet. "I've got a robe in there. And my gloves."

Before she fetched the robe and the gloves, Ivanova hung up Talia's evening gown from the night before. It seemed like another lifetime ago, thought the telepath, just those few hours. It was amazing how quickly your life could turn to junk.

Ivanova gave Talia her things with a brave smile. "Just stick to the truth."

"That's all I've got," answered Talia, pulling on her gloves. She stood up and pulled off the nightgown, momentarily nude. Ivanova didn't turn away. Talia slipped on the robe, and knotted it. Then she looked at Ivanova and waited for her to open the door.

Captain Sheridan and Mr. Garibaldi entered, both looking as if they had gone through their own set of traumas. Talia could see and hear the commotion outside the door, and a man in a black uniform was shaking his fist.

Garibaldi growled at them, "You'll get your chance!"

"Garibaldi!" snapped Sheridan.

Mercifully, the door closed, ending the angry shouts, for the moment. Sheridan and Garibaldi took deep breaths to try to calm themselves, but their anxiety was more unnerving to Talia than the ridiculous charges against her.

"Thanks for coming," she said, for no particular reason. It was doubtful they had come to rescue her, she told herself.

Sheridan tried to keep his voice even. "Ms. Winters, do you understand what's happened?"

"I didn't do it," she claimed. "I didn't take a bomb into that room."

"Well, then," said Garibaldi, "somebody slipped the bomb into your portfolio. My own forensic people will swear to that. We've got the residue of your handbag all over everything."

"Plus," said Sheridan, "you ran out just before the bomb detonated."

Ivanova stepped between them. "Excuse me, Captain, is this an interrogation, or a trial? You have to let her tell her side of it."

"There's nothing to tell!" shouted Talia. "I was as surprised as anyone when that bomb went off!"

"Why did you get up and leave the room?" asked Sheridan.

"I didn't feel well." Talia frowned, knowing how lame that answer sounded. "It's the truth."

"What did you have in your bag?" asked Garibaldi.

Talia shook her head in desperation. "Just some notes and cards, a conference program, a data crystal—nothing unusual!"

"A bomb is highly unusual," said the captain.

"I didn't know it was there!"

Garibaldi held out his hands, trying to calm everyone and think at the same time. "There are a lot of things wrong with this," he declared. "First of all, it was a very small, very sophisticated incendiary device. We think it was of alien design, because we don't have anything that small that would do that kind of damage, and leave so little trace.

"Secondly," he continued, "just moments after the bombing, that Free Phobos group on Mars was claiming credit for it! We hadn't released a single word about it, yet some jokers on Mars acted like they had won the World

Series. That's the same group who claimed the hotel bombing last week. They must have known about it, but how?''

"I'm not a terrorist," Talia insisted. "I don't even have any connection with Mars!"

Sheridan held up a finger. "Ms. Winters, that's not entirely true. While he was conscious, Mr. Bester gave us the rundown on Ted Hamilton, your uncle."

"No!" The telepath balled her hands into fists and slumped onto her bed. It didn't matter what she said—fate or some terrible power had beaten her to every signpost, turning every one of them to make her look guilty.

"Please," said Ivanova, "there's got to be some doubt in your minds! Had she died in the blast, you would have figured she was innocent. But since she had the misfortune to live, you think she's guilty?"

The first officer continued, very calmly, "Most of us have worked with Ms. Winters for over a year now—has she ever given any indication that she hated Psi Corps enough to blow up a roomful of them? Now, if it had been Garibaldi or me . . ."

Sheridan cast her a stern glare. "Please, Commander, the well-known animosity of my staff toward Psi Corps isn't helping matters."

"But she's right, Captain," said Garibaldi. "If Ms. Winters had an uncle who was in the Mars resistance, you never would've known it from her. I never heard her talk about Mars." He smiled at Talia. "Except once, when I asked her to do a favor for me."

Sheridan scowled. "She wouldn't necessarily broadcast the fact that she had an uncle who was a terrorist."

"Okay," said Garibaldi, "there's one more thing that's really strange. We've been over the conference room a hundred times, and we haven't found any remains of a timer or trigger device. So there must've been a filament or some kind of microscopic fuse inside the charge, and they must've triggered it remotely. But Ms. Winters had only gotten about five meters beyond the room when it blew, and she didn't have any devices on her. In other words, if she pushed the button, where's the button?''

"I didn't push any button!" moaned Talia.

Sheridan shrugged. "If I were the prosecutor on this, I could answer every one of these questions. The fact that this Martian organization already knew about the bombing shows that she had accomplices. So, she planted the bomb, and somebody else detonated it. Or she detonated it, and her accomplice took the device out of her hand while she was lying in the corridor.''

"I didn't do it," said Talia firmly. But nobody was listening to her. It was terrible the way they were talking about her as if she weren't there. As if she were already dead!

Of course, five people were dead, she reminded herself. Five fellow telepaths. She should be out in the corridor, demanding for heads to roll, instead of sitting helplessly on her bed, waiting for her own head to roll. Not only was she in danger of being falsely accused and convicted, but the guilty party was getting away!

She jumped to her feet. "You've got to stop them!"

"Who?" asked Sheridan.

"Whoever killed those telepaths!"

"Okay, Ms. Winters," said Sheridan calmly. "I'm getting the distinct impression that you plan to plead not guilty. Which is fine with me."

Talia lifted her chin and asked, "Are you going to arrest me?"

"We have to," answered the captain. "Everybody is fighting over jurisdiction of this case. If we don't arrest you and have the ombuds try you here, then Bester, Earthforce, or somebody will take you away. If you think you'll stand a better chance with them . . ."

"No!" snapped Ivanova. "If Psi Corps declares her to be a rogue telepath, they can deal with her however they please —without a trial. We can't let them have her."

Talia felt weak in the knees, and she sat down again. More than anything, she just wanted to crawl under her bedcovers and go back to sleep. There had to be some way to exit from this nightmare, if only she could think about it. If only she could remember everything. But it was all such a haze. She hadn't felt right the entire morning, and she had barely said ten words to anybody. Her presence at that meeting had been superfluous, as Bester had claimed it was. No, that wasn't it —he had called her a subterfuge.

Apparently, she was a better subterfuge than any of them had imagined. This was what she got for being ambitious and wanting to play with the big boys. She got used. Even now it seemed as if nobody—not her colleagues in the Corps or her neighbors on B5—really wanted to help her. They had their physical evidence and to hell with her! Somebody had to hang for this.

Talia had to flee from Babylon 5, she decided that moment, and find out who really did this.

"All right, it's agreed," said Garibaldi. "We'll have to arrest you, Ms. Winters. But we'll keep looking. I want to find that detonator, I want to know who's on the station from Mars, and I need to talk to all my people who were doing security on Green-12. Maybe you *did* have an accomplice, even if you didn't know about it."

He looked around her crowded quarters. "Sorry, but we can't leave you here, under house arrest. Bester's people are irate about it, plus all they're doing in the corridor is drawing flies. We'll have to take you to the brig, where we have better control over the situation. I'll give you five minutes to get dressed and pack a few things."

"She'll need a hearing before the ombuds to keep her in the brig," said Ivanova.

"I'll arrange it," answered Sheridan. "You sound like her counsel."

Ivanova nodded. "I am. Until I find her somebody better."

Sheridan rolled his eyes toward the heavens. "If you want me to say I was dead wrong about allowing the conference here, I will. I was dead wrong. Dumbest thing I ever did."

Ivanova glanced at Garibaldi and said, "We know that. I'm still her counsel."

The captain looked at the blond woman. "Is that all right with you?"

Talia nodded numbly.

"Come on, Ivanova," said the captain, "and let's get the paperwork started."

They opened the door, and Sheridan and Ivanova battled their way into an angry crowd, filled with floating video recorders. Garibaldi stared at them until the door closed, and the muscles around his neck tightened.

"Oh, brother," he moaned, "now the press has found us. Talia, what is this mess about? What happened?"

She shrugged and wearily shook her head.

"Who did you screw with?" he asked.

"Go away," she said in a husky voice. "I don't trust any of you. You know I didn't do this, but you're going to put me on trial!"

"That's to keep you on the station, until we find out who did it!"

She sniffed and untied her robe. "Right, you can tell me that when I'm convicted of five murders. Or tell me that when you turn me over to Bester. Or maybe you think I want to spend the rest of my life as the most famous prisoner in the brig of Babylon 5. You can sell tickets—there she is, the Psi Cop Bomber."

Garibaldi pointed at her and promised, "I'm going to find out who did this. You can bank on it."

"Get the hell out of here and let me find my clothes." The blond woman stood up and started to take off her robe, and Garibaldi hurried out.

"Doctor!" screamed a little man lying in the recovery room of a busy medlab. He started to thrash around in his bed, and then he winced and gasped from the pain.

"Doctor!" he cried through clenched teeth.

Dozing in the corner, Mr. Gray bolted to his feet and was the first one to the man's side. "Please be calm, Mr. Bester. It's wonderful to see you looking so . . . so awake, but you must remember your injuries." He rearranged some of the tubes and sheets that covered Mr. Bester.

The Psi Cop slumped back onto the bed, grumbling.

"Yes," said Gray, "your buttocks area was apparently very badly mangled, and the burns on your leg and arm—most unfortunate. Altogether, you were lucky."

"I don't feel so lucky," muttered Bester.

Gray swallowed. "Yes, but look at the alternatives."

Bester laughed sourly. "They can't get *me* so easily. Have they arrested Talia Winters yet?"

"Yes," answered Gray, "the last I heard, they were taking her to the brig. You know, she never struck me as being the violent type. I would have thought she was on a career track. I wonder if she really . . ."

"Don't wonder," said Bester, followed by a coughing fit. "She brought that bomb into the room, I know it! It was no accident that she ran out when she did. But who put her up to it? I don't know that."

"The Free Phobos group is claiming responsibility."

"I know," growled Bester, "but who are *they?*"

Gray looked down apologetically. "The conference has officially disbanded. Transports are taking most of the attendees out tonight."

"Damn," muttered Bester. "They'll get away."

"Who will get away?"

"Whoever put Ms. Winters up to it!" snapped the Psi Cop. "She couldn't have managed this by herself. Who *is* Free Phobos, and why do they want me out of the way?"

Gray cleared his throat. He wasn't about to say what he was thinking, that the number of people who wanted Bester out of the way was too numerous to investigate.

"You've never heard of Free Phobos?" asked the young telepath.

"Not before the first bombing. And not again until this second one. I've had plenty of people looking for them, too."

Bester grimaced in pain and tried to get comfortable in his hospital bed.

"Can I get anything for you, sir?" asked Gray with concern.

Through clenched teeth, Bester grunted, "Yes! Catch the bastards who did this to me! The ones who killed our people. You're still attached to my office—that's a direct order."

"Sir," said Gray, taken aback, "what about your own Psi Cops?"

Bester smiled with satisfaction. "We have Ms. Winters, or soon will have her. She's our dirty laundry, and we will wash it ourselves. We'll find out as much as there is to know from her, but there may be other leads. Follow them, Gray. Get to the bottom of it."

The young telepath felt a grip on his forearm, and he looked down to see burnt fingers wrapped in bandages, smearing blood on his sleeve.

"Promise me," rasped Bester.

"I'll find them," said Gray, removing his arm.

Garibaldi pulled open the door in slow motion, but the lights and the voices struck her in high-speed, strobelike bursts. Garibaldi grabbed her arm and dragged her out of her quarters, because she couldn't make herself move. Talia felt like she was staring at an oncoming train, the rush of people was so intense. The lights blinded her, the hands pushed in, while Garibaldi's security people pushed out. The black-suited ones stood on their tiptoes and shook their fists, shouting:

"Murderer!"

"Traitor!"

"Back!" snapped Garibaldi, like a lion tamer.

She could see a wedge of gray-suited backs forming before her and leading the way down the corridor. Garibaldi wrapped his arms around her like armor and steered her behind the wedge. People stood in doorways and clung like flies to the wall to get a look at her. The same people would have only given her a glance the day before.

The flying wedge swept through a bulkhead and down a ramp, and the crowd of people vanished. She was surprised to see only Garibaldi and his gray-suited security people. As they weren't needed to spearhead the charge anymore, the officers fell back to rear-guard positions. Soon it was just her and Garibaldi, followed by a man holding a PPG rifle.

Irrationally, she thought for a split second, *Can I get that rifle away from him?* But where would she go? How would she get off the station? Talia had to think about it—she just had to think.

Her inner voice was telling her to escape. It wasn't right or wrong, or even logical, but she had to listen. There was only one thing Talia Winters knew for sure—she had to get off Babylon 5 and exit from this nightmare!

CHAPTER 11

GARIBALDI pounded his knuckles together and looked at the bulk of his security staff, most of whom had been on duty the morning before in Green-12. He prowled around the briefing room, peering at their dour expressions.

"I know we're pretty down now," said Garibaldi, "but that assignment is over. Let's move on to the next one, which is to find out who had anything to do with that bombing. Now, who inspected Ms. Winters when she entered Green-12 that morning?"

"I did, sir," said Molly Tunder, a young woman who looked mostly Asian.

"What did you find in her bag?"

Tunder shrugged. "Nothing that struck me as odd. Cards, a conference program, notes on a transparency."

"And a data crystal," Garibaldi put in.

The young officer shook her head. "No, sir, I don't recall a data crystal."

"But she told me she had one," the chief insisted.

"I suppose," said the officer, "she could've been holding it in her hand."

"How did she appear to you?" asked Garibaldi.

"Out of sorts, distracted. But then, it was a stressful situation—the searches and pat-downs. And I couldn't spend much time with her."

Garibaldi knew the feeling. He would rather be down in the brig now talking to Talia, but he couldn't hold her hand and find the real culprits at the same time. There were a million things he wanted to do at once, but he had to calmly step through them.

"Detail one, you're at the beginning of your shift," he said. "As soon as we're finished here, you head Down Below and shake the trees. See if anybody knows anything about anything. And see if you can find Deuce, although I suspect he's already left the station. Deuce has the good sense not to get caught in a bombing."

His link buzzed, and the chief answered curtly, "Garibaldi."

"This is Rupel in the brig. Ms. Winters has a visitor, and she's demanding to see him."

"Who is it?"

"Ambassador Kosh," came the answer.

"Kosh," muttered Garibaldi. Relationships between humans and aliens were hard to explain, but he knew there was one between Talia and Kosh. Maybe the ambassador could help her get good legal counsel. On the other hand, the Vorlon often lived by his own rules, and who knew what they were?

"It's okay," he said. "But have someone present. I'm going to be down there in a few minutes to talk to Ms. Winters. Out."

He turned off his link and looked at the expectant faces. "I've already got Jenkins's report about finding Ms. Winters in the corridor after the blast. Did anybody else see anything?"

There were several seconds of uncomfortable silence before Garibaldi realized that even the professional observers hadn't seen anything. They were as mystified, sickened, guilt-ridden, and angry as he was.

"All right," he concluded, "you've got your assignments. We're looking for Martians, the forensic team is at the scene, and some of us are going Down Below. The good news is that all the telepaths are either gone or on their way off the station, except for the Psi Cops. There are still about fifty of them on B5, so stay away from them. Don't argue legalities with them. If they try to provoke anything, send them to me or Captain Sheridan."

Garibaldi nodded grimly to each of them in turn. "Dismissed."

The word "brig," decided Talia Winters, must have been a euphemism for a kennel. That was the way it felt to her—an airy, roomy, and bare cage for a person, with as much personality as a slab of concrete. She had lots of privacy due to the fact that there was nobody else in B5's neglected brig. Had the place been crowded and the dozen-or-so cells full— she didn't want to think of the bedlam.

Talia prowled her cell like a panther, ever moving, watchful, and ready to spring. At what? The cells were protected by a double cardkey system—first mechanical locks on each individual cell, then a barred doorway operated by cardkey. She didn't know how many guards waited outside the barred door, but she had seen several already.

Suddenly the door opened, and a massive figure filled it. Talia's heart pounded with hope, although this figure was a very strange savior. A bundle of exotic fabrics and armor as smooth as porcelain, Ambassador Kosh glided into the room and stopped a few meters in front of her cell. The head-gear nodded, and little tubes and orifices sniffed the air.

"It is the Hour of Longing," said Kosh in his twinkling, synthesized voice.

Talia snorted a derisive laugh. "You've got that right, Ambassador Kosh." She shook her head in amazement. "Everything going fine, and somebody lowers the boom on you. But I'm glad to see you. I've been thinking a lot about you, including a time just before the bomb went off."

She could see the guard edging closer to overhear them.

"Excuse me," she said, "can we have some privacy?"

"I'm afraid not," the guard answered politely. "Mr. Garibaldi's orders."

"Oh, is that right?" she seethed. "Bless Mr. Garibaldi for keeping the deranged terrorist under a close watch!"

"Anger is a blue sea," said Kosh.

Talia blinked at him, suddenly realizing that she could try to talk to Kosh in that cryptic language of allusions that he often employed. If only she understood it. Well, there was no time like the present to give it a try.

"This pickled herring would join the other ones," she said.

Kosh's bulk leaned forward. "The wings fly at midnight."

"I want to see the World Series," Talia remarked.

The guard squinted at both of them and leaned forward curiously.

"Apple pie," said Kosh, "and hush puppies."

"Inna Babylon, do you know Babylon?" she asked in a Jamaican accent.

"Gone, like the pickled herring."

"The eagle flies on Friday."

"Invisible Isabel," answered Kosh. He turned to the guard and bowed. "Our business is concluded."

The guard stopped scratching his head long enough to go back and open the door to the outer chamber. Ambassador Kosh swept out with grandeur, even in this place.

The guard gave Talia a quizzical look and said, "I don't know what happened there, but Garibaldi is on his way down. He wants to talk to you."

"I refuse to see him," she declared.

"I'll let you tell him that," said the guard.

"Tell me what?" asked Garibaldi, sweeping into the detention center.

"I refuse to talk to you without my counsel present," Talia claimed.

"Not even if it's to clear your name?" he asked incredulously.

She crossed her arms and regarded him warily. "If it's not, I'm going to clam up. I'm tired of talking, because nobody listens. What is it?"

"You told me you had a data crystal in your bag. Is that correct?"

She sighed. "Yes."

"Was it a real crystal, one you had accessed before?"

"Yes, it was," answered Talia. "It had statistics for the meeting, and I was studying it the day before."

Garibaldi frowned, as if he didn't want to hear that. He continued, "The officer who checked you in didn't find a data crystal in your bag. Did you have it in your hand, or a pocket that we might have missed?"

Talia frowned, trying to remember bits and pieces of that

terrible morning. "Oh, yes," she answered slowly. "Somebody had borrowed it and then given it back to me."

Garibaldi leaned forward. "Who?"

Talia started to speak but paused. After what she had gone through, she was reluctant to give out Emily Crane's name and put the poor woman through the same thing. Besides, she was certain that Emily Crane wasn't a terrorist bomber. In fact, the blast had nearly killed her beloved Authur Malten, and that let Emily out of the equation completely.

"I'll remind you," said Garibaldi, "whoever put that bomb in your bag meant for you to die, too."

Talia screwed her eyes shut and tried to keep from losing it. "Are you sure the data crystal was a bomb?" she asked.

"No," admitted the chief. "But it's an object that we know somebody else gave you. Since that's what you say happened . . ."

"It *is* what happened," she insisted.

"Okay, then," said Garibaldi, "this is information *you* need, for your defense."

"Listen," said Talia, "I don't want to unleash Bester and his people, plus all of Earthforce on this poor woman. I really believe she couldn't have anything to do with it."

"Maybe," conceded Garibaldi. "We think the same way about you, but . . ." He didn't finish the thought.

Talia nodded bitterly. "That's why I'm not going to put this woman through what I'm going through."

"Come on," begged Garibaldi. "I promise, I'll check her out personally. Listen, you'll need to talk to her, anyway, for your own defense. I won't give her name out until I've checked her out first."

"You really promise that?" asked Talia. "Because if I see her in this cell next door, and we're both innocent, I'm coming after you."

"I promise," said Garibaldi with a lopsided smile.

Hoarsely, the blond woman said, "Her name is Emily Crane. All I know about her is that she works in the Mix with Mr. Malten."

Garibaldi pressed his link. "Ivanova, it's me. Can you tell

me if Emily Crane has left the station? She was one of our recent guests, a commercial telepath."

"Hang on," said the second-in-command. Several long seconds ticked off before Ivanova reported, "She left in the first transport out. Her boss, Malten, was shaken up, and she was taking him home."

"And where might home be?" asked Garibaldi.

"The destination of the transport is Earth. That's as specific as it gets. They should be there in a day or so."

"Thanks. Out." Garibaldi shook his head. "Earth. Not much chance of me going there real soon."

Talia laughed nervously. "Me either."

"I'll look up her branch office," said Garibaldi. He leaned against the bars of her cell, looking like a sad basset hound. "I'd love to get you out of here, but we're in enough hot water already. Besides, you're safe here. So, is there anything I can get for you?"

"A hacksaw."

Garibaldi had a pained expression on his face. "How about some reading materials?"

She slumped onto her bed and yawned. "Not tonight, okay? I had my dinner, and I think I just need to sleep."

"I'll bring you some books in the morning," said the chief. He started out and turned. "I'm sorry about this. We'll find some way to get your life back to normal."

"Or what passes for normal," said Talia. She stretched out on a thin mattress resting atop a metal frame that was welded to the deck.

"Say, what time is it?" she asked.

Garibaldi checked his link. "Let's see, twenty-three forty."

"Thanks."

"Did you have a nice visit with Ambassador Kosh?"

"Good night."

She rolled away from him, and her eyes darted about frightenedly as she waited for him to leave. Finally, she heard the door ooze shut. She sat up in bed, looking around. There was a surveillance camera in each corner of the room, with its own area to cover, but otherwise, she was alone.

Or was she alone? What had Kosh meant by Invisible Isabel? That had been a game, right? A practical joke. There were no invisible people, really. Although who knew what there was in the Vorlons' advanced culture? She knew she had picked up the trace of a voice on Red-3, after she had eliminated all the visible people in the cafe. Whatever it was, it had been real to Kosh, too.

There were only twenty minutes left, she remembered, before Kosh was going to make his move. But what was his move? What was her part in it? How could she get off the station, even with the Vorlon's help? She had to calm down, Talia told herself, and stop asking questions for which there were no answers. If indeed Kosh had agreed to help her escape in twenty minutes, then he would. If she had misinterpreted his signals and he didn't help her, she was no worse off. One way she was a fugitive, but in the other way she was a prisoner with a celebrated murder trial ahead of her.

She half-expected some calm voice of reason and responsibility to take her aside and tell her that escape from Babylon 5 was crazy. Not only that, but it would make her look guilty. Even the people who defended her now would stop defending her, and probably chase her. But for some unfathomable reason, Talia knew that she could get off B5, and that she *had* to get off, if she wanted to stay alive. Moreover, she had to go to Earth if she wanted to clear her name. It was mad, but she had to do it.

In the clear light of madness, Talia stopped to think about Emily Crane. What did she really know about the small woman who stuttered? She was a licensed telepath specializing in the ad business, but maybe she had deep roots to Mars and the separatist movement. Maybe, in fact, the dark-skinned woman had actually tried to kill her, plus Bester, Malten, and the ones she had succeeded in killing.

What was that old expression, "the banality of evil." Ms. Crane was a banal person, a cipher among the rampant egotism of Psi Corps. Maybe that was just the sort of person a terrorist agency depended upon to infiltrate and do its dirtiest work.

Talia rubbed her eyes and plucked at the white jumpsuit and white gloves she was wearing. It had seemed a logical choice in clothing when she had put it on in her quarters—something comfortable for lounging about the cell—but now it seemed too flimsy and insignificant to get her all the way to Earth. What had she been thinking?

Without really knowing the time, Talia looked up, knowing that something was about to happen. If, she asked herself, there was an invisible being name Isabel in this detention center, what should Isabel be doing? That was easy—she should be unlocking the cell door.

The lock was on a box about two meters beyond the door, and it was operated by an electronic cardkey. In addition to the electronics, a mechanical bolt held the door shut. Talia concentrated on the bolt. Although she wasn't a locksmith, part of her espionage training at Psi Corps had involved the picking of locks and a few other counter-intelligence measures. She knew how a lock ought to work and how it ought to look inside. She couldn't get her hands inside the lock—but that was okay, she had Invisible Isabel. She was beginning to suspect that Isabel was tied to the telekinetic powers given her by Ironheart.

Concentrating very hard, Talia thought about being an invisible person who could slip into a small place and turn the tumblers. She could see her tiny hands running over the miniature components, bypassing the electronics to go directly to the mechanism. When the tumblers tripped, the bolt would spring back. *Move the tumblers, pull the bolt,* she told herself, *just the way you move your lucky penny.*

She ignored the sweat running down her face, slicking strands of blond hair to her pale cheeks. Talia thought only about Invisible Isabel and her tiny fingers. She was real, the telepath told herself; she was real, and she could move those small tumblers. She could, she could . . .

When the click sounded, it was like waking up from a dream. Talia heard her cell door creak open before she could even focus her eyes on it. She stood and pushed it wide open. There was no overwhelming sense of freedom as Talia stepped out of her cell, only terrible fear of what she was about to become. All her life, she had toed the line, done the right thing—a good daughter, a good student, a willing recruit to Psi Corps, and a hard worker ever since. There had been one or two romantic lapses, but youth had to be served. Since then, she had trod the straight and narrow.

She told herself that she was already considered a terrorist, a murderer, and a traitor, and she was about to add fugitive to the list. And rogue telepath. Of all the terrible labels, that one frightened her the most. Maybe she could clear herself of the other charges, but once a rogue telepath . . .

Talia had wandered to the front of the outer door, wondering if she was supposed to open it the same way. There was a small window in the door, and one of the guards jumped up and looked at her in amazement. She didn't hide from his startled gaze. What was the point?

The guard ran to his desk and started to pick up his PPG pistol and a cardkey, but he suddenly did a very strange thing. He started to move like a man who thought he was weightless, like a man who couldn't decide how to put his feet down. A second later he staggered and collapsed to the floor.

Talia pressed her face against the small window and could see two more guards lying unconscious on the anteroom floor. She looked instinctively at the air vents—if there was a gas, it was invisible. Just like her friend.

The seconds seemed to drag on, and there was nothing to do but stand there and wait for the next act of this surreal drama. In a few moments, the door on the other side of the anteroom—the one to freedom—opened, and Ambassador Kosh glided in. If the Vorlon was surprised by the sight of three guards lying unconscious on the floor, it didn't show in his movements. He went straightaway to the desk. When he stopped, a small mechanical claw issued from his ornate robe and picked up the cardkey. Then it extended over a meter to insert the card into the slot, and the door opened.

Talia walked into the anteroom. When she didn't faint, she knew the gas had dispersed even if its effects remained in force. She looked at Kosh, wondering what he would do next. The Vorlon's robe opened, and a little shelf slid out.

Upon the shelf was a Minbari robe and hood. She took the hood and put it over her head. It not only hid her face, but it hid the fact that her head didn't look like the hairless, crested dome of a Minbari.

"I'll be tall for a Minbari," said Talia with a humorless smile.

Mr. Bester was sitting up in his bed. He still looked terrible, thought Mr. Gray, and his mood was even worse. Gray almost felt sorry for the man who stood in front of him, getting a dressing-down.

"Captain Sheridan," growled Bester, "how dare you defy me! You cannot delay justice forever. I will get that woman in my custody—it is inevitable. If you persist in blocking me, it will mean the end of your career! After that pathetic show of security, I wouldn't be surprised if the Senate was already picking your replacement. And if you defy me, and the will of the Senate, by letting Talia Winters elude justice—nobody in the Earth Alliance will be able to save you!"

Sheridan's lips thinned. "Are you done?"

"No!" shrieked Bester. "I'm just beginning. By tomorrow morning, my people will have talked to the senators on the judicial committee. We will have a reversal of your foolish policy so fast that you won't know what hit you!"

"As a matter of fact," said Sheridan, "I've already heard from several Senators. They are putting the pressure on me, and so is Earthforce. But I told them exactly the same thing I'm telling you—this crime was committed on Babylon 5, and that's where we'll try it. We won't rush to trial either. Our investigation isn't complete, and Ms. Winters deserves the best legal counsel we can find. It may take weeks, or months."

Bester twisted in anger and followed it up with a grimace

and a howl of pain. Dr. Franklin, who had been hovering nearby, stepped between them.

"Captain Sheridan," said the doctor, "this man is due to receive artificial skin grafts in one hour. If you can't talk to him without aggravating him, I'm going to have to ask you to leave."

"But *he* summoned *me!*" protested Sheridan.

"That doesn't matter," said the doctor. "He's the one who's lying in bed, wounded."

Bester croaked, "It's okay, it's okay. I'm calm. Sheridan is fighting a losing battle here, and he knows it. If he wants to go down fighting, that's his business. I'll be happy to take him down."

There was some commotion in another part of the medlab, and Gray looked up to see Garibaldi and another security guard rush into the room. Garibaldi had been looking terrible for days, thought Gray, and now he looked worse than Mr. Bester.

"Captain," said the security chief, "we have a major breach in security."

Sheridan visibly blanched. "What's happened now?"

Garibaldi sighed and looked at Bester. "I guess we can't keep it a secret." He turned to the security guard who accompanied him. "Tell them what happened, Rupel."

The guard shook his head, as if he still wasn't sure. "It was peaceful at the brig, nothing was going on. And I looked up and saw Ms. Winters standing on the other side of the door, out of her cell!"

"What did you do?" asked Sheridan.

The man shook his head. "I started to go for my weapon and the cardkey and . . . that's all I remember. The next thing I know, I wake up on the floor, and the other two guards are out cold, too. She got clean away."

With horror, Gray glanced down to see if Mr. Bester had been seized by fits of anger, but the Psi Cop was unaccountably smiling. In fact, he looked pleased with the shocked expressions all around him.

"Thank you so much, Mr. Garibaldi," said Bester. "Your

incompetence has just ended a lot of pointless debate. A telepath who is fleeing prosecution is automatically classified as rogue."

Bester smiled with the delicious irony of it. "Now that Talia Winters is a rogue telepath, we don't need anybody's permission to go after her. Mr. Gray, call my subordinates in. We're going to bring down a rogue."

CHAPTER 12

"SIR," said Garibaldi desperately, "let me go after her."
Captain Sheridan and the security chief regarded each other with a mixture of confidence and uncertainty. They hadn't worked together very long, but they had been forced into a level of faith reserved for old comrades. Despite the way things had gone so far, thought Garibaldi, there had to be a way to pull this out of the fire. The captain had to trust him.

"How do you know she's left the station?" asked the captain.

"We're looking for her," explained Garibaldi. "My people are all over the docks, but we've been so backed up with the conference—and the mass exodus after the bombing—that we've got transports taking off every five minutes! We're eyeballing everything that goes out, but we could be missing something. In fact, we may already be too late."

Garibaldi rubbed his jaw. "To escape like this, she must've had help. I have a hunch about who helped her, and I have a hunch about where she went. There's a lead that only she and I know about—she might try to follow it up."

From his hospital bed, Bester was leaning forward with interest. "I'm a great believer in hunches, Mr. Garibaldi. Tell me, where is she going?" He cocked his head, as if listening, then he smiled. "You don't have to tell me. It's Earth."

The chief looked at the Psi Cop with disgust. "Your people are the ones who spooked her. They're the ones who made her run."

"I don't agree with that," said Bester. "I think fear made her run. But I agree that she had help. She's had help from the beginning, and just like you, I want to find out who's bankrolling this. So let's make a deal."

Bester grimaced as he shifted around to get a bit more height in his bed. "I will hold back my Psi Cops for a few days. Instead, let's send Mr. Garibaldi and Mr. Gray to Earth to find her. And her accomplices.''

Garibaldi turned his attention to the pasty-faced Gray. ''I don't want him coming with me.''

''Okay, Mr. Gray,'' said Bester. ''Let's alert my people on Earth—they can bring her down as soon as she steps off the transport.''

''Wait,'' said Sheridan, holding up a weathered hand. ''Mr. Bester is right about one thing—as soon as he calls the Psi Cops on her, it becomes an assassination. The local police will be after her, too. If we're going to find out anything, we want her investigated. We want all the leads followed up. Garibaldi, if you think you know where she's going, go there. And take Mr. Gray with you.''

Garibaldi shook his head, as if he couldn't believe what he was hearing. ''I work better alone.''

Bester smiled. ''I think you will find Mr. Gray is very little trouble. And he's *not* a Psi Cop—he's not authorized to take her out. He's just an investigator, like yourself.''

Garibaldi looked at Mr. Gray, who gave him an encouraging but nervous smile. He doesn't really want to go, thought Garibaldi; he just wants to get away from Bester, and I can't blame him for that. The security chief decided he would agree for the time being to take the telepath, and ditch him as soon as possible.

He scowled at Gray. ''All right. The last transport for Earth is leaving in an hour, docking bay five. Let's be on it.''

''Absolutely,'' agreed Gray. ''I have some theories of my own about this matter.''

Garibaldi started to tell him where to put his theories, but he decided to tell him after they were safely away.

Captain Sheridan took a deep breath and turned toward Dr. Franklin. ''Why don't you sedate your patient and get started.''

''Not a bad idea,'' said Franklin. ''Nurse, hypo!''

''Wait a minute,'' protested Bester, thrashing around in his bed. ''I need to report in! I need to call the president . . .''

Franklin administered the hypo.

Still scowling, Bester lay back in his bed. "Do a good job, you two," he murmured. "You don't want me to have to get out of this bed and come after you. . . ." His voice trailed off as he fell asleep.

"Mr. Garibaldi," said the doctor, "before you leave, we could use some extra security on the door."

"All right," scowled the security chief, "but having extra people hasn't solved any problems so far."

"We need to think like these terrorists," suggested Harriman Gray. "I have a lead of my own to follow up. I'll tell you about it on the flight. See you later, Mr. Garibaldi."

The slim telepath dashed off to follow his lead, and Garibaldi rolled his eyes at Captain Sheridan. "Sorry, sir, but why are you making me bring him?"

"Just like you said," answered Sheridan, "by ourselves, we haven't done much good so far. Maybe if we join forces with them—I don't know, it's worth a try. And I want to say, I know how you feel about Ms. Winters, but she's a fugitive. Bring her in, if you get the chance."

"I will," agreed Garibaldi. He lowered his voice. "I think it was Ambassador Kosh who helped her. I haven't got any proof, but he went to visit her half an hour before she escaped. Rupel, who's a linguist, listened to their conversation and couldn't understand a word of it."

"All right," said Sheridan grimly, "leave Kosh to me."

Talia sat in total darkness, wondering if she was going to her death, to her freedom, or just going mad. Under Kosh's orders, and against her screaming better judgment, she had ditched her Minbari outfit and crawled into a reinforced cargo box. And that's where she had remained for the better part of an hour now. There had been no instructions from Kosh, except to show her how the pins could be removed from the inside to let the straps work themselves free. Not even a proper good-bye from Kosh or anyone else, and she had been sealed up in this box. Even though Talia knew she could get out by pulling the pins, she had no idea where she would find herself.

She presumed she was on a vessel and that her rescuers had left Bablyon 5, because she had been knocked around by some pretty good g-forces. Or maybe somebody had simply tossed the crate down a stairwell—it was impossible to tell! In the absence of instructions or guidance, what was she supposed to do, stay in the box forever? Or until customs sold it for unclaimed surplus?

Worse yet, she had started to hear scuffling sounds outside in the—wherever she was. The sound was too heavy and massive to be rats, she hoped, but that didn't explain what it was. Could it be somebody moving the crates around? Or a heavy person just passing through? She had heard no voices, which for some reason made her think that it wasn't the crew. And if it wasn't the crew, who was it?

She had reached the level of endurance for breathing foul air and listening to strange noises in the darkness, while hunched in a terrible position. She had to find out where she was, or go crazy. So Talia reached for the pins that held the straps closed from inside. She already knew they would slide out easily, because she had been toying with them in the dark for the better part of an hour.

She felt the smooth sticks come out in her hands, and she knew the straps were now just lying across the top of the crate. All she would need was a swift push to be out of that stifling darkness. But once out, the secret of the box would be revealed. As with many boxes, there would be no putting back the surprise after it popped out. Whoever was shuffling around out there might view her as a stowaway and kill her. Or they might know Mr. Bester, who had to be looking for her by now.

It was the unknown either way, decided Talia, and she would rather die with light in her eyes, fresh air in her lungs, and her back straight. She pushed open the top and stretched.

A creature in rags gasped with fright and fell over a similar crate. Talia jumped out of her own crate and scrambled behind it. They peered at each other with fear and curiosity.

He had long, scraggly hair and a grubby beard, but he was at least human. She was about to welcome him with a big smile, when she saw his hand ease out from behind the box, and it was holding a PPG pistol.

"Suppose you just put your hands up," he said in a Southern drawl. "I didn't know I had company."

"Me neither," gulped Talia, raising her hands. She was instantly afraid she might be better off with aliens or Bester than this seedy character. She didn't want to tick him off by scanning him, and she had a feeling he'd been scanned before and would know it.

She wanted to get a good look at the place where she might die, so she glanced around. To her surprise, she was in another, much larger cargo crate with alien lettering running all around the top. It reminded her of a Dumpster she used to play in as a kid. But there was a naked lightbulb and some sort of ventilation system supplying them oxygen.

"I've seen you somewhere," said the man suspiciously.

She tried to smile. "Well, it's obvious we frequent the same places."

"Keep your hands up," he snarled. He didn't wave the weapon around like a maniac. In fact, he held it very steadily, as if it were an extension of his arm.

Talia looked around again, trying to see if there was any obvious way out of the Dumpster. There seemed to be a lid to the thing, and she could see what looked like a switch box amidst the alien lettering. But it didn't look promising.

Conversationally, she remarked, "I think we have more in common than a lot of people who have just met."

The man gave her a lopsided grin. "Well, maybe we do have some mutual friends. The question is—are you a plant put here to get me, or am I a plant put here to get you?"

He scratched his stubbly chin. "Since I know I'm up to no good, you must be a plant." He lifted the weapon and aimed it at her breastbone.

"I'm running away!" she shouted. "I'm a fugitive!" She put her hands over her face in case he blasted her anyway.

But he lowered the weapon and smiled. "Yeah, now I remember—you're B5's resident telepath. They got you for the bombing!"

He howled with laughter, and she thought for a second
about making a lunge for his weapon. She figured a second
would be as long as she lived, if she didn't make it.

He laughed so hard that he had to dab his eyes with his
dirty sleeve. "I guess you're in too much trouble to turn
anybody in. My name is Deuce."

"Deuce," she breathed. "The one from Down Below?"

He bowed mockingly. "One and the same. I see my reputation precedes me even in the hallowed halls of Psi Corps."

"I didn't do that bombing," she said, as if that made any
difference to a man like him.

"I know," he said, dabbing his eyes. "You were in the
wrong place at the wrong time."

"You know who did it?" she asked accusingly.

Deuce leveled the weapon at her again. "Lady, you were
in the wrong place yesterday, and you're still in the wrong
place. Ask me no questions, and I'll tell you no lies."

Talia was fairly certain that Deuce was going to kill her,
just as soon as she stopped being amusing. But they weren't
alone—wherever they were. Somebody was piloting this
ship, and somebody had made a deal with Kosh to take her
and deliver her somewhere. She and Deuce were not in a
vacuum.

Irrationally, Talia made a lunge for the switch box, trying
to get out. Deuce leaped to his feet right behind her and
knocked her down with a vicious punch to the shoulder.

"Stupid bitch!" he muttered. "Don't you know what
those signs say?"

Talia lay crumpled between the two crates, holding her
throbbing shoulder. She just stared at him, waiting to see if
he would kill her.

"I guess you don't know," he muttered, jerking his thumb
at the strange letters. "This here is a methane-breathers'
ship. We're in a self-contained cargo container with its own
atmosphere. In this case, it's set for oxygen. If you had
opened that hatch, we'd be rolling on the floor, bug-eyed and
suffocating, in about a minute."

"I'm sorry," said Talia, sitting up. "I've never been a fugitive before. I guess I'm not too good at it."

Deuce shook his head, as if he couldn't believe what he had gotten himself saddled with. He sat on the edge of a crate and just looked at her.

"Lady, the problem is, you can't do nothin' for me, and I can't do nothin' for you. You're poison, all the way around."

"That's not true," Talia insisted, shifting around to see him. "I won't ask you any more about the bombing—I don't care what you had to do with it. But I know you can get me a fake identicard and a new name, and some clothes. Maybe that's why my friend put me here with you."

Deuce rubbed the stubble under his chin. "Your friend must be awfully well connected to know my comings and goings. Yeah, I could arrange those things." He smiled at her. "What could you do for me in return?"

Talia wiped her face with her forearm and tried to think. "Isn't there something in your line of work that could use a telepath?"

The criminal leaned back and considered the offer. "There might be. But that doesn't change the fact that you're poison. By now you have Psi Cops, Earthforce, regular cops, and all the school crossing–guards looking for you. I'm small potatoes compared to you."

"Okay," she promised, "I'll leave whenever you say you want me to go." She couldn't believe she was making promises to a petty gangster, who had in some way arranged the bombing. What could she find out from him? She didn't want to think what it would take to gain his confidence.

"I'm going to regret it if I don't plug you now," said Deuce with all sincerity.

"Commander?" said the communications officer at the command center. "A Mr. Gray wishes to speak to you. He says it's the last time, and it will only take a moment."

Ivanova looked down from her station with a sour expression. As there was nothing pressing her for perhaps the next thirty seconds, she picked up a headset and put it on.

"Patch him through," she ordered.

"Is this Susan?" asked an uncertain voice.

"It is, Harriman. What do you want?"

"To say good-bye. I'm leaving on a transport for Earth in fifteen minutes with Mr. Garibaldi."

"So I heard," said Ivanova. "I don't know whether to wish you luck or not. I don't believe Talia Winters is guilty."

Gray replied somberly, "Whether she is or not, it's better we find her than Mr. Bester. This escape of hers doesn't look good, but we all know there's more to this affair than meets the eye. Garibaldi and I will get to the bottom of it. And, Susan . . ."

"Yes?"

"I'm determined to do something that will win you over."

Ivanova finally smiled. "That I would like to see. Take care of yourself, and Garibaldi."

"Thank you, Susan. Good-bye."

Ivanova took off the headset and laid it on the console. Garibaldi and Gray were such an odd pair, she thought to herself, maybe they really would do something useful. The way it was going, they couldn't mess things up much more than they already were.

"I'm sorry," said a synthesized voice, "Ambassador Kosh is indisposed."

"Well, you get him disposed right now!" growled Captain Sheridan.

"I'm sorry," said the voice, "Ambassador Kosh is indisposed. Please contact the ambassador at a later time."

Sheridan banged on the intercom outside the Alien Sector and cursed. Yelling at a computer voice wouldn't really do much good, he told himself, and he had no desire to storm Kosh's inner sanctum. Mainly, he had no desire to see the squidlike Vorlon warships come out of the jump gate and turn Babylon 5 into dust.

Everyone had warned him that Ambassador Kosh marched to his own drummer, but everyone had also said that contact with the advanced Vorlons was worth the occasional misunderstanding. However, in some of Kosh's actions there was no misunderstanding, just a willful disregard for convention. Of course, being unconventional meant being alien, thought Sheridan, and there was no doubt that Ambassador Kosh was alien.

He turned to go, and he nearly bumped into Lennier, Delenn's aide. The Minbari jumped sprightly to get out of the way.

"Excuse me, Mr. Lennier," said Sheridan, "I'm sorry. Did I step on your foot?"

"It's fine," said Lennier. "I keep forgetting, human hearing is not very good, and I should clear my throat when I approach."

"Well, if you're waiting to see Kosh, he's not receiving visitors."

"No," answered the Minbari, "I was waiting to see you, Captain Sheridan."

The captain shrugged. "I have a few minutes. But I warn you, it hasn't been a good week. So I hope you or the ambassador don't have some terrible problem."

They walked slowly down the corridor, and Lennier replied, "We have no complaints, but I'm very aware of your problem. This propensity toward violence is most regrettable."

Sheridan bristled slightly, knowing that was a gibe. He had seen the Minbari in warfare, close up, and he knew they could be as violent as anyone.

"Can you get to the point?" he asked bluntly.

Lennier stopped and gazed at him. "I may have some information for you."

"If it's about the bombing," said Sheridan, "I'm listening."

Lennier grimaced with minor embarrassment. "I became rather well acquainted with one of the attendees, a Mr. Barker. I gather he is a well-placed military liaison." The Minbari smiled. "He considers himself an expert on Minbari affairs, and he is indeed a wealth of information. Most of it over a decade old."

Sheridan waited patiently. He had learned a few things in his life, and one of them was that the Minbari could not be hurried. Whether you were listening to a story or setting up a counterattack against them, they would take their time doing whatever they were doing.

"At the reception," said Lennier, "Mr. Barker had a considerable number of refreshments, and he took me into his confidence. At the time, what he said to me sounded bizarre, but considering the events of yesterday, his remarks were eerily precognitive."

"What did he say?" Sheridan almost screamed.

"He said that he wasn't worried much about Mr. Bester and the Psi Cops, because they were going to be aced out. That was the exact phrase he used, 'aced out.' I asked him who would take their place in the pantheon of Psi Corps, and he said the commercial sector would come out on top, because they had the money behind them. Mr. Barker wasn't too happy about this one way or another, you understand. He envisioned the military getting the short end of the stick either way."

Lennier cocked his head and frowned. "He said that Bester was history, which at the time seemed mere wishful thinking. But the next day, Bester was almost history, wasn't he? And the suspected bomber is from the commercial sector."

"Yes," said Sheridan thoughtfully. "Everybody wants to blame Martian terrorists, but what is B5 to them? That's been bothering me this whole time. Thank you, Mr. Lennier, you've given me something to think about."

"Can I ask one thing in return?"

"Sure," said the captain, fearing the worst.

"Can you explain to me what that means, 'getting the short end of the stick.' A stick has only two ends and is joined at the middle—how can one end be shorter than the other?"

Sheridan sighed. "Actually, it means getting the short end when you draw sticks—I think. Why don't you walk with me to my office, and we'll figure it out."

* * *

Garibaldi gave a pained grin and held out his hand. "After you, Mr. Gray."

The slim telepath nodded his thanks and hoisted his flight bag onto his shoulder. Garibaldi followed several paces behind him on their way through the air-lock and onto the transport *Starfish*. It was the essential red-eye flight with about half the seats empty, and most of the other seats occupied by people who would soon be dozing.

The only passengers who looked wide awake were six black-suited Psi Cops sitting in the first row. They gave Garibaldi a look of unbridled malice as he walked past them with Gray, and he tried not to look their way.

The telepath stopped in the middle of the passenger cabin and asked, "Is this one all right?"

"No," growled Garibaldi, "in the back." He almost asked Gray if they had to sit together, but that would have been a churlish thing to ask in a half-filled cabin. Later on, he would claim to be tired, then he would head off in search of some privacy and elbow room.

They sat in the next-to-last row. Behind them a Centauri was already snoring, his hair sticking up from his pillow like a row of porcupine quills.

Gray opened up his briefcase and took out a stack of transparencies, dossiers, and photographs. Garibaldi couldn't help but watch the telepath arrange these materials in meticulous order. Then the telepath looked expectantly at Garibaldi and asked, "What have you found out?"

The security chief smiled smugly. "I haven't got a stack of files, but I've got one name. And that should be enough."

Gray pursed his lips. "The name is?"

The security chief smiled. "First, you tell me what you've got."

"All of these files," said Gray proudly, "are a record of the bombing at the Royal Tharsis Lodge on Mars."

"Mars?" mused Garibaldi. "I thought we were trying to solve the bombing on B5?"

"But they are related. The Free Phobos group claimed

responsibility for both bombings, and Mr. Bester and myself
were present at both.''

"You saw the bombing on Mars?''

"Thankfully, at a distance,'' answered Gray. "Although if
it hadn't have been for Mr. Bester's quick reactions, both of
us might have been casualties. Do you see why I think
they're related?''

"Yeah,'' said Garibaldi thoughtfully, "unless it's some
kind of conspiracy against the places themselves. What if
somebody had a thing against this hotel on Mars, and they
also had a thing against Babylon 5. So they picked the two
places just to wreak havoc there. What I'm saying is, whoever the idiot was who picked B5 may have also had something to do with the bombing of the hotel.''

"No,'' said Gray, chuckling. "That was *me*. I suggested
Babylon 5.''

Garibaldi jerked up in his seat. *"You* brought them here!''

His hands were reaching for the telepath's throat when a
feminine computer voice made an announcement: "Welcome
to Earth Transport *Starfish,* serving the routes between Babylon 5, Earth, and Centauri Prime. The first leg of our journey
—Babylon 5 to Earth—will have a duration of forty-eight
standard hours. Please settle back in your seats, and relax. A
robotic cart with food and drink will appear in the center
aisle after departure. You may signal for it by pushing the
service button on your armrest. Credits are accepted. Enjoy
your flight.''

Still seething, Garibaldi slumped back in his chair. Forty-
eight hours was too long to sit next to a dead body, and that
thought was the only thing that kept him from throttling Mr.
Gray.

The little man looked embarrassed. "In retrospect, it was a
mistake bringing the conference to B5. At the time, it seemed
a logical choice. Removed from Mars, good security, a new
place for most of them. I was very surprised when the violence followed us from Mars. This makes me believe even
more strongly that the two bombings are related, and not just

by the claims of a mystery group. I don't see how we can solve the second bombing without starting with the first.''

Garibaldi muttered, ''But Talia Winters was nowhere near Mars when the hotel bombing happened.''

''Precisely,'' answered Gray, ''which is an indication of her innocence, or the possibility that she was used as a dupe. Now tell me about that lead you have?''

Garibaldi smiled and closed his eyes. ''When you show me something really good, I'll show you mine.''

''Prepare for departure to Earth,'' purred the synthesized voice.

CHAPTER 13

TALIA screamed new nodules on her vocal cords as she felt the sudden sensation of weightlessness. At first she thought the ship had stopped until she heard the whistling of wind all around them. Deuce cut forth with a litany of swear words, and their voices were quickly drowned out by a rush of air against the Dumpster-like cargo container. They weren't just weightless—they were plunging through planetary atmosphere! Massive gravity had its grip on them.

Then the naked bulb burst, showering them with glass fragments, and the air ventilators stopped working—and both of them were screaming! Talia hardly noticed the way the cargo boxes banged against her, threatening to crush her in the free-fall. She just spun around in the darkness, her body a rubber ball cascading from one wall into another, swiping Deuce and the boxes in the process.

When she realized she might as well die calmly, Talia wrapped her arms around her head, tucked her legs in, and tried to still her galloping heart. Then the floor of the container abruptly rose up and crashed into her! She lay sprawling, gasping for air, as the big crate righted itself and shifted around. Now she heard groanings and creakings of a weirder sort, and air roared around the exterior of their strange vehicle.

"Damn," muttered Deuce in the darkness, "I wish they'd warn us before they cut us loose."

Still gulping air, Talia wheezed, "You *expected* that?"

"Old smugglers' trick. They plot their trajectory over the desert in North America and slow down just enough to push us out. With a parachute. It's not very accurate, but the *federales* are none the wiser that they dropped something."

Talia listened to the air whizzing past them, and she marveled at the fact that she was taking a parachute jump, albeit inside a box with bruises and welts all over her body. Blood was running through the hair on her scalp from a nasty cut.

"The chute is open?" she croaked.

"It had better be," mused Deuce, "or we'll be coyote dinner. But what if they would never find our bodies. We could be legends! Everyone would think we ran off together, you and me, and are living the good life on Betelgeuse 6."

"Yeah," said Talia with a gulp. "So where are we, anyway?" For all she knew, it could be Betelgeuse 6.

"You'll see," answered Deuce. "Brace yourself. I hear the wind changin'."

She had a second or two to curl up in a ball before the giant crate hammered onto something solid. She caught her breath, thinking they were safe, when the Dumpster began to move again. This time it tilted radically to one side and slid down an incline like a house on skis. She tried to scream, but her voice was too raw; she could only stare into the darkness and feel the rattling bumps beneath her. They thudded to another abrupt stop, and this one held, at least until Talia could start breathing again.

"Are we alive?" she rasped.

"Yeah," answered Deuce. "Cover your head—I'm gonna shoot my way out of here. Sometimes the metal starts to melt."

She didn't know Deuce very well, but she had learned to heed his warnings. Talia covered her head, but she kept one eye open to see what he was doing. She gasped when several plasm streaks shot through the darkness and punched holes in the lid of the container. Using the light from the discharge to aim, Deuce worked the smaller holes into a jagged hole about half a meter in diameter, or just big enough for a smallish person to climb out.

Talia squinted her eyes, expecting blinding sunlight to flood through the hole. Instead, soothing darkness greeted her eyes, plus the sight of nearly as many stars as a person saw in space. A city girl, she wasn't sure what all this meant.

"Where are we?" she asked.

"I told you," muttered Deuce, "you're gonna die here

real soon if you don't stop asking me questions. If you're going to be useful to me, you've just got to obey me, and that's it."

"Sorry," she answered. Talia knew she had a secret weapon in her ability to scan him, but she had a feeling that Deuce had been scanned before and would know it. Behind the rough exterior was a cagey and cool intellect, and she had every reason to believe that Deuce was as ruthless as he claimed to be. He would kill her for a slight provocation. So she opted to lie low and pick the time and place to scan him, knowing she might only get one chance.

In the dim starlight, she could just see Deuce scrounging around in his crate, the one in which he had been smuggled aboard the methane-breathers' ship. He finally pulled out a black briefcase and a dirty duffel bag. He opened the duffel bag and took out a crowbar, which he used to pound down the ragged edges of the hole he had shot open. His pounding turned the crate into a tin drum, and Talia had to cover her ears. Deuce finally stopped and took a flashlight out of his bag to study his handiwork.

"There," he drawled, "at least we'll have air. Want to go out and take a look around?"

Talia shook her head worriedly. She was beginning to feel that terrible panic she had felt upon waking up after the bombing—the shock, the disorientation, the feeling that she was stuck in a nightmare.

In fact, she told herself, she *was* stuck in a nightmare of the worst sort—reality. There was no waking up, so she might as well deal with it. She was in a shot-up Dumpster in the middle of the desert, chased by everyone, in the company of a murderer. No matter where they were, she was dependent upon this criminal for the time being, and it might get worse before it got better.

One thing Talia knew would never be the same—she would never again be smug about her life. Right now, being the lone human telepath on an out-of-the-way depot for aliens sounded just fine, the dream job. She would never again knock it or quest after anything higher. And if she could get back to that life, she would be eternally grateful. Right now, she wondered if it was even possible to recapture any shred of that past.

While she was musing in the dim light given off by a holeful of stars, Deuce turned on his flashlight again and began searching for something else in his duffel bag. He drew out a small electronic device, checked to see that it hadn't been damaged, then pulled out its antenna. He pressed a button on the device, and a red light began to blink on and off.

Talia was about to ask him what it was, but then she remembered: No more questions. Perhaps she should just stop talking altogether. Hobnobbing, being charming and gregarious, had only gotten her into trouble in the last few days. And when it had mattered, when she kept telling everybody the truth, nobody would listen to her. Maybe she should adopt Deuce's motto: Ask me no questions, and I'll tell you no lies. If she said nothing at all, she couldn't say anything wrong.

She was startled by a thud as Deuce turned one of the crates on end. Then he proceeded to climb up and peer out the hole. He made a low whistle.

"We are really in the middle of nowhere. I hope my boys have some decent coordinates."

Talia started to ask if this was really Earth, then she remembered not to talk. That device was some kind of homing beacon, it was clear, so somebody was out there, looking for them. She suddenly had a strong instinct to get out of the crate, and she pounded on Deuce's calf.

"Hey!" he shouted down. "What's the deal?"

She tried an experiment and told him telepathically to get off the crate.

He blinked at her and smiled. "All you had to do was ask."

Deuce climbed down and Talia climbed up. By standing on her tiptoes, she could just get her head, the top of her shoulders, and one arm out through the hole, but she was glad she had made the effort. Their little vessel was parked at an angle at the bottom of a dry wash, buried halfway under the sand, and surrounded by scrubby desert. Trailing behind them like a tattered bridal veil was the parachute that had saved their lives. It was ripped and streaked with dirt from the tumble down the wash.

In the blue starlight she couldn't see very far, but she could see gnarled trees at the rim of the wash and other ghostly shapes. Mesquite trees, Joshua trees, chollas, yuccas, prickly pears—she tried to remember all the spiny, weirdly shaped flora that grew in places like this. She was glad this desert wasn't just sand dunes but had some vegetation to it, even if the plants did appear stunted and misshapen.

She suddenly had an overwhelming desire to stand on the ground. After the nightmarish events of the last three days, she just had to get out and stand on firm ground. She began to squirm out, and Deuce put a hand underneath her foot to give her all the leverage she needed to get her hips through.

Talia screamed as she slid down the tilted side of the crate and plummeted into the sand. It got into her mouth and hair, but its grittiness felt wonderfully real, and the air smelled like perfume after that stifling container. After her scream, the desert was silent, but as she sat without moving for a few minutes, the twitters and chirps came back. She heard a distant howl. Unaccountably, Talia felt relaxed and unafraid for the first time since that awful morning of the conference.

The telepath was startled a moment later when a black briefcase landed in the sand not far from her. She reached over to open it, but the clasps were locked; it was a solidly built case. She pushed the briefcase away and ducked when the dirty duffel bag came flying out of the hole a moment later. The bags were followed by Deuce himself, squirming through the small opening. Like Kosh, he was an unlikely savior, she thought, but if she would ever end this nightmare and get her previous life back, she needed him. She would leave him his blood money in the briefcase. He had probably earned it.

She scrambled out of the way as she saw Deuce getting ready to slide down the crate and hit the sand. He rolled athletically off the edge of the crate and landed on his feet, never losing his grip on his PPG.

"Ah," said Deuce, "that's better. If we haven't been found by midday, we're going to regret getting out of there. But maybe we can crawl under it for shade."

He plopped down in the sand and fished a hat out of his duffel bag. "So," he drawled, "know any good jokes?"

She looked at him intently for several seconds, and he nodded. "You're not going to talk anymore, huh? Are you, like, suffering from some kind of trauma?"

Talia nodded, and it was the truth.

"So, when my friends show up, you're a mute, right? And you ain't no telepath."

She nodded again. "Not a bad cover," agreed Deuce, "because you can still communicate if you want to, with certain people. This ain't new to me, you know. I've had experience with telepaths before."

Talia nodded. She was almost certain of that.

Despite his best intentions to ignore the telepath, Garibaldi found himself peering over Gray's shoulder at his stack of files. As the transport *Starfish* made its way to Earth, Gray began to explain his documents in a conversational tone that the security chief found he could tolerate.

"These are the photos and dossiers of all the people who died in the hotel bombing. Twenty-seven of them, according to the reports, although not all the bodies were recovered."

"That's not uncommon on Mars," said Garibaldi. "In that atmosphere, an unprotected body can get desiccated very quickly. And the winds are strong enough to blow a body clean away, or it could fall into a crevice and disappear. Not to mention the difficulties of mounting a real search outside."

"At any rate," said Gray, "the police didn't investigate these people too thoroughly, because they think they're victims. They also found tracks outside the hotel, so they assumed the bomber came overland. This plays into the stereotype of the usual Martian terrorist, a madman who lives in the wilds and would be spotted immediately in polite company. But what if it was an *inside* job, like the bombing on B5?"

"You mean, the bomber is one of the missing employees?" asked Garibaldi doubtfully. "That's pretty farfetched, without some evidence."

"I've got some evidence. Remember, Mr. Bester and I were at the site when it happened. When a person is going through a psychic trauma, their mind sends out a sort of SOS —a telepath can hear it for miles. And these people were dying as they were being sucked out of the hole in the side of that hotel. We could hear their voices, screaming for help, just as well as I can hear your voice now.

"Mr. Bester told me that he counted twenty-six voices, and I think he's right. But the reports list twenty-seven deaths, or should we say, dead and missing. I trust Mr. Bester's talents, and I think one of those people lived."

Gray leaned forward in his seat and eagerly explained, "All they had to do was to carry a suit and a breathing mask with them when the blast went off, and they could just walk away! Maybe they would leave one or two footprints going in both directions to fool the police. It was night, and somebody could've had a rover waiting for them."

Garibaldi rubbed his chin thoughtfully. "I can see the advantages," he admitted. "You're working inside, and you have your leisure to plan it all, get the bomb in, and detonate it. They don't investigate you, because everyone thinks you're one of the victims."

"There is a modus operandi match, too," said Gray. "Ms. Winters would have been a victim, too, if she hadn't walked out when she did. Plus, that bombing on Mars made everyone take the Free Phobos group seriously, even though nobody knows anything about them. It was a setup for the B5 bombing."

Garibaldi smiled and asked, "Can I take a look at the photos of those hotel employees?"

"Certainly," said Gray, looking pleased with himself.

He handed over a stack of colored transparencies, and Garibaldi studied them intently. Most of them were what you would expect hotel waiters, cooks, and buspersons to look like—young, disadvantaged, with the pale pallor and surly expressions that typified people born on Mars. It was a hard place to live, and a lot of Martians resented having to bow and stoop to wealthy tourists to bring home a few credits. None of the employees' photos showed smiling faces, eager to prove themselves.

On his second pass through the photos, Garibaldi stopped. There was a young, dark-skinned woman in a hairnet, an assistant cook. He looked at her eyes. They were not sullen eyes like the others, but they were guarded, as if she were trying not to reveal anything. But she didn't fully succeed, because he knew he had seen her somewhere before.

More importantly, she had worked at the hotel for only a week when the bombing occurred.

"This is a possibility," said Garibaldi. "Do you recognize her?"

Gray turned the photo several different angles. "I'm not definite, but she bears some resemblance to the woman we flew to B5 with, the one who accompanied Mr. Malten."

"Do you know her name?"

Gray shook his head. "She was a mousy type—didn't stick in the brain too well."

Garibaldi sat forward and whispered, "If she's the one who flew in with him, then she's probably the one who flew out with him. I think her name, as a telepath, is Emily Crane."

Gray gave him a sidelong glance. "Is that the name you have?"

Garibaldi nodded. "Yep. She borrowed a data crystal from Talia Winters, and she returned it to her the morning of the bombing."

"Does anybody else know about her?"

The security chief shook his head. "No one."

"Uh-oh," said Gray with wide eyes.

"We can find her," said Garibaldi. "I promised Talia I would check her out myself. Besides, we don't want the regular cops or the Psi Cops shooting her, or spooking her, before she can clear our suspect.''

"No, that's not what I meant." Gray pointed down the aisle.

Garibaldi followed his finger and saw the six Psi Cops slouching their way down the aisle. In their black uniforms, they looked like a motorcycle gang from twentieth-century visuals Garibaldi had seen. Before he even had a chance to unfasten his seat belt, the six were leaning over him and Gray.

"You let our people get killed," snarled one. "And then you let that murderin' bitch get away."

"Leave Mr. Garibaldi alone," ordered Gray huffily. "He did the best he could."

"Shut up, worm," snapped another. "We don't think he did the best he could. If you know what's good for you, you'll stay out of our way."

One of them grabbed Garibaldi's collar and tried to hoist him out of his seat, but his seat belt held him fast. So instead he slapped the security chief hard across the face.

As Gray stared at him with concern, Garibaldi massaged his inflamed cheek. "Is it going to take the six of you to beat me up?"

"Yep," said another one. He put his foot on Garibaldi's toes and tried to grind them into the deck.

This time, the security chief yelped with pain and jerked his foot back. Gray was still staring at him, wondering what he would do.

"Keep your belt on," he whispered to Gray, "and hang on to your papers." The little man did as he was told.

"You're hot stuff on your own turf," said one of the Psi Cops, "but off it, you're nothin'. You're yellow."

"No," said Garibaldi, "I'm just smart. For example, did you fellows know that there's an emergency pull cord under the seats of this kind of transport? If you didn't know, there's a little sign over on the bulkhead that explains it."

But they weren't listening. A brutish Psi Cop gripped his collar again. "Now it's time to send *you* to the medlab."

Garibaldi reached under his seat and yanked on the emergency cord. At once, alarms went off inside the cabin, and another thing happened. The ship began to slow to a stop. With the absence of acceleration, the simulated gravity inside the cabin stopped also. The six Psi Cops, and anyone else who had been moving around the cabin, began to float weightlessly.

"Help!" screamed one, as he floated past Garibaldi, who was still strapped safely in his seat.

"Let me help you," said Garibaldi. As the man floated helplessly past him, the lanky security chief reached up and grabbed his collar. Holding him steady, he smashed him in the nose. Globules of blood went floating out of his nostrils. Clutching his documents, Mr. Gray watched all of this in amazement.

When the man tried to retaliate by swinging his fists, Garibaldi just gave him a shove, which sent him spinning into the bulkhead. There was a loud clang as his head hit the metal. The chief then calmly grabbed the leg of another Psi Cop who was floating past and pulled him down just far enough to punch him in a very sensitive spot. The man howled with pain, and Garibaldi sent him crashing into the ceiling.

By now the other four Psi Cops were trying desperately to get away from Garibaldi, but all they could do was float. They were saved by the captain's voice on the intercom.

"What's the matter back there?" she asked. "Who pulled the emergency stop?"

"I did, Michael Garibaldi, Security Chief of Babylon 5," he reported. "There was an altercation, and this was the simplest way to end it."

"I hope it's over," said the pilot. "Because you've cost us at least half an hour. That's the time it will take to get us back up to speed. Anybody floating will just have to keep floating until then."

"Too bad," said Garibaldi. A Psi Cop floated overhead, and Garibaldi flicked a long arm up and punched the man in the stomach. The Psi Cop groaned and rolled over.

The chief smiled at Mr. Gray. "There's a lesson in this—it's not good to be overconfident."

"I never am," Gray replied somberly.

The first rays of sunlight brought the slate-colored clouds to life, and they looked like the underbellies of a herd of buffaloes, slowly stampeding across the sky. Talia could see their woolly heads, their massive horns, their hooves, and the steam which shot from their nostrils. The crest of rugged mountains to the north was like a fence that penned them in, with the sun chasing them from behind.

Talia watched, fascinated, as the fiery dome of the sun rose over the desert floor. The vast desolation of this land was both frightening and soothing. It reminded her too much of her present life—drained and shot to hell, but filled with a strange promise of light that could chase away the darkness.

Deuce was asleep in the sand of the dry wash, clutching his briefcase and his PPG pistol across his chest. She could easily wrench one or both away from him now, but what good would that do her? Where could she go without Deuce and his friends, whoever they were? She did steal a few sips of his water, though, after she found a canteen hidden in his duffel bag. With Deuce's well-developed sense of self-preservation, he had failed to mention that he had any water.

Talia climbed out of the wash and watched the sun thaw the dew off the flat leaves and thistles of the plants which grew along the wash. It had been a long time since she had seen a sunrise on Earth, and the woman couldn't help but to feel a bit sad and homesick. She fought the temptation even to think about going to see her family. They would be watched. They would be hounded by newspeople, police, and the curious. Her family was undoubtedly going through hell, and that was just more incentive, if she needed any, to clear her name.

The distant mountains were taking on a reddish hue, and they reminded her of all the lakes, plains, and forests of this magnificent planet. Talia wondered if she would ever see those natural wonders again. She had thrived on an artificial satellite in a distant part of space, so maybe she could thrive anywhere, without her friends and family. Maybe she could be an expatriot of Earth. In truth, Talia wanted to join the migration of clouds across the sky, just a nebulous being who never had to worry about people, death, or detention cells.

She didn't know how long she stood there, watching the ragged horizon, before she saw them. At first, it seemed they were just another copse of misshapen trees in the distance, but the black specks kept coming closer. It was their unerring march through the wilderness that made her certain they were coming for her and Deuce. But who were they? What were they?

As the specks drew closer, she decided they were Hovercraft. She counted four of them, small ones. Talia supposed that a Hovercraft was a good vehicle for this type of terrain, which was treacherous but mostly flat. She heard some footsteps crunching the sand behind her, and she turned to see Deuce. He was drinking from his canteen, and he offered it to her without comment. She took a long drink this time. They were saved, so to speak, and there was no reason for Deuce to hoard his water any longer.

Talia glanced at the criminal, and he shook his head. "No, they're not like me. And they're not like you. Unless you lived about five hundred years ago, they're unlike anybody you've ever met. This is their home. Don't make fun of them, okay?"

Talia shook her head. She was not in any position to make fun of anybody, especially people who would consider this wilderness their home.

With reluctance, she removed her white linen gloves and folded them in the pocket of her jumpsuit.

CHAPTER 14

FROM his duffel bag, Deuce took out a pair of banged-up but good binoculars and handed them to Talia. She nodded her thanks and put the lenses to her eyes to study the approaching party. The four Hovercraft were clipping along at a good rate of speed, spewing up dust clouds behind them, and she realized with a shock that the pilots were all women!

As she looked closer with the binoculars, Talia decided that they weren't necessarily women but people with very long hair that whipped in the wind. Two of them were bare-chested, and she could see their bronze skin glistening in a halo effect created by the morning sun at their backs. It wasn't until she saw the stylized eagles painted on the noses of the Hovercraft, and the feathers flapping from the roll bars, that she felt certain who they were. In this wilderness, it made sense.

Indians, she thought aloud.

Deuce chuckled. "Well, real Indians wouldn't think so. Those are Bilagaani, as they call themselves. White Indians."

Talia nodded. She had heard of the White Indians, people who had forsaken their own culture to emulate the culture of another race that had flourished five hundred years earlier. They were shunned as pariahs by actual Native Americans, at least those who were trying to maintain their culture. Many Native American tribes had gotten rich and conservative from gambling enterprises around the turn of the millennium, and they had given up any effort to maintain their culture. The White Indians had picked up where they left off, often moving into deserted Indian villages.

"Don't be fooled," said Deuce. "This ain't a game to them. They take it real seriously, especially the religious parts. Some of them were born and raised this way, so they don't know any different. Others have come along, bringing

their big-city skills with them." Deuce smiled. "Those are
the ones I like."

The grubby criminal motioned at the vast desert. "They
live out here where nobody else will live, and nobody pays
them much mind. So they do little favors for people like
me." He smiled at Talia. "People like *us,* I should say.
You're a much bigger criminal than I am."

She glared at him, and the man laughed. "I won't tell
them who you are. But there should be a big reward for you
by now. Better watch your step."

Talia nodded somberly. After another twenty minutes, the
four Hovercraft came shooting out of a gully, skimming over
the crusty sand. She could hear the hiss of their powerful
propellers. Unlike wheeled vehicles, thought Talia, these did
little to disrupt the ecosystem, other than blowing the sand
around. The Hovercraft looked like blunt-nosed racecars,
with roll bars and a combination spoiler/solar panel in the
rear of each vehicle. The fanciful eagles and coyotes painted
on the craft did much to make them look authentic, but the
people driving them only succeeded in looking strange.

The Bilagaani stopped their vehicles and turned off their
engines, and the Hovercraft settled into the sand. One by one,
the drivers got out, stretching their legs. There were no cries
of greeting, no rush to shake hands with Deuce and Talia. In
fact, there was a deliberate reserve in their actions, as if a
rushed greeting would be unseemly. Their hair, driven into
ratty knots by their journey, hung to their waists. They were
wearing moccasins and thick flannel pants tied with draw-
strings; two of them wore crudely sewn shirts made from the
same material. From their necks hung leather pouches, and
there were short knives strapped to their arms.

One of the bare-chested Bilagaani was a tall, muscular
man with chestnut-brown hair. He was the kind of character,
thought Talia, who existed mainly in fiction—romantic,
handsome, although caked with dirt and sweat. The other
bare-chested Bilagaani was a middle-aged woman with
brown hair, and her breasts were as tanned as the rest of her.

The third one was an older man with white hair, and the fourth one looked like a boy.

Finally, it was the man with white hair and a creased face who approached them and held up his hand in greeting. "Brother Deuce," he said, "I hope all goes well."

"Brother Sky," said the gangster, "it is well to see you again."

Talia felt the others staring at her, and she stared right back. After her adventures of late, she was certain she was just as grungy and disreputable-looking as the rest of them. She could feel the caked blood in her scalp and on her forehead. And she felt bare without her gloves.

"What is your name, child?" asked Brother Sky.

Deuce shrugged. "She don't talk, and I don't know what her name is. But I would like to make some arrangements for her."

Sky smiled benignly, showing several missing teeth. "We will double your fee."

"What?" squawked Deuce. "You had to come out here, anyway! How can you double it?"

"Very well," said Sky, "we can leave her here, to feed Brother Coyote."

"All right," muttered the gangster. "But she needs everything I'm getting—new identicard, passage east."

Sky held up his hands in a token of peace. "The Creator will provide." He turned to the handsome one. "Make our peace with the land for this intrusion."

The young man leaped down into the wash and took only a few strides to reach the half-buried cargo container. He gathered up the parachute and stuffed it into the hole in the top of the container. Reverently, he took his pouch off his neck, opened it, and faced the east. As he spoke words in a language which Talia didn't recognize, he took bits of dried vegetable matter from his bag and tossed them into the wind. Everyone watched silently as he repeated this procedure facing the south, the west, and the north. Then he returned the pouch to his neck and climbed out of the wash.

"Father," he said, "we should return here and break down this container. There are things we can use."

Sky nodded. "Yes, my son. That is well." The old man motioned toward his Hovercraft. "Deuce, you will ride with the boy, as he is lighter. Your friend will ride with me."

The old Bilagaani studied Talia for a moment. "You will need a name, at least for the period you stay with us. Since you come from the sky, I will call you Rain."

Talia nodded and smiled. She liked the name Rain.

Boston was a strange city, thought Garibaldi, as he and Harriman Gray rode an autotaxi through the financial district. Mixed among the gleaming skyscrapers with mirrored surfaces were these old gray buildings with bay windows and skylights. The autotaxi shuddered up a steep hill, and they got a glimpse of the sparkling ocean and a sleek ocean liner at the dock. Then they plummeted down the other side of the hill and entered a grimy tunnel that looked as if it had been built at the dawn of time. The whole city seemed a dichotomy, thought Garibaldi, both modern and ancient, clean and dirty, with the usual big-city feature of way too many people.

They emerged from the tunnel, and the robotic car jerked sharply around a corner, following an invisible track in the street. Gray was thrown against Garibaldi by the centrifugal force.

"Sorry," said the telepath, straightening his shoulders.

"Why are you sorry?" asked the security chief. "You're not driving. We did tell this thing to go double-time."

Gray sighed and flicked on the viewer on the dashboard. He flipped stations until he found some news, and Garibaldi wasn't surprised to see a photo of Talia Winters.

". . . whose whereabouts are still unknown," said the newscaster. "The commercial telepath has been implicated in the recent bombing on station Babylon 5. She made good her escape three days ago and has not been sighted since. In addition to being wanted by authorities for the bombing on Babylon 5, Talia Winters has been declared a rogue telepath by the governing body of telepaths, Psi Corps."

"What?" growled Garibaldi. "I thought Bester was going to lay off for several days!"

Gray shrugged. "Maybe he woke up from his surgery in a bad mood."

"If you have any knowledge of the whereabouts of Talia Winters, please contact your local police or Psi Corps office."

Garibaldi flicked off the viewer. "Sheesh," he muttered. "If she lives through this, it'll be a miracle."

"I don't believe our chances of finding her first are very good."

"Yeah, but we're the only ones who know that she might be coming after Emily Crane. It's a long shot, but it's worth a try."

The vehicle came to an abrupt stop in front of one of the behemoth skyscrapers, not one of the charming stone buildings. Gray and Garibaldi looked at one another to see who would be the first to draw his creditchit.

"Your expense account has got to be better than mine," observed Garibaldi.

The telepath sighed and ran his card through the slot. "Thank you," said a synthesized voice. The doors opened, and they stepped out.

"Floor thirty-eight," said Garibaldi, looking at his electronic address keeper.

Garibaldi's Earthforce uniform and Gray's Psi Corps insignia got them past the security guards in the lobby without any problem, even though they didn't have an appointment. Garibaldi and Gray had agreed not to alert Emily Crane that they were coming; they wanted to surprise her and judge her reactions for themselves. Even though the rest of the universe thought Talia Winters was guilty, Garibaldi was going to prove them wrong. He just hoped he could do it before Bester and his goons got ahold of her.

The receptionist of the Mix office on floor thirty-eight was a dour-looking older man. At least he looked dourly at the two uniformed men as they approached his desk. His nameplate read: "Ronald Trishman."

"Hello, officers, what can I do for you?" he asked, while grabbing a keypad and trying to look busy.

Garibaldi tried to be charming but businesslike. "Does Emily Crane work here?"

"Who are you gentlemen?"

"I'm Michael Garibaldi, Security Chief of Babylon 5, and this is Mr. Gray, Psi Corps military liaison, currently under assignment to Mr. Bester. You've heard of him, right? We would like to see Emily Crane."

"Do you have an appointment?" asked Ronald Trishman, showing his displeasure.

"No."

"I'm afraid you'll need an appointment."

"That's a nice try," said Garibaldi. "Tell her she can talk to us or the Psi Cops. It's her choice."

The receptionist swallowed and touched a commlink panel on his desk. "Ms. Crane, there are two gentlemen here to see you. One is the security chief of Babylon 5, and the other is a telepath working for Mr. Bester. They say you can talk to them or to the Psi Cops."

"Please send them b-back," came the answer.

"Room two twelve," said the man. He buzzed open the door to the inner chamber, and Garibaldi was there in two strides, with Gray rushing to keep up.

When they found room 212, Emily Crane stood waiting for them in the doorway, a look of concern on her plain face. She was wearing a brown suit that was too long for her diminutive height, and it didn't do much to enliven her personality either.

"Hello," she said simply. "Come in."

She ushered them into an office that was a considerable contrast to her appearance. It had striking furnishings of a Frank Lloyd Wright influence, with ornate fractals carved into her Mayan-styled desk, conference table, and bureau. Emily Crane seated them in comfortable chairs decorated with a Mayan pattern in blood red.

Gray managed a smile and was the first to speak. "We're

sorry we have to bother you, Ms. Crane, but there's a matter we have to clear up."

Garibaldi crossed his legs and smiled benignly. They had decided in advance that Gray would do the questioning, because he was a fellow telepath. She might open up more for him. If he faltered, Garibaldi would step in and play good cop/bad cop. He was looking forward to being the bad cop.

Ms. Crane said nothing and waited for Gray to go on. Garibaldi realized that talking was not her strong suit, and she was going to do as little of it as possible.

"I'm assigned to Mr. Bester," said Gray, "and he is convinced that Talia Winters is guilty of the bombing on Babylon 5. She claimed to have certain items in her handbag, but her recollection does not match the recollection of the security officer who searched her on the way in."

Gray smiled rather charmingly. "This may seem like a trivial matter, but we need this information for the sake of completeness—to know exactly what was in her bag. Did you give Ms. Winters a data crystal sometime that morning?"

"Which morning?" asked Emily Crane. "We were passing a data crystal back and forth—m-myself to Mr. Malten and Ms. Winters. It was a very hectic t-two days."

Good dodge, thought Garibaldi. It wouldn't be easy to tie Emily Crane to this, especially with Talia on the loose, unable to testify and looking more guilty every minute. He had to remind himself that he was the only one in the entire universe Talia had told about Emily Crane.

"We're talking about the morning of the bombing," answered Gray. "After you had passed through security."

Garibaldi sat up with a start. He knew that he had seen Emily Crane before, but he hadn't remembered exactly when. Now he knew! He had checked her through himself that morning—in fact, he had held the bomb in his hand! That was twice he had held the bomb, if you counted his dream.

When he turned back, he found Emily looking at him in a strange way. She was scanning him!

"Stop it!" he barked. "You just answer the question, all right. Did you hand her that data crystal, the one I let you take through security?"

"No," she answered haughtily. "If you want to try to prove I did, good luck."

Garibaldi lost it and jumped to his feet. Leaning over her desk, he shouted at her, "You killed *five* of your own kind! And now you're going to let an innocent woman hang for it! I thought I had seen every kind of monster in Psi Corps, but, sister, you take the cake!"

Gray was holding his shoulders, restraining him more in symbol than reality. "We'll get her for it," he said with a sidelong glance at Emily Crane. "Remember, we can place her at the hotel bombing, too. We'll get her for that one, if not this one."

Now Emily jumped to her feet and pointed toward the door. "Get out!" she demanded.

While he was leaning over her desk, Garibaldi made a point of studying everything on it. Amid the billing statements, electronic gadgets, and printouts was one thing that caught his eye—a disposable transparency, the kind that self-destroyed after a brief period. It bore the logo of the Senate and several warnings of a classified nature. It seemed to be from the chairperson of the armed forces committee, a strange thing for a commercial telepath to be concerned about. He couldn't read more than that, but he did catch the number of a bill that was apparently under consideration.

"Out," she said, "or I will call security and my lawyer!"

Garibaldi pointed a finger in her face. "You get that lawyer, because you're going to need him."

"Come on," said Gray, pushing Garibaldi toward the door.

Once outside on the street, the agitated chief took a few deep breaths and looked at a morbid Mr. Gray. He felt pretty bad about it, as if they had blown the interrogation, but he couldn't think of another way they could've handled it.

Garibaldi shrugged. "Hey, at least we know who the bomber is."

"But we're the only ones who know," complained Gray, "and everybody else is looking for the wrong person. I suppose we could tell Mr. Bester, who would make Ms. Crane's life miserable, but somehow that's not the same as bringing her to justice."

"That's the last resort," said Garibaldi. "What do you think Crane will do? Will she fly?"

"As long as Ms. Winters is a fugitive, Ms. Crane is basically safe. If Ms. Winters gets killed, which is altogether probable, then Ms. Crane has nothing to worry about."

Garibaldi groaned. "We know *who,* but we don't know *why.* Who was she really trying to kill? Bester? Malten? Too bad for her, because she missed on both counts."

"If it's not personal," said Gray, "is it actually tied into the Martian revolution?"

"Listen, do you know anybody in the Senate?"

"A senator?" Gray asked doubtfully.

"It doesn't have to be a senator, it could be a clerk or an aide, maybe even a lobbyist. Somebody in the know. I saw a confidential memo on her desk, and it was from the Senate. I think it was about some pending bill. Maybe there's a connection with Mars."

The telepath pouted for a moment. "I would rather follow up my lead on the hotel bombing."

"Think about it, Gray. You would have to go to Mars to do that. You'd have to track down all the personnel data she gave when she was pretending to be a Martian domestic worker. If this thing takes us to Mars, I promise we'll do it."

Garibaldi patted the telepath on the back. "We're here in the East Coast metropolis. Let's check on stuff we can check out here. Also, we have to keep an eye on her in case she flies. You know, Gray, you have surprised me. You are doing a helluva job. We arrived here from two different paths, but we both got to Emily Crane."

Mr. Gray nodded somberly and made a fist. "We work well together. I say, let's nail whoever did this."

* * *

It seemed like a mirage, shimmering in the desert heat, a pile of adobe cubes; they looked like loaves of bread baking in the sun. After the long haul over the rugged terrain in the Hovercraft, without seeing anything except endless tracts of desolation, even these humble abodes looked miraculous. Talia rubbed her eyes, both to get a better look and to get the sand out. No, it really was a village, a low-level form of civilization to be sure, but Talia didn't think she had ever seen anything so beautiful.

"Bilagaani Pueblo!" shouted the old man into the wind, which ate most of his words.

Talia nodded and gripped the sides of the roll bar tighter. The sensation of metal against her bare hands felt strange. There really wasn't a second seat in the small Hovercraft, and she was hanging on for all she was worth.

As they drew closer, she decided the adobes looked like a pile of children's blocks, a smaller block piled on top of a larger block to form rudimentary second stories. The extra space also allowed walkways between various structures on the second story, and wooden ladders stretched to every roof in the pueblo, untilizing all the space. There were rounded wooden beams sticking straight out of the adobes at irregular intervals, and smoke curled from a chimney on the topmost structure.

Gathered around the pueblo were pens for animals—goats and chickens seemed to be the most popular—and there were several low-slung lodges, little more than a meter high. Some of these low lodges were skeletal structures, nothing but twigs with colorful bits of cloth tied to them. Near each lodge was an immense fire pit filled with gray rocks, and Talia wondered what so many fire pits were used for. Colorful feathers and handmade pennants decorated staffs and poles all over the village.

The dogs were the first ones to come running to greet the Hovercraft, and they were yapping and wagging their tails happily. They were followed by children, who were also yapping but had no tails to wag. Undaunted, they twirled clacking noisemakers over their heads, causing the chickens to scurry. Adults began to emerge from the adobes, and they exhibited only a mild interest in the new arrivals.

Talia now saw that the village was nestled against a small plateau barely taller than the tallest adobe and exactly the same color. This must make it difficult to spot from the ground, she thought. Atop the plateau was the incongruous sight of solar panels, microwave antennae, and satellite dishes; and in the distance were white windmills, churning in the breeze. She imagined that the solar panels and windmills generated all the power the pueblo could ever need. Maybe there would be a hot bath tonight, she thought hopefully.

Then she saw the muddy stream, barely a meter wide, skirting both the plateau and the pueblo as if it were trying to avoid them. She saw no other signs of water, and her hopes sank.

The strange caravan swerved to a halt near the other parked Hovercraft, and the pilots killed the engines. She gasped as the vehicle dropped to the ground. A moment later, Brother Sky was offering his hand to her.

"Come, Sister Rain," he said. "Do you need food?"

She nodded and got out of the Hovercraft. The dogs sniffed her, and the children ran around her in circles, giggling. Talia looked over and saw Deuce getting out of the boy's Hovercraft. The gangster managed to greet several people while keeping his black briefcase clutched to his chest. His duffel bag was slung over his shoulder.

She turned to see the bare-chested young man with the chestnut-colored hair. By himself he pushed the Hovercraft close enough together to loop a length of steel cable through their rings and chain them together. He glanced up at her and smiled, and she was instantly embarrassed about watching him. When she turned away, she found the middle-aged woman staring at her. The woman gave her a toothless grin and walked away, and she could see skin lesions and ruined skin on the woman's naked shoulders.

The people of the pueblo looked healthy enough, but many of them had the kind of simple ailments that come from living primitively: bad skin, bad teeth, limps, injuries, and one case of cataracts. Had they been in a city or a space station, they could have been cured of most of those ailments over the weekend. Those who weren't nude were dressed in similar dirty clothes and wore similar waist-length ratty hair. It was disconcerting to see all these Earthlings living in such primitive conditions, and Talia was glad when Sky escorted her inside a ground-floor adobe.

She had to duck her head to fit through the doorway, and she was surprised to find a tasteful electric floor lamp giving off a subdued bit of light. She was even more surprised to see a table, upon which sat a sprawling machine; it had various spools and feeds and looked like it was intended for small manufacturing. The smells of the room were also a strange mixture of industrial solvents and chile, cilantro, and onions.

"I will be right back," said Sky. He disappeared into the adjoining room, which Talia assumed was the kitchen. She could see no cooking utensils in the outer room.

A moment later, Deuce entered and slumped onto one of the mats on the floor. He kicked off his boots and groaned with relief. His feet added another odd smell to the room.

"Ever see anything like this?" he asked.

She shook her head in an honest answer.

Deuce grinned. "They bend the laws, but they're good people. They're on the edge, like you and me."

Talia nodded. Unfortunately, she couldn't argue with that generalization, given her present circumstances. The young man with the chestnut hair came in, and he was carrying a mangled pad of paper, a stubby pencil, and a measuring tape.

"Stand up, Brother Deuce," he said, motioning to the gangster.

Deuce complied, and the young man measured his height, as if he were fitting him for a suit. When he was done, he wrote his findings on his pad of paper.

"I'm going to guess on your weight," he said. "Our scale broke. But I'm pretty accurate." He tapped his pencil on his chin until he came up with a guess, which he also wrote on his pad. "Sister Rain," he said, "it's your turn."

She pointed to him and gave him a quizzical expression. "You want to know my name?" he asked. "It's Lizard."

At her startled expression, the young man chuckled. "It is our custom to name a child after the first thing the father sees. Sometimes this works out well, sometimes not. But we praise our grandparents and the Creator for giving us life, and we accept our name with their blessings. Turn around."

She obeyed, and Lizard ran the measuring tape from the crown of her head to the heels of her feet. In doing so, his fingers touched the bare skin at the nape of her neck, and it gave her a shock. For that split second, she glimpsed involuntarily into his mind and saw that his life out here was lonely. Painfully lonely, but he couldn't leave.

"Fine," he said, jotting down her measurements. "You look about the same weight as my sister—I'll use that. Thank you. I need to go back to my house and get on the microwave link. In maybe an hour, I'll have some matches for identicards. It's gotten too hard to do real forgeries, so I'll have to match you with a living person and download their data. You're just going to travel around with these cards, right? You're not going to apply for a job or a security clearance, are you?"

Deuce laughed hoarsely. "I don't think so."

Talia shook her head.

Lizard brushed his unruly hair back and gripped it in a ponytail. He waved to them and walked out, and Talia found herself watching his finely chiseled backbone and shoulders.

Deuce grinned. "You heard the rule against messing around with the chief's daughter? Well, that's the chief's son. Same rule."

Talia flashed him an angry look, but he ignored it. Nevertheless, she told herself, it was very good advice. The last thing she needed was to settle down out here in the wilderness, with a bunch of misfits who had stolen somebody else's culture. What did she really know about these people? She could wake up one morning and find Psi Cops staring down at her, while Lizard and Sky pocketed a nice reward. No, she was a shark now—she had to keep moving. She had to search out her prey, the same ones who had preyed on her.

That thought brought her back to Emily Crane. Ever since Garibaldi had elicited that name from her, Talia had wondered whether Emily actually had something to do with the bombing. If the bomb had been hidden in the data crystal—and she didn't know how likely or unlikely that was—then Emily had indeed not only tried to kill her, Bester, and Malten, but she had succeeded in killing five telepaths and casting the suspicions onto an innocent person! In other words, Emily Crane was an extremely dangerous and ruthless person. She had to be stopped.

Talia sat on the packed-dirt floor and wrapped her arms around herself. Having an identicard would make traveling possible, but it didn't mean she could travel with impunity. It didn't mean anything, except that she could risk her neck a dozen other places.

Sky came back into the room holding a handmade ceramic bowl. Its contents smelled good, and Talia sat up eagerly. The old man put the bowl in her lap, with no spoon, and she tried to ignore the strange things she found in it. There was a base of some sort of gruel, some vegetables which might've been bits of cactus, and some meat and black things.

Talia looked at Sky, and he smiled encouragingly. "Go ahead. It's all yours."

She apparently wasn't going to get a spoon, so she dipped her fingers into the potpourri and grabbed a glob of it. After her first hesitant taste, the weary fugitive was soon scraping the sides of the bowl with her fingertips.

"I'm glad you like it," said Sky, grinning. "You want some, Brother Deuce?"

"No, thanks," said the grubby criminal, stretching out on the mat. "But I could use a nap." He put his briefcase under his head as a pillow.

"Make yourselves at home," said Sky. "I have some crops to attend to."

He strode out through the low opening in the adobe hut,

leaving her alone with Deuce, who was quickly snoring. Taking a hint, Talia lay back on the hard-packed earth, thinking she could never get comfortable on bare dirt.

She was asleep in a matter of seconds.

CHAPTER 15

GARIBALDI stood on the concourse of Boston's Travel Center, staring at a blank viewer and waiting to link up with Babylon 5, as hundreds of commuters rushed behind him, headed toward bullet trains that would take them up and down the eastern seaboard. Gray stood to his left, fidgeting.

Finally, there was a chime and Captain John Sheridan's handsome face appeared on the viewer. Garibaldi sighed with relief. "Captain, I wasn't sure I'd be able to get through, but I thought I'd better report in."

"That's fine," answered the captain. "Have you turned up anything?"

Garibaldi glanced around to make sure nobody but Gray was eavesdropping. "Yeah, I think we found the bomber. But I don't know how we're going to prove it without having Talia Winters to testify. Her name is Emily Crane, and she works for the Mix in Boston. She handed Talia a data crystal just before they all went into that conference room."

"Interesting," mused Sheridan. "She's a commercial telepath, and that corresponds with some information that Mr. Lennier gave me. At the reception, he was talking to a military liaison named Barker."

Gray interjected, "He's high up."

"I gather that," said Sheridan. "He told Lennier that Bester would soon be history, and that the commercial sector was going to make a grab to control Psi Corps. I can't imagine how they would go about doing that, but it ties together."

Garibaldi frowned. "Unfortunately, it doesn't clear Talia, because she's also in the commercial sector. But it does let us concentrate our search."

The captain's link buzzed, and he lifted his hand to answer it. "Excuse me," he said. Over the long-distance connection, Garibaldi couldn't make out every word of the captain's conversation, but he clearly heard "Mr. Bester" mentioned several times.

"Out," said Sheridan. He turned back to the viewer and shook his head. "I've got to go. Our prize patient is making life difficult for everyone again. Now he's demanding to have his own doctor flown in! Dr. Franklin is about ready to walk. Keep me posted."

"Right, sir." Garibaldi pushed the button to sign off, then he nodded to Mr. Gray. "Time to call your friend."

"But he's only a clerk in the Senate," Gray protested.

"That's good enough. Those guys do all the work, and they know everything. Call him up, and ask him about Senate bill 22991."

Reluctantly, Gray pushed his creditchit into the slot and dialed some numbers on the commlink. After a few moments, a clean-cut, bookish-looking man about Gray's age came on the viewer.

"This is Senator Donaldson's office."

"Marlon, it's me—Harriman! How are you?"

"Harriman, what a surprise! My gosh, how long has it been? Was it the frat reunion in Montreal? Was that the last time I saw you?"

"I believe so," answered Gray. "You're an old hand now —five years working for the senator."

"And you look great," Marlon replied. "Where are you living these days?"

Garibaldi sighed and gave Gray a hand signal to hurry up.

"Berlin," answered Gray. "Listen, Marlon, I need some information about a Senate bill. I believe it's still in committee and hasn't gone to the floor yet."

Marlon smiled helpfully. "Whatever you need."

"I think the bill has something to do with telepaths. It's number 22991."

A pall fell over Marlon's face, and he looked as if he had been struck by a severe case of gastrointestinitis. He glanced around nervously and lowered his voice. "How do you know about that? I can't talk about it."

Garibaldi stepped into the picture. "Oh, I think you can,

Marlon, or we're going to come down to the senator's office and ask everyone who goes in and out until somebody tells us."

"Who are you?"

Gray rolled his eyes with embarrassment. "This is Michael Garibaldi, Chief of Security for Babylon 5. We're working on a case together."

"Is he serious about what he just said?"

"Yes," answered Gray with a sidelong glance at Garibaldi. "He's impatient, rude, and has very little tact."

"None," agreed Garibaldi.

The Senate clerk was still shaken. "I can't talk about this on a public comm. Do you still have my address? It hasn't changed since I've been in Washington."

"Yes," said Gray, consulting a small electronic device.

"I'll be home by six tonight. Why don't you meet me there? And don't go asking anybody else. I'll tell you what I know."

"Great," said Garibaldi, "we'll buy you dinner."

Looking very glum, Marlon signed off.

"Well done," said the security chief, slapping Gray on the back. "You just have time to buy me lunch before we hop the rails to Washington. Let's go."

Talia Winters felt somebody toying with her hair, and she woke up with a start to find a teenage girl leaning over her. The girl jumped away.

"I'm sorry," she said, "you have such beautiful hair. We're not allowed to cut our hair short like that. I wish we could."

Talia sat up, disoriented, and looked around the humble adobe hut, with the strange machine in one corner and the smells of cooking wafting from the other room. Once again she thought about how her life had taken on such a surreal quality that her dreams seemed normal by comparison. In her dream, she had been back on Babylon 5, conversing with tentacled aliens. Awake, she was a fugitive from the law, a rogue telepath, reduced to hiding out in the desert with a group of neo-primitives.

"My name is Rain," said the girl, stroking her honey-blond hair over her naked shoulder.

Talia almost answered the girl in spoken words, saying she was Rain, too. But she didn't have to say it. The girl laughed in a lilting voice.

"Yes, I know, you are Rain. When Brother Sky names the girls, they are almost always Rain. Some of the people place great significance in this, others say he is misogynistic, but I say he just doesn't like to remember names."

The teenager stroked her hair again, and her green eyes drilled into Talia's. "I think we should call you by your real name. It suits you so much better."

Talia almost cried out, but she forced her tongue back into her mouth as she stared into those vibrant green eyes.

"Winters," said the girl. "Sister Winters is so perfect."

The telepath fought back questions that tried to stampede out of her mouth. She shook her head vehemently, and the young Rain surprised her by nodding in sympathy.

"Yes, I know, you have to be Rain like all the rest of us. It's not fair, when Winters is better for you. I'm sorry." She shrugged and scrambled to her feet. As she dashed out the doorway, she whispered, "I'll see you later."

Talia tried to still her initial impulse to bolt from the pueblo and keep running. Where would she go? she asked herself. It's not surprising for the Bilagaani to know her real identity, she reasoned. They weren't as cut off out here as they seemed, not with that battery of antennae and dishes on the plateau. Lizard was out there now, stealing data off a secured link. It wasn't panic time yet, Talia assured herself, although it wouldn't take much to push her to it.

Young Rain had been so innocent about knowing her real name, and threatening at the same time. Talia couldn't believe they were scheming to do her harm. Would an adolescent be allowed to blurt something like that out, if the tribe was planning to turn her in? The Bilagaani simply knew who she was, and they didn't care if she knew it.

Hey, she reminded herself, these people were breaking serious laws themselves. They didn't want Psi Cops around. By running, she had naturally fallen in with people like Deuce and this weird offshoot of the underground. These were the people who lived in the cracks in the sidewalk, who lived in places like B5's Down Below. Like it or not, she was part of their world now, and she might visit more way stations in the underground before her journey was through.

If she didn't clear her name, she would have to live in the cracks forever.

No! she told herself. She wasn't going to let that happen. Talia wanted her real life back, and she resolved anew to keep her mouth shut, to keep to herself, and to keep moving. She wouldn't admit to anything. But she desperately needed to dye her hair or get a wig to go along with her new indenti-card. Hell, she thought, these people had enough hair to make her a hundred wigs! She wondered if they could improvise a wig or a dye-job for Sister Winters.

Talia glanced at the mat where Deuce had been sleeping and wondered where he was. She wanted to know how soon they would be getting out of the pueblo, and by what method. She might opt to make her own travel arrangements if what Deuce had in mind was too dangerous. Of course, she thought glumly, she didn't have any money. She could get Emily Crane's business address at any public terminal, and then she would at least know her destination. She figured she could play it by ear after she confronted Emily Crane, but first things first—where was Deuce?

She got to her feet and shuffled out the doorway. Shielding her eyes from the intense sunlight, Talia peered into the courtyard formed by the crude semicircle of stacked adobes. The courtyard looked brown and dusty, like an old coin, and nobody was visible. Even the chickens and goats were sleeping under mat lean-tos. It was hot, but it was the kind of dry heat that didn't leave her sweating so much as parched and enervated.

Talia sidled around the corner of Sky's adobe and saw a ladder leaning on the wall and leading up to the next level.

She heard some muted voices coming from above, so she decided to climb the ladder and try her luck. It was either that or sit around and go crazy, waiting for something terrible to happen.

The handmade wooden ladder creaked under her weight, but it was just the leather stretching; it never felt as if it was about to give way. She climbed up quickly to the next floor, which was the top of Sky's roof, and saw several scattered wooden toys—crude wagons, blocks, and noisemakers. Through an open door, she saw three children asleep, as she had been until a few minutes ago. It was siesta time, she concluded, the hottest part of the day when anyone with any sense would be sleeping. It was amazing how cool the adobes stayed compared to the outside temperatures.

"We build the adobe walls with bales of hay in the center," said Lizard.

She whirled around to see the handsome Bilagaani poking his head out of the low doorway of the neighboring adobe. His chestnut hair framed his face in sweaty ringlets.

"You were wondering how they stay so cool," he explained. "Everyone wonders that. Come inside before you roast."

Was Lizard a rogue telepath? wondered Talia. This would be the place for a rogue to hide out, she supposed, if there was such a place. She ducked into his cool adobe and was struck by a blast of air from a powerful fan; it blew her hair and clothes back and made her stagger. Lizard reached out a hand to pull her in.

"Keeps the dust out," he explained, as he motioned around the cramped collection of electronic equipment, most of it in no order that she could discern. He went back to his desk and looked at one of his four viewers, this one filled with data.

"Can you be thirty-two years old?" he asked. "I don't think you look that old, but this is the closest match. Height, weight, family background . . ."

She yanked at her blond hair, and he nodded.

"So you want to change your hair color, make it darker? I

thought you might. Then I've got one that will match even closer. I'll format that data, and we'll run you a card on the machine downstairs. Now, listen, these identicards are good for maybe four uses, about a week of traveling, and by then"
—he looked at the screen—"Frieda Nelson should be retired. You'll have to become someone else, because the system will eventually realize that Frieda Nelson can't be in two places at once."

He crossed his brawny arms and stared at the screen. "She's twenty-nine and hails from Eugene, Oregon. Remember, if you use it more than four times, you're taking a chance."

Talia nodded and tried to give him an encouraging smile. It was too bad that she couldn't stay and chat with this exotic young man, but she had to get organized. She had to get out of here—she could feel something already closing in, even if it was just her paranoia. Talia held up two fingers and shrugged.

"Deuce?" asked Lizard.

She nodded eagerly and shrugged again, as if to ask where he was.

Lizard chuckled and turned back to his screens. "I don't think you want to talk to Deuce at the moment. He is lying with one of the women of the tribe, Sister Morning. She's the one who came with us to get you."

Talia blinked at him, wishing she hadn't asked.

"Morning is a widow, and she took an interest in Deuce the last time he was here. She thinks she has a chance to convince him to stay, but I don't think so. Deuce likes a faster pace than Bilagaani Pueblo, I'm afraid."

Talia looked desperately around the little room with the huge fan, and her eyes lit upon Lizard's pad of paper and stubby pencil. She grabbed them, flipped to a clean page, and began to write. Lizard watched her with interest, a quiet mirth in his blue eyes.

After a few seconds, she handed him a sheet of paper bearing the scrawled words: "I need address for Emily Crane, works at the Mix."

Lizard rubbed his angular chin. "The Mix? Then she's a telepath, right? Are you sure you know what you're doing? Listen, you don't have to be in a hurry to leave. This is not a bad place to hang out, and we could get to know each other."

Would she get the same recruiting inducements as Deuce was getting? wondered Talia. She supposed there had to be some incentive to get people to live way the hell out here in this wilderness, and that might work with some people. But Talia couldn't imagine a life of nothing but sand, gruel, and Lizard. She had a life that she already enjoyed, and she longed to get back to it. The telepath pointed inflexibly at the sheet of paper bearing Emily's name.

"Okay," said the Bilagaani, punching in a few commands. "To get her business address will only take a moment."

Talia paced the cramped office. She didn't know why she was angry at Deuce for stopping to enjoy the local recreation. It was stupid to think that she had won that gangster's allegiance or loyalty. He was a cutthroat, pure and simple, and he would help her only as long as it didn't hurt him. Like the canteen he had hidden from her, Deuce would always save the best for himself. He had gotten her this far, but she would have to get the rest of the way on her own.

"Does Boston sound right for Emily Crane?" asked Lizard.

She nodded, and the young man printed Emily Crane's address onto a clear address card. When he went to hand it to her, his hand caught hers, as if to steady it, and their thoughts mingled disconcertingly. He told her, *It doesn't matter who you are.* She gripped his hand in return and told him telepathically, *It does matter! I am a hunted terrorist, and I will destroy you all if I stay. I have a life, and a purpose. Only death will stop me from clearing my name.*

Talia yanked the address card out of his hand and studied it. She memorized it all, including floor 38, and tucked the card into a zippered pocket of her jumpsuit.

"All right," said Lizard with resignation. "You'll need clothes, a disguise. Come with me."

He took her back out into the sunlight. Despite the heat, they climbed down the ladder and walked completely around the pueblo and toward the plateau that protected it. Talia wanted to ask where they were going, but she didn't dare. She saw the crops that Sky had talked about—neat rows of squash, corn, and various herbs she didn't recognize, all irrigated from the muddy stream. Tied to wooden stakes in the garden were colorful bits of cloth and miniature windmills; she supposed the purpose of the adornments was to frighten away the birds.

She also saw modern equipment connected to a concrete building. That had to be the collection center for their power transformer, Talia deduced, because of all the wires stretching from the building to the solar panels on the plateau and the windmills beyond. This was quite an operation they had here. Although the Bilagaani lived primitively by twenty-third-century standards, they weren't exactly nomads or monks who had taken a vow of poverty. They couldn't just get up and leave this pueblo. She wondered how it happened that they never got raided. Did they pay people off? Maybe they paid them off with information.

Before she could fully worry about such a prospect, Talia's attention was drawn to the extraordinary erosion on the plateau. Close up, it looked pockmarked and pitted, not the smooth rose-colored monument it had seemed from afar. Even Lizard appeared subdued by this sight, as if he could remember the plateau a million years ago, when it had been young and tall, a budding mountain. Now it seemed to mirror the tribe—a ghost of a grandeur long past, something more depressing than beautiful.

True to his name, the young man darted among the pockmarked cavities in the rock face and promptly disappeared. Talia hurried after him, and she almost cracked her resolve by calling his name. When she finally saw the low entrance to the cave, barely a meter high, she stopped. Ever since she was a little girl, she had been afraid of caves. Fortunately, she had never had much cause to come into contact with caves, growing up in a succession of urban areas. But here was one now. It had swallowed Lizard, and now it beckoned her.

Was he waiting inside to jump her? Talia thought fretfully. If he was the type to do so, she decided, she might as well confront him here and now. There was certainly something inside the cave he wanted her to see, and there was no time like the present to see it. Talia got down on her hands and knees in the caked sand and crawled into the hole.

The telepath was surprised to see a glimmer of light just ahead of her, but she didn't dare get to her feet until she saw how low the ceiling was. Then she rounded a corner and saw Lizard, standing upright and lighting an old lantern with some liquid floating in a glass bulb. She didn't know how it burned, but it gave off an amazing amount of light. She assumed that if the tall Bilagaani could stand upright in the cave, then so could she.

As she walked toward him, she saw the remarkable treasure hidden in the cavern. There were dozens of trunks, suitcases, and boxes filled to overflowing with clothes, hats, coats, belts, umbrellas, and other accessories. She moved from one box of treasure to another, surveying ancient things like fox stoles and brocaded bolo jackets. She remembered when those had been popular about a dozen years ago. This cave was like the world's largest emporium of antique clothing!

"The desert keeps these things very well," observed Lizard. "When people come to join us, they bring goods they cannot use anymore, and we store them here. We keep thinking we will burn them, but every now and then something turns out to be useful. You are welcome to anything you find here."

Talia nodded her thanks, although she felt a bit overwhelmed. She wanted a clean suit of nondescript civilian clothes, not trunkfuls of dirty, exotic, antique clothing.

"There is a mirror over there," said Lizard, pointing to what looked like a narrow doorway containing more people and another lantern. Talia jumped before she realized it was just their reflection.

"I will go finish your identicard," said the muscular young man. "Take your time."

Talia nodded her thanks and looked around with dismay at aged trunks full of dusty clothes.

Mr. Gray leaned forward in the autotaxi. "That's him," he said, pointing to a slim man walking down the sidewalk."

"He's late," muttered Garibaldi.

"Marlon has a very responsible job," countered Gray. He ran his chit through the slot on the dashboard, settling their debt with the robotic vehicle, and the doors opened to let them out.

Once they reached the sidewalk, Marlon glanced back at them, but he exhibited no inclination to greet them. It was cloak-and-dagger stuff all the way, thought Garibaldi, as they followed the man through the wrought-iron gate and into the courtyard of his apartment complex. This was one of those pseudo-Roman places, thought Garibaldi, with lots of chintzy columns and porticos. The pièce de résistance was a lighted swimming pool with a fake mosaic portrait of Neptune on its bottom.

Without saying anything, they followed Marlon to his apartment on the first floor, poolside. Garibaldi looked around as Marlon unlocked his door, figuring that if anybody was watching them they would assume that the guy was about to be mugged. But this strange procession had taken only a few seconds, and they were all safely ensconced in his apartment a moment later.

Marlon and Harriman Gray hugged each other like the old friends they were.

"Thank you for seeing us," said Gray.

Marlon gave Garibaldi an annoyed glance. "You didn't give me much of a choice, did you? How did you find out about bill 22991?"

"It's connected to the bombing on Babylon 5," explained Garibaldi. "So tell us about it." The chief sat down on the silk sofa, crossed his long legs, and waited.

The clerk sighed and went to his well-stocked bar. "I need some sustenance first. You want one?"

"Sure," said Gray.

"I gave up sustenance," answered Garibaldi.

Marlon collected his thoughts while he mixed the two drinks. He looked very serious as he delivered Gray's drink and took a seat beside Garibaldi on the sofa.

"It's like this," he began, "a lot of people hate Psi Corps."

"That's not exactly a news flash," said Garibaldi.

"Yes, but they *really* hate them, especially the Psi Cops and the intelligence groups. Only they're too afraid to say anything. I'm talking about senators here! You should see some of the things Psi Corps does to them—blackmail, intimidation, threats—it's terrible!"

Marlon took a gulp of his drink. It smelled like a martini to Garibaldi, a strong one, too. The clerk continued, "It's a secret proposal so far, but there's a bill under consideration that would privatize Psi Corps. Under the guise of saving money, this bill would take Psi Corps out of the military—which doesn't control it, anyway—and make the governing body of telepaths a completely civilian office."

He took another drink and went on, "Even though a lot of the same telepaths would still be around, the Senate hopes this will cut their ties to their allies, kill all their secret intelligence gathering, and basically neutralize them. All the good stuff they're doing, they can keep doing as a civilian entity that answers directly to the Senate. As far as the public is concerned, nothing changes—Psi Corps just becomes private instead of military. In reality, a lot changes."

Gray interjected a question. "This sounds like quite a windfall for somebody. Who would take over Psi Corps once it's privatized?"

Marlon shrugged. "Who else? There's only one firm of private telepaths that's big enough—the Mix."

Garibaldi and Gray looked at one another. They didn't need to be reminded who Emily Crane's employer was—the Mix.

"Does Arthur Malten know about this?" asked Garibaldi.

"Are you kidding?" scoffed Marlon. "He's been lining this up for years, going to all the senators who have been harassed by Psi Corps and making secret deals. When he has enough votes, and that may be soon, this bill will miraculously jump out of committee and go to the floor in the dead of night. It will be passed immediately, before Psi Corps has a chance to stop it. The president will sign it in his pajamas. When Psi Corps wakes up the next morning, Malten will be in charge."

"Does this mean that Malten's a good guy?" asked Garibaldi.

Marlon laughed cynically. "Hell no, he's doing it for the money. With the Psi Corps budget to play with, he stands to make a fortune! It's risky for Malten, but the Mix is already as big as it's going to get under Psi Corps. This is Malten's chance to grab everything." The young clerk drained his martini.

Gray cleared his throat and asked, "If you wanted to get away with this, would it be a good idea to kill Mr. Bester?"

"Well," answered Marlon, "they say the only way to kill a rattlesnake is to cut off its head. As long as Bester and his cops have carte blanche to deal with the telepaths as they want, he's in charge."

The clerk stood and went to the bar. "Harriman, would you like another one?"

"No, thank you," said the somber telepath. Garibaldi felt sorry for him. No one ever liked to hear about internecine warfare in their own ranks. This was telepath killing telepath for personal gain and power. Garibaldi might be content to let them kill each other off, but they were killing innocent people in the crossfire—twenty-six of them at the Royal Tharsis Lodge—and they were casting the blame on Mars separatists, who didn't need more grief.

Gray turned to Garibaldi and said puzzledly, "But Mr. Malten was in the explosion."

"He could've been wearing body armor. As I recall, he

didn't have a scratch on him, but his nerves were so shot that he had to leave B5 right away."

With determination, Harriman Gray rose to his feet. "I'm sorry, Marlon, we'd like to stay, but we should really see Mr. Malten as soon as possible."

"No need to rush off, then," said the clerk. "Malten is on Mars."

"How do you know that?" asked Garibaldi.

"He sent the senator a message from there just this afternoon. He's been letting us know his whereabouts in case we have to move fast on the privatization bill. These bombings are making everyone nervous, and that's actually playing into his hands. They're afraid that Bester is going to mount a real crackdown when he gets back on his feet. Say, you don't really think Malten is behind the bombings?"

"Keep that under your hat," ordered Gray. "We're following up leads, that's all."

"But I thought you had the bomber. What's her name, the blond woman who's been all over the news. They say her uncle is a terrorist."

Garibaldi shook his head with frustration. They had no shortage of suspects anymore, but they still had a shortage of evidence, and a more serious shortage of official cooperation. If only Talia hadn't run for it, all of this could've added up to some kind of a defense for her.

Where are you, Talia? he asked himself. *What are you doing to get yourself out of this mess?*

CHAPTER 16

TALIA Winters squealed with delight when she pulled the curly brown wig out of the hat box. She glanced behind her in the wavering lamplight of the cave to make sure that no one had heard her. It was a quality wig made from very good synthetic hair, and the hat box had kept it in decent condition. She put the wig on, tucking her blond tresses out of sight, and admired herself in the mirror. She saw that the wig was long and curled down her back, and she decided she would leave it that length. To complete the effect, Talia grabbed a beret and pulled it down on her head. Not only did the beret help to hold the wig in place, it gave her a slightly Bohemian look that went with the unruly hair and the old clothes.

Talia had chosen the most expensive outfit she could find to wear, even though it was ten years out of date, on the theory that expensive clothes always showed their quality. Better for a stranger she met in her travels to think she once had money, and didn't have it any longer, than to think that she had never had money. It was a designer pantsuit in navy blue, and she had found a plain black jacket to go with it. To see how the ensemble looked with the hair, she stripped off her white jumpsuit and tried everything on.

The effect was dramatic. Talia no longer looked her sophisticated, elegant self but more like . . . like Emily Crane. That is, she looked a bit mousy and frumpy. Was this the way Emily had mastered her deception, by trying on mismatched hair and outfits until she had achieved the requisite dowdiness? It depressed Talia to think that she had been fooled so easily, but more and more she couldn't think of any other explanation for a bomb being in her bag. Garibaldi was right—Emily was the only one who could have given it to her.

She could get confirmation about Emily from Deuce, but

she could also get shot between the eyes for asking him. She would just have to ask Emily herself. Damn, she wished Boston weren't so far away.

The telepath tried to imagine what kind of person Frieda Nelson of Eugene, Oregon, was. With these clothes, Frieda was probably an artist of some sort, maybe a person who wrote plays, painted pictures, or constructed homey crafts out of gingham and wood. She might even be the sort of person who would like hanging around at Bilagaani Pueblo with persons named Rain and Lizard. She was not Talia Winters, that was for sure.

"Knock, knock," drawled a voice. "Are you decent?"

She said nothing; she just waited for Deuce to crawl into the cave, carrying his ever-present briefcase and duffel bag. As soon as he got an eyeful of her, he burst out laughing.

"I'm sorry," he said. "You look like a teacher I once had. I didn't like her much, and I put a firecracker in her wastebasket. That was the last bit of official education I ever had."

When Talia said nothing, he reached into his pocket and pulled out an identicard. "Here's yours," he said. "I want you to know that this card and your transportation cost me a one-carat diamond. I don't know when you're going to pay me back, but I always remember my debtors. And I charge interest."

She snatched the card out of his hand but didn't promise him anything. At least now she knew what he carried in that black briefcase, and why he guarded it so closely.

"Lizard told me he already explained to you about these cards. They're okay to use a couple of times, but you're pushing it after that. We're supposed to be leaving at midnight, after their sweat."

She gave him a quizzical look.

"Sweat lodge," he explained. "Those small lodges out there—they heat up a bunch of stones, beat the drums, sing songs, and pray to their grandparents. And sweat. We'd be welcome to join them, I'm sure."

Talia shook her head.

"Deuce! Rain!" called a frightened voice.

They whirled around to see Rain, the teenager with the green eyes, come crawling into the cave. She looked worried, and she pointed to the sky.

"A black shuttlecraft just flew over," she said, panting. "Very high up. Brother Sky says it's Psi Cops!"

Talia felt as if she had been stabbed, the grip of panic was so strong on her chest. Deuce just looked disgusted.

"Bastards always spoil everything," he muttered. "If they find that cargo container out in the desert, we're pretty much had."

Talia suddenly realized that she was not going to change her clothes. She was going to make a run for it dressed like this—Cinderella before the ball. But where? How? There were voices in the narrow tunnel leading into the cave, and she waited tensely to see who it was. Nervously, she balled her hands into fists.

Sky entered, followed by Lizard, and both men looked equally grim. "We saw them," said the old man. "The buzzards are circling. You must leave now."

"How?" growled Deuce. "Do you want us to walk?"

"We'll sell you a Hovercraft," said the old man. "Two stones."

"Whoa!" the gangster wailed. "That's highway robbery! What the hell do I need a Hovercraft for? Just get me to a town, and I'll be all right." He pointed rudely at Talia. "I don't care what you do with *her*."

Lizard stepped forward, the muscles on his chest tight with anger, and he grabbed Deuce by the neck and shook him. "You came down with her, and you have to look after her! Remember, we could take all the diamonds and show the cops where your body burned up. There would be just enough left to identify."

When Deuce reached for his PPG, the old chief was quicker and grabbed his wrist. Talia also attacked Deuce, whirling around and punching him in the stomach.

"Okay, okay," croaked the petty crook. "Two stones it is!"

The Bilagaani dropped him to the floor of the cave, and he

scrambled for his briefcase. "I want a fast one, and I'm gonna pick it out myself."

Eyeing everyone suspiciously, Deuce extracted two diamonds from his briefcase and gave them to Brother Sky. The old man pointed toward the hole leading out of the cave and nearly pushed him through it.

Talia started to follow, and she felt Lizard grab her arm. She wrenched it away from him and glared at him. She wasn't in a mood to be friendly, especially to a guy who would kick her out into the midday desert with Psi Cops patrolling the air. She glanced around the graveyard of ancient clothes and decided it was more like a tomb.

Lizard shrugged helplessly. "We've got to get you out of the pueblo, that's all. Too many people's lives would be in jeopardy. Personally, I would like you to stay."

She nodded, softening a bit. It really wasn't his fault or the tribe's fault that she was a fugitive. It was her own damn ambition and foolishness. She touched Lizard's bare chest once, briefly, before she crawled out of the cave, and she hoped that would give him a strong enough impression to remember her by.

The sun was brutal, baking the pueblo and the plateau to a dusky brown. But she noticed that it had slipped substantially toward the west, and she guessed that it was about four in the afternoon. Talia didn't know much about fleeing across a desert, but she figured that nighttime was the right time. Well, it would be dark in a few hours, and maybe they could elude capture until then. She didn't want to count on her luck, because she hadn't had any lately.

Talia didn't know whether Deuce had picked the fastest Hovercraft, but he had picked the one with the loudest, brightest paintings on its hood. She guessed there was some logic in that—if they were spotted from above, it would be assumed they were Bilagaani. She was glad now that she had the long hair to fit the image of a Bilagaani plainswoman.

As Deuce was already in his seat, she climbed aboard without another word. The tribe was gathering around to see them off, and they were silent and noncommittal. Morning, the middle-aged woman who had comforted Deuce, was the only one who was crying. What a strange place this speck of North America was, thought Talia, odder than anything she had seen on Babylon 5.

"They were traveling west," said Brother Sky, pointing toward the sky. "If you travel northeast, you will find the town of Clement. Beware the salt flats."

"Thanks," muttered Deuce, not sounding like he meant it.

Lizard suddenly handed Talia a waterskin, and she gripped it for dear life. "Peace," he said somberly.

She nodded and tried to give him a smile. Deuce started the engine and gunned it, but the solar-powered turbine didn't make much noise. The Hovercraft lifted into the air a few centimeters and blew sand all over Lizard, Sky, and the others, but they stood their ground. A few even lifted their hands in a gesture of parting. Talia gripped the roll bars as they rocketed out of the Hovercraft pen and headed for the mountains to the northeast.

The crabcakes and sirloin tasted great, but they didn't sit very well in Garibaldi's stomach. He kept thinking about all the things he should be doing and all the places he should be running. The sedate Washington restaurant wasn't distracting him enough. The conversation of Marlon and Harriman wasn't doing him any good either, as they kept reliving fraternity pranks and trips to Fort Lauderdale. Then Gray launched into a description of his apartment in Berlin, and soon they were both discussing decorating ideas. Garibaldi wanted to climb the drapes.

"Excuse me," he said, rising from the table. "I need to take a little walk. We don't get rich food like that on Babylon 5, and my system is staging a revolution. Maybe I'll find a commlink and check in."

Gray gave him a quick look of concern, and Marlon paid no attention as the security chief slipped away from the table. He shot through the French doors and lacy curtains and found himself on the patio. He took a flight of curving stairs down to a meandering garden.

The out-of-doors smelled wonderful, and it began to lift his spirits immediately. There were gardens and open spaces on Babylon 5, but you had to seek them out. He seldom had time. The air of Babylon 5 was the best money could buy, but it couldn't compete with the pine aroma of the trees and the genuine steer manure on the lawn. It made him wonder how he could spend his days on a space station, revolving around a spooky, half-dead planet, when there was this planet, perfectly designed for the habitation of humans.

He thought about having to go back to Boston tonight, or first thing in the morning, and he realized what he missed about B5. It was self-contained. No running around in funny little vehicles trying to see people—everyone on B5 was a twenty-minute walk, or closer. And a quarter of a million people was considerably more manageable than four billion. Yes, the air smelled good on Earth, but it wasn't home.

After a few more sniffs of the real thing, Garibaldi went around to the front of the converted mansion. He thought he had seen a public commlink by the bathroom. Yes, he was right.

The commlink wasn't busy, and Garibaldi ran his chit through and punched in his commands. Then he leaned against the wall to wait, knowing it could take a few minutes. Some very elegant women were arriving with their dates, and they reminded him of Talia—thoroughbreds, smart, fast, gorgeous. He didn't know whether he would ever see Talia again, and that was beginning to depress him. Not that she had ever given him much more than the time of day, but she had been so assertive, confident, and proud of her accomplishments. It pained him to think she had been reduced to running like an animal, scared of every shadow.

He didn't know how it would be possible to find Talia before the others, but he had to try. There was always the possibility that she hadn't fled to Earth and had hitched a ride to the far ends of the galaxy. But he felt certain she had come to Earth. Not only was Emily Crane here, but this was familiar territory for her. People usually ran from the strange and to the familiar, not the other way around. Garibaldi often

thought that if he ever had to run from B5, he would go back
to Mars. He figured Talia would come here.

Earth was logical for another reason. If you were a human
and you wanted to hide, you didn't go where humans were
rare—you went where there were a lot of humans. Unfortunately, that just made his job more difficult, and nothing
short of finding her would help her now.

A synthesized voice startled him. "Hang on for your link
to Babylon 5."

"I'm hangin', I'm hangin'," he assured the computer.

An empty chair appeared on the screen, but presently Captain Sheridan dropped into it. "Garibaldi," he frowned,
"we've had a development here."

"Yes, sir."

"Mr. Bester has flown the coop. His supposedly private
doctor arrived, but they were really just a bunch of Psi Cops
who whisked him onto their ship. We never saw a doctor, but
we did see some orders that made it all official. Dr. Franklin
doesn't know whether to be angry or relieved."

"Can Bester get around?" asked Garibaldi.

"Not well. The doctor said that in a few days he could get
around on crutches or a cane. Since he's refused all medica-
tion, he won't be in a very good mood."

"What do you think his plans are?"

"To get Ms. Winters," answered the captain. "That's all
he could talk about. How are you coming along?"

Garibaldi glanced around and lowered his voice. "We've
got strong leads on both Arthur Malten and Emily Crane. It's
good stuff, but we can't pin them without Talia."

"That is a problem," conceded Sheridan. "We've got
some happy people now that the last of Psi Corps is gone,
but everyone feels badly about Ms. Winters. I wish we could
have handled it differently. What's done is done."

"Don't bet against me," declared Garibaldi. "I'm going
to bring her back, alive and free. Good-bye, sir."

"Good luck. Sheridan out."

Garibaldi signed off and paced around the foyer for a few
seconds. He had to do something! Go somewhere! After all,

they had learned everything they came to Washington to learn. Maybe he would go back to Boston right now and hang out in Emily Crane's front room. Was the woman from the Mix so confident that she wouldn't make a run for it? She and Malten had strong motives to stage these bombings, and that might inspire them to do something crazy.

Garibaldi tried to imagine a Psi Corps without the military trappings, threats, and overbearing nastiness, and he liked it. He liked it a lot. That thought made him realize that, philosophically, he was on the side of the bombers! Geez, why couldn't things be white and black, good guys and bad guys?

The main thing was that he couldn't sit around talking about Berlin, debutante balls, or frat parties. He had to ditch Gray right away. The telepath had been of surprising usefulness, being right about the Mars bombing fitting in with the B5 bombing. He had saved them a great deal of time by calling Marlon, but his usefulness was at an end. They knew everything they were likely to know without collaring either Emily Crane or Arthur Malten. For that they needed a bloodhound, which Garibaldi was. It could get rough, and Gray would just get in the way.

Garibaldi started out the front door of the restaurant, prepared to jog to the corner to catch an autotaxi, when he heard a loud, "Harrumph!"

He turned to see Gray, standing in the shadows with his arms crossed. "I wondered when you would run out," the telepath said accusingly.

Garibaldi shrugged. "Listen, I just heard that your boss, Bester, is on the prowl again. I thought maybe you might want to connect up with him, make a report or something."

"I thought we were a team," said Gray, clearly wounded. "My orders were to get to the bottom of this, and working together we were getting to the bottom of it. I'm sorry that you don't think our partnership is worthwhile."

"Aw, look," said Garibaldi with a smile, "I'm just antsy. I've got to do something. Tell you what, I'll meet you back at Emily Crane's office tomorrow morning at nine hundred hours. You can finish your dinner with your friend."

"You'll meet me tomorrow morning?" asked Gray doubtfully.

"Didn't I just say I would?"

"All right," said Gray. "Really, we're the only ones who know what's going on. We need to back each other up."

"Yeah, yeah," muttered Garibaldi, hurrying off. "See you tomorrow."

"What about your part of the check?"

"Thanks!" hollered Garibaldi, disappearing down the driveway.

Talia Winters peered out the rear of the Hovercraft with Deuce's beat-up binoculars. She wondered if she could spot the shuttlecraft before they spotted the Hovercraft. Probably not. Even if they did, that was only half the battle, because then they would still have to hide. They were skirting a ridge that had been formed by an old earthquake fault line, but it didn't really offer any hiding places. They had to face the fact that they were ducks on a platter out here in this desert.

"This trip was only supposed to cost me *one* diamond!" complained Deuce. "And now it's cost me *four!*"

As this was the two hundredth time he had complained about that particular injustice, Talia ignored him and pulled her wig and her hat down on her head. She guessed they were making good time for such a primitive craft, even if she was getting encrusted with sand; but it bothered her that she didn't know where they were going. Clement? It didn't ring a bell. They had to trust in Brother Sky's directions.

"You know, those kooks might not have seen anything!" snarled Deuce. "You didn't see a shuttlecraft, did you? Me neither!"

That thought hadn't occurred to her before, and Talia turned to look at the gangster. "Do you think they just wanted us out of there, so they made it up?"

"Sure, maybe they turn us in and say we stole their Hovercraft. I doubt if we're going to live to argue about it."

Talia banged on his shoulder and shouted, "Stop this thing! Park it somewhere!"

Deuce let up gradually on the accelerator, and the Hover-craft came to a stop and thudded into the sand. He wiped the sand off his face and demanded, "What's the matter with you?"

Talia jumped out of the craft and stretched her legs. "Stop and think about it," she said. "They got us out of the village because they know, one way or another, somebody is coming after us. Whether they sent for them, or they spotted us, or they intercepted a message, it doesn't matter. They know, and somebody's coming. There's no way to get across this desert by daylight without being spotted, so let's camouflage this thing and wait it out until nightfall."

Deuce stared at her for a moment, then stared into the unforgiving sun to the west of them. He grinned foolishly and scratched his stubbly chin. "Maybe we're doing this all wrong," he drawled. "Why should we run in a piddly Hover-craft, when they've got shuttles? Why should we run at all? Let's set a trap for *them*. How many of them can there be?"

"Well," said Talia, adjusting her wig, "assuming they're Psi Cops and they're after me, they won't alert any other authorities. They like to bring down a rogue themselves, without anybody interfering. They probably have several two-man shuttles spread out over this area."

Deuce grabbed the bumper of the Hovercraft and began to rock the vehicle. "Come on! Help me turn this thing over!"

"Why?" asked Talia, leaning down to grab the bumper.

"To make it looked like it wrecked."

CHAPTER 17

TALIA Winters watched a scorpion scuttle across the sand about a meter away from her face. The tan arachnid blended in perfectly with the sand, and she hadn't noticed it when she picked this place to lie down. Now its deadly tail was curving up and down, and its little pincers were looking for something to pinch. She was in horrendous fear that her nose would look delectable to the scorpion, but she couldn't possibly move or cry out. She would just have to let the scorpion sting her and take her chances with the venom.

Because a sleek, black shuttlecraft was about a kilometer away and swooping in for a landing.

Talia closed her eyes as the shuttlecraft landed and its thrusters blew sand all over her. After this sojourn in the desert, she wondered if she would ever feel clean again. She held her breath, waiting for the scorpion to get blown directly into the center of her face, stinger first. When that didn't happen, she held perfectly still, trying to look dead, or at least close to it.

She could imagine what the scene looked like from the air: an overturned Hovercraft which had skirted too close to the ridge, and the body of a woman lying a few meters away, broiling in what was left of the late-afternoon sun. It didn't look very threatening, she hoped.

Talia heard the door of the shuttlecraft open, and she heard their boots crunching across the sand. As she had guessed, there were only two of them, and she felt them probing her with their minds. Even though they were P12s and she was a mere P5, she had the advantage of all that contact with alien species; she was able to disrupt a casual mind-scan with bizarre images. Talia thought again about Ambassador Kosh and Invisible Isabel, knowing they wouldn't be able to make much sense out of that.

"She's alive," said one of them, "but she's delirious."

"Is that the rogue?" asked the other. "They said she had blond hair?"

"Hair color doesn't mean anything," said the first. "Besides, if we leave her here, she'll just die. Better take her in."

With her eyes closed, Talia wasn't able to see if they had returned their PPG weapons to their holsters. But they couldn't very well lift her, if they didn't. She heard their footsteps coming very close now, and it was time for her to give the prearranged signal.

She moaned loudly.

That drew their attention, and neither one of them heard Deuce as he rose up, covered with sand, and drilled the nearest Psi Cop in the arm with his PPG. The cop collapsed to his knees in shock, and the other one started to draw his weapon.

"Go ahead." Deuce grinned. "I promised the lady I wouldn't kill you, but I'm not great at keeping my promises."

Talia scrambled to her feet and grabbed the PPG out of the wounded Psi Cop's holster. Then she very carefully took the PPG from the other cop.

"You won't get away," said the black-suited telepath. "We'll bring you down."

Talia said nothing. She was busy gathering up the water bag and Deuce's briefcase and duffel bag from the fallen Hovercraft. As an afterthought, she left them the water bag.

"Oh, please let me kill them," begged Deuce. "Who would miss them? Even their mommas probably don't like them anymore."

Talia shot him a glare, and Deuce frowned disgruntledly and began to back toward the shuttlecraft. "Well," he said, "we are offering you gentlemen a great deal today—that perfectly good Hovercraft for this beat-up old shuttlecraft of yours. Now you just go northeast, and you'll get to civilization. I wouldn't go the other way, because we stole that Hovercraft from some folks, and they might shoot first and ask questions later."

Talia jumped into the shuttlecraft and kept her hand on the button to shut the hatch after Deuce.

"You got my briefcase?" asked the gangster.

"Yeah."

He nodded and jumped aboard. Talia quickly closed the hatch, and they scrambled into seats in the cockpit.

"Do you know how to fly one of these?" asked Talia.

Deuce laughed. "You think I never stole a shuttlecraft before? This is a hobby of mine."

Before she even had a chance to fasten her seat belt, he jammed the thrusters, and the little craft started to buck and shake. It wasn't a smooth takeoff, but they were soon in the air, with the dusty desert fading away beneath them.

Talia sighed and slumped back in her seat.

"Don't panic," said Deuce, "but you, uh, got a scorpion in your hair."

Talia panicked anyway—she screamed, yanked the wig off, and threw it on the floor. The startled scorpion tried to hide, but it was out of its element on the cold metal deck of the shuttlecraft. She took her shoe off to throw it at the arachnid.

"Don't kill him," said Deuce. "I'll take him with me to Guadalajara."

"Guadalajara," echoed Talia. "I need to go to Boston."

"Then I guess this is where you and I part company." To emphasize his determination, Deuce drew his PPG and aimed it at her.

"Can you let me off somewhere? A town, I mean."

"I'd have to let you off on the outskirts. You might have quite a walk."

Talia shrugged, too worn out to question whatever fate had in store for her next. "I haven't got any money," she added.

"Damnation," muttered Deuce, "what do I look like, a credit machine? This whole trip was only supposed to cost me *one* diamond, and now it's already cost me—"

"Four diamonds," she completed his sentence. "But you got a shuttlecraft out of it, and you wouldn't have gotten that without me."

"Yeah," Deuce conceded, putting his weapon away. "I guess you paid your debt. Hand me my case."

She handed him his briefcase, and he put the craft on autopilot as he rummaged through it.

"Here's a one-carat diamond," he said. "That should get you wherever you want to go. You know, you really should've let me kill those Psi Cops. As soon as they get to a link, everybody on Earth will know you're here."

"I know," said Talia somberly. She took the diamond from him and tried to smile. "Thank you."

"You're a tough one," said Deuce admiringly. "If we ever run into each other again—say, at my hanging—will you tell them I'm not totally bad? That I once did a favor for somebody, and let two Psi Cops live."

Talia gave him a real smile. "I will. I once heard somebody on B5 say that nobody is what they seem. I never knew what that meant before, but now I know—we have lots of people inside of us. Good, bad, right, wrong, it all gets blurred together. I'll never forget that you helped me, Deuce."

He smiled boyishly, and for a moment she could see the little kid who had put a firecracker in a teacher's wastebasket. Was that the moment he had gone bad? If it hadn't been for that incident, or if it hadn't been for the bombing, might they both be upstanding citizens now instead of fugitives on the run? She didn't know. She would never know.

"Phoenix coming up," said Deuce.

It was almost dark by the time Deuce landed the black shuttlecraft behind a grain elevator on the outskirts of the sprawling city.

"No time for long good-byes," he said, opening the hatch. "This is busy airspace around here."

Talia straightened her wig and her beret and made sure she had her only two possessions, the diamond and Emily Crane's address. She had thought about taking one of the extra PPGs, but shooting it out with the authorities was not really her style.

She paused in the doorway. "Bye."

"Good luck," drawled Deuce. "You'll need it."

Talia jumped out of the craft and ran for cover as he shot

the thrusters. A second later, the shuttlecraft and Deuce were gone, and she was alone again, surrounded by darkness and crickets. It felt soothing, like the darkness was a natural place for her these days. She saw the arcing lights of the city in the distance, and she found her way to an overgrown road and began walking.

Michael Garibaldi stood alone on the bridge, looking at the lights of Boston Harbor as they glinted off the black water. He had rushed back to Boston, for what? His efforts to find Emily Crane's home address had gone for naught, and he had no friends in the local police department to help him. The last thing he wanted to do was to try to explain all of this to a local cop—commercial telepaths pretending to be Martian terrorists in order to blow up Psi Cops on a space station several light-years away. You had to be there. Plus, they would keep him tied up in the squad room for days, making statements, checking statements.

With Malten having already skipped to Mars, Emily Crane was the only lead he had. Despite Gray's opinion that she wouldn't skip, he didn't trust her. As long as Talia was at large, they couldn't move against Crane, but she wasn't in the clear. If Talia showed up, protected and talking to the right people, Crane was in serious trouble. If only he could corner her at home, he reasoned, maybe he could throw enough fear into her to get *her* to confess to the police. But how could he get her unlisted address?

He snapped his fingers just as a barge announced its approach through the black waters with a woeful moan. Maybe he should go see the receptionist at the Mix office—what was his name? It had been right there on his nameplate: Ronald Trishman! A receptionist, even a sour one like him, was likely to have a listed address. Garibaldi dashed to the end of the bridge and into a bar along the waterfront.

The smell of booze was inviting—it always was—and the sight of all the lowlifes made him feel right at home, but Garibaldi had chosen another poison tonight. He went to the viewer and waited for a large guy with tattoos all over his arms to finish talking to his kids somewhere in Australia, then he grabbed the link before anybody else could. He punched up the information index and entered Ronald Trishman's name.

There were two Ronald Trishmans, but that wasn't bad for a city the size of Boston. The security officer jotted them both down in his electronic address book. It wasn't all that late, about 22:00, so he decided to pay these two Ronald Trishmans a call. One of them was bound to know where Emily Crane lived.

He knew the first one was wrong as soon as he got off the autotaxi. The place, called Flag Hill, was far too ritzy, a collection of townhouses built to look old but really quite elegant, with bay windows and a neo-colonial look. Well, he thought, maybe Ronald slummed by working as a receptionist.

He buzzed the outer door, and a sleepy woman's voice answered his call. "Yes?"

"Excuse me," said Garibaldi, "I need to speak to Ronald for a moment."

"He's taking a bath. What is it? Who are you?"

"I work with him at the Mix."

"Mix?" she asked. "He's a doctor." She rang off.

When Garibaldi got back to the street, he saw that his autotaxi had taken off. Well, he supposed, maybe he hadn't tipped it enough. He looked around the maze of dark streets and townhouses, all of it coated with a halo of city lights. After the sweltering closeness of Babylon 5, Boston seemed like an immense wilderness park, far too large to make sense out of and filled with exotic humans. He wondered what that said about his life—that Londo, G'Kar, and their alien brethren seemed normal compared to this mass of humanity.

The security chief had a pretty good sense of direction, and it was a pleasant night, so he decided to walk. He knew the second Ronald Trishman lived up some street named Beacon, and he wasn't far away from there. He would ask directions as he went. Within about three blocks, the oak trees thinned out to a standard urban sprawl of office buildings and shops, and he wasn't the only pedestrian anymore. The others looked better dressed, more affluent, and he felt like a soldier home from leave in his uniform. As he drew closer to a casino, his attention was snagged by a row of screens in the window.

Once again, there was Talia Winters's face. It was a good face for the screen—angular and confident, with lovely eyes —he could see why they liked to show it so much. This time they did a computer animation on Talia's face to turn her sleek blond hair into long, brown, curly locks. He couldn't hear the audio, so he ducked inside to see what the report was about.

"Based on the officers' description," said the newscaster, "Talia Winters was traveling with a man and wearing a dark hairstyle, probably a wig. She was last seen in Arizona, although she could be many kilometers from there by now. She and her companion are believed to have a shuttlecraft."

Traveling with a man, thought Garibaldi. She had found a protector. *That should be me,* he thought. Well, he was doing the best he could, building a case against the real bad guys. But he felt guilty about not doing more to find her. All he could think of doing was to stake out Emily Crane's office, believing she would find her way there, eventually. But what if she was just running and not trying to find Emily Crane?

At any rate, it was definite that she was on Earth, as he had figured. She would be lucky to escape from the planet before the Psi Cops got her. He wasn't going to count on her being able to testify on her own behalf, so the pressure was on him to find the real culprits. He wasn't telepathic, but he tried to send her a message:

Keep running, Talia.

"I have a diamond," said the tall woman with the curly brown hair.

She batted her eyelashes at the pawnbroker, hoping he didn't notice how filthy she was. Then she nearly swallowed her tongue as she caught sight of herself on the viewer behind him. It was her public relations photograph, taken last

year for the brochures—only in this photo she was wearing
the wig she was actually wearing! She gripped her beret
tighter and looked down, waiting for the pawnbroker to yell
for the cops.

"Yes?" he asked. "A diamond?"

He had been talking to another customer when she entered, Talia recalled, so he probably hadn't seen the news-
cast. She sighed and took the cut diamond out of her jacket
pocket. With a hopeful smile, she handed it to him, and he
placed it on the velvet pad.

"One carat," she said. "Gem quality."

"I'll be the judge of that," answered the pawnbroker,
reaching for his scanner. He passed the diamond under the
light beam for a few seconds, glanced at the readouts, and
nodded. "Yes, it's top quality. Nothing like that left on
Earth. Where did it come from?"

"Do you want it, or not?"

"Eight hundred credits."

She tried to stay calm. "I want to sell it, not a loan."

"Same price either way."

"I think it's worth more than that," Talia said slowly.

"Then go somewhere else."

She took the jewel off the velvet, but he called out to her
before she could put it in her pocket. "Eight-fifty, no more."

She looked at him and thought how weary and dirty she
was. At least with some money she could get a bath. This
was robbery, anyway, but at least she would die or be captured with some money in her pocket.

"Yeah," she said, "eight-fifty."

"All right," said the man, "if you'll hand me your
creditchit, I'll add it to your account."

She shook her head and looked down. "I don't have any
credits. That's why I need to sell the diamond."

"All right," said the man, eager to conclude the deal any
way he could, "give me your identicard, and I'll make you a
creditchit. That's one of our services. It adds only one percent."

Another rip-off, she thought, but beggars can't be

choosers. At least she had an identicard. She handed it to the man, and he disappeared with both the card and the diamond.

She looked around the pawnshop, and she couldn't remember whether she had ever been inside a pawnshop before in her life. She imagined they hadn't changed in hundreds of years, with an odd assortment of jewelry, collectibles, small electronics, musical instruments, anything that was easy to carry and might be worth a few credits. There were also four teller windows for the various financial services that the shop offered.

"Here you go, Ms. Nelson," he said, returning her identicard and a new creditchit. "Thank you for coming in." She finally let out a breath and glanced at the two cards. It seemed for a moment almost that she was a real person again, even if she did have someone else's identity.

"Thank you," she said. "If I wanted a bullet train or shuttle to the east coast, where would I find it?"

"There's a U-rail at the corner that will take you to the bullet station. The trains leave frequently, so that would be the quickest way."

"Thank you," she said, feeling a bit woozy but straggling out the door. If it had been possible, she would've stretched out on the sidewalk and gone to sleep. *No,* she told herself, *you're a shark. Gotta keep moving. Keep moving.*

This was more like it, thought Garibaldi, surveying the nondescript skyscraper. It was the kind of silver monstrosity that housed a thousand families at once, and it already felt more comfortable to him than all that open space. The gate had a security lock, but so many people went in and out that anyone could time his approach to slip in with other tenants. Garibaldi did exactly that and slipped in with a family of Sikhs wearing turbans and white robes.

"Home on leave?" asked the patriarch of the group.

"Yes," said Garibaldi, "going to see my dad, Ronald Trishman. Do you know him?"

The family shook their heads in unison and headed for the escalator. Garibaldi checked his address keeper as if he were looking for the apartment number, but he hit the index screen as soon as they were out of sight. He found Ronald's apartment number on the forty-sixth floor, west wing, and he took a combination of escalators and high-speed elevators to get there.

It was getting late, he reminded himself. This was a planet, and they didn't live on a twenty-four-hour clock like he was used to, with no particular day or night. He had better not sound threatening when he asked for Ronald, or he might end up talking to regular cops after all.

He stopped in front of the correct door, found Trishman's name under the doorbell, and buzzed. A small viewer built into the door beeped on, and he could hear sounds of the apartment's built-in security coming alive. He buzzed again, figuring armed guards would be summoned if Ronald Trishman didn't answer the door soon.

Finally a puzzled face squinted at him from the view-screen. "Who the hell is it?"

He lowered his head apologetically. "I'm extremely sorry to bother you. I'm Michael Garibaldi, security chief of Babylon 5. We spoke today."

"Well, good God, what do you want at this hour?"

"We're extremely worried that Emily Crane may be in physical danger."

"What?" muttered the older man. "Why would you come here? Oh, what the hell, I'll let you in. I'll wake up all the neighbors if I don't."

He heard clicking sounds, and the door slid open. Garibaldi smiled to himself as he ducked inside. Trishman was wearing an expensive bathrobe and slippers; all he lacked was a pipe.

"Listen," said the receptionist, bustling around nervously, "if we're going to talk, I'm going to make some tea. Do you want some?"

"No, thanks," said Garibaldi, "you go ahead. I never liked tea much."

He heard Ronald knocking about in the kitchen, making a terrific amount of noise. The old man must've been nervous, thought Garibaldi, and he wondered if he knew something about the Mix's big ambitions. He took a seat on the sofa, marveling at the size of the living room, which was decorated tastefully all in white.

After living on Babylon 5 for a year, rooms in even the dinkiest apartments looked huge. This room even had a tinted picture window that gazed upon a small window of ocean between two similar apartment towers. It wasn't a thrilling view, thought Garibaldi, but it was better than a bulkhead.

After a few minutes, Ronald Trishman came back with a tray, a teapot, and two cups, as if he was still hopeful Garibaldi would try some tea.

"I made enough for four people," he said, "so you're welcome if you want some." Trishman leaned forward and asked in a gossipy way, "Now, what is this about Ms. Crane?"

"We just want to make sure she's safe, but we can't find her."

"Isn't she at home?" asked Trishman.

While Garibaldi was trying to decide how to finesse that question, Trishman clicked his fingers and added, "No, of course she wouldn't be at home. She's on her way to Mars, or maybe she's there by now."

"Mars," repeated Garibaldi without much surprise. That figured. "Are you sure?"

The older man shrugged and said, "That's my job. A receptionist knows who's in town and who isn't."

Okay, thought Garibaldi, he had gotten what he had come for. Now if he got anything else it would be gravy. "Do you know anything about a bill before the Senate that would place the Mix in charge of Psi Corps?"

The old man's eyes twinkled. "No. Do tell?"

Garibaldi started to say more, but then he realized that his job was to ask the questions, not answer them. Let this guy pontificate. "Is Mr. Malten around your office a lot?"

Trishman shook his head. "Not an exceptional amount.

Perhaps half a dozen times a year. Surely you can't suspect *him* of doing anything wrong."

"Well," said Garibaldi, "putting a bill before the Senate isn't doing anything wrong. I suppose changing Psi Corps wouldn't be all that wrong either."

"Then you're with us," said Trishman with satisfaction.

"Wait a minute," said the security chief. "We're not talking about a political debate—we're talking about two fatal bombings! If you know anything about this, I expect you to tell me."

"I think you know about as much as I do," said the old man, rising and taking his cup to the kitchen. "Do you want to spend the night?"

"What?" asked Garibaldi.

"It's the middle of the night, Mr. Garibaldi. This is not the time to go running around knocking on doors. Don't they have night where you come from?"

"Is that a rhetorical question?" asked the security chief. He yawned and decided that he was getting tired. He had to meet Gray in the morning, in all likelihood to fly to Mars. No, he didn't have a hotel room; it just hadn't occurred to him to get one. On the other hand, could he trust this guy?

"I don't think so," he said, rising to his feet. "So are you in favor of the Mix taking over Psi Corps?"

"Instead of the other way around, like it is now?" asked Trishman. "Who wouldn't be? That doesn't mean I know anything about how this takeover is going to happen. I don't."

"Well, that's a relief," said Garibaldi. "Do you know where Ms. Crane is staying on Mars?"

Trishman smiled. "I'm afraid not. You're welcome to that couch, or not. But I'm going back to bed."

Garibaldi felt as if he had been dismissed, so he moved to the door and pressed the panel to open it. As he strode out, he was looking over his shoulder to say good night, when strong hands gripped his arms and shoulders. They dragged him back into the room.

He struggled, but there were three of them. They took him

by surprise and squirted some stuff in his face that made him swoon. Garibaldi staggered backward, losing his senses, but he managed a lucky swing that caught one of them in the stomach and doubled him over. The other two were still in his face, and one of them squirted him again with the sedative. Garibaldi windmilled his fists in the air, but he wasn't connecting.

He was slipping, falling, going where no one could reach him.

CHAPTER 18

THE lure of the bullet station and immediate passage to Boston was strong, but the lure of a bed and a shower was stronger. When Talia passed a homey, old-fashioned hotel before she reached the station, she couldn't stop herself from going in and pressing the buzzer on the check-in counter. It was the middle of the night, but she hoped she would still be able to get a room.

A kindly older lady finally appeared. "What can we do for you, miss?"

"A single," she said. "Do you have one?"

"Yes, my dear, only sixty credits for a single. Interested?"

Talia found herself nodding before she even thought about it.

"Fine. I'll need your creditchit and your identicard."

Talia passed them over, thinking that was the second time she had used the fake identicard. She only had two more times. But she was so dirty and weary that she would risk facing a million Psi Cops to be clean and rested. Tomorrow would be time enough to get to Boston, she told herself, time enough to confront Emily Crane, clear her name, and get her life back.

She dragged herself to the room and ripped off the dirty clothes and the wig. Talia felt like throwing the entire outfit away, but she doubted if she would get very far naked. In the shower, she let the lukewarm water run over her hair and body, and she watched a river of sand snake from her feet to the drain. She was too weary to even adjust the water to make it warmer, although she had the strength to rub some shampoo in her hair.

When she staggered out of the shower, she collapsed into the droopy bed with beads of water still clinging to her back. She fell immediately into a sleep that was so deep it was beyond dreams.

* * *

Garibaldi, however, was having a dream. A nightmare, to be
exact. In this dream, people were tying his hands behind his
back, tying his feet together, and stuffing a gag in his mouth.
He wanted to wake up, but he couldn't open his eyes. It
wasn't until he began to squirm against his bindings that the
dream turned really ugly. Someone slapped him across the
mouth, knocking him to the floor, and his eyes bugged open.
Unfortunately, the dream didn't end—he was still bound and
gagged.

He was also still in Trishman's white living room, only the
older man was not in sight. Instead, there were two brawny
young men, well dressed in suits. One of them was standing
over Garibaldi, glowering at him. Ah, yes, he thought, that
was the guy he had punched in the stomach. Well, why was
he upset? He wasn't the one bound and gagged, lying on the
floor with a drugged-out hangover.

The man looked like he wanted to slap him again, when a
woman's voice intruded. "Don't even think about it."

Garibaldi craned his neck as best he could to see who had
entered from the bedroom. Lo and behold, it was Emily
Crane! Only she wasn't dressed in her usual frumpy outfit
but in a sleek gray jumpsuit, with her hair pulled back severely. He tried to ask her how her trip to Mars had been, but
everything he said came out a mumble.

"Get him back on the couch," ordered the woman. The
two goons complied and lifted him back into a semicomfort-
able position.

"Mr. Garibaldi," she said, "if you promise not to cry out,
I will remove the gag."

He nodded. Crying out wasn't really his style, but he was
looking forward to kicking the crap out of these guys at the
first opportunity. She snapped her fingers, and the gag came
off.

"That was a quick trip to Mars," he croaked.

"Don't blame Ronald for lying," she said, sitting beside
him on the couch. "Or for calling us. We only have another
twenty-four hours before we can put our plan into effect, and

then we stage a bloodless coup of Psi Corps. Don't you want that—to get rid of Bester and his ilk?''

"Sister, right now, your ilk doesn't seem much better." One of the goons moved forward with his fists balled, and Garibaldi winced, awaiting the blow.

But Emily Crane waved the man off and looked back at Garibaldi. "Do you see why we have to keep you quiet for twenty-four hours, until the bill is passed and signed? Your detective work was quite good, but we can't let years of planning go down the drain to save one telepath."

She smiled pleasantly. "I'm hopeful you'll come around to our way of thinking. In twenty-four hours, after you see all that we've accomplished, you might want to forget about your investigation. The public is happy with Martian terrorists as the bombers—why can't you be?''

Garibaldi wasn't going to argue with the lady, because the alternative to agreeing with them was probably winding up as fish food in the harbor. "What are you going to do with me?" he asked.

Emily Crane got up, strode to the picture window, and looked out at the sleeping city. "Maybe we should move Mr. Garibaldi while it's still dark outside. If something happened to him here, it would reflect badly on Trishman. Gag him, untie his feet, and keep a PPG in his back."

The thugs untied the rope around Garibaldi's ankles and hauled him to his feet. They shoved the foul-tasting rag back into his mouth, but he was willing to give up his voice in exchange for having his legs free. His hands were still tied behind his back, but he could kick, he could run! He saw one of the goons pull a PPG out of his jacket pocket, and he felt the metal in his back. Maybe he wouldn't kick or run right now, thought Garibaldi.

Emily Crane opened the door and checked the corridor to make sure it was clear, then she motioned for them to follow her. Garibaldi stumbled out, sandwiched between the two thugs, one of whom had a PPG in his back. The only reason they were letting him walk, he decided, was to keep from having to carry his dead body. Nevertheless, he couldn't think of any way to get away from them, and he behaved himself all the way down the elevator and the escalator.

In the street, he told himself, maybe someone would see this obvious kidnapping and call the cops. But there was no one in the street in these dead hours just before dawn, nothing but a silent row of electric-powered vehicles. If he ran, thought Garibaldi, he was trying to decide how many meters he would get before the guy with the PPG drilled him. He figured three.

Suddenly, a strange voice seemed to speak in his head. It told him to duck! Garibaldi had nothing to lose, so he pretended to trip. He stumbled to the pavement a split second before a PPG blast ripped the head off the man behind him. The other goon was drawing his weapon when three blasts from entirely different directions turned his midsection a fiery orange. The two pieces of him fell to the ground.

Emily Crane ran for it, and her short height let her elude the first shots directed at her. Then two black-suited Psi Cops jumped out of the bushes directly in front of her. As she stumbled away from them, begging forgiveness, they executed her.

Strong arms picked Garibaldi off the pavement and guided him to a black shuttlecraft that awaited them in an adjacent parking lot. They tossed him in like a bag of potatoes, the hatch slammed shut, and the thrusters blasted the craft off the ground and into the black night.

"Hold still," said a familiar voice, and Garibaldi felt hands untying the ropes at his back. Once his hands were free, he ripped off the gag and rolled over to greet his saviors.

The first thing he saw was the relieved and smiling face of Harriman Gray. Behind him, swathed in bandages and holding a cane, sat Mr. Bester. The only other person in the shuttlecraft was the pilot, and she was concentrating on getting them through the skyscrapers of Boston.

"It would be polite to say 'thank you,' " suggested Bester.

"Yes, thank you," croaked Garibaldi. "You . . . you wasted them. Damn it, Emily Crane was the only one who could clear Talia Winters!"

"Rogue telepaths," said Bester. "All perfectly legal, although I doubt if we'll claim credit. Actually, you owe your life to Mr. Gray here. He got worried about you last night and contacted my office. When I spoke with him, he told me all about Emily Crane and the Mix. We just managed to get a tail on her before she came over here with her friends. We've been hoping you would come out soon."

Garibaldi touched his partner's arm. "Thanks, Gray."

The young telepath looked a bit sheepish. "I wasn't planning to tell Mr. Bester last night, but I got worried about you."

The security chief looked out the cockpit window at the vanishing lights of the city. "Did you warn me to duck?" he asked.

Gray nodded, and Garibaldi cleared his throat, thinking about what would have happened to him if he hadn't ducked. He lifted his hand, and it was still shaking.

"We'll leave the bodies there," said Bester contentedly. "I always say, if you can't talk to the person you want, leave a message."

Garibaldi rubbed his dry lips and looked back out the window. He shouldn't be an ingrate, because they had probably saved his life, but he felt rotten about the cold-blooded executions. That could be Talia lying down there in the street, he reminded himself.

"The person you want is Malten," he said hoarsely.

"It certainly is," agreed Bester. "I want to thank you two, you've done a wonderful job on this case. Beyond my expectations. You led us right to the rattlers' nest."

Garibaldi remained single-minded. "Then you'll let Talia Winters go now, right?"

Mr. Bester frowned. "That is a concern. To let her go would be to admit we made a mistake, and we don't like to air our dirty linen in public. Plus, we want to keep the Mix healthy and in place, with a few more controls and minus Malten. The Free Phobos group will never be heard from again, so what is the harm in letting them keep the blame?"

"Talia Winters!" barked Garibaldi. "Read my lips. She's not guilty, and you know it."

Bester swallowed and looked past him. "I've arranged for your passage back to Babylon 5, and Mr. Gray's passage to Berlin. There will be commendations for both of you in my report."

"Mr. Bester!" snapped Gray. "That is patently unfair! You know very well she is innocent."

The Psi Cop shook his head in amazement. "Don't you know how many agencies are after her now? I couldn't call them off even if I wanted to! If she turns herself in—to the right people—she might stand a chance."

"Then I'm going to keep after her," vowed Garibaldi.

"It is no longer your concern!" Bester seethed. He winced in pain as he shifted in his seat.

"Not true," said Garibaldi. "I'm bringing back a fugitive who escaped from Babylon 5. I can do that all day long. Put this shuttle down! I'm getting off."

"Me too," said Gray, jutting his chin.

"All right," snapped Bester. "Put them down."

"Is Miami okay?" asked the pilot. "That's the closest big city without backtracking."

"Fine," responded both Garibaldi and Gray. The security chief gave his partner a nod and glanced out the cockpit window. He saw that they were in space, in reentry, and half the globe was shimmering in the sunlight of a new day.

"One more thing," said Bester through clenched teeth.

"Yeah?"

"Stay away from Mars."

Garibaldi chuckled and looked at the Psi Cop. "You're talking about my old stomping grounds. Is that where Malten really is? On Mars. Why don't you get him?"

"We know he's on Mars, but we don't know where. If you find out where he is, call us. Let us handle him."

"Sure," said Garibaldi, "and if you find Talia, call me. Let me handle her."

They felt the thrusters of the shuttlecraft kick on, and the noise level increased. They strapped themselves into seats and braced for the descent into Miami.

Talia lay in the swaybacked bed, just watching the sun stream through the dirty lace curtains of the old hotel. It was not the kind of place she would have stayed a week earlier, but it felt so warm and friendly that she never wanted to leave. She knew she had to get up, keep moving, but her body told her to rest. It creaked with protest when she forced it out of the bed.

She strolled past the viewer and wondered if she should put the news on. She couldn't bear to see herself in that wig again, either in a computer mock-up or in real life, so she had decided to trim her regular hair a bit and stuff it all into the beret. Even though she dreaded seeing her face on the screen again, she couldn't resist the masochistic impulse to turn on the viewer. She dialed the news, hoping against hope that something good might have happened while she slept.

Thankfully, she caught the tail end of the report on her, which summed up that she was still at large. This came as some relief, she thought ruefully, just in case the hotel room was really an ingenious prison. At large, thought Talia. What a strange phrase—it sounded as if she were everywhere and nowhere at once, which was sort of true.

She was about to turn the viewer off when she heard the announcer mention a name, Emily Crane. Talia jumped back as if she had been shocked, and she stared at the image on the screen. It *was* Emily Crane, the one who had turned her into a hunted fugitive. Only she was dead, and her PR photo was replaced by a more grisly shot of a limp body on a sidewalk. Talia concentrated on the announcer's words:

"There are no suspects, and police are asking that anyone with information on the murder of Emily Crane, Michael Graham, and Barry Strump please come forward. Once again, three commercial telepaths from the Mix were brutally murdered about five o'clock this morning. There was no apparent robbery or motive. In sports, we have a new champion in field hockey . . ."

Talia punched it off and slumped back into the bed. Now, what the hell was she going to do? The one person who might be able to clear her was dead! She felt like curling up in the droopy bed and just staying there until her money ran out, or the Psi Cops found her, whichever came first.

After a moment, Talia sat up and wiped her eyes. She stared at the morning light as it streamed through the window, knowing what she had to do. She had to run for real. No more running *to* somewhere, just running away *from* everything. The one person who might have cleared her was dead, and she would never get a break.

Where could she go? In all the exotic places she thought about, such as Minbar, she would stick out and be easily recognizable. Earth was just too risky, and she couldn't get near where she really wanted to go—her childhood haunts. She needed someplace that was chaotic, with a thriving underground, because she was firmly a part of that social strata now. She could think of only one such place.

Mars.

Uncle Ted had been part of her undoing, so maybe he could help her now. Plus, Mars would be cheap to get to. She hurriedly put on her clothes and stuffed her hair under her beret. A glance in the mirror warned her that she looked too much like herself, and she resolved to do something about that later. First, she had to figure out a way to let Uncle Ted know she was coming.

She ran her chit through the viewer slot and punched in her mother's address. Then she entered her E-mail: "Hobo, Uhkhead."

It might be a message Ambassador Kosh would appreciate, she thought with a grim smile. Talia was sure her mother would get it, because "Hobo, Uhkhead" was her baby-talk way of saying "Hello, Uncle Ted." She had seen herself say it often enough in old home visuals. She wanted to say a lot more to her mother—like "Mom, I'm innocent!"—but that would have given away the sender. She hoped the cryptic message would look like garbled junk to whoever was reading her mom's mail.

Before she left the hotel, Talia took the card with Emily Crane's address on it and ripped it up.

"Now boarding shuttle 1312 for Clarke Spaceport," announced the computer. Gray and Garibaldi were already in line for the trip to the orbital spacedock, from where they would grab a flight to Mars.

Garibaldi glanced around the Miami Interstellar Port, marveling at the odd choice of colors. He had never seen a transportation center painted all in turquoise before. Ah, well, maybe they had gotten a deal on the paint. At any rate, the pastel color softened the hard look of many of the passengers in line with them.

He turned to Gray and said, "You know, you don't really have to come with me. You could just wipe your hands of this and go enjoy your place in Berlin for a few days."

"No," said the telepath, "we're a team. I was glad to have been of assistance this morning, when you needed it."

"There's something I didn't tell Bester," remarked Garibaldi, lowering his voice. "Emily Crane said that the plan would be put into effect within twenty-four hours. So if Bester doesn't find Malten by tonight, by tomorrow Malten may be his boss."

They shuffled ahead a few more steps in the line, and Gray replied, "That would be fittingly ironic, but I think Mr. Bester will be at the Senate today, twisting arms. His problem is how to bring down Malten without bringing down the entire Mix."

The two men strolled down the rampway and onto the shuttlecraft. It was a medium-sized craft and seated about forty people. Gray stopped midway down the aisle and pointed at two empty seats, then he remembered and shook his head.

"The rear, right?"

Garibaldi nodded, and they found seats once again in the next-to-last row. "You can see everybody from the back," he remarked.

"What makes you think that Ms. Winters will go to Mars?" asked Gray.

The chief shrugged and looked out the port window. "I don't know. It's close by, and that's where *I* would go if I were running. She needs to find an underground organization to hide her, and there are plenty of them on Mars. It's a good haystack, if you're a needle."

"She might be very useful to the Martian separatists," said Gray. "She's a telepath with a full knowledge of Psi Corps, plus she has her experience with aliens. I often wonder, what would we do if the Mars separatists allied themselves with an alien power?"

"Let's not think about it, okay?" asked Garibaldi. "Mars is a mess. We ignored it for too long, and now we don't know what to do with it. You wonder why the hell the alliance tries so hard to hang on to it."

"Yes, don't you," Gray remarked dryly.

In the gift store at Sky Harbor Travel Center, Talia bought an expensive print scarf, which she tied around her beret. Now it looked less as if she were tying to hide her hair color, she hoped. She bought some sunglasses, which were tinted lightly enough to wear indoors, and she glanced in the mirror at Frieda Nelson, the eccentric artist from Oregon. The real Frieda was probably a straight-laced professional, and she hoped that she wasn't destroying the woman's reputation.

"Announcing the departure of shuttle 512 to the Clarke Spaceport," droned the computer voice.

She glanced at her ticket—yes, that was her. She was booked all the way to Central Mars, and she wondered how often she would have to show her identicard. There would probably be a check-in when she reached the Clarke Spaceport, because space stations wanted to make sure that people were coming and going, not sticking around. Then she would have to show the card again when she disembarked at Mars. That would make four uses, right at the limit.

Talia tightened the scarf under her neck and headed for her gate. She walked briskly, to make it look as if she were a busy person, not a fugitive skulking about. She had become a bit more optimistic as she realized that there were other people who could clear her name. Deuce, for one; and surely Emily Crane had other accomplices. Some of them might be on Mars, and she would keep her eyes and ears open.

She darted importantly between two police officers, daring them to look at her. They did, but despite her thumping heart, they didn't rush after her. If she could make this last jump to Mars, and not get nabbed, maybe she could catch her breath. Unfortunately, she had begun to figure out who had killed Emily Crane. That was one way the Psi Cops handled rogues—to slaughter them in the street. Talia shuddered, but she shook off the panic attack and marched down the ramp to her shuttlecraft.

CHAPTER 19

"IDENTICARD, please?"

Talia took a breath and handed the card over to the security guard at the gate. If she got caught up here in the Clarke Spaceport, there wasn't anywhere for her to run. She adjusted her sunglasses as she waited for him to slide the card through his scanner.

"Thank you, Ms. Nelson," he replied, handing the card back to her. "Will you be staying long?"

"I'm catching a flight to Mars right away," she answered.

"Thank you," he repeated like a parrot. "Have a pleasant stay."

Talia moved past him, walking like a zombie with no particular sense of where she was going in the sprawling spaceport. She saw a bank of screens running news highlights, and she made a beeline in the opposite direction. She never wanted to see herself in the news again—from now on she would lead a life of quiet obscurity. She figured she had about fifty credits left on her creditchit, and food was the most logical thing to blow it on. If the Psi Cops brought her down, at least she would die with a full stomach.

She entered the restaurant as Gray and Garibaldi walked by. They didn't see each other.

"She may be traveling with a man," said Garibaldi. "At least, that's the report I saw."

"Then maybe she's run in a completely different direction," replied Gray. "After all, Mars is a stronghold for the Psi Cops. If I were running, I would certainly *not* go to Mars."

Garibaldi smiled. "I'll remember that if I'm ever chasing you." He looked back at the restaurant they had just passed. "You want something to eat?"

"No, thank you," answered Gray with a sour expression. "My stomach has been acting up. Too much excitement, too many quick takeoffs and landings. You go ahead. I'd just like to sit down until they announce our flight."

Garibaldi turned to go, and then something caught his eye. He gripped Gray's arm and pointed. "What are they doing?"

About thirty meters away, a team of four black-uniformed Psi Cops had stopped a young blond woman and were checking her identicard. She was protesting, but it didn't do her much good.

"Spot-checking," said Gray. "They're still looking for her."

Through clenched teeth, Garibaldi muttered, "Even though they know she's innocent."

"Those four men don't know she's innocent. Only Bester knows, and it's useful to him to blame Ms. Winters. If we could find Malten, maybe we could get him to testify on her behalf."

"If he's still alive," added Garibaldi.

The Psi Cops bowed and offered apologies to the woman, who scurried to get away from them as quickly as possible. They strode down the corridor, four abreast, scrutinizing every woman they passed.

"I just lost my appetite," growled Garibaldi. "Let's go find the gate and be the first ones on for a change."

At the counter in the restaurant, Talia had just started to eat her tuna fish sandwich when she saw the four black-suited Psi Cops stop in the doorway. They entered and confronted a young woman seated close to the door. Talia quickly lowered her head and wrapped the sandwich in her napkin. When they headed her way, she bolted for the rest room, hoping nobody would notice her quick departure. Fortunately, it was the kind of place where people often had to run and eat at the same time. At least, that's what she told herself as she burst through the swinging door into the women's rest room.

Talia took refuge in one of the stalls and sat on the toilet lid. Glumly, she unwrapped her squashed sandwich and tried to eat it. But she only got through a few bites before she dissolved into tears. Was this the life she had to face? Running from the sight of a uniform, eating in a bathroom stall? She was so pathetic. Maybe she should just march up to the Psi Cops and turn herself in. They could only kill her once, but this way she was dying every minute.

The telepath hadn't realized how loudly she was sobbing until she heard a knock on the door. "Are you all right?" asked a kindly voice.

She grabbed some toilet paper and dabbed it at her eyes. "Yes, yes," she lied. "I'm all right."

"Can I help you?"

This was ridiculous, talking through the door of a bathroom stall. "Just a second," she said. Talia stood up and tossed the remains of her sandwich into the toilet, which she loudly flushed.

When she emerged, she saw a kindly old lady, smiling sweetly at her. "What's the problem, dearie?"

As Talia was trying to figure out what to say, she heard a synthesized voice announce, "Transport *Bradley* to Mars is now loading at docking bay three. Repeat, transport *Bradley* to Mars is now loading at docking bay three."

"It's . . . it's my boyfriend!" Talia blurt out. "He beats me, and I've been trying to run away from him. But everywhere I go, he follows me!"

The old lady frowned. "That sonofabitch. Let's sic the police on him!"

"No," said Talia, "that will only bog me down in more legal problems. I've got a ticket for the flight to Mars, and if I can just get on it, I'll be rid of him for good. I've got family who will protect me there."

"Is he out there now?" asked the lady, pointing to the door leading to the restaurant.

"Yes," breathed Talia. "Perhaps if there was a diversion, I could get past him."

The woman nodded thoughtfully. "You mean, like if a little old lady ran out there, saying some guy was trying to flash her?"

"Yes, that would do it," said Talia. "Direct everybody's

attention toward the back of the restaurant, if you can, and I'll run out the front. Thanks so much.''

"Fine," said the older lady, fluffing her hair in the mirror. "I like to act."

She walked calmly out of the rest room and went to the rear of the restaurant, where she commenced screaming. "Help! Help! He flashed me! He's naked! He went that way!"

Talia edged out the door and skirted along the wall, as far as possible from the direction the lady was pointing. Even the four Psi Cops stopped their interrogations long enough to see what the fuss was about, and two of them moved to intercept the old lady.

"He doesn't have any pants on!" she screamed.

No one noticed Talia as she slipped away from the restaurant.

At the gate, there was a long line waiting to board the transport to Mars, and at the end of the line were two different Psi Cops, questioning a young woman and her male companion. Talia nearly bolted in the opposite direction, but her reasoning faculties overruled her panic button. There had to be teams of Psi Cops all over the spacedock, the voice of self-preservation said. Hanging around here was suicide. She fished her ticket out of the pocket of her blue pantsuit and charged to the front of the line.

"Harold, Harold!" she called, waving her ticket. "Yoo-hoo! Wait for me!"

She stepped right in front of a middle-age couple waiting to board and stomped her foot. "Oh, that man? Didn't he get my message?"

"Go ahead," said the man, motioning her to go first.

"Thank you," she said with a curtsey.

She stepped in front of the gate agent and offered him her ticket.

"I'll need to run your identicard, too," said the young man with a sigh.

"Oh," she answered, trying to sound nonplussed. "I didn't think they carded you on this end."

"Just for today. Extra security precautions. That's why the line's so backed up." He took her card and ran it through. When he handed the card back, he didn't bother to call her Ms. Nelson, but he did wave her through.

Twenty meters away, midway down the line, Harriman Gray clicked his tongue. "Did you see that woman cut in line? Some people have no class."

"Hmm," murmured Garibaldi. He had been watching the two Psi Cops roust all the young, attractive women. Some job they had. He wondered whether either of them had been part of the execution squad that had wasted Emily Crane in the wee hours.

Their patience was eventually rewarded, and Garibaldi and Gray boarded the *Bradley*. This was a big transport with a full complement, as the jump between Earth and Mars was a popular one, and Garibaldi panned the sea of faces as they made their way to the back of the craft. Gray didn't even question the seating rule anymore. For once, they settled in at the very last row, and Garibaldi stretched his long legs in the aisle.

Talia had been studying her identicard for several seconds, wondering if it was still a pass to freedom or a death certificate. She had used it four times, the last unexpectedly, and she would be asked for it again when she disembarked at Mars. She didn't have any other card she could use, and they wouldn't let her off without it—so she was going to use it a fifth time, like it or not. She hadn't planned to spend the entire flight in anguish over her identicard, but that's how it looked.

Then she saw two Psi Cops enter the transport and stop near the front of the cabin. Talia slouched in her seat, glad she had picked a row toward the rear of the craft, about two-thirds of the way back. She was in the last seat, against the bulkhead, and she leaned away from the aisle and put her chin in her hand to hide her face.

But the Psi Cops hadn't come on board searching for her; they were passengers traveling to Mars. They were among the last to find their seats. Great, thought Talia, two Psi Cops sitting a few rows away from her and a bum identicard that she couldn't use anymore. She gnawed on her thumbnail and wondered what else could go wrong.

"It's a full ship," observed Mr. Gray.

"There are still two Psi Cops," muttered Garibaldi. "Damn, they were beginning to get on my nerves back there. Who the hell do they think they are?"

"Psi Cops chasing a rogue telepath," said Gray. "You think we're only hard on you folks, the nontelepaths. We're much harder on ourselves. By running, Ms. Winters brought this on herself, remember that."

"We've got to find her first," vowed Garibaldi, although he realized that if hundreds of Psi Cops and a whole planetful of police couldn't find her, what chance did he have? Maybe her male companion was good; maybe he had gotten her out of it. After all, there was a lot of space out there, and maybe she could find a safe chunk of it. Garibaldi wished her well if she was running for daylight. But he would miss her.

"Please prepare for departure," said a computer voice. "Fasten seat restraints; stow all documents and carry-on items."

A few meters away, Talia relaxed in her chair. It was definite now—if she was going to be arrested, it would be on Mars. Of course, that would just feed the publicity mill that was grinding out stories about her connections to Mars. It couldn't be helped. This nightmare wanted to create its own internal logic, and she had to go with it.

Garibaldi settled back, crossed his arms, and closed his eyes. He told Gray, "Wake me up when we're there."

Halfway through the trip, Garibaldi got jostled awake by the man sitting across the aisle from him, who got up to stretch his legs. Gray was snoring softly to the right of him, and the lights in the cabin had been dimmed by half. Most people were asleep, but a handful were standing, milling about. He was just about to fall back to sleep when he saw the lithe figure of a woman moving about seven rows in front of him.

She was just the type he liked, classy and cultured, and she was wearing a pantsuit that hugged her slim torso. She was wearing a scarf and dark glasses, and he wondered if perhaps she wasn't older than he imagined. Ah, well, even if she was eighty, she still looked pretty good.

You pig, quit staring at her, he told himself. But the woman had almost struggled to the end of her row and was about to hit the aisle, so he thought he would hold on to catch her rear action. Garibaldi wasn't disappointed—it was the finest can he had seen in a long time. In fact, it was reminiscent. He sat up in his seat and stared at the woman's buttocks as she sauntered away from him. Then he gripped Gray's arm.

"Wake up!" he whispered. "Wake up!"

"What is it? What is it?" mumbled Gray.

He bent so close to Gray that it probably looked as if he was kissing him. "She's here on this transport with us," he whispered, "Talia."

"You saw her? You made positive identification?"

"Well," admitted Garibaldi, "all I saw was her rear end, but that's enough."

Gray wrinkled his nose. "Really, Garibaldi, that is disgusting! You see a woman's rear end, and you fantasize that you can identify Ms. Winters from *her* rear end? I hadn't realized you were such close associates."

"Trust me," claimed Garibaldi, "I have been watching that can very closely for the past year, and I know it by heart. But I want you to verify the ID—we'll be able to see her face when she comes back."

"I don't need to stare at her," said Gray with distaste. "All I have to do is scan her."

"No, don't do that. There are two Psi Cops on board, and I don't want to alert them. If she gets a mind-scan, she'll think it's them and she'll freak. The best we can do is let those two guys get off and try to approach her where we have some privacy."

Gray shook his head. "What am I doing? I'm talking as if you could identify a woman from her bottom!"

"Just look at her when she comes back, all right?"

Gray shook his head with disbelief and began to shut his eyes. That didn't last long, because Garibaldi elbowed him in the ribs.

"There she is!" he whispered.

With a look of contempt on his face, Mr. Gray peered around the seat in front of him. Garibaldi was holding the seat card with flight instructions in front of his face, in case she looked his way. The woman in the blue pantsuit stepped briskly back into her row, and she looked up only once. When she did, Garibaldi saw the chiseled features—a little more gaunt than before—and the determined eyes—darting and wary behind the sunglasses. She was a frightened woman, running on the edge, and he fought the temptation to leap out of his seat and wrap his arms around her. Hang in there, Talia, he told her with his thoughts.

She glanced up again, looking puzzled, as she made her way over people's knees to her seat. Finally she collapsed into the seat and molded herself into the shadows along the bulkhead.

"All right," admitted Gray, "that is either her or a very close proximity. And I'll pay more attention to women's rear ends in the future."

"You do that," whispered Garibaldi. "How should we handle this?"

"As you say, if we approach her in this crowded cabin, it might cause a scene. I suppose we have no choice but to wait until we get off the ship, then play it by ear. I suppose, if she's gotten this far, she has a fake identicard."

"Can you tell if there's someone with her?" asked Garibaldi.

"Somebody is sitting next to her. But all the seats are full, so that doesn't mean anything."

The man who was sitting across the aisle from Garibaldi chose that moment to return to his seat. The security chief smiled pleasantly at the passenger, knowing this was the end of his candid conversation with Gray. Besides, there was nothing left to say. They just had to sit tight until they could get Talia alone.

But at least they had found her! She was still in trouble, but she had friends around her.

Talia glanced behind her, thinking what a weird sensation that had been. She had been concentrating so hard on blocking her thoughts as she walked by the two Psi Cops that she had been stunned by a thought coming from the other direction. She hadn't been able to read it, because she had been blocking, but it troubled her to think that someone behind her was also watching her. Thinking about her.

She wanted to stare into the crowd of faces behind her, but she didn't dare. What if they were still watching? Really, was there anybody back there? It was probably just some guy giving her a leer, like Garibaldi always gave her on the lift. She even missed that part of Babylon 5. What was she doing to herself, wondered Talia, letting her paranoia get to her? Hadn't she come this far without a hitch? She would make it all the way. The worst part of running, she decided, was that the paranoia never let up. It only got worse.

Talia tried to sleep, knowing she wouldn't be able to.

Garibaldi sat nervously through the reentry into Mars' thin atmosphere. The transport was capable of docking on the Red Planet, with its fraction of Earth's gravity, so they didn't have to transfer from an orbital spacedock. As the long journey was about to come to an end, there was excited conversation in the cabin, and people moved about in their seats, anxious to be off the crowded vessel. But not him. The safe confines of the shuttle had been just fine; now they would have to chance the craziness of Mars. As far as he knew, Talia considered him the enemy, and she might freak when she saw him.

He could feel Gray tensing beside him, too. The timing of their actions would have to be perfect. There could be Psi Cops at the dock, eyeing everyone, rousting the attractive women. Maybe somebody would be meeting her—maybe the man she had traveled with. Or maybe that man was somewhere else on the craft, making it look as if they weren't traveling together.

No, he decided, it would be best to let Talia get through the security check-in alone, then they would make contact. But they had to be ready to move immediately if things went wrong. They might have to fight for jurisdiction over her. Despite being so close to her, he felt far away from Talia. What was her mental state like after the bombing, the accusations, and then running for her life? Not good, he imagined.

"This is where it all began for me," mused Mr. Gray. "About a week and a half ago, I got off this flight, and Mr. Bester was there waiting for me."

"Well, let's hope there's not a repeat of that," muttered Garibaldi.

They heard a heavy clanging and a thud as the air-lock mechanism latched on to the ship's hull. Everyone else heard it, too, and they rose from their seats in unison, ready to bolt from the transport as quickly as possible.

"Welcome to Mars," said a synthesized voice. "The time is 13:11, and the temperature is 379 degrees Celsius. It is hot and dry. Please watch your step as Mars has thirty-eight percent of the gravity of Earth."

The people in Talia's row began to file out, but she hung back, stricken with fear. She knew her identicard was going to get her arrested, and she couldn't go through that again! Not the lights, the accusations, the raised fists, and the angry shouts from people who wanted to punish her! Talia's heart was starting to do flip-flops in her rib cage, and she couldn't make her legs move. She felt ill, physically ill. *Come on,* she told herself, *you've felt ill for days now. If this is the end of the race, then so be it. Face it like a woman.*

For a moment, Garibaldi got excited, thinking that Talia would hang back in the cabin long enough for him and Gray to approach her there. But she suddenly got a determined look on her face and leaped from her seat, inserting herself forcefully into the herd of passengers moving toward the hatch. With maybe twenty people between them, he and Gray had to push and shove just to keep up. Even then, Talia's lithe body moved through the crowd faster than they could.

"She's getting away!" whispered Garibaldi.

"I can always send her a message," said Gray, "as long as she's in my line of sight."

"Hold off," ordered Garibaldi.

At least the two Psi Cops were already off the vessel, Talia noticed as she worked her way down the line. She hoped they got waved through the check-in and were long gone, but there was no such luck. When she reached the gate area, she could see the Psi Cops standing patiently to show their identicards to security. There were two more Psi Cops standing beyond the barriers, waiting for them.

Once again, Talia almost bolted, but there was no place to go. She held up her identicard and looked at it, hoping that Brother Lizard had outdone himself when he had chosen Frieda Nelson as her identity. Maybe Frieda was the stay-at-home type who never went anywhere, never had any call to use her real identicard. Maybe the system was not yet wise to there being two Frieda Nelsons. Right, she thought cynically, and maybe she would live to see her next birthday.

Behind her, two men inched forward, straining their necks to see what was happening. They were so close yet so far away, thought Garibaldi. With a few strides, he could touch her—and scare the daylights out of her. Her shoulders were hunched, and she moved as if she had aged ten years. More than anything, he just wanted to wrap his arms around Talia and tell her it was okay. There would be a happy ending.

He only hoped that was true.

The two Psi Cops met their friends, and there were hearty handshakes among gloved hands. To everyone's relief, they wandered off, apparently not on duty and not particularly interested in their fellow passengers.

Talia swallowed what was left of the saliva in her mouth. She would get through this—she would. The card would work one last time. Somehow, the people in the line in front of her melted away, and she found herself gliding forward in the light gravity, confidently presenting her card to the waiting security guard. The dock area was so much like B5's dock that it almost felt like home. Home, she thought wistfully. There's no place like home, except when they take it away from you.

"Thank you," said the security guard, taking the card from her trembling hand. "Are you all right, miss?"

She sniffled and gripped her hands to her chest. "Yes, just a bit air-sick."

"I get that way myself," remarked the guard pleasantly. He ran her card through the slot in his scanning device, and her heart and her breath held perfectly still.

"Hmm," he said puzzledly. "You are Ms. Frieda Nelson, aren't you?"

"Yes," she gasped.

"From Eugene, Oregon?"

"Last time I looked." She tried to sound disdainful, but she felt as if she was going to be stricken by a heart attack.

"Could you please step to the side for a moment while I finish with these other passengers." His tone wasn't so pleasant anymore, but it wasn't angry either. "There's an irregularity on your card. These glitches happen." To make sure she wasn't going anywhere, he put the card in his pocket.

Talia stood to the side, as ordered, and she wondered if she dared to send him a telepathic suggestion to the effect that her card was really okay. That was the sort of thing Mr. Bester could do with ease. Unfortunately, she felt so shaky and distressed that she didn't know if she could concentrate well enough to pull it off. Well, nothing ventured nothing gained.

Just as she had screwed up her courage to send the guard a message, an outside voice invaded her mind. Very clearly, it stated, "You are among friends. Do not panic."

Then, a monstrous explosion ripped the building!

CHAPTER 20

TALIA screamed, along with hundreds of others, as she staggered to the floor. She saw a flaming refreshment cart go rolling down the middle of the mall, spewing great clouds of choking, black smoke. The security guard was trying to hold back a panicked line of passengers while yelling into his link, and he wasn't paying any attention to her. She jumped to her feet and dashed through the smoke.

She bumped hard into a strange man, who wrapped his arms around her. Talia shrieked at his bizarre appearance, but then she realized he was a regular man wearing goggles and a breathing mask. She looked closer and saw his long white hair, like the mane of an old lion, and the devil-may-care smile under the mask.

"Hiya, Talia!" said his muffled voice.

"Uncle Ted," she gasped, and she dissolved into a coughing fit.

"This gas won't last forever," he warned, grabbing her arm and yanking her down the corridor. She staggered after him, her senses overcome by the smoke, shouts, and noise. Then a competing voice sounded in her head.

"Talia!" it called. It was a real voice, yelling above all the others. "Wait for me!"

She pulled away from Uncle Ted and whirled around. A telepathic voice popped into her head, saying, "Do not panic, Talia. It's Garibaldi and a friend."

Her uncle regained a grip on her arm and tried to pull her along. "What's the matter with you!" he growled.

"Stop!" she demanded. "I'm not alone!"

Two men came charging out of the smoke, hands over their mouths, coughing. A Psi Cop rushed by in the other direction, waving his PPG. Uncle Ted drew his own PPG and looked as if he was about to blast Garibaldi and Gray.

"No," she said, grabbing his arm. "Please wait."

"I don't want to shoot them!" He pulled on her arm, but Garibaldi reached her that same moment and started to pull on her free hand. The bare contact sent a shock of distracting intimacies through her mind.

There was no time for greetings or explanations, and Talia knew it. She pulled her hand away and saw the shock of the contact register in Garibaldi's eyes. "We've got to go with my uncle *now,*" she told Garibaldi. "Don't speak, just follow."

"But . . ."

She let her uncle drag her away, and she barely had time to glance over her shoulder to make sure Garibaldi and Gray were following. They were! As she and Uncle Ted approached a clearing in the smoke, he whipped his mask off and stuck it into the pockets of his greatcoat. As always, she marveled, he was quite a dashing figure. Even in his sixties, he had that handsome boyishness that had always gotten him into trouble. She hoped that she would age that well, although she felt as if she were aging fast at the moment.

Uncle Ted whipped out a cardkey and got them into a door marked EMPLOYEES ONLY. Talia stopped to hold the door open for Garibaldi and Gray. When the two men tried to talk, she put her fingers to her lips and glared at them. The telepathic message she sent them wasn't subtle either—it said they could follow or not, but they were not to stop her and Uncle Ted.

Garibaldi followed without question, and Gray looked around like he needed some encouragement. But with the others rushing away from him, he sprinted to catch up. The strange caravan of a dashing figure, a frightened woman, and two confused men swept through a sweltering kitchen where workers were baking doughnuts. The bakers glanced up from their work with minor interest, as if they were prepared for such intrusions.

After they rushed out another door, the group found themselves in a gray, unfinished corridor full of conduits and ducts for ventilation and life support. Uncle Ted suddenly pulled his PPG and pointed it squarely at Garibaldi.

"Honey, I wasn't expecting you to have friends from Earthforce."

Garibaldi just tried to ignore him. "Listen, Talia, we caught the real bombers—we all know you're innocent."

Talia scowled. "Oh, now you know! And I see what happens when you 'catch' someone—shot to pieces all over the sidewalk." Self-consciously, she pulled on her gloves. Garibaldi's eyes followed the action with fascination. She turned to Gray. "Are the Psi Cops still after me?"

"Yes," admitted the telepath.

"Then I'm still running."

"Please, we've got to talk," begged Garibaldi. "Let us come with you!"

"Out of the question," declared Uncle Ted.

"If you come with us," said Talia, "you've got to swear that you won't turn us in."

"I swear," he answered. "Besides, I know your Uncle Ted."

The flamboyant man squinted at him. "From where?"

"Here. It was almost two years ago, and I arrested you for creating a public nuisance, remember? You were railing against the new emigration rule—good speech. I was supposed to rough you up, if you'll remember, but I let you go with a warning."

"Yes, yes! Thank you!" beamed Uncle Ted. Then he frowned. "Those were the days when I could still speak in public. So, are you with the movement?"

"Not exactly," admitted Garibaldi. "But I'm not gonna let your niece out of my sight again. We have to talk somewhere about what to do next, and it might as well be at your place. Right, Gray?"

Mr. Gray looked stricken with fear at the thought of continuing with this dangerous group, but he didn't say no. Uncle Ted motioned for them to follow, and he took off at a jog down the dimly lit corridor. Talia could hear nothing but a rush of air coming from the ducts overhead, plus their pounding footsteps, echoing between the narrow walls.

Uncle Ted stopped at a large hatch in the center of the floor and motioned to Garibaldi. "Help me with this."

The security chief put his back into it, and the two men managed to twist the wheel enough to open the hatch. They threw back the cover, and Uncle Ted took a small flashlight out of his pocket. He turned it on and blinked the light three times into the hole. There was an answering beam of light that flashed three times across what looked like a river of coffee at the bottom of the conduit.

Talia leaned farther over the edge and peered down. She saw the flashlight beam sweeping eerily over the black water, and it was followed by the noses of three inflatable rafts gliding into view. The first raft had a young woman in it, and she was steering the other two rafts with her hands.

"With two people in each raft," grumbled Uncle Ted, "we'll probably all get wet. Don't worry, it's clean water. Or as clean as recycled water gets on Mars."

A metal ladder descended from one side of the cavity, and Uncle Ted started down. The woman floating below carefully positioned an empty raft underneath him, and he dropped into it with hardly a splash. He motioned for Talia to come down, and she did so without question. What was her fear of caves and tunnels anymore, when hundreds of Psi Cops were chasing after her?

She wasn't as adept at getting into the raft as Uncle Ted, and water came sloshing over the sides, coating the seat of her pants. Thankfully, it was warm water, almost the temperature of bathwater, although it did smell strongly of chemicals. Garibaldi came down next, and the young woman expertly guided the last empty raft underneath him. He alit in fine shape, only swamping it a bit. He grabbed a paddle and began to position the raft for Gray.

"You!" called Uncle Ted to Gray. "Shut the hatch before you come down. Don't worry about getting it tight."

Gray did as he was told, getting the hatch closed with no problem. He descended the ladder cautiously, doing everything right, but Garibaldi overshot him as he tried to position the raft. Gray landed half-on and half-off the inflated rubber,

and he finally gave up and slid into the water when he realized how warm it was. He treaded water until Garibaldi extended the paddle to him and pulled him aboard, swamping
the raft and getting both of them soaking wet.

"Earthlings," muttered Uncle Ted.

The young woman laughed heartily and said, "You're
lucky. A lot of Martians don't know how to swim."

"Keep your voices down," ordered Uncle Ted as he put
his paddle in the water and angled the raft into the current.
With powerful strokes he took off, and the others followed,
trembling flashlight beams leading the way. Soon the only
noise in the darkness was the sound of paddles slipping
through liquid and the steady drip of condensation over their
heads.

After about an hour of steady paddling, it began to get extremely warm in the conduit, and the air was thin and dry.
"Don't worry," Uncle Ted told the strangers. "We'll get out
of the aqueduct before all the air is gone."

"That's good to know," said Garibaldi. "Does this
aqueduct go outdoors?"

"Yes," answered Ted. "It's just a short stretch, and it's
well insulated. Or we'd be cooked. We're getting out just
before the turbines."

"Was that a real bomb you set off?" asked Gray with
disapproval in his voice.

"Not really," answered Uncle Ted. "It was mainly sound
and smoke, although I think we used one concussion cap.
I'm not into violence anymore."

"Uncle Ted," said Talia, "I want you to know I'm innocent of that bombing on Babylon 5."

"Of course you are, honey," answered the charismatic
figure with a toss of his leonine hair. "I'm innocent of sedi-
tion, or perdition, or whatever they've accused me of this
week. But that doesn't matter—they have to have their vil-
lains."

He slapped his paddle on the water and said, "I plead
guilty to wanting a Mars that is free from Earth's govern-

ment and their greed. What are they to us? Do they know us? Do they care about us? Or do they want only what they can take out of our soil and our sweat?''

Uncle Ted chuckled. ''Stop me before I start making a speech. I'm a Jainist now, a follower of Gandhi, and I truly have disavowed violence. Gandhi is sort of ancient history, and you young people probably don't know who he was.''

''I do,'' said Gray. ''If you are really following the precepts of Mahatma Gandhi, I salute you. Many Martian revolutionaries do not.''

''Yes, I know,'' muttered Ted. ''But we can't win by fighting Earthforce. We can only lose people and lose the moral high ground. What I do is organize nonviolent protests and tell my followers to resist passively. But it's hard being passive, when people are trying to kill you.''

He turned and smiled at his niece. ''Sweetheart, I know what it's like to be in hiding, to run from every shadow. You and I can never be free, but then *none* of Mars is free. Maybe one day, you and I—and every Martian!—will be able to walk in the sun, free citizens.''

His lady friend lifted a fist and chanted, ''Power to Mars!''

''This is Moira,'' said Uncle Ted. ''She keeps me together.''

''What do you know about the Free Phobos movement?'' asked Garibaldi.

''Nothing!'' said Ted with a scowl. ''I never heard of them before now. But those two stupid bombings sure brought us a bad crackdown and a lot of biased media coverage. I'd like to have a word with this Free Phobos bunch, before they do a third bombing.''

''A third bombing?'' asked Garibaldi.

''Yes, Free Phobos released a statement this morning that they're planning a third bombing soon.'' He chuckled. ''I have to admit, the threat of a real bombing made my little smoke bomb at the dock all the more effective.''

''We know who's behind Free Phobos,'' said Garibaldi. ''If we put the right guy in jail, Talia can go free.''

''Right,'' muttered Ted sarcastically. He shined his flashlight on a grating that protected a line of pumping equipment recessed into the side of the aqueduct. They could hear a cascade of water somewhere in the darkness ahead of them, plus turbines churning. Uncle Ted steered his raft toward the pumps.

"Tie up on the grating," he ordered. "There's a narrow footpath—just try to follow me. Remember, we have to take out the rafts and deflate them, so don't let them get away. We can't leave anything that will give us away."

"Talia," said Garibaldi, "Arthur Malten is behind all of this. We've got to find him to clear you."

She looked back at him, stunned and hurt. Maybe she didn't want to hear that Arthur Malten had set her up to die, but he couldn't spare her the truth. Talia lowered her head and appeared to be thinking about it. After what she must have been through, thought Garibaldi, could anything surprise her?

"It's good to see you," she said finally.

"You, too," he admitted.

Uncle Ted grabbed the grating and hoisted himself onto a narrow ledge in front of it. He tied up his raft and helped Talia step out, then he caught the other two rafts and tied them at the grating. After everyone was safely on the ledge, hanging by their fingernails to the grating, Ted and Moira dragged the rafts out of the water and deflated them.

Very carefully, they skirted the narrow ledge. Through the soles of his shoes, Garibaldi could feel the heat rising up from the metal. They squeezed through a gap cut in the grating and walked carefully among the high-compression pumps, kerchunking away. Finally they reached a secured doorway, and Uncle Ted produced another keycard that opened the door.

They went through and found themselves in a storage room lined with shelves containing pipes, washers, fittings, and tools. There was a spiral stairway leading upward, and the air and temperature in the room were normal, or at least as normal as they got on Mars.

"I think this room is as far as I'm going to go with you boys," said Uncle Ted. "You can talk to Talia here."

For emphasis, he took his PPG out of his pocket. He studied the weapon for a moment before handing it to Moira. "I'm a pacifist, but I would fight to protect my Talia, after what they put her through."

"Believe me," said Garibaldi, "we came here to save her. In order to do that, we have to find Arthur Malten—he's the key to this Free Phobos group and everything else. Does anybody have any ideas?"

Gray stroked his chin thoughtfully. "Do your people have the ability to send out press releases to the media?"

"Of course," answered Ted, "that's about the only way I can make myself heard these days."

"Then let's expose him. Tell the press that Arthur Malten of the Mix is the man behind Free Phobos and the bombings. Coming from you, they're liable to believe it. Besides, it happens to be the truth."

A smile crept across Garibaldi's face. "That won't make Mr. Bester very happy. He wanted to keep that a secret."

"Well," answered Gray, "let's make them both unhappy, shall we? Once Malten is exposed, there's no reason for Bester to keep blaming Ms. Winters and the separatists. And Malten won't have to set off another bomb just to give his sham terrorist group some credence."

"What is this all about?" asked Talia wearily.

Briefly, Garibaldi told her, Ted, and Moira about Malten's attempt to privatize Psi Corps and have himself installed as head. They listened in rapt attention as he explained about the secret Senate bill, the fate of Emily Crane, and how closely the coup within Psi Corps had come to happening.

"In fact," said Garibaldi, "it might still happen if we don't move on it. I'd like to see Psi Corps disbanded, not fall under another tyrant."

"I'll be damned," muttered Uncle Ted. "Hey, I've got to tell this story right away, the whole bloody mess. And I think it's better Talia come with me, until she's officially absolved."

"Fine," agreed Garibaldi, turning to the blond woman in the dirty beret. "I just wanted to make sure you were safe, and that you knew we were trying to help you."

Talia stood up and gave him a grateful hug, allowing her head to rest on his shoulder for a moment. That made it all worthwhile for Garibaldi.

"Give us five minutes," said Uncle Ted, heading for the staircase. "Then come up after us. You'll find yourselves in a factory up there—just ignore everyone and keep climbing stairs until you find a monorail stop."

"Okay," said the security chief. "Give 'em hell."

Uncle Ted shepherded Moira and Talia up the stairs, and the weary telepath looked back one last time to give Garibaldi a smile. He waved until she was out of sight.

"What an experience she must've had," observed Gray with sympathy. "It's like she can barely talk."

"She doesn't need to talk," answered Garibaldi. "Just the way she is, I would walk across Mars for her."

"I know what you mean," Gray sighed. "Well, shall we go somewhere and wait for Mr. Bester to call us? He won't be very happy."

The two men grinned at one another.

With nowhere else to go to wait, Garibaldi and Gray took refuge in a nearby canteen devoted to military personnel from Earthforce. They arrived just in time to catch the news.

The newscaster raised an eyebrow as he reported the story, but he got it essentially correct when he said, "There has been a dramatic development in the Psi Corps bombing story. Noted Martian revolutionary Theodore Hamiliton is claiming that the Free Phobos terrorist group is actually one man—Arthur Malten, founder of the Mix!

"According to this report, Arthur Malten was poised to take over the leadership of Psi Corps with the passage of a privatization bill in the Senate. Details of this bill have now been verified by independent sources in the Senate. According to Hamilton, who is also Talia Winters's uncle, the bombing on Babylon 5 was really an attempt by Arthur

Malten to rid himself of political opponents within Psi Corps.''

In the canteen, there were gasps of surprise and an occasional "I told you so!" Everyone put down their Ping-Pong paddles and pool cues to listen to the gruesome details, which included two fatal bombings, dozens of deaths, and the murder of Emily Crane. Garibaldi frowned, because the report stuck it to the bad guys, but it didn't clear Talia. With Ted being her uncle, the news reports made it seem as if the information was coming from her. Public opinion would still figure her to be in the thick of it.

He looked at Gray and asked, "Are you sure Bester knows where we are?"

"I was very clear about it," answered the telepath.

The commlink on the wall buzzed, and the closest officer answered it. After a moment, he called out, "Is there somebody named Gray here?"

"That's me!" called the telepath.

"There's a shuttlecraft on its way for you," reported the man, and he returned immediately to watching the news.

Gray and Garibaldi smiled at one another.

Because of Mars' thin atmosphere, every shuttlecraft had to dock with an air-lock, and most small shuttlecraft had a hatch at the bottom for that purpose. So Gray and Garibaldi had to climb up a ladder through the air-lock in order to board the black shuttlecraft through its underbelly. If Mr. Bester was surprised to see Garibaldi, he didn't say so, and Garibaldi certainly wasn't surprised to see him.

"I hope you two are proud of yourselves," he sneered. "I ought to arrest you for collaborating with the enemy."

"What are you talking about?" asked Garibaldi. He and Gray looked innocently at one another.

"Thanks to you, there is no way we can handle this quietly now. The whole Alliance will know. . . ."

"That you made a mistake," offered Gray. "That you're fallible."

"No," muttered the Psi Cop, "that Psi Corps is vulnerable to attacks from within. That's the one place we fear the most, attacks from within. And that's why we Psi Cops are so important to the Corps.''

"Aren't you forgetting one thing?'' asked Garibaldi. "If it hadn't been for me and Gray, by this time tomorrow you would've been out of a job! I'll have second thoughts about that for a while, I can tell you.''

Bester narrowed his eyes angrily. "I know what you want from me, and I'm not going to give it to you. Ms. Winters will remain a suspect *and* a rogue telepath. I imagine she will soon go on the list of known Martian terrorists.''

Garibaldi nearly jumped out of his seat to strangle the pompous twit, but his inner voice warned him to keep calm. This was the only man who could remove the most damning of the charges against her—rogue telepath.

"I will testify in Ms. Winters's behalf,'' vowed Gray. "And when we capture Malten, he can testify.''

Bester chuckled humorlessly. "Do you think I would let Arthur Malten go on the stand to testify? His trial would become a trial about Psi Corps itself, and the Mix would get destroyed in the process. To save us all a lot of embarrassment, we're negotiating with Arthur Malten.''

Garibaldi sat up in his seat. "You know where he is? Why don't you bring him in?''

"Yes, bring him in!'' echoed Gray.

"Well, we don't exactly know where he is. Mars is a big planet, and he's very clever. The Mix has a private underground transmitter, and we've been communicating over that. So we have a vague idea what area he's in.''

Gray was sputtering with anger. "How . . . how can you negotiate with Malten? The man tried to kill you, remember, and he succeeded in killing two dozen innocent people!''

Bester scratched his nose. "There is that, of course. But we have some things we need from Mr. Malten. We need him to sign a confession, thanks to your loose lips. It'll have to be worded carefully to make it clear that he, Emily Crane, and those other two were the only telepaths involved from the Mix. His supporters in the Senate will have to officially condemn him. Then Malten will have to address the Mix employees—give them a pep talk and appoint a successor. We have several good candidates in mind.''

The Psi Cop paused in thought. ''In exchange for saving the Mix, there will be a plea-bargained conviction, and he will be paroled to some distant planet.''

''Then you'll kill him,'' said Gray.

Bester smiled but did not correct that assumption.

''What about Talia?'' insisted Garibaldi.

Bester was distracted by his pilot, although she hadn't moved or said a word. ''What did you just receive?''

''Finch is reporting that Malten broke off negotiations. He may be running. There was an echo on his last transmission, and we think we may have pinpointed his hideout. I have coordinates—we can be there in fifteen minutes.''

''Go!''

CHAPTER 21

GARIBALDI stared out the starboard window of the shuttlecraft and watched the barren terrain of Mars streak by.
Mars never looked real from the air, he thought to himself,
with all those lifeless and craggy hills, broken up by the
occasional dusty habitat, monorail tube, or factory dome.
Mars was a place that couldn't possibly exist, yet here it was,
a monument to humanity's determination to bring life to a
dead planet. No matter how many buildings they put up, the
edifices of man always looked tenuous on Mars, like vines
trying to cling to a smooth metal door.

The terrain didn't look real from ground level either, he
recalled. From that perspective, the mountains, chasms, and
sheer cliffs looked too large and too vivid to be real. They
rose at odd angles out of the pockmarked, reddish soil, like
crystals growing in a culture. The mountains looked like
sand castles, as if they would crumble in a strong wind.

"I hate this place," muttered Gray beside him.

"Yes, Mars is an acquired taste," agreed Garibaldi. He
looked at Bester. "Psi Corps has certainly acquired it."

Bester was ignoring them as he leaned forward intently.
"Status?"

"I'm running sonar," reported the pilot. "The readings
indicate that there is a structure where we picked up the
echo. It's the size and shape of a bunker."

"Underground?" asked Bester.

"Yes, but not too deep. I can hover over it and turn on the
thrusters. That might blow away some of the camouflaged
covering."

"Do it," ordered Bester.

Garibaldi braced himself as the pilot—who was damned
good, he had to admit—positioned the craft directly over a
small mound between two jagged mountains. The mound
looked like a mogul on a ski slope, and he had seen hundreds

of similar protrusions on Mars, formed by the pressures of lava flow. The pilot came so close to the mound that she nearly landed, then she popped the thrusters. The shuttlecraft rose like a shot between the two mountains, shuddering and rattling until she could regain control of it. Then she banked the craft away from the peaks and swerved around for another view.

True to her word, she had blasted a star-shaped hole in the artificial surface covering the mound. Under the singed material, sections of gray metal shone dully in the sun.

"Can you raise anybody in there?" asked Bester.

"I've been trying," she answered. "So has Mr. Finch. Malten has either left, or is keeping quiet."

"Damn," muttered Bester, "if we've lost him—if he ran for it—well, there will be no more negotiations!"

"I can land on the mound," the pilot offered. "We might be able to cut through, or find a hatch."

"If you've got a suit," said Garibaldi, "I'll go out and take a look."

"They're in the storage bin in the back," answered Bester. "Right beside the air-lock chamber. You can exit there."

Garibaldi started off, then stopped. "You won't leave me out here, will you?"

Bester scowled. "Leave you alone with Malten, or maybe a batch of his secret files? Not bloody likely."

Garibaldi found four environmental suits in the closet, and he was glad to see they were all roomy and optimized for use on Mars. With the low gravity, nobody had to worry about carrying around too much weight, so a Martian environmental suit could carry the maximum amount of high-grade insulation, plus cooling and air-processing equipment. He stripped off his uniform, figuring the pilot had seen it all before, and squeezed into the suit.

He lowered the helmet onto his head, locked it, and waved to the pilot. She set them down carefully on top of the camouflaged bunker, but they could still hear the grinding of metal against metal. There was a scary moment as something crunched and the ship shifted, but it settled down at an angle that wasn't too terribly dangerous. Garibaldi guessed that a few more pieces of the camouflage material had broken away under the weight of the shuttlecraft.

He pressed the button to open the air-lock chamber, then crammed himself into the tiny space. With a deep breath, he pressed the second air-lock and opened the hatch to the outside.

The brightness of the Martian landscape startled him at first, and he lifted his eyes to the dark sky until they could adjust. A few seconds later, he was scrambling like a mummified mountain goat over the top of the bunker, trying to find a way in. With his foot, he kicked off more chunks of the soil-colored camouflage material until he finally discovered a docking hatch.

He activated the radio inside his helmet and waved at the shuttle pilot in the cockpit. "I found a docking hatch. Do you want me to go in, or do you want to fly ten meters over here and try to dock?"

Garibaldi waited a few seconds, and the pilot replied, "Get clear. We're going to dock."

He bent his legs and jumped about twenty meters to the ground, landing so lightly that he had to run a few steps to slow himself down. That was when he saw the fresh rover tracks in the red soil. The sight of the tracks gave Garibaldi a very bad feeling in his stomach. He didn't know why, but he didn't think Malten would flee overland by rover. He just wasn't the survivalist type.

But it was too late to suggest caution, because the shuttlecraft lifted up again and came down expertly atop the hatch he had uncovered. Whatever Bester's bad qualities, thought Garibaldi, he had attracted a very good pilot for his shuttlecraft. When the thrusters went dead, Garibaldi jumped back on top of the bunker with one effortless leap. He peered under the shuttlecraft and saw the robotic mechanism of the air-lock twisting around by itself to find the hatch. They finally paired up and locked with a solid clunk.

He tapped his radio again. "Do you have atmosphere in the bunker?"

"Positive on that," answered the pilot. "Come back in. Mr. Bester is opening the hatch."

Garibaldi hurried as fast as the bulky suit would allow to the chamber at the rear of the craft. By the time he got through the air-lock and was stripping off his suit, Mr. Bester was halfway down the hatch. The Psi Cop groaned with pain at every rung of the ladder, and he pounded the head of his thick metal cane on the ladder.

Gray looked at Garibaldi and shrugged. "He insisted on going down."

The chief began putting on his uniform. "Be careful down there! I saw fresh rover tracks outside."

Bester's head disappeared into the hatch, and he was gone. Gray scrambled down after him, and Garibaldi tried to be patient as he waited his turn. He glanced at the young pilot.

"Keep the motor running," he advised her.

Then he heard a shout. "Oh, my God—stay back!"

Garibaldi was so anxious to see what was happening that he dropped the last few meters of the ladder onto very plush blue carpeting. He was amazed when he saw the vast layout of viewers, computers, and editing equipment—it was truly a decked-out communications bunker. There were hardly any other furnishings in the room, except for a workbench and a few chairs. It was one of the chairs that Bester and Gray were staring at.

Arthur Malten, wide awake but looking haggard, was tied to one of the chairs, with a bomb strapped to his head. He was trying to hold perfectly still, but the sweat was running a marathon race down his face. Pinned to his chest was a note that read: "Compliments of the real revolutionaries."

"They came in," he gasped. "Martians! I didn't see them!"

Garibaldi edged forward. "Can we disable it."

"No, no!" screamed Arthur Malten. "It's got a motion detector on it. You get too close—*kaboom!* If I move too much—*kaboom!* They explained it to me in loving detail. They also have a remote!"

That last admission made Bester start hobbling toward the

ladder with his cane. "Listen, Malten, we're not the bomb squad. I'll send for some specialists."

"Bester!" called the desperate telepath. "I didn't mean it personally! You understand, it was politics."

"Of course," said the Psi Cop. "It was a damn good try, too. You took me by surprise and nearly succeeded. I'll remember that."

"The Mix," croaked Arthur Malten. "Try to save it."

"We will. Come on, gentlemen."

"But we just can't leave him here," Gray protested. "Garibaldi, do something!"

The security chief rubbed his hands together and tried to think. "We need some small clippers, but if we can't get close to him . . ."

"Mr. Bester!" called the pilot from above. "An unidentified man is telling us we have thirty seconds to get off . . . or else!"

"I am sorry about Talia Winters, too!" wailed Malten from the chair. "And *Emily!*" He began to sob, and his head bounced around, which made Bester squirt up the ladder.

"That's a deathbed confession," said Garibaldi, pushing Gray toward the ladder. "Let's move it!"

"There's no hope for him?" asked the telepath.

"Not unless we get help. Move it!"

The light gravity allowed them to bound hand-over-hand up the ladder, as Malten's sobs grew louder and more pitiful. When they reached the shuttlecraft cabin, Bester was already strapped in, and the pilot was going through her preignition checklist. Bester stumbled to his seat, and Garibaldi struggled to get the hatch shut. He fell backward as the robotic link broke and the mechanism retracted into the shuttlecraft.

"Five seconds!" called the pilot.

They heard a low rumble beneath them, and Garibaldi shouted, "Now!"

She jammed on the thrusters as a fireball and concussion rocked the little craft, sending it spinning around. Garibaldi was tossed into Bester's legs, and the Psi Cop screamed in anguish. The pilot bore down and never gave up on the bucking craft, yet Garibaldi could see one of the jagged peaks looming ever closer in the window. He braced himself for impact, but the pilot hit the thrusters again and spun them away from the mountain.

She picked up altitude as quickly as she could, and everyone craned their necks toward the ports to see what had happened. All that was left of Arthur Malten's secret bunker was a huge, black crater with a few smoldering sparks at its edges. Debris and twisted bits of metal were scattered for half a kilometer around the site.

"Oh, my," murmured Gray, slumping back in his seat.

Bester looked reflective. "Maybe it had to end this way. Well, I suppose we can tell the press that he died constructing a bomb."

Garibaldi scowled and shook his head. "You never want to give the right people credit for anything, do you? The revolutionaries found him before you did, and they weren't in a negotiating mood. Face it, Bester, you have been one step behind everybody this whole chain of events."

The Psi Cop bristled. "I'm still going to take down Talia Winters and her uncle."

"No, you're not," said Garibaldi confidently. "I didn't want to use this, because I'm ashamed of it, but you force my hand. Do you remember the reception on Babylon 5 the first night of the conference? It was our only successful event."

"Yes, what of it?" asked Bester, sounding wary.

"That night I made a visual of several of your Psi Cops *gambling* in the private quarters of Ambassador Londo Mollari. I believe he was teaching them three-card monte."

Mr. Bester looked pale, but he still managed a smile. "That can't be true. You're bluffing."

"Am I?" Garibaldi countered. "You can ask Ambassador Mollari for confirmation. He was, shall we say, my accomplice."

Bester's lips thinned, and he stared hard at Garibaldi. But Harriman Gray inserted himself between the men and warned, "Don't scan him, Mr. Bester. I will help him block it. Suffice to say, Garibaldi told me about this incriminating visual, but I begged him not to use it.''

Gray looked with disgust at Garibaldi. ''He must feel you gave him no choice.''

The security chief picked some Martian dirt out of his fingernails. ''You will drop all charges against Talia Winters, especially the rogue telepath. And you'll do it right this minute, or the next thing you'll see on the news will be Psi Cops gambling. Won't the press enjoy that right after this juicy scandal with the Mix? Maybe the Senate will have enough courage to throw you out on their own.''

''I don't believe you did it,'' muttered Bester, ''but it's the kind of thing Ambassador Mollari *would* do.'' He called out to the pilot, ''Get me a channel to headquarters.''

''Yes, sir. You're on-line.''

''This is Mr. Bester with a final report on the Babylon 5 bombing. This information is cleared for immediate release to the media. Arthur Malten confessed to forming a terrorist organization called Free Phobos, and his only accomplices were three other telepaths from the Mix—Emily Crane, Michael Graham, and Barry Strump. Unbeknownst to anyone, they were Martian sympathizers. Mr. Malten died this afternoon, the victim of an accidental bomb explosion.

''In light of this new information, all charges against Talia Winters have been dropped. She is to be taken off the list of rogue telepaths, with all her duties and rights as a member of Psi Corps restored to her, effective immediately. Bester out.''

Garibaldi nodded, leaned back in his seat, and closed his eyes.

At the Clarke Spaceport orbiting Earth, two men stood among the crowds, shaking hands. One man wore gloves, and the other didn't. One was catching a quick shuttle to Berlin, and the other was headed in the opposite direction to catch a two-day transport to Babylon 5.

''Are you sure you don't want to come back with me?'' asked Garibaldi. ''If you've blown your expense account, I'll put you up on my couch.''

Gray chuckled. "I *have* blown my expense account, thanks to you. But that's not the reason. I don't want to go back to B5 just to see Susan—that would be making a nuisance of myself. I'll have business on B5 again someday, and I'll be looking forward to seeing all of you."

"Just don't bring Bester with you."

The two men laughed, and Gray lowered his head. "I have one request. Will you tell Susan that I did something worthwhile. Something that would win her over."

"You bet I'll tell her," said Garibaldi. "I plan to get a lot of free meals out of this—by recounting our adventures over and over again. I'll leave out the part where you fell in the water."

"That was *your* fault," Gray reminded him.

"That's why I'll leave it out."

"And how is Ms. Winters?"

"Still a little shaken," answered Garibaldi. "I understand she's staying with her parents for a few days before she goes back. I bet she'll have some pretty good stories to tell, too." He sighed. "These are classy women we're talking about, and we're a couple of lugs. We may never stand a chance with them."

"I know," said Gray.

A synthesized voice announced, "Transport *Starfish* is now boarding for Babylon 5."

"That's me," said Garibaldi. He started off but stopped to wave back. "You're okay, Gray."

"You too."

Two hundred kilometers below them, a young woman with sleek blond hair stood watching the stars from her parents' porch. The nightmare was finally over, but she still didn't feel like talking much, about her escape or anything else. So much of what had happened to her in the last few days Talia didn't understand. She had to parse it slowly in the light of time, and pick out those pieces that were worth saving, and worth puzzling over.

As she watched the stars glimmer, she marveled at the fact

that she lived among them. She called them home. Talia had
seen enough of both Earth and Mars to last her for a while,
and she looked forward to going back to the cold blackness
of space. She longed to see the aliens, who were less judg-
mental and prejudiced than her own species. Among aliens,
you could be whoever you were, she realized, but among
humans you had to be whoever they wanted you to be.

And nobody was what they seemed.

Out of all the weirdness, the duplicity, the good masquerading as bad, and the bad masquerading as good, there was
one piece of her journey she wanted badly to understand. It
was Invisible Isabel. She wanted to talk to Ambassador Kosh
as soon as possible, but she knew the Vorlon would speak in
riddles and tell her nothing outright. Kosh would want her to
figure it out for herself.

The part of Invisible Isabel she recognized was her nascent
telekinetic abilities, a gift from an old friend; but it was
Isabel's voice that was new to her. That voice was confident
and independent, and it could get her out of tough scrapes.
She couldn't hear it all the time, but she would like to hear it
more often.

"Talia, honey, we're going to have some ice cream!"
called her mom, sounding a lot like her Uncle Ted. His nightmare was still going on, but at least he had chosen it.

And what about the dogged persistence of Garibaldi? That
was something. She had to think about all of it, but not
tonight. Tonight she would eat ice cream and listen to stories
about her extended family and parents' friends. Then she
would return to her home, Babylon 5.

Book 2
Accusations
by Lois Tilton

Historian's note: This story takes place after the events in 'The Coming of the Shadows', and before 'All Alone in the Night'.

CHAPTER 1

Observation Dome, Babylon 5: When it was quiet, with no ships departing or approaching the station, an observer could look out through the curved windows and see the stars glowing silently against the black backdrop of space. At such times it might be possible to contemplate the infinity of the cosmos and wonder at humanity's place among the sentient races of the universe.

But such peaceful meditation was rarely possible in the Observation Dome. This was the Control Center of Babylon 5, and Commander Susan Ivanova was intent on her console, not contemplating the view from the window. The surface of the large curved control console was black, as space was black, but its data screens glowed in vivid electronic hues as the figures constantly flickered and changed. On the central screen, icons represented the ships filling the station's traffic lanes, pulling away from the station, coming in to dock. One in particular was highlighted: a crippled cargo transport coming in, three days behind schedule, with damage to its stabilizers that predicted an interesting docking experience to come.

Ivanova stood with hands clasped behind her back, considering the computer-projected trajectory of the incoming freighter on the screen. The colors of the lighted displays played across her face, its skin pulled taut by her tightly braided hair.

Then she ordered crisply, "Centauri transport *Gonfalion,* this is Babylon Control. Your trajectory is erratic. I'm ordering you to cut your engines. We're going to tow you in. Do not, repeat *not* attempt to dock under your own power. Do you read me, *Gonfalion*?"

The face of the alien pilot on the communications screen did not look happy on hearing this order. There would be towing charges added to the station's usual docking fees. But the fines for noncompliance would certainly be a lot stiffer yet. "Acknowledged, Babylon Control. I'm cutting power to the thrusters now."

The scan technician checking her own instruments confirmed, "Their engines are shutting down, Commander."

Ivanova acknowledged with a short nod. Still intently watching the screen, she ordered, "Get a couple of shuttles out there to tow her into cargo bay eight. Divert all incoming traffic away from that traffic lane. Give them plenty of room."

It was a slow and tricky job, to lock grapples onto a ship the size of an interstellar freighter and maneuver it into the narrow chute of the station's docking bay. Ivanova would oversee the operation from here at her console, as insurance against something else going wrong. Not that she mistrusted the skill of the station's pilots, but there was only one desirable outcome and an infinite number of disastrous ones. Under such circumstances, she preferred not to rely on luck. It was the Russian in her coming out, she sometimes said.

There were other, smaller annoyances trying to claim her attention: the communications screen on her console now showed three more new messages waiting in the queue. Ivanova already knew what most of them were about. In the corridors outside the sanctuary of the Observation Dome, where they weren't allowed entry, prowled a small pack of shipping factors, insurance agents, hopeful salvage operators, and others who wanted news of the damaged freighter and its cargo. But they'd just have to wait until the ship was safely docked. She had no time and less inclination to deal with them now.

On the screen, the shuttles were closing in on the mass of the cargo ship, deploying grapples.

"Got it, Control," the pilot of shuttle A reported. "Locked on."

"Well done," Ivanova commended her.

"Commander," Communications broke in, "there's another message. Sender says it's urgent and personal."

"If it's personal, then it can wait," Ivanova said curtly. Several months ago, such a message would have instantly aroused concern about her father, dying in a hospital on Earth, but that phase of her life was over now. Mother, brother, now father, all of them dead, and there was no one else she could think of who might be calling her on a matter both personal and urgent enough to interfere with duty.

Now both shuttles had the cargo ship fast, and Ivanova ordered, "All right, take her in."

There was one tense moment after that when a departing Narn fighter cut too close to the crippled ship's path, but Ivanova instantly ordered it, "Narn fighter 42, reduce your speed and return to your assigned traffic lane."

The maneuver had been deliberate, Ivanova suspected. The Narn and the Centauri had been at war intermittently for over a century, and the hostilities between them were always close to the surface, even here on Babylon 5, this station whose very reason for existence was peace between all sentient races. Lately, with war between them now breaking out in earnest, that goal was seeming further and further remote, but for the moment, the balance of power held, precariously. And it was simple commonsense self-preservation to obey the instructions of the traffic controller on a station as crowded with ships as this one was now.

The rest of the docking maneuvers were uneventful, even tedious, and from time to time Ivanova's thoughts wandered to the waiting message: urgent and personal. Who could have sent it to her? What could they want?

With the crisis finally averted, she returned control of traffic operations to the technicians on duty, then after a slight hesitation, she queried the computer for the name of the sender of that one particular message.

"The sender's name is J. D."

"J. D.?" she wondered aloud. "Just J. D.?"

"There is no other name or identification with the message."

But Ivanova had already remembered. Ortega. J. D. Ortega. But what was he doing here on Babylon 5? And what urgent business could he have with her? As far as she knew, Ortega had gone back home to Mars, turning down a career in Earthforce, choosing to go back to the mines while Ivanova went on to be promoted full commander before she was thirty. His face was coming back to her now: the blue-black curly hair, the warm smile.

There hadn't been anything between the two of them. It would have been wrong for a number of reasons: J. D. was her flight instructor, he was fiercely loyal to his wife back home on Mars. Ivanova remembered how he kept her picture with him all the time—what was her name? Constanzia? Ivanova had always suspected that it was for Constanzia's sake that he'd left Earthforce. It was hard to imagine him down in the red cavern of some Martian mine instead of the freedom of a Starfury.

But he'd taught her everything she knew about flying. Yes, she remembered.

"Let's see the message," she finally ordered the computer.

"Playing message now."

The face that appeared on her communications screen was and was not J. D.'s. His father, maybe, or a brother, she thought at first. This was an older face, with the laugh lines deeper and somehow not so much like laughter. Ivanova had to suppress a sudden urge to stare at her own face in the mirror surface of her console. *Have we changed so much? Has it been so long? Ten years?*

But the voice was the same. The message was brief, hurried. "Susan, I'm in trouble. They say you're Number Two here on this station. I don't know anyone else who might be able to help. There's something I have to tell you. Please, meet me in the Alpha Wing ready room at 20:00 hours."

"J. D.?" Ivanova asked aloud, but it was the computer that responded: "End of message."

20:00 hours. Ivanova thought quickly. She'd be off duty by then. Of course she'd meet him. But what kind of trouble was he in? Why did he seem so nervous, even fearful? What was wrong?

"Computer, what time is it now?"

"21:55 hours."

Ivanova stood up, paced the width of the room, sat down again. The ready room was empty, which it usually was at this hour, when Alpha Wing was off duty. She'd been here almost two hours, first watching the news on the wall screens, then reading a few of the old newspapers lying around the place, finally resorting to a holographic game that she found under a seat cushion, sending a tiny image of a Starfury zipping around the room on the tail of a Minbari fighter. It probably ought to be confiscated, she thought. Earth was at peace with the Minbari now, it couldn't do any good to go bringing up the war again, especially here on Babylon 5 where running into a real Minbari fighter was a frequent occurrence. On the other hand, it was a fairly good game.

She was still in uniform, her hair pulled back into the braid she usually wore on duty, contributing an edge to the headache she could feel now, throbbing above her temples. Almost two hours! Where was J. D.? Her concern had progressed from "Why doesn't he show up on time?" to "What's keeping him?" and by now to "What's happened to him?"

"Computer, what time is it now?"

"22:02 hours."

More than two hours. And in all that time, no one had come into the room. Only one other person had been here at all, a large man with Oriental features who'd come out of the rest room and brushed past her just after she entered the main waiting room.

So what had happened to J. D.? In his message, he'd said he was in trouble. Had seemed afraid. Hard to believe that J. D. Ortega could have any enemies at all, let alone here on Babylon 5, where he'd never set foot until—

Until when? How long *had* he been on the station? Why hadn't he contacted her until now?

"Computer, when did J. D. Ortega arrive on the station?"

"Station registry shows there have been eight individuals named Ortega arriving at Babylon 5 since it first went on-line. None of them had the initials J. D."

"What? That's impossible!"

There was a computer console at a battered table in one corner, and Ivanova went to it now and queried the registry again. A list of names scrolled down the screen. It was true. *Ortega, J. D.* wasn't listed.

Now, that was wrong, just plain very wrong. If J. D. was somewhere on the station, he had to be in the registry. She called up his message again and queried its origin.

"Message was sent from Gray 18 at 13:08 hours."

So he was on the station. That *was* J. D. Ortega's face on the screen. His voice: "I'm in trouble."

Ivanova was starting to wonder just what kind of trouble. "Something's going on," she said to herself in a low voice. But maybe the registry was the wrong place to be looking.

"Computer, search all files for the name J. D. Ortega," she ordered.

The response wasn't quite what she'd wanted to hear. "This file is restricted."

Ivanova scowled. She input her password, identifying herself as the station's executive officer.

"Password is valid. Security clearance is valid. Accessing file: J. D. Ortega."

And there was his image on the screen, but this time it was flagged for all Earth Alliance Security Forces: FUGITIVE ALERT. RED LEVEL. WANTED FOR SUSPICION OF TERRORISM AND CONSPIRACY.

J. D. Ortega? A terrorist? A part of Ivanova's universe shifted on its foundations. No, that was impossible, it couldn't be true, it had to be some kind of error. Mistaken identity. But the face on the screen—it *was* J. D.'s.

Shaken and anxious, she touched her personal communications link to switch it on. "Garibaldi? This is Ivanova."

With relief, she heard the familiar voice of Babylon 5's security chief answering, "Ivanova? What's up?"

"I know you're not on duty—"

"Hey, there's no rest for the wicked, and that's me. Spill it, Ivanova."

But that was harder than it sounded. Ivanova started to explain, "Earlier today I got a message from an old friend. My old flight instructor. He asked me to meet him in the Alpha Wing ready room at 20:00 hours. I've waited all that time. He never showed."

Garibaldi's voice was amused. "Stood you up, huh? You want security to track down your date for you?"

Ivanova shook off the remark. Michael Garibaldi was notorious for his bad jokes, but she wasn't in the mood for him to start now.

"In his message, he said he was in trouble." She hesitated. Was this betraying J. D.? "When he didn't show up after more than two hours, I queried the computer. First, it said there was no record of him in the station registry. Then . . . it said there was an alert out for him. On suspicion of terrorism."

Garibaldi's voice was suddenly serious. "What's your friend's name?"

"J. D. Ortega."

There was a pause. Then Garibaldi said grimly, "I think you'd better meet me in Security Central, Commander."

He was waiting for her, waiting in his usual swivel chair, surrounded by banks of screens and instrumentation that took up half the space in the office. Garibaldi's gray Earthforce uniform was, as usual, not quite as crisp as a career officer's might be. He'd been around a long while and come to believe that results were what counted, not image. Ivanova had come to learn that he usually got the results.

On the main console, a file was displayed on a data screen. Garibaldi waved Ivanova over to it. "Is this your friend?" he asked her. "Does he come from Mars Colony?"

With a slight feeling of reluctance, she nodded. "That's J. D."

"It looks like your friend Ortega's gone and gotten himself involved in Mars Colony politics. Separatist politics, the Free Mars movement. Earth Central put out the alert for him ten days ago."

"No." She shook her head, reading through the file, stunned by the revelations. "No, Garibaldi, this can't be right. Not J. D. You don't *know* him—how he is. I mean, his wife, his family mean everything to him. He gave up his career for them, so he could stay home on Mars. He went back to work for the mines. He wouldn't . . ."

Ivanova's voice trailed off, silenced by what she was reading. "Do you have him in the lockup? Is that where he is?"

Garibaldi shook his head. "Until now, I had no idea he might even be on Babylon 5. This was just a general alert, sent out to all Earth Alliance security officers. Tell me, how well do you know this guy? He was your flight instructor? Have you seen him since then? Met with him recently?"

"No, not since he left Earthforce. That was before I took the assignment on Io. Where I served under Captain Sheridan the first time." She paused abruptly, looked at Garibaldi with an altered expression, suddenly aware that this was an interrogation. Then she went on in the same controlled voice she used at the command console. "I haven't seen him since then. A few messages, the kind of thing you send on the holidays. The last few years, no, nothing. I don't think I've thought of him in the last few years—until today."

Garibaldi said quietly, "I think you'd better show me that message you got today."

Ivanova felt a strange sensation of being torn in half. J. D. had come to her for help. But she had no choice, not as an Earthforce officer. And besides, she realized at once that Garibaldi didn't really need to ask her permission. As head of station security, he had access to almost any message he wanted to see. "Of course," she said quickly, covering up the momentary hesitation.

This time, viewing the message on the screen, she couldn't help seeing J. D. Ortega's expression as furtive, the face of a man on the run. "I'm in trouble," he was saying. That was certainly an understatement, Ivanova thought.

"That's him," she confirmed it again, shaking her head. "I just can't understand it. Not J. D."

"But we do know," Garibaldi reminded her, "that he

managed to get onto Babylon 5 and send at least one message without being identified. That's what worries me. How did he manage to get onto the station without triggering the alert? And if he could do that, what else was he involved in? We've got no idea how long he's been on the station. Or if someone's been hiding him. If we have a branch of the Free Mars organization on Babylon 5, that's a problem.''

Ivanova wasn't quite ready to give up. "But if he was a terrorist, then why would he come to me for help? He must have known my position on the station. If he was involved in Free Mars, why not go to them? Maybe they're the ones who were after him. He said he was in trouble.''

"I'd certainly like to know, too. Which means we have to take him in for questioning. Whenever he contacts you again.''

Wordlessly, she agreed. But there was still that gnawing doubt.

Ortega's face was still displayed on the screen. *J. D.? What kind of trouble are you in? What happened? Where were you tonight?*

CHAPTER 2

The distress signal was going out on all frequencies, to all ships in Epsilon Sector as well as Babylon 5. On the communications screen in the station's Observation Dome, the pilot's frantic face was sweating as he sent, "Mayday! Mayday! We're under attack! Raiders closing in fast! We need help out here! This is the transport ship *Cassini,* coordinates Red 470 by 13 by 16! Mayday! Mayday!"

Captain John Sheridan was at the command console. Instantly, he ordered, "Commander Ivanova, scramble Alpha Wing! We've got raiders! Red 470 by 13 by 16! That's out by the secondary transit point in Section 13!"

Ivanova was already heading at a run for the Cobra bays where her fighter stood prepped and ready to go, while in the Observation Dome Sheridan continued to deal with the endangered transport ship. The main force of raider ships had been eliminated last year, but there were still small pockets, independent units functioning alone. "*Cassini,* this is Babylon Control, we have a fighter wing scrambling now. Are you hit? What weapons do you have? Can you hold them off till we get there?"

"We're trying to make it back to the jump gate," the desperate pilot reported. "It's our only chance; we can't run from them. There's too many of them and they're too fast! But I don't know if we'll make it. They've got us cut off. They were on us almost as soon as we came through the gate. Waiting for us! It was a setup!"

"Try to hold on, *Cassini,* help is on the way!" But when he turned away from the communications screen,

Sheridan's expression was grim. He knew, as the transport's pilot had to, that there wasn't much hope of Ivanova reaching the endangered ship before it was too late. After Alpha Wing came out of hyperspace into Section Red 13, the fighters would still have almost three hours in normal space before they could reach the transfer jump point where the transport had been ambushed, even at a Starfury's maximum acceleration.

The Cobra bay doors stood open wide, ready. C&C had already cleared them for immediate launch, priority. Ivanova ran quickly through her preflight check. "Alpha Wing, ready for drop?"

With all nine ships signaling readiness, "Prepare to launch. On my mark, Alpha Wing. Let's go! Drop!"

The cradle swung down, and the F23 Starfury dropped free of the station, falling out into space in the curved trajectory imparted by the station's spin. Then Ivanova fired the thrusters, and the fighter blasted away from Babylon 5. One by one, the rest of Alpha Wing joined in behind her, falling into formation as they accelerated toward the jump gate.

Ivanova's hands were tight on the fighter's controls, as if she could propel the ship by the sheer force of will. Time was the crucial element in these situations—time to launch the fighters, to get to the jump point, even more time to reach the endangered ship once they were through. Through her command helmet, she was monitoring Sheridan's exchange with the *Cassini*'s pilot, and she could already tell the situation wasn't good. The transport was too far away, the raiders were too close on its tail. By the time Alpha flight got there, it might already be too late.

Too often, lately, they'd been too late. Angrily, Ivanova thrust away the memory of what they'd found on those occasions.

Ahead was the jump gate, the permanent hyperspace installation maintained by Babylon 5. "This is Alpha Leader, prepare for jump," Ivanova ordered, heading for the gate's center at the head of the fighter wing. As her Starfury entered the gate, an immense power surge opened the hyperspace vortex, warping space, time, light, pulling the ship in and through. Simultaneously it disappeared into the jump point's infinite black center and into the dark red nightmare of hyperspace, and emerged from the blue-shifted funnel of energy into Section Red 13, light-years from Babylon 5 in normal space. One by one, in order, the rest of Alpha Wing followed, taking up formation again behind Ivanova.

"This is Alpha Leader, let's get to that transport! Maximum burn," she ordered. "ETA to the *Cassini*'s last recorded position 166 minutes. Warm up your weapons. Let's be ready for the raiders when we get there!"

But when she tried to raise the transport to report that she was on the way, there was no response. "Any transmissions from the *Cassini*?"

"Negative," reported Alpha Two, Gordon Mokena, her wingman and the designated scan/communications ship for the mission.

Damn, she said under her breath. Not good, not good at all.

She opened up a direct subspace tachyon channel to Babylon 5. "Babylon Control, this is Ivanova, we're out in 13, and I can't raise the *Cassini*. Are you still in contact? Do you have a current fix on their position?"

Sheridan's voice responded, "Ivanova, we lost contact with the *Cassini* about the time you went through the jump gate. Their last reported position was 470 by 13 by 18. They were trying to make it back through the jump gate."

Grimly, Ivanova made the course correction, just as if there were still a realistic odds on the transport's sur-

vival. There was no question of turning back. You had to
see it through, no matter how bad it looked. For the
chance that some other ship might come onto the scene
and manage to chase off the raiders. For the chance of
saving a survivor. And if all that failed, for the chance of
revenge, of getting just one raider ship in your sights and
seeing it disintegrate, lit by the brief flare as its fuel went
up with the oxygen from its ruptured tanks.

Vengeance was supposed to be something you left to
the Lord, or so she'd been taught as a child, but Ivanova
didn't care. She wanted those raiders.

Sometimes it seemed they would never be able to
stamp them out. Wipe out one nest of them, another
would pop up in a different sector of space. The more
trade grew between the stars, the more the opportunities
for piracy, the more the profits in it, feeding the black
market. *Humans and aliens—greed seems to be one
thing we have in common,* Ivanova thought grimly.

The raiders were typically hit-and-run operators,
snatching what was valuable from the transports they hit,
killing the crews, and abandoning their victims to the
cold void of space. They had started out as opportunistic
pirates, roaming the shipping routes and hitting whatever
random targets they came across, but after the destruction of their main force, they were becoming more desperate. These days, they didn't like to leave their profits
to chance. The remaining pirate consortiums operated
from mother ships large enough to create their own jump
points in space. And they preferred to choose their
targets in advance, relying on bribes to obtain cargo
manifests and routing schedules. There didn't seem to be
any information that wasn't for sale if the price was high
enough.

Angrily, Ivanova diverted her mind from this train of
thought by querying the computer for the current ETA at
the *Cassini*'s position.

"ETA for coordinates 470 by 13 by 18 is twenty-four minutes."

Close enough. She opened her command channel. "This is Alpha Leader, all ships activate long-range scan," she ordered. "Let's see if we can pick them up out there."

For several minutes she watched the screen while the scan turned up nothing. Then Alpha Two reported in: "I'm getting something! Looks like raiders! Four . . . no, I think five of them!"

"I'm getting more! They've got another ship with them! Something big, like a transport!" Alpha Five announced.

"Location?"

Both pilots sent the coordinates and other scan data. The data matched with what Ivanova's own instruments were picking up. The raiders were obviously heading for the Red 13 jump point. Then they didn't come from a jump-capable carrier.

"What about the *Cassini*?" Ivanova asked, but there was still no communication from the ship they were trying to save.

At their current acceleration, the raiders would be at the jump point in less than fourteen minutes. They were close, but the transport they were escorting was clearly slowing them down. Alpha Wing's Starfuries, with thrusters on maximum burn, could make it there in twelve minutes. But what about the *Cassini*? Had the raiders captured the freighter, taken her in tow?

Then, from Alpha Two: "Commander, I'm picking up a mass of about 850K tonnes at 470 by 13 by 18. Reading just mass, no acceleration, no life sign."

The *Cassini*. Ivanova knew it. Her worst-case outcome, realized again.

Now it was decision time. "Alpha Two, Six, Ten—

check it out. If it's the transport . . . you know what to do.

"The rest of you, close up formation. Activate weapons. We're going to cut those bastards off at the jump point and burn them down."

As the three designated Starfuries pivoted out of the main formation, the remaining fighters closed up as ordered, following Ivanova's thruster flares on an intercepting course, to reach the jump gate before the raiders and their hijacked cargo. If she could do it, cut them off at the jump gate, the raiders were already hot ash, with nowhere to run. The Starfuries were faster, and there was no sanctuary in empty space, no safety but engines and firepower, and Alpha Wing had the raider ships outgunned. Their situation would be as hopeless as the transport *Cassini* had been when they attacked it.

Ivanova's voice over the command channel never lost its clipped, cool tones, her orders were by the book, her hands on the controls were steady, but there was a tightness in her jaw, a look in her eyes that promised no mercy on the raiders once she got them in her sights.

Because it was procedure, she opened a wide-band comm channel. "This is Earthforce Commander Ivanova to suspected raider ships. Cut your engines or I will attack."

There was no response. Then it was all or nothing. The raiders continued their flight toward the jump point, and Alpha Wing's formation, a fusion-powered spearpoint, flung itself at its targets, phased plasma guns fully charged, closing in.

But the targets weren't blind or helpless. As soon as they detected the Earthforce fighters bearing down on them, the raiders reacted, a half-dozen of the small wing-shaped fighters peeling off to engage their pursuers. On her screen, Ivanova could see the transport and its remaining escort begin to increase acceleration as they raced for the safety of the jump gate.

Whatever was in that transport, whatever they were guarding, had to be valuable if the raiders were willing to risk themselves to save it. "This is Alpha Leader. Three, Four, Nine, Twelve—engage their rear guard. The rest of you stay with me. We're going to take out that transport. Open fire as soon as you're in range."

The larger ship was not, she could see clearly now, the *Cassini,* but a leaner, faster type of freighter, designed for the rapid loading of stolen cargo and a fast escape, and undoubtedly armed. A fleeting thought passed through Ivanova's mind that the raiders had been well prepared to grab this cargo, whatever it was. But she had no time to think of anything but the coming fight as soon as the ready indicator on her weapons system finally showed the closest fighter in range.

"Lock on target. Fire."

Superheated plasma shot from her guns, intercepted by the transport's defensive weapons. From the formation around her came more fire as Alpha Wing engaged the enemy. A raider ship bore down on her from straight ahead, but Ivanova had it in her sights, fired, and had the savage satisfaction of seeing the incandescent gases of its death-explosion fill her screen. Another raider took a hit, spun crazily for a brief instant, then disintegrated into flying debris.

Ivanova's command channel was filled with voices.

Raider at ten o'clock.

I've got him, Ten!

I've lost an engine, Alpha Leader. I'm falling back.

About twenty degrees away and behind them, Ivanova's tactical screen showed the smaller formation of Starfuries led by Alpha Three engaging the raiders' rear defenders. Around her, the main body of Alpha Wing was in pursuit of the rest, taking out the raider fighters one by one. With some part of her brain she was aware of all this activity, tracking it, making the correct responses. But most of her attention was focused on the raider transport, the rapidly decreasing distance between it and the jump point, and the slower rate with which she was inexorably closing the gap between them. The transport ship was well armed. As it fired one of its rear guns, Ivanova's Starfury was rocked by a plasma burst a lot closer than she found comfortable. But she returned the fire, and one of her shots made a direct hit, blowing away a rear cargo section and one of the transport's thrusters.

Seeing that, the rest of the raiders seemed to figure that their hijacked cargo was lost and it was time to save themselves. The leading pair of raider ships accelerated ahead, through the jump gate, passing into hyperspace with sudden successive flares of light. *Damn!* Ivanova cursed to herself, but they were beyond her reach now.

Now panic started to spread through the surviving raiders. They broke off the fight, racing each other for the gate, followed at a rapidly increasing distance by the abandoned, limping transport. "Damn!" Ivanova swore again in frustration as one more passed through and escaped her, then another.

There was still the transport, crippled and outgunned, with Alpha Wing closing in. Ivanova opened the channel again to call for its surrender. But before the cargo ship could respond, two of the last raiders, both diving for the jump gate at the same time, collided, both fighters obliterated in a single explosive fireball. A third was unable to veer away in time to avoid the blast wave, which slammed it into one of the jump gate's extended arms.

"Pull up!" Ivanova ordered her ships urgently, and they broke off the pursuit, evading the massive energy surge that flashed out from the damaged gate's power node.

Ivanova's scan readout broke into static as the energy

level went off the scale. She watched in a kind of horrified awe to see the disabled transport, out of control and unable to change course, slide inexorably into the intensely charged field. There was a blue-white flash that struck at her eyes even through her polarized viewscreen, and then the ship was gone.

She let out a breath. "This is Alpha Leader, all ships return to formation. Let's check out the damages."

Mokena in Alpha Two had reported somberly, "We've found the *Cassini,* Commander. The crew's dead. They gutted the ship, tore the cargo section open to get at it."

Now Ivanova was seeing the devastation for herself, the ruined, lifeless ship, the gaping hole in the cargo hold. Her fighter drifted almost motionless past the wreckage, close enough that she could see the carbon-scoring from the raider's blasts along its hull, the ruin of the flight cabin's interior, the empty hold. What had it been carrying, what was worth so much destruction, so many lives?

There were sometimes moments, like seeing the raider transport drift helplessly to its destruction, when Ivanova would start to feel doubt, to wonder if the killing could be justified. Sights like this one made the doubts disappear. Some things had to be fought, had to be put down.

The other ships had already taken the *Cassini* crew's remains onboard, salvaged the ship's records, its log, the black box. Once they got back to Babylon 5, they might reveal something.

Ivanova activated her command channel. "This is Alpha Leader. Form up. Nothing more we can do here. Let's go home."

CHAPTER 3

They started out looking for a fugitive. Not such an easy job, not with Babylon 5's population crowding a quarter million sentient beings. Eliminate the methane-breathers, narrow it down even further to humans, and the scale of the problem still was a lot to contend with. The alien sectors of the station still had to be included in the search, just in case this Ortega fellow might be hiding in there, maybe inside an environment suit.

But this was part of Michael Garibaldi's job description, and there was no one who knew the ins and outs of Babylon 5 better than he did. He wouldn't deserve to be chief of security if there was, would he?

The job meant just about everything to Garibaldi. He figured it was his last chance, and he'd given up most everything he had left to come here and take it. Given up Lise and any chance of working things out with her—and now he'd never know whether they might have made it together. She was married now, and he supposed he wished her well.

But he'd been on the long slide down for a long time, ever since the mess on Europa. Came close to hitting the bottom more than once. And then Jeff Sinclair had pulled him off the slide, given him this job, this chance —Chief of Security on one of Earth Alliance's most sensitive outposts. Only now things had changed again. Jeff Sinclair wasn't commander of Babylon 5 anymore. He was ambassador to the Minbari, and Captain John Sheridan had the commander's desk now, and Sheridan had seen Garibaldi's file, had to know the kind of man who was holding this job—almost certainly not the kind of man he would have chosen himself.

So here was the bottom line: Garibaldi knew he couldn't afford to screw up. This Ortega case was a big one—Priority One fugitive alert. Earth Central wanted this guy real bad. Garibaldi called in his entire security staff on it.

"All right, listen up. This is our man. J. D. Ortega. You all have a copy of his file, right? Study it carefully. You can see that he's wanted for terrorism and conspiracy on Mars. Probably related to last year's uprising, Free Mars, the separatist movement.

"Now, somehow, he got onto Babylon 5 without triggering our scanners, and that brings up the possibility that he may have some kind of forged identicard. Also possibly confederates here on the station. You'd better believe we're going to be looking into *that*. But right for the moment, our job is to find J. D. Ortega and take him into custody. That means we search this station until we've crawled through every ventilation duct and unbolted every wall panel, if that's what it takes. All right, you all have your assignments. Are there any questions?"

There weren't any, to Garibaldi's relief. Because of the nature of the charges, because of Commander Ivanova's involvement, there were aspects of the case he didn't want to discuss with his whole staff. Just as there were parts of the file he hadn't distributed to all of them —a matter of security clearances. Earth Central wanted this one kept shut tight.

They were looking for a fugitive, and so when Command and Control called in on his link that someone had reported a body in one of the fighter maintenance bays, Garibaldi deputed one of his subordinates, Ensign Torres, to check into the matter.

A few minutes later, Torres called back. "Chief, it's him. The body—it's him!"

"Him? You mean Ortega? He's dead? You mean he was killed?"

"That's what it looks like, Chief."

Garibaldi's first thought was that this didn't really solve anything. So they'd found Ortega; now they had to look for his killer. And what about Ivanova? When she found out her old friend was dead?

But he reacted according to the book. "All right, Torres, I hope you have the area sealed off. Good. Keep it that way. No one in or out, nobody says anything to anyone until I get there. You've got whoever reported the body? Good. I want you to hold them for questioning. Whoever's seen the body, whoever knows it's there. Got that? I'm on my way. Remember, nobody into that area except me and Dr. Franklin from Medlab. I'm calling him right now."

Garibaldi's priority call got him through to the head of medical services on Babylon 5. "Doc, this is Garibaldi, I've got a dead body here, and I need you to examine it right away."

"Look, Garibaldi, I've got an experiment in progress here. I'll send—"

"No, I need you, personally. This is a security matter. Something Earth Central wants kept quiet. You've got the highest security clearance on the medical staff."

"A homicide?"

"Could be. Most likely it is. But that's one of the things I want you to find out."

A sigh of resignation. "All right, Garibaldi, I'll be right there. Where did you say you put this body?"

"Fighter maintenance bay one." Which, he suddenly realized, was Alpha Wing's maintenance bay.

* * *

They gathered around the equipment locker: Garibaldi, Franklin, and Garibaldi's best evidence technician, Popovic. Franklin and Popovic were busy with the corpse, running scanners up and down the length of the body, taking samples from the locker and the floor around it. Garibaldi took a few steps away, leaving them to their macabre work. He'd seen the dead man's face for a moment, long enough that he was mortally certain it was J. D. Ortega. That was as much as he needed.

So. They'd been looking for a fugitive, but they'd found a corpse. And a mystery. No, Garibaldi didn't think this was going to simplify the case.

He opened his link to C&C. "This is Garibaldi. I'm calling off the search for J. D. Ortega. We've found him."

Then he turned to the other end of the bay, where Torres was holding a small unhappy group from leaving. There was the maintenance foreman, the technician, who'd actually found the body, and an unfortunate fighter pilot who'd shown up to check on the progress of the repairs to her ship just as the discovery of the body was made.

Or was it really luck? Maybe the pilot was involved in some way, maybe she was planning to move the body and the ship was just an excuse? Garibaldi didn't mean to leave any questions unasked.

He started with the mechanic, who was not at all unwilling to talk.

"I came in a little early, to get to work on this ship. Got to rebuild the upper starboard engine."

Garibaldi glanced briefly at the impatient pilot. So she was with Alpha Wing, Ivanova's group. Stuck here with a crippled ship while the rest of them were out chasing raiders. He wondered if that had any significance for the investigation.

The mechanic was saying, "So I get my brazing arc,

and somebody else's been using it, got the feed line all clogged. I hate that, people using my tools! So I go to the locker to look for a new feed line. And there he is.''

"The body?"

"Yeah. All stiff and staring at me. So I call Brunetti to come see, he calls security, and then you guys all show up.''

The foreman nodded, silently confirming this account of the events.

"No one else?" Garibaldi asked.

"Only her.'' The mechanic looked at the pilot, who said, "Look, I just came in here to check on my ship, all right? I came in, these guys were looking at something in the locker, I came over to see, and there was this naked dead guy. But I just came in to check on my ship!''

"All right, one at a time. Now, do any of you recognize this man? Any of you ever seen him before on the station? Or anywhere else?''

Three heads shook vigorously in the negative.

"You're sure? Never seen him before? A long time ago, maybe? During the war? On Earth, Mars?''

They were sure.

"All right, so he was a total stranger.'' Back to the mechanic now. "He was like that when you found him? No clothes?''

"Not a stitch.''

"And you didn't see his clothes around on the floor or anywhere? In another locker?''

"Nope.''

"All right, what time do you usually come on duty? Were you late this morning or maybe a little bit early? Who was the first one into the bay?''

He wasn't halfway through with the questioning when Franklin came over to him. "I've done everything I can here. For the rest, I'll have to take him to Medlab. I've ordered a cart to come pick him up.''

"Sure, Doc, that's fine. You and Popovic have everything you need?"

"Yes, we're finished. There's no need to keep the site secured. This isn't where he was killed."

The fighter pilot was on her feet. "That means we can go, right?"

"Not quite yet," Garibaldi stopped her. "I still have a few more questions."

The next time he saw J. D. Ortega's body, it looked much different. The corpse in the locker had been stiff, contorted into a grotesque position to fit it inside the confined space, teeth bared in a rictus, eyes staring. Now it lay covered as if the dead man were asleep, and Garibaldi didn't turn away when Franklin pulled off the cover to expose it to view.

"He looks better already," Garibaldi said dryly.

"I used a compound to reduce rigor," Franklin explained. "Makes it a lot easier to conduct the autopsy. So here's what we've got. These bruises and abrasions are posthumous. They were probably made when the body was being forced into the locker. Now, *these* marks are not. There was a struggle. He tried to fight them off."

"Then it was a homicide."

"Oh, yes." Franklin flashed a pointer at a small livid spot in the crook of Ortega's arm. "This is where they injected the poison."

"Ah. So what was it?"

"Chloro-quasi-dianimidine. Injected directly into the bloodstream."

Garibaldi frowned. "I thought that couldn't be detected, that it broke down within a few minutes after death. Or am I thinking of something else with a longer name?"

"No. That's the general belief. As it happens, recent

research has come up with a more sensitive test. It's not widely known."

"Maybe a good thing that it's not."

"True. Now, as to time of death, I put it at around 20:00 hours yesterday."

Garibaldi frowned, remembering what Ivanova had told him. "How sure are you about that time?"

"Give or take an hour either way. No more than that. The breakdown of the drug is a good guide, besides the usual signs, rigor and all that. No way to pin it down much more closely, though."

"And you're sure they killed him someplace else, then brought him into the maintenance bay to hide the corpse? Any idea how long ago that was?"

"I'd say within a couple of hours after he was killed. No longer than that."

"And obviously, they took off his clothes before that. To search him, I suppose." Garibaldi wondered, *What were the killers looking for?*

Franklin echoed his question aloud. "I wonder if they found whatever they were looking for. I suppose it was something fairly small, easily concealed."

"Like a data crystal," Garibaldi said, speculating. He had a sudden thought. "It couldn't still be . . . inside there?"

Franklin shook his head. "I scanned him. Not a thing."

"And I suppose the killers could have scanned him, too."

"It's not hard to get that equipment," Franklin said, covering up the body again. "Well, what do we do with him now?"

"Wait. Until I contact Earth Central. They may have specific instructions. I don't know what they're going to think about this. Orders said they wanted him taken alive and shipped to Earth."

"All right, then. I'll try to keep him fresh for them."

"Um, before you put him away . . ."

Franklin paused.

"I think there's someone else who ought to see him. Someone who can give us a definite ID. After she gets back."

CHAPTER 4

Ivanova was just leaving the briefing room when she saw Garibaldi waiting outside. "Garibaldi. What is it?"

"Commander, I know you're just back from a tough mission, but I think there's something you should see."

Ivanova shut her eyes wearily. All through the long debriefing, she'd been anticipating the moment when she could fall into her bed. Or maybe into a stiff drink first and then to bed. But her eyes flew open again when she heard Garibaldi say, "We've found your friend Ortega."

"Ortega? J. D.? You have him in custody?"

He shook his head. "I think you'd better see for yourself."

Garibaldi looked at Captain Sheridan, standing in the doorway behind her. "Maybe you want to see him, too, sir."

Sheridan sighed. "Maybe I should."

Ivanova was numb with exhaustion and shock as the small group headed toward Medlab, and she didn't react when they showed her the covered form on the treatment table. Dr. Franklin's grave expression would have prepared her for the sight, even if nothing else had. "Go ahead."

They were all stiff, standing almost to attention as the doctor pulled aside the cover and exposed the dead face. "Commander, can you identify this man?"

She blinked. It was strange. At her first, brief glance, the face on the table was almost the face of the J. D. she'd known ten years ago, not the man who'd sent her the message to meet her last night. The harsh lines of strain were softened. They looked like laugh lines again. She could almost imagine his eyes opening, his mouth breaking into one of those smiles.

But in the next moment the signs of death were all too obvious—the discoloration of the skin, the slackness of the flesh. She turned away abruptly, glad the eyes had been closed. "Yes, that's J. D. Ortega. What happened? How did he die?"

"Murdered," said Franklin, frowning as he covered the body again. But the head of Medlab took all death seriously. It was his enemy, as the raiders were hers.

"Murdered how?" Her voice had recovered its usual crisp tone.

"An injection. Poison. The death itself was probably painless. But he tried to fight off his attackers beforehand.

"I see." It wasn't all. She knew from the way they were all looking at her that it wasn't all.

It was Garibaldi who told her. "We found him in an equipment locker out in fighter maintenance bay one. He'd been moved there after he was killed."

Ivanova knew what he was saying. "That's our maintenance bay. It's just one level down from the Alpha ready room. Where he was going to meet me."

Garibaldi nodded. There was more. "The doc here estimates the time of death at around 20:00 hours, yesterday."

"20:00 hours. Yesterday?" Ivanova shivered suddenly. At the exact moment she'd been in the ready room, waiting for Ortega, wondering why he was late, someone had been stabbing a lethal poison into his bloodstream. She'd been waiting for a dead man all that time.

"At least now we know why he never showed up," Garibaldi said. "They got to him before he could get to you."

Captain Sheridan interjected, "Commander, you say you have no idea why this man wanted to meet with you?"

"No, sir. I assumed, from his message, that he needed my help, that he might have enemies on the station."

"Which obviously he did," Garibaldi interjected.

"You didn't know he was a wanted fugitive, then?"

"No, sir. Ortega was an old friend, from after the war. I didn't know he was on the station until I got his message. When he didn't make the meeting, I queried the computer. That was when I found out about the alert and contacted Mr. Garibaldi."

"I see." The captain looked distinctly unhappy about this situation that had fallen into his lap. "Well, according to Mr. Garibaldi, it looks like he might have had friends on Babylon 5 as well as enemies. I hope you can help us find both of them."

"Of course." Ivanova's already-straight back went slightly stiffer, her shoulders squared. "Anything I can do."

Sheridan nodded in approval. "But I suppose it's a matter for security right now. Why don't you get some sleep, Commander? Unless there's anything else?" he asked Garibaldi.

"No, sir," said Garibaldi. "Not yet. We're still investigating. Questioning the witnesses who found the body."

Ivanova turned to him. "Let me know if you find anything."

"Of course."

After she'd left the lab Sheridan said, "Mr. Garibaldi."

A muscle in the side of Garibaldi's face twitched. "Yes, sir."

"Tell me I'm wrong, tell me these latest developments

aren't going to make this case more complicated than it was before.''

"Sorry, sir, can't do it. Before, all we had to do was nail Ortega, turn him over to EA, and be done with him. And maybe find out how he got onto the station. Now, it looks to me we've got to find whoever killed him and whatever they were looking for when they did it.''

"Whatever they were looking for?''

"The body was stripped. To me, that means searched —real thoroughly. Yeah, I think they were looking for something.''

Sheridan sighed. "Garibaldi, I've gone over the files on this case since you first reported it to me. Earth Central seems to consider it highly sensitive stuff. I have every confidence that you'll give it your highest priority. Have you sent them a report about finding the body?''

"Not yet, sir. I thought I'd wait until Commander Ivanova got a look at him. Positive ID.''

"Well, now she has.''

"I'll get on it right away.''

"And you'll keep me informed.''

"Absolutely, sir. As soon as I find anything, you'll know about it.''

"Good.'' Sheridan started to leave the lab, then paused. "I can't help wondering—why did he come here? Why did he want to see Ivanova?''

"Maybe we'll learn that when we find out who killed him.''

"I hope so. I really do.''

On his way back to the maintenance bay, Garibaldi encountered one of the people he wanted to see, Ms. Talia Winters, registered telepath, the station's only representative of the Psi Corps. While she wasn't a member of his security department, her duties included assisting in difficult investigations. And in this one Garibaldi was using all the resources he had available.

"Ah, Ms. Winters! So you're finished with the witnesses? Did they all agree to be scanned?"

She nodded gravely, slightly stiff in her long, unattractive skirt and jacket. She smoothed down the skirt with gloved hands. It was something Garibaldi often noticed about her, that contact with other minds didn't seem to make the telepath very happy. It was like she carried around some secret cloud of grief.

The Psi Corps made Garibaldi just a little nervous. It made most people he knew a little nervous. Someone knowing what was going on inside your head . . .

But Talia's tone was dry, businesslike. "They all agreed, yes. They seemed to feel a scan was the quickest way of putting an end to the questions."

"Well, I'm glad they cooperated. So, what did you find out?"

"Nothing. I'm sorry, I mean none of the witnesses know any more than they've told you already."

"The truth."

"Yes, the truth," she agreed. "The fighter pilot just came into the bay to check on her ship—she very much resents your trying to link her to your investigation, by the way."

"That's just too bad for her," Garibaldi replied, unrepentant.

"The mechanic who found the body and his foreman have told you everything they know, too. I'm sorry, but there just isn't anything more."

"Well, thanks anyway, Ms. Winters. Every bit of information helps, even if it isn't what we wanted to hear." She turned to go, still stiff, untouchable. "Um, Ms. Winters?"

"Yes? Mr. Garibaldi?"

"I was just wondering. Just . . . hypothetically.

There wouldn't be any way of doing a telepathic scan after a person's dead, would there be?"

She recoiled visibly. "No! And even if there were, I would certainly never want to attempt such a thing. I can't imagine anything more . . ."

He shrugged, a wry grin on his face. "Oh, well. It was just a thought. Thanks again, Ms. Winters."

The door to the maintenance bay closed behind her.

"Damn," said Garibaldi.

CHAPTER 5

There were raider ships everywhere. She kept firing, firing, but the raiders kept coming at her. From above, behind. She had to protect her wingman. He was in trouble. She could hear him calling her: "Commander Ivanova!"

Strange, it was Garibaldi's voice, not Mokena's. Garibaldi wasn't her wingman? Was he?

"Commander Ivanova!"

Groaning, she struggled to open her eyes. C&C? No, they couldn't be calling her already, she was just back from a mission, she wasn't supposed to be on duty yet, she had to sleep.

"Commander Ivanova!"

"Uh . . . Ivanova here," she mumbled, still too much asleep to speak clearly.

"Commander, this is Garibaldi. Are you awake?"

"No," she said, letting her face fall back onto the pillow.

"Ivanova, sorry to wake you, but there's something I'd like you to see."

"Garibaldi, in case you didn't know, I was just out tangling with about a hundred raiders. I just got to sleep, it's the middle of the night—"

"Actually, it's 10:30 hours."

"Um . . ." Ivanova shook her head and opened her eyes. Was it really? "So, what is it?"

"We found another piece of evidence in the Ortega case. I think it involves you."

"I'll be right there."

A life in the military had taught Ivanova how to get

herself quickly into uniform while still asleep, but this time Garibaldi's news had galvanized her awake. What was this new evidence? How could it involve her?

"That was quick," said Garibaldi approvingly as she came into the briefing room. Ivanova was taken slightly aback to see that Captain Sheridan was there as well. The security chief took an evidence packet from his pocket and removed a small slip of paper, security sealed.

Ivanova handled it cautiously. The paper had been tightly folded at one time, then opened and smoothed out. She could easily read through the clear seal: *S I – hardwır*. She shook her head slightly, not understanding.

"You've never seen this before? You don't know what it means?" Garibaldi asked.

"*S I*: I suppose that could mean Susan Ivanova. But I don't know what the rest of it means. I never saw this before. Where'd you find it?"

"In the ready room. Where you were waiting for Ortega. We put it through some pretty fine scans and managed to pick up enough to make it certain. This was Ortega's. He'd handled the paper, at least, even if he didn't write the note."

"In the ready room?" There was disbelief in Ivanova's voice. "He left me a note?"

"On the floor. Near the door to the rest room."

"But I never saw . . . You mean, it was there while I was waiting for him? All that time?"

"You probably wouldn't have noticed it. My team was going over the place a centimeter at a time. It was under a counter. And you know how pilots are—they don't always toss their stuff into the recycler. There was other trash on the floor."

She remembered slowly that it was true, the newspapers thrown here and there when people were done with them, wrappers on the floor.

Garibaldi rubbed his forehead, right where the hair was receding. "Tell me, Commander, were you on time for that meeting with Ortega? Or maybe five, ten minutes late?"

She closed her eyes to recall it. "All right, I got there, the room was empty, Ortega wasn't there. No, there was this guy—"

"What guy?" Garibaldi demanded eagerly.

"I don't know. No one I knew. Just this guy. Just when I came in the door, he was coming out of the rest room. He looked like he was in a hurry, he left."

"Do you think you could identify him?"

"I don't know. I didn't really look at him, once I was sure it wasn't Ortega."

"All right, we'll check on that later. What about the time?"

"I checked the time. I remember. Right after I came in and saw the room was empty. It was . . . I can't remember exactly. I was maybe four or five minutes late, I think. No more than that. I queried the computer, it'd be in the log, wouldn't it?"

"You first queried the time from that location at 20:04 hours," Garibaldi confirmed.

"Then that was right after I came in. I remember, when he didn't show up, I kept checking the time."

Sheridan interjected, "Commander, that note—do you know what it means?"

She read it again: *S I hardw r.* Shook her head. "No, I don't."

"No idea at all?" Garibaldi asked.

"Well, I assume it means 'hardware.' Maybe, military hardware, weapons? That kind of thing?"

Garibaldi took it, peered at the handwriting. "Or 'hardwar' maybe? Whatever that would mean?"

He passed it on to Sheridan, who had held out his hand to see it. "Looks more like an 'i' there. Like it was supposed to be 'hardwire'?"

Garibaldi took the paper, examined it again. "Yeah, it does, now that you mention it. Hardwire. So what does that mean? Computer?"

The voice responded: "Hardwired: Primary reference: obsolete, primitive electronic computing machines: instructions permanently embedded in physical structure of computing device.

"Secondary references: instinctive behaviors, genetically encoded behaviors.

"Tertiary references: late-twentieth-century futuristic fiction. Derivative references: wetware, cyberware.

"Do you wish expanded information on any of these references?"

The others looked at her. Ivanova shrugged. "Sorry."

"Maybe he didn't have time to finish what he was going to write. He heard someone coming," Garibaldi suggested. "But if he wrote it to you, it ought to mean *something* to you."

"I'm sorry, it doesn't," Ivanova said again with a touch of irritation in her voice. Hadn't she already said so? "Is that it? Is there anything else?"

"Not yet," Garibaldi answered her. "Nothing definite. We're still trying to find just where Ortega was killed. Checking out the ready room first, though it isn't very likely, not if you were there at 20:04 hours. Of course, I'll let you know if anything else turns up."

"Thanks."

Sheridan stood. "Well, I tell you what, Commander, now that you're up, how about I treat you to breakfast before you have to go on duty? I think I have some news you'll be a little happier to hear."

"That's a very good idea, sir. I accept."

* * *

Breakfast turned out to include a rare and much-appreciated treat: real coffee, imported from Earth. Eyes closed, Ivanova held the cup to her face and inhaled the fragrance, deeply, then rolled a single sip around in her mouth before swallowing it. "Oh, that's good! The real thing. I don't know if I'd have decided to go into space if they'd told me how hard it was to find real coffee. I don't know how Earthforce expects people to wake up in the morning and function on that synthetic stuff."

"It was a gift from my father. Shipped out here for my last birthday. Two pounds of it, direct from Earth. I thought I remembered how much you liked it. It was even harder to get back when we were stationed off Io, right after the war."

"I remember."

"Anyway," said Sheridan, putting down his empty cup, "I've got the information you asked about, on the *Cassini*."

"Ah! The cargo!" She'd simply been too tired to check the records after debriefing—and the trip to Medlab to view J. D.'s body.

"Their cargo. What was so valuable it cost all those lives. It was morbidium ingots. Shipped from Marsport."

"Morbidium. That's a strategic metal. Trade restricted."

Sheridan nodded. Morbidium was vital in the production of phased plasma weapons, an essential element in the alloy that made up their central coils. Difficult and expensive to manufacture. Earth Alliance restricted trade in all the strategic metals, setting prices and prohibiting sale to all unapproved buyers. The predictable result was a strong interest on the black market, where weapons and components were among the most heavily traded commodities. The temptation for pirates was obvious. The profits would be enormous.

"You think there was a leak," Sheridan said. "Somebody slipped them the routing information."

"You remember, Captain, it's what the *Cassini*'s pilot said: 'It's a setup.' They were waiting for that transport, they knew where and when and what it was carrying. They even brought their own transport along to haul off the cargo. Now, that takes advance planning."

Sheridan agreed. "I know. No matter what you do to tighten security, as long as raiders are willing to pay for the data, it gets out. Tell a routing clerk she can earn five thousand credits for just one bit of information. You'll get it. And the more they steal, the more they can afford to pay to bribe someone else."

"Raider activity seems to go in cycles. We hurt them last year, cut off their source of heavy weapons. Now it's starting to look like they're back again. Too many incidents the last few months. There's got to be something behind it. A new bunch of raiders on the scene. A new supplier of information. Something. If we can just find out what it is . . ."

"You want to look into it?"

"Just to see if there's something I can pick up. With the jump gate in 13 down for repairs, there'll have to be some wholesale rerouting. Maybe a pattern will show up. Of course, what we should have are regular Earthforce patrols of all the jump points and shipping routes."

"With the current political climate on Earth, we'll be lucky if they don't cut back funding. Space isn't exactly the most popular budget item on the new administration's agenda. I wouldn't hold my breath and count on the ships for more patrols."

"I know," Ivanova said glumly. "Even though you'd think they'd want to protect strategic metals shipments, at least. Maybe if there are more losses, or the shipping companies start to complain, something will be done."

"Well, good luck with it, Commander. I'll look forward to seeing your report if you find anything significant.''

"Thank you, sir. And thanks for the coffee." Ivanova started to stand up. It was just about time to go back on duty, already.

"Ah, Commander? This other business? This murdered terrorist suspect. I know it's rough, when it's someone you haven't seen in a long time. The way people can change.''

She sighed, sat back down. "I still have a hard time believing it. That J. D. Ortega could be mixed up in something like that. You know, I kept thinking, before they found his body: when we find him, when we investigate, we'll find out it was all a mistake. Mistaken identity, or . . . something. But now—I just don't know. He was *murdered* . . .''

"Well, I hope it's all cleared up as soon as possible. When Garibaldi finds who killed him.''

"So do I.''

Things were already busy in the Observation Dome when Ivanova arrived. A lot of outgoing traffic had to be rerouted away from the Red 13 transfer point until the damaged gate could be repaired, and that meant schedule changes all the way down the line—absolutely necessary if you didn't want to have two ships occupying the same space at the same time in some sector three jumps away.

Ivanova noticed several curious looks aimed in her direction as she came into the dome. It made her wonder, what were they thinking about? Her engagement with the raiders or Ortega's murder? Of course, no one was supposed to know about the murder, and she didn't really want to talk about it. She was glad the technicians were professional military personnel, who knew better than to ask personal questions while on duty.

Lieutenant Nomura did offer a brief "Glad to see you

back in one piece, Commander," as she relieved him at the control console, but no more than that. No congratulations on her victory over the raiders. They were both professional enough to realize that Ivanova hadn't won a real victory, and no congratulations were in order when even now arrangements were being made for the disposal of the bodies of the *Cassini*'s crew.

"I'm glad we all made it back," was her response.

After that, it was all business as Nomura briefed her on the ongoing operations. It wasn't a pretty picture. "Every pilot or shipowner who's been delayed by even five minutes is demanding to talk to 'someone in higher authority.' To Captain Sheridan, to Earth Central . . ."

"I'll try to handle them," Ivanova said dryly.

"Good luck." Nomura turned over the console and left the problems in her lap. He'd coped with them long enough. Ivanova very quickly realized there was going to be no spare time today to check out her speculations about the recent raider activity. Not with all the questions, complaints, and demands the rerouting was generating. Nomura hadn't exaggerated. Schedules, deadlines, perishable goods, guaranteed-on-time clauses in delivery contracts: everyone was convinced the rerouting was a conspiracy designed to affect their business alone, and that their own case deserved priority over all others.

Ivanova was soon heartily weary of the words: "Don't you understand? I have a *schedule* to meet!"

It wasn't long before she had to restrain herself from shouting back: "Don't *you* understand? Someone may have already sold your schedule to the raiders! This delay may just save your precious cargo." But of course her actual reply was more on the order of: "I appreciate your scheduling difficulties, pilot, and I personally promise to make sure your departure is given the highest possible priority, consistent with station regulations."

Which was simply another way of saying that they could take the schedule she gave them.

But worse by far than the commercial interests were the diplomats and their staffs. Like the pilot of the Minbari courier ship—arrogant, warrior class down to the bone—who all but suggested the war would break out again if Babylon 5 delayed the delivery of his dispatches by as much as an hour. If he weren't given clearance *immediately,* he might even call in a war cruiser more than capable of opening a jump point on its own power. Ivanova crisply suggested that he go ahead and do just that, since it would solve quite a few of her scheduling problems.

Or the Narn captain who expressed doubt that there even was a breakdown of the jump gate. "This could be some kind of trick, a plot on the part of our enemies to delay us at this station! I *demand* clearance! Now!"

At which Ivanova took a deep breath. "Captain Ka'Hosh, I was there when the damage was done. I can personally attest to the fact. Now, if you don't want your flight to be rerouted around that point, then you're going to have to wait until the repairs are completed. We estimate the jump gate will be back on-line within thirty-eight Earth hours. At that time, you'll be given all the proper priority, I guarantee it. And in the meantime, if your enemies are here on this station, they're not going anywhere through that gate, either."

Which seemed to satisfy the Narn, for the moment.

Ivanova checked the time, suppressed an urge to groan. It'd only been two and a half hours since she came on duty.

It looked like it was going to be a very long day.

CHAPTER 6

Later—much, much later—Ivanova sat at the computer screen in her own quarters. "Computer, I want the records of all raider attacks on cargo vessels in Earth Alliance space within the last year. Graphic display mode."

"Accessing."

"Display by type of cargo. How many attacks on ships carrying strategic metals?"

The information appeared on her data screen. Strategic metals—yes, there they were." Ivanova closed her eyes for a moment. They were tired. She was tired. It had been a perfectly harrowing day, coping with the mess caused by the damaged jump gate. At least, after tomorrow, it ought to be fixed. But then who knew what new crisis would erupt?

Now that she was finally off duty, she ought to be able to relax, but the matter of the raiders had been nagging at the back of her mind all day. She knew it would chase her through her dreams if she didn't get some kind of answer first.

She opened her eyes again. "Compare hijacking of strategic metals with previous years, back, oh, ten years. By total tonnage stolen and by number of attacks." When the display changed, she nodded. Yes. Both figures were up, starting a little over a year ago. But was the increase in all strategic metals, or just certain ones? The *Cassini,* she recalled, had been carrying morbidium.

"Break the figures on strategic metals down by type of commodity."

And there on her data screen, the answer leaped out at

her. Total tonnage of morbidium hijacked had gone up dramatically beginning about sixteen months ago. An increase of 184 percent during one year alone. That was hard to believe.

Maybe there was simply more of the metal being shipped. But when the computer displayed the figures, it was clear that although there was an increase of tonnage shipped, this by no means could account for the amount being hijacked. And no one at Earth Central had noticed? With a strategic commodity?

To Ivanova, morbidium meant armaments. Specifically, the power coils of phased plasma weapons. And unfortunately, these days, trade in armaments was at an all-time high since the Earth-Minbari war.

Ivanova rubbed the sides of her forehead with her fingertips. "Computer, can you give me a breakdown of the price of strategic metals on the black market over the past two years?"

But at this point, the computer was unhelpful. "Those data are not available," the voice said primly.

"Damn," Ivanova muttered. But she supposed the black market didn't issue regular financial reports. Not, at least, into the Earthforce databanks. She supposed Garibaldi might be able to find out something. He seemed to have contacts with certain underworld types. She made a note to herself to ask him, later, maybe tomorrow.

Maybe another approach. Like, where were the raiders getting their information? Was there some common factor? What kinds of persons had access to the data?

"Computer, display all raider attacks on strategic metals shipments during the last year. Break down the data by transport company."

She stared at the screen. No pattern seemed apparent. "Highlight shipments of morbidium." She shook her head. Still no pattern. Then she was frustrated by the fact that the station's databanks didn't contain the information on ownership or the insurance company covering the cargo on all transports, only those logged through Babylon 5. Finally, "Display the data by point of origin of cargo."

And there it was! A distinct, sharp increase in total hijacked cargoes originating from Marsport, beginning sixteen months ago, at just about the same time as the increase in hijacked morbidium shipments. The *Cassini* had shipped out of Marsport. Just to be sure, "Highlight attacks on cargoes of morbidium originating from Marsport."

Yes, that was it. She had the answer. Marsport shipped a load of the strategic metal every two to three days. In the last sixteen months, twenty percent of those cargoes had been the object of raider attacks, most of them successful.

There was her leak. No doubt about it. Someone in Marsport was leaking transport routing data to the raiders, and the commodity they were targeting was morbidium.

Incredible that no one had picked up on this so far. Or —maybe "incredible" wasn't the right word. Maybe "suspicious" was.

She leaned back from the desk, stretched stiff muscles. Well, it was a beginning, at least. And it was good to remember there was more than one way to hit at the raiders besides plasma fire. Without information, they were blind. "Just plug that leak," she said aloud.

The computer, always literal-minded, replied, "No leak detected at this time."

Ivanova shut her eyes. "No more input," she told it. "I'm finished for tonight. I'm going to bed. Hold any calls."

*   *   *

The mess hall at breakfast—dozens of uniformed figures hurrying with full trays to their tables, getting ready for the morning duty shift. Ivanova spotted Garibaldi heading for the empty seat next to her. He sat down with a heavily loaded tray.

"Planning to skip lunch?" she asked, raising her eyebrows at the sight of his meal. "And dinner?"

Swallowing a generous mouthful, he said, "You know, I've noticed that about women. You never like to see a man enjoy a good hearty meal."

Her eyebrows went up again. "You call that hearty? A few more meals like that, you won't have a functioning heart left."

He put down his fork. "See what I mean?"

"By the way," she asked him, "any more news on your investigation?"

He slapped his forehead. "Oh! I forgot I meant to tell you. You were off-line last night. Well, we found out where Ortega was killed. In the head."

She drew back in dismay. "You mean, the head right off the ready room? He was killed right there? Then he must have been in there all that time! Are you sure?"

He nodded. "We found traces of the poison on the floor. And slight traces of Ortega's blood."

Ivanova shivered. "Then . . . that man, the one who brushed past me. He must have been—"

"The killer. Right."

"And he was probably just outside the room all that time, just waiting for me to leave."

"Or for someone else to show up," Garibaldi agreed. "That guy must have been sweating blood, wondering what else was going to go wrong. Here he'd planned a nice, peaceful private murder, and you walk in on it."

"I just wish I could have been a couple of minutes earlier," she said regretfully.

"I don't. Or we might have had two corpses down in

the equipment bay. That guy was a pro. That particular poison isn't something amateurs can get ahold of.

"Anyway, it looks like you're the only witness who can identify him. Sometime soon I want you to come into my office, try again to identify this guy."

"Of course." She shuddered again, her appetite gone.

"If you want me to put some security on you, just to be safe—"

"No, I don't think it's necessary, is it? Nobody else knows about this, do they?"

"Nope, this is strictly need-to-know stuff. Ultraclassified, though I'm not quite sure I know why." Garibaldi gave an interested look at her tray. "Say, by the way, the captain says you're doing a little investigating of your own?"

"Just running down some data through the computer. I was wondering where the raiders are getting their information. Now I know."

"And?"

"Marsport. Someone in a shipping office in Marsport is selling transport routing data."

Now he was the one to raise his eyebrows. "That was easy."

"Easy? I was up half the night!" She shook her head. "No, you're right. Once you look at the figures the right way, it's obvious. And the station's computer doesn't even have all the data available. Someone on Earth or Mars should have spotted this months ago. Maybe even as much as a year ago. Someone, for whatever reason, hasn't been doing their job.

"Anyway, I'm putting a report together to send on to Earth Central later today."

Garibaldi prodded a piece of fruit with his fork. "Are you sure that's such a good idea?"

"What do you mean?"

"I mean stirring around in someone else's anthill.

Suggesting that people in other departments might be negligent—or worse.''

She stared at him in indignant disbelief. "Garibaldi! I don't believe you! Raiders are hitting ships out there, crews are being killed!''

"Yeah, I guess you're right. Just be careful, all right? I've seen these things turn ugly. It could be you'll be stepping on some toes a lot higher up than yours." He took another look at her tray. "Say, aren't you going to finish that?''

He was starting to reach toward the tray when his link sounded. "Garibaldi here.''

"This is Captain Sheridan, Mr. Garibaldi. Something's come up. Could you meet me in the briefing room?''

"I'm on my way." He looked up to see Ivanova carrying her half-finished breakfast tray away and sighed in regret.

Garibaldi came briskly into the briefing room. Sheridan looked up at him. "Mr. Garibaldi, I've been reading your latest report on the Ortega case. Good work. I have to say, you've been very thorough in investigating this. So I don't want you to think that this is because I have any reservations with the way you're handling the job.''

What is? Garibaldi wondered silently, thinking that this didn't sound good at all.

"But I have to order you to terminate your investigation.''

"What? Close the case? A murder investigation?'' He couldn't believe what he was hearing. "Sir?''

Sheridan looked slightly uncomfortable. "Like I say, this doesn't reflect on you. And it wasn't my decision. I have orders directly from Earth Central. They're sending a special team of investigators to take over the case. Apparently, with the connection to the Free Mars movement, they consider it too sensitive for the regular Babylon 5 security staff to handle.''

Garibaldi started to open his mouth to say something which probably would have sounded like "Horsehockey," but he closed it in time.

Sheridan went on, "So, as of now, you're ordered to pull all your staff off the case, seal all your files and records, and be ready to hand them over to the special investigators when they arrive on the station.''

"Which will be when?''

"They're already in transit onboard the *Asimov*.''

"They didn't lose any time, did they?''

Sheridan looked up at him, started to say something, then decided against it. "If you have no more questions, that will be all. Thank you, Mr. Garibaldi.''

CHAPTER 7

"Oh-oh," Garibaldi said to himself. He was checking the monitors from Security Central as the passengers from the *Asimov* started toward customs, and he was getting his first glance at the special investigation team from Earth Central. "Bad news."

It was impossible to mistake them—stiff and ultramilitary in their Earthforce blues. Three officers, two men and a woman, but they all had flinty, hard eyes that said, *We know you're guilty of something, and we'll find out what it is, no matter how long it takes.* One look, and the security guard at the customs gate jumped to attention like she'd just touched a hot wire. Even through the monitor, Garibaldi could almost see her sweat as she followed the prescribed routine: take the identicard, check the face on the card against the holder, run it through the scanner, confirm the data, welcome the passenger to Babylon 5 if and only if the check is positive.

Once past the checkpoint, the three of them passed out of sight of the monitor, heading for the lift tubes. Heading, Garibaldi realized, for him.

So he was ready when they came into the security office like a three-man assault team—one on point, one securing the door at the rear, and the main force, flashing the insignia of a commander's rank, heading straight for the primary objective: the computer console.

Garibaldi moved to put himself in the way. "This office is a restricted area," he announced firmly. "Do you have authorization?"

The Earthforce commander, a wiry man of around forty with short-cropped blond hair and sharp, thin features, took another step forward, with a scowl built on order to intimidate. "Are you Garibaldi?"

"I'm Michael Garibaldi, Babylon 5 Chief of Security."

"You're required to turn over all your records and files on the Ortega case. I'll need your passwords," he snapped, a lot like a short-haired terrier or one of those other kinds of small dogs that bite.

Garibaldi stood his ground, which happened to rest on Earthforce regulations. "I have to see your ID and authorization first."

The commander's lips thinned to a straight line, but he produced the documents, slapped them into Garibaldi's hand. Garibaldi scanned through them, nodded. Identicard in the name of Commander Ian Wallace. The authorization, of course, was all in order, security clearance up to ultraviolet and maybe beyond. "Commander," he acknowledged crisply, handing them back, but also adding, "I'll need their ID, too."

"You've seen my orders, *Mister* Garibaldi. You know I have full authority here."

"Not quite, Commander," Garibaldi insisted firmly. "You have full authority over the Ortega case, but this is the Babylon 5 security office, and my files hold references to other classified matters that aren't related to that case in any way, so I have to make sure anyone who's going to have access has got the proper clearance."

Angrily, Wallace gestured for his aides to come forward, and they handed their ID cards to Garibaldi, who noted that they were Lieutenants Miyoshi and Khatib. Miyoshi was a full-bodied woman who looked like she was wearing a stiff corset under her uniform. To Garibaldi she seemed rather old for her rank. Khatib—Khatib was one of the coldest-looking men he had ever seen. Black eyes, a sharply beaked nose, a lipless mouth like a snake's. Garibaldi almost expected to see a forked tongue flicker out. *Very bad news.*

But his ID was in order, and his security clearance. Garibaldi took a step back from the computer terminal. "Clearances are all in order. I'll get you the passwords." As he handed them to Wallace, he grinned insincerely. "Welcome to Babylon 5, Commander. I hope you enjoy your stay."

"Damn, I hate those stupid games," Garibaldi said, jamming his hands into his pants pockets.

"What games?" Ivanova asked, with half her attention on the command console.

"Power games, status games. Like a couple of dockyard dogs snarling at each other over a bone."

Ivanova was dubious. "But you were right. Following procedure. Are you sure you're not just talking about one of those male things? Chest-thumping, testosterone?"

Garibaldi shook his head. "No, it's more than just that. I know this kind of bastard. First time you meet him, it's got to be a test. I *know* I was right. That's the whole point. He doesn't like me now, but I tell you, if I'd given in, it would have been worse."

He paused to look out through the Observation Dome at the bright, distant flare of the jump gate as a ship passed through into the vortex. Ivanova's attention was still on her console. "Anyway," he continued, "I'm off this case. But you're still an important witness. You're probably going to have to talk to these guys sometime soon. Be careful, all right? These guys are serious trouble."

"Garibaldi, you worry too much. Remember, I've survived ten years in the military. I know the type you're talking about. I don't think I'll have too much trouble with them."

"Well, sometimes there's reason to worry. All I know

is, someone up in the brass-hat department is really interested in this case."

Now she turned away from the screen to face him. "*That's* what really bothers me, if you want to know the truth. We have raiders out here, we have ships being attacked, crews killed, and what do they do about it? They cut our budget. They won't send out more patrols. They ignore reports of corruption and inefficiency in the bureaucracy.

"But push the right buttons, when they hear words like 'terrorism'—when it threatens them politically—then they send up a team of investigators on the next ship, don't spare the trouble, to hell with the expense."

"Ah, I take it you haven't heard back about your report on the leak of the transport routes to the raiders?"

She shook her head, then turned back to the console. "Of course, I only sent it out the day before yesterday. These things take time."

"Well, just be careful, that's all. If you do get into trouble I don't know how much I'll be able to help you. These guys are setting up their own little private kingdom on the station, outside Security Central. Wallace says he doesn't want interruptions or interference. I've got to assign a team of security agents to him—they follow his orders, nobody else's. He's got his own command center in briefing room B, he's brought in his own computer system—ours isn't secure enough for him—and he's even setting up his own lockup facilities." Garibaldi scowled. "I don't like it."

Ivanova had seen that look before. "So what are you going to do?"

"Do? Nothing. Those are orders."

"Well, you be careful, too," Ivanova said. She knew Garibaldi.

* * *

There was a part of Babylon 5 that they called Down Below, down in Brown Sector, although officially there was no such place, but officially didn't much matter in Down Below. It was a place where you had to crawl through maintenance hatches to get where you were going, where power and water came from illicit taps on the station's lines, where people slept in empty cargo drums and lived in corners behind a screen made out of rags.

With a population the size of Babylon 5's, there were always people who would slip through the cracks, who existed in the marginal habitat along the edge of legality. Some slipped over that margin, and they were Garibaldi's business. The rest of them—it was a case of live and let live.

You could buy almost anything in Down Below; the commerce covered the spectrum from off-white to black. People sold their bodies—that was a given. There were regular business establishments and there were furtive characters in the hallways with hidden pockets in their coats. Information, like any other commodity, was for sale here, too, which was one reason Garibaldi tolerated the place. This was his ear on the black market, on the coming and going of persons and goods who might not belong on the station.

But all the business, no matter how technically legal, tended to pause when Garibaldi entered the area. Goods were quickly put away, people found that they had business elsewhere, urgent transactions were no longer so urgent. The station's chief of security was not a popular customer in Down Below.

Wherever Garibaldi looked, people acted even more furtive than usual. His usual informers had evaporated.

But there was more than one way to hunt for information. Garibaldi decided to capitalize on the effect of his presence. He wandered. He lingered. He examined, one by one, the counterfeit jewels on the tray of a very reluctant vendor. He asked to see the entertainment licenses of a trio of corridor musicians and the customs certificates of a rack of imported skink-skin boots which the proprietor of a makeshift shop had tried to hide under an equally dubious rug. He was very bad for business, and he showed no inclination to leave.

Finally a sallow-faced figure came up to where he sat at his ease, sipping mineral water at a table in the Happy Daze Bar, an establishment not licensed to sell intoxicating beverages, where he was presently the only customer. "What you wants, Garibaldi?"

It was Mort the Ear, purveyor of information, finder of things, and current owner of the bar.

"Want? Oh, I don't want anything in particular, Mort. I just thought I'd do a little shopping, see the sights, visit a few old friends."

"How comes you gots lot time on you hands now, Garibaldi? Two, three day ago, big investigating, big case. Now . . ." Mort paused, grinned crookedly.

Garibaldi wondered how long it would take the news about Wallace and his investigative team to get out. If it wasn't already all over the station. Wallace hadn't exactly been an inconspicuous arrival on Babylon 5. He grinned back with a show of teeth. "Well, I just thought I'd take some time off to come down here and look up an old friend of mine. Louie. Yeah, Louie's an old buddy, haven't seen him in years. He moved to Mars a few years ago, worked around here and there. Now, what do I hear but my old friend Louie's right here on Babylon 5!

"So I say to myself: Mike, you've got to go look up your old friend Louie, you used to be so thick together. So I go to look him up, and—guess what? The station registry doesn't have any record of Louie coming onto the station! None of the checkpoints recorded old Louie coming through! Now, isn't that crazy?

"Because, you know, it's real nice when people come

in customs the right way and we put their identicard through the scanner and their name in the registry. See, then we know who's on the station. We know where to find them when we're looking for them. So I say to myself, Mike, why don't you just go hang around the station for a while, look around, and maybe you'll run into old Louie. We can have a few laughs, talk about old times, and then maybe I can find out what happened with his ID when he came onto the station, so it won't happen again. Then I can look up old Louie anytime I feel like it, and I won't have to come down here, looking for him."

"You not makes sense, Garibaldi."

"Then let me make it more clear, Mort. Somebody's been coming onto this station through the back door. Maybe with fake ID. I don't like that. I want to know what kind of a counterfeit identicard can fake out our scanners. I want to see it for myself."

"You wants fake ID?"

"You got it, Mort."

"I gots lot fake ID, you want it." He started to reach into a pocket somewhere in the interior of the layers of clothing that didn't conceal his scrawny frame, but Garibaldi stopped him.

"Huh-uh, Mort. Not that junk you peddle to the tourists. The real thing."

Sullenly, "Maybe I asks around."

"That's good to hear. And maybe I might come down here and do some more shopping in a day or two. After all, I have all this time on my hands now, like you say."

He strolled off. It was a fishing expedition, but something might come of it, you never knew.

He hesitated before taking the next step, because it was treading awfully close to Wallace's investigation, but, dammit, people sneaking onto Babylon 5 cut right to the heart of station security. And if there were forged identicards floating around, he needed to find them.

Up in a more respectable section of brown deck, a woman named Hardesty ran an establishment called the Wet Rock, a place where station workers came after their shifts to have a beer or two or three. The beer was as cheap as beer can be on a space station off in the middle of nowhere, and the food she served with it was a little bit heavy on the starch and the grease. Garibaldi liked it.

"Hardesty, how you doing?"

"Doing all right," she said, in a tone that meant: Is this call business or pleasure, Garibaldi?

"You haven't seen Meyers around lately?"

"Think he left the station. Went out on an ice hauler a couple, few days ago. Maybe."

"How about Nick?"

"Nick Patinos?"

"The one."

"Think he works the swing shift now. Awfully hard to get hold of him."

"He still come in here sometimes?"

"After work, yeah. Mostly he's at that stupid game parlor, though. Or the gym."

Garibaldi knew where the game parlor was. Nick was one of about a dozen participants seated at tables where immaterial ground cars raced each other around a virtual track and ghostly holographic figures sparred in gladiatorial contests. Garibaldi joined the spectators for a while until one of the figures fell to its knees and expired, after which a new challenger sat down to contend with the winner.

"You're getting better with that broadsword, Nick," Garibaldi remarked.

The man looked up from a beer. He was a dockworker with dark eyes and hair turning gray on the edges. "Hey, Mike. Yeah, I can go ten minutes sometimes with Cass these days."

"Maybe we can play a round sometime. Or go over to

the gym, spar a round or two in the lo-grav. Like we used to, on Mars.''

''Yeah, maybe.'' He paused, gave Garibaldi a look. ''But you didn't come down here today to play holo games, did you, Mike?''

His silence admitted it.

''What I heard was, you're looking into things.'' Nick looked back down into his beer. ''Maybe the kind of thing that's going to cause a lot of trouble.''

Good news sure spreads fast, Garibaldi thought sourly. ''You heard that, did you?''

Nick made an offhand gesture. ''Here and there.''

''Well, there was a fugitive alert a couple days ago. A suspected terrorist—''

But Nick slammed his beer down angrily on the table. ''Terrorists! You know what, ever since the uprising last year, you Earthforce types have got nothing on your brains but goddamn terrorists! I'm sick of it! You show your ID card, and every time it's 'Oh, you're from Mars, we've got to check your stuff, check you out just in case you've got explosives in with your dirty socks.' I'm tired of it, Mike!''

''Hey! Look, Nick, you know me. I'm not just 'Earthforce,' all right? Maybe somebody's probing into the terrorist thing, but it's not me. Not now. Hey, you can believe me, can't you? We knew each other on Mars for, what, three years?''

''Yeah, but things are different now. You've been out of touch.''

Garibaldi was, for an instant, bitterly reminded of Lise. She wouldn't come with him to Babylon 5, he wouldn't stay with her on Mars. Yeah, he'd been out of touch too long, 'til it was too late.

''All right,'' he said, forcibly putting her out of his mind, ''we're not on Mars now, we're on Babylon 5: a space station, a closed environment. I have the safety of this place on my hands. All I want to know is: how does a guy get onto the station without going through customs? Does he get smuggled in with the cargo or use a fake identicard, or what? Nick, think about it. Forget politics for a minute, Earth and Free Mars and all the rest of it. Nobody wants a crazy getting onto the station, running around with explosives, biohazards, whatever! Come on! Help me out here!''

"I'll think about it, Mike. I'll ask around. But this really isn't a good time right now. Things . . ." He shook his head. "I'll see."

"If you know anything—"

"I don't know about any threats to the station. I can tell you that right now."

"Or illegal entries? Or counterfeit identicards?"

Nick shook his head, put down the empty glass of beer, stood up to leave. "I'll ask around. But it really isn't a good time."

You could say that again, thought Garibaldi. It was a lousy time. And he had a feeling it was going to be getting a lot worse, real soon now.

CHAPTER 8

The interview did not start out on a cordial note.
Lieutenant Miyoshi barely looked up when Ivanova came into the briefing room.

Ivanova waited a moment, then, "Lieutenant, judging from the number of messages you sent while I was on duty today, I assumed you had some questions to ask me. But if you're busy, I can certainly come back later."

When Miyoshi did look up, her expression reminded Ivanova, too late, of Garibaldi's warning this morning. "Not at all, Commander. I'm glad you can finally spare the time to help with this investigation."

Ivanova sat down opposite her, uninvited. "I'm sure you can appreciate, Lieutenant, that my duties on this station can't always be dropped at a moment's notice. I am the executive officer. We've had a transit point jump gate out of commission recently, and a number of other urgent matters that I had to deal with."

"Yes, I understand you were involved in that . . . accident. However, in the interim, I've had time to review your file—in particular, your correspondence with the fugitive terrorist J. D. Ortega."

Correspondence? Ivanova frowned. She didn't like this. "Don't you mean 'alleged terrorist'?"

"If you insist. So, how long have you known this 'alleged terrorist,' Commander?"

"About ten years. Since shortly after the war. He was my flight instructor when I was in training."

"You were close?"

"No closer than cadets and instructors usually are."

Miyoshi raised a dubious brow. "And after the war, you maintained a correspondence."

"Not really, not after he went back to Mars, no."

"Indeed? What would you say if I told you we had records, notes signed by you, in your handwriting?"

Tightly, "If you want to call a couple of holiday greeting cards a 'correspondence,' then I suppose we did, for a year or two."

"And can you produce any of the notes he sent to you?"

"I'm an Earthforce career officer, Lieutenant. I've been posted a half-dozen different times in those years. I don't save holiday cards from all my old buddies."

"So, since the time of your last known meeting with the suspected terrorist, you've disposed of all written records of your correspondence."

Furious now, Ivanova got to her feet. "I don't have to sit here and take this—"

But it was as if Miyoshi had been waiting for her outburst. A smile spread across her broad face. "Commander, yes, you do. Let me remind you, we have full authority here to conduct this investigation. *Full* authority, Commander. I could, at this moment, have you arrested until you agree to answer my questions."

Glowering, Ivanova sat back down.

"Now, to continue." But having made her point, Miyoshi kept the rest of her questions closer to the facts. "You claim that when Ortega contacted you, you had no idea he was a terrorist suspect or a fugitive."

"That's right."

"But there was a priority alert sent out by Earth Central."

"That alert was sent out to all Earth Alliance installations. To their security offices. There was no particular indication that he might be here on Babylon 5."

"But Mr. Garibaldi recognized the name."

"Mr. Garibaldi is head of security on the station. That's his job. Not mine."

"And when you became aware that he was the subject of a fugitive alert, you immediately contacted security, is that right?"

"That's right. I called Mr. Garibaldi."

"But why the delay? Why wait until Ortega had already been dead for almost two hours?"

"What do you mean?"

"I mean that we have a certain number of facts here. Ortega was supposed to meet you in ready room one at 20:00 hours. According to Dr. Franklin, whose credentials are more than adequate, he was killed at approximately that time, probably in the adjacent rest room. The log of the station's computer places you on the scene intermittently from 20:04 to 22:06. And by your own admission, you were near the body for over two hours."

"That's correct."

"Approximately twenty-three hours after the murder, Ortega's body was found in an equipment locker in an aircraft maintenance area just one level from where he was killed. His body was stripped, and his clothing and personal effects have not yet been recovered."

"That's right. So just what are you implying?"

"I'm stating the facts, Commander. These facts are consistent with a number of different interpretations. Let's look at some more facts. From the time of Ortega's death to your meeting with Mr. Garibaldi over two hours later, you have no witnesses to your presence in the ready room. No one saw you there—except for one man you claim to have seen leaving just after you came in. But you haven't been able to identify this man, am I correct? You'd never seen him before, you haven't seen him since. In *fact*, there's no reason to suppose the existence of this mysterious figure, is there? Except for your testimony."

Ivanova was too stunned to reply.

"Now, we have one other piece of evidence, Commander. A note, addressed to 'S.I.' We all suppose we know who S.I. is, don't we? Susan Ivanova. This note, addressed to you, Commander Ivanova, says, 'hardwir.' You claim, don't you, that you have no idea what this might mean. 'Hardwir.' "

Miyoshi leaned forward a little in her chair, closer to Ivanova. Her hair was black, pulled back away from her face, and shone with what seemed to be some kind of perfumed oil. "This note is one of our very few tangible pieces of evidence, Commander. It's been positively linked to Ortega—our own forensics tests confirm this as well as the scan performed by your station security office. And I don't think there's any argument, is there, as to the identity of S.I.?"

She leaned even closer. "He wrote this to you, Commander Ivanova. He meant for you to understand it. Do you still claim you don't know what it means?"

Ivanova couldn't think of the words to say, she was so furious and confused. Finally, stiffly, "You already have my testimony."

"Yes, we do." Miyoshi sat straight again, spent a few moments glancing back at the data screen in front of her. Then, "It would be a very good thing, Commander, if you could manage to recall the significance of this note. A very good thing for you and for all of us.

"That will be all, for the moment."

Ivanova stood, still too shaken to speak, and stalked out of the briefing room. She was alternately flashing hot and cold—anger, disbelief, and a trace of real fear battling for control of her reactions.

What was happening? What was going on? Reality seemed to be shifting beneath her feet.

Could they really do this to her?

Garibaldi. He warned me. He tried to warn me.

He said that it was something they did deliberately—
try to make you so angry you'd make a mistake, say
something you hadn't planned to. But why? Could they
really think she'd murdered Ortega? Been involved in his
murder? But only a few minutes ago Miyoshi was almost
outright accusing her of conspiring with him, carrying
on an illicit correspondence! It just didn't make sense!
So why were they doing this to her? What did they want?
What side did they think she was on?

CHAPTER 9

Something was going on.

Michael Garibaldi had been in the security business for a long time. Over the years, he'd developed the instincts. Sometimes you could see it out in the open, the way it had been last year when the dockworkers were working up to go on strike. Trouble coming on and nobody trying to hide it. But this was something else. It was in the way people wouldn't look at you straight—down at the floor, out into the distance, anything to avoid meeting your eyes. They knew—but they wished they didn't.

The only problem was, he was dead certain it was connected to the Ortega thing, and that meant terrorism, separatist politics, the Free Mars movement—stuff way up out of his league. Sheridan had told him straight out, "Earth Central is taking over the Ortega case. It belongs to Wallace now. Stay out of it."

Good advice. Maybe he should take it.

But, hell, since when had he been any good at taking advice?

Take Nick Patinos, now. A good guy. Life-support systems engineer. Worked on all the big domes on Mars in his day. Been on Babylon 5 since the construction phase. Garibaldi had met him originally in Gerry's Lo-G Gym in Marsport, where they'd worked out together some. He'd developed into a good, reliable source. Garibaldi could always count on Nick to put him straight. Not that he was an informer, no. You had to be clear on that. Guys like Nick didn't turn in their own. But: Hey, Nick, I hear there's a lot of skimming going on out of the warehouse in Syrtis. You suppose organized crime's got a hand in it? Or: Nick, there's a rumor that Biggie Wiszniewski is back on the docks, starting up his old operation—you hear anything about that? And Nick would set him straight. A good contact.

But now Nick wasn't talking—Nick was *afraid* to talk, and that meant something was seriously not right.

Back at his office in Security Central, Garibaldi called up Nick's file from the computer, just to see if he could stir up a hunch, reading through it. What he didn't expect was the prim computer voice saying: "That file is not available."

Garibaldi sat up straight at his console. "That's the file on Patinos, Nick. P-a-t-i-n-o-s."

"That file is not available. The information is restricted."

"What?"

"The security file on Nick Patinos, spelled P-a-t-i-n-o-s, is restricted. No access is permitted."

"This is Chief of Security Michael Garibaldi. My security clearance is ultraviolet-alpha, the current passwords are Ginseng, Rabbit, Arawak. Acknowledge? Or do I have to key it in?"

"Clearance and passwords acknowledged. The information you have requested is restricted. No access permitted."

"Restricted to whom, dammit?"

"That information is restricted."

"It's Wallace, isn't it! That bastard has locked up my files!"

"That information is restricted."

He thought for a moment. "Give me a list of the unrestricted files on all station personnel—No, that'd be too long. Give me a list of the unrestricted files on all persons known to have worked on the Mars Colony."

It was a very short list. His own name was on it. Two others—security personnel. That was all.

Garibaldi stared at the data screen. "The bastard—he's locked up my files!"

Captain Sheridan had placed himself between Wallace and Garibaldi, which was probably a good thing, unless his Chief of Security tried to go through him to throttle the Earthforce investigator.

Garibaldi was livid. "He has all my official passwords! He has access to all Babylon 5 security records! He's gone into the station database and put a lock on the files! Not just Ortega's—he's locked up every damn file of all station personnel who've ever worked on Mars! I can't access any of them! He's crippled the security operations on the whole damn station!"

Wallace only gave him a cold, narrow look and directed his reply to Sheridan. "How does he know? How does he know Ortega's file is restricted if he hasn't tried to access it? Or the files on these other suspects? This simply proves my precautions were necessary. There are *very* sensitive aspects to this case, which neither Mr. Garibaldi nor anyone else on this station have a need to know. I don't want every file clerk and security grunt accessing the records of my investigation. And, quite frankly, I have serious doubts about some of the personnel on Babylon 5."

"If something affects the security of this station I damn well right have the need to know what it is!" Garibaldi snapped back.

But Sheridan interrupted with a sharp chop of his hand through the space separating them. "All right! Let's get this sorted out! Commander Wallace, you admit you've restricted access to these records? You've restricted access to Babylon 5 security files from Babylon 5's own security chief?"

"My authorization—"

"Commander, your authorization does *not* give you full control over Babylon 5! That happens to be *my* position. You're here to investigate the Ortega case, not take over the security functions of this station and hamper its officers in the performance of their normal duties."

"Let me correct you, Captain. My authorization covers more than the case of one mining engineer's death. We're here to investigate a serious terrorist conspiracy, a threat both to this station and to the established government on Mars Colony."

"That may be the case, Commander, but I can't let the security requirements of Babylon 5 be compromised. You've exceeded your authority here, and I'm ordering you, as the commander of this station, to restore access to those records."

Wallace replied tightly, "I have to insist that the files on the Ortega case itself remain sealed. Even from Mr. Garibaldi. I have my reasons."

"All right, but *only* those files directly concerning Ortega. The rest are to be restored immediately. And I don't want to see you pulling this again, Commander. Is that clear?"

"Captain," Wallace acknowledged with stiff formality.

"And as for you, Mr. Garibaldi," Sheridan went on, "you will, as ordered, *not* involve yourself in Commander Wallace's investigation."

"Yeah, but how far does that go? If there are people sneaking onto this station, I need to find out about it, I need to be able to plug up the holes before more rats crawl onboard. And what if we've got guys with counterfeit identicards? That affects security on the whole station. I'm not supposed to investigate it? Some of my best contacts happen to come from Mars. I'm not supposed to meet with them? Just because it might happen to interfere with *his* investigation?''

Sheridan shook his head. ''I have to agree with the Commander on this one, Mr. Garibaldi. Probing into the way Ortega got onto the station could well interfere with the investigation of this case. Now, if you find other evidence that somebody on Babylon 5 is churning out counterfeit identicards, then that's your business. But not if it involves Ortega. Let it go.''

How can I find evidence if I can't investigate? Garibaldi thought but didn't ask aloud. At least he was getting his records back. That was the main thing.

But Wallace wasn't finished. ''There's one more thing, Captain. A serious matter. One reason, in fact, why I saw fit to restrict access to these sensitive records. In my opinion, the security of this station is compromised. Seriously compromised. You have an officer on your command staff who is gravely implicated in this case. I have to insist—''

Garibaldi was the first to catch on to whom he meant. ''Now you just wait one damned minute—''

Wallace ignored him. ''I have to insist, Captain, that this officer be placed under arrest pending the completion of our investigation.''

Sheridan's eyes widened. ''If you mean—''

''Confined to quarters, or, at the very least, suspended from her duties.''

''—Commander Ivanova—''

''You've got to be crazy!'' Garibaldi exploded.

Wallace was impervious. ''You've ordered me to restore access to highly sensitive files, on the grounds of maintaining Babylon 5's security. This means that Commander Ivanova, as a member of your command staff, would have access to them. Commander Ivanova, let me make it plain, is a suspect in this case. She has maintained a correspondence with a suspected terrorist. She arranged a clandestine meeting with this terrorist and was present at or about the time he was killed, under extremely suspicious circumstances. A note addressed to her by this terrorist was found near the scene of his death. It's obviously in some code, but Commander Ivanova has refused to reveal what it means. The commander was hostile when questioned by my investigator. She only agreed to answer questions under threat of arrest. She claims to have seen a suspect in the murder, but there are no other witnesses to identify this man. In fact, there are no witnesses to support her version of events."

Garibaldi furiously interrupted, "You haven't got a scrap of evidence—"

Ignoring him, Wallace continued. "Most important, we also have reason to believe that when the suspected terrorist J. D. Ortega came onto this station, he brought with him some information: vital information concerning a matter I am not authorized to reveal. When his body was discovered, there was no sign of this information. His clothing and personal effects have not yet been located, which gives us reason to believe that this information was taken from him and is now in the possession of some other party. He may have passed it on to a contact before his death—or it may have been taken from him, either by his killer, or someone who discovered the body after the killer left. We think it is quite possible that Commander Ivanova may be one or another of these persons. Given the circumstances and the extremely sensitive nature of the information in question, I think it imperative that the Commander be placed in custody. Certainly, it's unthinkable that she be allowed to remain in her current position, with access to sensitive records."

Garibaldi was staring at him as if he'd grown scales and a tail, but Sheridan looked disturbed. "You have these charges in your report?"

"They aren't charges, Captain. Not yet, at least. But,

yes, all our findings to date are in our report. Read it, Captain. Ignore your previous ties to the commander and read it with an objective mind."

Garibaldi burst out, "Captain, you can't let him—"

But Sheridan cut him off. "That'll do, Mr. Garibaldi. And you, too, Commander. I'll give the matter my consideration and let you know what I decide. That will be all."

Sheridan was alone. Alone with Wallace's report on his desk.

A lot of hard things he'd had to do in the course of his career. Writing those letters to the families of the men killed under his command—that was the worst, hands down. But this wasn't much far behind.

He'd read the report. Read it, as Wallace intended him to, the way Earth Central would certainly read it when it showed up on their desks. It twisted the facts. Twisted them until they bent backward in both directions, sometimes. But—the facts were there. Indisputable. Ivanova was—compromised.

His link chimed softly. "Captain? This is Ivanova. You wanted to see me?"

Sheridan forced himself to meet her eyes when she came into the command office. The anxious look on her face—she knew what this was about.

"Sit down, Commander. I won't keep you hanging. I'm not happy about it, but Commander Wallace's report really leaves me no choice. Until further notice, you're suspended from all duties as a member of the command staff of Babylon 5."

It hurt her. He could see it. Her face went white and she remained on her feet, eyes front, almost at attention. No matter how much she thought she was prepared, it hit her hard.

"Do you have anything you want to say?"

"Only . . ." She swallowed. "Do *you* believe the charges, Captain?"

He shook his head. Emphatic. "No. I don't. But what I believe isn't the point. Commander Wallace's position is . . . probable. The way he puts it. And, unfortunately, he's right—it's just your word that things didn't happen the way he insinuates."

"My word . . . as an Earthforce officer . . ."

"Is enough for me. Absolutely," Sheridan said firmly. "But the position of executive officer, in a command like this one, has got to be above all suspicion. And—you are compromised. Until we find evidence to the contrary. I'm sorry, Susan," he added gently.

But Ivanova stiffened to full attention. "If the Captain would excuse me now?"

"Of course."

"Damn," he said aloud once she'd gone. Why did a thing like this have to happen to an officer like Ivanova? He knew her kind. All these years with a perfect record. The military was her life. Her career was everything to her. She'd been on the track to flag rank—up until now.

Now—face it. No matter whether Wallace filed formal charges or not, the suspension was on her record. The suspicion. Every promotion board that looked at it from now on would see it, would pass her by. She would never have a command of her own.

Her career was effectively over.

What a damn shame.

CHAPTER 10

Garibaldi stood in the corridor outside the closed door. "Ivanova. C'mon, I know you're in there. It's me, it's Mike Garibaldi. Let me in, all right?"

Silence. He cursed under his breath. "Look, Ivanova, this isn't going to help."

No response.

"I'm not going to go away, you know. I'll just wait out here and clutter up the corridor—"

From inside came a muffled, "All *right*! Come in, if you're not going to go away."

The door slid open. Garibaldi stepped cautiously inside. Ivanova's quarters were dimly lit. She stood up from the couch to face him. She was wearing, he could see, a plain collarless shirt, rather rumpled, and nondescript civilian pants. Her shoulders were slumped, and Garibaldi could just make out the redness in her eyes.

"So," she said dully, "now you're inside, cluttering up my quarters. Is it an improvement?"

"Look, Ivanova, you can't just sit in here in the dark like this. Come on. You have to face this thing. You can't let it lick you."

"I'm already done for, Garibaldi. I've been suspended. My security clearance has been revoked. I'm compromised. It's on my record. No matter what happens now, it'll stay on my record. Every time I have to go through a security clearance, they'll see the red flag there. Did you know that, up to now, I had a perfect record?"

She turned away. "I just don't see how the captain could go along with it. I mean, he *knows* me. I served under him on Io, he knows what kind of officer I am. If it were some other commander—''

''Listen to me,'' Garibaldi intervened in Sheridan's defense. ''I was there. In the Command Office. I heard what Wallace said. He wanted you put under arrest at first. Confined to quarters. He would have gone to Earth Central on this, I'll just bet on it. Him and his authorization. Is that what you would have wanted? Sheridan was trying to protect you from that. What else was he going to do?''

She shrugged. ''He says he believes me, of course. He says he trusts my word.'' She looked away—up at the ceiling, over at the corner. ''I hear that I'm going to be assigned to some other duty—something 'less sensitive.' Not as part of the command staff. I could be a shuttle pilot, maybe. Or sit a tech post in C&C. I'm qualified for that, anyway. I guess when they ship me back to Earth, I can find some kind of job . . .''

''Now, come on! I can't believe this! Are you going to let the bastards get away with this? Let Wallace beat you without fighting back?''

Suddenly the pent-up emotion flooded into her voice. ''But *why*? That's what I want to know. Why are they doing this to me? Do they really believe these crazy charges? Do you know what they're saying? It doesn't even make sense! One minute they say I've been conspiring with Ortega; the next minute they decide I'm the one who killed him. What's going on, Garibaldi? Why . . .''

But at that point she choked up, and Garibaldi found himself holding her, feeling her body shake as she fought down the sobs. After a moment, he was disturbingly conscious of her body heat, the softness of a female form pressed against his own. Out of uniform, with her hair down . . . he found himself wanting to stroke her hair to comfort her.

But that—no, that would be the wrong—very, very wrong thing to do. Not Ivanova. No.

Awkwardly, he made himself pat her shoulder. She pulled back, straightened, wiped her eyes. "Sorry."

He let her take the time to pull herself back together, wondering why it was somehow all right for women to cry—or maybe why men had to find it so hard. There'd been enough times in the last few years when he'd wanted to cry, when he'd even almost wished there was someone to hold him like that while he did it. And maybe that was the worst part—there wasn't, and he was starting to think maybe there wouldn't ever be anyone like that in his life again.

But that was another train of thought he didn't want to get onto right now.

They both sat down. Garibaldi gathered his words. "Look, Ivanova, I know what it's like to be framed, all right? I've seen it done. This—looks like a frame job."

"But *why*?"

"Well, I hate to say it, but if they were looking for a suspect, you're the obvious one. I mean, who else are they going to pick? No one else on this station seems to have any connection to Ortega. So say they're trying to cover up for someone. Say they don't want it getting out who really killed Ortega. Best way is to pin it on someone else. You're available, they can make the evidence fit. So the case is closed.

"Now, I know you might not want to hear this, but if you could *prove* you were telling the truth—"

"No." She stood, agitated. "No, we've been through this before. I won't submit myself to that. Someone probing around in my mind. Even if Psi Corps was allowed to scan defendants in these kinds of investigations, and they're not."

He sighed. He knew all about Ivanova's aversion to the Psi Corps, which she held responsible for her mother's death. She often had to make an effort even to be polite to a telepath. "All right. Then there's just the other alternative."

"You mean—find out who really killed Ortega?"

He nodded. "Which of course *shouldn't* be a problem. That's my job, after all. Only now . . ."

"You've been ordered off the case."

"Not just off it. I'm not supposed to go anywhere near it. Sheridan handed me a direct order. Stay away from Wallace's investigation. Don't interfere. Did you know— the bastard had locked up half the station's security files? Not just Ortega's. The records on just about everyone who ever worked on Mars were restricted. They *really* don't want anyone to know what's going on with this case. Damn! I wish I could get into those files!"

"I thought they were restored."

"All but Ortega's. That one's still restricted. Anyway, I'll bet if I so much as sneeze in the direction of that file, it'll set off alarms so loud they'd hear them at Earth Central. *And* I'll bet Wallace is just sitting there waiting for me to try it, the bastard."

She sat beside him. "Do you think they were trying to frame Ortega, too? I still do have trouble believing he could be involved in something like terrorism."

He shrugged. "Who knows? Unless we can find out why he was here in the first place."

Ivanova went thoughtful. "You know, Miyoshi said . . ."

"Said what?" Garibaldi asked.

"She said they had reason to believe Ortega had smuggled information onto the station. And passed it on to someone."

"Such as you."

"That's what she seems to think." Ivanova was starting to look worried. "You know, Garibaldi, I think I can almost make sense of it. Listen: Ortega sends me a message. I meet him at 20:00 hours, as arranged. He gives me the information. As soon as I have it, I kill him, drag his body into the head, wait two hours, querying the computer about the time, to make it look like he never showed up—''

"And then run straight to me and report him missing, to establish an alibi . . .''

"Whose side are you on, anyway, Garibaldi?''

He was glad to see she was recovered enough to joke about it. "No, but really. You needed those two hours. To search him, to strip off his clothes—''

"For what? If I already had the information?''

"All right. So maybe you didn't. Maybe he refused to give it to you, and that's why you killed him. Then you searched him, found the information, dragged the body off to hide it—''

"Did I have time to do that? In the two hours?''

"I think you did. According to Doc Franklin, the body was moved into that locker when it was still fairly recently dead. Afterward, you were with me, you didn't have time.''

She shivered. "This is starting to scare me. Do you think they really believe this? Do they think I have that information, whatever it is, and they're trying to force it out of me?''

He patted her shoulder again, a safe, brotherly gesture. "Don't know. I do wish . . .''

"What?''

"I wish you could figure out what Ortega meant in that note. 'Hardwir.' He must have thought it would mean something to you.''

"Maybe he never finished what he was going to write. Maybe he didn't have time? He was worried. I've been over it again and again in my mind. He was worried. Someone was after him. Suppose he thought they knew about the meeting place. He couldn't contact me, but he wanted to be sure I got the information. So he came early, started to write the note, to leave it where I'd find it. But whoever killed him got there first, before he could finish writing it.''

"And didn't see the note?"

"I didn't. Nobody else did, 'til your security team swept the room. It was on the floor, crumpled up. He knew it was too late and he didn't *want* them to find it."

"Could be," said Garibaldi glumly. "But so far, whatever happened, that note seems to be the key to this whole mess. If you could just remember—"

She pressed her hands to the sides of her head. "I just can't! Don't you think I've tried?"

"Well, I'm going to find out."

"What do you mean?"

"I mean getting to the bottom of the whole thing. From the beginning."

"But you can't do that!"

"Why not?"

"Sheridan gave you a direct order."

He snorted. "Hell, do you think I'm going to let something like a stupid order stand in my way, when it's your career at stake? Maybe even more?"

Maybe even more. The words stopped her automatic protest. But . . . "What about your career?"

"Hey, let me worry about that."

"No! Garibaldi, I can't let you—"

"Look, I'm already involved in this thing. Wallace has got me on his hate list. So the only way to make sure both of our careers are safe is to find out what's going on."

"I suppose," she said dubiously.

"I *know*," Garibaldi insisted.

"So what are you going to do?"

"Ask around. Wallace may have the records, but I have something he doesn't—contacts. Although," he added, "it's not going to be easy getting anything out of them. People are worried. Scared."

"Of what?"

"If I knew that . . ."

"And what do I do?"

"Think. Try to remember. Everything about Ortega you can. Write it all down for me. And listen. *Don't* trust the computer. Not even your own personal log. I don't know what kind of access level Wallace has, but he has all my passwords and maybe some we don't even know about.

"The bastard," he added.

CHAPTER 11

First you set out the bait. Then you go around and check your trapline, see what picked it up.

Garibaldi liked the trapper image, which he'd picked up from an old book. There were times in the security business when you had a lot of time on your hands to sit and read. Not, however, since he'd come to Babylon 5.

The station was like the old Earth frontier, though, when he thought about it. Out on the edge of the new. Full of risks and hazards, yes, and some of them unknown. But that was how he preferred it. Without too much time on his hands to sit and brood about the past.

And so, thinking of traps and bait and what he might catch, he strolled down into the Down Below section, to see what had been stirred up by his recent conversation with Mort the Ear. At first he didn't notice anything much out of the ordinary, just the usual sullen and hostile looks directed at him by the usual sullen and hostile denizens, upset at having their business interrupted by the intrusion of station law. But after a while he began to notice—things weren't quite the same today. He looked around at the sign that advertised the Happy Daze bar. Someone had finally fixed the flickering D.

Frowning, he slipped inside the hatch and made his way through the smoke and haze that passed for an atmosphere in the place, up to the bar. Instead of Mort, there was a new bartender, one of the Drazi who seemed to be opening up a lot of new businesses in this section. "Say, friend, have you seen my buddy Mort—Mort the Ear? Owns this place? I was hoping to run into him down here today."

"Mort gone."

Garibaldi frowned. "What you mean—gone? Gone where?"

The Drazi made a sweeping gesture. "Gone. From station. Took transport yesterday. Sold business. Took big loss," he announced with a smug expression.

"What?"

The Drazi made a gesture of confirmation-of-improbable-circumstance. "Mort say, too much trouble here now. Sell bar. Move to Euphrates Sector for peace and quiet."

Garibaldi swore. This was one thing he hadn't expected—to find his trap empty. Things must be worse than he'd thought. Maybe a lot worse.

But just as he was wondering how, a call came in through his link. "Mr. Garibaldi."

"Garibaldi here."

The call was direct from Security Central. Immediately he was alert. "What is it?"

"We may have had another murder."

"I'll be right there."

There were no cemeteries on Babylon 5. But people did die, and when they did, their mortal remains had to be disposed of in various ways, according to the customs and beliefs of several dozen races, with more than a hundred major religions among them. Sometimes their bodies were shipped home for the proper rites, sometimes they were shot into the heart of the nearby sun. In certain rare cases, they were ritually consumed by the friends and relations of the deceased, a practice tolerated by the station authorities, tolerance being policy on Babylon 5.

But it was a general rule that the remains of sentient beings were never dispatched to the inevitable destination of all other organic waste on the station: the recycling system.

And yet—Garibaldi, the recycling tech, her supervisor, and the two security agents who'd first responded to the report had all examined the object. All concurred in their judgment: it was a humanoid foot, cleanly severed at the ankle joint. Best bet, a human foot.

"Got the evidence pouch?" Garibaldi asked.

"Here, Chief." One security agent held it out. Garibaldi, using a set of tongs provided for the purpose by the recycling supervisor, inserted the evidence into the container, sealed it. "Get that to Medlab, give it to Doc Franklin for analysis. He's already expecting it."

The agent hurried away with obvious relief to be out of the noxious atmosphere. Garibaldi looked at the recycling supervisor, a man about his own age, named Ryerson. "Is that it?"

"As far as we can tell."

"Then maybe we can get out of this place?"

They went back across the catwalk above a huge vat, Ryerson leading the way, then the remaining security officer, the petite young ensign named Torres. Garibaldi followed them down a narrow flight of stairs, crossing the network of color-coded pipes, each greater in diameter than a man's body, that led to it. It was a place as impressive in its own way as the fusion power plant. And larger, in order to serve a population of a quarter-million in a closed environment.

"Does this kind of thing happen often?" Garibaldi asked, taking a breath of the cool air on the other side of the door. It certainly hadn't happened here on Babylon 5 before now.

"More often than you might think," Ryerson said, nodding. "People don't like to think how the recycling system really works. Stuff goes in *here* and comes out the other end *there*. All automatic, untouched by human hands, unseen by human eyes. Nice and clean, nice and sanitary.

"And that's so, just as long as people follow the recycling regs like they're told. But they don't, see. They never do. Blockages happen all the time. We got to know where the problem is, where to shut the system down. And nine times out of ten, it's people not following the rules, throwing stuff in where it doesn't belong, throwing in stuff that has no business in the system. You wouldn't *believe* some of what we've dragged out of those pipes. Out of the alien sectors, especially. Sometimes I wonder, I really do."

"Like a human body? Blocking the pipes?"

"No, a body isn't going to make that much trouble. Not if you cut it up right so it fits. Human body's one hundred percent organic matter, system ought to handle it just fine. No, what made that stoppage was about sixty pounds of silicon solar sheets that some dipwit stuffed into the organic disposal system and *didn't* put through the shredder, like the regs say. Happens all the time, though. You can't teach some people. *Then* we gotta go in there, open up the lines, clear it out. Your foot here just got caught up in it."

"But don't you have scanners? Wouldn't they spot something like body parts in the system?"

"Hell, yes, there's scanners! But they're mostly used to check for trouble, for blockage. Or, say, somebody flushes a data crystal with all the station's defense codes in it—we could scan for it. But do you know how many kilometers of line we've got in this whole system? You know what it would take to scan and monitor every piece of waste that comes through, every second of every day? Oh, sure, it could be done, but you know what it would cost? You imagine Earth Central springing for the cost?"

"All right! So you're saying you can stuff a human

body down the recycler and the monitors won't pick it up?''

"Toss it down whole and they will, sure they will. Whole body'll block up a pipe somewheres. But you chop it up into small enough pieces, it'll go through. System's *designed* so stuff will go through, if people just follow the regs. Now, I do remember one time, on Luna Colony, woman killed her husband and his girlfriend, caught them together, you know? Chopped them up with the kitchen knives and stuffed them into the system. Husband's head, though, got stuck in the line, and they pulled it out, traced it to her. But that must have been a small line. Or the guy had a big head—''

Ryerson stopped as his link went off. "Yeah?''

"Boss, how soon can we get that line moving again? We're getting backup in the shunt from section Brown 62.''

Ryerson turned to Garibaldi. "Well?''

"You're sure you've checked? There are no more body parts in there?''

"Not in the main line. Not upstream of that stoppage. Downstream, now, things get a little harder to sort out. Past the digestion vat there. If your foot had made it past that junction—''

"I get the picture," Garibaldi said quickly. "So I guess there's nothing more we can do here.''

His assistant, Torres, looked vastly relieved to hear him say that. Together, they left the recycling facility. Garibaldi rubbed his forehead, where his hairline had lately retreated. "Just when you think you know everything, seen it all, something like this comes along.''

"It makes you wonder, doesn't it, how many more bodies get tossed in there and never recovered," Torres remarked.

"Yeah, it does," Garibaldi said thoughtfully.

They went up the lift tube to Medlab, where Dr.

Franklin told them to wait, he was just finishing up his analysis of the remains. "If this keeps up," Franklin said, finally coming into the office, "security's going to have to hire its own forensic pathologist. Not that this consulting sideline isn't interesting, of course, but I do have my own research, and a patient or two . . ."

"All right," said Garibaldi, "just tell me what you found."

"It's human, that's the first thing. Human and male. And I got a reasonably decent plantar print, considering the condition of the specimen."

"DNA?"

"Still analyzing."

"Cause of death?"

"Unknown."

"What about time of death, that kind of thing?"

Franklin shook his head. "Not with this one, Garibaldi. Cell structure shows that the tissue was frozen first before it went into the system. No telling for how long. Maybe as much as a year."

"Anything else?"

Franklin nodded. "They used a laser to sever the foot. You can see clearly where the tissue was seared."

"So. First freeze the body, then cut it up. Not bad, not much mess that way. You can keep the pieces on ice as long as you want, dispose of them one by one through the recycling system, one piece here, another piece there . . . This is just great!"

"It could be a serial killer!" Torres exclaimed with some enthusiasm.

"Just what we need around here," said Garibaldi with less. "A serial killer, a professional assassin—civilian or military, alien or human, just take your pick."

Franklin gave them a quizzical look. "Isn't that a lot to assume, just from one body?"

The computer interrupted. "DNA analysis of the specimen is complete."

Garibaldi asked quickly, "Computer, can you identify the specimen?"

"Accessing." Everyone in the room waited.

Simultaneously: *"What?"*

Obediently, the computer responded: "DNA pattern is identified as belonging to Fengshi Yang. Arrived on Babylon 5 on 04/18/59, departed 04/20/59."

Torres was the one who asked the obvious question: "He left without his *foot*?"

CHAPTER 12

Garibaldi retreated to his own console in Security Central to continue to probe the mystery of Fengshi Yang. Unless there were two Yangs (an identical twin?) or the man, as Torres suggested, had left the station with only one foot, then something was seriously wrong.

It turned out to be easy enough to find out, when Garibaldi checked the passenger lists of the ships arriving and departing the station on the dates in question. Yang had in fact arrived on Babylon 5 five days ago, on the eighteenth. The very day, as Garibaldi wasn't likely to forget, when J. D. Ortega was killed. But although the station registry had him leaving on the *Asimov* two days later, there was no Fengshi Yang listed in the *Asimov*'s own passenger list when it departed on the twentieth. At the very least, there was a discrepancy in the records.

Now, the head of Babylon 5's security section didn't like discrepancies in his records on general principles. He didn't like the idea of people being on the station when they weren't supposed to be, when they weren't in the registry at all or when the registry said they'd left three days ago. And he most especially didn't like it when the subject of the discrepancy was chopped up in little bits and tossed into the station's recycling system. Such circumstances tended to make him suspicious. By the time Yang was officially leaving Babylon 5, Garibaldi was willing to bet, he was probably already dead, frozen, and on his way to being reduced down to his basic chemical elements.

But none of that was what had captured Garibaldi's

attention. What had jumped out at him from the passenger list was Yang's port of departure: Mars.

Garibaldi believed in coincidence about as much as he believed in the tooth fairy. Two men murdered, both of them from Mars. Except that according to Yang's file, he wasn't from Mars. He was an import-export rep for a clothing firm on Earth. All right, but at least he'd been on Mars, right before he came to Babylon 5.

Two murdered men, both from Mars, both with discrepancies in their files in the station registry.

Coincidence? Garibaldi snorted.

All right, first assumption: they were both killed by the same agency. But maybe not. Disposition of the bodies was different. Ortega's was hidden almost in the open. Unless, Garibaldi wondered, the killers hadn't meant to leave it there. Did they mean to come back for the body later? To freeze it and send it down the recycling system the way they'd done Yang's?

Maybe that was assuming too much. What else?

He thought a moment, then tapped his link. "Doc? This is Garibaldi. I've got one more question for you on this murder business. Yang."

"Yes?"

"When you said you couldn't determine the cause of death, did you try that test you told me about before—for that poison, chloro-quasi-dia-whatever?"

"Dianimidine. I tried it, yes, but with the condition of the tissue, I couldn't get a reading."

"So it could have been that same stuff as you found . . . in another case we had on the station once." He was deliberately not referring to Ortega's murder and hoped Franklin would pick up the hint.

"That's right, it could have been. But there's just no way to tell, one way or the other. Not unless you find some other part of him that's better preserved."

"Not much chance of that, according to Ryerson. Thanks, Doc."

"Anything else?"

"No. Not right now."

Garibaldi thought for a moment, then called in Ensign Torres. She was young, bright, very enthusiastic, although her enthusiasm did have its limits when it came to the recycling system. Certainly she was ready for more independent responsibility.

"Chief?"

"Torres, it looks like the records on our Mr. Yang have gotten mixed up."

"That's for sure. You know, actually, I was wondering if this case might be related to that other one—the other murder? You know, neither of them in the station registry correctly?"

Maybe even too bright, Garibaldi thought. Very deliberately, he said, "I really don't think there's any grounds for supposing any similarity between the two cases, Torres. After all, if there were, it might involve matters we're not authorized to investigate."

Her expression sobered. "Yes, Chief, you're quite right. Now that I think about it, I don't see any similarity between the two cases at all."

"Well then, since that's so, how would you like to do some digging into the Yang case?"

Now her face brightened again. "Yes, Chief!"

"Good. Now, here's Yang's file. As you can see, there's not too much to go on. But he was in the clothing business, so that might be a good place to start. Check out the merchants on the station, find out who he might have been dealing with, who his associates were, if he had any enemies. Was he carrying valuables? You know what kind of questions to ask."

"I'll get on it right away. And thanks, Chief!"

"Fine. I'll be looking forward to your report."

Torres left the security office, full of proud enthusiasm. Garibaldi told himself he ought to be ashamed of himself, pulling a trick like that on a nice bright kid like Torres. But the experience in investigation certainly wouldn't hurt her, and, who knows, she might even turn up something useful.

And while she was looking into that—Garibaldi turned back to his own screen where Yang's official file was displayed, next to the passenger list from the *Asimov*. One entry, one word that could be the key to it all: Mars.

This time he wasn't just fishing . . . or baiting traps or whatever. This time he meant business. He had questions and he by damn wanted answers.

He found Nick Patinos in the Lo-G Gym, doing tae kwon do exercises with a tall dark alien woman who danced and drifted with slow-motion grace as she parried and returned the strikes of Nick's wooden staff. Their steps and leaps in the low gravity were deliberately slow, controlled. Every movement seemed elongated. Nick was having a hard time keeping up with his opponent, but Garibaldi, watching, knew enough about martial arts to be able to see that his old friend had gotten a lot better since the last time the two of them had sparred. He doubted that he could beat Nick now and regretted that a thousand things—pressures of the job—had kept him from staying in shape the way he knew he should have. Not, of course, that he'd call himself *out* of shape, not exactly . . .

The match ended, and Nick bowed to his partner, then propelled himself with a long, slow roll in Garibaldi's direction, landing about two meters in front of him. "Mike." He held out the staff. "Ready to try a round or two?"

Garibaldi shook his head. "Not this time. I'm here on business, Nick."

Nick turned away as abruptly as possible in the low gravity. "Look, Mike, I thought I made myself clear, before. I'm not talking. Not now. Not about this."

"Not about *what*?" Garibaldi struggled to lower his voice as he saw people in the gym turning their heads in their direction. "Dammit, what's going on around here that nobody will talk about?"

Nick led him away, into the locker room where the sound of showers and blowers would cover their voices. "I'll tell you, Mike, I don't know what's going on. All I know is—I don't want to know. It's safer that way. What I don't know, no one can pry out of me."

"What are you talking about? I'm the Chief of Security on this station!"

"Yeah, but those guys from Earth Central aren't working for you on this, are they? They're working for somebody a whole lot higher up. They've been all over the station, dragging people in for questioning—people who've done *nothing*. They don't say why, they don't say what they're looking for. I don't want these guys picking me up and reaming out my brain for something I don't know anything about."

"What are you talking about? Reaming out your brain?"

Nick looked uncertain. "That's what I've heard."

"You mean they've got a telepath working for them? But there's only one telepath on this station." He hesitated. Was he sure about that?

"Look, Mike, I don't care how many telepaths they've got." He paused, looked around, but the locker room was empty at the moment. "You want to know what's going on? All right, I'll tell you what it's like. You weren't on Mars last year, were you? During the uprising? You were safe on this station."

"So were you."

"Yeah, but I've got a brother and sister at home. What they told me—it was bad there, Mike. Troops all over the place, making arrests everywhere, not asking questions before they did, either. My sister's two kids were in school—Olympus University. There were demonstrations. Troops moved in, closed the place down, detained everyone they saw. They held my sister's kids for three months. No charges, they didn't have anything against them, only they were in the wrong place when trouble broke out. But that was enough to make them 'suspected terrorists.'

"Now do you hear what I'm saying? I know those kids, I halfway raised them, after their own dad died in the mining accident. So they might have joined a peaceful demonstration, but there's no way they would have joined Spear of Ares, or any of those Free Mars groups. But did that matter to Earthforce? No, they held them for three months.

"And now you've got these guys on this station, hauling people in for interrogation for no other reason except they come from Mars, talking about 'suspected terrorists.' You want to know what's going on, that's what's going on, and, yeah, it's got people scared.

"And I'll tell you something else, too. Some of the people they've talked to—haven't come back."

"What are you saying?"

"Just that. A friend of mine had a date for dinner last night—she's a clerk in one of the survey offices. She told him she wasn't sure if she could make it, she was supposed to go see this Earthforce officer to answer some questions, she didn't know about what. Well, she never showed up for dinner, never answered her calls. He checks, she's been shipped back to Earth. Shipped back this morning. No reason."

Garibaldi was appalled. Not that it was going on—he

was no innocent. It was Wallace, of course it was. But why didn't he know about this? Why hadn't anyone told him?

Of course, he'd been trying to help Ivanova, and then this Yang murder coming up. Still . . .

"Nick, I swear, I didn't know! I'll look into this for you, I promise. Your friend, what's his name?"

"Nope."

"*Dammit!* Nick!"

"Hey, I don't turn in my friends, Mike. I never have. I've maybe set you straight on a couple things before, but that's it."

"So your friend might be involved in this?"

"I didn't say that. I don't know. All I know is, he doesn't want his name mentioned to anyone from Earthforce Security."

"All right," Garibaldi sighed, "let's start over. Look, the guy I'm looking for now has no connection to . . . this other thing. Like you said, I'm off that case. This is a completely separate investigation." At least, officially it was.

Nick frowned, waited. Garibaldi took out a projector and clicked on the holographic image of Fengshi Yang as taken from his official file. It hovered in the space between them like a ghost. "Do you know this guy? Have you ever seen him?"

Nick shook his head. "Seen him where?"

"Here on the station. Or maybe on Mars."

"Sorry. Can't say I have. Why? Who is he?"

"Who was he, is more like it. His body turned up early today."

"You mean he was killed?"

"Looks like it, yeah. We're trying to trace down his movements, who he might have seen, you know."

"Well, why come to me?"

"He might have come from Mars. At least, his last port of departure was Mars."

Nick exploded. "You're telling me this doesn't have anything to do with that other thing? You expect me to believe that? 'A completely separate investigation'? C'mon, Mike! A guy gets killed, and the only lead you've got is that he might have come from Mars? What, was he a suspected terrorist, too? Who's next?"

"I don't know! Why do you think I'm trying to find out? If the killings are connected, I want to know, too. But I've got nothing to go on! I don't even know if his name's really Yang. Somebody's messed with his file in the station registry. Only thing I've found out so far is that he came here from Mars. So I go with what I've got. And if this case turns out to be connected to the first one, and this Earthforce guy Wallace finds out, the guy who's been hauling in all your friends for questioning, then he takes over and leaves me nowhere."

Nick shook his head. "Sorry. I really can't help." He turned to leave.

Garibaldi tried once again. "Um, I don't suppose this friend of yours, this guy you were talking about, might know who Yang was?"

"I'll ask him, all right? I'll ask around. That's as much as I can do, Mike. Even for you."

"Thanks," Garibaldi said. Nick pushed his way through the door and was gone. A couple of men came into the showers, gave Garibaldi a questioning look. He put away the projector with Yang's holo image.

He didn't like what he was starting to hear. And Nick —was he still holding something back?

If he was, though, maybe he had a good reason.

And that reason was Commander Ian Wallace.

CHAPTER 13

Reaming out my mind.

Garibaldi sometimes wondered what it would feel like. People were afraid of telepaths—most of them were, anyway. Having all your weaknesses exposed, all your worst secrets, the things about yourself you never wanted anyone to know. He certainly had enough secrets like that. And even with all the Psi Corps regulations and restrictions, he still sometimes had the uncomfortable suspicion that Talia Winters could tell what he was thinking.

The lift tube door opened, and there she was. Coincidence again? She glanced at him, then shut her eyes. She looked drawn-out, exhausted, pale. But from what?

Garibaldi had a good idea. Officially, at least, Ms. Winters was the only telepath currently on Babylon 5. So if anyone was reaming minds, she had to be the one doing it. Only, that didn't fit what he knew of Talia Winters. She just wasn't the mind-reaming kind. Not that they didn't exist. Garibaldi had met at least one Psi Cop who'd burn out your brain as soon as blink at you. But Talia, as much as she might like to present a cool, impervious exterior, was a sensitive. To have to probe into a cruel or deviant mind was actually a painful experience for her. But—it was her job. If it needed to be done, it was her duty. The Psi Corps took care of its own, but that was the cost.

And tonight it looked like the cost had been high.

Garibaldi had left his interview with Nick in a mood to bite off heads. Wallace's by preference, but he could think of a lot of other heads that would do. People being arrested all over his station and he didn't know about it?

But suddenly another source of information had presented itself. "Um, Ms. Winters? Talia?"

She opened her eyes wearily. "Mr. Garibaldi?"

"You look tired. Would you maybe like a drink?"

"I don't know—"

"There's something I'd like to ask you."

She sighed. "I could use a drink, actually. It's been a long day."

In the restaurant, she sank down into a chair and brushed back her blond hair away from her paler face with a gloved hand while Garibaldi went to get both their drinks, her wine and his water. "Thanks," she said, taking the glass.

"A hard day, huh?" Garibaldi asked. "I don't suppose it involved monitoring interrogations for Commander Wallace?"

She straightened, managed to look stern. "Mr. Garibaldi, you know I can't talk to you about that. If that's what you had in mind."

"Look, Ms. Winters, I'm not asking for a transcript of the questioning, I'm not trying to interfere with his investigation . . ." A slight pause, while he recalled that she could tell if he was lying—if he was thinking about her knowing he was lying . . .

"Look, I've talked to some people, and they're scared. People are being arrested, pulled in for questioning. Someone mentioned telepaths, 'reaming out your mind.' So, if it's not you . . ."

"I see." She sighed again. "All right, Commander Wallace has asked me to assist in his investigation. But nobody's reaming out anyone's mind. I simply report if the witnesses are telling the truth. Just as I would in any investigation of this kind."

"And they've all agreed to this? The witnesses? They aren't being coerced?"

"Mr. Garibaldi, I can't say—"

"But they are scared, aren't they?"

"It's perfectly natural for a person being questioned by the authorities to be apprehensive. You ought to know that."

"But the findings of a telepath aren't admissible in court."

"I don't believe . . . that a court of law is the question here," she admitted reluctantly.

"Have you heard anything about certain witnesses being shipped back to Earth for more questioning?"

"No, I don't know anything about that."

"And what about Commander Wallace? Is he telling the truth?"

"Mr. Garibaldi!"

"All right!" He admitted defeat with poor grace.

"I don't even know why you're asking me all these questions. After all, a man's been killed, there's a serious terrorist threat—"

"Is there? Really?"

"I don't know what you mean."

"Don't you?" He was genuinely curious.

"I've *told* you, it's against Psi Corps rules to intrude on a person's thoughts."

"All right, so you don't know what I mean. Tell me, do you think Commander Ivanova could really be involved with the Free Mars movement? With terrorists? That she had anything to do with Ortega's death?"

"I can't really say—"

"But Wallace wanted her suspended from her command. Do you know why? Does *he* believe it?"

She shook her head, turning away from him. "You *know* I can't talk about that! Why do you keep asking me?"

"Because I want to help Ivanova. And find out the truth about what's going on around here. That's why."

Winters found her wine on the table, took a drink of it. "I'm not even sure if she'd want my help," she said slowly. "I'm not exactly Commander Ivanova's favorite person."

"You know, it's not personal," Garibaldi said.

"Oh, I do know. And I understand her reasons. I know how she feels about her mother and what the Psi Corps did to her. She looks at me, and all she sees is Psi Corps. I know that. But it doesn't make it any easier to deal with her. I've tried."

"You'd want to help her, though?"

"If I could. But I can't. Not if she doesn't agree. You do understand? I'd *like* to help her . . ."

"I understand."

"There are rules."

"I know."

Winters twisted her fingers together, looked at her half-empty glass of wine. "You're that sure she isn't involved in . . . any of this?"

"As sure as if I'd read her mind," Garibaldi said firmly. "She's being set up. Framed. Wallace is doing it. I don't know the reason, but I'm sure."

"I see," Winters whispered, looking down into her wine. "I think I see."

It was early in the morning, but Captain Sheridan was already in the Command Office. So much to do. Babylon 5 was different than any command he'd ever held, diplomatic at least as much as military, and with so many civilians coming and going it was almost like commanding a city. At least he'd had an experienced executive officer—up to now.

He missed Ivanova's support. There were other junior officers on the station, of course, but there was no one,

really, to take her place, no one with the experience that
she had of running this place. Without her, there seemed
to be ten times as many calls, ten times as many emergencies he couldn't delegate to anyone else, had to handle himself, even when he recognized that he didn't
really have all the necessary experience yet, either.

If only Ivanova hadn't gotten herself mixed up in this
damned Ortega affair. *That* was something he wished
would get cleared up and over with as soon as possible.
He had enough problems right now, new to this command, without a terrorist threat hanging over the place.

Garibaldi had been in late last night, breathing fire,
complaining that Wallace was establishing a police state
on Babylon 5. That there were rumors spreading all over
the station about people being arrested for no other reason than being from Mars. Rumors about forced telepathic probes, even torture, drugs.

But were the rumors true? Sheridan had asked. Were
they even substantiated?

"I'm not sure yet how much they're substantiated,"
Garibaldi had said. "They're not groundless, I do know
that. But even if they are just rumors, this points to substantial unrest on the station. The workers, the people we
count on to run this place, are scared. They're scared and
they're angry. In my opinion as Chief of Security, these
rumors constitute a serious threat to order and safety.

"And another thing," he'd gone on, as if that much
wasn't enough, "I understand that Commander Wallace
has ordered the members of the security staff assigned to
him *not* to take orders from me, not to report to me any
details on what he's doing on the station. All these arrests going on—my own men were ordered to keep them
from me. Hell, half the station knew about it before I
did!''

So that was another problem Sheridan knew he was

going to have to deal with sometime today—Garibaldi
and Wallace fighting over jurisdiction again. He sighed.

"Captain Sheridan?"

Sheridan swore to himself, then took a breath. He
might as well give up. Once it started, it wouldn't stop.
"Yes? What is it?"

"Captain, Ms. Winters would like to meet with you.
Are you available?"

Resigned, he said, "Yes, have her come in. Are there
any other calls?"

"Not yet, Captain."

The telepath entered the office. She looked anxious,
nervous about something. He smiled to put her at ease.
"Ms. Winters. Come in, sit down. Is there a problem I
can help you with?"

"Well, Captain . . ." She sat straight and forward in
the chair. "I'm sure you must know, Commander Wallace has asked me to help him question witnesses in the
Ortega case. I know that it's part of my duty to assist the
authorities in this kind of thing, but I really . . . Captain, can he require me to do this?"

Sheridan frowned, remembering what Garibaldi had
said last night. "Why? Is there something wrong?"

"I don't know. Some of these people don't seem to
have consented freely to being probed. Commander Wallace calls them witnesses to Ortega's murder, but most of
them don't know anything about it. He talks about terrorism, but it seems to me that he's the one doing the terrorizing. I'm just not happy being involved in all this."

"I see. Well, Ms. Winters, if you mean can Commander Wallace order you to cooperate with him, the
answer, strictly speaking, is no, he can't. You're not under military orders. On the other hand, as you know,
your license as a telepath does require you to cooperate
with the legally constituted authorities. You can refuse,
but then Commander Wallace would have the right to

complain to Psi Corps and possibly request the assistance of another telepath. You probably know better than I do how Psi Corps would react in that case."

Winters looked unhappy. "Well, yes, I'm aware of that. What I suppose I was wondering . . . I mean, you outrank him, you're in charge of Babylon 5, can't you order Commander Wallace to conduct his investigation some other way? Besides dragging in all these innocent people?"

"I see," Sheridan said, more slowly this time. "There, we have a problem. I am in command of this station, but in the matter of this investigation, Commander Wallace's orders come directly from Earth Central. They give him full authority in the matter. So if you're asking exactly where my authority ends and his begins, that's kind of a gray area. What neither of us wants in this situation is to have to appeal to Earth Central."

"I understand."

"I can talk to the commander, of course. I can express your concerns."

"Thank you, Captain."

"I'm sorry I can't be any more help, Ms. Winters, but I'm afraid that if the commander insists on your cooperation, in the end, this will be between you and Psi Corps."

She stood. "I'm glad you could take the time to hear me."

Sheridan watched her leave, glad he wasn't a telepath. Psi Corps had its own discipline, different from the military. Secretive. The strongest telepaths assigned as cops to control the others. He supposed that was the way it had to be, but there was something sinister about it, definitely something sinister about the Psi Cops in their black uniforms.

He hoped Ms. Winters would be all right, but he'd

only told her the truth: he couldn't really intervene to help her. Not, at any rate, without challenging Wallace.

But maybe Wallace would agree to see reason. He hoped so.

He toggled his link. "This is Captain Sheridan. Commander Wallace, I'd like to speak with you at the earliest possible opportunity today."

There was no reply. Sheridan ordered C&C: "Contact Commander Wallace for me, please. Have him call me. Make it a priority request."

But a moment later there was a reply. "Captain, there is no response from Commander Wallace."

Sheridan's expression hardened. "Contact him again. Keep trying until you do. I'm ordering him to report to my office. Now."

Wallace didn't show up in the next minute, or in the next ten minutes, but two hours later he was at the door to the Command Office. Sheridan could see the cold anger at being summoned. He didn't care.

"Commander, I called you some time ago. You didn't respond."

"I was interrogating a witness. I ordered all communications held."

"Commander, I'm starting to have some questions about your use of your authority on this station. You're adding to them right now. As commanding officer of Babylon 5, I'd appreciate a response when I try to contact you. Or do you consider yourself exempt from the requirement to observe normal Earthforce regulations and procedures?"

Wallace said stiffly, "No, I do not."

"In that case, I'll expect that in the future you'll make yourself available for emergency communications. Now, as I've said, there are starting to be some questions about the way you're conducting your investigation. There are rumors that you've been using unauthorized methods of obtaining information, and they're causing unrest on the station, to the point where it raises concerns about security. And the station's registered telepath has expressed reservations of her own.''

But Wallace's expression was implacable. ''Captain, I am not answerable to you about my conduct of this investigation. If your station has security problems, then Mr. Garibaldi will have to deal with them. That's his job, as he repeatedly insists.

''And if you want to question my authority, Captain, I suggest you contact Earth Central.''

''I'll do that, then, Commander.''

''Is there anything else, Captain?''

''No. You can go. But . . . stay in touch. That *is* an order.''

CHAPTER 14

Somehow, it seemed a lot easier to breathe in the Command Office with Wallace gone. But Sheridan had an uneasy feeling he might have made a mistake. No doubt that he'd lost his temper, which was an effect Commander Wallace seemed to have on people. But now he was going to have to ask Earth Central to clarify just where the lines of authority lay, and there was no guarantee at all that he was going to like the answer when he got it.

But maybe it had been inevitable all along, ever since the first moment Wallace stepped foot onto Babylon 5. Garibaldi had seen it coming, tried to warn him.

Well, if it was inevitable . . .

"I'd like a Gold channel opened for a transmission to Earth."

He might as well get it over with.

Talia Winters paused before she opened the door of the interview room. Interrogation room was how she thought of it, part of Commander Wallace's private interrogation system, what he called his command post.

There was a man seated in a chair in the center of the room, and at her desk Lieutenant Miyoshi, who looked up with her flat black eyes. "You're late."

"I had other business. And an appointment with the captain."

"Every minute you're late delays this investigation." Miyoshi glared at her. "From now on, you *don't* have other business. You're the only registered telepath on this station. Our investigation requires your services. We were assured that you'd be available.''

"Now, just wait a minute!"

"No, I've already been waiting! More than a minute! I have four more witnesses to examine today. They're all probably lying." Miyoshi turned back to her desk, unlocked a drawer, and took something from it. "I want you to look at this, Ms. Winters. Commander Wallace told me you've been questioning our authority.''

Talia took the object reluctantly. It was a viewer card, and at the touch of her gloved hand, the PSI symbol took holographic form and rose, glowing, from the card. Simultaneously, the message forced itself into her mind: *Obey. No questions. Obey.*

Talia recoiled with a soft sound, and the card returned to its flat, featureless state. Miyoshi, watching her, had a faint smile on her lips. "Now do you question my authority, Ms. Winters?''

She shuddered. "No," she said faintly.

"Good," Miyoshi snapped. "Now, let's get to work. I've already wasted too much time, and I've got a lot of questions to ask.''

"Commander Ivanova reporting as ordered, Captain.''

Sheridan sighed inwardly. Reporting on time, correct, in uniform. Her salute could have been put into a textbook. Only her eyes were different, a different look in them, like defeat. He tried to pretend he didn't notice it.

"Commander. Please sit down. You know that I've been thinking about a temporary assignment for you, until things get straightened out. Now, I've been reading your report.''

He paused, seeing her expression turn puzzled. "Your report on the current situation with the raiders," he explained. "How they're targeting strategic metals shipments. Very good analysis there. And some excellent suggestions."

"Then, have you . . . heard back from Earth Central about it?"

"Ah, no. Not yet. There was no reply except that they'd be studying the matter further."

"Oh."

"Well, as I said, there are some excellent suggestions here. I especially agree that if your analysis is correct it ought to be easy to identify the transports at highest risk for attack and supply them with an escort. I know—your report stressed the fact—that our resources are too thin to provide escorts to every freighter who comes through into Grid Epsilon. But if we do as you suggest, identify the transports coming out of Marsport with these cargoes of morbidium and other strategic metals, I think we'll see results that more than justify the effort." He paused. Ivanova looked suddenly stunned. "Commander?"

"Uh, yes, sir. Transports coming out of Marsport. Shipments of morbidium. That's right."

"Yes. Now, what I want you to do is take command of Alpha Wing and pursue this strategy as vigorously as possible. Once the vulnerable shipments are identified, the routing and scheduling information plotted, you'll be able to intercept the transports and escort them in.

"Do you have any questions?"

"No, sir. I appreciate your giving me this assignment, very much."

"I want to see results, remember."

Her smile was slightly crooked. "Well, I always did say I wanted to see more flight time, didn't I? Thank you, sir."

The first thing she did was turn on her link to contact Garibaldi. "This is Ivanova. I think . . . I know what it is!"

"What what is?"

"The . . . connection. The real reason they're trying to frame me! It's Mars!"

Garibaldi had a sudden paranoid image of Wallace, listening in through some patch in the station's communications system. "I think we'd better talk about this—face-to-face," he warned Ivanova.

A moment of puzzled silence from the other side of the link. Then, "I'm just outside C&C."

They met there, decided to talk in Ivanova's quarters. Before he would let her say a word, he deactivated her computer and swept the rooms for bugs. "All right," he said finally, "what's this about Mars? You mean Ortega, that he was part of the Free Mars movement?"

"No! You remember, that report I did—the raiders, the hijacked transports. What you warned me about. Well, those transports all shipped out of Marsport!"

"You mean the . . ."

"Morbidium shipments. Morbidium shipments from Mars! *That's* the connection, I'll bet on it!"

Garibaldi's eyed widened. "I think you just might have hit on it. Why did Wallace and his crew pick on you when we all know there's no real connection between you and Ortega. When you're not from Mars, you've never been on Mars, there was *nothing* to link you to Mars, just a couple of holiday cards."

"Until you went and figured out that somebody on Mars is leaking shipping information to the raiders."

"Not just that," Ivanova explained. "Or they would have figured it out a year ago. Somebody in charge is sitting on the information. Keeping it quiet. Whoever's involved in this is someone high up in Earth Alliance."

"All right," said Garibaldi enthusiastically, "so where's the link to the terrorists? Where does the Free Mars movement come in? And your friend Ortega? How does it all fit together—morbidium . . . raiders . . . terrorists.''

"Weapons," said Ivanova. "Terrorists need guns, and morbidium is essential in the production of plasma weapons. And the sale is restricted.''

"Except on the black market," Garibaldi added. "Where terrorists would buy. Terrorists with a link to the raiders. Somehow they get the transport information, pass it to the raiders, who hijack the morbidium, sell it on the black market, and Free Mars takes their pay in the finished product.''

"So maybe I stumbled onto something bigger than I thought." Ivanova shook her head. "But if this is true, you know what it means!''

Garibaldi nodded slowly. "Wallace. He might be a part of it. If Earthforce officials are involved, even just in covering this up, then the first thing he's going to do is try to get rid of the person who uncovered it.''

Ivanova raised a hand. "But wait a minute. That can't be it. Earth Central sent Wallace here to investigate even before I sent that report. They couldn't have known about it.''

Garibaldi frowned in thought. "All right. They didn't know at first. They just sent Wallace to investigate Ortega's death. Then they get your report. They don't know how much you know, but you're a loose cannon. Too dangerous to be allowed to go around probing into things they don't want to get out.

"But that's another thing!" Ivanova said eagerly. "If Wallace is part of the cover-up of the link between the terrorists and the raiders, then why go to so much trouble to track down Ortega? It has to mean that J. D. wasn't involved with the terrorists at all!''

"Maybe . . ." Garibaldi shook his head in confusion. "It turns everything around backward. All right, let's think it through. Say that Ortega's a good guy, like you say. He's found out something. About this link between the terrorists and the raiders. He contacts the authorities, but they're involved, too. They try to shut him up. He runs. They put out a fugitive alert on him. He comes here to Babylon 5, tries to contact you, you're the only honest Earthforce officer he knows. But he gets killed before he can pass you the information. Only, the bad guys don't know that. They think you know what it is."

"That makes sense," said Ivanova slowly, "except—who was the murderer? It can't be Wallace or either of his aides, they were on Earth. And . . . if they killed him, then wouldn't they *know* I didn't have the information? So why all this?"

"Yeah, what are they still looking for?" Garibaldi asked himself. "And why did they kill the other guy?"

"What other guy?"

"Oh, I forgot, you don't know—now we've got two murders."

"By the same murderers?"

Garibaldi's voice betrayed his frustration. "I wish I knew! I'm not any closer to knowing who killed Ortega since the day we pulled his body out of that locker. And I won't be, if Wallace has his way.

"And as for this other guy, Yang, I don't know anything for sure about him except that part of him's missing. His name might not even be Yang. But I *think* he came here from Mars."

"He was killed after Ortega was?"

"We don't even know that. They had him frozen. Who knows for how long?

"I hate this, you know. Here I am, head of security on this station, and I'm groping around in the dark, blind and deaf. I can't try to connect Yang's murder to the Ortega case, because if I do, Wallace will come down out of the sky like a harpy and snatch it away."

Ivanova couldn't resist. "I thought harpies were supposed to be women."

"You know what I mean."

"So what can we do?"

"You? Be careful, that's what. Watch your back. I'm going to be watching it, too."

"And you?"

Garibaldi took a breath. "So far, I've kept the Yang thing quiet." He bit his lip. "I mean, I've kept it out of the computer files."

"Because of Wallace?"

He nodded. "Once he finds out, once he makes the connection, then it's all over. I won't have anything to go on. So it's a race. I've got to find out who killed Yang before Wallace does. I've got to dig so deep I might just end up in the fusion core, but that's the only way."

Ivanova frowned. "You could get in trouble. Your job—"

"Never mind my job. I'll take care of that. Remember, I've been in this business a long time, and I'm still around. I've learned a few tricks. Trust me on this, all right?"

Ivanova still looked dubious, but she was interrupted by the sound of his link. "Mr. Garibaldi, would you report to the captain in the Command Office."

"I'll be right there." And to Ivanova as he left, "Just trust me."

Alone in the lift tube, on the way to see Sheridan, Garibaldi wondered how much he should say about Wallace. What he and Ivanova had cooked up between them was raw speculation, nothing but. He didn't want to go to Sheridan with no proof, no evidence, nothing but a crazy conspiracy theory. The captain would probably kick him out of the Command Office, and rightly so.

No, this was something he was going to have to handle

on his own, his own way. For Ivanova's sake. She was young, she still had everything ahead of her—a brilliant career if he could just prove those charges were part of a frame-up. As for himself, he knew the risks. But Mike Garibaldi had had his chances and, mostly, blown them. What he had to look forward to—didn't really look all that inviting, the closer he got to it.

If he could have made it up with Lise . . . but that was over.

For Ivanova's sake, then.

He paused in front of the door to the Command Office, making sure he knew his own mind.

"Captain Sheridan, you wanted to see me."

The captain turned slowly in his chair. "Mr. Garibaldi. Have you ever seen a Code Ultraviolet message?"

"Not too often, sir."

"Well, take a look." He keyed a code into the computer console. The ultraviolet security logo appeared on the screen, and a familiar face.

"That's . . ."

"Captain Sheridan, this is Admiral Wilson of the Office of the Joint Chiefs. Commander Ian Wallace has been sent by this office in order to conduct an investigation of the utmost importance to the security of Earth Alliance. As commander of Babylon 5, you and your staff are to afford him every degree of cooperation. His authority in all matters pertaining to this investigation is not to be questioned.

"I trust this clarifies the concerns you expressed."

The image blanked on the screen, leaving Garibaldi stunned. "Direct from the Joint Chiefs?"

"You saw it for yourself. The personnel of this station are ordered to cooperate with Commander Wallace in the conduct of his investigation. That's a clear order. Isn't it, Mr. Garibaldi?"

"Yes, sir. Very clear."

CHAPTER 15

There was trouble in the casino, a fight had broken out, and it was still going on when Garibaldi arrived on the scene, despite the security agents already pulling the combatants apart and threatening them with shock sticks. The security chief himself waded into the middle of it, hurt his knuckles on some alien's bone-armored gut, and after a few more minutes, order was restored to the point where he could try to find out what the hell was going on.

"All right, what is it? What's the problem here?"

Accusations from all sides: "He started it."

"No, he did!"

"She cheated!"

"I cheated? I? You cheated! You're the one!"

"You were reading my mind! That's cheating! That's against the law! She oughta be under arrest!"

Garibaldi didn't have anything against aliens, not really. But there was something about poker—plain, old-fashioned Earth poker—that in his opinion made it a human game. Human mind against human mind. You got aliens playing poker, especially with humans, and this kind of thing always seemed to happen. This time, the argument was between a human and an alien tourist, a Hyach. The Hyach was a female, backed by a larger version in male who seemed to be her mate. The female had claws. Her human antagonist's face had bleeding scratches, which he was wiping with the sleeve of his shirt.

From the senior security guard on the scene, Garibaldi learned that the fight had spread to the spectators and other casino patrons, basically along racial lines—human against alien. This factor increased the potential for further violence and made a quick, fair, open solution imperative—now.

"He was cheating!" the Hyach kept insisting. "He was making marks on cards!"

"You see any marks on those cards? Huh? You see any?" the human yelled back with considerable heat, playing to the spectators. "She's the one who cheated! Crawling around inside my mind, spying on me, reading my hand! Sneaking, cheating telepath!"

As the crowd pressed in, muttering in hostile tones, Garibaldi noted the number of credit chips spilled over the table—and more on the floor. He made a *look out* gesture to the nearest security guard, who nodded and stepped over to keep the space clear, shock stick held openly across his chest.

As for Garibaldi, he didn't need to be a telepath to know that the human gambler had been cheating, and how. On one of his fingers there was almost certainly an E-Z MarkR implant, favorite device of amateur cardsharps. A matching implant behind his eye would pick up the faint electromagnetic trace left as the player marked the cards. More sophisticated gambling establishments on Earth scanned the players as they came through the door, and anyone caught with a MarkR implant was usually taken out to the back of the casino for a short, painful discussion on gambling etiquette.

But this was Babylon 5, and Garibaldi had his own views on dealing with gambling etiquette. He grabbed the protesting gambler by the wrist and dragged him a short way across the floor of the casino to the manager's office. "I think we've got a MarkR implant here, do you have a scanner?"

The scanner was duly produced, and when Garibaldi

switched it on, the flashing light and loud alarm as much as branded the gambler on the hand: CHEAT.

Immediately a small group of people began loudly demanding their money back, as Garibaldi turned the squirming gambler over to one of the security staff. *Dumb amateurs, they never learn. The only people who ever make any money with those implants are the cheats who sell them.*

But there were still a number of voices loudly declaring, "Hey, what about her? What about the telepath? Yeah, I'm not going to gamble with any telepaths around."

Followed by the manager, Garibaldi intercepted the Hyach as she was starting to gather credit chips from the card table. "Wait just a minute." Her mate behind her glared. Garibaldi glared back for an instant before he turned to the female. "Lady, are you aware that house rules in this casino prohibit telepaths from taking part in games of chance?"

"What you mean? You prove it yourself. He was cheating, he was the one. Not I. Not I."

She reached again for the chips, and again Garibaldi stopped her. "But are you a telepath? Because if you are, I'm afraid your winnings will have to be forfeited."

"What is this *four-feet*? What do you mean? He was the one who cheat!"

"Just because he was cheating, doesn't mean he was the only one." Garibaldi tapped on his link. "Ms. Winters, this is the chief of security. We have a situation here that may involve a telepath. Can you come to the casino, please?" He glanced up at the surly crowd, clearly unwilling to disperse before the issue was settled. "Yes, I'd say it was a sort of an emergency. All right, yes, definitely an emergency."

While they waited, the Hyach continued to protest, shrilly demanding to see her ambassador, the com-

mander of the station, a lawyer. On Garibaldi's other
side, the casino manager made nervous noises. He kept
sending urgent mental messages to Talia Winters: *Hurry
up, will you? Before this situation gets out of hand?
Before she ruptures my eardrums?*

On Earth, of course, or in any territory under Earth
Alliance law, this situation would have been unusual.
The Psi Corps ruled its members with a firm hand, and
activities like poker were strictly forbidden. No one
wanted to gamble with a telepath.

But this was Babylon 5, where the rules were different.
Earth law wasn't the only system that counted here, and
the Psi Corps had no authority over an alien telepath. But
the house rules of the casino applied to everyone, even to
members of alien races who considered telepathic powers perfectly normal and placed no restrictions on their
use.

Finally Ms. Winters arrived, looking fragile and
weary. Garibaldi realized she'd probably been asleep
when he called her. But as the surly crowd parted to let
her through, her expression grew serious.

"Sorry to bother you, but I was afraid this situation
might get out of hand. I don't want to have to put down a
riot," he apologized. "This lady just won a lot of money
at poker, and she denies that she's a telepath."

Talia turned to the Hyach, met her eyes, held them a
moment. Then the alien furiously turned her head away.

"She's a telepath," Talia said flatly.

Garibaldi nodded. He'd had a hunch it was so.
"Sorry, lady, but I'm afraid you can't take that money.
Using telepathic powers is considered cheating here.
You're forbidden to enter the casino again as long as you
remain on Babylon 5." He gestured for a couple of
guards to remove her from the room, screaming and protesting all the way to the door, her surly mate following
in silence.

The crowd, mollified and under the eyes of the rest of the guards, began to subside.

"Thanks, Ms. Winters," Garibaldi told her, sincerely grateful. "I wanted to settle this thing down without using weapons. We don't need more human-alien tension around this station." He paused. "It's a good thing they were both cheating."

"You're sure she was cheating?"

Garibaldi's eyebrows went up. "She wasn't?"

Talia rolled her eyes back. "Oh, of course! Why else would a telepath ever want to play cards? What other amusements do we have, besides prying into other people's minds?" She sounded bitter.

"Hey, sorry. But I was fairly sure she was cheating some way or other, even before I knew she was a telepath," Garibaldi said cautiously.

Talia pressed her hands to her eyes. "I'm sorry, I'm a bit on edge lately. But, no, I don't know for sure if she was cheating. We don't probe—not even each other. Not without permission."

"I know. You've told me that. I guess I just thought . . . I don't know."

"I could feel her shielding, and her anger, and that's all I needed to know—that she was a telepath. That was all you needed to know, wasn't it?"

"You're right. And I am sorry. Look, if you want to get back to your quarters, I'll walk you there—or at least to the lift tube. Unless you'd like a drink?"

She shook her head. "No, I do need some sleep."

He walked with her through the crowd, now mostly returned to their own various devices. As they reached the lift, he said, "If there's anything I can do, any way I can help . . ."

"No. It's an internal matter of the Psi Corps. Thank you, though, for asking."

The lift door opened, and she stepped inside. As it

closed, Garibaldi wondered: why was she so exhausted? It was Wallace, he was sure, but what was the bastard doing with her? What kind of secrets was he fishing out of people's minds?

With order restored, Garibaldi decided to stroll down to the lockup and check out his newest prisoner. If the guy didn't have a prior record for gambling offenses, he'd just as soon simply kick him off the station as haul him in front of the Ombunds for formal sentencing. And he didn't really think this particular cardsharp had a prior record. He just wasn't good enough at it.

But Garibaldi also wanted to make sure that whoever sold him the stupid implant wasn't operating here on Babylon 5. That was one more kind of trouble he didn't need.

A call-up of the guy's record revealed no priors for gambling offenses, several arrests for brawling, and one conviction for taking indecent liberties. He was an asteroid miner named Welch, his ship was stopped-over here on Babylon 5 for a crew R&R, he came from the Mars Colony, he had no war record. A more-or-less typical spacer. But—he came from Mars Colony. It was a long shot, but maybe he knew something.

Welch, when Garibaldi got another look at him in the interview room, did not look happy. He tried to conceal his hand behind his back when the security chief remarked, "E-Z MarkR implant, huh? I'll bet you saw their ad: *Make Colossal Credits playing cards with your friends! They'll never know your secret!* Is that so?"

Welch squirmed.

"Look, friend," Garibaldi said, deciding to teach this fellow a few of the basics, "do you know how lucky you are that you didn't try to use that thing in some high-powered casino on Earth or Mars? The enforcers in those places aren't nice guys, like I am. First . . ." He grabbed hold of Welch's hand, forced it down flat onto the table. "First they'd whack this thing off. Then they'd feed it to you. One finger at a time. Whether you were hungry or not. Next . . ." He pressed a thumb up next to Welch's eye where the visual implant was. "They'd pop this right out. And feed it to you for dessert. And after that, if you were lucky, they might leave one or two working parts. Do you get my drift, Mr. Welch?"

He nodded quickly.

"That's good. But, like I said, I'm a nice guy. And you're a lucky guy, because I've looked at your record, and I don't find any prior convictions for gambling offenses, which means you just got this thing or you haven't been caught yet." He lifted Welch's hand by the wrist, rotated it to get a clearer view. "No fresh scar. I guess that means you haven't been caught yet. So you've been lucky. Let's see how lucky you're going to be now. We can handle this two ways, Welch. One, you're in trouble. Two, you're in a hell of a lot of trouble. And that depends on how you answer my questions. So which will it be?"

Welch squirmed again, trying unsuccessfully to pull his hand from Garibaldi's grip. "I din't know. Din't think it was against the law."

Garibaldi shook his head. "Fraud: Obtaining goods, services, or other items of value by deceptive or misleading means." He tapped the gambler's hand against the table. "This is a deceptive means. A damned cheap one, too. Now, where'd you get the implant?"

"This guy. He has a clinic, out in the Belt. I owed him some money I couldn't pay back. And he told me—that's all right, 'cause he could help me. He'd sell me this implant, and I could win money playing cards with the guys on the ship, pay him back the next time I was in port."

Garibaldi sighed. Why didn't they ever have a different story? Something interesting for a change? "How'd you lose the money in the first place? Gambling?"

Welch nodded miserably. "So I did what he said. Except when I went to pay him back, he said I still owed him for the implant, it was real high-tech stuff. But the guys on the ship, they weren't playing with me anymore, and so I figured it was time to get out of the Belt. I signed on with this out-system operation. And ended up here."

This guy has a vacuum for brains, Garibaldi thought. "And I suppose you ended up in the Belt after you got in trouble on Mars? Except it really wasn't your fault?"

"Something like that, maybe."

"All right, I tell you what you're going to do now. You're going to our Medlab, where a nice technician is going to remove that implant and throw it away like the piece of trash it is. Then you're going to sit in our lockup until your ship pulls out, and then you're never going to set foot on Babylon 5 again as long as you know what's good for you.

"Oh," he added, "and there'll be a charge for removing the implant. Our medics don't work for free."

"A charge?"

Garibaldi sighed again. "Don't tell me you don't have the money?"

"Well, I mean, I did, but it was all on the poker table, before that snake-eyed, telepath, alien bitch—"

"Never mind that. So you don't have the money. I'll contact your ship, then, and they can take the cost out of your pay. Unless you'd rather tell it to the Ombunds?"

"Aw, sheesh, look, can't you give me a break? I never woulda done it if I had the money. . . ."

"If you want a break, you've got to earn it. Now, let's start with the name of this guy out in the Belt?"

Welch didn't want to say, he squirmed a lot more, he whined, he was going to get in trouble. But Garibaldi was persuasive. When he had the information on the source in the Belt, he went on, "Now, how would you like to talk about Mars?"

"I don't know no names on Mars. I mean, it's been five, six years since I was there. Who can remember?"

"Try," Garibaldi urged him. "For example, what do you remember about a guy named Yang? Fengshi Yang?"

"I dunno. Never heard of him." But Welch's eyes were evasive.

"Let me jog your memory a little." Garibaldi pulled his viewer. "Here. This is what he looks like. Remember him now?"

"Maybe."

Yes! Garibaldi exulted inwardly. *Finally!* But he kept his expression blank as he pressed for more information. "Maybe what? Maybe you saw him on the Mars Colony once? Or twice? Maybe he worked for Earth Alliance?"

"Maybe I did. Back when I was working the deep mines I mighta seen him. Back before I got into space."

"Yang was a miner?"

"Nah." Welch was starting to squirm again. "But he worked around the mines. Maybe for one of the companies, I don't know. Metallicorp, maybe. Or AreTech. I think . . . people said he was like an enforcer. If, say, you owed money to somebody. Or somebody didn't much like you."

"I see. So this Yang would have been the kind of guy to have a lot of enemies?"

"Yeah, I guess so. I wouldn't want to mess with him, though. Not from what I heard."

"I see. And do you think any of these enemies might have been political?"

"I don't know what you mean."

"Sure you do. Was Yang involved in the Free Mars

movement? Do you think he could have been involved in any of the terrorist activity?''

Vehement head-shaking. "I dunno. I don't. That was after my time. I took off from Mars Colony six, seven years ago. Never was involved in any of that stuff. Far as I know, Yang worked around the mines, that's all. I didn't try to cross his path, you know what I mean?''

"I know what you mean." Garibaldi took a moment to decide. It was a direct order. All the way from the Joint Chiefs. Then he asked the question: "What about a guy named Ortega? J. D. Ortega. Did you ever see him when you were on Mars Colony? Working in the mines?''

"Nope. No, I don't think so. Name doesn't mean anything.''

And that, for all that Garibaldi kept pressing him, was about all the information he could get out of Welch. But at least it was something. At least the guy had heard of Yang, and placed him on Mars.

Garibaldi made a decision. "So," he said, "I tell you what. I'm going to give you that break I talked about. 'Cause it sounds to me like you might have reason not to want to run into this Yang character. Right?''

Welch's eyes got very wide and the pitch of his voice went up. "Here? On B5? You mean he's *here*?''

"That's what I thought. So I'm going to do you a favor and let you go back to your ship now. You stay there 'til you pull out of the docking bay and you don't set foot on this station again. Got it?''

Vigorous nod of the head.

"I'll make sure no one knows you were ever here. And you'll do the same, right? You'll never mention to anyone that we had this little talk.''

"Yeah, right.''

Garibaldi called a guard to come and escort Welch to Medlab and then back to his ship. He hoped the guy had enough sense to keep his mouth shut. Because if Wallace ever found out he'd been asking questions about J. D. Ortega and the Free Mars movement, he was going to be in deeper trouble than Welch could ever imagine.

CHAPTER 16

Ivanova ran through the preflight check like a litany, secure in the familiar space of the Starfury's cockpit, suited up for space, hands on the controls. It felt good. It felt right.

"Escort Wing, ready for launch."

Sheridan had given her back what she needed. A command, if not the command they had taken away from her. And more than that: flight.

"Escort Wing launching. On my mark. Drop!"

The ship fell away from the station through the open door of the bay. As soon as she was clear, Ivanova hit the ignition, and the thrusters roared into life. She could feel their power, the force of acceleration trying to press her back into her seat. The rest of the escort formed themselves up behind and around her, and the six ships headed as one into the jump gate's infinite vortex.

Six Starfuries. Not the whole of Alpha Wing, but they were still going out in force, expecting a fight. Hoping, at least in Ivanova's case, for one. Hoping to splash some raiders, hit them where it hurt. And if she had a mental image of Commander Ian Wallace as the target when the plasma hit, well, so much the better.

The gate flung them out of hyperspace with Ivanova coolly ordering, "Hold your formation, Escort Wing." Their rendezvous was two and a half hours away, across Blue Sector, with the heavy hauler *Kobold* as it came through the transfer point carrying raw ingots of iridium, titanium, nickel, and morbidium from the mines of Mars.

No problem getting a ship like that to show up on the mass detector, Ivanova thought. Almost as heavy as a small planet, with the inertia to match. Flying it would be about as exciting as a tug pushing a barge up a slow stream.

Her hands hovered over the fighter's controls, just to feel the temptation, just for a second, to cut loose with the afterburners. Yes, it was good to be back.

"2:20 hours 'til estimated time of rendezvous," she said, because she had no orders to give now that they were through the gate and still so far from their destination. The fighters were all in formation, all on course. You couldn't have aimless chatter in the cockpit when the ships were out on patrol, but sometimes on the long stretches space could seem like an awfully big, dark silent place and a friendly voice was good to hear.

"Copy that, Alpha Leader," Mokena replied from Alpha Two.

By the time the jump gate showed up on the long-range scan, Ivanova was ready for the confrontation she expected and hoped would happen. "Weapons systems on. Keep on the alert for raiders," she ordered, but the fighter pilots had all been briefed on the nature of this patrol. They knew what was likely to show up, and they were ready for it.

Then there was a sudden massive energy surge showing up on her instruments, a blaze of blue light from the jump gate, and the transport came through from hyperspace at the maximum acceleration for a ship of her class.

Ivanova made immediate contact. "This is Earthforce Commander Susan Ivanova, commanding Escort Wing Alpha. Are you the *Kobold*?"

"Affirmative, Commander. Earth Alliance transport *Kobold*, out of Marsport. We're glad to see you out here."

"Glad to be here, *Kobold*. We've come out to give you

an escort as far as Babylon 5. We've heard raiders might be taking an interest in your cargo.''

"Thanks, Commander. I've got to say, it's about time, and then some.''

"Take escort formation,'' Ivanova ordered her command, and they fell into place around the transport, matching velocities, heading back in the direction of Babylon 5.

It was too easy. Ivanova found herself almost wishing the raiders would show up. Once they were all on course, the transport's pilot came on-line through Ivanova's comm channel. "Commander, can I ask—you said you heard raiders might be taking an interest in our cargo?''

"That's right.''

"Well, could I ask—where you heard this? Your source?''

"Meet me once we're on Babylon 5,'' Ivanova told him, "and we can talk about it there.''

"It's a date, Commander.''

Alpha Two broke in: "I'm picking up something on scan. Bearing 80 by 44 by 122.''

"I've got it, too,'' reported one of the other fighters.

Ivanova checked the screen. A trio of tiny points, at the limit of scan range, but closing in fast. Raiders, she thought at once, and the computer confirmed the probability: small, fast ships—certainly fighters of some kind, and in this sector, that meant raiders. "Heat up your weapons,'' she ordered. "Keep alert. Any more of them out there?''

"Negative, Commander. Just those three.''

"Well,'' the *Kobold*'s pilot said, "it looks like your information was correct, Commander.''

But where are the rest of them? Ivanova wondered. The raider ships were small and usually operated in packs.

"Are we going to take them on?'' Alpha Three asked

as the three ships closed the distance while remaining well out of the Starfuries' range.

"They're trying to draw us away," Ivanova declared. "Three and Six: take off after them, get them if you can, but don't let yourselves get separated or drawn into a chase. Our job is escorting this transport."

At her order, the two fighters spun about with a burst of their thrusters and headed after the raider ships, which suddenly fled, leading them away. "Diversion," Ivanova said, mostly to herself. It was easy to follow the chase on her tactical display, as the pair of Starfuries bore down on the smaller, boomerang-shaped ships. Silently, she was cheering them on, her hand poised above the button of a phantom plasma torpedo, aching to fire. *Go! Get them!*

The raider pilots had judged the distance and their opposition well. As soon as Alpha Three and Six started to come within firing range, the three ships split up, attempting to divide the pursuit. "Don't do it!" Ivanova was about to order, but Alpha Three read the situation the same way she did.

"Stick with me!" he told his wingman. "We're going after the one heading off at ten o'clock!"

Together they pinned down their target. Alpha Three got off one good shot that singed the raider's tail and left him vulnerable to the next burst of plasma from Six, which finished the job.

In the meantime, the other two raiders had fled out of range. "Alpha Leader, should we continue pursuit?" Three asked Ivanova.

"Negative, Alpha Three, break it off and return to escort formation. Good shooting, you guys."

"Commander, do you think they'll try it again?" the transport pilot asked, but the question was answered before Ivanova could, as one of the other fighters reported, "I've got more of them on scan. Four this time."

"Hold escort formation," Ivanova reminded her command. "They're trying to draw us away. Remember, it's the transport they want."

But this time the raiders kept a more respectful distance. "They're looking for their friends," Ivanova conjectured. But of the first raiders, one was splashed and the other two turned tail, and eventually these newcomers retreated out of scan range, giving up on their anticipated prey. Ivanova watched their images disappear from her display. There was a sharp stab of regret for the opportunity lost, the chance to take off after them, weapons hot and ready. But, as she knew full well, the transport was her primary responsibility.

"It looks like clear sailing back to Babylon 5," she announced to the *Kobold*. "Just sit back and enjoy the ride."

"Commander, you have no idea just how good that sounds," the pilot said in a very sincere tone.

When Garibaldi started to add up the facts he had so far, one minute it seemed almost conclusive, the next minute it had all vanished to a handful of threads so thin you couldn't hang a feather from them. It felt strange to be working without the computer, but ever since Wallace had wiped his files, he wasn't sure what kind of bug the Earthforce investigator might have placed in the system. Generally, he considered himself sharp enough when it came to computer security, but he had to figure that Wallace had come from Earth Central with passwords and override codes to override anything he might have.

But before they had computers, they had paper and pens, and so did Garibaldi.

So, adding it all up, so far he had Mars Colony, with Free Mars terrorists, with morbidium mines, with the raw material for plasma weapons. Out here in Grid Epsilon, he had raiders, hijacking the cargoes of morbidium.

Linking them together, he had J. D. Ortega, maybe part of the Free Mars movement and maybe not, turning up dead on Babylon 5 with some mysterious, now-missing piece of information. He had Susan Ivanova, investigating the hijackings, sent a message by Ortega that might or might not have referred to that mysterious information. And now: Fengshi Yang, again from Mars, again showing up dead on Babylon 5. Yang, whose records were not what they should be: an "enforcer," somehow connected with "the mines."

Was he an agent of the Free Mars movement? A terrorist? Welch didn't seem to think so, but Garibaldi didn't think much of relying on Welch's mental powers. An agent of the raiders, maybe? The agent who passed on the shipping data? Had he come to Babylon 5 to meet Ortega? To work out a deal? Pass on a warning?

To kill him?

Garibaldi pushed squares of paper around on his desktop, arranging them in different configurations. Which arrangement made it all make sense? A square of paper marked X for whoever had killed Ortega. Another X for whoever had killed Yang. But was X one person, or two? Maybe one X had killed another X. Then there'd be only one X left. What side was X on? Or should that be what sides?

His data screen stared at him blankly. Damn! It would be so easy just to access the computer and ask it to search the records for anyone on the station with a previous involvement in mining on Mars. Yeah. And how much do you want to bet that won't bring Wallace down on your head, Garibaldi?

Well, there was more than one way to search. This sure as hell wasn't getting him anywhere. He flashed the squares of paper. He had all that stuff in his head, anyway. What he needed now was to have another talk with someone.

* * *

It hadn't been easy to set this up. Garibaldi still didn't know the guy's name. Just that he was Nick's friend, whose lady friend had worked in the survey office, been interrogated by Wallace, and shipped back to—presumably—Earth. Mineral surveys, assays. Did that have anything to do with mines? With morbidium shipments? Terrorists? Fengshi Yang?

Nick's friend was a nervous-looking guy. Claimed he didn't know anything, he wasn't involved, didn't want to be involved. But he had, Nick had grudgingly admitted it, been involved with mining. Or at least with mining machinery, a company that built the big loaders.

The meeting place was down in the machine shops, one of the dozens of different divisions of the Engineering Department on Babylon 5. The man—he still wouldn't give his name—had his fists clenched inside grease-stained coveralls and wouldn't take them out. Garibaldi got the feeling there was something in his background behind it, maybe something in his record he didn't want to come out, some incident in his past that had made him generally hostile to the kind of authority Garibaldi represented, to Earthforce.

"I only agreed to this because Nick asked me to. And mostly because he said maybe you could do something about Sonia. Find out . . . something. Where they took her. What they did with her. Why."

"I can try. I'll do what I can. But I've got to tell you up front, whatever happened to your friend is out of my control."

A frown. "You're Earthforce, you're security, aren't you? Nick said you were the head guy."

"I'm head of Babylon 5 security, yes. But there's an independent investigation going on that I'm not directly involved in. Nick should have told you that. I'm not mixed up with what this Commander Wallace is doing on the station. But I'll try. And if I do find out what I'm looking for, it could help your friend.''

"So what is it you're looking for?"

Garibaldi handed him the viewer. "This man. Whatever you know about him. We think his name is Fengshi Yang. He might have called himself something else, though."

A frown. "You think Sonia might have been involved with this guy?"

"I don't know. I don't know what Sonia was involved in. If you told me, you know, that might help."

But he abruptly gave back the viewer. "No. No, never saw him before."

Garibaldi thought he had the sudden intuition of what it must be like to be a telepath and simply *know* when someone was lying. "What I've heard," he said, "is that he worked as a kind of enforcer on Mars. Around the mines."

Quickly, "I wouldn't know. I wasn't a miner. Look, I've got to go. I don't have anything to say."

Garibaldi tried to stop him, but the look in the guy's eyes—he was scared. He dropped his arm, let him go. Damn, there was another lead that went nowhere. More time wasted. Everyone was scared, no one would talk. A dozen interviews so far, and only Welch had talked, and Welch had dead space for brains.

Now what? There were other workers in the machine shop area. A few of them gave him a curious glance. Garibaldi wondered if he ought to go over, show them Yang's holo, ask if any of them had ever worked in the mines on Mars. But he already knew what they'd say: No, sorry, never saw him before, never heard of him. No, I wasn't a miner. I don't know anything.

Would they rather have Wallace asking the questions? he wondered, leaving the shop area. Would they rather have a telepath probing around in their minds, digging out the truth?

Garibaldi knew he was looking at a dead end. If he didn't find any leads soon, he was going to be the one facing the real trouble—failing to file proper reports, concealing the truth about his investigation. As soon as Wallace found out.

Well, maybe Torres had uncovered a lead. He could hope. He was supposed to meet her now, anyway.

Preoccupied, he didn't notice the guy who came up behind him, the other one from his side, didn't notice the shock sticks they pulled, didn't see—

Then pain radiated through his entire nervous system, short-circuiting all thought processes, all other functions. His muscles spasmed out of control, and he didn't even feel it when his head connected with the deck.

CHAPTER 17

He came to slowly, conscious only vaguely of pain, a general, body-wide hurting. It was dark. He tried to reach out, to grope for a surface, but he couldn't move his arms. He tried again, realized they were tied somehow, fastened behind him. And—yes—his legs, too, tied together at the ankles, bent up against his chest. His back was pressed up against some hard, unyielding surface, his arms trapped between them, cramped, circulation cut off. He tried to shift to a different position, to ease the discomfort, but there was no room to move. His back was against one wall, his shoulder against another, and if he leaned over to the other side, he hit a third wall. And his feet and knees were pressed up against the fourth. He was crammed into this dark place that was almost too small to hold him, tied up—why?

Fear made his heartbeat race. It was hard to breathe in here. The air felt hot and stale, as if there wasn't much oxygen. And that thought instantly triggered the sensation that he was stifling, choking— No, wait. In his mouth, a gag.

So where was he? A dark, small, enclosed place. A locker?

A locker . . .

Ortega! Now real panic hit him, making him kick out and strain against his bonds. This was how they'd found J. D. Ortega's body, crammed into a locker just like this! Garibaldi couldn't help remembering the sight of the corpse, stiff with rigor mortis, knees bent up against the chest to fit it inside. Was this why he was tied up in here?

Was he supposed to die in here the same way, in this dark, airless place?

No! He kicked out with both feet together, as much in protest as a serious attempt to break out of his confinement. He could just manage it, just draw his feet back far enough to make an impact.

He kicked out again. *No!* they weren't going to get away with this. *No!* he wasn't going to let them. *No!* not like Ortega. *No!* he wasn't going to die in here. *No! No! No!*

He paused, falling back, aching, sweating, gasping for breath that wouldn't come through the gag in his mouth. His head throbbed and his ears were ringing from the din of the repeated kicks against the locker walls. It was too much.

Get ahold of yourself, Mike! All right, calm down. Think.

He remembered then that J. D. Ortega hadn't suffocated in the locker, that he'd been poisoned and shoved inside after he was dead. Didn't mean, of course, that he couldn't die in here, but at least it wasn't the same, not quite the same. And if they'd meant him to die, they would have killed him already. Wouldn't they? Unless they thought he was dead before they put him in here.

All right, all right. It didn't help to dwell on any of that, did it? After all, he was alive, and that's what mattered. And staying that way.

If he could reach his link, he could call for help. Shouldn't be too hard, his wrists were tied together. He groped for the link, found his wrist, the back of his hand —but no link. It was gone. Damn!

Now what?

All right. Let's think this through, Mike. Problem: My link is gone, I'm tied up and shut into this locker. Assuming it is a locker. So let's assume it is. Then it should have a door. Four sides, one of them should be the door.

*Can't tell which one, it's too dark. Can I kick it open?
Well, the lockers on the station aren't all that strong. I
should be able to. But I was just kicking the hell out of it,
and it's still shut tight. So maybe that side isn't the door.*

To say that Garibaldi couldn't move at all was to exag-
gerate the facts by just a bit. He had freedom enough to
move his bound legs enough to kick. And, he now discovered, he could manage to twist and rotate his entire
body a centimeter at a time until he was facing another
one of the locker's walls, which he hoped would prove to
be the door.

It was a slow, exhausting process that again left him
breathing hard, as if he were running out of air. The
locker must be airtight, then, he thought. Or maybe it
wasn't really a locker at all, maybe it was something a
whole lot harder to break out of.

Desperately, he kicked out. The locker's sides rang
with the impact, hurt his ears again. Loud.

Someone ought to be able to hear that. He paused.
Again, his ears were ringing. It was like his whole skull
was vibrating with the sound. Made it hard to think.

*No, have to think. All right. If I'm making so much
noise, why doesn't anyone hear it? Maybe there's no one
around. Or maybe they're making so much noise themselves they can't hear me.*

But the way his ears were ringing, he couldn't tell. It
didn't matter, though. He had to keep trying. Someone
might come by and hear him. Or he could finally manage
to kick the door down. Only if he kept trying, though.

So he kept trying.

On the main communications display in the Observation Dome Commander Ivanova was saying, "No, I
don't expect another attack. The first one was just a feint,
to see if they could draw us off. The second time they

didn't even come into range. No, we've scared them off."

"Good work," Sheridan said enthusiastically. "I think we'll be able to show Earth Central that this approach can work. Results, Commander. That's what counts."

"Yes, sir. We'll be bringing the transport in. ETA in 3:50 hours."

"Good work," Sheridan said again, pleased for her, pleased for the safety of the transport and the success of this approach to fighter escort patrols. A good officer, Ivanova. Innovation, initiative, just the right degree of aggression. Good qualities.

"Captain Sheridan?"

He turned to see another officer standing slightly behind him, an ensign, security insignia on her uniform. Short, red-haired. Seemed to be upset about something, but controlling it. "Ensign Torres?" he recalled her name.

"Yes, sir. Could I speak with you, sir?"

"Of course."

She glanced around the busy center of the Observation Dome. "In private?"

"Of course." Once behind the closed door of the briefing room, he asked, "So what's the trouble, Ensign?"

"Sir, it's Mr. Garibaldi. I'm afraid he's missing. I can't locate him."

Sheridan reached for his link, but Torres shook her head. "He doesn't answer his link. And C&C can't trace it. I've already tried. And . . . I have reason to believe he may be in danger."

"Better tell me about it, Ensign."

"We've been investigating a murder—"

"Not the Ortega case?"

"No, sir. A different murder. A man was found . . .

that is, part of him was found in the recycling system. We were able to ID him through his DNA code. His name was listed as Fengshi Yang, but there's a mix-up with his file in the station registry, inconsistencies. We've been 'rying to trace him, determine his true identity.''

Sheridan frowned. "I don't think I was informed about this, Ensign. Why not?"

Torres's small white teeth bit down on her lower lip. "I don't know, sir. But Mr. Garibaldi wanted this case kept quiet, in case information got out to the wrong parties, I suppose. I think I was the only one working directly on it with him. But . . . I didn't know you hadn't been informed."

The captain's frown deepened. Torres was having trouble keeping her eyes straightforward. There was something she wasn't saying, at least. "Go on," he said impatiently.

"Yes, sir. He was supposed to meet me more than three hours ago. To discuss our results. When he didn't show up, I tried to reach him on his link. I supposed at first that there might be some reason why he might have gone off-line. But he never does that. And then when I asked C&C to check on him, they reported no trace to his link at all. Sir, I'm worried, but because this could be a sensitive case, I didn't know if I should issue a stationwide search alert."

"What do you mean, a sensitive case?"

Torres looked away for just an instant. "Well, sir, we weren't sure . . . I mean, there was no evidence, and Mr. Garibaldi told me not to mention anything, but it's possible there could be a connection between this murder and the Ortega case. And I think that may have been what he was investigating."

"You think?"

"Sir, he didn't tell me. He *said* there wasn't a connection, but I think . . . he thought there might have been. And he didn't want anyone else involved. I wasn't sure what to do—"

"I see," said Sheridan shortly. "Do you have any idea where he might have gone, where he might be?"

"No, sir. If I had, I'd have checked myself. But he didn't tell me. I don't think he told anyone what he was doing."

Sheridan nodded. Time enough to get to the bottom of the mystery later, time enough to get the true story out of Garibaldi—once they found him. "This is Captain Sheridan, I'm calling a general stationwide alert. Mr. Garibaldi is missing."

"Come on, Ensign Torres. I haven't been on this station very long, but after we get through taking it apart, I may know every square meter of it. We're going to find Garibaldi."

How long had it been? Wearily, Garibaldi kicked again at the side of the locker. Was it starting to give? If it was, he sure couldn't tell. Why'd they have to make the lockers on this station so damn strong, anyway? His hips ached, his back. His shoulders were agony, with his arms twisted back behind him. His head throbbed with pain.

He twisted himself around again until his back was pressed up against a new surface. Got to keep trying. He kicked out. Was this the door?

Got to keep trying.

No, wait. What was that? A sound? A voice?

He tried to call out through the gag, choked, then kicked the side of the locker again—I'm here!

Did they hear him?

Yes! Relief flowed through him. Oh, yes! Someone calling his name! *Garibaldi?*

He kicked twice. *Once for no and twice for yes. Where did I hear that?*

"Garibaldi? Is that you? Where are you?"

Here! he wanted to yell, but the gag prevented it. Two kicks again. Not so hard this time, not so loud. Just so they could find the locker he was in.

"Garibaldi? Are you in here?"

The captain's voice. Sheridan. *Thank you, Captain. Thank you.*

"He's in here! In this locker! Get it open, now!"

There was a grating, wrenching noise. "Dammit, then try the next one! I know he's in here!"

He kicked out again, to be helpful, but suddenly there was another loud ripping sound of metal tearing, and the wall on his left side gave way and he was falling, couldn't catch himself.

Blinding light. Hands grabbing hold of him, easing him down to the floor.

"Get him untied! Garibaldi, are you all right?"

The gag was pulled from his mouth. He gasped, tried to swallow, managed to croak an inarticulate response. Swallowed again. "Fine. Just fine."

Even managed a grin. "Real . . . happy to see you . . . Captain."

They took him to Medlab. Garibaldi didn't really want to go to Medlab, but they didn't ask his opinion in the matter, and the captain ordered it, and so it was done.

Dr. Franklin examined him, gave him something that made his aches and pains fade away, peered into his eyes with an instrument and said he was lucky he had a hard head, but one of these days he was going to hit it too many times.

"Concussion?" the captain asked.

The doc shook his head. "No, I don't think so. It was a glancing blow, like he struck it when he fell. Now, *this* is a shock-stick burn." He pointed to a place on the side of Garibaldi's neck.

Funny, he couldn't remember that place hurting before, in the locker. But it was coming back to him now. A shock stick. Yeah. That's what it must have been. Not the first time he'd been shocked. It wasn't the kind of experience you forgot. Yeah, first the shock. Then coming to in the dark. He remembered it now.

Experimentally, he shook his head. It almost didn't hurt. He sat up, to Doc's protesting "Hey, take it easy."

"I feel all right. I'm just sitting up." He turned to face Sheridan. And there was Torres, behind him. Torres? "Thanks for pulling me out of there, Captain."

"You had us a little bit worried there for a while."

And Torres, apologetic, said, "I'm sorry, Chief. I wasn't sure what you wanted me to do, but after I couldn't raise you on your link, I told the captain. I hope—"

"I think that was a good decision," Garibaldi said sincerely. "Thanks, Torres."

Sheridan was looking at him. "You want to tell me about it now?"

Franklin started to protest that his patient had just been hit on the head, but Garibaldi sat up straight. His head felt clearer now, though he knew that was probably the drugs.

"I don't know how much there is to tell, Captain. I was interviewing a possible witness, who didn't have very much to say. I left him, I was heading back to the lift tube, to meet with Torres, and then—'zap!"

"I understand you're investigating a murder. A man named Yang? Is there a connection? Do you think it was Yang's killer who zapped you? Someone who didn't want your witness to talk?"

Garibaldi closed his eyes a moment. Maybe he wasn't really ready for this. But it was too late now.

Sheridan's expression was starting to take on a more severe look. "According to Ensign Torres here, there might be a connection between Yang's death and the Ortega case. But there's nothing to that effect in the file on Yang's case. In fact, there's almost nothing in that file."

Torres, still behind the captain, looked pained and guilty.

Garibaldi shook his head, winced. "It was only a hunch. No facts. No evidence. Nothing to put into a file. All I really know is that Yang departed for Babylon 5 from Marsport on date 04/18 and died sometime within the next five days."

Sheridan looked dubious. "That's your hunch?"

"One more thing. According to the station registry, he left Babylon 5 on 04/20. Passenger manifest says he didn't. Fact that we found his body three days later says he didn't. So somebody must have tampered with his file in the station registry. That's my hunch. That's it."

Garibaldi was earnestly glad there wasn't a telepath in the room at the moment. He was thinking of Welch, and the information that Welch had given him, tying Yang to Mars and the mines there. But Welch was safely back on his ship, with nothing in his record to suggest he was anything but a gambler thrown off the station for cheating at cards.

Sheridan started to say something, then turned his head. There was noise out in the corridor, someone shouting. Franklin looked furious, strode to the door. "Keep it down! What's all this about? I'm not having my patients disturbed!"

But Garibaldi shut his eyes. Suddenly his headache was coming back. He recognized the furious voice demanding that someone get out of his way and stop obstructing his investigation if she didn't want to face "very serious charges, Technician."

Just what he needed right now. His favorite head-hunter, Commander Ian Wallace, had come to visit him.

CHAPTER 18

Wallace burst into the treatment room followed by his aide Khatib and a seething Franklin. "All right, Garibaldi, this is it—"

But he was stopped short by the sight of Sheridan standing at Garibaldi's bedside, a Sheridan who did not look like part of a welcoming committee. "I *hope,* Commander, that you have some reasonable explanation for barging into Medlab like this, disturbing the patients?"

Wallace drew himself up straight. "Captain, I have reason to believe that your chief of security has been interfering in my investigation, in defiance of both my orders and yours. And I believe you understand *now* how important my findings are to Earth Central."

But if this last remark was intended to intimidate Sheridan, it had the opposite effect. Babylon 5's commander did not like being reminded of Wallace's knowledge of his personal, restricted message from the Earthforce Joint Chiefs. "What I understand at the moment, Commander," he said tightly, "is that you have one minute to either justify your presence here or leave Medlab."

"Very well, Captain. We can continue this discussion in your office. Where I intend to demand that you relieve Mr. Garibaldi of his duties as head of Babylon 5 security and hold him under arrest. He was ordered explicitly and repeatedly not to get involved in the Ortega case. Now I discover that he's been questioning *my* witnesses! Getting himself involved in a situation that he *clearly* isn't capable of handling." He flashed Garibaldi a brief unsympathetic glance. "In fact, removing Mr. Garibaldi from his position might be said to be for his own good."

Sheridan had seen the look. He snapped, "That won't be necessary, Commander. Your request is denied. Mr. Garibaldi has just been injured in the course of carrying out his duties as head of security, investigating a murder on this station. He has every right to question suspects or witnesses to this crime, whether or not you consider them 'your witnesses.' Particularly since it seems that you've been questioning every other man, woman, and alien on Babylon 5."

Wallace blinked, looked back at Khatib. He seemed uncertain. "What murder?"

"A salesman from Earth was killed recently. A man named Yang."

"Yang?"

"That's right. Why? You don't know anything about this case, do you? This man named Yang?"

Quickly, too quickly, shaking his head, "No. The name means nothing to me."

Garibaldi's head lifted a few centimeters from his pillow, staring at Wallace with avid interest.

Sheridan went on, unnoticing, "Then it won't interfere with your own investigation if the Babylon 5 security office tries to track down his killer? Since the two cases aren't related. As you claim."

Wallace took a slight step backward. "Of course not. I can see I might have . . . been misinformed."

"Yes, you might have," said Sheridan. He looked at Torres, who was standing motionless and looking like she wished she were invisible. "Lieutenant, you can escort the commander from Medlab."

Gratefully, Torres said, "Yes, sir. Commander, if you'd come with me?"

Wallace turned to leave, ignoring Torres, but Garibaldi, sitting up on the treatment bed, couldn't resist. "Say, Commander. If you do come across any leads on the Yang case, you'll let me know, won't you?"

Wallace said coldly, "Of course."

"I'll do the same for you, too. We ought to help each other out, shouldn't we? Seeing as we're in the same line of business."

Wallace didn't answer, but Khatib shot Garibaldi a silent, deadly look.

"That's a nasty one," he thought to himself as they left, followed at a safe distance by the lieutenant.

"Thanks, Captain," he said out loud.

Franklin looked satisfied to see Wallace leaving. "I think we should all leave Garibaldi to get some rest, sir."

"Just a few minutes, Doctor. If I can speak to Garibaldi alone."

"I think I'm feeling dizzy," Garibaldi muttered, closing his eyes.

"Flash it, Garibaldi. And to hell with Commander Wallace. I want to know what's really going on! I talked to Torres, and she says you do think this Yang case is related to the other one. You know something, and I want to hear it!"

"I swear, Captain! I've got next to nothing! Every time I think I've got my hands on a lead, it turns into smoke." Garibaldi paused. "All right, you want to know why I think there's a connection? Because I can't find out a thing! No one will talk.

"This is my station. I mean, I have connections here, people that I can talk to, who'll talk to me. But this time, when I was still looking into the Ortega case, before you ordered me not to, I got nowhere. Nobody knows nothing. They won't talk. All right, so when I started asking around about this guy Yang, I got just the same thing. Nothing. Nobody's talking. They're afraid, Captain."

"Afraid of what?"

"That's what I don't know! Only it all seems to point to Mars. I did find out one thing, that Yang was from Mars. He was involved in something people don't want to talk about. And Ortega was from Mars. He was a suspected terrorist, no one wants to talk about that. He came to Babylon 5, he was killed. Yang came to Babylon 5, he was killed. One more thing. We've got no record of Ortega coming onto the station; the station records on Yang were falsified."

Sheridan said nothing, but he was listening, at least.

"Everything else is just crazy speculation."

But the captain wasn't going to let him leave it at that. "What kind of crazy speculation?"

Garibaldi rubbed his head. "Like, who Yang really was. What he was here for. Look, it's just a crazy theory, all right? But I've been talking with Ivanova. You know how she traced the leaks in that transport routing data back to Mars? Well, she figures there might be somebody from Earthdome in on it, covering it up. So it could be that Ortega wasn't a terrorist, that he found out about the deal, and the bad guys in Earthdome tried to shut him up. So they send an enforcer after him, but something goes wrong, the enforcer gets killed, too."

"And Yang was the enforcer?"

"That was his line of work, from what I've heard."

Sheridan was frowning in thought. "But then, after all the probing around he's done, questioning everyone on the station who's ever been to Mars, why wouldn't Wallace know about Yang?"

"I think he does."

Sheridan looked at him and the shock snapped his eyes wide.

Garibaldi nodded. "Just then. When you mentioned Yang's name. I was watching Wallace's face—and that snake, Khatib's. They *knew*. They knew about Yang, all right. They just didn't think *we* knew. And they weren't happy about it."

For a moment, they both considered the implications of that in silence.

Then Garibaldi went on, "So say we've got Earthforce officials mixed up in something dirty. Some guy finds out about it. He's got, say, names, dates. He's dead, the enforcer's dead, but the information hasn't shown up. You don't know if he's passed it on. So maybe you send another enforcer to find it. An enforcer with authorization—"

"Direct from the Joint Chiefs? Come on, Garibaldi!"

"Hey, didn't I say it was crazy?"

Sheridan paced a step away from the bed, stopped, turned around again to Garibaldi. "I mean, I wondered about Wallace, I admit it. His tactics. Enough to question Earth Central about him. And you saw what I got back! I mean, the Joint Chiefs, Garibaldi. Direct from Admiral Wilson. You're spinning conspiracy theories all the way up to the High Command!"

"Yeah, I know. Why do you think I didn't write it up in an official report? Why do you think I tried to keep the whole Yang business quiet?" Garibaldi sighed. "Only, there's one more side to it."

Sheridan looked as if he didn't want to hear it, then waved for Garibaldi to go on.

"All right, the bad guys send their investigators. They discover that the guy with the information met with a certain Earthforce officer. And it's the same Earthforce officer who just filed a report with Earth Central pointing right to their dirty dealings. And the first thing the investigators do is call for that officer's arrest."

Sheridan clenched his fists. "I *can't* go to Earth Central with this! You know I can't! I've got my orders! Direct from—" He didn't say it. "Dammit, Garibaldi, this *is* crazy! I don't believe it. You said it—you don't have any facts to back this up."

"Yeah, I know." Garibaldi sighed again, rubbed his head where it ached. "And there are other problems.

Like, who just zapped me with a shock stick and stuffed me in that locker? And who killed Yang?"

"The same group?"

Garibaldi shook his head, winced. The drugs were starting to wear off at the edges, letting the pain in. "No. I had a lot of time to think about it, in there. And I don't think so. They could have killed me easy enough, if that's what they'd meant to do. No, it was a warning."

"You mean, stop asking questions, or you'll end up like Ortega, stuffed into a locker?"

"Something like that, yeah." Garibaldi paused a moment, thought about it. "No. Whoever took care of Ortega was a pro. Whether it was Yang or not. But he didn't care much about the body being found. In fact, he might even have meant it like they did me—as a warning."

"To someone," Sheridan agreed.

"But whoever killed Yang, they *didn't* want the body found. In fact . . ." he paused again, "in fact, they'd probably be real upset if they knew it was identified. And that somebody was investigating the murder. I'll bet that'd be kind of a shock."

He met Sheridan's eyes, knew they were both thinking the same thing.

"And that kind of changes everything," Garibaldi said slowly. After a moment, he asked, "So now what do we do?"

Sheridan's jaw tightened. "I don't know about all this other stuff, Garibaldi, all these conspiracies. But we still have an unsolved murder on Babylon 5. That's a fact. And, like I told Commander Wallace, I can't overlook a murder on the station where I'm in command."

"And Wallace just admitted that the Yang case isn't related to his investigation," Garibaldi added with a certain tone of satisfaction. "So I guess it's up to us to find the killer."

"And I *won't* tolerate an attack on one of my officers," Sheridan went on, his course firmly set. "That's another fact. Now, first thing is to bring in this witness you were talking to just before it happened. What's his name?" He raised his hand to call security on his link, but lowered it when Garibaldi said, "I don't know."

"Don't know his name?"

Garibaldi shook his head, carefully this time. "The way it was set up, he wouldn't talk if I knew his identity. He didn't have that much to say, anyway."

"So how'd you contact him?"

"Through . . . other contacts. Look, Captain, I'm not sure I want to say who it was. These people talked to me because I promised confidentiality. And they know they can trust me. What am I supposed to do—break my promise? Turn them in?"

"What else do you think they did? They turned you in, Garibaldi! They set you up, they turned you over to . . . whoever it was! You could have been killed. These are the people you want to protect?"

"Yeah, it sounds crazy, doesn't it?" Garibaldi closed his eyes and let his head drop forward. The headache was getting worse again now. And the trouble was, he did want to protect them. Nick, and the others who'd trusted him enough to spill their guts. It was part of being what he was—you stood up for your sources, you didn't give them away. "Look, I'd just rather . . . do this my way. It's my job, after all."

But Sheridan was unmoved. "Your way just almost got you killed. And you're still not fit for duty. No, Garibaldi, this time, things are going to be done my way."

CHAPTER 19

On approach to the docking bay, Escort Wing Alpha pulled back to let the transport enter first, then docked themselves. Ivanova cracked her canopy and climbed out with stiff, cramped legs after hours in the cockpit. She nodded cheerfully to the docking crew and headed to the ready room to take off her flight suit. But first she linked-in to Sheridan.

"Captain, this is Ivanova. We're back, escort mission a success. Transport *Kobold* safely delivered, no casualties or damage, one raider flamed. Would you like me to report for debrief right away?"

"Can we put that off for a while, Ivanova? We have a situation here. There was an attack on Garibaldi—he's all right; he's resting in Medlab. But there are some security-related matters I want to take care of first."

"He's all right? Can I see him?" she asked, alarmed.

"Dr. Franklin says not to worry. But he's tired now. He got kind of banged up. It might be better to let him rest."

Now what was going on? Ivanova wondered. Who had attacked Garibaldi? At least he was going to be all right.

As she went to her own quarters to change, it occurred to her that there was time, then, to meet with the *Kobold*'s pilot. She was curious to know what he had to say.

His name was Pal, a thin, dark man, and he insisted on buying her a late dinner, which Ivanova didn't refuse, as the confrontation with the raiders had restored the edge to her appetite.

"You have no idea, Commander," he said, leading the way to a table in the open-air restaurant, "no idea what a relief it was to come out of the jump gate and find you there waiting for us. Though there were a few seconds—before you identified yourself—that I thought your ships might be the raiders themselves."

"You were expecting an attack, then?"

"Gods, yes! we were expecting an attack. I'll tell you —things have been so bad lately, the Transport Pilots Union has been threatening an action. Ground all transports until Earthforce starts to do their job and give us some escort through raider territory." He frowned, cleared his throat, then said nothing as the waiter came up to bring them plates of pancakes rolled around a mixture of chopped vegetables and spices. Pal poured a generous amount of hot sauce over his, bringing the dish to near the combustion point. Ivanova, familiar with the sauce, served herself a much smaller amount.

After the waiter had left, Pal lowered his voice. "The thing is . . . I'm on the union's Central Committee. And so I happen to know that as of the date we left Marsport, Earthforce was still 'studying our demands.' That's why I said I was surprised to see you out there. They keep telling us they don't have the resources to provide the escorts we need. They say they don't have the ships. So that's why I'm curious. What's going on?"

"I see," said Ivanova, swallowing a cautious bite of her meal. Hot, but good. "No, there's been no policy change on the Earthforce Command level, I can tell you that. It was Captain Sheridan, here on Babylon 5, who ordered the patrols, just for the territory we cover in Grid Epsilon. And only for certain transports judged to be high risk."

Pal's eyebrows raised. "And just what do you consider a high-risk transport?"

Ivanova hesitated. How much should she reveal? "We've done a computer analysis of the pattern of recent attacks. Certain routes seem more vulnerable than others.

Certain cargoes that are particularly valuable on the black market. The computer indicates the transports that are most likely to be attacked, based on that analysis, and we send out an escort wing to meet them. So far, at least, it seems to be working."

Pal leaned closer across the table. "And does your computer analysis say anything about data leaks, about routing information being sold to the raiders, about the way they know where these valuable cargoes are going to be coming through the jump gates, and when? Come on, Commander, don't tell me about a random computer analysis! We know better! Someone out there is making a profit by selling us out, making a profit off dead ships and crews! Don't tell me Earthforce doesn't know a thing about it!"

Ivanova swallowed. So she wasn't the only one who'd noticed this pattern in the attacks! "Mr. Pal, I'm only a wing commander at the moment. Earth Central doesn't confide in me at the policy level." She paused. "But, just personally, I think you're right. I'm sure you're right. The raiders have got to be operating on the basis of inside information."

"Oh, they know about it," Pal said darkly. "Earth Central. They just won't admit it. Not to us. And after a while, you know, you start to ask why."

"And?"

"Some of us wonder if they maybe have a reason to look the other way."

Ivanova put down her fork. She *wasn't* the only one to suspect it! "Mr. Pal," she asked carefully, "do you have any proof for this accusation? Any evidence?"

But Pal shook his head. "Not . . . directly. No. But we've made complaints. Many complaints to Earthforce. Nothing is done. Nothing is ever done! So I think—one or two officers, highly placed, in a position to derail an investigation, put questions on hold, file complaints where they won't be found?

"And there's another thing," Pal went on. "Some of us have started to wonder about those cargoes. The ones the raiders have targeted? The ones so valuable on the black market, as you say?"

She nodded. "Strategic metals, primarily, these days. What you were carrying—iridium, morbidium—"

"If that's what we really are carrying. Some of us would like to go back in our holds, crack open those crates, see what's really inside. Is it strategic metals—or slag?"

"Slag?"

"Worthless mass." Pal was using his fork now to punctuate his remarks. Ivanova had forgotten about hers, about her meal. "Think about it, Commander. How much is an ingot of iridium worth? A whole crate of ingots? A ship's hold full of them? What insurance value would you place on a cargo like that?"

"I believe the value is determined by Earth Central, isn't it? The price of strategic metals is restricted."

"Exactly!" Pal exclaimed, stabbing the table. "And if you have this commodity to sell at the official price, and the price on the black market keeps going higher and higher, what do you do? How can you make a greater profit?"

"So they sell to the black market? They bribe Earthforce officials to overlook certain shipments? But what does this have to do with the raids?" she asked, intrigued but confused.

"This is what we think," he said, leaning closer across the table. "For each cargo, there are two ships. One with the real cargo. The other with slag. They pay the raiders to take the false shipment. The real one, they ship to the black market. They get the higher price for the metal, and, for the false cargo, they collect the insured value.

"Simple, isn't it?"

Ivanova, who had already suspected much of this herself, was speechless for a moment. "What does your insurance company think about this?" she wondered finally.

"They also have their suspicions. I've been in contact with the insurance agent here on Babylon 5. We've discussed possible measures to confirm what we suspect." He frowned. "I'm telling you this in confidence, Commander."

"You have my word."

"When we reach our destination, we intend to have the crates unsealed, the contents checked before we deliver it. The insurance agent is trying to arrange for this now. If you like, I'll let you know what we find."

"I would appreciate that," Ivanova said eagerly. "I'd really like, personally, to get to the bottom of all this."

Pal's expression went grim. "Well, I warn you, Commander, the union won't stand for it much longer! Our people are dying out here—ships and crews are being sold out to satisfy the greed of rapacious corporations and corrupt officials! We're not powerless, Commander Ivanova. They're making a mistake if they think they can get away with this!"

By this time, Pal had raised his voice, and half the tables were looking in their direction. Ivanova quickly stabbed her fork into a slice of pancake in an attempt to pretend the conversation was of no particular importance. But her hand froze as she lifted it. There in the restaurant doorway, glaring at her, was Lieutenant Miyoshi.

"Uh-oh," murmured Ivanova. "There's trouble."

But it was too late now to pretend nothing was going on.

In a spirit of defiance, she turned back to her dinner companion. "I think I'll have some more of that hot sauce, Mr. Pal."

Because things were certainly getting hot enough around here lately.

An hour or so later, after meeting with the captain, Ivanova came into Garibaldi's room in Medlab to find him seated on the edge of his bed, contemplating the floor. "I thought you were supposed to be resting."

"So I rested. I feel fine now. Time to get back on my feet."

She looked him over. "You don't look so fine. What's that on your head?"

His hand went to the place. "This? Oh, that's nothing, it looks worse than it is. I just hit my head when I fell."

"When they zapped you with a shock stick."

"I guess you've been talking to someone."

She nodded. "The captain."

"What else did he tell you?"

"Not too much. Somebody grabbed you, stuffed you in a locker. Made it look like the way we found Ortega. He thinks it's a warning not to go around asking questions. Thinks it was a terrorist group. Only . . ."

He heard the hesitation in her voice. "What?"

"Well, I found out something today. If it's true. I still don't know what to think. But I just had dinner a while ago with the pilot of that transport we brought in this evening. His name is Pal, he's some kind of official with the Transport Pilots Union. They're suspicious of the raider activity, too. *And* a cover-up. But . . . they think it's some kind of major fraud on the part of the mining corporations. That certain transports are set up with a fake cargo, something that has mass but no real value. Then they file a false insurance claim and sell the real cargo on the black market. Garibaldi, if he's right, the profits could be in the millions! More than I ever thought.''

"He has proof of this?"

She shook her head. "That's the problem, he says they don't. But they're going to try to get it. Crack open the cargo crates and see what's really in there."

"Isn't that illegal?"

"I think they're trying to arrange something with their insurance company. Anyway, I got the impression they don't much care by now. All the raids, all the losses they've taken, no one doing anything about it."

Garibaldi sank back onto the bed. He rubbed his head. "They're going to open up the crates? But wait a minute. That doesn't make sense. They couldn't count on every raid being successful, could they? So what happens when these fake cargoes get to where they're going? What happens when the buyers open the crates and find junk? Wouldn't that expose the whole scheme?"

Ivanova's expression sobered. She hadn't considered that. But . . . "Unless the buyers were in on it?"

"Maybe," Garibaldi admitted.

"But the main thing is, they suspect the same thing we do. Someone is selling out those transports. And somebody from Earth Alliance is covering it up."

"Yeah," Garibaldi agreed, "but it still doesn't tie in the rest of it: Ortega, Wallace, Yang."

"Yang?"

"The other guy who was killed, remember? I told you about him. We found his foot in the recycling system?"

He briefly explained the recent confrontation with Wallace and his discussion with Sheridan afterward. "He thinks the whole thing sounds crazy. You've got to admit, a conspiracy going all the way up to the Joint Chiefs?"

But Ivanova had seized on one fact. "Wait a minute! If this Yang worked for the mines—so did J. D.! He was a mining engineer, I think. So, you see, there *is* a connection!''

"Maybe," Garibaldi admitted slowly. "I don't know. My source wasn't what you'd call real reliable. But there's one more thing."

"What?" Ivanova demanded when he didn't say anything.

"Wallace made a mistake," Garibaldi said slowly. "He was caught by surprise when the captain mentioned Yang's name, and he said he'd never heard of him. And he was lying. I'll stake my career on it, he's lying. But the thing is, he denied there was any connection between Yang and Ortega, between the two cases. We've got orders from high up in Earth Central not to interfere with the Ortega case. But Babylon 5 security is free to track down whatever we can find out about Yang."

Garibaldi started to get to his feet, but Ivanova put out her hand to stop him. "What do you think you're doing?"

"They hid my uniform somewhere around here."

"You're not leaving here?"

"No! I just want something in one of the pockets."

Ivanova told him to stay put and searched out the uniform herself. "All right," she said, handing it to him, "what is it?"

"This," he said, pulling out the holo card with Yang's picture. "I meant to ask you before if you could identify this guy."

She activated the viewer and gasped suddenly as Yang's holographic image coalesced. He was a man with Oriental features, middle-aged, with a heavyset face and dark eyebrows. "That's him! That's the man in the ready room! He brushed right past me as he came out of the head!"

"Where he'd just left Ortega's body," Garibaldi said,

nodding. "This is it. This is the guy who killed him. Now we know for sure."

Ivanova snapped the image off, shuddering. "If I could only just *remember*," she said in a whisper. "If I only knew what J. D. was trying to tell me. Then we'd know."

"But we don't. We don't know for sure. Not yet." Garibaldi's face was set into lines of grim determination. "But I'm going to find out."

CHAPTER 20

"Commander Ivanova!"

She looked around to see who was calling her. It was the next morning, she was just crossing the Zocalo, and the first thought she had was a recollection of Garibaldi's warning. But she dismissed the thought of assassins attacking her in the middle of the most public place on the station.

And the person approaching was an unlikely assassin, wearing a business suit, a young woman with severely cut black hair, with the look of the up-and-coming junior corporation soldier, putting in her time in space to earn a transfer to the seats of power on Earth. "Commander Ivanova?" she asked again.

"Yes, what can I do for you?"

"I'm Luz Espada, agent for Universal Underwriters here on Babylon 5. Could I speak with you about an important matter? I think Mr. Pal has already mentioned it to you. Perhaps if I could buy you a cup of coffee?"

Even without the offer of coffee, Ivanova would have agreed at once. Espada got them a secluded table in a small, expensive cafe.

"Commander," she got right to the point, "I spoke last night with Mr. Pal, and he suggests you might be able to confirm some suspicions which have come up lately concerning the raids on shipping. That there may have been insurance fraud on a very large scale."

"That's possible, yes," Ivanova admitted cautiously. "You understand, though, anything I say is unofficial, unconfirmed by Earthforce. In fact, they might even deny it."

"Which makes the whole situation rather more complicated, yes," Espada agreed. "But anything you can contribute would be appreciated."

Briefly, Ivanova outlined the data search that had led her to conclude that information on shipping routes was being sold or transmitted to the raiders. "It wasn't really very hard to dig this out, once I started asking the right questions," she concluded. "That's when I started to wonder if there was any official involvement, someone in Earthforce in on the deal, helping cover it up."

"Yes," Espada nodded, "that's essentially the same conclusion we're starting to reach."

Ivanova frowned, confused about something. "If I'm right, the pattern I found shows that this has been going on for at least a year. Would it take the insurance companies so long to start to notice a pattern of fraud? I thought your industry was on the watch for this kind of thing."

"Well, of course we are. But as a matter of fact, the *Kobold*'s cargo would have only been the third such loss for Universal within the last year. Two losses would have been consistent with the general level of raider activity lately. I don't believe there was an investigation. Or, if there was, it was inconclusive. Three times, though. That starts to look like a pattern."

"You only insured the cargo? Not the ship itself?"

"That's correct."

"Is that usual? To have the ship insured by one company and the cargo by another?"

"Oh, very common." She tapped her wrist link, a design very similar to the Earthforce model. "Computer, do we have the data on the *Kobold*?"

"The cargo transport vessel *Kobold*, 1,500 tonnes, is owned by Instell Shipping, Inc., a subsidiary of Aegean Enterprises. It is insured by the TransGalactic Assurance Corporation."

"And who shipped the cargo?" Ivanova asked tensely.

Espada queried her computer and got the answer, "Property of AreTech Consolidated Mines."

"Is that a Mars corporation?" Ivanova asked.

"Their operations are all on Mars," Espada told her. "The company headquarters is on Earth."

"What about the other two raider losses you mentioned? Did their cargoes both include morbidium? Were they shipped from AreTech, too?"

Espada looked at her. "As a matter of fact, they were."

"But Universal doesn't insure all AreTech's cargoes, does it?"

"No, I don't believe so." Espada pulled out a portable data screen from her case and plugged it into her link. Figures scrolled onto the display. "No," she said slowly, "it seems that AreTech deals with a number of different companies."

"Is that . . . usual, too?"

"It's not unusual, no," Espada said. "In cases of cargoes so valuable, and vulnerable, a company might ask several insurance carriers to bid on the coverage of each shipment, to minimize costs. Also, from our side, it tends to minimize the risks, spread them out."

Ivanova had a strong sense that she was onto something, that any moment now it was going to break through—the key to the whole situation. "Then no single insurance company would be likely to notice a suspicious pattern of losses?"

"Not unless they compared figures," Espada agreed. "And industry policy is to keep that information confidential. To keep the other companies from undercutting our bids."

"So a company like AreTech Mines would know about this policy?"

"I'm sure they would be aware of it, yes."

"Ms. Espada, what Mr. Pal spoke to me about involved a rather . . . far-reaching conspiracy, if it's true. He mentioned selling strategic metals on the black market. How much money might be involved in that? An amount large enough to bribe Earthforce officers?"

"Commander, the current official price of a single ingot of morbidium is twelve hundred credits. On the black market, you could probably get six times that price today. And we're talking about tons. Shiploads."

"I see," said Ivanova.

Espada's lips compressed with worry. "Commander, unsettled times are very bad for the insurance industry. And lately, things aren't looking very settled at all. There are governments preparing for war. Alien races attacking each other. The demand for strategic materials is likely to be insatiable, and that will keep driving the prices higher. This doesn't look good."

Ivanova was about to agree wholeheartedly, but before she could say so, a voice came over her link: "Commander Ivanova. Security wants you to come to docking bay 18 right away. There's an incident with the crew of a transport, and they've asked for you."

"I'll be right there." Then she asked, "What transport is it? The *Kobold*?"

"That's it, Commander."

"I'm on my way." She stood up quickly. "Excuse me, an emergency."

"Of course," said Espada. As soon as Ivanova had turned to go, Espada returned her attention to her data screen and started to go through the figures again.

Ivanova took the tram down to the docking bay, wondering how serious the disturbance was, if she ought to stop and get riot control gear—a flak jacket, at least, or a weapon. But the security officer in charge, Ensign Torres, told her over her link that it wasn't necessary.

"The situation isn't violent—not yet. But they want you here. The transport's crew asked for you specifically. As an intermediary, I suppose."

She could hear the uproar almost as soon as she reached the docking area, angry voices raised, echoing in the vast spaces where the largest ships were docked. There was a security detail on the scene, she saw when she came closer, but none of them had weapons drawn, which was a good sign. Ivanova was glad to see that Garibaldi hadn't somehow dragged himself out of his bed in Medlab to take charge of the situation. They probably had him sedated.

Torres beckoned her over, looking relieved. "Glad you're here. Do you know what this is all about?"

"No!" She had to shout to be heard over the shouts of the ship's crew, gathered at the cargo hatch in an attitude of repelling boarders, do or die. "What's going on?"

Torres pointed across the bay to the dark, menacing figure of Lieutenant Khatib. "He's got orders from Commander Wallace to search the transport's cargo. But the crew claims we've abducted their pilot and they won't let him into the ship. Khatib orders his own security detail to use force, but the detail won't do it without confirmation from Babylon 5 command. Khatib says it's mutiny. I think he'd shoot the whole squad if he could."

Mutiny? Ivanova thought. "Where's the captain?"

"He's in conference with the Narn ambassador. There's been another incident with the Centauri. They're talking about declaring war or something. The captain's mediating."

"And Garibaldi's in Medlab." *And I'm no longer in the chain of command,* Ivanova added to herself, but Torres certainly understood the situation well enough. "So you're in charge?"

"I'm senior security officer on duty. But *he*—Khatib —won't take my order to leave the docking bay. He wants me to order my team to attack the transport. Of course, I won't do it. And *they*—the transport crew—refuse to disperse. They're armed, Commander, but so far they haven't done anything. And they've been asking for you."

"Right." Ivanova nodded, grasping the situation in its simplest terms: one more crisis. Fine. She knew how to deal with a crisis. "Who's their speaker?"

"The tall dark guy. Copilot. Name's LeDuc."

"Right." Ivanova said again, advancing past the security line to confront the *Kobold*'s representative. "Mr. LeDuc, I'm Commander Ivanova. You asked for me?"

"Commander! Yes! I'm glad you're here. Mr. Pal said he trusted you. Now they've got him somewhere. What's going on around this station?"

"I'm not sure yet. But I'm trying to find out. What happened to Mr. Pal? Who's got him where?"

"Security! They took him away!"

"Under arrest, you mean?"

LeDuc pointed in Khatib's direction with a look of open hostility. "He comes up to Pal, says he's from security, a special investigator, wants to ask a few questions. Pal says he doesn't have time, we've got a scheduled departure, we're already off schedule, he's already talked to one of the officers on the station, he doesn't have anything more to add.

"*He* says that doesn't matter, his questions are different, and if Pal doesn't cooperate he'll order our departure canceled. Can he do that, Commander?"

Ivanova frowned. "Not on his own authority, no. Not directly, at least."

"That's what Pal told him, told him to flare off. Then this guy says Pal's under arrest, and he grabs him like *this*." LeDuc demonstrated, bending his own arm back. "Some of the crew was with him, they say, hey, what's going on, but this security guy pulls a weapon and says if they interfere, they're under arrest, too, for obstructing justice.

"So they go back to the ship, I call the security office to protest, they say they'll check on it, but I don't get any answers, just a runaround, you know what I mean, Commander?"

Ivanova nodded.

"So, about an hour later, *he* shows up at the ship with this security detail, and now he says he's going to search the *Kobold*. Well, *I* say he's not going to set one foot on our ship until we get our pilot back, and our clearance for departure, because, I tell you, Commander, you saved our butts out there at the jump gate, and I was glad to see you then, but now I can't wait to get off this station, if you know what I mean."

Ivanova thought she felt the same way, sometimes. This might be one of them.

But LeDuc went on, "So *he* says the ship isn't leaving this docking bay 'til he checks out the cargo, and *I* say he's not coming on board the ship until they release Pal—"

Ivanova figured she had the general picture. "So what we have here is a standoff, right?"

"Right. And we decided to call you in, because Pal said you could be trusted, at least."

"Right."

Ivanova looked across the security cordon at Khatib, who glared back at her. Right. "Look," she told LeDuc, "the officer who arrested Mr. Pal isn't in charge here, the ensign over there is. And she's not going to order our security forces to do anything drastic. There won't be any violence unless you start it."

LeDuc shook his head fervently. "We don't want trouble, Commander, we just want our pilot back and our clearance off this place."

"Fine. I'll see what I can do." Without much hope of

success, she went up to Wallace's aide, who stood with folded arms as close as he could get to the ship's cargo hatch. "This isn't getting anyone anywhere, is it, Lieutenant Khatib?"

Khatib sneered down at her from his superior height. "You have no authority here, Commander Ivanova. You're not in command."

"No, I'm not, but neither are you, Lieutenant. Ensign Torres is the officer in command here, and I know she's not going to order Babylon 5 security to use force in a situation like this. So it seems to me that it's time to negotiate, and the crew of the *Kobold* have asked me to speak on their behalf. They want to know where their pilot is and they want him back with all his working parts in order, if you know what I mean."

"The pilot will be released when Commander Wallace is finished with him. And *after* I've searched this ship. I have my orders, and they don't include negotiation."

"And just what kind of questions does the good commander have for Mr. Pal, anyway?"

"The subject of our investigation is confidential," Khatib sneered.

Ivanova wished Captain Sheridan were there. Only Sheridan outranked Wallace, and even so she wasn't sure he had the authority to order him to release his reluctant witness. She walked over to speak to Torres again. "I'm going to try something. But first I need to know, has the *Kobold*'s clearance for departure actually been canceled?" It rankled to have to go through the ensign for the information that should have been hers with a single query through her link, but Ivanova was determined to play this by the book as long as Khatib was watching her.

"I'll check, Commander," Torres replied, and opened her link. "No, they're still set for departure, as far as C&C is concerned."

Ivanova nodded. Good. She knew C&C would never

revoke the *Kobold*'s clearance on Wallace's orders. It
would take someone on the command staff, and the command staff was thin on the ground right at the moment.

She went back to consult with LeDuc. "I have a tactic
to propose," she told him. "Now, as you know, your
pilot Mr. Pal confided in me about some very sensitive
matters. Do you know what I'm talking about?"

Gravely, the copilot acknowledged that he did.

She went on, "Because of what he told me, and because of other incidents that have happened here on Babylon 5, I'm concerned about leaving Mr. Pal in the hands
of these particular Earthforce officers. Concerned about
his safety."

"I know! That's why we're protesting this!"

"Yes," Ivanova agreed, "but, because of other things
Mr. Pal told me, I think he wouldn't object, himself, to
having a thorough search made of the cargo. Would he?"
LeDuc's eyes widened in comprehension as she went on,
"Of course, it would be illegal for anyone else to break
open sealed shipping crates, but it's different in the case
of a search conducted by the proper authorities, right? In
that case, the broken seals would be accounted for."

"I see what you mean," LeDuc said slowly.

"So it's probable that if Mr. Pal were here, he
wouldn't actually object to this search."

"Yeah, I see what you mean."

"Now, this is the hard part," Ivanova went on. "If
I'm right, then the investigators who are holding Mr. Pal
want to examine this cargo very badly. I don't know
why, exactly, but I know they're looking for something
and they think it might be on this ship. It's a risk, but I'm
willing to bet that they want to search the ship even more
than they want to keep Mr. Pal for more questioning. The
question is—are you willing to take that risk?"

"What do you mean?"

"I mean that I'd like to offer Lieutenant Khatib over

there a deal. If he produces your pilot, free and un-harmed, you'll let him and a security detail onto the ship to search it. Uh, I'm assuming you don't have anything to hide?''

"No! We've got nothing to hide. This is a straight-up transport ship, we don't do smuggling deals on the side."

"Good, then."

"But what if he doesn't go for it?"

Ivanova grimaced. "That's the hard part. You take off."

"Without the pilot? No! We're not running out on Pal!"

"Listen," Ivanova urged him. "It's a bluff. I *think* Khatib will give in. If I'm right, they want something on this ship more than they want Pal. But you've got to convince them you mean it. You've got to be ready to go through with it. No backing down, not even at the last minute, not even at the jump gate. You go through."

"And what happens if you're wrong, Commander? What happens then? To Mr. Pal?"

Ivanova took a breath. "All right. Good question. In the first place, Captain Sheridan isn't available now, but when he knows what's going on, I'm sure he'll take steps to make sure Mr. Pal is safe. I guarantee, myself, to make every effort to see that he is."

"Can you guarantee it'll work?"

She shook her head. "No. But this is the alternative: to keep the standoff going, to wait until Captain Sheridan is finished mediating a dispute between a couple of alien races, however long that takes, to wait while he tries to negotiate with Commander Wallace, the officer who's holding Mr. Pal. It's a matter of time, don't you see? If we take the risk, we stand a chance of getting Pal out of there *now*. Not tomorrow, or the day after that."

"I see what you mean," LeDuc said again. "I got to talk to my crew."

He stepped back to the hatch, and there was a brief huddled discussion. Then LeDuc nodded to Ivanova. "Go for it, Commander. I'll go heat up the engines."

"Right." Back to Khatib. "This is the deal, Lieutenant."

"My orders don't include deals," Khatib said loftily.

"The deal is—you get in to inspect the ship, search the cargo, whatever you have in mind. As soon as the pilot is released."

Khatib scowled. "I don't have the authority to agree to that."

"Then why don't you get on the link to your boss and ask for the authority, Lieutenant? Because this is the rest of the deal. If you don't produce Mr. Pal, unharmed, in twenty minutes, you can forget about searching the cargo because the *Kobold* will be departing Babylon 5, on schedule."

"You can't do that!"

"I'm not doing anything, Lieutenant, I'm just a speaker for the *Kobold*'s crew. This is their offer."

"I'll revoke their clearance to depart!"

"No, you won't. You don't have the authority, Lieutenant Khatib. Commander Wallace doesn't have the authority. And I'll just bet that by the time you find somebody who does have the authority, the *Kobold* will already be through the jump gate and gone. So what's it going to be, Lieutenant? Do we negotiate, or do you stand here until that ship takes off?"

"You wouldn't dare."

Ivanova raised her eyebrows. "Me? I told you, Lieutenant, I'm just an intermediary here. Lieutenant, I'm not involved. This is the *Kobold* crew's decision."

"They wouldn't dare. We have their pilot."

Ivanova's brows lowered. "That wouldn't be a threat,

would it, Lieutenant Khatib? You wouldn't be planning to harm Mr. Pal?''

Glaring at her, Khatib stepped back and toggled on his link. She could hear him briefly describing the situation to Wallace, and at one point he raised his voice a little: "I *can't*! I've tried, but C&C won't take my orders! All right, you try it." Interested, she tried to hear more, but Khatib had lowered his voice again and all she could catch were snatches: "Twenty minutes . . . no, she won't take my orders either . . . I can't! . . . dozen people watching . . ."

"Commander Wallace is considering the matter," he finally snarled to Ivanova.

Her lips quirked in a half-grin, knowing that Commander Wallace was probably on the comm right now, trying to browbeat C&C into revoking the *Kobold*'s clearance. But she knew Torres had briefed the duty staff on the situation, and she didn't think they'd give in. They weren't eager to take Commander Wallace's orders. He hadn't endeared himself to Babylon 5 personnel during his stay on the station.

Ivanova waited. Torres waited. The security cordon, still alert for trouble, waited. The transport's crew continued their preparations for departure.

Several minutes later there was another heated exchange between Khatib and Wallace over the link. Khatib shut it off and glared again at Ivanova. "You say they agree to allow the search?"

"After Mr. Pal is safely onboard the ship." She added, "And they want Ensign Torres, as security officer in charge, to be present, to make sure there are no irregularities. And representatives of the crew, since they're legally responsible for the condition of the cargo. And the agent of the company insuring it."

"Agreed," Khatib snapped. He took a step toward the

cargo hatch, but Ivanova held up a hand to stop him. "*After* Mr. Pal is onboard."

"The commander is on his way."

"He'd better hurry," Ivanova remarked casually. "In . . . eleven minutes this bay will have to be cleared for takeoff. I don't think you want to be standing here waiting for him after the blast doors are sealed shut."

Khatib made an inarticulate sound of rage in the back of his throat. Ivanova grinned smugly back at him. Enjoying this.

But a few minutes later they could see Wallace approaching, accompanied by a security man and a smaller figure between them whose walk was slightly unsteady. Ivanova stepped up to take him from them and saw that Pal's expression was somewhat glazed, his pupils wider than they should have been. *Drugs,* she thought. Drugs and a telepath. They weren't leaving anything to chance, were they?

Wallace recognized her, drew back, made a gesture as if he were about to drag Pal back, but there were clearly too many people watching for him to pull out of the deal now. "Commander," he said coldly, "I didn't know you were involved in this. But I should have realized."

Ivanova smiled at him politely. "I'm simply here to speak for the *Kobold*'s crew. At their request. They were concerned about Mr. Pal." She grasped the pilot's hand reassuringly and led him toward the crew hatch, where his copilot was waiting.

"Are you all right?" she whispered urgently.

"Fine," he said, "but I talked, I told them things. They . . . gave me something."

"It's all right," she said, hoping it was. "I think he'll be fine once he sleeps it off," she told LeDuc, "but he's in no condition to be on the bridge."

Wallace and Khatib had been consulting. "Now I suppose there will be no objection to our searching the hold?'' Khatib asked.

"No objection," Ivanova agreed. "Ensign Torres, you'll be an official observer? And the crew representatives?" She had already called Espada, who was on her way down.

"Our purser, Mr. Kim. And Commander Ivanova."

"She's not a member of your crew!" Wallace objected.

"She's still our representative," LeDuc insisted. "And I will be present as well."

But Wallace didn't seem to care who else was in the hold as long as he got in to search it. Khatib, picking up a bag of equipment, followed him as the ship's purser solemnly unsealed the door of the hold.

Ivanova's first reaction on stepping into the space was —*How are they going to check out all this!* Hundreds of sealed cargo containers filled the hold. Cargo was usually shipped in containers—crates or canisters or drums—for ease of loading and unloading, for load stability. And for reasons of security, since most goods sent through space were valuable, most containers were sealed. But Wallace and Khatib seemed to know what they were doing. With their instruments, they scanned the crates, one by one, followed by the attentive purser, Mr. Kim, with his notebook listing each container's contents, owner, port of origin, and other pertinent data. Espada, at his side, compared her own records to his. Ivanova, Torres, and LeDuc trailed after them, as if they fully understood what was going on.

Wallace stopped, pointed to a particular crate, and said, "This one."

Kim stepped up and cracked the seal, making a note in his records. As Wallace and Khatib inspected the contents, Ivanova looked over her shoulder at Espada's display. *Container # 7794. Contents: morbidium ingots, approx 96% pure; property of AreTech Consolidated Mines; port of origin, Marsport . . .*

She exchanged glances with LeDuc, who held a whispered consultation with Kim. What did an ingot of pure morbidium look like, anyway? she wondered. How could you distinguish it from an ingot of, say, tin or iron?

Kim made more notes. Wallace and Khatib continued their search, looking dissatisfied. It took quite a while. It took a very long while. The cargo crew eventually had to be summoned with equipment to shift the crates. For each one they opened, Kim the purser made his own inspection, and another note in his records. LeDuc had a consultation with his bridge crew, relaying a query from Babylon 5 C&C. No, he didn't have any idea how long this would take, departure would have to be delayed indefinitely.

When he was done with the hold, Wallace insisted on searching the rest of the ship, including the bridge and crew quarters. But it was finally done, and Wallace, looking as if he'd just swallowed something bad, retreated from the *Kobold,* followed by an equally dissatisfied Khatib.

"Whatever it was, I don't think they found it," Torres remarked, sighing.

"No," Ivanova agreed thoughtfully. Whatever it was. But she had a good idea. Something that might have been passed on from J. D. Ortega, to her, to the transport pilot. Something Wallace had been terrorizing the station's population trying to find.

But it was LeDuc who looked the most relieved. "Now we can get out of this place! Not to accuse you of inhospitality, Commander. But I want the first slot for departure *off* Babylon 5!"

"I understand. But what about the cargo? Is it genuine?"

Kim looked up from his notebook. "Morbidium. Every crate they opened contained morbidium. Between ninety-four and ninety-eight percent pure metal. Every ingot I checked."

"Well," said Ivanova, slightly disappointed. "So much for that theory."

"Apparently so," Espada agreed. "I still want to thank you, Commander. Your insights have been very helpful."

"Then you'll continue to investigate?"

"Oh, yes."

"Tell Mr. Pal that I'm sorry for all his trouble," Ivanova said to LeDuc.

"I will. And thank you, Commander Ivanova. You got him out of there."

But not in time, Ivanova thought to herself as she left the ship with Espada. Whatever Pal knew, everything she'd told him—Wallace probably knew it all now.

Occupied with her thoughts, Ivanova heard a familiar voice call her name as she left the *Kobold*'s docking bay. She looked up. There was Captain Sheridan on the deck, in consultation with Ensign Torres.

She went over to them. "The ensign tells me that this situation is under control now. I'm glad to hear it," Sheridan said. "I understand you were of some assistance in the negotiations."

"I was just a speaker on behalf of the transport's crew," Ivanova said again. "It wasn't much trouble. Really."

CHAPTER 21

"So now we know," Ivanova admitted, setting down her tray on the table in the mess hall. "Damn, I was *so* sure that Pal had to be right! The insurance fraud scheme and everything! But the morbidium cargoes aren't fake, after all."

She went on glumly, "And now Wallace has pumped Pal full of drugs and found out about the whole thing."

"Except that what he found out is wrong," Garibaldi added.

"Some comfort." Ivanova looked at her breakfast with distaste. "And the captain is still convinced that whoever knocked you on the head was involved with the Free Mars movement?"

"Yeah." Garibaldi gingerly touched the healing contusion on his forehead. "What do you think"—he grinned—"does it give me that romantic, wounded look?"

"It'd help if you lost your appetite and went all pale and thin instead," she replied with a pointed look at the amount on his tray, rapidly being diminished.

"Forget it, then," Garibaldi said firmly. "I'm probably not the type, anyway."

Ivanova finished her own meal, looked up to see him assessing what was left, rolled her eyes. He was the incorrigible type, is what he was.

"Going back out on patrol?" he asked.

"Right." She sighed. "I know this raider thing was my idea, but if things ever get back to normal around here, you won't hear me complaining about lack of flight time for a while."

"It's good for you," he remarked. "Keeps your reflexes sharp. People won't sneak up on you, zap you with a shock stick. Especially not while you're off somewhere in space."

"I'll remember that," she said dryly. And left Garibaldi the tray.

He pulled it over to him, but once Ivanova had left the mess hall he showed no real interest in the fruit or biscuits she hadn't eaten. In fact, he pushed his own tray away. It was hard, he thought, having to live up to your image all the time, what people expected of you.

There across the room, at a table by herself, was Talia Winters sitting over a cup of some synthetic coffee-substitute. She looked thin. She ought to eat more, but he didn't know how to approach her to tell her so. Which was really dumb, he told himself, because she was a telepath, she'd *know* how he felt. Still, he didn't trust himself not to say some stupid thing.

Besides, he decided, abruptly getting to his feet, he had work to do. See what kind of a mess had piled up in the security office while he was flat on his back over in Medlab.

There was, as he'd suspected, a backlog of messages, memos, and reports waiting for him. Garibaldi sighed, sat down in front of the display, and called up the first ones. A few moments later his eyes met a familiar name on a list of persons detained within the last twenty-four hours. "Hey! What's Nick Patinos doing in the lockup?"

The computer obligingly replied, "Nick Patinos is being held for questioning."

"On whose orders, dammit?"

"The detention was ordered by Captain Sheridan."

He called over to the clerk on duty at the lockup, "Kennealy, what do you know about these arrests?"

The clerk looked up from his own display. "The captain ordered them. He said he was personally taking over the case while you were in Medlab.''

"What case?" Garibaldi demanded, exasperated. Who did Sheridan think he was, taking over his job? Maybe he'd like it on a permanent basis?

But to Kennealy it was self-evident. "Your case, Chief. The case of whoever zapped you with that shock stick. Assault on a station officer. The captain was really flamed about it, that's for sure.''

"I see." Garibaldi went back to sit at his console and try to think this through. The thing was, he'd meant what he'd told Sheridan about confidentiality. His sources. It was a basic thing, underlying all his work in security, all throughout his career. If your source couldn't trust you —trust you to go to the wall before you'd say a word to implicate him, to break his cover—then you didn't deserve his trust. It was that simple. He'd done a lot of things he wasn't proud of, but that wasn't one of them. He'd never given up the name of a contact.

And Nick—he'd gone back a long way with Nick Patinos. Would even call the man a friend, an old friend. Now what was Nick going to think of him? How could he ever ask Nick to trust him again?

And where had Sheridan gotten Nick's name from, anyway?

Kennealy didn't know. He'd just processed the order, then the record when the man was brought in. That was all. Why, was there a problem?

"No," Garibaldi said curtly.

Yes.

He was halfway ready to call up Sheridan and ask him what the hell he thought he was doing, detaining his contacts, violating their confidentiality, breaking his *word,* dammit. But he hesitated, because Sheridan wasn't his old friend Jeff Sinclair, and it might mean his job.

Sheridan was a different type of commander. Garibaldi remembered what the captain had said back in Medlab yesterday, that he wasn't going to tolerate assaults on his station's officers. It meant something to Sheridan—his officers, his people. Slowly, Garibaldi thought about the last time he'd been hospitalized, only then he was in a coma, dying—or so Doc had told him, later. And Sheridan had been the one who'd saved his life, donating his life-force to a man he'd never met but who was one of his officers. Sheridan had done that, the very first day he set foot on the station.

It was a somewhat subdued head of security who finally called up his commanding officer. "Captain, there are some names on the detention list that I didn't authorize. These are sources of mine. I promised to protect their identities."

Sheridan's expression on the screen was firm. "We had this discussion already, Mr. Garibaldi. I respect your position, but I want you to appreciate mine. I have reason to believe these individuals had knowledge of, or possibly participated in, a wanton assault on my head of security. I can't, I won't tolerate it. Now, if you don't want to conduct the investigation in this case, I can assign it to someone else. But I'm going to find these people, Garibaldi, and this station is going to see that they can't get away with this kind of act."

"Yes, sir, I do appreciate your position. I'd just like to know this, though—where did you get the names? How did you find these people? I didn't . . . in Medlab, with the drugs, I didn't say anything, did I?"

Sheridan paused, and a look of understanding crossed his face. "I see. No, you didn't give anything away. I asked some of your officers. I had them go through your files. Quite a few names surfaced, and we ran them through a computer analysis. And, Chief, I'm not charging them with anything, not yet. For the moment, they're just being held for questioning."

"I see." *Which one of my officers?* Garibaldi wondered. *Torres?*

"Will you be wanting me to assign this to someone else?" Sheridan asked. "It might be better, considering your involvement."

Garibaldi shook his head firmly. There was no more pain. "No, sir. I'll take care of it myself."

"That's your call."

"It's my job."

Garibaldi stared for a while at the blank screen. It occurred to him that maybe the captain was right and he was wrong. That if he'd been set up—but, hell, of course he'd been set up! Who else could have done it? He'd been asking people to trust him, but didn't that have to go both ways? Who'd betrayed whom?

He finally pulled the witness files from the computer and started to go through them all, one by one.

Nick Patinos gave a short, bitter laugh on seeing who'd just come into the lockup. "Well, Mike. I wondered when you'd be showing up. Hey, if you'd wanted to talk, you could have sent an invitation. Or, hell, I'd have invited you to my place."

"And how many guys with shock sticks waiting for me when I got there, Nick?"

Nick looked down, muttered, "You weren't supposed to get hurt. It was a warning. That's all."

Garibaldi said heatedly, "So you were in on it! You set me up!"

"I didn't—"

"*Dammit,* Nick! I thought you . . . I didn't think you'd—"

"*I didn't know!*" Nick shouted. Then, looking away from Garibaldi again, "I mean, I didn't know what was going to happen, what they were going to do." He looked up again to meet Garibaldi's accusing eyes. "I told them. I said, you weren't a part of it, you weren't working with those other bastards. But Earthforce is Earthforce, Mike. That's what it comes down to, doesn't it? And you're Earthforce.'' He shook his head. ''I told them, I didn't want to know about it, whatever they were going to do. Just to make sure you weren't hurt. And that's what they said, it was just to warn you off.''

Nick clenched his fist, then brought it down on the table between them. ''You couldn't just let it go! You had to keep coming around, coming back, asking more questions. Dammit, Mike, I tried to warn you, I told you what was going on. But you had to keep coming back!''

But Garibaldi's anger was equal to Nick's. ''Yeah, I had to keep coming back! That's my job! There's been at least two people murdered on the station and a lot of transport crews murdered out in space, there's a good officer with her career ruined, there's God-knows-what kind of conspiracies and collusions maybe all the way up to Earth Central. So, what, I'm supposed to forget about all this just because my good buddy Nick says people don't feel like talking about it? I'm in charge of security around here. I have responsibilities! I can't just forget about things like that.''

''No matter who it hurts?''

''You think people aren't being hurt now? You really believe these guys when they tell you nobody'll get hurt? Nick, I thought you had better sense than that!''

For a few moments they just stared at each other, the atmosphere between them heated by high emotions. Nick was the first to lower his eyes. Finally he said, ''Look, Mike, I don't know about the rest of it, but I am sorry it had to be you.'' A shorter pause. ''I hope it wasn't . . . you know . . .''

''I've had better experiences.'' Garibaldi struggled with himself—the friend versus the security officer. ''Oh, I guess I'll live.''

"For what it's worth," Nick's voice was earnest, "I really didn't know what they were going to do. I just hope you can believe that."

Garibaldi said nothing. He wasn't sure if he could or not. Maybe it'd take time.

He took a breath. "The thing is, Nick, I'm going to have to have their names."

Nick drew back, stiffened, and the friend became the prisoner, the man on the other side of the divide. "Nothing doing, Mike."

Garibaldi hadn't supposed he would say anything else. Still, he had to ask. "All right, then, Nick. But I can't let you go, at least not until this thing is over. Understand— it wasn't just me who was assaulted, Mike Garibaldi—it was the head of Babylon 5 security."

"I guess you've got to do your job," Nick said coldly.

"That's right. I do." Garibaldi turned to leave, then stopped. "I want you to know one thing, though. It wasn't my order to have you brought in. It wasn't me they got the names from. That's all I ask you to believe."

But his old friend Nick said nothing in reply, only turned his back.

The guy from the machine shop was named Williams, Val Williams.

Garibaldi had dug out the name himself, the way he'd question any witness—going through the computer, having it sort through the files for men of the approximate physical description of the man he'd met with in the machine shop. It hadn't even taken very long, less than an hour, until he recognized the guy's face out of the hundreds of faces the computer pulled up and displayed. He noted that Williams didn't work in the machine shop, after all.

Garibaldi figured it was better this way. He hadn't wanted to have to resort to forcing the name from Nick or anyone else who'd trusted him, once. Not unless he had to.

Yeah, it was better this way.

He closed down the computer search without flagging Williams's file, then sent out a team of security agents to bring the suspect in. But the man's assigned quarters were empty, and he hadn't been seen at his job since the meeting in the machine shop. Garibaldi wasn't surprised. He sent out an alert to check departing ships and went through the passenger lists of ships that had already left since the attack. Nothing. So, if he was lucky, Williams was probably still hiding on the station somewhere.

By this time, Ensign Torres had come on duty again. "It's good to see you back, Chief," she told Garibaldi, a bit uncertain in her manner.

"You did good, Torres," he reassured her. "You used your best judgment under the circumstances." He grinned. "You were probably even right."

She still seemed uncomfortable. "About those names. Of your contacts. Captain Sheridan ordered me to track them down."

"I understand." Garibaldi didn't blame Torres. He didn't even really blame Sheridan. They were only doing their jobs. Neither of them had made a promise to the men they'd brought in, and no one had breached a confidence.

It was true, his contacts would probably never believe it. Never trust him again. Nick Patinos, maybe—he might. One of these days. But at least Garibaldi knew he hadn't broken his word.

But it was done now, and Torres had done a good job getting all those names. He told her so, adding, "I hear you did great handling that incident down in the cargo bay, too. It could have turned into a riot."

"It was Commander Ivanova who settled it," she said, deprecating her own efforts.

"But you were in command," he insisted. "I'm going to make sure it goes into your file."

"Thanks, Chief," she said. "Um, what about my report? On Yang? Did you get a chance to read it?"

"Damn!" Garibaldi almost slapped his forehead, caught himself in time. With everything that had happened, he'd forgotten all about it. "Sorry, I was interrupted by a shock stick and it completely slipped my mind. So what did you find out?"

She shook her head. "Well, I checked with all the merchants, all the import-export agents. None of them had seen him. His credit record—nothing. Almost no transactions. He paid for his quarters, had his meals there. Whatever the man was doing on Babylon 5, he didn't leave a trail."

Garibaldi nodded. "Which tells us what we thought all along. This guy was no import-export merchant. If he was here on business, it was the kind of business he didn't want anyone to know about."

"The only thing I did find out is, he's not from Earth. We ran a routine identification request to try to find a next-of-kin, and they couldn't find a record of any Earth resident matching the ID we have for Yang."

"That helps, Torres, that helps a lot. Good work."

"So now what do we do?" Torres asked, more confidently now.

"I'm going to check out our Mr. Yang with Earthdome on Mars," he told her. "As for you, how'd you like to go track down Val Williams? Here's all the stuff we have on him. According to the records, he hasn't left Babylon 5."

"But according to Yang's records, he'd already left the station, when he was here, dead. I mean, we can't really trust the records, can we?"

"You're right," he agreed, adding to himself, *And who had access to the records, who could have changed them?* "So let's not count on them, but let's assume he's still here. Make sure everyone in Security sees Williams's picture, that they can identify him by sight, *not* just to rely on the ID scanner, that he might have a counterfeit identicard. Check all outbound passenger ships—and transports. You know what to do."

"Right, Chief. And thanks." She left, confident and eager to be on the hunt. Garibaldi envied her enthusiasm. But that was youth. He used to have that, too. When he was Torres's age. It was unsettling to realize the size of the gap that lay between his age and Torres. She was young enough to be his daughter—if he'd ever had one.

Dismissing *that* unwelcome thought, he got back to work, calling up a communications channel to Mars and contacting Earthdome to put in a request for all information on a Yang, Fengshi, known to have arrived from Marsport on the *Asimov* on 04/18/59. He advised them that possibly the information given on Yang's ID might be incorrect.

After that, he got down to all the work that had accumulated while he was laid up: the messages, memos, reports, the requests that needed his authorization, all the chicken tracks a bureaucracy ran on.

There was Torres's official report on Yang in the queue, and he read it through, just in case there might be one piece of data in there that might match up with some other piece and amount to a clue. There wasn't. The man had moved on Babylon 5 like a ghost, leaving no tracks to follow him by. Or rather, Garibaldi corrected himself, like a pro. And a pro, almost by definition, is working *for* someone. So who was it? Was he working for someone in Earth Alliance? The AreTech mining company? The Free Mars organization?

The call from Mars came in much sooner than he'd expected, interrupting this well-worn train of speculation. He answered, "Garibaldi here. What do you have for me?"

But the face on the screen didn't belong to a mere data clerk. This was an Earthforce major, security. "I'm sorry, Mr. Garibaldi," she said, "but your request for information has been denied. That file is classified."

"What?" He recalled himself, lowered his voice. "Excuse me, Major, but what do you mean? I'm head of security on Babylon 5, I have an ultraviolet clearance to see classified files."

The major shook her head. "As I said, I'm sorry, but not this file. It's classified ultraviolet eyes-only."

"Well, just whose eyes are we talking about, Major? This isn't just a casual request, you know. I'm conducting a murder investigation here. This Yang character was killed, chopped into little bits, and shoved into the recycling system. Now, I'd say that constitutes need-to-know, wouldn't you?"

The face on the screen looked grave, even concerned. "I don't know about that, Mr. Garibaldi. It sounds like you have a point. But I just can't release this information without authorization."

"Whose authorization? Who ordered this file classified, anyway?"

"I'm afraid that information is classified, too."

Garibaldi controlled himself. He didn't swear out loud. "Well, I'm putting in an official request for access to the files on Yang. Take it as far up as it has to go. This is a murder investigation and it may involve other illicit activity, too."

"I'll make that request, Mr. Garibaldi. Through the official channels. But until I receive authorization, there's nothing else I can do."

Garibaldi thought for a moment. If Ivanova was right, someone in Earthdome, someone most likely in

Earthforce security, was involved in a cover-up. Was this major part of it? Or was she just following orders?

"Can you tell me this: how long has that file been restricted? What's the date on that eyes-only classification? Or is that information restricted, too?"

A slight smile lit her face, and there was a look in her eye that Garibaldi liked. She checked something on a screen out of his sight. "No, that information is not classified, Mr. Garibaldi. The file was restricted as of 22:45 hours, 04/26/59, Earth standard time."

Garibaldi felt his heartbeat quicken. Yes! Yang's file had been restricted less than an hour after Wallace had declared in Medlab that he knew of no connection between that case and Ortega's. Commander Wallace had made one big mistake—and now he was trying to cover it up!

"Can you tell me," he asked the major on Mars, "whether the classification of this file was requested by a Commander Ian Wallace?"

Garibaldi wasn't a telepath, but he could see the major's eyes go to the unseen terminal and open in surprise. "I'm sorry, that information is classified."

Oh, he thought, *but you've given me the answer, anyway.* "That's all right, I understand. You've been very helpful, Major. I want to thank you for your cooperation."

"And good luck with your murder investigation, Mr. Garibaldi."

"You'll transmit that request?"

"Right away."

"Thanks again."

Garibaldi signed off, then leaned back in his chair to consider the implications of what he'd just found out. First, it was true—Wallace had lied about Yang, that he didn't know anything about the case. He'd lied, then immediately acted to cover it up. "That's your second mistake, Wallace," he said softly to himself. "You should have classified that file from the beginning."

So why hadn't he? Because a classified file was like a red flag, telling everyone who saw it that there were secrets inside. Wallace hadn't wanted anyone to know there was a secret about Fengshi Yang. As far as he figured, no one ever had to know Yang existed. But what he hadn't counted on was—someone finding the body.

Just one stroke of bad luck.

It would have certainly stayed a secret, otherwise. For one thing, Yang's secretive ways worked against him. There were only the bare records of his arrival and presence on Babylon 5. He might almost not have existed. Certainly, there was no reason for anyone to notice him missing, to report it to the authorities. Especially if his records said he'd left the station—who would doubt it? Who would suspect that someone would have altered those records?

There were still questions—too damn many questions. Who had Yang been working for? What had he known—or found out—or failed to find out?

Ivanova thought Yang must be an agent of the corrupt officials in Earthdome, but Garibaldi wasn't so sure. Yang had certainly killed Ortega, but who had killed Yang? Wallace was covering up evidence, but whose side was Wallace on? Captain Sheridan refused to believe in a conspiracy that went all the way up to the Joint Chiefs. And what was Garibaldi, as head of security, supposed to do about all this? Hand over his evidence to Wallace? Arrest him, for obstructing justice in the Yang case? What kind of proof did he have, what kind of evidence? Is it evidence when the suspect has the evidence classified?

Garibaldi knew when he was in over his head. Normally, he supposed, the thing to do would be to call Internal Investigations. Maybe, if he had a case. But he didn't have a case. He had part of a body, a file he couldn't access, and a big pile of suspicious circumstances, but that wasn't a case.

Yeah, he could just hear it, the kind of questions *they'd* ask him: "And how do you know Commander Wallace was lying, Mr. Garibaldi? Isn't it possible that he felt you simply weren't entitled to know the details of his investigation? How can you claim you know that the commander ordered Yang's file to be classified? Do you have clearance for that information? Don't you think you're overstepping the bounds of your authority, Mr. Garibaldi? Weren't you given explicit orders not to get involved in the Ortega case, Mr. Garibaldi?"

Yeah, he'd be the one ending up in the lockup, after all that.

So what could he do? Nothing? At least until he could find some proof. Do nothing, while Wallace still didn't have whatever he was looking for and in the meantime there'd been two deaths . . . at least two deaths . . .

Garibaldi tapped his link. "Torres, this is Garibaldi."

"Torres here."

"What's the status with Williams? Any fix on him yet?"

"Negative, we're still searching, but we haven't found anything yet. Um, we have had an encounter with the competition."

"Commander Wallace?"

"His aide, that Lieutenant Khatib."

"Keep looking, Torres," Garibaldi said grimly.

He shut down his console and got to his feet. A few moments later he was in the lockup, confronting Nick Patinos. "Look," he said urgently, "maybe you know something I don't, maybe you have reason to know that Val Williams is safe in hiding on Luna Colony and everything's fine. But security hasn't found him yet, and I'm starting to think about what happened to the last missing person we found on this station. At least, we found a piece of him. That's all that was left. One piece of him.

"So unless you're sure, Nick, unless you're very sure that Williams is safe and sound someplace where neither Wallace nor I can get at him, I strongly suggest you tell me where you think he is. Or the name of someone else who knows. Unless you'd rather see him melted down to sludge in the recycling system and coming back as breakfast in the mess hall. Because if I don't find him, I'm afraid someone else is going to. And if he does, I don't think anyone will ever see him again."

Nick paled. "I can't tell you that, Mike," he said finally, but it was obviously hard.

Garibaldi's jaw tightened. "If that's the way you want it. Your choice. I thought maybe you might have figured out the difference by now between me and that bastard Wallace—"

"Dammit . . ."

"Your choice."

"All right!" Nick held his head in his hands. Then he looked up at Garibaldi. "His real name is Nagy. Josef Nagy. He might try to get off the station using his own ID."

Garibaldi frowned. "What else?"

"That's it, Mike. All I know."

"The truth?"

Eyes met. "The truth."

Garibaldi nodded, toggled on his link. "Torres, this is Garibaldi—" Then he stopped himself, remembering Wallace, the possibility of a bug in communications. This was one name he couldn't afford to leak to the opposition. "I have some information for you. Hold on." He was going to have to run it down to her himself.

He looked at Nick. "You'd better hope we find him first."

CHAPTER 22

"Distress call coming in, Commander!"

"Get the coordinates, Alpha Two!" Ivanova ordered Mokena, picking up the call.

The signal came through unevenly. ". . . raiders . . . We're under attack! . . . help! Is anyone out there?"

Ivanova immediately transmitted, "Vessel under attack, this is Earthforce Commander Susan Ivanova. Give me your location."

"Earthforce? Is it Earthforce out there? We need help! Raiders attacking!"

"They must be having communications problems," Ivanova sent to Alpha Two. "Did you get that? Can you get a fix on them?" But what ship was it? They were out here to meet and escort the *Duster,* another ore carrier out of Marsport, but it wasn't scheduled to come through the jump gate for another hour.

To the ship under attack she sent again, "This is Earthforce. We're trying to help you! Transmit your coordinates!"

"I've got it, Alpha Leader! Coordinates Red 477 by 36 by 10."

"Heading to Red 36," she ordered her patrol. "Keep formation. Thrusters on max burn. We've got raiders out there. Be ready to open fire on my orders."

With a surge of power from her engines, Ivanova's Starfury shot forward, changing course for the location of the endangered ship. The ready indicators for her weapons array glowed red. As one, the other fighters in the patrol turned with her, maintaining the formation.

After a moment, she established clear communication with the ship and asked for their ID.

"This is Earth transport *Cyrus Mac,* out of Luna. We've got raiders on our tail! How soon can you get here, Earthforce?"

"We're on our way, *Cyrus Mac*! I estimate eighteen minutes. How many raiders? Can you hold them off? Is your ship crippled? Are you having communications problems?"

"Four . . . no, five of them! They're closing in fast! They're almost in range. Hurry, Earthforce, or we may not make it!"

Ivanova swore under her breath. She wondered if the raiders had made a mistake, pouncing on a ship that had come through the jump gate ahead of the *Duster.* Just how accurate was their information?

Or was this a diversion?

"Alpha Wing, stay alert!" she warned her patrol. "This could be another trick."

But the pilot or communications officer, whoever was transmitting from the *Cyrus Mac,* seemed on the verge of panic now. "They're firing! They're . . . we're hit! Earthforce, we're hit!"

With a firm grip on her fighter's controls, silently cursing the raiders, Ivanova pressed for more power, but the Starfury was already burning at the maximum. Damn! It was going to happen again. She knew it. They were going to be too late again. She *hated* this helplessness, knowing that only a few minutes could make the difference between saving a ship or losing it, and there was no way to get there any sooner.

Alpha Two reported, "Alpha Leader, we've lost communications with the transport."

But she'd already heard the channel go to background static. Damn!

They could only keep going, in the hope there might

be something left to save. In a few more minutes Ivanova picked up the image of the transport on her tactical screen. No raiders. They must have picked up the Starfuries on the way. "I've got the ship," she said. "Alpha Two, check the transport. The rest of you, wide scan, see if you can pick up the raiders."

"No sign of life, Commander," Alpha Two reported. "That ship is dead."

As the patrol came closer, the image of the transport clarified. Ivanova swore again. Wreckage. Crumpled, blasted, twisted metal. No sign of life, no survivors.

"Commander, I've picked up the raiders!" came a transmission from Alpha Six. "Heading 120 by 19."

Automatically, Ivanova started to give the order for pursuit. No, wait. Heading 120 by 19 was away from the jump point. This was another diversion. She was sure of it. Again, she scanned the wreckage of the dead ship. Dead and cold. It radiated no more warmth than the dark, empty space surrounding it. No telling how long it had been drifting here lifeless—days or months or maybe years. But it had been a lot longer than ten minutes.

"No pursuit," she ordered her patrol. "This is Alpha Leader, I repeat, no pursuit. It's another trick. This wreck is cold. We're heading back to the jump point."

After marking the wreck with a beacon for the salvage team, she spun her ship, and the Starfuries reversed direction, re-formed, and followed their commander toward the rendezvous with the *Duster*.

They knew we were going to be here, Ivanova thought to herself. The raiders had their diversion planned in advance, knowing exactly when we'd show up. It sure looked like their information was up-to-date.

Only the deception hadn't worked, and now it was too late for the raiders, for a change. But that was enough to give Ivanova an idea. The raiders weren't the only ones who could set a trap. "Alpha Two," she sent, "this is

Alpha Leader. Proceed to the vicinity of the jump gate
with Four and Five and meet up with the *Duster*. Alpha
Three and Six, you stay with me."

If this went the way she planned, then the raiders lurking near the jump point, ready to pounce on the *Duster*,
would think their deception had worked, that Ivanova had
split the patrol and sent half the Starfuries off in pursuit
of the attackers of the dead *Cyrus Mac*. She hoped it
would make them overconfident. She hoped she was
right.

She was using the jump gate itself as a shield, coming
around it from the other direction, hoping the residual
tachyon emissions would mask the presence of her fighters on the raider's tactical displays. She kept a channel
open to Alpha Two, but they maintained radio silence in
case the raiders were monitoring their communications
lines. So she heard: "I've spotted them, Alpha Two.
Raider ships! Must be, nine . . . ten of them!"

"Any sign of the transport yet?"

"Negative, Alpha Two."

"They're coming in! They're attacking!"

Ten of the raider ships against three Starfuries. The
odds just barely favored the raiders. But Ivanova was
about to change that. She led the rest of Alpha Wing into
the fight from around the other side of the jump gate,
coming in from the rear of the raiders, trapping the pirates between them. She and the two fighters on her
wings each took out one of the raiders before they had
time to react to the sudden appearance of another enemy
attacking, and now the odds that had prevailed just a few
minutes ago were reversed. One-on-one, the Starfuries
had the decisive edge.

The dogfight was a fast, furious action. It took quick
reflexes and a cool head to be a fighter pilot. Both sides
had computer-assisted targeting, but even so, with twelve

ships involved in the fight, there was always a chance for one to get flamed by friendly fire.

Several of the raiders spun around and tried to flee the action, but those were shot down almost instantly. The rest, seeing what chance they had, formed up and tried to defend themselves. A couple of them were good, Ivanova noted with that part of her brain that always remained cool and detached in a firefight.

But the rest of her was fully engaged in the combat mode. "On your tail, Four!" she shouted, and the raider ship fired, but Alpha Two took it out before it could take another shot. Alpha Six, on her wing, blasted another raider coming in from above. Space around them was filled with incandescent metallic gases and flying, glowing shards.

Then Ivanova saw two more of the raiders converging on Alpha Two. Alpha Four, his wingman, was engaged with another of the enemy, but Six fired, got in a strike that sent one ship spinning away. Two's weapons were still operational and he got in a shot that finished the raider off. But it was his last. The second raider, coming in on his other side, turned the Starfury into a glowing ball of death only seconds later.

Ivanova saw her wingman's ship explode, saw him die, and rage boiled up in her throat, a scream she couldn't release. She bore down on the raider with her weapons burning hot, fully charged. Six followed after to back her up, but Ivanova sent through clenched teeth, "He's *mine*!"

The raider fled, with nothing but black space ahead of him and Ivanova on his tail like divine vengeance. No matter which way he turned, twisted, ran, he couldn't shake her. The Starfury's thrusters were burning at max, closing the distance, and Ivanova counted down the seconds he had left to live. Her tactical display showed him in range, she locked on the target, fired, and scored a direct hit on the raider's right wing. Superheated plasma fused the discharge tubes, the wing buckled, crumpled, and the ship went spinning crazily, out of control.

"Got him!" Ivanova exulted in a fierce whisper, diving after her prey, heading in for the kill.

She had him in her sights again, her weapons locked on, her hand closed on the firing control, when she suddenly heard the signal for surrender coming from the raider's ship. "Eat plasma, you bastard!" she shouted back, and fired. But at the very last instant, she pulled her aim and the shot only grazed the tip of his other wing as she went streaking past, so close she had a clear sight of the ruined ship on visual. One wing was gone, the other twisted and half-melted away. It was completely helpless, unable to move under its own power or fire its weapons. Only the cockpit looked as if it might be intact. Maybe.

Ivanova circled back in a tight loop, cutting power to her thrusters. In the distance, Alpha Six had turned back to the fight, now that Ivanova had taken care of the enemy. She scanned the raider. The cockpit wasn't quite intact, after all. Atmosphere was boiling out of a crack. But there were life signs. The bastard was still alive. Still sending the surrender code. *Damn!*

Her guns were still hot. She wanted to fire. She wanted, very simply, to kill the bastard, to blast him into superheated steam. For vengeance, for the sake of all the dead ships, for the *Cassini,* for the cold wreck still drifting out there with the salvage beacon on it. And most of all for Lieutenant Gordon Mokena, her wingman. For the sake of Alpha Two.

There were no witnesses. No one would ever know.

She circled back again, almost drifting now, the damage to the raider ship stark and violent ahead of her. Scan showed the cockpit atmosphere almost dissipated, and as it came into view, she could see the raider himself, suited and helmeted. She wondered how much oxygen he had, how long he'd last if she fired up her engines, took off, and left him there alone to die.

But the surrender signal was still going. Then the raider opened his comm channel. "Well, Earthforce, what's it going to be?"

Ivanova swore again to herself and opened the channel. When she spoke, her voice was crisp, as if she were handling routine traffic in the Observation Dome back on Babylon 5. "This is Commander Susan Ivanova. You have five seconds to say why I shouldn't melt down what's left of your ship with you inside it."

"How about Earthforce regs, Commander? Like the one about not firing on a disarmed enemy who wants to surrender?"

"Those are the Articles of War. They apply to an honorable enemy, not a glob of scum like you." But she already knew she wasn't going to do it. Maybe no one would ever know—but she would, and she'd never forget it, either.

But she did, for her own satisfaction and to make sure all his weapons really were disabled, put one more shot on her lowest power setting through the remaining half of the wing. The wreck of the raider's ship lurched and spun in reaction, and over her comm channel Ivanova could hear his choked-off curse, then the gasping intake of his breath as he realized he was still alive.

"Hey . . . Commander. Look. Maybe we can make . . . a deal?"

Though Ivanova had no intention of firing again, she paused before answering. "What kind of a deal?"

A shaken laugh. "Hell, any kind of deal you want, Earthforce! You want to know where our base is?"

Contemptuously, "You'd sell out your own side?"

"Hey, like you say, I'm scum. They're all scum. What difference does it make to you, one piece of scum more or less?'' And when Ivanova didn't answer, ''So c'mon, what do you say, Earthforce?''

The tone of his voice was almost enough to make her regret her decision not to shoot. But this was an opportunity she hadn't looked for. Slowly, she replied, ''That'll do for a start. Then I want to know where you get your information about the transport schedules. How you know what ships are going to be coming through the jump gate and what they're carrying. Where the information originates, how you receive it, how the targets are picked—all of it.''

A pause. ''You don't think small, do you, Earthforce?''

''Well, c'mon,'' she mocked him, ''what'll it be?''

He exhaled in resignation. ''So what do you want to know first?''

CHAPTER 23

The first thing Garibaldi did after leaving Nick in the lockup was make sure the rest of security was notified about Josef Nagy's real identity. But he was interrupted by a call from Mars.

It was his security major from Earthdome, and her expression was very stiff, even grave. "Mr. Garibaldi, in response to the request that you made, I'm afraid the answer is 'No.'"

"Just like that, so fast? Just 'No'?"

"I relayed your request up to the highest levels. The information you want is restricted *to* the highest levels."

"By 'the highest levels' you mean . . ."

"The very highest levels. I'm sorry, Mr. Garibaldi."

Even the fact that the Joint Chiefs office itself had disapproved his request was classified. Garibaldi shook his head in disbelief. Maybe something was going on he had no idea about.

"I'd like to ask one more question, if I can?"

"Of course. If the information isn't classified," she replied with a faint return of her smile.

Garibaldi sighed. She had a sense of humor, his major on Mars. "I'd like any information you have on a Josef Nagy. May have been involved in the Free Mars movement. Age, oh, between twenty-five and thirty." He played a hunch. "He may have worked in the mining industry."

Out of his view, she checked her records. "Yes, we have a file on a Josef Nagy. Wanted on suspicion of membership in a terrorist group, wanted for sabotage, wanted for conspiracy to commit treason. Is this Nagy on Babylon 5?"

"We have no record of him on the station," Garibaldi didn't quite lie. That was according to the rules of this game. "His name was brought up in the course of an investigation into another matter. I figured I ought to check it out. Of course, without the file, I have no way of knowing if it's the same Josef Nagy. I don't have ID on him, just the name."

"I'll send you the file right away."

"Then this one isn't classified?"

She smiled. "As head security officer on Babylon 5, your clearance is sufficient. Is there any other way I can help you, Mr. Garibaldi?"

"No, that's it for today. Maybe we can talk again sometime, though. Thank you, Major."

The screen blanked to the BABCOM logo. A few moments later, the computer notified him, "Data file arriving, transmitted from Earthdome on Mars. The file is restricted, please input password."

He tapped out "bastard" on the keys of his console, having changed all his passwords since Wallace released the station's files.

"Access granted."

Immediately a man's image appeared on his data screen. It was Williams. That is, Williams was Nagy, all right, although the longer hair and mustache he'd worn on Mars made him look younger than the bitter, suspicious worker Garibaldi had interviewed in the machine shop.

He scrolled down the rest of the information and exclaimed aloud, "Yes!" A year ago, Nagy had been employed by AreTech Consolidated Mines as a data analyst. During last year's insurrection on Mars, there'd been a system crash which wiped out a number of the company's personnel records. Nagy was a prime suspect. An alert had gone out for his arrest, but he remained missing.

Garibaldi switched from Nagy's file to the list of scheduled departures from the station. The passenger liner *Heinlein* was scheduled to depart, but that was too obvious. He knew Torres would check it out, of course, anyway. Also departing: the Minbari ambassador. A Narn cargo ship. The *Redstone 4*, a supply transport heading back to Earth by way of Mars and Luna. The name struck him, made him think of Mars. He called up more data on the transport and hit it immediately. Red Stone Shipping, Inc. And the pilot, Edwin Cooper—from Mars Colony.

Garibaldi quickly got on the link to Torres. "The *Redstone 4*," he said, "have you checked it out?"

"Not yet. Departure isn't scheduled for another eight hours."

"I'm going down there. I'll meet you. I've got a feeling about this one."

"I'll be there."

They arrived at the loading dock while the *Redstone 4* was still taking on cargo. Garibaldi briefed Torres on the situation and then, accompanied by a team of security agents, they asked for permission to board the ship and speak to the pilot.

He met them on the bridge. Torres stepped forward. "Mr. Cooper, I'm Ensign Torres, Babylon 5 security, and we'd like to take a look through your ship. We have reason to believe there might be some contraband items on board."

Cooper scowled. "I hope this doesn't cause a delay, Ensign. As you can see, we're busy loading."

"I certainly hope it doesn't, Mr. Cooper. Now, if I could see your records, the bill of lading, customs statements . . ."

Garibaldi, standing back with the rest of the security

team, could observe Cooper while Torres went briefly through the records. The man looked itchy, nervous. Like he wanted them off the bridge. Torres logged off the ship's computer, having gone through the items mentioned plus the roster of the crew. She shook her head slightly. "Everything seems to be in order, Mr. Cooper. Now we'll just take a look around." But as a precaution against the pilot calling to warn Nagy—if Nagy were in fact on board—she left one security man on the bridge as a guard.

"He's not on the crew roster," she said, once they were off. "Under the name of either Williams or Nagy. But they could have just smuggled him on board. How should we do this?"

"Why don't you check the holds, and I'll take crew quarters," Garibaldi suggested.

The men and women who crewed the *Redstone 4* did not live in luxurious quarters, but they were better than some barracks Garibaldi had occupied during the varied course of his career. Bunks were fold-down, wardrobe space adequate, entertainment systems minimal. The rooms were all quiet, apparently empty, which was normal with cargo loading underway. All hands would be at work. All legitimate crew members, at least.

Garibaldi went up and down the corridors, checking each room with his scanner for life signs. One room, another, another. Then he was picking up something. Not from this room, but the one next door, marked Laundry. And with departure only a few hours away, this was definitely not the time for someone to be washing out his unmentionables.

Garibaldi took out his PPG, adjusted it to the lowest power setting. He didn't want to blast this guy Nagy, he wanted him alive for questioning. On the other hand, Nagy was probably desperate and might be armed. Garibaldi took a breath, then abruptly kicked open the door.

There was a gasp of breath, a movement in one corner, and Garibaldi had his gun trained on the man backed into it, partly hidden behind some bags of dirty clothes. "Hold it! This is Babylon 5 security! Come on out of there—slow."

The man in the corner froze for a few moments, as if Garibaldi might have not seen him, or might have meant someone else. Then he slowly straightened, and Garibaldi got a good look at his face. It was Williams, all right. Or rather, Josef Nagy. "Put your hands up," he ordered him. "Step out here."

Nagy did it, taking one step, then another into the center of the narrow laundry room. But Garibaldi saw his eyes darting wildly—to the PPG, to the corridor behind him. He was prepared for the desperate lunge, the last-ditch, futile attempt to break away. He sidestepped, turned, and met the onrushing fugitive with a fist in the gut. Nagy's breath exploded out of him. He folded up and collapsed onto the deck, where Garibaldi pinned him.

But the fight seemed to have gone out of Nagy. He'd taken his chance and lost it. Garibaldi opened his link. "Torres, this is Garibaldi. I've got him."

He pulled his prisoner to his feet. "Come on, Nagy, let's go have another little talk."

Torres and her men showed up when he was halfway down the corridor. "Should I take him to the lockup?" she asked.

But Garibaldi had been thinking about that, and other things, like classified files and who had access to them, even with new passwords. "No, I don't think so. I'll do it." He went on, looking hard at each one of them at a time, "Look, I know this is irregular, but I'd like this arrest kept quiet. No official file on it. No prisoner named Nagy in the lockup. I think you know why. Can I count on your cooperation?"

After a moment's hesitation, Torres said he could count on her, and the others agreed.

Garibaldi marched Nagy out with him through the *Redstone 4*'s cargo hatch, toward the lift tube. "You can't do this!" his prisoner protested in a low voice that lacked real conviction. "You can't get away with this!"

"Shut up," Garibaldi told him without rancor. "I'm doing this for your own good, whether you believe it or not."

Nagy clearly didn't believe it, but he shut up anyway and went without a struggle, the path of least resistance. He seemed completely defeated as Garibaldi brought him into an interrogation room and shoved him down into a chair, taking the seat opposite.

"All right. *Now* we're going to talk. For real this time."

Nagy said nothing, looking around warily, as if he were wondering when the instruments of persuasion, the drugs, the Psi Corps were all going to materialize.

Garibaldi knew he had to shock him into speech. "First of all, where's the real Val Williams? What'd you do with him—knock him over the head, take his ID?"

Nagy's head jerked up. "No! I mean, there is no real Williams. It's just a name. Made-up."

"Where'd you get the ID, then? From your terrorist pals in the Free Mars group?"

"That's a lie!"

"That was a *question*."

"Free Mars isn't a terrorist organization! I'm not a terrorist!"

"So what are you, Nagy? Why did you come to Babylon 5, anyway? What were you planning to do here? Sabotage? Blow up the station, maybe?"

"No! I'm a patriot! Only my homeworld is Mars, not Earth! Is that so hard to understand?"

"I don't get paid to understand. I get paid to enforce

the rules and stop trouble. Right now I'm getting paid to figure out why two men are dead here on this station. And at least one of them was a suspected terrorist from Mars. J. D. Ortega. Funny thing. He worked for the mines, too, just like you.''

Nagy shook his head.

"What does that mean?" Garibaldi prompted him.

"Ortega was no terrorist, either. He wasn't even part of the organization.''

"You knew Ortega?"

"Who he was. He worked for the company.''

"What company? AreTech?''

A nod.

"What did he do there? Wasn't he an engineer, something like that?''

"Metallurgist, I think. One of the guys in white coats, worked in the lab. I don't know exactly what he did, I was just a clerk. I kept the records.''

"Do you know why someone would charge him with being a terrorist?''

A shake of the head.

"Why someone was trying to kill him?''

"No. I don't know about any of that stuff. Look, when you worked for the company, you didn't want to know about anything that wasn't your business, all right? You didn't want to ask questions. There was always talk— about under-the-table deals, bribing the safety inspectors, closing down the whole mine. But if they found out about it . . .''

"Would that maybe be when a guy named Fengshi Yang would step in? Company enforcer? His job to keep the workers in line, stop the rumors? That kind of thing?''

A sullen nod.

"So if Ortega had gotten into trouble with AreTech, they might have sent somebody like Yang after him?''

Another reluctant nod.

Garibaldi pressed on, "So Ortega could have come to Babylon 5 because he was in trouble with the company, not because he was a terrorist."

"If they sent Yang after him, yeah."

"But you didn't think it was a good idea to tell me about any of this when we talked before in the machine shop, before you had me mugged. I suppose you knew there was a team of special investigators nosing around the station, probing into Ortega's death. But you talked to me. Why?"

"They took Sonia! And . . . I heard . . . that you weren't part of them. The ones who arrested her."

"So you decided to talk to me. But right after that you decided it was a real good idea to send a hit team of your friends out after me, to stuff me into that locker. Just like Yang did with Ortega's body. You knew about Yang, didn't you? You knew he killed Ortega."

A very slight nod.

"So the question is, who killed Yang? Was it you, Nagy?"

"No!" The prisoner's face paled with shock.

"Then who did? Someone else who worked for the company? Some more of your patriot friends from Mars? Did they kill the company enforcer, chop up his body, stuff him into the recyclers?"

"I don't know! I swear! I don't *know* who did it!" Now Nagy was volubly eager to talk, to deny it. "All anybody knew was, he was here on Babylon 5. He'd already killed one guy, no one knew who else he was after. Anybody could have done it!"

Garibaldi nodded in understanding. "So somebody figured they had to get rid of Yang. But I kept coming around, kept asking questions. Better get rid of me, too. Isn't that right?"

There was a slight new sheen of nervous sweat on

Nagy's forehead. "Like I said, some people said you weren't part of it. That you were . . . all right. But, then, you knew about Yang, about the mine . . ."

"Part of what?" Garibaldi asked.

"The whole thing! The company! Earthforce! All of you! You're all in it together! God knows what they've done with Sonia—"

"That's right. Your friend. From the assay office. The one they took away. Did she know about you? Your background?"

"No! God, I don't think so, I was careful. If she knew, I'd have been dragged in days ago. She . . ." Nagy dropped his head into his hands for a minute, then raised it, took a breath. "I never knew her on Mars. We only met after I got here and started to work. As far as she knew, I was Val Williams, from Earth, I was a clerk for a survey company."

"She never worked for AreTech?"

"No, she worked in the assay bureau. That's a government office."

"What about Ortega?" Garibaldi asked. "Do you know how he came onto Babylon 5? Did he have a fake identicard like you did? Under another name? Where do you think he might have gotten such a thing if he wasn't mixed up in the Free Mars organization?"

"I don't know." A pause. "Maybe. If he knew the right people."

"What right people?" But Garibaldi's link interrupted him. "Mr. Garibaldi, you're wanted at the Shuttle Bay. There's been another killing. It's Lieutenant Khatib."

Khatib? Murdered? As if things weren't already complicated enough!

Jumping up, he said, "I'll be right there." But he

paused, turned back to Nagy. "You're a lucky man, Nagy. He was out there looking for you, too. And, take my word for it, you're glad he didn't find you before I did."

CHAPTER 24

"Alpha Leader, this is Alpha Three. Are you all right out there?"

"Everything's under control, Alpha Three. I'm just stopping to pick up a piece of . . . salvage. What's the situation there?"

"Raiders are all scragged. Alpha Four sustained minor damage, but Moy is all right. And we've made contact with the *Duster*, we're going to rendezvous with her now." He gave the coordinates.

"I'll meet you there, Three."

Ivanova returned to her work, making the grapples fast between her ship and the raider. She meant to tow the crippled hulk over to the *Duster*, now that it had shown up, and transfer her prisoner to the transport for the trip back to Babylon 5. She was worried that her prisoner's sudden willingness to talk might take on less urgency, now that he was no longer at immediate risk of being hosed with charged plasma.

Not, she thought sourly, that he'd stopped talking yet.

"Say, Earthforce, how long's this little trip going to take? I haven't got all the oxygen in the universe, you know. Even scum like me needs to breathe. What are you going to do if I start to run short on air?"

"Watch you turn blue," Ivanova snapped, which she regretted a moment later. It only seemed to encourage him.

"Kinda hard to talk without air, Earthforce."

"Then why don't you start saving it?"

"I got a lot to say, you know. About our operations,

contacts. It'd be too bad if I ran out of breathing room before I got a chance to tell you all about it."

But when she no longer responded, the raider eventually went silent. In fact, he was quiet for so long that Ivanova finally started to worry: maybe it hadn't been a bluff, maybe he'd really run out of oxy. She ran a quick scan, saw he was still alive. And the *Duster* was just ahead now, just about ten minutes away.

"Alpha Three, this is Alpha Leader, how do things stand?"

"This is Alpha Three. The *Duster* has room in its shuttle bay, so we're stowing Alpha Four in there for the trip back."

"You say Moy is all right?"

"She's fine, Commander. But her ship's got one wing that doesn't look like it wants to take a lot of stress."

This suddenly appeared to Ivanova as a solution to her problem. "Do you think she's in shape to fly my ship home?"

"One minute, Alpha Leader, I'll check." A moment later, "She says no problem. Are you all right, Commander?"

"I'm fine. I just want to stay with my salvage on the way back to the station."

"We'll be expecting you, Alpha Leader."

A few minutes later, Ivanova cut thrusters and came in on a slow approach to the *Duster*, with the three intact Starfuries clustered around its bulk. The *Duster* was definitely in the supersized class of carriers.

She opened a channel to the transport's bridge. "This is Earthforce Commander Susan Ivanova, from Babylon 5. I'd like to speak to the pilot of the *Duster*."

"This is Bogdonovich, Senior Pilot. We were sure glad to see your reception committee."

"Glad to hear it, Mr. Bogdonovich. I understand you're taking one of our crippled ships onboard?"

"We've got plenty of room, Commander, it's no problem."

"Good. I'd like to know if you also have some kind of secure room onboard that I could use as a lockup."

Bogdonovich had obviously scanned the wreck of the raider ship she had in tow. "Prisoner, Commander?" he asked curiously.

"Let's say an item of salvage, Mr. Bogdonovich."

"If you say so. Sure, I have a place where you can stow your salvage. You can dock and bring it onboard through cargo hatch D."

"Good. And be careful loading it. I suspect it's still hazardous."

"I read you, Commander."

Ivanova opened the channel again to the raider ship. "This is Commander Ivanova. We're going to be bringing you onboard the transport shortly. This is just a reminder not to try anything. If you still want to keep on breathing."

"Whatever you say, Commander."

The raider's voice was a whisper now. Maybe he was really short of air. But Ivanova didn't waste time wondering about it. With practiced efficiency, she let loose the grapples to the raider and docked with the transport ship. She'd let the experienced crew handle the job of taking on the cargo. Before leaving her fighter, she took out her handgun and powered it on.

Moy was waiting, suited and helmeted, at the lock. "You're sure you're all right?" Ivanova wanted to know. "No problem with flying my ship back?"

"I'm fine, Commander. No problem at all."

The transport's crew had already gotten the hulk of the raider's ship onboard through a cargo hatch when Ivanova arrived. She noted with satisfaction that she wasn't the only one armed. The crew seemed to have a security officer, that was good. She nodded at him, and he came over, spoke to her through his helmet radio, since the cargo bay was still unpressurized. "I'm Massie, Commander. Anything I can do to help?"

"Thank you, Mr. Massie. Just keep an eye on him for now."

While they were securing the wreck of the raider's ship and closing up the cargo hatch, Ivanova spoke to her prisoner again. "All right, as soon as your ship is secure, you can climb on out of there. Just remember, everyone here has more than sufficient reason to want to blow you out of that cockpit."

There was no reply, but the canopy of the pirate ship slid open slowly. Ivanova watched with her PPG trained on the cockpit as a helmet emerged, then the rest of the suited figure. He hung for a moment at the edge of the canopy, hesitating, then jumped down. For a moment his knees didn't seem to be able to hold him, then he grabbed hold of the remains of a wing strut and pulled himself upright with one hand. As soon as he did, he unlatched his helmet and pulled it off, taking great gasps of air, despite the fact that Ivanova's indicator showed the air pressure in the hold wasn't quite completely equalized yet. So maybe he did almost run out of air, she thought. The business end of her PPG still didn't waver in its aim, even when she unlatched her own helmet, handing it over to a crew member. "Can you keep this for me?"

"Sure, Commander."

She stepped up to the raider, who saw her approaching, straightened up, and turned to her with a wan, bloody grin. "So you're Ivanova, huh? Hey, from what I'd heard around, I was figuring on an old ice-axe. I'm Zaccione, but everybody calls me Zack."

Ivanova had no trouble recognizing his type and dismissing it. "Are you in need of medical attention?"

He waved a hand nonchalantly. "Hell, no. Just a

scratch, like they say." But with his other hand, he was still clutching the base of the wing strut.

The transport's security officer had come up on the other side of the prisoner so they both had him under guard. "Commander Ivanova? What do you want done with him?"

"Does your ship have a medic?"

"Yes, we do."

"Good, we can get him patched up and scanned to make sure he has no hidden weapons."

"I have a scanner here with me." Massie ran the instrument up and down the raider's body. "Nope, he's clean."

"Good," Ivanova said again. To the prisoner, "Last chance. Do you want to see the medic, or not, before we talk?"

"If you insist."

Zaccione's injuries proved to be cracked ribs and a broken nose. "Clean him up," Ivanova ordered, "but don't be too generous with the painkillers. He's got a lot of talking to do and I don't want him nodding off."

"Thanks a lot," the raider said, wincing as Massie secured his wrists in restraints.

"Mr. Massie, I understand you have a secure room?"

"That's right."

"Let's go, then."

Massie was reluctant at first to leave her locked up alone with the raider, but he made no more objections after she told him the subject of the interrogation was classified and might in fact be dangerous to know.

"So now we're alone together, huh, Earthforce," Zaccione said, grinning up at her with a set of very white, even teeth.

"Let's get this clear, scumball," Ivanova said tightly. "You're facing a short walk out into some very cold vacuum as soon as we get back to Babylon 5. For a man who likes to breathe as much as you do, you're wasting a lot of air with this line of crap."

"I thought Earth Alliance law reserved the death penalty for treason and mutiny."

"You've attacked Earthforce ships, and that's treason enough in my book." Ivanova wasn't sure if this was so, but she managed to sound convincing anyway. She wasn't concerned with penalties at the moment, she was concerned with information.

"Whatever you say, Commander. So what is it you want to know?"

"How do you pick the particular transports you attack? Where do you get your information? Is it always morbidium?"

"You've been doing homework, Commander. Yeah, that's it."

"Why morbidium? Why not some other strategic metals?"

He started to shrug, then stopped himself. "I dunno. The deal is for morbidium, that's all. If there's something else shipped with it, that's dessert, right? Hey, it's all right with us. You know what that stuff's *worth*?"

"I have a rough idea, yes. So what do you pay for the information?"

"Used to be, we'd pay the fixed rate. You know, the official price. Lately, with the price going up, the price we get, they've been wanting more. Greedy bastards. They turn around and collect from the insurance, too."

"Just what greedy bastards are you talking about?"

"The mine."

"Your information comes directly from the mine?"

"Yeah, that's right."

"That's the mining corporation, the owners? Not just some clerk that you're dealing with?"

"Yeah, they're selling out their own cargoes. Don't ask me why."

"So they sell you the information at the fixed rate, then collect the insured value. And you get the rest of the profit?" Ivanova recalled Pal's suspicions. "Some people have wondered if maybe the cargoes are just slag— empty mass. That all this is just part of an insurance fraud scheme."

"Hey, Earthforce, this isn't what you'd call a low-risk enterprise, is it? We'll pay for the information, but the cargo has to be worth it. We're not going out after slag!"

"All right, let's get back to where you get the information. From the morbidium mines. Just one company, or all of them? Just who's passing it to you? I want names."

The raider wasn't grinning anymore. "Look, Commander, like you said, once you take me in, all I see waiting for me is an open air-lock and a lot of vacuum. If I tell you everything I know now, then what kind of a guarantee do I have?"

"The only thing I guarantee right now is that you'll keep breathing long enough to make it back to Babylon 5," Ivanova said grimly. "Then you won't have a choice whether to talk or not. There's a team of special investigators waiting for you. They'll suck every scrap of information out of your mind and leave it as empty as a broken eggshell. They'll throw what's left out the air-lock and you won't even be in there to know it."

The raider blinked at the threat. He searched her face —did she mean it?

Ivanova stared back. "Or you can talk to me now and have it on record."

"AreTech," he finally, reluctantly, said.

"The big mining company? They're the only one?"

"Right. The information comes from their main office on Mars. We have an agent there. He passes it on. We know where the cargo's routed, when it's scheduled to come through the jump gates, when we can hit them. It's real convenient. Or, at least, it used to be.''

Ivanova thought about what Espada, the insurance agent, had told her, about the shipments all being insured by different companies, to divert suspicion. "You never wondered why they were doing this?''

He shrugged, winced. "Uh, Commander, you know those painkillers the medic talked about?''

"Later," she said, pitiless.

"Look, all right. We're always on the lookout for data. Makes our job easier, you know what I mean? So, one day a while back, this guy makes contact with one of our agents. He says he's got information, routing details on a real valuable shipment of strategic metals. Are we interested? And the best thing is, he doesn't want anything for it. Just for us to hit the transports where and when he says.

"So, well, sure everyone automatically thinks this is some kind of trick, the guy's an Earthforce agent, you know? Too good to be true? But our guy checks him out, he's legitimate, works for the mining company and all that. Some of us decide, well, we'll check it out. The ship comes through, just like the guy said it would. We hit it, get the stuff, sell it, and suddenly this is looking like a good idea. So we're in business, we make a deal with the guy for regular information. It's worth what we pay for it. By now we're one of the major suppliers of weapons-grade morbidium in eight sectors.''

"Who do you sell to?''

"The highest bidder, who else?''

"Aliens? The Narn, maybe?''

"Hey, it's a free market! Not like Earth. Supply and demand, you know. Right now, demand is real high. We've got buyers for every shipment we take.''

"Why don't they just sell the morbidium on the black market themselves, then?''

"Don't ask me, Earthforce. Maybe it's the E A inspectors, the way they check each shipment, count every ingot before they seal it up. I don't know."

"Wouldn't it be easier to just bribe the officials? Would you know anything about that? Earthforce officers on the take? Covering this business up?"

"I've heard . . . maybe they've got somebody paid off, yeah. But I don't really know. What I've heard is, people around the mine who start asking questions don't last very long. You know what I mean?"

"I still want names. Does the name J. D. Ortega mean anything to you? Was he involved in any of this?"

"Never heard of him."

"How about Yang? Or Wallace?"

"Look, Commander, I said I don't know. Not any of those names. I'm not involved in that. I'm just a fighter pilot, just like you are, that's all."

Ivanova almost hit him. "Don't you *ever* say that," she said fiercely. "Don't you ever say that again."

"Whatever you say, Commander."

CHAPTER 25

Sheridan and Garibaldi waited, watching while the shuttle pilot brought in Khatib's body. On the other side of the bay were Wallace and Miyoshi, rigid, speaking to no one.

Under his breath, Garibaldi remarked, "Would you believe I didn't think this situation could possibly get any worse?"

Sheridan only looked angry and muttered something about not planning to tolerate any more murders on Babylon 5.

Garibaldi raised his eyebrows. "This one is going to be a lot of fun, I can tell you. Khatib was a real, real popular guy. I can't think of anyone on the station with more people who had reason to want to do him in. I guess I'm lucky I'm such a nice guy, or else I might have been out the air-lock instead of just shoved into that locker."

The shuttle door opened, and the pilot emerged, looking around for someone to help him bring out the body. Dr. Franklin and one of his medics were standing by, but Commander Wallace shoved them both out of the way.

Sheridan swore and moved to intervene, with Garibaldi following after.

"This man was my aide," Wallace was insisting with particular vehemence. "This murder is connected to my investigation and no one—"

"Commander Wallace!" Sheridan glared at him. "Are you a licensed medical examiner or forensic pathologist? If not, you *will* stand back and let Dr. Franklin take the remains to Medlab for a proper examination.

Whatever questions you have, I'm sure he can answer them.''

As Wallace sullenly moved back to let the medics at the body, Sheridan got a good look at it. Not a pleasant sight. The limbs were frozen into contorted, outflung positions, the jaw hung open as if Khatib was still screaming aloud when his murderers shoved him out the air-lock. But when Sheridan saw where Franklin's attention was focused, he doubted that Khatib had had a chance to scream at all. Dark-red crystalline blood had filled a distinct depression in the side of the dead man's skull. As they moved him, sparkling flakes of it fell from his hair onto the deck.

While the body was being transferred to Medlab, Wallace objected again to anyone but himself having access to the results of the examination. At that, Garibaldi protested, ''Hey, wait a minute! This is the third murder on this station in the last ten days! If that's not a matter for Babylon 5 security, I don't know what is!''

''I can't allow interference with my investigation! The information is restricted!''

Garibaldi snorted angrily. ''Just what is it you've got to hide, Wallace? You know, it's getting awfully suspicious when records and evidence start to disappear whenever you show up, or files are all of a sudden reclassified the minute somebody tries to take a look at them. Maybe we'd better check for blood on your hands, too, while we're at it.''

At that, Wallace went white with anger, but Captain Sheridan stepped between the two before they were at each other's throats again. ''No one is going to be interfering with the results of this examination. I want the truth out in the open for once.''

Wallace started to protest again, but a glance at the expression on Sheridan's face stopped him. He paused, pulled Miyoshi away from the rest, and gave her some orders in a low voice that Sheridan couldn't make out.

"All right, *Captain,* as you so often point out, you're in command of this station. At the moment."

Sheridan ignored the threat. He was heartily sick of Commander Wallace, his constant threats, his investigation, his disruption of the station. In fact, he briefly allowed the subversive thought: if anyone had to be put out the air-lock . . .

Garibaldi could tell that Dr. Franklin wasn't real happy at all the witnesses gathered around his examination table. "What is this, a medical-school class?"

It took a short while to restore the body from its flash-frozen state, during which Franklin made a number of superficial observations, something about whether Khatib had already been dead when they put him out into space. Wallace, Garibaldi noticed, kept having to avert his eyes from the corpse. Squeamish, he thought. Sheridan watched the proceedings without outward emotion. Garibaldi supposed that the captain had seen enough of the effects of decompression on human flesh during the Earth-Minbari war.

But his thoughts kept returning to the murders, the pattern of them—whether there was any pattern. Three bodies, he thought. If you're the killer, what do you do with them? One in a locker, one recycled, and one out the air-lock. Three different sets of killers? Or different circumstances?

Ortega had been killed by a pro. The deed had been premeditated, but rushed, and the body left as an example, if Nagy was right, to other employees who might dare defy the AreTech mining company. Yang's killer, on the other hand, had gone to a great deal of trouble to try to keep the body from being discovered.

And now Khatib. Again, this one had the look of a

rush job. The killer wasn't a pro, if Garibaldi knew anything about it. Just hit the guy over the head, dispose of the result any which way, as soon as you can. A human body floating outside a station like Babylon 5, with its heavy traffic load, wasn't likely to go overlooked for very long.

Garibaldi was distracted from this line of thought as Wallace got a call over his link. From Miyoshi, Garibaldi supposed. Whatever the news was, Wallace seemed agitated. He stepped back away from the examining table, all the way back to the door, where he continued the whispered exchange. Garibaldi wondered what was going on, but his attention was drawn back to the examining table when the medical tech picked up a laser and started to cut away the victim's clothes. Garibaldi took a step closer, picked up the pieces of Khatib's uniform and quickly ran his hands over the pockets, recognized the familiar shape of a hologram viewer card in one.

He glanced over in Wallace's direction again, but the investigator was still distracted. Good. He carefully shook the contents out of the pockets, to seal the items away in evidence bags. What was on the viewer? He turned it on and saw the familiar face of J. D. Ortega materialize. No surprise there. But there was more information on the viewer. He scrolled down, saw files appear, personnel files, clearly marked as the files of AreTech Consolidated Mines. But on the bottom? Whose signature was it? He turned up the resolution.

"Give me that!" Wallace reached to grab the viewer.

Garibaldi automatically pulled it away. "Watch it! This is evidence!"

"This information is classified!" Wallace screamed. "You have no authority to view that! Hand it over!"

"This is evidence," Garibaldi insisted again. "Evidence in a murder investigation. What happens if I hand it over? Does it just conveniently disappear? Will it ever show up in court? Or will the court ever be allowed to see it?''

"That's none of your concern, Garibaldi! This is *my* investigation—"

Garibaldi appealed directly to the commanding officer. "Captain, this evidence has a direct bearing on the Yang murder case. Which, if you remember, Commander Wallace and Lieutenant Khatib claimed to know nothing about. Well, this proves they lied. It may prove a lot more."

"All right, I'm taking custody of all this material," Sheridan said decisively. "Commander, if you want to appeal my decision, go right ahead. All the way to the Joint Chiefs. But I'm getting just a little bit tired of people getting killed every other day on this station and nobody admitting they know what's going on!"

"You'll be sorry," Wallace started to threaten, but his link interrupted him again.

"What?" he shouted. Then, lowering his voice only slightly, "Not right now, Sumiko! . . . What? Well, can't you handle it yourself? Get more security?"

"What about more security?" Garibaldi demanded, but just then his own link cut in.

"Mr. Garibaldi! Can you come up to Red Central right away? There's trouble here, a crowd of people—it looks like it might turn into a riot!"

"I'll be right there!" Garibaldi glanced at Sheridan, but the captain had heard. His expression was grim.

"Dr. Franklin, can you keep these items of evidence secure here in Medlab?" he asked.

"Completely secure," Franklin assured him.

"Then let's go," he told Garibaldi.

There was, indeed, a near-riot in progress by the time they came on the scene, both Garibaldi and Sheridan in black combat armor. Security agents had their shock sticks out and were using them where necessary. The crowd as far as Garibaldi could see amounted to about a hundred, all human, and as far as he could tell mostly station workers. And they were clearly worked up to a mad froth about something. Shouting, they surged forward in waves against the cordon of security agents, clashing, falling back to regroup and gather their fury for another advance. Things were being thrown, too—sections of grid panels wrenched off the walls, chairs, components of shattered comm screens.

Garibaldi grabbed the nearest security man he could reach. "What's the situation? Are any of them armed?" he shouted over the noise of the mob.

"No, sir, at least we don't think they have guns. But they've got pipes, conduit, tools—they're starting to tear things up, throw stuff."

At which point a metal shard came flying overhead, close enough that Sheridan swore out loud.

"Do you think we're getting it under control?" Garibaldi asked.

"No, sir, I wouldn't say so, not really. Orders are not to use guns, not unless it looks like somebody's going to get hurt. But if this keeps up—"

The agent broke off his remark and went after a pair of rioters who were trying to drag down another security man. Garibaldi and Sheridan ran after him, and the rioters retreated, yelling curses.

The two security agents returned together, breathing hard. The second one had a visible bruise discoloring the edge of a cheekbone. He recognized Sheridan and Garibaldi. "Getting mean out here, sir."

"What's this all about?" Sheridan demanded.

"Not quite sure, sir. They're demanding the prisoners be released, that's all I know."

"What prisoners?"

"I heard there was some kind of sweep, lots of arrests, bunch of people started to protest—it turned into this."

Sheridan shook his head. "There were no orders—"

But Garibaldi said curtly, "Wallace!"

"Damn!" Sheridan swore. He toggled his link. "This is Captain Sheridan, get me the senior security officer assigned to Commander Wallace."

"Contacting Lieutenant Kohler," the computer voice serenely replied.

Almost at the same time, "Kohler here," came through Sheridan's link.

"Lieutenant, what's going on? How'd this get started?"

"Sir, I got orders from Commander Wallace to bring in a long list of people. Suspects in the murder of Lieutenant Khatib. There was a confrontation. One group on the docks tried to keep us from taking a suspect out. That seems to be what started all this. I guess it must have moved up to Red."

"Lieutenant, you take no more orders from Commander Wallace, not unless *I* order it. Is that clear?"

"Yes, sir!"

"Damn!" Sheridan said again.

Garibaldi felt a twinge of alarm. He told Sheridan, having to raise his voice to be heard, "That may not be the only thing going on. I just arrested that guy who set me up to get zapped the other day. He admitted it. He's involved with the Free Mars movement somehow. I was just questioning him when the news came through about Khatib. Could be his arrest has something to do with all this, too. And those other people you had brought in for questioning."

"Well, it's time to get it stopped," Sheridan said decisively. He started to edge toward a more central location where he could be seen by the whole crowd, and Garibaldi went with him, shotgun position, trying to keep himself as much as possible between the station's commander and the furious mob.

It was hard going, ducking the thrown missiles that came flying from the hands of the angry rioters, but eventually they reached a place where Sheridan could swing up on a catwalk and be several feet above the heads of the surging throng. Unfortunately, it would also make him a target for every hand holding something to throw, or even a weapon. Garibaldi pulled the captain back. "Let me get their attention first."

He picked a convenient nearby power junction, aimed his gun, and the sudden blinding flare of sparks caused by the high-energy plasma burst did indeed get the instant attention of the mob.

Sheridan lost none of the opportunity, immediately climbing up to the catwalk and shouting, "I'm Captain John Sheridan, commander of Babylon 5! What the hell is this disturbance all about? If you people have a grievance, tell me about it! Now! So what's going on?"

Several dozen people began yelling all at once. Sheridan shook his head, waved for silence. After a few moments the voices quieted down and a couple of people stepped forward. "We want all the arrests stopped! All the prisoners released!"

Someone from farther back in the milling throng yelled, "Or else we take this station apart to get them out!"

Several dozen of the crowd cheered that remark, and Garibaldi took a firmer grip on his PPG.

"What prisoners? What arrests?" Sheridan demanded again. "You want me to release murderers, is that it? Traitors?"

"Not criminals! Innocent men and women!" There was even louder agreement with this statement, but a few voices also added, "Patriots! Not traitors!"

Garibaldi reached up to get Sheridan's attention.

"Nagy," he explained. "The guy I arrested, the guy with Free Mars. That's what he called himself, a patriot."

"This isn't getting us anywhere." Sheridan took a worried look at the restless mob. Raising his voice again, he said, "I want to meet with your representatives. Bring me a list of names. If innocent people have been arrested, I'll personally see that they're released."

There was a long moment as the speakers in the front of the crowd turned back to consult with the others. People were shoving forward to try to be heard, calling out names. Some were angrily demanding more concessions. One man yelled, "It's like a police state!" and that comment again was greeted with approving cheers.

Garibaldi tensed, and security agents braced themselves, but there was no new outbreak of violence. Sheridan got on his link and contacted Kohler again. "Lieutenant, meet me in briefing room three with that list of people you just arrested. And bring Commander Wallace with you!"

Four people stepped forward again, three men and a woman, and one of them said, "All right, Sheridan, we've got the names. Let's meet. Let's see what you do about this!"

A cordon of guards cleared the way to the briefing room, with the crowd surging behind them, willing for the moment to wait to see what came of the meeting. Garibaldi wondered how long their patience would last and hoped they could resolve the issue quickly.

The foremost spokesman was a man Garibaldi recognized as Hank Ndeme, proprietor of the largest food-service operation on Babylon 5, and a native of Mars. He got right to the point before Sheridan could say a word, holding out a notebook in his hand and shaking it in the faces of the Earthforce officers. "Here are the names!

I've got them all right here! Now let's see them released!"

"*If* they're innocent," Sheridan reminded him. "Let me inform you, in case you don't know it already, that there've been three murders on Babylon 5 in the last ten days, plus an assault on the station's chief security officer. If you think I'm going to tolerate that, you're going to find out otherwise."

"Is that any excuse for turning this whole station into a police state?" Ms. Connoly, the Dockworkers Union Rep, demanded, repeating the phrase. "Is that any reason to pull men and women out of their quarters, off their jobs?"

"I'm checking into that right now," Sheridan told her. "There may have been excesses. If so, they'll be rectified."

But Ndeme shook his head. "This has got to *stop*," he insisted. "Every man, woman, and child from Mars on this station is treated like a criminal, like a terrorist. What is it, a crime to be born on Mars? You come from Mars, you've got no rights? Is that how things are?"

"Not just from Mars," Connoly protested. "They took three people from my section, none of them ever set foot on Mars—"

Garibaldi interrupted, "Let's hear those names."

Ndeme activated the recorder. The first couple of names no one recognized; the third was "Val Williams."

Garibaldi said, "Val Williams is a pseudonym for Josef Nagy, who was taken into custody earlier today. Mr. Nagy has confessed to complicity in the attack on an Earthforce officer."

Ndeme seemed taken aback by this information, but only for an instant. "What about Allen Rodgers, then? Irene Hardesty? Nick Patinos?"

"None of these people is currently being charged with

any crime. They were taken in for questioning in the case of the assault on Mr. Garibaldi," Sheridan said.

"Taken in for questioning, under arrest—what's the difference?" Ndeme demanded. "All we know is, security comes and drags them away to the lockup. You ask why, and no one gives you any information, everything is classified, and then they start to ask: What connection do *you* have to the suspect, anyway?"

Sheridan and Garibaldi looked at each other, both thinking the same thing: *Wallace.*

Sheridan looked irritably at his link, but just then the briefing room door opened and Lieutenant Kohler came in, looking agitated and slightly the worse for wear. With him was a hostile and truculent Lieutenant Miyoshi. "Sorry, sir, I couldn't reach the commander. I did bring the lieutenant, though."

Sheridan's jaw tightened. "C&C, this is Captain Sheridan. I want Commander Wallace to contact me *now,* and that's an order!" To Miyoshi, he said, "Where's your superior, Lieutenant?"

Defiantly, "The commander doesn't want to be disturbed!"

"Lieutenant Miyoshi, you *will* get on your link and contact Commander Wallace."

"You don't have the authority—"

"Or I'll have you under arrest for insubordination and refusal to obey a direct order."

Miyoshi, glaring at Sheridan, toggled her link. "Commander, this is Miyoshi. Captain Sheridan has ordered me to call you. Are you there, Commander?" She looked up from her wrist with a smug and bitter expression of triumph. "He doesn't answer."

"You'd better hope it's not because someone shoved him out an air-lock," Garibaldi said uncharitably.

But Sheridan decided to give up on Wallace for the

moment. He asked Kohler, instead, "Do you have that list of names?"

"Yes, sir." He took out a data crystal, handed it to Sheridan, ignoring Miyoshi's shrill protest: "You can't do that! Those names, all that information is classified!"

"To hell with that!" Sheridan said decisively, inserting the crystal into the reader. The list of names appeared on the screen, and Ndeme and the other representatives crowded around it, saying, "Yes! That's him! There they are!"

There were at least fifty names. "These were all arrested in connection with Lieutenant Khatib's murder?" Sheridan asked Kohler.

"Well, no, sir. That's just the list of suspects. We didn't bring all of them in yet. The disturbance broke out—"

But Sheridan had already found the second list, the names of people actually in custody. "There'll be no more arrests," he reminded Kohler, and Miyoshi as well. "Not without my express order. No more people dragged in for questioning without my authorization."

"I understand, sir," said Kohler. Miyoshi said nothing.

Sheridan went back to the first list, muttered to himself, "This is too much."

Garibaldi added, "If you wanted to bring in everyone on this station who might have wanted to shove Khatib through an air-lock, you couldn't hold them all in the main docking bay."

"All right," said Sheridan. "Lieutenant Kohler, I'm ordering every person on that list to be released, immediately. Monitor their whereabouts, but let them go." To Miyoshi, anticipating her protest, "If Commander Wallace can show any cause to connect them with Khatib's murder or any other crime, we'll pick them up again."

"I think, with Nagy in custody, we can release these

others," Garibaldi added, meaning Patinos, Hardesty, and the rest brought in for questioning about his assault.

The civilian representatives, skeptical, were still going through their list, comparing them with the names on the screen. "There's still more," Ndeme insisted. "More names aren't on that list." He named some of them. Connoly added several more.

Sheridan took a breath. "I have to explain something. Commander Wallace and his aides, from Earth Central, have been conducting an independent investigation into a terrorist incident which occurred on Babylon 5. The specific details are classified, but I know that they include at least one murder. You understand, the commander is operating directly under the authority of the Earth Central. If Commander Wallace has authorized arrests, I don't have direct knowledge of them. All I can promise you, and I *do* promise you, is that I'll do whatever I can to find out what's happened to these people.

"But I warn you, I'm not about to let the murderers of an Earthforce officer get off free. This crime will be investigated and the guilty parties will be punished according to the law. I hope that's clear."

The representatives consulted with each other. Finally, "I guess that'll do, Captain," Ndeme said.

"*If* the rest of these people are released," Connoly added.

"They'll all be released unless we find specific, concrete reason to hold them," Sheridan promised. "And there'll be no repetition of today's incident. All arrests in connection with this investigation will have to be authorized by me." He fixed Miyoshi with a hard stare. "Do you understand me, Lieutenant?"

"I'll inform Commander Wallace," she said stiffly.

"Mr. Garibaldi, will you take those names?" Sheridan ordered.

In a few moments more it was done, the lists of names

recorded and cross-checked, everyone but Miyoshi agreeing that they were satisfied for the moment.

As the civilian representatives left the briefing room, Garibaldi held Sheridan back for a moment. "Sir, you're taking quite a risk, aren't you? Wallace is bound to try to take your head for it."

"I did what I had to in an emergency," Sheridan insisted. "To disperse a riot. This damned witch-hunt of his is disrupting the entire station, interfering with normal operations. There's got to be a limit."

"Well, I have some information that I think will help." He explained, "I just found some of this out. Anyway, you remember, when we found Yang's . . . remains, that Wallace said he knew nothing about the case? And I said he was lying? Well, it seems that Yang was an enforcer from a company on Mars, looking for J. D. Ortega. In fact, the evidence points to Yang as the one who killed him."

Garibaldi took a breath. "Just now, when I was going through Khatib's uniform, I found a holo card with Ortega's personnel file, taken from the company he and Yang both worked for. And the signature authorizing the transfer of the file was *Fengshi Yang*." A pause. "There's only one way Khatib could have come into possession of that card."

"So Yang killed Ortega, then Khatib . . ."

"Killed Yang. I'd put my money on him, anyway. And Wallace knew about it, at the very least. That's why he lied, so we wouldn't connect him with the murder."

"So that's murder and complicity, and concealment of the crime," Sheridan said. "But is it proof?"

"We'll have proof for sure if we find Yang's prints or other traces of him on that card, as soon as we can do a forensic scan . . ." He stopped as the thought occurred to him, only an instant before it occurred to Sheridan, too: the evidence implicating Wallace, still in Medlab.

Where they'd left Wallace. And Wallace, nowhere to be found.

Garibaldi had his link on first. "Dr. Franklin! This is Garibaldi! It's an emergency!"

"This is Franklin, what is it, Garibaldi?"

"The evidence! Khatib's effects! Are they still secure? Listen, whatever you do, don't let Commander Wallace—"

"You're too late, Garibaldi, he was already here."

Only the tone of amusement in Franklin's voice kept Garibaldi from cursing out loud. "And the evidence? Is it safe?"

"Come and see for yourself."

"I figured it must be important, whatever it was, the way you and Wallace were fighting over it," Franklin was saying. "So I put it in the most secure place around here, the biohazard lab. Not too long after you left, Wallace pulled out a gun and demanded I turn over the evidence. He said he was the only one authorized to have access to it. Well, I don't argue with a gun in my face, so I opened the lab and let him in."

Franklin was grinning. Neither Sheridan nor Garibaldi quite got the joke. "You might remember, I just recently upgraded the security for the biohazard lab."

"Yeah," said Garibaldi, "I remember you said something about adding more fail-safes."

Franklin nodded. "Now there are two sealed air-locks, each one leading into the next compartment. Unless you activate the override sequence, the locks don't open until the person in the chamber has undergone a prescribed decontamination procedure and put on an environment suit. And if someone doesn't wait for the procedure and tries to force the lock . . ."

Now Garibaldi was grinning. "And you didn't hit the override switch when you sent him in there, did you?"

Franklin looked pleased with himself. "I don't much like it when people force their way into Medlab and wave guns in my face, no."

The air-lock door with the biohazard warning was clear, and Sheridan looked through, then Garibaldi. Commander Wallace lay unconscious on the floor. The inner seal of the air-lock showed signs that it had taken and withstood a direct burst from a PPG.

"That's one seriously sealed lock you've got there, Doc," Garibaldi commented.

"Biohazard contamination is a serious potential problem on a space station," Franklin replied in a humorless tone of voice. "The knock-out gas is released automatically when someone tries to force the seal. And that's the outer compartment. If someone tries to leave the inner chamber without going through decontamination, the gas that's released is lethal."

Garibaldi gave him a look of respect. "And the evidence bags are in there?"

Franklin nodded, stepped to a console, and input a command. "Of course, with the system deactivated, there's no risk. Do you want to go retrieve the evidence?"

Garibaldi hesitated. "You wouldn't want to go first? Just in case?"

CHAPTER 26

"Commander Ivanova, we're cleared for docking at Babylon 5. ETA twenty minutes."

"Thank you, Mr. Bogdonovich. Could you get me a clear channel to the station?"

"Here you are, Commander."

Ivanova was on the *Duster*'s bridge, her prisoner under guard back in the ship's small medlab. When the channel opened she said, "This is Commander Ivanova, could you put me through to Mr. Garibaldi?"

But C&C replied, "I'm sorry, Commander, but Mr. Garibaldi isn't available at the moment. There's a disturbance on the station."

Ivanova swore to herself in Russian.

"What was that, Commander?"

"Never mind. Can you contact me with someone in security, then? Ensign Torres, possibly?"

"I'm sorry, Commander, but there's really no one available in security right now."

"How big of a riot is it?"

"It's sort of a big one, Commander, from what I hear. Unless you have an emergency—"

"Not an emergency, exactly, no," Ivanova admitted. "But it is important. I suppose the captain is unavailable, too?"

"Sorry, Commander."

"Well, please have Mr. Garibaldi contact me onboard the *Duster* as soon as he's free."

"Trouble, Commander?" the transport's copilot asked.

"Some trouble on the station, it looks like. I don't have the details. A disturbance of some kind."

"I hope it doesn't mess up our docking."

"I doubt it. They wouldn't have cleared you if there was trouble in the docking bays." She thought a moment. "Could I borrow your guard after the ship docks? Massie, that's his name, isn't it? I'd like some more security when I take the prisoner onto the station, especially if there's trouble going on."

"Duke Massie, sure. Go right ahead and borrow him, Commander. If it weren't for you and your fighter squad, we probably wouldn't be docking now or anytime."

Things got busy then on the bridge as the crew prepared for docking. It was no simple maneuver with a ship as large as the *Duster,* and for a while Ivanova watched Bogdonovich's work on the bridge with professional interest. But halfway through the process she left to take charge again of her prisoner.

The raider didn't look so very dangerous in the custody of Massie, whose size had probably been one important qualification for his job. Zaccione wasn't so subdued, however, that he couldn't look up when Ivanova came into the room. "Hey, Earthforce, you're back! Missed me, did you?"

"Shut up, slimeball," said the guard.

Ivanova ignored both of them, saying to Massie, "I'd like you to help me take the prisoner to the lockup after we've docked. There's a disturbance on the station, and no security available."

"Sure, Commander, be glad to. He won't give you any trouble while I'm along."

"Thank you," she said uncomfortably, a little stiffly, while the raider grinned.

Ivanova uncharitably observed that his swollen, broken nose rather negated the intended effect of his boyish charm. She counted the minutes until the transport was docked and she could get rid of both prisoner and guard. She stood quickly when the announcement came over the comm system: *Docking procedures completed. Passengers may begin disembarking now.*

"That means us," she said briskly. "Let's go."

"Let's go," Massie repeated to the raider, gesturing with his weapon.

Zaccione got more stiffly to his feet. "Whatever you say."

The *Duster* did in fact carry a few passengers in addition to freight. Ivanova encountered them on the way to the boarding hatch. When the civilians saw the armed Earthforce officer, the massive armed guard, and the prisoner between them, they quickly stepped back to give them plenty of clearance.

The Babylon 5 customs guard also raised her eyebrows at the sight of them. "Welcome back, Commander." She looked at the prisoner, the guard.

"Nothing to declare, Fitch," Ivanova said briskly. "Just a worthless piece of salvage. How are things on the station now?"

"Settling down. Cleaning up to do yet."

"Thanks." Ivanova frowned, wondering why Garibaldi hadn't contacted her if the disturbance was over. Had he gotten her message?

Once they got to the lift tube, she raised her link, not taking her eyes from her prisoner. "Garibaldi, this is Ivanova. Are things under control?"

"Ivanova! You're back!"

"Can you meet me in Security Central? At the lockup? I think you'll want to see what I brought back."

"I'm there now. I think you'll want to see what I've got, too."

She frowned, recognizing the amused tone in Garibaldi's voice and wondering what surprise she had waiting for her this time.

Getting off the tube at Red level, she was shocked to see the condition in which the riot had left the place. Wall panels had been battered, even quite a few of them ripped off. Lights were smashed, equipment broken, and debris littered the floor. A maintenance engineer was up on a scaffold doing repairs to a power junction that looked as if it had been blasted with fire from a PPG. Which, knowing Garibaldi, Ivanova figured it probably had.

The raider emitted a low whistle. "Some wild parties you guys must have around here, Earthforce."

Ivanova gritted her teeth. Without comment, she led the way to Security Central, back to the lockup area, where both Garibaldi and Sheridan were waiting for her. "Captain," she said in slight surprise. Then, gesturing at Zaccione, "Garibaldi, will you please have someone take this off my hands? Mr. Massie, thank you for your assistance."

A guard came to lead the raider away, but Zaccione turned to call back, "It's been fun, Earthforce!"

Garibaldi rolled his eyes back. "Who's that?"

Ivanova exhaled in relief. "One of the raiders who hit us out there. I managed to run him down and persuade him to surrender." Then, turning back to Sheridan and straightening to attention, "Sorry, sir. Mission was completed successfully. Transport safely escorted to dock. Nine raider ships shot down, one captured. But we lost Lieutenant Mokena."

Captain Sheridan's face seemed to tremble for an instant, before his expression set. He'd heard those words too many times, too many men and women under his command gone to their deaths. "Any other casualties?" he asked at last.

"No, sir, just slight damage to Alpha Four. Moy brought in my ship, and I came back in the transport with the prisoner."

The dead pilot's memory hovered like a ghostly presence among them, reducing speech to set formulas. Finally Garibaldi asked, "And your prisoner? Sorry, I got your message, but I didn't have time to contact you before this. We had a few problems on the station."

"So I saw," she said dryly. But then she recalled a little of the excitement of finding out what Zaccione knew. "The prisoner, right. I got him to talk. He knows *all* about the morbidium deal! It's a company called AreTech behind it."

"AreTech Consolidated Mines?" Garibaldi asked with great interest.

"They pass the routing information on to the raiders. It's a scheme to sell morbidium on the black market. I'm sure there are Earth Alliance officials involved, too. To keep the whole dirty mess quiet."

"And this guy knows about it?"

"He knows a lot. More than he's already said, I'll bet on it."

"So that's what it was all about," Sheridan said, shaking his head.

"And that must have been what Ortega knew, the reason they wanted him killed," Garibaldi added.

Ivanova looked at him. "Ortega? You found a connection?"

"Oh, I forgot, you don't know. J. D. Ortega worked for AreTech mines. The guy who killed him, Yang, worked as an enforcer for the mining company."

"That's what Zaccione said! People who asked too many questions about the mining operations would turn up missing."

"Yeah, that sounds like Yang, all right," Garibaldi agreed.

"So that's it! That was the information they were after!" Ivanova's excitement heated with hope. They had the answer! Finally!

"And then Wallace's gang came onto the station to find out what Ortega knew, who he'd passed the information on to. They found out about Yang, took care of him—"

"Commander Wallace killed Yang?"

"Actually, it was probably Khatib, if you ask me. At any rate, we found evidence decisively linking Khatib to Yang's death."

"Has he confessed?" Ivanova asked doubtfully.

"He can't. He's dead," Garibaldi said.

"Khatib is dead?" Ivanova shook her head. "Wait a minute. Just what exactly has been going on around here while I was gone?"

Garibaldi grinned. "It all started when I got a lead on that guy who set me up to get zapped. I put him under arrest—he has an interesting story to tell, too, by the way —and I tried to keep it quiet, but apparently word got out. Some of Nagy's Free Mars pals panicked. They must have figured somebody talked and they were next to be arrested. They killed Khatib—I guess they didn't like him as much as me—and shoved his body out the airlock. We retrieved the body, took it to Medlab, and that's where we found the evidence linking him to Yang's murder."

"That's all?" Ivanova asked, eyebrows raised.

"Not quite. So when Wallace found out Khatib was dead, he went a little unhinged. He ordered a general sweep, started to pull in people from all over the station —people from Mars, people who'd worked with Nagy, people who had any connection to mining. And that was just the last straw. People had just had enough of the arrests. Somebody tried to intervene, it turned into a fight, the fight turned into a riot.

"And while we were all busy trying to put out the flames, Wallace sneaks back into Medlab to try to steal the evidence linking Khatib to Yang."

"And did he?" she asked, ready to believe anything by this time.

Garibaldi's grin widened. "Nope. But he did manage to give us sufficient cause to charge him with complicity in Yang's murder. After the fact at the least."

Ivanova slowly understood. "You mean—"

"That's right. Wallace and his little mouthpiece Miyoshi are locked up right down the hall from your pirate."

CHAPTER 27

The raider wasn't cooperating. He wasn't joking anymore, either, at least.

"He insists on seeing the Ombunds," Sheridan told Ivanova. "Says he's not saying a word unless he does. Says he's got the right."

"He has the nerve to talk about *rights* . . ." she fumed.

"Well, he does," Sheridan told her. "And the fact is, he doesn't have to talk at all, if it comes to that. If we want his testimony, that's how we're going to have to play it."

"Put him out on the other side of the air-lock, see how long it takes him to decide to talk," Ivanova said stubbornly. "I've got it all on record, what he told me on the transport."

"That's another point," Sheridan said firmly. "It could be argued—and when he goes to trial and·has a lawyer it probably *will* be argued—that everything he said at the time was coerced. That you threatened him. Now, I understand how it was—Mokena getting killed, the heat of combat. You got carried away. But if we want his testimony to hold up this time, we've got to do it by the book."

"So he gets to see the Ombunds. To cut a deal." Ivanova was disgusted.

"We need what he has to say," Garibaldi said, looking up from the display where he was going over the raider's records. "We're all pretty far out on a limb here if Earth Central wants to start sawing. J. D. Ortega still officially has the status of a wanted terrorist, and you're still under suspicion as his associate. We have to prove those charges were false, that Earthforce officials on Mars were corrupt, that Wallace was engaging in a cover-up, not a legitimate investigation.''

''Or else we're in for a long, hard fall,'' Ivanova said under her breath, reverting to pessimism.

Communications broke in. ''Captain Sheridan, there's a Gold level transmission for you, from Earth. Admiral Wilson.''

Oh-oh, Garibaldi's expression said, and Ivanova nodded agreement as they both stood to leave the briefing room and give the captain privacy to take the call.

Sheridan faced the comm screen alone, like a man facing an execution detail. He straightened his shoulders, said, ''Put the admiral through.''

Wilson's face was high-colored with agitation. ''You've really done it this time, Sheridan. You had your orders. *Explicit* orders. You were warned. *Not* to interfere with Commander Wallace's investigation in *any way.* I thought I made myself clear. You've exceeded your authority this time, Sheridan.''

''With all due respect, sir, I believe I have not. I believe that my actions were justified. Sir.''

''*Arresting* the investigating officer? For murder? For conspiracy?''

''Sir, if my authority in commanding this station does not include the authority to place a murder suspect under arrest, given adequate cause, then I hereby tender my resignation, immediately.''

''Now, you just hold it, Sheridan. What are you talking about?''

''Sir, we have proof that Commander Wallace's aide, Lieutenant Khatib, murdered a man named Fengshi Yang. We have additional evidence that the commander knew about this murder, that he abused his authority in order to cover it up, and that he finally tried to destroy the evidence, pulling a lethal weapon on my senior medical officer."

Wilson looked dubious. "This is a serious accusation. You said you have *proof*?"

"I hope so, yes, sir. We do have proof of the murder, and who committed it. And in addition, we may have additional evidence that involves the commander in a another conspiracy which has cost the lives of over one hundred transport crew members over the last sixteen months."

Now Wilson snorted in disbelief. "Wallace? In a conspiracy?"

"Sir, we have strong evidence that AreTech Consolidated Mines has been engaged in a systematic conspiracy to sell out its own cargoes to raiders, in order to profit from the increased price of the metal. We believe Earth Alliance officials were part of this conspiracy. We have reason to believe that the actual purpose of Commander Wallace's investigation was not to pursue Free Mars terrorists but to eliminate a threat to this conspiracy."

Wilson's face slowly lost its color. "You say you have evidence of this?" he asked slowly. "This conspiracy?"

"We have some evidence. In the case of the murder, conclusive evidence. Our investigation into the other matters isn't concluded yet."

Wilson looked grave. "Captain, you've stumbled onto matters you know nothing about. It may be that you've uncovered some valuable information. I'm going to consult with my superiors about this. I'm not authorized to disclose any further details. In the meanwhile, let me warn you—this information is to go no further than it's already gone. Is that understood?"

"Yes, sir. And what about Commander Wallace? He hasn't yet been officially charged with murder—"

"Forget about that, Captain. You do nothing about the

commander. It will be taken care of. A ship will be coming to take him back to Earth.''

"I understand."

"I'll get back to you about the rest of this. Wilson out."

The screen blanked. Sheridan sat for a moment watching the BABCOM logo scroll across it, as if it carried a message for his execution. Finally he stood and went through to where Garibaldi and Ivanova were waiting for him, both looking concerned.

"Do we keep our heads," Garibaldi was the one to ask, "or not?"

"We keep them." But before the expressions of relief could take hold, he added, "For the moment."

"And Wallace?" Ivanova asked.

"Gets shipped back to Earth." Sheridan glanced around at security agents coming and going, making reports and taking calls. "Maybe we'd better talk about this back inside."

"He's going to get away with murder?" Garibaldi demanded with some heat once they were back behind the closed doors of the briefing room.

Sheridan answered him slowly. "I get the distinct feeling that Earthforce Command thinks a single murder is insignificant, in comparison."

"To what?" Ivanova asked.

"To what they won't say yet." Sheridan paused to remember what Wilson had said: "We've stumbled onto matters we know nothing about. That we're not supposed to know anything about, either."

"So what are we supposed to do, then?" Ivanova demanded.

"For one thing, not to let this information, whatever it means, go any further than it already has. That's an order. And the other thing is, if we have any chance of finding more evidence, we'd better find it now."

Ivanova sighed. "In that case, we'd better call in the Ombunds."

Ombunds Wellington's position on the matter was quite firm. The station's chief civilian judge might be old and white-haired, but his air of authority was sufficient to transform the utilitarian setting of the interrogation room into a court.

"No matter what you might think of Mr. Zaccione's alleged crimes, nothing he could have done negates the fact that he still has the right not to incriminate himself. And it seems clear that what you're asking him to do, to testify about these matters you can't disclose, would in fact require him to admit to his involvement in a number of crimes that carry the highest penalties our law allows —short of the death penalty, that is," he added, with a reproving look at Ivanova.

She flared back, "I don't need his confession. I have enough proof to convict his tail a dozen times over. I *saw* him flame my wingman—"

"But that isn't the point, Commander, as we all know," Sheridan reminded her. "It's not Zaccione we want to convict. Not now, at any rate."

She exhaled sharply. "I know. Of course. Sorry. It's just the thought of that scum, getting off—"

"You don't want to convict him now," Wellington reminded them, "but Mr. Zaccione has to consider that he will be put on trial later, in the future. When what he says now can be held against him."

"What's the deal, then?" Garibaldi asked, getting as usual to the bottom line. "If he thinks he can just walk—"

"I managed to convince him that option was unrealistic," Wellington said dryly. "As Commander Ivanova points out, the evidence against him is quite overwhelming. He has agreed to testify for you under two conditions: first, that none of his testimony will ever be used as evidence against him in a court of law. Second, that you agree not to seek either the death penalty or brainwipe if he's convicted of any crimes."

Ivanova was about to protest, but Sheridan said, "Remember, Commander, from what Admiral Wilson said, I don't think it's likely that Earth Central will allow the facts to be made public in a trial, no matter what. And if we have any hope of proving . . . what we need to prove, your raider is it."

"I know. I know. All right. If it's the only way."

"Tell him it's a deal," said Garibaldi.

"No, wait!" They all looked at Ivanova. "All right," she said through clenched teeth, "it's a deal, but I want something else. I want a guarantee that his testimony is really the truth. I want a telepath to scan him during questioning. I want the truth out of him, no matter what."

Garibaldi stared at her. "You want to call in the Psi Corps?"

"Ivanova has a point," Sheridan agreed. "Can we get Ms. Winters in to scan the raider while we question him?"

"I'll see if she's available," Garibaldi said, lifting his link. "This is Garibaldi, get me Ms. Winters."

But he still couldn't quite believe Ivanova had asked for her. Not Ivanova.

Two guards brought the prisoner between them into the briefing room, sat him in a chair, and at a nod from Garibaldi, left the room.

The raider looked around, from one of them to another, and when his eyes lit on Ivanova a faint grin came onto his face. "Hey, Earthforce, I guess you missed me, huh?"

But the joke was halfhearted and fell predictably flat

in the company present. Garibaldi took the place of the guards, leaning back in the corner with his arms crossed, watchful eyes on the prisoner.

Captain Sheridan, ignoring the remark, began the proceedings by sitting down opposite the raider. "Mr. Zaccione, this session is being recorded. You've freely agreed to make these statements on the condition that they won't be used against you in any future legal action, is that correct?"

"Yes, that's right," he replied.

"The woman standing next to you is Ms. Talia Winters, registered telepath. She'll be scanning you during the questioning to monitor the truth of your statements. You've freely agreed to this, is that correct?"

"Right."

"Mr. Zaccione," Talia took over, "I want you to relax and try not to think about my presence. Simply answer all the questions openly. Remember, I'll only be scanning the surface level of your thoughts, just far enough to determine whether you're telling the truth. You probably won't even be aware that I'm here, unless you attempt to lie."

"Oh, I think I'd always be aware of *you* in my brain, Psi Corps," he said, turning the grin on the telepath, who ignored it.

"I'm ready, Captain."

"All right, Zaccione, you can start by telling us everything you know about the scheme by AreTech Consolidated Mines to have its cargoes apprehended by raiders. How did you obtain the shipping schedules from the company?"

The raider went through the entire story again, essentially what he'd already told Ivanova on board the *Duster*: how a contact from AreTech had met with an agent of the raiders to pass on the shipping routes and schedules, the company selling out its own cargoes. But Sheridan pressed for more details:

"How often did your agent meet with the company representative?"

"Did you know the names of the ships? The exact nature of the cargoes? The exact tonnage?"

"How many freighters did you attack every month as a result of this information? How many in total? What was the total tonnage of cargo lost?"

Most questions the raider answered, occasionally saying he didn't know the exact details Sheridan was asking for. In a few cases, he seemed reluctant.

"The name of the AreTech representative who supplied this information to you?"

"I'm not sure . . ."

"Previously, you told Commander Ivanova that your organization had verified his identity."

"Forrester, I think. Or maybe Forrestal—something like that."

"Ms. Winters?" Sheridan asked.

"I believe the name Forrestal is correct, Captain. As far as he knows."

"And the name of your agent on Mars?"

Zaccione shifted uncomfortably in his chair. "I . . . don't—"

"That's not true, Captain," Talia said crisply. "He does know the name, but he's reluctant to disclose it."

"Answer the question," Sheridan ordered.

The raider's eyes shifted from Sheridan to the telepath. "You'd better answer, Zack," she told him. "It'll be a lot easier on you than if I have to go in after the name."

"King," he finally said in a low voice. "Wally King. He works as a shipping clerk in a freight office in Marsport."

"That's the truth," Talia confirmed.

"Good. Now," Sheridan went on, "do you believe there were Earth Alliance officials connected to this conspiracy? Officers in Earthforce?"

"Somebody had to keep Earthforce off our backs." He glanced briefly, resentfully at Ivanova. "They were supposed to, anyway."

"What are the names of these corrupt Earthforce officials?"

Zaccione shook his head. There was a noticeable increase of tension in the room. Ivanova held her breath. Garibaldi leaned forward.

"I don't know."

"Their names," Sheridan insisted. "Ms. Winters?"

She looked over at the captain. "He's not lying."

"Go deeper," Ivanova insisted. "Dig them out of him."

"He doesn't know their names," Talia said firmly.

Sheridan scowled. "Does the name Yang mean anything to you?"

"Yeah, but he's not Earthforce. He works for the company. Leans on people who ask questions."

"To your knowledge, did Yang ever kill to keep people from asking questions?"

"One time I know of, at least. Guy from an insurance agency came around. They found him outside the dome without his breather."

"And what about the name Wallace?"

The raider shook his head.

"He doesn't know," Talia supplied.

"Are you sure?" Ivanova demanded.

"Quite sure. He doesn't know the name."

Sheridan's expression was worried. He looked at Ivanova, shook his head. He continued the questioning a while longer, eliciting a few more facts about the raiders' operations, but no more details about the Earth Alliance officials who were supposed to be involved in the cover-up. Zaccione didn't know their names. He'd never been in direct contact with them. They worked behind the scenes, he explained.

Eventually Sheridan pushed back his chair. "I guess that'll be all," he admitted.

Garibaldi left his corner, led the prisoner away, back to the lockup.

"I'm sorry," Sheridan said to Ivanova. "I don't know how much this will help. Without the names. Without a direct connection to Wallace."

"Oh, well." She grinned weakly. "I guess you can't get turnip juice from a stone. We tried."

"We did the best job we could," Sheridan agreed. "And thank you, Ms. Winters, for assisting."

Ivanova hesitated a moment, then stepped closer to Talia. "Yes, thank you. I know it had to be unpleasant, stepping into that kind of mind."

Talia shook her head, produced a faint smile. "Oh, he wasn't so bad. Not compared to some."

Ivanova's brows raised. "Scum like him? With what he said to you?"

"Oh, a lot of people say that kind of thing—men, especially, when they're trying to mask anxiety. It didn't mean anything."

Ivanova looked skeptical. "Anxiety? Him?"

Now it was Talia's turn to hesitate. "I know you don't . . . care for what I do, Commander. But I've learned that most minds really aren't evil. Some of them—yes, some of them are. But mostly what I see is fear. And loneliness. And self-doubt. I know that this raider shot down your wingman, that you must be very angry. But there was nothing you could have—"

Ivanova held up her hands in front of her face, shook her head. "No," she said, "you don't know that, you don't know anything about it . . ."

She rushed from the room.

Talia sighed in dismay. "I'm sorry," she apologized to Sheridan. "I almost thought there, for a moment, that she could accept what I am, that I'm not a threat to her."

"It's all right," Sheridan said. "It didn't take a telepath to see it. It's hard when you lose a wingman, you know. Even when you know there's nothing you could have done, there's still this voice inside you, saying if you just could have been there a little sooner, tried a little harder."

Talia turned to a different subject. "Is it true? Has Commander Wallace been arrested?"

Sheridan frowned. "I supposed you'd know sooner or later. It's true. But that's confidential."

"Of course." She nodded slowly. "I'm glad. Doing this for him, invading all those poor people's minds while he questioned them . . . Their consent was coerced, you know. He threatened them with arrest, shipping them back to Earth. In some cases, they never consented at all."

"Well, he won't be doing it anymore," Sheridan assured her. "Not on Babylon 5."

CHAPTER 28

"Captain Sheridan, there's a Gold level communication, from Admiral Wilson."

Sheridan had been expecting it. "Put him on."

It was in fact an Ultraviolet level transmission, which required Sheridan to input his code before it would commence. Then Wilson's face appeared on the wall display. "Well, Sheridan, I expect that Commander Wallace and his aide will soon be on their way back to Earth."

"Yes, sir, their ship leaves Babylon 5 in about half an hour."

"Good. And I'm sure you'll be glad to know that your recent actions have been reviewed by the Joint Chiefs, and they've decided that under the circumstances, you were justified in what you did. It seems on further examination that Commander Wallace didn't conduct his investigation with the greatest possible amount of discretion."

"And the other charges against him?"

The admiral cleared his throat portentously. "I've been authorized to disclose certain facts which were previously restricted—with good reason. The conspiracy involving AreTech Consolidated Mines is indeed quite real. In fact, your investigation into the matter will prove quite helpful in tracking down a number of matters you don't need to know about. But some arrests have already been made on the basis of what you've sent.

"However, your suspicions concerning the involvement of Commander Wallace, no matter how well founded they might have seemed in light of your limited knowledge of the situation, are incorrect. Commander

Wallace is an agent of the Joint Chiefs office. The matter which he was sent to investigate is something that must remain classified, but it involves information of vital importance to Earth's defenses. Vital importance.

"This information is believed to have been obtained by the man named J. D. Ortega, who was employed by AreTech. We still aren't sure what he intended to do with it. Suffice it to say that he could have gotten any price—any price he wanted to name—for it. AreTech sent their agent to get the information back. Our agents were searching for him at the same time. As you're aware, the agent from AreTech got to him first.

"Commander Wallace's orders were to retrieve that information by any means necessary. Naturally, his suspicion centered on the AreTech agent, Yang. Unfortunately . . . well, you know what occurred. At any rate, the information has never been recovered. We can only conclude it must have been destroyed—or that it's already gotten into the wrong hands. This is unfortunate, but there doesn't seem to be any value in pursuing it further."

"Then the investigation is over?"

"I'm afraid it is. But you'll be glad to know that there will be no reprimands for you or your staff. We understand that you had to proceed according to the information available."

"Yes, sir, that's very good to hear. Then I assume Commander Ivanova will be reinstated as second-in-command here?"

Wilson frowned. "At this time, the Joint Chiefs don't think such an action would be advisable."

Sheridan stood halfway up in his chair. "What? It was Commander Ivanova who uncovered the conspiracy—"

"True, Captain. The Joint Chiefs have taken this into consideration."

"Into consideration of *what*?"

"The possibility of terrorist associations—"

"There *was* no terrorist activity involved! You just admitted it yourself. J. D. Ortega was taking some secret information from AreTech Mines, he wasn't a terrorist!"

"Captain, you're out of order!" Wilson's color rose as his scowl deepened. "As the evidence from your own security department clearly shows, this Ortega did have a connection to the Free Mars movement. It was this terrorist organization that arranged for him to leave Mars and come onto Babylon 5 with false credentials. It was individuals connected with this organization who conspired to attack your head of security and who most probably murdered Lieutenant Khatib, in order to protect their own identities. Isn't this correct?"

"But that has nothing to do with Ivanova!" Sheridan insisted vehemently. "She had nothing to do with J. D. Ortega. He was her flight instructor, years ago—that's all."

"That may be true, but nevertheless, the decision of the Joint Chiefs is that it would be best if Commander Ivanova did not occupy the rather sensitive position of executive officer of Babylon 5. At this time, at least. The matter is scheduled for a review."

"A review? When?"

"A decision on that has not yet been made. You'll be informed of the results in due course."

And with that, he cut the transmission while Sheridan could only sit and swear at the logo on the screen.

The worst part was—he still had to tell Ivanova.

The liner Asimov *will be departing for Earth at 09:00 hours, with scheduled stops at Mars and Luna colonies. Passengers can now proceed to boarding area. We hope you've enjoyed your stay on Babylon 5.*

Sinclair nodded absently at the announcement. Sometimes it was reassuring to hear the normal sounds of the station going about its regular routine—business as usual, no emergencies, no disturbances.

The lift tube opened, and a pair of security guards stepped out, escorting a prisoner in prison coveralls and wrist restraints, Garibaldi following them. Sheridan watched the raider Zaccione being taken past the customs guards and into the ship before the regular passengers. Garibaldi stopped to join him. "Lucky guy," he commented.

"Not too lucky. He'll be spending the rest of his life in prison on Earth."

"Better off than brainwiped," Garibaldi insisted. He rubbed his forehead. "But sometimes I think Ivanova's got the right idea, just shove them out the air-lock. Easier on everyone."

"Maybe," Sheridan said. "When you've seen enough good men die, it's hard to get real worked up about a bad one. But I think she's taking it all fairly well. Considering."

Garibaldi nodded. "She was fine at the trial. I was glad to see that. For a while, I was worried she was kind of obsessed with this raider."

"I know. He was the one who killed Mokena. And, you know, it's a lot easier when you have someone to take the blame, instead of wondering if there was something else you could have done."

"Yeah, but a good commander always does."

Neither of them said anything else for a while, just stood there, watching the traffic moving through the station.

"It was a raw deal they gave her," Garibaldi said finally, meaning the Joint Chiefs, not the raiders.

"When I could send her out on those escort patrols," Sheridan agreed, "it was one thing. A mission. Something she could get her teeth into. But now—they could have reassigned her. But to just leave her like this . . ."

"I could use her in security, but that's no job for someone with her rank. It's just a raw deal," Garibaldi said again.

But there was nothing either of them could do. There was no higher level where the decision could be appealed. They were both aware that promises of a future review were just that—empty promises. Earth Central would simply let Ivanova wait until she finally got tired of hanging in the vacuum and turned in her resignation.

"Commander! Commander Ivanova!"

Ivanova turned around. It was Espada calling to her, the insurance agent. She waited until the other woman had caught up.

"Commander—Oh, I'm out of breath!—Commander, I just wanted to thank you and let you know Earthforce has finally released the information we needed for our case against AreTech Mines! We have proof now that we can take to court—AreTech *was* feeding the shipping routes to the raiders! We're suing to invalidate all their claims." Espada was beaming with elation. "I don't know how you knew it, but you were right. They've already stopped trading in AreTech stock. They say the corporation directors are all going to be indicted, not just the officials directly involved."

"I suppose Universal stock would be a pretty good buy now, then?" Ivanova asked wryly.

Espada suddenly sobered. "Well, strictly speaking, to say that would be a violation of the statutes on disclosing insider information. But if anyone deserves to profit from all this, it's you!"

"Well, I'll certainly keep that in mind when the next big financial windfall drops at my feet," Ivanova replied. She apologized for having to rush away, citing urgent duties and deeply feeling the irony of the lie. *"Urgent duties,"* right. As urgent as polishing the silverware in the mess hall. Taking an inventory of the inventory-control forms. Or maybe the forms for officers tendering the resignation of their commissions. Which she was afraid it was going to come to, sooner or later. Couldn't go on like this forever, that was for sure.

What was on the agenda for today? Another training flight?

She knew she couldn't blame Sheridan for her situation. He had his orders. And part of the problem was, by capturing that raider, she'd just smarted herself out of her own job. Taking out those escort patrols, going head-to-head with the raiders, that was one thing. But routine training flights, day after day?

She went to her locker in the ready room, started to suit up. Still no replacement for Mokena, she noted as the others pulled on their flight suits.

No, she couldn't blame Sheridan. The fact was, and she knew it, Earth Central just didn't trust her. And it was nothing to do with terrorists on Mars, either, though they still used that convenient excuse. They still thought she knew something, had something to do with that secret information Ortega had—whatever it was, if there ever really was secret information. Maybe it was lost, maybe it wasn't. No one knew. All Ivanova knew was that Ortega wanted to pass it on to her, have her save it for him—something. And that *damned* note. "Hardwir," she said out loud. Never had figured out what it meant.

Climbing into the cockpit. Sealing the canopy. Instrument check. "Alpha Flight, power on."

The routine she could do in her sleep. Training flight. Close-formation flying. Basic maneuvers. She dropped back and let Moy take over the leader position, give her some experience, see how she did with it. Then back to the warm red tunnel of the docking bay, back to Babylon 5.

That damned note was still on her mind. "Hardwir."

What was it supposed to mean? Why had J. D. thought she'd remember? Earth Central probably thought it was a secret code.

Back in the ready room. The place was a mess, as usual. The little old woman mopping the floor wasn't doing a very good job cleaning up.

Maybe Sheridan would let her have that job—scrubbing floors.

It sure didn't look like she was ever going to get a better one here on Babylon 5.

Garibaldi was still on duty when he wandered into the casino, just to check things out. Ivanova would have been on duty, too, in better times. At the moment, though, she was out of uniform—very much so, in fact. Hair down, red dress obviously cut with display in mind, drink in her hand.

And the guy next to her had his hand where Garibaldi had rarely ever seen a guy put his hand—and survive the experience. But Ivanova was laughing. Laughing a little too loud. And leaning back against the guy, so his hand slid farther down, across the surface of one breast . . .

Garibaldi's eyes narrowed. He didn't like this. Ivanova could take care of herself, under normal circumstances. Hell, he'd seen her close down the bar, just because some idiot made a remark suggesting he might like to do what this guy was doing right now. Garibaldi thought he'd frankly almost rather see her exorcising her demons that way, in a good brawl, not like this.

He wandered purposefully in her direction. Forcing a cheerful tone, "Hey, Ivanova! This a friend of yours, is he? I don't think we've met."

"Garibaldi! Hi! This is Rick." She blinked through an alcoholic haze. "It is Rick, isn't it?"

"Sure is, Susie. Rick Morrison, remember?"

Garibaldi almost boggled openly as the guy stroked

her throat, and downward, where the dress invited it. *Susie?!* Ivanova? As Londo would say, *Great Maker!*

"Pleased to meet you," Garibaldi managed to say with the minimum necessary civility.

But a few moments later; when Ivanova had briefly left the table, he had his chance. Taking the guy by the elbow hard enough to let him know he meant business, he said, "Look, *friend,* I just want you to know something. Susan Ivanova *is* my friend. And I wouldn't be happy to hear that she ends up doing something she's going to regret the morning after. You understand me?"

"Hey, what's it to you? I'd say the lady's old enough to know what she wants. What are you, anyway? Her keeper? Her father, maybe?"

That one hurt. But if Garibaldi was maybe old enough to be Ivanova's father, he could at least show this slimy punk how easy it would be for the old man to break his arm. The guy blanched as he applied just a little more force to his elbow. "I'll tell you who I am. I'm head of security on Babylon 5, that's who. Now, maybe you're right and Ivanova's old enough to choose who she wants to party with. That's fine with me. But is she sober enough? That's the question. So I tell you what. You can either pretend to be a gentleman and walk her back to her quarters and shake her hand good night. Or you can take your chances. But if you hurt her, you'll by God wish you were never born."

He released the arm just as Ivanova came back to the table. The guy pulled it away and rubbed his elbow, looking frightened. Ivanova had a glazed look in her eyes. "I'm getting kind of sleepy, Dick, I think I'd like to go back to my quarters and go to bed."

The guy swallowed nervously. "I'll walk you back there," he said.

Garibaldi watched them go. So maybe he'd been out of line, maybe Ivanova was entitled to a little harmless

fun. Maybe this Rick Morrison or whoever was really a
nice guy.

And maybe the Narn and the Centauri would kiss and
let bygones be bygones.

God, he hated to see Ivanova like this! But how else
could he help her? What could he do?

Commander Ivanova, the time is now 06:05 hours.

The mercilessly cheerful computer voice repeated the
time again. Ivanova moaned.

"Commander, your reply was not understood. Would
you repeat?"

She tried to raise her head, moaned again, and finally
managed to form a couple of semicoherent words: "Go
away."

"Acknowledged, Commander. Have a nice day!"

Ivanova hoped that if she only lay very, very still, she
wouldn't be sick. Or was it that she'd already been sick
and was just waiting to die? She hoped in that case it
wouldn't be long.

There was a foul taste in her mouth, her stomach was
threatening to heave itself inside out, and her head refused to lift itself off the pillows. She made herself think
of the medical dispenser in the bathroom. Relief, if she
could just get herself there without being sick on the
way. She managed to sit up, to stand, to grope her way
across the room, because opening her eyes would have
been too much.

"Sobertal," she groaned, and clutched the tablet released by the dispenser. She swallowed it dry, stood
holding herself upright, waiting for the pill to take effect.

At last she could open her eyes. She confronted her
image in the mirror and quickly shut them again. Oh, no!

What was I doing last night? she asked herself.

A cold shower helped some. Enough to get her brain
powered up to remember the night before. Going to the

casino. By herself. Feeling *damned* sorry for herself. A sympathetic someone. His nice, warm hands supporting her as he brought her to the door . . .

Only suddenly the notion didn't seem all that nice at all. The conviction that she'd been acting like a fool was taking firm hold in her mind.

On her way back across the room she almost tripped over the dress lying on the floor. The red dress. Ivanova closed her eyes. Why did I decide to wear *that*?

Sober enough by now to feel completely disgusted with herself, she got into her uniform, braiding her hair as tightly as possible until it felt like it was pulling the remains of her headache out by the roots. She ignored the rest of the crowd still in the mess hall for a late breakfast and headed mindlessly to the line for coffee, only remembering at the last minute as the bitter, chemical-flavored synthetic poured into her cup that there was no real coffee.

She shuddered, but took it, unable to face this particular morning without something containing caffeine. At least it was hot. And equally unable to stand the thought of company, she sat down at a table by herself.

She only glanced up when her half-lidded eyes caught sight of a cheerfully replete figure heading in her direction. She closed her eyes completely. *No, not Garibaldi, not this morning!*

He grinned wickedly. "Well, Ivanova, how was your night out?"

She didn't look up. "I don't want to hear about it, Garibaldi, I really don't."

"Really?"

There was something in his tone. Now she did look up. "What did I do? Take off all my clothes? Challenge the Minbari Wind Swords to a duel? Has the casino got a warrant out for my arrest?"

His voice went more serious. He pulled out a chair and

sat down across from her. "Nothing like that. Really. I was worried about you, that's all. That guy you were with—"

"What guy?" she demanded defensively, vaguely recalling that there was some guy or other, but not who.

"Hey! I'm sure he was a perfect gentleman! Look, I'm not saying you can't go out and have a good time. You've earned it. I just . . ." He hesitated. "I just remember when I started thinking that a few drinks might help me face my problems. I don't like to see you . . ."

He looked down at the table; she stared into her coffee mug. Finally, "He was a perfect gentleman, huh?"

"After I promised to break his arm." He paused, saving the best for last. "He was calling you 'Susie.' "

Ivanova winced, took another sip of black synthetic stuff. "Thanks," she said at last. "For caring what happens to me now. Sometimes . . . I'm not sure I do, anymore."

He stood up with a squeal of chair legs. "That's horsehockey. And you know it." And left her there to think it over by herself.

Alone again, she watched the last tendrils of steam from the mug die away. Garibaldi was right, she still cared. That her career was ruined, yes, there was nothing she cared for more than that. If there was only something she could *do* about it . . .

As she stared glumly into the black sludge in the mug, she saw another figure sit down at a solitary table with her tray. Talia Winters. Garibaldi's polar opposite in the food department. She probably had two pieces of dry toast on her tray, at the most. And these days she was looking so thin she was almost gaunt.

But now Ivanova recalled what Garibaldi had said about what Wallace had put Talia through, what a strain on her the ordeal had been. At least they had one thing in common, she thought—neither of them could stand Wallace. Guiltily, she remembered how she'd added to the telepath's workload, insisting that she should scan Zaccione, the raider. And how she'd reacted, afterward.

She lifted the mug, shuddered, put it down again and went back to the line for a fresh mug. She stopped at Talia's table. "Do you mind if I sit down?"

The telepath looked up sharply, startled. "Uh, why, no! Please do. You're just having coffee?"

"If you can call it that." Ivanova stole a glance at Talia's tray. Two pieces of toast. Not dry, though, there was some kind of spread on it. And a dish of fruit.

"I want . . ." Ivanova's throat closed up. This was hard. "I want to thank you again. For helping out during that testimony. I'm sorry I . . . reacted."

"That's all right, I understand. I didn't mean to criticize. Your personal life."

"No. I guess I was thinking, if I could just drag the truth out of that guy, it'd all be solved, all the conspiracies, everything. It'd all be *over*. Make up for everything. And then, it wasn't."

"I'm sorry it didn't all work out. I mean, for you."

"For my career. I know. That's what I want . . ." She swallowed. "I want to ask you. If you could help me again."

"If I can, yes, of course," Talia said, puzzled.

"I suppose you know that Earth Central doesn't want me reinstated. I think it's because they don't trust me, because of Ortega, because of that note he wrote, the information nobody's ever found—I think they still think I know something about it." Ivanova's speech was hesitating. She wondered if she was making any sense at all. Normally, with Talia, she did everything she could to push her away, away from her mind. Now . . .

"What I want is, what was on that note. It was just one word. I'm sure it should be something I remember, but I just don't. And the harder I try, the more it just doesn't mean anything. And I was wondering . . ."

Her hands were sweaty, and she put down the coffee mug before she dropped it. She could feel the rapid stutter of her heartbeat, the nervous tingle of fear. "I was wondering if you might be able to . . . find it . . ."

Talia spoke very softly, carefully. "I think I probably could, yes, if it's part of your memory. The mind retains many, many memories that the consciousness can't access." She looked dubiously at Ivanova. "But it would require something more than a simple surface scan. With Zaccione, for the most part, I was only skimming the outer surface of his thoughts. In your case, in the case you're discussing, I'd need to go deeper than that. Do you understand?"

Ivanova couldn't speak. If she could, she would have wanted to scream, to run, or strike out with every power she possessed: *Keep out of my mind!*

But instead, she stiffly nodded that she understood.

"It would be best to do this in a place where we can have complete privacy, with no interruptions. May I suggest my quarters?"

Ivanova nodded again, managed to whisper, "That would be fine."

Talia looked down at the half-eaten breakfast on her tray. "Do you want to go now?"

"No!" Ivanova took a quick, nervous sip from her mug. "Finish your breakfast. Please. I still have this coffee." Anything, she thought, to put it off, just another couple of minutes. She took a deeper drink from the mug and shuddered. *God, this stuff is awful!*

Ivanova had never been in Talia's quarters, and she looked around with some curiosity while she moved around the room, adjusting the placement of pillows, pulling a dead leaf off a plant. The telepath seemed almost as nervous as she was.

"Well," Talia finally said, "should we start this?"

Ivanova would have rather stepped out the air-lock. But it was her career. The only thing that could save it. "Yes," she said.

Talia gestured to a couch. "I think this would be the best place." As Ivanova stiffly sat down, Talia began, self-consciously, to remove her gray gloves. "Direct touch makes the mental contact easier," she explained, slightly embarrassed.

Ivanova nodded as the other woman sat down next to her. "Sit back, please. Try to relax. Close your eyes. Try not to resist my presence." They were almost the same words that Talia had used when preparing to scan the captured raider, but this time her tone was different, less impersonal.

The telepath carefully placed a hand over Ivanova's. It felt warm and slightly damp from the glove. Talia closed her eyes for a moment. "Now, I want you to think of the time you spent with J. D. Ortega. Don't try to remember any specific thing. Just picture his face in your mind, listen to some of the things he used to say to you. He was your flight trainer. Think about the time you spent with him in the cockpit of the training ship. Think about learning to fly. Yes, that's good."

Ivanova kept her eyes closed. Talia Winters's voice was very soft, a soothing voice. There was no reason for her to be nervous about this. She was going to help her remember, that was all.

She couldn't quite discern the moment when the spoken voice ceased and gave place to the voice in her mind. The touch of Talia's hand was warm, comforting, and reassuring. It was as if Talia were sitting with her in the cockpit of the training ship, with J. D. in the copilot's seat. Talia's bare hands were on the ship's controls, but they were also her own. They were wearing the gray cadet uniform instead of those long, concealing dresses that Talia always wore. *You don't like the way I dress? I'm sorry. I've always been sorry you didn't like me, Susan.*

Next to them, J. D. was talking about the use of the tactical screen. "You all know how to use a computer screen. But you can't use this the way you do an ordinary data screen."

He's really quite good-looking, I think. Too bad he was so much in love with his wife.

"You don't see the screen, you don't see through the screen. You see *with* the screen. It's like your eyes—do you stop and think about how to use your eyes? You don't, you simply see. Well, the screen is your eyes and the screen is your brain. The processing has to be immediate, instantaneous. You don't have time to stop and think."

He was a good pilot. But he didn't like the military. Just the flying.

"You know how they're saying that one day there'll be a direct interface hardwired between our brains and the ship's computer? Well, here's the secret: you have to learn to fly as if there already were—hardwired into the ship, all together."

Susan, isn't that it? The key to the message? Hardwired?

And now Ivanova heard the words, distinct from the thought in her mind: "Susan, isn't that it? The key to the message? *Hardwired?*"

Talia Winters's hand squeezed hers tightly. Ivanova jerked it away, jumped up. "Yes! Yes, that's it! I remember now!"

"I'm so happy for you! What does it mean, though?"

"It means . . . it means the secret is somewhere in my ship! My fighter! On the tac screen! It means he put it someplace where a pilot would see it and not really see it!''

She was almost at the door before she turned around and said awkwardly, "Thank you. Thank you—very much.''

CHAPTER 29

Ivanova ran all the way to the Cobra bay, barely able to stand still while the lift tube descended. *No wonder,* she was thinking, *no wonder I couldn't remember.* "Hardwired." It was J. D. who was always interested in strange new technologies, things like direct ship/brain interfaces. In those days, all she could think of was getting into the cockpit of a fighter, somehow taking over from her brother and avenging his death all mixed up together in her mind.

She ran past the startled dockworkers, who yelled, "Hey, Commander! Is there an alert on?"

"No, it's nothing!" she shouted back. "Is my ship ready?"

But there was no need for them to answer, she could see it there, the familiar ship in the familiar cradle. She had a thought, turned around to see the shift foreman looking at her with a concerned frown. "Everyone knows which one is my ship, don't they?"

"Why, Commander?" A look of sudden alarm. "Are you thinking of sabotage?"

"No! I mean, there's been no sabotage threat or anything like that. I was just wondering."

"Good. Then there's nothing wrong?"

"No, I just wanted to check out something I forgot last time I was out."

She slid into the seat inside the cockpit, stared around her at the controls and display screens, more than familiar, almost extensions of herself by now. The tac display was dark. She closed her eyes, then opened them again.

She switched on the computer, and the screen glowed

into life: rows of controls, the targeting array. J. D. had been desperate. He wouldn't have had much time. Whatever he'd hidden, it was too dangerous to keep it on him, too valuable to risk its loss . . .

Suddenly, she knew. "Computer, keyword search: Hardwired."

"No file accessed."

She thought an instant. "Keyword search: J. D."

"Accessing: file J. D."

"Display file."

But what flashed into sight on her screen was nothing she could comprehend. A diagram of some kind. A code. Maybe the map of a new star system. So complex that the pattern only emerged after she fined down the resolution. It meant something, certainly. But she had no idea what, and the tactical computer knew no more than she did.

So this is it, she thought. *J. D., this is what you died for? And the rest of them? What secret could this possibly be to be worth so much?*

He'd known she was on the station, somehow found out which ship was hers (from some secret Free Mars sympathizer on the Cobra bay's crew?). And he'd copied the information—as a backup—to her tac computer. Hidden in with all the other files, where no one would ever be likely to notice its existence—unless they had the keyword to search for it.

Ivanova felt a profound sense of loss and sadness. What had happened to her old flight instructor? What kind of person had he become, that he was involved in all this? "Dammit, J. D.!"

But this wasn't getting her anywhere. She had the computer transfer the data to a crystal, then slipped it into a pocket of her flight suit. Now to find out what exactly she had here.

The same old janitor was mopping the hall outside the

Cobra bays, and Ivanova stepped aside to get out of her way. She barely caught a glimpse of sudden movement in the corner of her eye before the blow struck—shock stick, not mop handle—shorting out her entire nervous system, reducing all her senses to blinding white static.

When they returned, the first thing she felt was hands on her, someone tearing at her uniform, tearing it off. And her first incoherent thought was rape—some maniac had attacked her. But then the voice came clear, and she recognized it.

"Where is it? I know you've got it! I knew it all along! Ms. Perfect Record! Ms. Full Commander at twenty-eight! Ms. Hero, capturing raiders single-handed! He passed it on to you! I knew he did! I knew—

"Yes! This is it! This is it, isn't it! The crystal! You knew the code, I knew you did! I knew it!"

Ivanova forced open her eyes. For a moment, she thought her brain wasn't functioning right after the shock, because the voice was Miyoshi's—it had been in so many of her recent nightmares—but the face was the little old cleaning woman from the ready room. Then they merged, the old woman's face and Miyoshi's, and she could see through the fake wrinkles, the disguise, to the lieutenant from Earthforce Command standing over her, the data crystal clutched in her hand, and her eyes bright and face glowing with triumphant success.

Of course. Khatib's crime and Wallace's failure had tainted Miyoshi. Her own career was ruined—at least as ruined as Ivanova's. Finding this data crystal was the only way to redeem herself.

And Ivanova's career? There didn't seem much of a chance that Miyoshi was interested in redeeming it, too.

Up to me, then, she thought groggily. But how could she do anything now, with the effects of the shock still barely worn off? She wondered how much she could move, slowly flexed the fingers on her right hand, then her left. If she could switch on her link . . .

But Miyoshi's eyes were on her like a hawk's. She bent down, held the crystal out, directly over Ivanova's face. "*I've* got it now! I watched you! I watched you go to the telepath, I knew it'd come out, sooner or later! If you only knew how long I waited . . ."

Suddenly she straightened, snatched the crystal away, tucked it into one of the inside pockets of the Maintenance coverall she was wearing. Then, from another pocket, she took out something else, which Ivanova couldn't quite make out, a thin cylinder. Miyoshi was smiling, and Ivanova didn't like the looks of that smile, didn't like it at all.

"You know where we are, don't you?"

Wherever it was, Ivanova didn't think she was going to be as happy about it as Miyoshi was. She blinked her eyes, turned her head, trying to place the plain, utilitarian walls—of one of the heads. And she'd been on her way to the Alpha Wing ready room . . .

"Yes, I thought you did. Nice touch of irony, isn't it? And just think how much fun your friend *Mr.* Garibaldi will have, figuring out this one! He likes to play detective, doesn't he?"

Ivanova knew she had to take her chance now. She swept with her legs, not sure until the last instant if they even worked yet, and sent Miyoshi staggering. At the same time she reached for her link, to call for help, to call Garibaldi—

It wasn't there. The back of her wrist was empty, bare.

And the strength in her legs hadn't been enough to do more than send Miyoshi stumbling into the wall. The lieutenant was still on her feet, and she quickly regained her balance, spun around to turn on Ivanova, saw her still on her back on the floor, groping for her link. The smile returned. Miyoshi slowly reached into another coverall pocket, came out with another object that she held up, out of Ivanova's reach. The link.

"Looking for this?"

The missing link, and Ivanova would have broken out into laughter if she weren't so sure Miyoshi meant to kill her. But now Miyoshi frowned and put the link back away, and with a wary eye on Ivanova she bent down to pick up the cylinder from the floor where she'd dropped it as she lost her balance. An injector, Ivanova recognized it now, and she wouldn't want to take bets that it wasn't loaded with some kind of poison.

There was going to be another murder on Babylon 5, another unsolved killing, because of course Miyoshi wasn't still on the station, Miyoshi had been shipped back to Earth with her boss, so who could have done it? Sheridan would be furious, Ivanova thought with irrelevant clarity. He was sick and tired of murders.

But Miyoshi's frown deepened while she fiddled with the tube, and finally she threw it back down on the floor with an expression of disgust. "Now, that's a nuisance! It's broken."

Still carefully watching Ivanova, she picked up a shock stick where it was propped up next to a washstand. "You know," she said in a too-casual tone, "these things are supposed to be nonlethal. But you've worked in security some, I'll bet you know better. It takes some *work,* but you can do the job with this if you have to. And now it looks like you've left me no choice. Too bad you weren't carrying a weapon, you know. I could have used it."

She firmly twisted the shock stick's handle until it was turned to the highest setting. Ivanova knew with the certainty of desperation that she was only going to have one more chance. She wished she weren't still lying here on her back.

Miyoshi approached with the shock stick held like a

sword. Ivanova braced herself, knowing Miyoshi was watching for her reaction. They were both combat trained, and they watched each other like a pair of fencers, each looking for an opening, for a feint. One touch with the stick and Ivanova would be helpless again. She pivoted to keep Miyoshi in front of her. She was at a disadvantage in this position, but she knew at least that she was recovering quickly, that every minute she was regaining her strength and coordination.

But Miyoshi clearly knew it, too. She lunged forward, and Ivanova countered with a twist to the right, to get to her feet. But she was too slow, her muscles hadn't still quite recovered their quickness, and the stick jabbed her hip, the shock instantaneous, the nerves overloading all at once, seeming to explode . . .

Garibaldi heard the call come in over his link and the security channel simultaneously. "Security! Mr. Garibaldi! It's Commander Ivanova! She's in terrible trouble! You have to find her!"

"Call an alert!" he ordered. Then, recognizing the voice, "Talia? What's going on?"

"I don't know! I just know she's in danger! Please! Hurry! Find her before it's too late!"

"Get me a trace on her link," Garibaldi ordered again. "Contact the captain. Let him know what's going on."

The computer voice broke in, "Commander Ivanova traced to Alpha Wing ready room."

"That's—" He didn't complete the statement out loud. That's where J. D. Ortega had been killed. "Tac Squad B, with me! All available security to the Alpha Wing ready room. Hurry!"

* * *

Garibaldi burst into the ready room at the head of his squad, but he wasn't the first on the scene. An officer pointed to the door to the head. "They're in there."

He hurried to the door. There was the unmistakable lingering scent of a recent plasma discharge. Three security officers knelt on the floor where there were two unconscious forms. Ivanova—

He started forward in alarm, but the closest security man looked up and said, "She's alive, Mr. Garibaldi, just stunned. We've already called Medlab."

Another stood up, holding a shock stick. "She was using *this* on the commander. I ordered her to drop the stick and put up her hands. She turned on us."

From the floor the officer bending over the other inert figure straightened. "She's dead."

Garibaldi stepped closer to see who it was. "Miyoshi!" he exclaimed in shocked astonishment. "Lieutenant Miyoshi!"

The security agent who'd shot her seemed slightly uncertain of himself. "She was attacking Commander Ivanova, Chief. She didn't drop her weapon when I ordered her to."

"Good job," Garibaldi assured him. "You can put it all in your report."

He looked at Ivanova, who seemed to be having some kind of slight spasm. "Where's Medical, dammit!"

But just then the medical team rushed into the room, Dr. Franklin at their head. "Ivanova's hurt?"

"Shock stick," Garibaldi said tersely, standing back out of the medics' way with the rest of security, their job finished for the moment.

"This one's dead," the other medic reported from Miyoshi's side. "Plasma burst. Hit point-blank."

Franklin was applying an injector to Ivanova. "She's coming around," he announced. "Commander? Commander Ivanova? Can you hear me? Can you say something?"

Now Garibaldi edged closer again. Ivanova was stirring. Her lips moved. He made out, "Mi . . . yo . . . shi . . ."

"It's all right," he assured her. "Miyoshi's taken care of. You're all right now. You're safe."

"Ga . . . ri . . ."

"That's right, it's me. She got you with a shock stick, but you're going to be just fine, isn't she, Doc?"

But Franklin wasn't about to let the security department make the diagnosis for him. He pulled back Ivanova's eyelid and aimed an instrument into one eye, then the other. "Mmh," he said finally, "looks all right. But we'll just go up to Medlab for a neurological scan, just to make sure."

But Ivanova blinked, tried to lift her head. "No! Wait! Miyoshi. Data. Crystal."

"Miyoshi has a data crystal?" Garibaldi asked.

"Ortega. I. Found. It."

Now Garibaldi understood. "Don't worry. I'll find it. Here, wait a minute, don't move that body."

He knelt down, started to go through the pockets of her coveralls. They were maintenance department issue, he noticed. And the makeup on her face made her look almost twice her real age. He *hoped* he wouldn't have to make a body check. He hated that, when people swallowed data crystals and you had to get them back the hard way. But then maybe he could just leave that up to Franklin.

Nope, no need. The crystal was there in an inside pocket, and he slipped it into a pocket of his own, then hurried after the team of medics who had taken Ivanova to Medlab, to give her the news that he'd found it.

She was sitting up by the time he arrived, recovering quickly with Franklin's treatment. Captain Sheridan was there questioning her, but when she saw Garibaldi come in she almost tried to jump to her feet before the medic could restrain her. "Did you find it? Do you have it?"

"I've got it right here," he assured her. "Do you know what it is?"

"No. It's not like anything I've ever seen. I have to think it might be alien, even."

"Hmm." Garibaldi looked speculative, taking the crystal out of his pocket and turning it around in his fingers, as if he could see into the data matrix.

"Can I see it?" Sheridan asked, and Garibaldi gave it to him.

Suddenly Talia came hurrying into the treatment room, slightly out of breath. "They said you found her! They said— Susan, are you all right?"

Ivanova's head jerked back as if she'd been slapped. "I . . . I'm fine, quite fine," she said rapidly, but Garibaldi could see her face color with confusion. And at the same time Talia's face went pale.

Garibaldi took her aside, asked in a low voice, "I wanted to ask you, when you called in, just how did you know that Ivanova was in trouble?"

Talia stammered, "I don't know, I . . . She had just finished consulting me on a . . . confidential matter. I suppose the connection . . . there must have still been a connection. After we were . . . that close. I don't know, but I *knew* she needed help."

Garibaldi stared in disbelief at Ivanova. "She went to you? As a telepath?"

"I believe she was desperate," Talia said, flipping her hair back. Her tone was more detached now.

Ivanova had heard. "Yes, I did consult Ms. Winters in her professional capacity. I felt it was necessary . . . to recall the significance of Ortega's note." She hesitated visibly. "I'm grateful for Ms. Winters calling in for help when she did."

"I'm glad you weren't seriously hurt," Talia replied, her voice even more clipped and cool than Ivanova's. "But I can see there are already too many people in here."

She spun sharply around and left the room, while Sheridan questioned Garibaldi with an unspoken *Do you have any idea what this is all about?* and Garibaldi shaking his head that he didn't. Neither of them had dared interfere between the two women, and Ivanova's expression didn't encourage any questions now.

"The crystal," she insisted, "we have to see what's on it."

Sheridan looked down at it, still in his hand. "So this is what everyone was dying for," he said quietly. "I wonder what could possibly be worth it."

He popped the crystal into the nearest computer console, saw the pattern come up onto the screen, and shook his head. "Now, what's *that*?"

To the computer, "Analysis."

"Analysis underway," it replied.

"Hey!" said Ivanova, "that's my crystal! I get to see it!" Garibaldi helped her onto her feet.

Franklin, always curious about new technology, came to watch the screen with them as the analysis progressed. "What that looks like to me," he said slowly, "is an atomic diagram. Of one hell of a *big* atom!"

A few moments later, the computer agreed with him. "Most probable analysis: the information represents a schematic of an isotope of an unknown metallic element. Analysis suggests an element of Group VI b, atomic number of 156, with anomalous electron shielding and the presence of an unknown subatomic particle—"

"That can't be right!" Franklin exclaimed. "There is no element 156! And, if there were, it'd be so radioactive it'd have a half-life measured in nanoseconds. It'd be too unstable to exist! And, see there—the atomic weight is twice what it should be for an isotope of an element in that range.''

"Most probable analysis," the computer replied, "the element is artificial, not capable of existing in nature. This appears to be the result of the presence of an anomalous subatomic particle, an unknown nucleon, stabilizing the nucleus.''

"An unknown subatomic particle? A new, artificial element?" Sheridan said in wonder. "This can't be anything produced by human technology.''

The computer agreed. What they had was the schematic for an utterly unknown metal, produced artificially by a technology that had to be alien.

"But what's it good for?" Garibaldi asked, almost suspiciously. "Why is everyone murdering people left and right to get their hands on this?''

"Estimated analysis yields a probable melting point: 6,180 degrees; boiling point: 11,500 degrees; conductivity index: 0.42—''

"It's a supermorbidium!" Ivanova exclaimed. "No natural metal can withstand that kind of heat! I'll just bet I know what it's good for—the phase coils of plasma weapons!''

Everyone in the room stared at the display in silence. "This would revolutionize weapons technology," Sheridan finally said in a low voice. "The strategic advantage could be enormous.'' He was recalling the admiral's words: *Vital importance to Earth's defenses.*

"The sort of information governments would kill for," Garibaldi added.

"And it would make morbidium obsolete for strategic purposes," Ivanova said slowly. "And if morbidium were your primary source of revenue . . .''

"You'd kill to keep the information from getting out," Garibaldi completed the thought.

But Ivanova wasn't so sure. "Maybe. Or maybe you'd

try to get in on the ground floor with the new technology. But for that, you'd need capital. And the minute word got out about this new metal, the price of your stock would fall . . . you'd want to sell out before that happened . . . snatch whatever profits you could . . ." She shook her head. Economics wasn't a clear-cut science, like astrogation or hyperspace field theory.

A lot of things weren't clear-cut. She realized she might never know what J. D. had intended to do with the crystal. Had the temptation of fabulous wealth been too much for him? Or had he been trying to turn the information over to Earthforce and gotten caught up in the corruption surrounding AreTech's conspiracy? Or had he been a member of Free Mars all along and intended to use the discovery to support his political goals?

Captain Sheridan, however, was quite certain of one thing. "Commander Ivanova," he said firmly, "I want you to come with me to the Command Office. We're going to be making a call to Admiral Wilson of the Joint Chiefs. I think we have something they've been looking for."

CHAPTER 30

It was quiet in the Observation Dome on Babylon 5, a rare hour when there were no ships scheduled to depart or arrive at the station. Only the skeleton crew of duty technicians sat at their consoles, intent on their work.

On the dome's upper level, Commander Ivanova stood in front of the control console, hands clasped behind her back. The glowing colored lights of the displays reflected off the curved window above them, but Ivanova was looking past them, out at the black immensity of space and the silent stars.

All her eyes could see were peace and stillness. But the instruments controlled by her console could see further, deeper, into ranges of energy inaccessible to merely human senses. There were wars out there among those stars, contesting that space. There were ships and weapons—and the weapons were always more powerful, capable of more destruction.

Now Earth was reaching out for alien power, to put alien weapons in human hands. Ivanova had the fleeting thought that she didn't know which frightened her more: the destructive potential of technology, or what humanity might do if they obtained it.

But there was no more time to wonder, because at that moment the scan technician called out, "Commander Ivanova! Getting a sharp rise in tachyon emissions! Something big is coming through the jump point!"

"I've got it!" she said quickly, turning her attention back to the main display. In command.

Book 3
Blood Oath
by John Vornholt

Historian's note: This story takes place prior to the
events in 'The Coming of Shadows'.

CHAPTER 1

THE DATA crystal was dark, like a smoky quartz, and Ambassador G'Kar twisted it between his fingers. He marveled at the way its subtle facets could absorb and access data at speeds that rivaled the Narn mind. The best data crystals were grown on Minbar, and this one had the look of top quality. Something caught G'Kar's eye, and he furrowed his spotted cranium and squinted at the crystal's metallic connector. That was odd. The date and microscopic identity pattern had been removed by a laser beam, making the crystal all but untraceable. Who would want to send him an untraceable data crystal in his regular mail pouch?

Intrigued, the ambassador stood up and slipped the crystal into the viewer on his wall. A female Narn appeared on the screen, and what a female Narn she was! Young and slender, she was wearing a flowing gown of blood-red material, and it was cinched with a belt and scabbard which accentuated her curves. Her red eyes gleamed with intensity and arrested G'Kar to the spot. He didn't know what the young Narn was going to say on this recorded message, but she certainly had caught his attention.

"Hello, G'Kar," said the woman imperiously. "Do you recognize me? I am Mi'Ra, daughter of Du'Rog. I speak for my mother, Ka'Het, and my brother, T'Kog. We are all that is left of the family you destroyed. Yes, G'Kar, we are beaten, and our titles and lands are gone. Our father is dead, his name disgraced, and his attempt to kill you from the grave was a failure. To our shame, every assassin has failed."

G'Kar swallowed hard and leaned closer. He dreaded what was coming next.

Mi'Ra's lovely face contorted into rage. "You think

you are safe within the Third Circle and the Earth space station. You are wrong! The widow, the son, and the daughter of Du'Rog have sworn the *Shon'Kar* against you! No more will you face inept assassins but the very family you destroyed! The Prophets willing, by my own hands you will die. From this day forward, the purpose of our *V'Tar* is to kill you. Let this mark show my will."

With that, Mi'Ra pulled a short but vicious-looking sword from her scabbard and pressed the blade to her head. At once, the blood streamed from the wound and flowed down her delicate cheekbone to her neck and shoulder, where it mingled with the identical color in her gown. Involuntarily, G'Kar reached up and touched his own scaly brow.

The viewer blinked off, and he snatched the data crystal from the viewer. He half-expected his tormentor to leap out of the closet with her bloody knife. No, she was not here this moment, but she would be here – someday. If he didn't do something about Mi'Ra, daughter of Du'Rog, she would strike him down in the middle of dinner or smother him while he slept. Knowing that, he would never sleep again.

G'Kar dashed to his terminal with the impulse of ordering her arrest. He stopped himself, realizing that he couldn't bring the full weight of his position down upon the family of Du'Rog. The *Shon'Kar* was a tradition that was central to the heart of the Narn; if he squashed them, it would only win them sympathy. Even Narn law would prevail against him. Worse yet, an action against Mi'Ra, Ka'Het, and T'Kog would bring to light the whole unsavory business of his ascendency to the Third Circle, his treachery, and Du'Rog's disgrace. He had let this wound fester too long, and now the infection was about to spread – unless he took his knife and cut it out.

G'Kar sighed and slumped back into his chair, the stiff leather of his waistcoat squeaking against the pelt covering the cushion. He would have to do something – already the family of Du'Rog had made two serious attempts on his life, and here was the daughter threatening more! He could count on some protection from Garibaldi and his security forces for as long as he remained on Babylon 5. But who wanted to live like a hunted animal? Besides, the station was a sieve, with aliens and strangers of all types filtering through by the hundreds every day. If Mi'Ra was as determined as she sounded, she would find some way on to Babylon 5 and would stalk him until her Blood Oath was fulfilled. Only death would stop her.

Therefore, thought G'Kar rationally, Mi'Ra would have to die. Ka'Het and T'Kog might listen to reason if that firebrand in the red dress was gone. Who could he ask to help him? No self-respecting Narn would take his side against such a well-deserved *Shon'Kar*, and he couldn't share his secret with humans, Minbari, or other races. If only he could kill Mi'Ra himself and make it appear as if somebody else had done it. G'Kar glanced around his quarters, just to make certain that his foe wasn't hiding behind the curtains. He remembered well the other attempts on his life, and how both had nearly been successful.

The order of business was first to put the daughter of Du'Rog off the scent, then make sure she was not hunting him faster than he could hunt her. When she was at ease, he would strike.

The ambassador tapped the link on his desk. "Good morning, Na'Toth."

"Good morning, Ambassador," his assistant answered crisply.

G'Kar cleared his throat importantly. "A special dispatch has just come in, and I must return to Homeworld immediately. I will pilot myself in my personal transport."

He could imagine her puzzled face as she said, "Ambassador, the cruiser *K'sha Na'vas* is arriving tomorrow for a courtesy call. They could take you home in half the time of your transport."

"The *K'sha Na'Vas*," said G'Kar thoughtfully, "and my old friend, Vin'Tok. That is tempting, but I prefer to pilot myself. I need some time alone – to think. I will be leaving in four hours, and I will do my own packing. Cancel my appointments, make my apologies, and do whatever is necessary. If anybody asks, this is personal business."

"Yes, Ambassador," said Na'Toth, not letting her surprise affect her efficiency.

"G'Kar out." He tapped the link and sat back in his chair. He wished he could tell Na'Toth his plans, but he knew her feelings regarded the *Shon'Kar*. Perhaps he could tell her when it was all over, if he was victorious.

Commander Ivanova shifted on the balls of her feet as she surveyed her domain: Command and Control, an air-filled bubble on the tip of the station. The commander's hair was pulled back from her attractive face in a severe on-duty hairstyle, and she felt tense, although she didn't know why. The 50,000 kilometers of space surrounding the station were peaceful, even though departing traffic had fallen somewhat behind schedule. The only one complaining was Ambassador G'Kar, which figured.

"Ten seconds to jump for the *Borelian*," said one of the techs behind her.

Ivanova gazed at her monitor in time to see the jump gate blossom into pulsating rays of golden light. Like a tunnel into infinity, the lights stretched along the length of the latticework and swallowed the Centauri transport like a whale swallowing a minnow. Then the tube of light faded into blackness, leaving nothing but the skeleton of the gleaming latticework.

"Captain in C-and-C," announced a voice.

"As you were," replied the cheerful voice of Captain John Sheridan. Ivanova turned around to see the captain as he strode along the crosswalk, nodding to subordinates. His hands were clasped behind his back, which she had come to recognize as his nonintrusive approach. There was no emergency or urgent business to discuss, but Sheridan still looked concerned about something.

She gave him a brief nod. "Hello, Captain."

"Commander." He smiled boyishly. "How's traffic tonight?"

"Moderate. Departures are slightly behind schedule, but only one ship is complaining."

Sheridan frowned. "That would be Ambassador G'Kar, wouldn't it?"

"Yes," she answered. "He's in his personal transport, and he seems to be in quite a hurry to get out of here."

Sheridan scratched his sandy-gray hair. "I just found out he was leaving. This is rather sudden, isn't it? G'Kar isn't noted for leaving like this, without any ceremony."

"No, sir, he isn't. He was recalled to Homeworld unexpectedly. None of us knows why."

The communications officer broke in. "Commander, the ambassador wants to know if he's been cleared for jump."

"Patch him in to me for a moment," said the captain.

At once, the Narn's spotted cranium and jutting jaw appeared on the monitor in front of Sheridan. He looked agitated. "What is the delay?" demanded the ambassador. "Oh, hello, Captain Sheridan. Is there some difficulty?"

"That was going to be my question," said the captain. "It's not like you to leave as suddenly as this, and I wondered if there was a problem. Is there anything we can do to help?"

The Narn shook his head impatiently. "I left word that this is a personal matter, which I must handle by myself. I'll be checking in with Na'Toth, and you can consult her about my return. Am I cleared to leave?"

Sheridan hesitated. "Have a safe trip, Ambassador. You know, it's a long way for someone to be flying solo in a small craft."

G'Kar's eyes narrowed. "We all have responsibilities, and some of them we must face alone. Goodbye, Captain."

"Goodbye," said Sheridan.

Ivanova felt an odd apprehension as she went through the pre-launch checklist. "Goodbye" was such a simple word; yet depending on how it was said, it could mean the cheerful parting of a few minutes or the anguished parting of forever. There was something ominous in the way G'Kar and Sheridan had exchanged those simple words. She glanced at Captain Sheridan, who was trying so hard to understand the alien ambassadors and, at the same time, keep his distance from them. Sheridan had yet to learn how futile it was to try to think like them, or how difficult it was to keep from being drawn into their intrigues.

She wanted to tell G'Kar good luck, but all she said was, "Narn transport, you are cleared for departure."

As the small cigar-shaped vessel disengaged from the dock and glided into the starscape, Captain Sheridan shook his head. "Was he in any kind of trouble with his government?"

"I don't know," Ivanova said with a shrug. "Contrary to popular belief, I don't know everything that goes on here."

"Thirty seconds until jump," said a tech.

Captain Sheridan was just turning to leave when it happened. The instruments tracking G'Kar's one-man ship shot off their scales.

"Reactor breach! Narn transport!" shouted a tech.

A colleague added, "Radiation increase of four hundred percent!"

Ivanova pounded her communications panel. "Narn transport, come in! G'Kar!"

The small ship continued to drift for a second until it exploded into a searing cloud of subatomic particles. The explosion blossomed outward through space, until it vanished like a rainbow chased by the sun. In less than two seconds, there was nothing left of G'Kar's personal transport but ever-expanding space dust.

"Oh, my God!" said a tech behind Ivanova.

Captain Sheridan leaned on a panel, gaping with amazement at the glimmering starscape, where there had been a ship a few seconds earlier. He swallowed hard and yelled, "Scramble a Starfury. And a rescue team!"

"Starfury One," said Ivanova, "scramble for reconnaissance – code ten – grid alpha 136. Also, search and rescue, go to grid alpha 136."

"There's nothing left of it," said one stunned tech. "There's not enough left to fill a thimble."

Nobody was going to rescind the order to send a Starfury and a rescue team, but it certainly looked pointless. A few seconds later, a tech announced that the Starfury was away and circling the coordinates. The rescue team was getting suited up for a space-walk.

Captain Sheridan tapped his link and spoke into the back of his hand. "Sheridan to Garibaldi, come in."

"Yes, sir," said the security chief, sounding a little groggy, as if he'd been taking a nap.

"There's been a terrible accident." Sheridan glanced at Ivanova. "At least we *think* it's an accident."

"A plasma charge on the main reactor would do that," she said.

Sheridan heaved his shoulders. "Anyway, Chief, G'Kar is dead."

"What!" blurted Garibaldi. "How?"

"Meet me in C-and-C," grumbled Sheridan. "Out."

"Starfury One reporting." Everyone's attention turned to the sleek, quad-winged fighter on the overhead screen. A moment later, that image was replaced by a young man in a helmet. Warren Keffer's face was obscured by the reflections on his faceplate, but Ivanova could still see the worry under the plexiglass.

"Report," she said.

Keffer studied his instruments. "I'm picking up lots of

trace elements, residual gases, and a pocket of radiation.
I see exactly where the explosion took place, but if
you're looking for survivors . . . forget it. We'll be lucky
to find any debris at all."

Ivanova nodded grimly, having expected the worst.
She glanced at Captain Sheridan, and his usually un-
ruffled face looked shocked and gaunt. That confirmed
it.

G'Kar of the Third Circle, the Narn Regime's first
Ambassador to Babylon 5, was dead.

CHAPTER 2

SINCE G'KAR often worked in his quarters, Na'Toth used her access to go in and organize his transparencies, data crystals, and documents. G'Kar could be messy and disorganized when left to his own devices, and she was looking for commitments he hadn't told her about, perhaps even a clue as to why he had left so suddenly.

Could he be in trouble with the council? G'Kar's allies in the Kha'Ri were supposed to keep him out of the political fray, to leave him free to do his job, but they were not always successful. G'Kar was outspoken, short-tempered and secretive – he could have enemies and battles she didn't even know about. Na'Toth sunk into the chair at his desk and saw half-a-dozen data crystals strewn across the desktop. She scooped them up and shoved them into a corner, still wondering about his mysterious departure, going alone and piloting himself.

The door chimed, and Na'Toth lifted her formidable jaw. Temporarily she was the sole representative of the Narn Regime on Babylon 5, and she had to conduct herself in a certain manner. The visitor was probably a constituent having travel difficulties, or someone making a complaint about some incident of Narn brutality. She had a special data crystal with autoerase for those complaints.

"Enter!"

To her surprise, it wasn't a confused tourist but Captain John Sheridan, followed by Security Chief Garibaldi and Commander Ivanova. Na'Toth bristled in her chair, thinking that they were after information. But even if she knew anything, which she didn't, she wasn't about to discuss G'Kar's personal affairs with a bunch of Earthers.

"Can I help you?"

Captain Sheridan halted and straightened his shoulders. He looked back at his subordinates, but they both looked dazed and unable to offer him any help. Na'Toth turned slowly in her chair, realizing that they weren't after information – they had come to deliver it.

"The ambassador . . ." Sheridan said hoarsely. "Ambassador G'Kar is dead. His ship exploded just before reaching the jump gate."

"*What!*" shouted Na'Toth, leaping to her feet. She brought her fist down on the desk with a thud, and the data crystals bounced out of the corner and rolled around.

"We're conducting an investigation," Garibaldi said. "We're wondering if you can tell us anything."

Na'Toth shook her head like a maddened wildebeest and went stomping around the room. "Have you searched the area? Is there any sign of him?"

"None," said Sheridan. "We've sent reconnaissance, rescue crews, repair crews to check the airlocks, everything we can think of . . . but his craft was obliterated. He couldn't have survived it."

"The debris pattern is consistent with a bomb," Ivanova added.

Na'Toth finally straightened her back, lifted her chin, and said calmly, "You must tell me everything you know. If he has been murdered, I will swear *Shon'Kar* against his murderers!"

"*Shon'Kar*?" asked Sheridan puzzledly.

"The Blood Oath," said Garibaldi. "Look, Na'Toth, there won't be any vigilante justice – Earth has got plenty of laws against killing people. If you want justice, just tell us who might have wanted him dead. If they're still on the station, we'll get them."

"If I knew who did it," Na'Toth answered, "I would be there right now, with my fingers around his throat."

"Then tell us what you do know," said Sheridan. "Did anybody threaten G'Kar recently? What was this trip back to Homeworld all about?"

The Narn shook her fists in frustration. "I don't know why he was going home. It could have had something to do with the Kha'Ri, his wife. Who knows? He said he received a dispatch and was leaving on personal business. As for having enemies, you know that G'Kar has his share. He has a few right here on the station, such as Londo Mollari. I would look first at that sniveling Centauri if I were you."

"He's on my list," Garibaldi assured her. "But Londo has had years to try to kill G'Kar, if that's what he wanted to do. That's really not his style. Maybe it was somebody G'Kar recently met. Did he have any new associates? Did he seem worried about anything?"

Na'Toth wasn't really listening. The true weight of what had happened was finally descending upon her. G'Kar was dead, and she would have to devote the rest of her life to his *Shon'Kar*, the finding and killing of his murderers. These pathetic Terrans with their outraged sense of justice were not important, not when G'Kar's death must be avenged.

"Perhaps," she said, "it was bound to come to this. On Babylon 5, G'Kar was too prominent and surrounded by too many enemies. He risked his life to promote Narn interests, and this is what he got in return."

Sheridan cleared his throat. "Who else had access to his private transport? Try to help us here."

"His private transport has been docked for months, unused. Dozens of maintenance people had access to it, and most of them were *your* people. He actually believed he was safe here." Na'Toth snorted a derisive laugh. "Foolish man. He actually thought he was safe here."

Ivanova moved toward G'Kar's desk and picked up a data crystal that was perilously close to falling off the edge. She picked up the other data crystals, too, and leafed through the pile of transparencies.

"Is this the way he left his desk?" asked the commander.

Na'Toth shrugged. "Unfortunately, yes. He left everything as you see it. Perhaps there is something useful here, but I worry that he was lured by this message into a hasty departure."

Garibaldi took an evidence bag from a pouch on his belt and opened it. "Commander, could you please drop those crystals in here. And the transparencies."

As Ivanova dropped the evidence into the bag, Garibaldi told Na'Toth, "We're going to have to remove all his documents and seal off his quarters. I'll give you a receipt for this property, and I'll give it back to you after I've had a look."

"It doesn't matter," answered Na'Toth. "What are the leavings of a dead man but twigs on a dead tree?"

"I feel terrible about this," said Captain Sheridan. "Allow me to contact the Kha'Ri for you."

"No," snapped Na'Toth. "I will do it. There are several matters I must attend to right away. I will be in my quarters."

Garibaldi watched the woman square her shoulders and march out of the room. Na'Toth's reaction had been about what he'd expected – no tears, no denial, no accusations, and not much help either – just pure anger. Some people might have considered Na'Toth a suspect, but not him. He knew how much she admired G'Kar.

"Does she mean it with this *Shon'Kar* thing?" asked Sheridan.

"Oh, she means it all right," said Garibaldi. "If you remember from reading the reports, she had her own *Shon'Kar* against Deathwalker. Na'Toth nearly killed that woman with her bare hands the moment she stepped off her ship. They take the Blood Oath very seriously."

The chief tapped his link and said, "Garibaldi here. I want a security detail and a forensic team at Ambassador G'Kar's quarters. On the double."

"Let's freeze departures," said Sheridan.

Ivanova started to the door. "I'm on my way to C-and-C."

The two men watched Ivanova leave, and Garibaldi felt like he was in suspended animation. His shock and grief had put him into a sort of lethargy. He knew they should be taking action, but they could do nothing to bring G'Kar back to life. That made every action seem pointless. Still, justice had to be served, whether one called it *Shon'Kar* or revenge. If the perpetrator was still on the station, they had to open every hatch until they found him.

"I've got condolences and reports to send," said Sheridan. The captain winced. "There will have to be a station announcement, then a press conference. Don't worry, I'll keep the press away from you. You just pursue your investigation."

"Thanks," said Garibaldi.

The captain strode out, and the security chief dropped the bag of documents and data crystals on to G'Kar's desk. Looking for more clues, he glanced around G'Kar's quarters, which were almost Mediterranean in appearance, with heavy furnishings of dark metal and leather. On the walls hung embroidered tapestries of hunts and battle scenes, with bloodstone standing in for the blood. Garibaldi turned his attention to the desk drawers and added a few stationery items to his evidence bag.

"Welch here, Chief." Garibaldi looked up to see the security detail he had called for.

"Ambassador G'Kar is dead," the chief reported simply. "His ship exploded, and he was the only casualty. I can't give you any more information than that." Garibaldi frowned. "I'm worried about his aide, Attaché Na'Toth. She's not a suspect, but she could be a victim. And I think she knows more than she's telling us. You and Baker go to Na'Toth's quarters and keep an eye on her. Tell her you're just checking in, to see if she needs anything. If she goes anywhere, follow her and advise me."

"Yes, sir," said Welch. He and a woman officer hurried down the corridor.

Garibaldi pointed to the other two officers. "You seal off these quarters and wait for the forensic team. Except for them, nobody is to go in or out. All Narns trying to leave the station should be held for questioning."

"Yes, sir." The officers took positions on either side of the door.

Garibaldi thought about taking his bag of evidence to the laboratory, but he wanted to view the data crystals first, and he had a viewer only a meter away. He reached into the bag and brought up a handful of data crystals, which varied in shape and color. Their connectors were exactly the same, although they had different serial numbers and notations etched upon them.

That is, all but one had serial numbers and notations. One data crystal was so dark that it looked as if it had been irradiated, and it had no identifying marks. Slowly, he placed it into G'Kar's viewer.

A female Narn appeared on the screen, and she was breathtaking. She had on a clinging red dress that hugged her slender body. This couldn't be G'Kar's wife, could it? Garibaldi dismissed the idea out of hand, because if this was G'Kar's wife, he wouldn't have left her for months at a time.

"Hello, G'Kar," sneered the woman. "Do you recognize me? I am Mi'Ra, daughter of Du'Rog. I speak for my mother, Ka'Het, and my brother, T'Kog. We are all that is left of the family you destroyed. Yes, G'Kar, we are beaten, and our titles and lands are gone. Our father is dead, his name disgraced, and his attempt to kill you from the grave was a failure. To our shame, every assassin has failed."

Garibaldi grumbled a curse under his breath, because he had never heard of any of these murder attempts. The delectable Narn got really angry at that point and went on to threaten G'Kar's life. She vowed a *Shon'Kar* against him, as if they didn't have enough of those. Well, thought Garibaldi, this certainly qualified as a personal problem.

When she pulled out a sword and sliced open her own forehead, Garibaldi's jaw flopped open. The viewer blinked off at the same time that his link chimed. Garibaldi yanked the data crystal from the viewer and put it in his pocket before he answered his link.

"Garibaldi here."

"Welch," came the reply. "We have a problem, sir. Attaché Na'Toth is not in her quarters."

The security chief headed for the door. "All right, *find* her. In fact, I'm sending out a security alert. Detail *all* Narns for questioning!"

Ambassador Londo Mollari preened in front of his vanity mirror, shaping thick strands of black hair into dagger-like spikes. They framed his rotund face like the rays of Proxima Centauri. He touched a manicured finger to his tongue and ran the saliva over an unruly eyebrow, then he adjusted his sash and the medals on his burgundy jacket. He had to look good tonight – it was a holiday on Babylon 5! Summer Solstice, they called it, and he'd had no idea that solar astronomy was so popular on Earth. At a holiday commemorating the sun, what could be better than having one's hair look like the rays of the sun?

Londo chuckled and took a sip of chardonnay wine, which he was drinking in honor of Earth's fiesta. Then he checked his purse to make sure he had his casino tokens, his winnings from the night before. But he didn't plan to gamble too much, not when the ladies were in a holiday spirit and there were exotic refreshments to sample. His experience with Terran beverages had proven them to be sweetly innocent in taste yet quite intoxicating in effect. A perfect drink with which to woo the ladies, he thought with another chuckle.

Slapping his ample belly and thinking about his wonderful meal of woolly embryo and brain pudding, Londo strode to the door. He began to hum a waltz melody, thinking that he might do some dancing tonight, and he was still humming when he stepped into the corridor. He didn't know there was someone waiting for him until the hand cupped his mouth and the knife slipped under his double chin.

"Quiet," hissed Na'Toth. "Your life depends upon it."

Londo's first instinct was to fight back, but the strong female was thirty years younger than he, and she had the advantage. Still, he couldn't remain quiet. "You fool!" he sputtered through her fingers. "What's the matter with you?"

The knife point pricked his chin, and it felt as if he had cut himself shaving. "Open the door," she whispered.

The Centauri did as he was told, because he didn't wish to be slaughtered in the hallway, for all to see. If he was to die, at least let it be privately and with some dignity. He jabbed his identicard into the lock, and the door slid open.

Na'Toth guided him into his quarters, taking a glance down the hallway to make sure they weren't seen. As soon as the door shut behind them, she pressed the knife closer to his throat.

"What's the matter with you?" he asked again in his peculiar accent. "If you need to go to this much trouble to kill me, just kill me and be done with it!"

She gripped his ornate collar and shook him. "You killed G'Kar, didn't you?"

He laughed at the absurdity of it. "Kill G'Kar? Many times in my dreams, but he's still alive, isn't he?" He stared at her wary eyes. "Do you mean G'Kar is dead?"

She glowered at him. "You don't know anything about it, I suppose."

"I swear I don't! How did it happen?"

"Much more quickly than your death will." Na'Toth pressed the knife into his throat.

There came a door chime, followed by a banging on the door. "Londo!" called Garibaldi. "Are you in there?"

The Centauri grinned at his attacker, showing a pair of sharp canine teeth. "Do you wish to be a fugitive or not?" he whispered to Na'Toth.

She pulled back the knife and stuck it into her sheath. "I can't kill you without proof. But if I ever find any proof . . ."

"It will be false," claimed Londo. He straightened his jacket and wiped a few beads of blood off his chin. Then he went to his control panel and opened the door.

Garibaldi rushed in, followed by two more security officers clutching PPG rifles, and the chief didn't look surprised to find Na'Toth there.

"I thought you had things to do," he said to the Narn.

"This is one of them," she answered.

Londo cleared his throat and loosened his collar. "I told her, and I'll tell you, Garibaldi – I had nothing to do with G'Kar's murder. In fact, I just found out about it."

"Yes, he was gunned down while walking along the mall," said Garibaldi.

Londo shivered. "Ooooh, disgusting. I hope it didn't spoil your Terran holiday." Then the Centauri thought about what he had just heard. "You mean, the Narn ambassador was shot down in plain view, like a dog, and you don't know who did it? You are slipping, Garibaldi."

The security chief looked sheepish. "That's not really how he died."

"Oh!" said Londo with disappointment. "Now you're playing games with me, hoping to trip me up. It won't work. In this matter, I am as dumb as you are!"

Na'Toth scowled. "If it wasn't you, if it wasn't one of our enemies, then who was it?"

Londo cocked his head, trying not to smile. The idea of never having to see G'Kar's smirking face again had its appeal, but there would be a price for such relief. First, there would be the inevitable suspicion cast upon him and all Centauri, and that would grow worse if no one was arrested. Second, there was bound to be much

gnashing of teeth and rattling of swords from the Narn
Regime. And finally there would be a *new* Narn ambassador to B5, one who might prove more unpleasant and
pig-headed than G'Kar, if that was possible.

The ambassador lowered his head. "Of course, I will
relay my condolences to the Narn Regime, but I ought
to wait until there has been official confirmation."

G'Kar pointed toward the Centauri's desk. "Check
your terminal in a while, and there should be an
announcement from Captain Sheridan. He scheduled a
memorial service for G'Kar at 18:00 hours tomorrow in
the theater on Green-9. Don't expect a lot of details about
this – we really don't know what happened. It may have
been an accident."

Now Londo permitted himself a smile. "I don't think
so. A man like G'Kar always dies badly."

Na'Toth glared at him, and her hand flew to the hilt
of her knife. Londo laughed. "Did you really think G'Kar
would die of old age, in a soft bed somewhere?"

"No," Na'Toth admitted, letting her hand drop from
the hilt of the knife.

"I have sources of information," said Londo Mollari.
"Permit me to ask around a bit, purely in the interest of
aiding Mr. Garibaldi. Perhaps I can uncover some tidbit
of knowledge that has gone unnoticed."

"Just watch yourself," Garibaldi cautioned him. "We
don't want to lose any more ambassadors."

That wiped the smile off Londo's face. "Thank you for
spoiling my evening."

"Think nothing of it." Garibaldi turned to the Narn
attaché. "Na'Toth, I think you had better come with me.
I have a few questions for you, based on some new information."

Na'Toth said nothing to apologize for the unprovoked
attack on Londo; in fact, she glared at him for a moment
before brushing past the security officers. Garibaldi and
his officers followed her out, and the door clamped shut
behind them.

Ambassador Mollari heaved a worried sigh and poured himself another glass of wine. The death of an ambassador, even a *Narn* ambassador, was bound to create wounds that might take years to heal. It could set back the peace negotiations that staggered forward in starts and stops, and scare away the League of Non-aligned Planets. The death of more than one ambassador could doom the entire mission of Babylon 5.

Londo set down his wine glass and hurried to his communications panel. He pressed the panel and snapped, "Vir! Come to my quarters immediately."

"But, sir," answered the voice of his portly aide, "I thought we had agreed to meet in the casino." Londo heard a shriek of laughter in the background.

"The fiesta is over for us. We have intelligence to gather. I take it you do not know that G'Kar is gone?"

"Is he here yet?" asked Vir, having a hard time coping with the noise in the casino. "No, I haven't seen him."

"Never mind," said Londo. "You'll hear about it soon enough. Come to my quarters, as I ordered. And look out for suspicious persons, especially suspicious *Narn* persons. Mollari out."

Hmmm, thought Londo Mollari with a wry smile, *they suspect another Narn*. But they hadn't made any arrests or even admitted that it was murder, so their case must be lacking. He would help them if he could because he didn't want to feel any more Narn blades at his throat. On the other hand, if this incident were to mushroom out of control and cause chaos on the Narn Council, that could lead to a weakened grip on some of the Narn colonies, which was not such a bad thing. It might be a good time to foment insurrection on those colonies stolen from the Centauri.

Londo Mollari sipped his wine thoughtfully.

CHAPTER 3

"I HAVE THINGS TO DO!" said Na'Toth as she planted her feet firmly in the center of the corridor and refused to budge.

"Like roughing up the ambassador," said Garibaldi. "If you really want to find G'Kar's murderer, you'll make time to come with me."

She lowered her jaw slightly. "You know who did it?"

"Let's just say, I have a pretty good guess. Come on, the captain is waiting."

When Garibaldi and Na'Toth reached the captain's office, Ivanova was just completing her report. Basically, the repair crew, the rescue crew, and the reconnaissance ship had uncovered a whole bunch of nothing. There was nothing wrong with the docking mechanism or the airlock, and there was nothing left of the small craft and her pilot, except for a billion particles scattered through space. It would take days to gather enough of these particles to analyze them, and she had assigned crews to the task.

All eyes turned to Garibaldi, and he extracted the unmarked data crystal from his pocket. "This is one of the crystals G'Kar left on his desk. I popped it into his viewer because it didn't have any serial numbers or markings on it."

"I always clearly label our data crystals," said Na'Toth, bristling at the idea that she would be such an inefficient administrator.

"I'm sure you do," said Garibaldi, "but I don't think you've seen this crystal."

He activated the captain's viewer behind his desk and inserted the crystal. He heard several intakes of breath when the vibrant Narn woman in the red gown appeared on the screen.

"Hello, G'Kar," she began. "Do you recognize me? I am Mi'Ra, daughter of Du'Rog. I speak for my mother, Ka'Het, and my brother, T'Kog. We are all that is left of the family you destroyed."

Na'Toth slammed her fist on the back of Sheridan's chair and cursed colorfully. Garibaldi instantly paused the playback.

"I take it you know this woman?" asked Captain Sheridan.

Na'Toth's lips trembled, whether from anger or sorrow it was hard to tell. "I know what is coming next."

Garibaldi resumed the playback, and the Narn in the red dress swore the *Shon'Kar* against the dead man. She invoked the Prophets to allow her to kill him with her own hands. Garibaldi didn't warn them that she was about to cut a gash in her own forehead, and there were more abrupt intakes of breath. The playback ended, leaving the room in silence.

"Charming," said Ivanova.

Na'Toth stalked to the door, and Garibaldi headed her off. "After what's happened, I don't want to make things hard for you, Na'Toth, but I want you to tell us everything you know."

The angry Na'Toth stared from one human to another, and Garibaldi had a terrible fear that she would smash his head and bolt for the door.

Finally Na'Toth growled deep in her throat and began to pace Sheridan's tasteful office. "I had just arrived on Babylon 5. I had never met G'Kar, but I was excited about my new position and eager to prove myself. At that time, Du'Rog, her father, was dying. As his dying wish, he hired an assassin from the Thenta Ma'Kur to come to the station to kill G'Kar. To make sure that G'Kar suffered and knew why he was to die, Du'Rog sent him a message like that one, on a data crystal."

She laughed without humor. "In fact, G'Kar thought *I* was the assassin! What a fool Du'Rog was, as his assassin would have succeeded without the advance warning."

"Why didn't you tell me about this murder attempt?" said Garibaldi.

"It was the time of the religious festival," answered the Narn, "and you had your own problems. Besides, this was a private affair. G'Kar did cause grave wrong to the Du'Rog family, and their vengeance was justified. We managed to stop them the first time, but this time they apparently . . ." Na'Toth bowed her majestic head, unable to finish the thought.

Captain Sheridan scowled. "So this is another incident of *Shon'Kar*? I had heard the Narns were civilized, but vengeance killings and blood feuds went out with the Middle Ages! They won't be tolerated on this station."

Na'Toth said, "Why don't you tell that to Mi'Ra. She obviously doesn't know that rule."

Sheridan came out from behind his desk, letting his anger subside. "Listen, Na'Toth, we're all angry about this, and we all want to see the killers brought to justice. This message is almost a confession, but we still don't have any proof. But one thing I want to make clear – I won't have this Blood Oath business on my station."

Na'Toth moved her head from side to side, as if forcing her thick neck muscles to relax. She was still enraged, thought Garibaldi, but now G'Kar's death made some kind of sense according to her view of the universe. It wasn't inexplicable or random anymore – there was a face to it.

"The Du'Rog family should be easy to find," declared Na'Toth, "on Homeworld. And guess where I am going."

"We're not letting any Narns leave the station," warned Garibaldi.

Na'Toth straightened. "I have diplomatic immunity. They can't stop me, can they, Captain?"

Sheridan shook his head. "No. You and G'Kar can leave the station anytime." The captain looked saddened for a moment when he realized that he had used G'Kar's name in the present tense.

"What exactly did G'Kar do to Du'Rog?" asked
Ivanova.

Na'Toth's shoulders slumped. "It's not a pleasant
story, and you won't think highly of my superior when
you hear it. After the first murder attempt was foiled,
G'Kar told me the truth as a reward for earning his trust.
It began when he wanted to succeed to the Third
Circle."

At Sheridan's puzzled expression, she explained,
"You see, Narn society is highly regimented. We have
circles – you might call them social classes. The Inner
Circle is what you would call the royal family. The
Second Circle is made up of our spiritual leaders and
prophets, and the Third Circle is the highest to which a
commoner can aspire. As you can see, to aspire to the
Third Circle is very ambitious, and G'Kar was very
ambitious."

Na'Toth gazed at the blank viewer as if remembering
a school lesson from long ago. "There are a number of
chairs in the Third Circle; the number is always constant.
To be seated, a chair must be empty."

She glanced back at them. "Someone in the Third
Circle died, and there was an opening. G'Kar and
Du'Rog vied for it, lobbying their friends and allies.
Du'Rog was the elder man, with more experience, but
G'Kar was more ruthless.

"During this time, there was a famous war crimes trial
against a revolutionary named General Balashar. The tri-
bunal had been hammering at him to know where he had
obtained certain weapons, but he knew he would be sen-
tenced to death no matter what he said. Then one day,
out of nowhere, the general said Du'Rog had sold him
the weapons. Although there was no evidence, a hue and
cry went up and Du'Rog was ruined. He was removed
from the Council.

"After General Balashar was executed, G'Kar laid a
substantial sum upon his family and had them relocated
for this little favor. Du'Rog was banished, and G'Kar

succeeded to the Third Circle and has his choice of plum positions. He chose to become ambassador to Babylon 5."

"Okay," said Sheridan, "but it didn't end there. Is this woman, Mi'Ra, capable of carrying out her threat?"

Na'Toth lowered her head and looked at the captain through hooded eyes. "Captain, the *Shon'Kar* is not an idle threat – it is a life's ambition, a goal for which you would gladly sacrifice your life. I do not know Mi'Ra, but I saw her draw the blood. She had determined that the most important thing in her life was to fulfill her *Shon'Kar*, and she would do so or die."

Sheridan cleared his throat uneasily. "There were two more terms I didn't understand. You said Du'Rog hired the Thenta Ma'Kur. What is that?"

"A league of professional assassins," answered Na'Toth. "Expensive but extremely reliable, under most circumstances. We were lucky to foil them the first time."

"And what is the *V'Tar* she mentioned?"

"The purpose in life." Na'Toth lifted her chin. "Mi'Ra is saying there is no higher purpose in life than to fulfill the *Shon'Kar*. That is as it should be."

The captain shook his head. "If you don't mind, can you explain a little more about how Narn society works? I'm trying to understand all of this."

Na'Toth said, "Narn social structure is very old, nearly as old as our race itself. When the Centauri conquered us, they made us all equal – slaves. They killed many in the Inner Circle, as you can imagine, because a conqueror always kills the leaders first. We have learned that lesson well."

Her jaw clenched tightly. "I cannot tell you what it does to a people – to have a race from the stars enslave you. It was the defining moment in our history, because it made us strong and ruthless. Children were hidden from the Centauri, papers were forged, and the bloodlines continued. When we cast off the Centauri, we returned to our old class system with a vengeance. Only those in the Inner Circle can govern, with the help of the Kha'Ri."

Softly, she added, "Before the Centauri landed, we were farmers – simple people. If they hadn't invaded, we would probably still be living in sod houses and plowing fields."

"Now you're the conquerors," said Garibaldi, "and the Centauri are a fading power."

Na'Toth smiled. "That is by design."

"But you don't have to continue this Blood Oath, do you?" asked Sheridan. "You're a civilized people now. Can't you let it end?"

She glared at the captain. "You haven't understood a word I have said." With that, the Narn shouldered her way past Garibaldi and strode out the door.

The chief called after her, "Let us handle it!" She ignored him and marched down the corridor.

When Na'Toth started out nobody could think of a reason to stop her.

"How soon can she leave?" asked Garibaldi. "Are there any Narn ships in dock?"

"No," said Sheridan, "but there's one docking tomorrow. I didn't get a chance to tell you yet, but I talked to members of the Narn Council. They don't like our explanation for G'Kar's death, or rather our *lack* of an explanation. They haven't exactly accused us of negligence, but they want to know how this could have happened. I offered to send a delegation to answer questions and show them vidlogs, maintenance reports, whatever pertains to the case. That crystal should help – it makes it clear that this is probably a Narn internal matter."

"They'll let her go," said Ivanova.

Sheridan stiffened. "If this Mi'Ra person is off the station and back on Homeworld, it's out of our hands. One more thing – there's going to be a big memorial service for G'Kar on Homeworld, and there's no way for dignitaries to get there from Earth in time. So our delegation will also have to attend that service. Make sure you take your dress uniforms."

Garibaldi gulped. "I beg your pardon, sir?"

"You mean *we're* going?" said Ivanova.

Captain Sheridan managed an encouraging smile. "Commander, you're the best one to answer questions about launch procedures and C-and-C. Chief, you're the best one to answer questions about security, and you also have that data crystal. You're part of my staff – on short notice, you're the best I could do for dignitaries."

"The murderer may not have left the station," said Garibaldi.

Sheridan glanced at his computer terminal. "The *K'sha Na'vas* doesn't dock for almost twenty-four hours, so you have some time. But get packed – you will be on that ship when it leaves."

"Bring your heavy coat and your speedo," said Ivanova.

"Why?" asked Garibaldi.

"The Narn Homeworld has thin atmosphere, low humidity, and very little air pressure. In one location, temperatures can vary sixty degrees in one day, between freezing cold and broiling heat. Ever see a Narn sweat?"

Garibaldi shook his head. "No."

"Me neither," said Ivanova.

Garibaldi grabbed the data crystal and headed to the door. "But I'm going to make some Narns sweat right now."

The giant red sun glowed high in the sky, making it a warm afternoon in the Homeworld city of Ka'Pul. It was in the upper forties of the Celsius scale, G'Kar estimated. Odd how he kept thinking in Terran terms – he must really try to get away from that blasted Earth station more often.

"Good afternoon, Ambassador," said an acolyte, passing him on the catwalks stretching between the cliffside hotel on one side of the canyon and the university annex on the other side. It was a metal catwalk, enclosed against accidents, and it spanned a rugged depression of steaming pools and jungle growth about fifty meters below. This remote canyon was one of the few places on the planet where the vegetation hadn't been destroyed by the Centauri. Thanks to the red sun, the leaves had a copper glow to them.

G'Kar nodded curtly to the acolyte. Since he was one of the guest lecturers, it was rather impertinent of the acolyte to address him at all. He walked on, content that the young man had felt his displeasure. There were fewer people than he imagined would be out on a beautiful day like this, but then he remembered that it was Feastday. Many of the acolytes had returned to their homes and would not be coming back until the evening. He would give his first address that night at the faculty dinner.

Two more acolytes entered the catwalk near the annex, and they humbly lowered their heads as they walked toward him. Seeing the acolytes dressed in their crude, unadorned robes reminded him of when he had studied for the Eighth Circle. He remembered it as an austere time of life, full of discipline and study. Still, he had made valuable contacts in the university, contacts which served him well once he reached the Eighth Circle. After that, there was no formal training as one moved up the ranks, just hard work, self-discipline, and ambition. Always ambition. Perhaps a little luck was useful, but G'Kar had always felt that a person should create his own luck.

He took a deep breath that included the fragrance of the *tibo* blossoms wafting up from the steaming jungle below. Ah, it was good to be alive and back in a simple place with real air. Babylon 5 could be so claustrophobic at times. The pagoda that housed the annex was in sight, and it was gilded with gold and encrusted with gemstones. He quickened his step, because he was slightly late for an appointment with the regent.

The two acolytes were coming closer now, and the cat-walk wasn't really intended for more than two people to walk abreast. To G'Kar's approval, the acolytes formed a single file and melted against the metal meshing, allowing the ambassador to pass. He gave them an approving smile as he walked by.

One of them moved a hair too abruptly, which caught his attention, and G'Kar's peripheral vision caught the other one lifting his arm. The reptile center of G'Kar's brain told him to duck, and he did so before the knife could strike his neck. It glanced harmlessly off his leather waistcoat. He whirled around to catch the arm of the second assailant, and a small hand weapon clattered on to the walkway.

The two of them were frightened now, and their panic betrayed them. The unarmed man froze, and the one with the knife lunged for G'Kar's throat. The old self-defense training came back, and G'Kar gripped the man's knife hand and snapped the small bones of the wrist, eliciting a yelp of pain. The unarmed man finally dove for the gun on the walkway, but he was too late. G'Kar lashed out with his foot and sent the weapon sailing, then he threw the attacker with the broken wrist on top of the other. The would-be assassins sprawled on the walkway like helpless infants.

"Plebeians!" he spat at them.

He was looking forward to permanently crippling them when their accomplices reacted. From the jungle below came a familiar pop. The blast from the PPG cannon hit the catwalk and warped its molecular structure, and the floor literally melted beneath G'Kar. He dropped through a hole up to his waist, hanging desperately to singed metal, his legs dangling in space.

This gave his foes on the catwalk another opportunity. The one with the broken wrist was still howling in pain, but the other one snatched up the knife. Grinning with pleasure, he was about to carve G'Kar's head into a jack-o-lantern, when the pop sounded again. The sniper had picked the wrong target, however, and a wavering beam ripped through the man with the broken wrist, turning him into smoldering pulp.

This indiscriminate killing spooked the man with the knife, and he leaped over G'Kar and ran toward the pagoda. Struggling frantically, G'Kar managed to extricate his legs from the hole. He had just regained his feet when another PPG blast severed the walkway behind him. The stressed metal groaned ominously, and G'Kar was pitched backwards. He clawed for a handhold, but the dead man rolled on top of him. G'Kar screamed in horror as the lifeless form careened into space and dropped through the branches below with barely a sound.

G'Kar lost his grip and started to fall. The jungle swirled beneath him . . .

With a shriek, he bolted upright on a dirty cot. Confused and disoriented, the Narn gaped at his surroundings, which looked like a shack made of rusty sheet metal and old tablecloths. The smell was some atrocious mixture of curry and ground *aryx* horn. He nearly gagged, but at least he realized that he had only been dreaming.

An old Narn poked his head through the flap of the doorway. "Will you be quiet!" he hissed. "Even in Down Below, people can recognize your voice."

"Sorry," he whispered, rubbing his eyes. "I forgot where I was. Had a bad dream, too. What time is it?"

"Just after midnight," said the old Narn, whose name was Pa'Nar. He was one of G'Kar's operatives, stationed in Down Below to gather information. From nearby came the sound of drunken voices, and the old man slipped inside the shack. "You've only got about fourteen hours to go. Don't start panicking on me, or you'll get us both killed."

"I didn't panic." G'Kar looked down. "I was dreaming, that's all. I was reliving a terrible experience that actually happened to me."

"We don't have any control over dreams like that," admitted the old Narn. "The Prophets send those dreams, to keep us on our toes."

"Well, they did a good job," said G'Kar. "I'm as nervous as a *pitlok* on Feastday." He stood up and banged his head on the metal sheet that formed a sort of roof.

G'Kar groaned and slumped back on to the cot. It was the middle of the night, or what passed for night on Babylon 5. "I don't know if I can stand this for fourteen more hours."

"It was your idea," said Pa'Nar. "Although I can't understand whatever gave you the idea to pretend to be dead. You must be in considerable trouble."

Even dressed in rags, the ambassador had a regal gaze. "I pay you to do my bidding, and my reasons are none of your concern. You just make sure I am safe."

Pa'Nar chuckled. "How much safer can you be? You are *dead*." The old man scooted out the door and tied the flap behind him.

G'Kar moaned and lay back on his cot. He might as well sleep, for there was nothing else to do in the dismal shack. But sleep didn't sound appetizing after that horrible dream, which was all the more horrifying because it had been real. He couldn't remember what had happened to him after he lost his grip on the catwalk and fell into the branches, but he had woken up in the infirmary, with only a concussion and superficial wounds to show for all the mayhem. To avoid having anyone pry into the past, he had hushed up the attack and returned to Babylon 5 without saying anything to anyone, including Na'Toth. The assassins had escaped, and the dead man had never been identified.

But G'Kar didn't need to be told who they were or who had hired them. It was the Du'Rog family. They had become unhinged! After engineering two attempts on his life with paid assassins, now they had sworn *Shon'Kar* and were coming after him themselves.

Had they no respect for his rank and position? He supposed no, since he had destroyed their father to get his rank. That desperate act had troubled him more than once over the years, but he had always thought it would fade from importance with the passage of time. His crime had not been ambition – Du'Rog was just as ambitious as he – his crime had been impatience. He could have let Du'Rog have that chair in the Third Circle while he bided his time. Another vacancy had recently come open, and he would have gotten it, with his wife's help. But then Du'Rog, or someone else, would have become ambassador on Babylon 5. The last few years of his life would have been radically different.

G'Kar snorted. Considering his present circumstances – hiding out in the slum of Down Below, pretending to be dead – changing the past didn't sound like a bad idea. It just couldn't be done. G'Kar's only choice was to change the future, to kill the remnants of the Du'Rog family before they killed him. He had taken a chance leaving the data crystal behind, but he wanted to leave some record – in the hands of the humans – in case genuine death was imminent.

He felt movement on his skin, and he opened his eyes to see a cockroach scuttling across his wrist. He caught it in his hand and studied the squirming insect for a moment.

"I am G'Kar, Third Circle," he told the bug. "Who are you to annoy me?"

When the roach didn't answer, he squashed it, pretending that it was Mi'Ra, daughter of Du'Rog.

CHAPTER 4

THE ALARM WENT OFF, and Susan Ivanova rolled over and swatted the panel button like it was an annoying tarantula. A few seconds later, an overly cheerful computer voice informed her, "Downloading messages and schedule."

She stared bleary-eyed at the ceiling, wondering if it would be possible to grab an extra forty winks. Then she remembered – she had a full shift of work ahead of her, followed by the station's memorial service for G'Kar, and then a visit to the Narn Homeworld, which would probably take at least a week, counting travel time.

How much blame would Narn officials place on the personnel of Babylon 5 for this tragedy? Ivanova already felt considerable guilt, because the murder – or accident, in the unlikely event it turned out to be an accident – had happened on her watch. It had happened within her sphere of control, in the space between B5 and the jump gate. Was there anything she could have done to prevent it? In hindsight, it was easy to say that they should have prevented G'Kar from taking off on a long trip in a solo craft, but what could they have done to stop him?

G'Kar's transport had sat idle for months, and there was no way of knowing when it had been sabotaged. It was clear from the story about Du'Rog that G'Kar had been courting disaster. Even his most trusted subordinate had admitted that he deserved to be killed for what he had done to Du'Rog. Vengeance was a strong emotion, as Ivanova knew from first-hand experience. If she had been raised in a culture that honored revenge killing, she might have hunted down those responsible for her mother's death.

She dragged herself out of bed and made a small pot of coffee. It was important, she decided, to win back

Na'Toth's trust. In all likelihood, the Narn attaché would be on the same ship with her and Garibaldi, and they would desperately need a guide on Homeworld, somebody they could trust. She glanced at her clock and saw that she had an hour-and-a-half before the start of her shift. Much of her day would be spent scheduling senior techs to act as her replacement in C-and-C, which was work she hated to do. She didn't like to think the station could function without her, especially for an extended period of time.

Ivanova adhered her link to the back of her hand and touched it. "I would like Attaché Na'Toth's quarters."

To her surprise, the strong-willed Narn answered, "Na'Toth here."

"This is Susan Ivanova," she said quickly. "We had a stressful meeting yesterday, and I would like the opportunity to make it up to you. Could I buy you breakfast? I promise not to dissuade you from your *Shon'Kar*."

She held her breath during the long pause that followed. "I suppose," said Na'Toth warily.

"Shall we meet in the café on Red-3? Say, in twenty minutes?"

"Very well."

She found Na'Toth waiting for her in the busy café on Red-3, and the Narn attaché was drumming her fingers impatiently on the table as Ivanova approached.

"You are two minutes late," she said.

"Sorry." Ivanova slipped into her chair. "I didn't allow myself enough time to get dressed and check my messages. Have you ordered yet?"

Na'Toth nodded. "Yes, smoked eel. It was the most expensive item on the breakfast menu."

"I like smoked eel," said the commander without hesitation. "Perhaps I'll have the same." The waiter appeared, and she ordered smoked eel, a bagel, and some more coffee.

"What did you want to see me about?" asked Na'Toth. "It wasn't really to make up for yesterday."

"As a matter of fact, it was," said the commander. "You've got to understand that humans are a very guilt-ridden species. We feel guilty all the time, about everything. Since G'Kar died outside our station, we feel it's our responsibility. Garibaldi is turning the station upside-down looking for Mi'Ra."

Na'Toth lifted her spotted cranium and regarded the human with piercing red eyes. "He needn't bother. G'Kar was a Narn, and his murderers were Narn. He brought the *Shon'Kar* on to himself through his actions. You need feel no guilt, nor do you need to do anything, except to stay out of our affairs. Our society will not punish his murderers if they were fulfilling the *Shon'Kar*. You must know that if you expect to come with me to Homeworld."

Ivanova blinked at the Narn, marveling at how quick she had gotten to the point of the meeting. "You don't mind that Garibaldi and I are going with you?"

"If your purpose is to honor the memory of G'Kar, how could I mind? If your purpose is to deprive me of my *Shon'Kar*, I mind a great deal. This will not be easy for me, because I will be accused of negligence in letting G'Kar die."

"That's hardly fair."

"Fair or not," said the Narn, "an attaché is also a body-guard. That is one reason why my vow of *Shon'Kar* is so important to me. I am shamed by his murder."

"Now who's feeling guilty?" asked Ivanova.

"I am," admitted Na'Toth. The waiter brought their plates of eel, and the two women ate in silence.

In a shanty shack in the depths of Down Below, the dead man washed his face in a shallow pan of grimy water. He had never realized what Pa'Nar had to go through to live down here – he would have to give the man more money.

He took a ragged bit of cloth and dried his prominent chin and brow. This banishment to Down Below would be over mercifully soon, he told himself, and he would

be safely aboard the *K'sha Na'vas*, headed back to
Homeworld. He would arrive in disguise and attend to
his business with the Du'Rog family, ending it once and
for all.

There was another commotion outside in the grimy
corridor, but he had learned to ignore the petty thievery
and drunken brawls that typified life in Down Below. He
had occasionally ventured down here for amusement, but
he would never come here again, if he could help it. The
shouts grew louder outside the shack, and he nearly
threw open the flap to order them to be quiet. No, he cautioned himself, this was not the time to be assertive.

Suddenly, the flap flew open, and Pa'Nar crawled in,
looking distraught. "You must hide!" he hissed.

"Hide?" growled G'Kar. He glanced around at the dismal shack. "I *am* hiding!"

"It's Garibaldi!" warned the older man, glancing over
his shoulder. "His officers are making another sweep,
looking for your killers. We caused a disturbance to
delay them, but they are searching everywhere!"

G'Kar grabbed his PPG pistol and looked around.
There was no rear door to the pathetic shack, and no
place to run even if he got out. He climbed back on to
the cot and clutched the weapon to his chest.

"Throw the blanket over me," he ordered. "Tell them
I am sick."

They both jumped when a fist pounded on the corru-
gated metal wall, nearly bringing the shack down.
"Excuse me," barked a voice, "is this a Narn household?"

"I am coming!" called Pa'Nar. He threw the blanket
over G'Kar, who turned his back to the door. Trembling
with fear, the older Narn scurried out.

G'Kar could hear their conversation. "Sorry to bother
you," began the officer, "but we're looking for undocumented Narns in connection with Ambassador G'Kar's
death. Are you listed on the station roster?"

"I should be," said the Narn. "My name is Pa'Nar. I

came here on the *Hala'Tar* about a year ago. Lost all my money gambling, and now I'm stuck here. You couldn't help me get off the station, could you?"

"'Fraid not. Can I see your identicard, please?"

G'Kar suffered a few tense moments while the security officer presumably checked Pa'Nar's identicard on his handheld terminal. "Yes, I have you listed," he agreed. "Any other Narns in your household?"

Careful, G'Kar though in panic. The wrong answer could be disastrous. But what was the right answer?

"Only my brother is here," said Pa'Nar loudly. "He is very sick."

"I'll have to see him," insisted the officer. "I'll just take a look inside and check his identicard. Excuse me."

G'Kar kept his back to the doorway, wondering if he could possibly be lucky enough to encounter a security officer who didn't know him on sight. Probably not. As one of the four alien ambassadors on the station, he wasn't exactly an unknown quantity. He could feel his heart pounding as the security officer shuffled through the flap.

"Excuse me," he said, "we're looking for undocumented Narns in connection with Ambassador G'Kar's death. Are you on the station roster?"

G'Kar coughed and wheezed and tried to sound very sick. He pulled the blanket tighter around his broad shoulders with one hand and gripped his PPG weapon with the other.

"Did you hear what I said?" insisted the officer. "I need your name, and your identicard."

"Ha'Mok," wheezed G'Kar. From his waistcoat he pulled out his fake identicard and tossed it on to the floor behind him.

"Thank you," said the officer sarcastically. G'Kar could envision him bending down to retrieve the card, then running it through his machine. G'Kar had no problem feigning labored breathing during the moments that followed.

"You are listed on the roster," said the officer. "But I have to see you to make positive identification. Turn over, please."

That, decided G'Kar, he could not do. He cursed himself – why hadn't he donned his disguise earlier? It was too late now, and this young man had put himself squarely in the way.

"I don't wish to vomit all over you!" croaked G'Kar. "I have a virus . . . a potent one! It is liquefying my intestines."

The security officer rose up and banged his head on the low roof. G'Kar wheezed, "It would kill a human in a day or two!"

Now the officer was lifting his hand to his link to call for instructions, just as Pa'Nar crept up behind him and smashed a crowbar on the back of his skull. The officer crumpled to the grimy floor in a gray heap.

"I hope you didn't kill him," said G'Kar, rolling to his feet. He bent down and retrieved his fake identicard from under the officer's nose. Warm moisture on the card revealed that the officer was still breathing.

"We'll have to kill him, won't we?" asked Pa'Nar.

"No," snapped the ambassador. "This action is not his concern. His death would dishonor my actions even further. Besides, I have to come back to B5 someday, after I step forward and admit to this deception."

G'Kar brought the heel of his boot down upon the officer's handheld terminal, smashing the case and grinding the chips into silicon. Then he bent down and ripped the link off the back of the man's hand and thrust it into the trembling hands of the old Narn.

"Take his link far away from here, so they can't trace him by it," ordered G'Kar. "While you're at it, you had better keep going, Pa'Nar. Clean yourself up and get off this station on the first public transport."

"We're just going to leave him here?" gasped Pa'Nar.

G'Kar scowled. "If you want to carry him out, be my guest."

The old Narn gulped, stuck the link in his pocket, and scurried out. G'Kar turned his attention to the unfortunate Earthforce officer sprawled on the floor and said, "Your boss, Mr. Garibaldi, is very thorough. I must remember that."

The Narn began to undress, replacing the disgusting rags Pa'Nar had provided with the humble robe of an acolyte. The choice of the acolyte had been his, in memory of the deceit employed against him by the assassins at Ka'Pul.

From the pocket of his robe G'Kar produced a mirror and the most important piece of his disguise – the skull cap. The thin layer of artificial skin covered his entire cranium and matched his skin color perfectly except for one thing – the spots were completely different. Where pools of dark pigment had blossomed on his head, the skull cap had seas of bronze, and vice-versa. It was surprising how much the appliance changed a Narn's appearance, and he supposed it was like a human exchanging ebony hair for golden hair.

Then he applied another piece of his disguise, the contact lenses that turned his eyes from their usual vibrant red to a dull brown. A Narn who met him would think that his eyes were quite unusual, but tests had shown that the effect of brown eyes on humans was just the opposite. They perceived a face that was bland and friendly, a forgettable face, much like one of their own. The final part of his disguise was an attitude adjustment – instead of his usual arrogance and bluster there would be a subservient timidity that required his head be lowered most of the time.

G'Kar jumped when a groan issued from the floor. Without a moment's hesitation, he scooped his old clothes off the floor and threw them into a cloth bag. He checked to make sure he had the proper identicard and the proper attitude as he lowered his head and ducked through the flap hanging in the doorway.

CHAPTER 5

"**O**FFICER DOES NOT respond," came Lou Welch's report from the Brown Sector of Down Below.

"What?" answered Garibaldi into his link. Some crazy derelict in an access duct overhead was hollering just to hear the echo, a phenomenon that was typical when a person consumed too much dust. Everyone had shouted at the guy to be quiet, to no avail, and now two of his security officers were on their way to grab him and take him to medlab. This interruption had slowed down Garibaldi's search through the Green Sector of Down Below, putting him in an even worse mood. He was dreading all the diplomatic schmoozing he would have to be doing in a couple of hours, and he could barely hear himself worry.

"I said, 'Leffler doesn't respond!'" shouted Welch. "He was working a corridor alone, and now he's just disappeared. We're trying to trace his link, but it's not where it should be. I'd like permission to give up the search for Narns to search for Leffler. We may need to do a house-to-house."

"Permission granted," answered Garibaldi. He winced at the howling that reverberated over his head. "We're stalled here, too, so I'm coming over there. Garibaldi out!"

He turned to his subordinates in Green Sector and yelled, "As soon as you get him quiet, keep checking Narns until you're relieved, or you hear from me. I'll be in Brown Sector."

The chief jogged to get away from the din, but he didn't find it any quieter in the connecting corridor. The explosion of G'Kar's ship and the rousting of the Narn derelicts had unleashed a kind of sullen resentment in the bowels of Down Below. There was some incidental ranting about heavy-handed Earthforce, and a few Drazi glared at him. No one looked like they particularly wanted to see him.

With a start, Garibaldi realized that this might not be the best time to be wandering alone through Down Below. Leffler was missing and not responding, and he had been working alone, too. The chief didn't make a big deal about it, but he slowed down his pace long enough to give every doorway, corridor, and alien a thorough inspection before he drew close. His hand dangled near the PPG weapon on his belt.

He was beginning to get the feeling that somebody in this collection of interstellar misfits knew something about G'Kar's death. Something was hidden down here, as it usually was. Garibaldi tried to concentrate on Mi'Ra, the Narn in the blood-soaked dress. She was the key. Could she be brazen enough to sneak on to the station and use Down Below as her base of operations? To kill an ambassador, you would need a place like this to wait, to bide your time. Hell, *everybody* in Down Below was biding their time, and the cost of living was low. The cost of dying was also low, and she could hire accomplices if she needed them.

There was just one thing wrong with this theory. Mi'Ra was a rather striking-looking woman, and Narns were comparatively rare in Down Below. She wouldn't blend in easily, not like a Drazi or a human.

Garibaldi's attention was snagged by a Narn male skirting the other side of the corridor; he was wearing a cloak that looked as if it were made out of burlap. The man's head was lowered respectfully, and he moved slowly, as with age. Garibaldi got the distinct impression that he knew the Narn, so he permitted himself a closer look and wondered whether he should take the time to identify the man and check his identicard. The Narn glanced briefly at him then lowered his head, and Garibaldi realized that he didn't know him. In fact, he seemed a harmless sort, probably some kind of monk.

Well, Garibaldi mused, Down Below was a good place to live out a vow of poverty. He let the Narn go without hassling him.

His link buzzed, and he lifted his hand. "Garibaldi here."

"This is Welch," came the familiar voice. "We found Leffler's link in a really foul latrine, but he's not in there. We're breaking up to go house-to-house now. There are a lot of boiler rooms and shanties around here."

"Buddy system," said Garibaldi, glancing around at sullen stares. "No more singles. I'll be there in five minutes."

Garibaldi signed off and continued his wary stroll through the byways of Down Below. The security chief knew these mean corridors as well as anyone, and he kept to the best-lit routes, the ones closest to the exits and lifts. He couldn't help but feel that time was getting away from him in this investigation. His instincts told him to clamp down, but he had to dash off to the Narn Homeworld – to turn the case over to them, knowing they wouldn't do a damn thing with it. He looked around at the squalor and knew that it wasn't doing his mood any good. It was time to turn the grunge work over to his subordinates and start doing his packing.

He veered toward an exit when his link buzzed. "This is Garibaldi."

"We've found Leffler," said Welch with relief. "He's out cold, and he may have a cracked skull – but he's breathing. A medteam is on its way. We got lucky with a tip from some kids, and we found him knocked cold in a shanty."

"Question those kids," ordered Garibaldi. "What exactly did they see? Who went into the shack with him?"

"We can't find them," said Welch apologetically. "They yelled down from the top of a catwalk, pointed out the shack, then ran off. We've been looking everywhere for them, but they're gone. At least we have Leffler. Want us to break off and look for those kids?"

Garibaldi stopped, thinking that he was just spinning his wheels no matter what direction he ran in. "No, just concentrate on the Narns. Ask them if they've seen an attractive female Narn."

"With pleasure," said Welch a little too cheerfully. "But we'll keep looking for the kids, or anyone else who might've seen what happened to Leffler. Welch out."

Garibaldi rubbed his eyes, wondering what the hell he could've been thinking. If the secret was in Down Below, they would never find it, anyway. This place was a black hole. People, information, stolen goods – they just sunk into the muck and were never seen again. Better admit it, thought Garibaldi, he was going to leave B5 for a few days and be out of the loop.

He pushed the exit door open and headed up a ramp. As he walked, he tapped his link again. "Could I have Talia Winters' quarters?"

Luck was with him, and he caught the telepath on the first try. "This is Talia Winters."

"Hi, this is Garibaldi. I've got a favor to ask."

"Ask away," she said. "With G'Kar dead, nobody's in much of a mood to conduct business. What happened to him?"

"That's what we're trying to find out. Could I call you later to do a scan on one of my men? A fellow named Leffler. Something happened to him in Down Below, and he may need help remembering."

"I plan to stay close to home," promised Talia. "The only place I'm going is to G'Kar's memorial service."

"Can't forget about that," said Garibaldi, snapping his fingers. "I'll call you as soon as I get a report on Leffler. The medteam is just getting to him – he isn't even conscious yet."

"I'll be waiting," said the telepath.

Garibaldi signed off and headed to his quarters to start packing.

Commander Ivanova checked her uniform in a shop

window on the mall, content that it was as straight as it was going to be. She couldn't guess how the Narn delegation from the *K'sha Na'vas* would react to the news that G'Kar had been murdered, complete with self-incriminating suspects but no one in custody. Would they shrug? Would they declare war? She had to be prepared to be diplomatic whatever their reaction.

A shadow fell over her, and she turned to see Ambassador Londo Mollari strolling to her side. He was smiling, although his black uniform was rather reserved and funereal, even if it did look like a braided tuxedo. "Good afternoon," he said. "Mind if I accompany you, Commander?"

"No, Ambassador, although I don't know if I'll be great company. I'm not looking forward to this memorial service, or the next one."

"I should say not." Londo's smile dimmed only slightly. "I heard you were going to the Narn Homeworld. Good luck in your travels. It's such a dismal place."

"Yes, well, it'll only be for a few days," she answered. A few *pointless* days, she almost added.

"But you *do* have a suspect," Londo said matter-of-factly.

Ivanova glanced at the Centauri and his thick crown of ebony hair. Was he fishing for information, or was this common knowledge by now? Maybe she would fish back.

"Who do you think killed him?" she asked.

Londo shrugged. "It wasn't us. More than likely, it was one of his own kind. You know, they have this ghastly tradition called the *Shon'Kar*, where they kill each other for the slightest offense. You will learn, under that cultured exterior, the Narns are beasts."

She wasn't about to reply to that slur. A Narn would have argued that the Centauri were a hundred times more brutal, especially to other species. It did seem as if Londo had found out or guessed at the motive behind G'Kar's murder. But on this day, hearing him dump on G'Kar and his race was more than she could handle.

"Why are you bothering to come?" she asked.

"Why, my dear Commander," he said, feigning shock, "I am *speaking* at the memorial service. Both myself and Ambassador Delenn have volunteered to speak about our colleague, and Captain Sheridan has agreed. You needn't worry – during this somber occasion, I won't sully his reputation with the truth."

Ivanova turned away from the ambassador, annoyed at his jovial good humor. It seemed that at every funeral she had ever attended, there was always somebody in a good mood. She darted ahead of him into the monorail car that ran along the spine of the station. Glancing at her timepiece, Ivanova realized that they would arrive at the dock in plenty of time to meet the *K'sha Na'vas*, so she contented herself to watch the girders and reflective panels whiz by. Londo respected her silence and said nothing during the high-speed ride through the core of the station.

To her relief, he was frowning gravely as they stepped off the car and made their way through a throng of people clustered around the docking bay. Wordlessly, Ivanova and Londo took their positions among the other dignitaries, which included Delenn and Lennier, Na'Toth, Dr. Franklin, and representatives from the Nonaligned Worlds. Ambassador Kosh was conspicuously absent, and so was Garibaldi. Captain Sheridan gave her a brief nod and a pained smile. It was a full day after the tragic event, and the captain still looked stunned.

Life never seems so fragile, thought Ivanova, as when a vibrant person like G'Kar suddenly disappears from this plane of existence. One moment he is here – an unpredictable, exasperating force in the universe – and the next moment he is gone. Ivanova resolved to sit a short shiva for G'Kar, perhaps during the journey to his Homeworld, and to honor him by lighting a kaddish candle. She wiped her eye, unable to fathom how all this grief could bring any peace to the broken Du'Rog family.

She spied Garibaldi dashing down the corridor, fastening the buttons on his dress uniform. Before she could get his attention, she heard a whooshing sound, and she turned to see four Narns striding out of the airlock and down the ramp. Their heavy boots tromped along the ramp like syncopated drums. The two men and two women were dressed in military finery, and their somber faces matched everyone else's.

They saluted Na'Toth with a fist to the chest, then they bowed stiffly to Captain Sheridan. Ivanova glided her way through the crowd to get closer to Sheridan. He was bound to want to introduce her early on in the proceedings.

"And here she is," said Sheridan with relief, "my first officer, Commander Susan Ivanova." She nodded and met their eyes. Narns, like humans, were one of the few races who liked eye-to-eye contact, especially upon introductions. Considering the circumstances, she didn't smile.

"Greetings," said the tallest Narn, who had a cadaverous hatchet-face profile. "I am Captain Vin'Tok of the Fourth Circle. This is my first officer, Liege Yal'Tar." A husky woman nodded curtly at them. "Our military attaché, Tza'Gur, and my chief engineer, Ni'Kol." He motioned to an older pair of Narns, female and male, respectively. There were a flurry of introductions as the four Narns met Londo, Dr. Franklin, Lennier, and Delenn.

The Narns blinked curiously at the diminutive Minbari ambassador. "What I had heard about you is true," marveled Captain Vin'Tok, reaching out to touch Delenn's streaked hair. His fingers stopped and trembled.

Delenn nodded sympathetically. "Everyday we find we have more in common with other races. Today we share your grief."

"Yes," said Vin'Tok. "Captain Sheridan, we haven't received many details about this incident. Could we go somewhere to talk?"

"That was going to be my suggestion." Sheridan mustered a polite smile. "Before the memorial service, we're having a reception in the café on Green-3. Ambassador Delenn will be happy to show your party to the reception, and you can come with me, Captain, for a briefing."

"I insist upon going with you!" said Attaché Tza'Gur. The older woman had seemed the grandmotherly type until her sharp voice cut through the murmur.

Sheridan smiled uneasily. "Very well. My office is this way." He pointed into the crowd and it magically parted, helped by Garibaldi's security. While the smaller party of two humans and three Narns headed for the monorail, Delenn rustled through the crowd in her silken robe, and the larger contingent followed her to the free food.

No one noticed a hunched Narn in a simple cloak who walked up the ramp and mingled with the crew of the *K'sha Na'vas*.

In Sheridan's office, they stood in silence as they watched the visual replay of the wrenching explosion that blasted G'Kar's transport into space dust. There was very little to say, thought Ivanova, except that if it wasn't a bomb, it was a very faulty reactor that should have been discovered during routine checks. Captain Vin-'Tok's face never betrayed the slightest emotion, but Tza'Gur could be heard muttering under her breath.

When the vidlog ended, Captain Sheridan held up his hand to quiet the murmurs. "Before we jump to any conclusions, I have one more thing to show you. This is taken from a data crystal that was discovered on Ambassador G'Kar's desk after his death."

With that insufficient warning, the captain played the visual of Mi'Ra, daughter of Du'Rog, vowing the *Shon-'Kar* against the dead man. Both Vin'Tok and Tza'Gur watched intently as the young Narn woman slit her scalp and let the blood flow down her face. When it was over, Tza'Gur was breathing so heavily that she had to find a chair to sit in.

"So that is it," said Vin'Tok with bitter acceptance. "Naturally, when we heard of the ambassador's death, we feared the worst. We feared that his murder was politically motivated, which would bring terrible repercussions. Now we know it was a personal matter."

"Under our law," said Garibaldi, "if we catch the murderer on Babylon 5, we're going to bring him to trial."

Vin'Tok sighed and looked at Na'Toth for help. "Have you explained the *Shon'Kar* to them?"

"I have," Na'Toth said dryly. "They are stubborn in their beliefs."

"I have studied Terran law," a cracked voice broke in. All eyes turned to the older woman, Tza'Gur, as she rose from her chair. "Under Terran law, the *Shon'Kar* would be called 'justifiable homicide.'"

"I hate to correct you," said Sheridan, "but that's something entirely different. Justifiable homicide is when a person is attacked and is fighting for his life. This is a revenge killing, pure and simple. We call it premeditated murder."

"Come now," said Tza'Gur. "You Earthers are not pacifists. You have many instances where murder is permitted – justifiable homicide, warfare, capital punishment. What is the difference between the *Shon'Kar* and your justice, where you catch a murderer, try him, and space him?"

Sheridan shook his head and tried not to look exasperated. "In one case, there's been a fair trial that removes all doubt that the accused could be innocent. In the other case, it's vigilante justice, which we don't condone."

"There is no doubt in a *Shon'Kar*," said the old woman. "It is never sworn unless there is certainty, and the end result is the same."

Sheridan sighed. "Then it's true, even if the Du'Rog family is guilty, nothing will happen to them?"

Vin'Tok glanced at the captain and smiled. "I

wouldn't say that exactly. The ambassador had many
friends. The Du'Rog family knew they could be sacri-
ficing their lives to fulfill the *Shon'Kar*. We appreciate
your diligence and concern in this matter, and after seeing this crystal, I am sorry that you must send a
delegation to Homeworld."

"We wish to go – to honor G'Kar," said Ivanova.

Vin'Tok nodded in a courtly manner. "Understood. It
will be our honor to transport you. Now if you'll excuse
us, I think we should join the others at the reception."

"Come," said Na'Toth, motioning towards the door,
"I'll show you the way." With that, the three Narns filed
out of the captain's office.

Sheridan's lips thinned. "I wish we could catch the
murderer on the station."

"I sent you a report about one of my officers," said
Garibaldi. "I don't know if it's related to this, but Leffler
had his head bashed in while we were sweeping for
Narns in Down Below. He's in a coma, but the doc
thinks he'll be all right. Somebody didn't want to be
carded."

"I read your report," answered the captain. "Don't
worry, Garibaldi. I'll follow through while you're gone,
and we'll catch them, if they're here."

Ivanova said, "Big 'if.'"

"Oh, one more thing." Sheridan bowed his head apologetically. "You can't take any weapons to Homeworld or
aboard their ship. In exchange for that concession, I got
you diplomatic immunity."

"Great," said Garibaldi, brushing back his short-
cropped hair. "We'll be unarmed and unable to do
anything if we meet the murderer face to face. In fact,
she can *brag* about killing G'Kar if she feels like it!"

Sheridan straightened. "Let's do the only thing we can
for G'Kar – show how much we miss him."

The small amphitheater in the Green Sector had seen a
number of plays and concerts, recalled Ivanova, but it

was doubtful whether it had seen any greater drama than
the memorial service for G'Kar. Mourners and the curious were packed in, clogging the aisles, hanging from the
rafters. She could see Garibaldi and his officers trying to
keep the aisles clear and the riffraff out, but it was a losing battle. At least they managed to keep a row of seats
roped off in the front, and that was where Ivanova was
sitting with Captain Sheridan, the ambassadors, and the
visiting Narns.

The doors to the theater slammed shut, and the unruly
crowd began to quiet. From the seat beside her, Captain
Sheridan rose to his feet and scanned the audience. When
he was content that they were finally settling in, he strode
to the stage and stepped behind the podium. His commanding presence brought the audience to a gradual
hush.

"Thank you for coming," he began, "to the memorial
service for Ambassador G'Kar of the Narn Regime. I
know the shocking and sudden nature of his death has
left all of us feeling stunned. We wish we could do something to turn back the clock, to prevent it from
happening. But we can't. And we can't become obsessed
with the tragedy – we must move on to our real purpose
in gathering here today. We have come here to remember G'Kar as one of the founders of Babylon 5, a driving
force in its creation and success."

Sheridan cleared his throat and let his gaze fall on
Londo Mollari. "G'Kar used to say that serving on
Babylon 5 was a great honor because he was facing his
enemies. But I don't think even his enemies considered
him the enemy. Underneath his warrior exterior, he was
a peacemaker, a person who was helping us search for
reasons to have peace instead of war. I won't claim that
G'Kar and I were old friends or knew each other well,
but I always felt that G'Kar was trying to make things
better."

The captain bowed his head. "Humans often say a
prayer in a situation like this, which is a way of talking to

our creator, so you'll excuse me if I indulge. Dear God, we wish G'Kar a swift journey to the afterlife, in whatever form he believed. We wish a minimum of grief to those he leaves behind, and we hope You can heal the call of revenge in our hearts. Finally, we pray that G'Kar's search for peace will have an everlasting effect on Babylon 5 and the governments which support her. Amen."

"Amen," Ivanova repeated with the Jewish intonation.

Sheridan looked momentarily nervous as he realized what was coming next. "Being an ambassador on B5 means being on the point for your entire culture, and it takes a special person to do that. G'Kar had few peers on this station, but we are fortunate to have two of them with us today. Before Ambassador Delenn speaks, Ambassador Mollari has a few words."

There were shocked murmurs throughout the hall, and the Narn delegation glared at Londo as he ambled importantly toward the podium. He smiled knowingly, which came out looking like a sneer.

"You do not know my race," he began, "if you think we have no respect for our enemies. We have enormous respect for the Narn Regime, even though they keep stealing our ancestral holdings; but that is a discussion for another day. In fact, that is a discussion I often had with my departed enemy, G'Kar. There was *nothing* we agreed upon, yet we understood each other as few friends do. We knew the difficulties of our position on this station – the way our governments expected us to be wise and brilliant, when we were only mortal. Both of us felt our allegiance to home mixed with a strange sense of belonging to something bigger, something we found here, on Babylon 5. As few others can say, he was my equal – this G'Kar of the Third Circle – and I will miss him."

Londo shrugged fatalistically. "They will send another, but he will not be G'Kar. I will miss seeing the veins pop out of his neck when he is yelling at me, or the way he sputtered when he did not get his way. The next ambassador will certainly not yell or sputter as zestfully as G'Kar." The Centauri touched his fist to his chest in the Narn salute. "Goodbye, my enemy."

Like several people in the audience, Ivanova was sniffling, and she had to fish a handkerchief out of her pocket. This memorial service was turning out to be just what she feared most, a heartfelt tribute to a person who had gone before his time. G'Kar had died just when he was making his greatest contributions – all to satisfy a primitive urge for revenge. She wanted to scream, but she couldn't. So instead she cried.

Ivanova looked up to see Delenn sweep across the stage and stand next to the podium, which would have dwarfed her had she stood behind it. Her shocks of auburn hair gave her a softer appearance than she'd had before her transformation; it added to her beatific presence. Today, however, her fragile face looked angry and determined.

"The death of G'Kar is an outrage!" said Delenn, drawing hushed breaths from the crowd. "I came here to remember my colleague, but I don't truly want to do that. Instead, I want my colleague to be *alive*, as he always was. I do not feel like forgiving his murderers and moving on, although I know that is the prudent thing to do. You must excuse me while I vent my outrage first, because my friend, G'Kar, is not here to do it for himself."

The Narns squirmed in their chairs, and Delenn apparently took some comfort in that. "When I came here, Babylon 5 was just a collection of people from different worlds. It had no personality, no identity, not much chance of survival. Then I met Ambassadors G'Kar, Kosh, Mollari, I renewed my acquaintance with Ambassador Sinclair – and my mission became real to me. It is not an easy thing to willfully submit oneself to an experiment, but that is what we have done here on Babylon 5.

G'Kar firmly believed in our mission, and he accepted
Babylon 5 as his home. This was a great inspiration to
me and many of us who had strong ties to our home-
worlds. I took strength from G'Kar, and I am weakened
now that he is gone."

Delenn's anger gave way to a nostalgic smile. "G'Kar
could be belligerent and difficult, but I remember him for
his moments of kindness, openness, and generosity. For
him not to be here anymore – in the Council meetings or
at official receptions – is unthinkable. I have a sense of
overwhelming loss, when I know that I should be feeling acceptance. So let us acknowledge the fact that
G'Kar has transformed, while we have remained the
same."

Delenn folded her hands and looked at the Narns. "The
candle is a universal symbol of the light that even one
small soul can cast in this lifetime. Would you permit a
small procession of candles?"

Captain Vin'Tok nodded, and the lights were dimmed.
Lennier stepped forward, accompanied by six Minbari
priests, each bearing a long, tapered candle. Lennier
waved a spark over each candle, and they seemed to burst
into flame simultaneously. The lights were dimmer further, and the candlebearers moved in a circle around the
stage while a melancholy flute sounded from somewhere
in the balcony. The procession was simple and unhur-
ried, six white lights floating through the darkness while
the flute mourned aloud for everyone.

After what seemed like a brief but healing time, the
house lights were brought back up, and the six Minbari
priests and their candles formed a line leading out the
door. Despite the pandemonium that had ensued when
everyone was entering the theater, the somber audience
filed out in respectful silence, gazing at the candles as
they passed them. Ivanova swallowed back a lump in her
throat, thinking that B5 was probably strong enough to
survive the passing of G'Kar, but it was still a tremendous blow.

"Are you up on your Mark Twain?" she heard a voice ask.

She turned to see Londo Mollari looking expectantly at her, a half-smile on his face.

"I've heard of him, but I'm no expert on early American writers," she admitted.

"Too bad," said Londo. "You could enjoy this more."

Before she could question him further about the odd literary allusion, Captain Vin'Tok stepped between them. "We leave in forty-six minutes," he told her. "We expect punctuality."

"You'll get it," said the commander, "as long as you have some coffee on board."

"We recently added coffee to our stores," replied the Narn with a slight smile. He started to follow Na'Toth out the rear exit, then stopped. "I suggest you bring both warm and cool clothing."

"I've done my research," she assured him. "I'm prepared for anything."

Vin'Tok gave her a curt bow. Several security guards stepped in and escorted the Narn delegation through the backstage area. Ivanova turned to look for Londo, and she saw his spiked hair cutting through the sea of alien heads like the dorsal fin of a shark. She was too far away to catch up with him, so she let her eyes wander. Finally she spied Garibaldi, leaning over the railing of the balcony and looking down on the mourners like a vengeful angel.

She tapped her link. "Ivanova to Garibaldi."

"I see you," said the chief with a wave. "What's up?"

"I just wanted to tell you that we leave for Homeworld in forty-five minutes."

"Do you have any idea what we're getting ourselves into?" he asked with concern.

"Nope," she admitted. "But I did hear one bit of good news."

"What's that?"

"They have coffee on board."

"But at night I expect hot chocolate," said the chief. "I've got a million things to do before we leave, but I'll be there. Garibaldi out."

A dust devil swirled through the copper-colored sand, across pockmarked walls, up a cement post, and finally found a street sign to play with. The sign twisted and squeaked on its corroded metal rings, tossing rust confetti to the playful dust devil. Mi'Ra, daughter of Du'Rog, paused under the sign, which read simply "V'Tar." She had to laugh that such a poverty-stricken street, squeezed dry of all life and hope, could be named after the spark of life.

Street V'Tar consisted of two rows of three-story buildings, each one more weary and forlorn than the one before. Even in this wind, she could smell the burning rubber. The only light came from clay pots that swung in the wind, casting shadow races on the dilapidated buildings. With frightening sameness, Street V'Tar stretched down a hill until it was mercifully swallowed in darkness. Mi'Ra shivered, knowing this drained section of the border zone was her home, worse than a plebian's.

"Hurry!" she called into the wind, wondering where her lazy brother, T'Kog, was hiding now. T'Kog was a grave disappointment to her, and she found she was wasting too much energy keeping him focused on the *Shon'Kar*. He still acted as if life was going to change, get better of its own accord, and she knew it was not.

"Mi'Ra! Mi'Ra!" he screamed, stumbling out of the darkness.

She drew her compact PPG, thinking T'Kog was being chased. When the Narn saw that her younger brother was laughing and waving some bits of newspad, her sharp features bent into a scowl. "Stop using my name!"

"Do you see what this is!" he said, shoving the newspad in her face. "G'Kar is dead! G'Kar died in an explosion launching from Babylon 5!"

Mi'Ra grasped the sheets out of his hands and stared

at them, each symbol registering on her smooth reptilian face. Her spotted cranium throbbed, and her lips twisted back. *G'Kar the destroyer was dead!* Their hated foe, killer of their father, defiler of their name, and object of their *Shon'Kar* – he was dead. Killed in a suspicious explosion. Clearly, somebody had gotten to him, but who?

She shouted at the night sky, "Why wasn't it *me*?"

"Hush, sister. Let the fate have some play here," T'Kog cautioned her.

"Who gave you these?" she demanded, flashing the newspads in his face.

T'Kog pointed innocently behind them. "A man down there, he was giving them away. Several people seemed to know about it already."

Mi'Ra had already leveled her PPG and was scanning the shadows when she heard a voice spring from inside a dust devil. "Don't be afraid, my dear," it crooned.

She knew this disembodied voice was a trick – some said the Thenta Ma'Kur had learned it from the technomages – but the assassins had made it their own. The young Narn woman moved in a crouch with her pistol drawn, trying to find the source of the voice. She had reason to hate the league, and they her – but she knew that if they wanted her dead, they would strike without issuing a warning.

"You haven't come to kill us, have you?" she asked.

"Not at this time, my lady," said the voice. "Come to the nearest archway in the wall."

T'Kog was slinking away from the confrontation, but Mi'Ra grabbed him by his shabby collar and thrust him against the wall. He hit the pockmarked cement head-on and moaned as he massaged a knot on his dotted cranium.

"You picked up the message," she told him. "So you come with me."

Mi'Ra dragged him the rest of the way and threw him against one side of the archway, while she leaned against the other. She holstered her weapon and watched the light in the clay pot sway back and forth. "We're here!" she shouted into the wind.

A slim man wrapped in black shawls eased out of the shadows and slumped against the wall beside her brother, who gasped. Slinking back T'Kog managed to get control of himself and face up to this apparition. The black shawls covered every part of him, including his face, and they flapped leisurely in the wind that groaned around them.

"You've been making trouble for us," said the man in a cultured bass voice. "Telling people that we don't fulfill our contracts."

"Well, you don't!" Mi'Ra spit at the ground. "The Thenta Ma'Kur is a sham, and that's all I tell them."

The man swaddled in black flinched for a moment but settled into the archway. "You cannot say that anymore. We have fulfilled our contract with your father. G'Kar is dead."

Mi'Ra narrowed her blazing red eyes at the assassin, knowing that he and death were familiar friends. "Is this true? G'Kar is truly dead?"

"Go to Jasba," said the man. "Find any public viewer. You will see, G'Kar is dead. The newspads are real."

Mi'Ra breathed deeply and sunk against the ancient archway. "Then it is over?" she asked in disbelief.

"Not for you," said the assassin. "Many suspect you because of your brave but indiscreet *Shon'Kar*. Next time, leave this work to the professionals."

Mi'Ra glared at him. As much as she despised the cold-blooded scavengers of the Thenta Ma'Kur, she was ready to accept the fact that they had fulfilled their contract.

Still, the Narn woman straightened her shoulders and declared, "I am proud of my *Shon'Kar*."

"Of course you are, my dear, but the humans of Babylon 5 do not appreciate the *Shon'Kar* as much as we do. G'Kar also has many friends, important ones. Our advice to you is this – neither admit nor deny your hand in his murder, and do not mention us. Your Blood Oath is well-known, and all will come to accept it."

Mi'Ra bowed. "I will do as you wish. From now on, I will speak highly of your fellowship."

The black-shrouded figure bowed in return. "Earthforce personnel are coming to Homeworld to answer the Council's questions. We will stay close to them and watch them, in case they interfere too much. As of now, our business with you is concluded."

With that, the black-shrouded man stepped from the light of the archway and strode into the darkness, which accepted him without hesitation.

CHAPTER 6

MICHAEL GARIBALDI stayed behind in the theater balcony, watching the mourners depart after the memorial service for G'Kar. He wasn't the sentimental type, except when it came to old friends and young ladies, but the memorial service had been oddly touching. Even Londo had risen to the occasion. As Delenn had said in her address, it was easy to be angry and deny what had happened, and it was much harder to accept the fact that G'Kar was gone. It was like a whole section of the station was suddenly missing.

He leaned over the balcony again, wondering if there was a murderer in the well-behaved crowd. The security chief had no idea anybody was watching him.

"Hi, my name is Al Vernon!" crowed a loud voice directly behind him. The security chief whirled around to see a human male approaching him from the back of the balcony. He was a portly fellow dressed in a checkered sportcoat, and sweat glistened on his florid face. He held out a pudgy hand as if it was the most important thing in the world that he shake Garibaldi's hand.

"Do I know you?" asked Garibaldi.

"No, sir, you do not," answered the man cheerfully, but that didn't prevent him from grabbing Garibaldi's hand and yanking for all he was worth. "My name is Al Vernon, but I already said that. You're Garibaldi, the security chief of this fine station, am I right?"

"That's no secret," growled the chief. "Listen, I've got to leave the station soon, and I'm busy." He glanced down and saw Talia Winters filing out of the amphitheater with the others, which reminded him of another matter still up in the air – Officer Leffler. "Do you think you could get to the point?" he demanded of his chubby acquaintance.

"It's quite simple, sir." He stood on his tiptoes to whisper to the taller man. "Rumor has it that you're going to the Narn Homeworld aboard the *K'sha Na'vas*. I'd like to tag along, if I could. I've been trying to get there for six months, and I was hoping you would prevail upon the Narns or Captain Sheridan to get me aboard."

Garibaldi gaped at the man. "You've got a lot of nerve. If you know all of that, then you also know that we're an official delegation. The *K'sha Na'vas* is not a transport – you can't just buy a ticket on her."

Al Vernon laughed nervously. "That is one reason why I must appeal to you, sir. I've managed to come this far – I only just arrived – but I find myself short of funds for the journey to Homeworld. However, I've got excellent lines of credit there, plus many business associates who will vouch for me."

"You've been to Homeworld?" asked Garibaldi, sounding doubtful.

"Been there, sir? Why, I lived there for ten years! Have a wife there, I do. Well, she's an ex-wife by now, I should imagine. Darling little thing, except for when she used to get mad at me." He whispered again, "Don't marry a Narn unless you can stand a woman with a temper."

Now Garibaldi was intrigued. "Do they often marry humans?"

"No, not often," admitted Al. "The number of humans living on Homeworld is very small, but a family with too many daughters might see fit to marry one off to a human who was prosperous. Children are out of the question, of course, but sexual relations are not. No, indeedy."

Garibaldi scowled at the man's sly grin, but he was still intrigued. "What kind of business did you do there?"

"Importer of alien technologies," answered Al. "The Narns are crazy for anything from outside the Regime. Toys, kitchen goods, communications . . ."

"Weapons," suggested Garibaldi.

The man bristled. "Nothing illegal, I can assure you. In fact, had I not been so scrupulous, I would have avoided the business reversals that have kept me away from Narn for so long."

Garibaldi rubbed his chin. "You know, it might not be a bad idea to have a guide along, somebody who knows the territory. We've been summoned to answer questions about G'Kar's death, but we don't want to be held up in a bureaucratic nightmare for days on end."

"I still have some friends in high places," Al assured him. "I could save you considerable time and help you to avoid many pitfalls."

"You would be part of the official delegation – no weapons, no funny business – and you would have to attend a memorial service for G'Kar."

Al Vernon rubbed his chubby hands together. "I would be honored to attend a service for Ambassador G'Kar, whom I met many years ago. What a tragic loss."

"Yeah." The chief tapped his link and spoke into the device. "This is Garibaldi to C-and-C."

"Lieutenant Mitchell on duty," came a sprightly female voice. "Go ahead, Chief."

"I would like the complete records on a human male who's here on the station. He goes by the name of Al Vernon. I also want to know how long he's been on B5, and what his financial status is. And I want to know if there is any record of him ever living on the Narn Homeworld."

Garibaldi smiled at his new friend, who seemed to be sweating just a little bit more. "You only have half-an-hour on this, so get back to me as soon as you can."

"Yes, sir. C-and-C out."

Al Vernon chuckled and tugged at his collar. "You're a thorough man, aren't you, Mr. Garibaldi?"

"I just want to make sure you are who you say you are. I'll talk to the captain and do the best I can. Meet me in forty-three minutes in dock six, and be ready to go."

"Yes, sir!" said Al, snapping to attention and thrusting his stomach out.

Garibaldi winced at the man's eagerness and strode to the steps leading down from the balcony. He didn't feel as if he had made much of a commitment, because if Al Vernon's story didn't check out, he wasn't going anywhere. If by some miracle Al did check out, he could be a valuable ally, a human who knew his way around the Narn Homeworld. Garibaldi wanted to trust Na'Toth to be their guide, but he was afraid that the attaché had her own agenda.

Maybe if he was lucky, thought the chief, there would be a break in the investigation before he had to board *K'sha Na'vas*. Maybe they'd find Mi'Ra in Down Below, or Leffler would jump up in bed and identify both his assailant and the murderer. *Get real*, thought Garibaldi, knowing that he would never have a lucky streak like that.

He stopped in the corridor and watched the last of the mourners, who were breaking up into small groups and going about their business. After a moment, the chief tapped his link and said, "Garibaldi to medlab."

"Franklin here," came the response. "Are you checking up on your officer?"

"Yeah, Doc. Has Leffler regained consciousness?"

"I just got back from the service. Let me check." A minute later, Franklin reported back, "Leffler gained consciousness briefly, but he became agitated and we sedated him. His vital signs and EKG look good, but you can't be too careful with head trauma."

"Can we wake him up to be questioned?" asked Garibaldi.

The doctor's tone was cool. "I think he's several hours away from that. Perhaps tomorrow."

"Thanks," said Garibaldi. "I'll be off-station by then, so could you contact Captain Sheridan as soon as Leffler is well enough to be questioned about his attack?"

"I'll make sure. Anything else?"

"Nope. Garibaldi out." He tapped his link again. "Garibaldi to Welch."

"I read you, Chief."

"Any luck down there?" he asked, expecting the worst.

"Afraid not. We've checked every Narn in sight, and we've found a handful with expired identicards. But we've made positive ID on all of them, and none of them are recent arrivals to the station. No one seems to have any connection with the Du'Rog family."

"What about the attack on Leffler? Anyone see anything?"

"No, sir. But then nobody ever sees anything down here."

Garibaldi frowned at the back of his hand. "All right, Lou, call it off for now. I'm off the station in about forty minutes, but there is one thing I want you to follow up on."

"Sure, chief."

"When Leffler comes to, question him. If he can't remember who hit him – and people often lose their memory after a head injury – contact Talia Winters. She can do a scan on him and help us fill in the blanks. She's already agreed to do this, so all you have to do is call her."

"Gotcha. Have a good trip."

"Yeah," said Garibaldi. "Out."

After stopping at his quarters to pick up his duffel bag and rescue his heavy coat from mothballs, Garibaldi headed toward Captain Sheridan's office. He was about ten meters from the captain's door when his link buzzed.

"Garibaldi here!" he snapped at the back of his head.

"This is Lieutenant Mitchell in C-and-C, and I have that data for you on Al Vernon. Want me to upload to your link?"

Garibaldi checked the time and saw that he was running out of it. "Send it to Captain Sheridan's terminal. I'm just outside his office. Garibaldi out."

Be there, Captain Sheridan, he muttered to himself as he pressed the chime. To his relief, a voice called, "Enter!"

Garibaldi ducked through the door and was relieved to see that Sheridan was alone in his office. He was peering at his flat-screen terminal, a bemused expression on his face.

The captain barely looked up. "Hello, Garibaldi. Ready for your trip?"

"Not really, sir," admitted the security chief. "I hope I haven't caught you at a bad time, but this will only take a moment."

Sheridan frowned at his screen. "Would you believe I'm looking at Narn legal texts? Most of them are centuries old and predate the Centauri invasion. It seems as if they prefer debating the meaning of these old laws, most of which are irrelevant to a spacefaring society, to writing any new laws. Their beliefs are mired in the past. This *Shon'Kar* business reminds me of Earth a few centuries back, when it was legal to fight duels to the death."

Garibaldi stepped to the side of Sheridan's desk. "Sir, I was expecting a download from C-and-C, and I had them send it directly to you. Could I take a look?"

Sheridan pushed his chair back and motioned toward the screen. "Go ahead."

Garibaldi angled the screen and punched in some commands. As information and a photograph blossomed on the screen, he began to read aloud, "Full name is Albert Curtis Vernon, a.k.a. Al Vernon, and he hails from Mansfield, Ohio." He stopped and pointed to a window of text. "This is interesting, sir – he's done a lot of traveling around, but you can see that the Narn Homeworld was his legal residence for almost ten years. He was registered with both the embassy and the trade commission. Yeah, he seems legit."

"Is this man a suspect in G'Kar's murder?" asked Sheridan.

"No, sir. This may sound crazy, but I would like to take Al Vernon with us to Homeworld, to be sort of a guide."

Sheridan blinked at him. "How well do you know this man?"

"I just met him. He came up to me after the service and said he wanted to get back to Homeworld. He agreed to be my guide if I arranged passage on the *K'sha Na'vas*."

"That's not our ship, Garibaldi. I can't order them to take a stranger on board a military vessel."

The chief cleared his throat. "Begging your pardon, sir, but it's your prerogative to pick the people for the official delegation. I don't remember volunteering, yet there I am. You could put Al Vernon on the list. Since he's married to a Narn, he is sort of a pioneer in Narn-Terran relationships."

"How long has Al Vernon been on the station?" In answer to his own question, the captain glanced at his screen and said, "He just arrived here two hours ago, so he couldn't have been involved in G'Kar's death. He didn't waste any time getting to you, did he?"

"No sir. I don't intend to trust him with my life – all I know is that he fell into my lap, and I'd feel like a fool if I didn't take him. He said he was broke – how many credits does he have?"

Sheridan gazed at his screen. "He hasn't used a credit chit on the station, so we have no record of his financial status. Look at all the places this guy has been – Centauri Prime, Mars, Antareus, Betelguese Four, not to mention ten years on the Narn Homeworld. Look here and here – there are a lot of gaps where we don't know where he's been. If you take this man with you, he'll have to be your responsibility. I'll hold you personally accountable for his actions."

"Yes, sir," Garibaldi answered gravely, wondering if he was taking leave of his senses. He had absolutely no reason to trust Al Vernon, just a hunch that providence had dealt him a trump card in a plaid sportcoat.

Captain Sheridan pressed his console, and the main viewer on the wall blinked on, showing a communications graph. "This is Captain Sheridan to the

Narn cruiser *K'sha Na'vas*. I would like to speak to Captain Vin'Tok, if he is available."

The graphic was replaced by a view of the bridge of the Narn heavy cruiser, *K'sha Na'vas*. The lights were dimmed drowsily, as if take-off were hours away instead of ten minutes. Vin'Tok sat down in front of the screen, and his face was half-bathed in shadows.

"Hello, Captain," he said. "May I be of help?"

"Captain, I wish to include one more dignitary on the list of delegates from Earth. His name is Al Vernon, and he's a civilian."

Now Vin'Tok sat up abruptly in his chair and scowled at Sheridan. "This is highly irregular, adding a passenger only ten minutes before we depart."

Sheridan smiled pleasantly. "We are only trying to show our respect to Ambassador G'Kar by sending a worthy delegation. I can upload to you the records of Mr. Vernon, so you can see for yourself that he's a fitting symbol of the cooperation between our worlds."

"Very well," muttered the Narn captain. "I trust this will not delay our departure. Out." He punched a button, and the screen went blank.

On the dimly lit bridge of the warship *K'sha Na'vas*, G'Kar's sharp chin jutted out of the shadows. "You fool! Bringing a complete stranger on board!"

"What was I to do?" asked Vin'Tok. "A three-person delegation is still small. How was I to refuse the humans? Believe me, they have been quite genuine in their grief over your demise. The memorial service was heartwarming. When this is all over, my friend, you will have to tell me why you have taken such a desperate action."

G'Kar sat stiffly in his chair, his lips tight. Dead men have little influence, he was beginning to find out.

"Data download from Captain Sheridan is now complete," announced a Narn tech.

"You'd better get below," Vin'Tok told G'Kar, a note of dismissal in his voice.

G'Kar wanted to protest, but his power and prestige

were evaporating before his eyes. No longer was he
G'Kar of the Third Circle. He was a dead man – a nonentity. His lot was to be hidden away, hunted, and now
ignored. When he had hastily devised this scheme, he
had never realized the jeopardy in which he was placing
himself. He had assumed that his associates would treat
him as they always had, realizing that he was still G'Kar.
But G'Kar was officially dead; he had no strings to pull
and no teeth to his bite. He was dependent upon the kindness of friends, and they seemed more curious than
helpful.

He would try to arrange being discovered floating in
space, and still alive, as soon as his mission to
Homeworld was over. And he would conclude that business as quickly as possible.

With armed guards at his back, G'Kar marched toward
the ladder that would take him down into the hold. There
his furnished cell awaited.

Garibaldi was ambushed just as he was coming off the
lift on the docking level. Ivanova stopped him with a
palm to the chest and peered at him with eyes that were
darker and more intense than usual.

"What is this about a stranger coming with us?" she
demanded.

"You mean Al Vernon," Garibaldi said sheepishly.
"He's a stranger to *us*, but he's no stranger to
Homeworld. We'll need someone who knows their way
around."

"What about Na'Toth? I took her out to breakfast this
morning – bought her smoked eel! She's agreed to help
us."

Garibaldi scowled. "Until she catches sight of Mi'Ra
and goes for her throat. I want to get in and get out with
the least amount of trouble, and I think Al will be a big
help."

He struggled with his duffel bag and his heavy coat
while trying to check on the time. Damn it, he didn't

want to go someplace where he had to wear a coat, where the temperature shot up and down the thermometer like a yo-yo. He liked it on B-5, where the temperature was regulated for optimum comfort.

Ivanova hefted her own luggage and bulky jacket. "We'd better keep moving."

"Mr. Garibaldi!" bellowed a voice. They turned to see a squat man in a loud sportcoat waddling towards them, dragging a huge suitcase in each hand.

Ivanova gave Garibaldi a raised eyebrow. "Don't tell me that's him?"

"I'm sure he'll tell you himself." Garibaldi managed a smile.

His round face beaming, Al Vernon dropped his suitcases in front of Ivanova. "I'm Al Vernon," he said proudly, "and you must be Commander Ivanova. This is a real pleasure, yes, indeedy!"

The commander frowned darkly. "I wasn't consulted about you coming with us, and I'm not sure I agree with it. This is a delicate mission, and we may need to be tactful." She glanced at Garibaldi. "On the other hand, neither one of us knows how to be tactful. How about you?"

Al dabbed a handkerchief at his moist forehead. "I don't know how tactful I am, but I do know Narns. With them, you have to deal with a position of strength. If they sense weakness, they'll eat you alive. Have you got anything to bargain with?"

Garibaldi looked at Ivanova and shook his head. "No, all we've got is a data crystal, some vidlogs, and a desire to get home. If we're sticking to the truth, why should we have to bargain?"

"One hand washes the other. That's a human phrase, but the Narns could have invented it." Al picked up his suitcases and grinned. "I hate to be late! Shall we be going?"

With Mr. Vernon plunging ahead in the lead, the Terran delegation made their way to bay six, where the

K'sha Na'vas was docked. Waiting for them was Na'Toth, who gave the three humans a disdainful look.

"I hope you aren't turning this into a circus," she said.

Nonplussed, Al Vernon looked at her and smiled. "The flower of Narn womanhood is the thorn."

Na'Toth blinked at him in surprise. "Where did you learn that?"

"From my lovely wife, Hannah. Well, that's what I called her; her real name is Ho'Na. She was a great student of the *Vopa Cha'Kur*. I have always been attracted to powerful women, Narn women." He shrugged. "It is a terrible weakness. I cannot wait to return to the land of thorny women."

Na'Toth laughed, a rich, ribald sound. "Under the thorn is the softest fruit," she added.

"How well I know," agreed Al Vernon.

Garibaldi and Ivanova looked blankly at one another, neither one of them being an expert on Narn double entendres. On the plus side, Al Vernon seemed to have made his first conquest among their hosts.

He bowed formally to Na'Toth. "May I have the pleasure of serving you dinner tonight?"

Na'Toth frowned at the invitation. "I'm sure we'll all eat together. If you'll excuse me. I'll tell the captain that the Terran delegation is here." The lanky Narn strode through the airlock.

"I'm afraid to ask," said Garibaldi, "but what is this *Vopa Cha'Kur*?"

Al smiled. "It's equivalent to Earth's *Kama Sutra*. Required reading on Narn, old boy."

With that, the portly man gripped his bags and rumbled up the ramp. Ivanova and Garibaldi struggled along in his wake. The air-lock door whooshed open, and they walked down another ramp into the receiving compartment, where Captain Vin'Tok, his first officer, Yal'Tar, and Na'Toth stood waiting. A crewman bolted the hatch behind them and made ready for departure.

With importance, Captain Vin'Tok proclaimed, "On

behalf of the Narn Regime, welcome aboard the cruiser
K'sha Na'vas of the Second Fleet of the Golden Order."

"It is our pleasure," said Commander Ivanova. "I just
wish it were under happier circumstances."

A communications panel on the wall made a chirping
sound, and the first officer rushed to answer it. "This is
Yal'Tar."

"Our escort has arrived," came the reply. "We have
completed the checklist, and we are cleared for departure."

"Escort?" muttered Garibaldi.

Vin'Tok shrugged. "Two smaller cruisers. It is nothing
– just three ships with the same destination. We Narns
like to travel in packs."

"Ah, yes" Al Vernon beamed – "I always feel safe on
a Narn vessel. They take the extra precaution."

Vin'Tok narrowed his eyes at the colorfully dressed
human. "I did some checking. You disappeared from
Narn two years ago – listed as missing, presumed dead."

Al laughed nervously. "Well, as the great Mark Twain
said, the reports of my death were greatly exaggerated!
I will tell you of my adventure over dinner tonight,
Captain. Suffice to say, I am happy to be returning to the
land that cries in bloodstone."

Vin'Tok cocked his head and smiled, apparently taken
off guard by another Narn homily. He issued some orders
to his crew, and Garibaldi looked at Ivanova only to find
that her brow was deeply furrowed in thought. "Are you
trying to make sense of this?" he whispered.

"No, he mentioned Mark Twain." She frowned in
thought. "That's twice I've heard the name today."

Garibaldi looked around. "I'm more worried about
why we need three warships to get to Homeworld."

A hatch opened, and two crew members came in to
pick up the passengers' luggage and coats. Captain
Vin'Tok led his guests through the hatch and down a
short walkway that was surrounded by ducts and access
panels. They went through another hatch and entered a

chamber that contained about sixty seats arranged in a
semicircle, facing center. To Garibaldi, the room looked
like a combination troop transport and briefing room.
With no troops present, the chamber seemed oddly hollow, like the inside of a tomb.

Vin'Tok motioned to the empty seats. "You will be
comfortable here. Please strap yourselves in with the
restraining bars, as there will be an increase in g's and
weightlessness for a few minutes. After we have entered
hyperspace, I will escort you to your quarters."

Na'Toth immediately took a seat, as if showing that
she was a passenger who knew her place. Al Vernon hustled to the seat beside her and unnecessarily helped her
pull down her restraining bar. With about fifty empty
seats, Garibaldi had a wide range of choices. He always
liked to sit at the back of a vessel, where he could keep
an eye on everybody else, so he wandered in that direction. Still embedded in her own thoughts, Ivanova trailed
after him.

Garibaldi pulled the molded bar down over his head
and lifted his eyebrows at Ivanova. The Narns kept watch
on their four passengers until each one was safely
strapped into his or her own seat. Only then did they
leave them alone in the transport section.

A few aisles away, Na'Toth and Al were chatting like
old friends, although it sounded as if they were now talking about restaurants instead of sex.

"What do you know about Mark Twain?" Ivanova
asked.

"Plenty," said Garibaldi. "I love Mark Twain."

Suddenly Garibaldi heard a hollow clanging sound
that reverberated around the empty chamber. *We're
pulling away from the station*, he thought. The skin on
his face stretched back, his hair follicles tingled, and he
could feel a flurry of butterflies in his stomach. They
were on their way to the Narn Homeworld.

As the three Narn cruisers approached the jump gate,
they looked like a school of stingrays with twin tails. In

formation, the sleek ships darted into the jump gate and were swallowed in a blaze of light.

CHAPTER 7

DR. STEPHEN FRANKLIN bent over his prized patient, Dan Leffler, and smiled at the man. "Just relax. Don't try to move. It's especially important to keep your head still."

"Okay," muttered Leffler, gazing around at medlab. The blinking lights and instruments blinded him, and he twisted his head from side to side. That gave him a terrific headache, so he stopped doing it and just screwed his eyes shut.

"Lower the lights, please," said Dr. Franklin very calmly. He placed his dark hands on Leffler's chest, and the disoriented man felt a wave of comfort. "Don't move around, please. Just try to stay calm."

"Chief Garibaldi," croaked Leffler. "I . . . uh . . . the Narns . . ."

"Chief Garibaldi has left the station, but Captain Sheridan is on his way here, and so is your friend, Lou Welch." He smiled pleasantly. "You're a popular fellow, Leffler. I hear that our resident telepath, Talia Winters, wants to see you, too. You just try to collect your thoughts, and don't move around too much. Okay?"

The doctor stood up, looking confident, calm, and authoritative all at the same time. "Be sure to tell me if you have any serious pain anywhere. We can sedate you again."

"All right," said the officer, taking a deep breath and starting to feel more like a human being than a blob of confusion. He tried to collect his thoughts, but they seemed to be rather nebulous — just a few scattered images floating weightlessly beyond his grasp.

Leffler didn't know how long he lay there, getting reacquainted with his various appendages and assuring himself he wasn't seriously hurt, except for the foamcore bandage around his head and the dull throbbing that would not go away. Somebody had sure dinged his rocker panel, but he couldn't remember who, only that it had something to do with Narns. Well, his brother, Taylor, always told him he had a hard head. He guessed that was better than the alternative.

When he heard voices speaking softly nearby, he opened his eyes and saw the good doctor conferring with Lou Welch, Captain Sheridan, and Talia Winters, who looked like an angel with a halo of blonde hair around her head. "Lou!" he croaked.

His fellow officer rushed to the bedside, his sardonic face creasing into a smile. "Yeah, Leffler, we send you to do a simple job, and you get your head busted open."

"Lou, I don't know who did it. I can't tell you anything."

"Relax," Dr. Franklin cautioned. "You won't remember it all at once. Your memory will come back in bits and pieces – it may take days." He looked pointedly at Captain Sheridan. "Your health is the primary concern."

"Of course," said Sheridan. He smiled at Leffler with his ruggedly handsome face. "Soldier, do you think you're up to answering a few questions?"

"Yes, sir." Leffler tried to relax. "I'll do the best I can."

Sheridan glanced at Welch, who consulted a handheld device. "Let me tell you the details that we have so far, and maybe they will jar your memory. You were in Down Below, corridor 112 of Brown Sector, checking for undocumented Narns among the lurkers. This was in connection with the death of Ambassador G'Kar."

"Yes," said Leffler slowly, the assignment coming back to him. "I remember all of that. We were looking for some family . . . "

"Du'Rog," answered Welch. "That's right, Zeke. You're doing good. That stretch of corridor has a lot of small shacks made out of all kinds of discarded stuff.

You were checking around, running ID on Narns. Some kids told us that you went inside one of those shacks. Do you know what happened next?"

"I went inside one of them," Leffler repeated to himself, squinting into their faces. Then he grew frustrated. "I went inside several of them, running lots of identicards. I don't remember one in particular – I don't remember what was so special about it."

"Let me ask you this," said Captain Sheridan, "do you remember anything odd happening to you? Anything unusual?"

Leffler shut his eyes, hoping it would improve his memory. His mind did possess one odd image – an old Narn, lying in bed with his back to him. "There was a Narn who was sick," he said. "I never saw his face."

Sheridan leaned forward. "You never saw his face. So you never verified his ID?"

"I guess not," admitted Leffler. "Or I did, but I just don't remember it."

"May I try?" Talia Winters asked softly. Sheridan nodded and motioned toward the patient. The telepath, dressed elegantly in a gray suit with leather trim, stepped to the edge of the bed and smiled sympathetically at Leffler.

"I'm reluctant to scan you in your condition," she said, "but if we can find out what happened to Ambassador G'Kar . . ."

"I understand. It's okay," said Leffler, trying to appear brave in the presence of the beautiful telepath. "What have I got to hide?"

"I won't find that out," said the telepath. "This scan is going to be very specific, concentrating on what happened to you in Down Below. But if the pain becomes too great, for either one of us, I'm going to break it off."

"Okay," agreed Leffler, taking a deep breath.

Slowly, Talia Winters pulled the black leather glove off her right hand, revealing a delicate appendage that was even whiter than her porcelain face. She explained,

"I want you to concentrate on an image in your mind from earlier today, when you were in Down Below. It could be a person, like that sick Narn, or a place, or a number on a bulkhead. Just think of something that you clearly remember from earlier today."

Leffler tried to remember the sick Narn who was lying on the cot, his back toward him. He seemed important for some reason. Then he felt Ms. Winters' cool fingers on his wrist, and the image became crystal clear, populated by a mob of people and impressions vying for his attention. All kinds of memories came cascading into his consciousness, including some from years ago, but Ms. Winters' cool, white hand was there to push most of them away. With her calm assistance, he suddenly knew where he was – in the corridor, outside the row of dilapidated shacks in Down Below.

He heard words, but they were hollow, slurred, and badly amplified – as if he were hearing them over a blown speaker. Then he realized they were his own words, saying to someone in Down Below, "Sorry to bother you, but we're looking for undocumented Narns in connection with Ambassador G'Kar's death. Are you listed on the station roster?"

An old Narn looked queerly at him, his face fading in and out of memory. Suddenly Ms. Winters' hand reached forward, grabbed the Narn by his patchwork collar, and pulled him into sharp focus. "I should be," answered the Narn. "My name is Pa'Nar. I came here on the *Hala'Tar* about a year ago. Lost all my money gambling, and now I'm stuck here. You couldn't help me get off the station, could you?"

"'Fraid not. Can I see your identicard, please?"

In indelible slow motion, every movement magnified, Leffler saw himself checking the Narn's identicard. He saw the readouts in blazing letters on his handheld terminal. "Yes, I have you listed," warbled the hollow voice. "Any other Narns in your household?"

"Only my brother is here," echoed the words as loud

as a scream. "He is very sick."

Leffler felt himself backing away, as if he didn't want to pursue matters further. He knew he should insist upon seeing the sick Narn, but he also knew there was lurking danger inside the dilapidated shack. The white hand pushed him in the back and urged him to do his duty.

"I have to see him," came his own hollow voice. "I'll just take a look inside and check his identicard. Excuse me."

Pushing back a dirty canvas flap, Leffler plunged into the darkness of the shack. He cringed at the certain danger, and he wanted to run – but the white hand again pushed him firmly ahead.

"It's all right," said a soothing female voice. "We're only going to look."

Then the vivid image of the sick Narn lying in the cot returned to his mind, and Leffler felt as if he had arrived somewhere, at some kind of understanding. "Excuse me," he said, "we're looking for undocumented Narns in connection with Ambassador G'Kar's death. Are you on the station roster?"

The Narn coughed and wheezed and sounded very sick, as he pulled his blanket tighter.

"Did you hear what I said?" insisted the officer. "I need your name, and your identicard."

"Ha'Mok," wheezed the sick Narn. *Ha'Mok, Ha'Mok, Ha'Mok*, echoed the voice in Leffler's mind, replayed at various speeds and pitches. What was there about that voice? he wondered.

An identicard clattered to the grimy floor, and Leffler bent down to pick it up. Every motion continued to be magnified in importance, scrutinized down to the last detail. "Thank you," moaned the voice, sounding like it came from inside a cave. He saw the identicard sliding through his terminal like a sailboat slicing across the waves. The little letters danced for a moment then spelled out the message, "ID confirmed."

One last step, Leffler knew. What was it? *Oh, yes, his face. His face!* But there was no record of his face, even though the white hand swirled around the dingy shack trying to find it. There were only voices.

"You are listed on the roster," a voice roared in his ears. "But I have to see you to make positive identification. Turn over, please." *Turn over please. Turn over please.* But the figure was as motionless as a stone.

Like a slap to the face, the Narn's words struck him: "I don't wish to vomit all over you! I have a virus . . . a potent one! It is liquefying my intestines. It would kill a human in a day or two!"

Leffler tried to stagger away, to escape from the faceless danger and the inhuman voice, but the white hand jerked his head around and made him listen again. *It would kill a human in a day or two! It would kill a human in a day or two!*

Leffler's own intestines didn't feel so good. He lifted his hand to speak into his link, but the confounded slow motion of the dreamworld betrayed him. He felt a horrible darkness descending, and he was unable to move quickly enough to avoid it. His head felt as if it were caught in a vice, and he screamed with terror.

Instantly, the contact on his wrist vanished, and the strange voices floated away on a gentle breeze. As his eyes fluttered open, images became indistinct and blended into the quiltwork of lights in medlab. The first thing he saw distinctly was Talia Winters; her angelic face was troubled as she hurriedly pulled her glove over her naked right hand.

"It'll be okay," he assured her. "I won't feel a thing." She gave him a friendly smile. "You can rest now."

"Excellent idea," agreed Dr. Franklin, pushing Captain Sheridan, Ms. Winters, and Lou Welch away from the bed. Franklin motioned to a nurse, and the patient felt a sting in his shoulder where she gave him a hypo. A friendly darkness descended, and Leffler was snoring within seconds.

"First, I have some names," Talia Winters told Sheridan

and Welch. "Two Narns named Pa'Nar and Ha'Mok. I'm certain they're the ones who hit him. At least, I'm sure the attack occurred in the shack where these two were living."

Welch entered the data on his handheld terminal, and the three of them waited for the results. "Hey," said Welch, "this Pa'Nar guy is listed as a passenger on a transport that's boarding right now! Headed for Earth."

"Go get him," ordered Sheridan. "I'll hold the transport."

As Welch rushed out the door and Sheridan contacted C-and-C, Talia Winters tried to collect her thoughts. Memory wiped clean by a trauma to the head was often the most difficult to probe. It was like trying to resurrect computer files that had been disrupted by a strong magnetic field. There was just no way to fully trust what you found.

"Do Narns sound the same to you, Captain?" she asked.

He gave her a puzzled look. "Sound the same as what?"

"Their speaking voices. Does one Narn sound a lot like another?"

Sheridan shook his head in frustration. "I'm not a good one to ask. Why? Did you recognize one of their voices?"

"I thought so," she answered with a shrug. "That is, a voice reminded me of someone I knew, and it reminded Leffler, too. But I don't think it could be him."

"How do you know? Who are you talking about?"

Talia Winters smiled sheepishly at the captain. "Ambassador G'Kar. But he's dead, isn't he?"

Captain Sheridan stared at her, and she went on, "Officer Leffler remembers talking to a Narn, whose face he didn't see but whose voice sounded like G'Kar. But two Narn voices might sound the same, especially to a human."

"Yes," Sheridan answered thoughtfully. "That is, we

saw his personal transport blow up, but we never saw a body. How certain are you of this?"

Talia laughed, shaking her blond hair. "I'm not certain at all. I'm telling you this based on a scan of memory that has been damaged by trauma to the head. I wouldn't give it much credence – it's just an impression I had. But I would ask one thing, Captain – if you find these two Narns, I'd like to be there when you question them."

"Certainly," answered Sheridan. "Thank you for your help."

Talia Winters sighed. "I hope it helps."

In the transport section of the *K'sha Na'vas*, Michael Garibaldi stared at the hatch, expecting it to open, but the door refused to budge. It must have been ten minutes since they entered hyperspace – he could feel the return of gravity caused by the rapid acceleration – yet their hosts hadn't returned. Normally he would enjoy passing the time chatting with Ivanova, but she kept babbling on about Mark Twain.

"I remember hearing about Tom Sawyer and Huckleberry Finn," said Ivanova, "but I don't remember the details. I knew I should have read more Mark Twain and less Dostoevsky."

Garibaldi frowned. "Are you trying to recall a book by Twain, a short story, or one of his essays?"

"I wasn't thinking about Mark Twain at all," admitted Ivanova, "until Londo mentioned it at the memorial service. And now this man quoted Mark Twain."

"The quote Al gave, about reports of his death being greatly exaggerated, is famous. Anybody from North America would be likely to say that, if they were mistakenly accused of being dead. I hate to ask, but what exactly did Londo say about Mark Twain?"

"Only that I would enjoy the service more if I was up on my Mark Twain." She gave Garibaldi a quizzical frown.

"Okay," said the chief. "Let's think about that. What

could he mean? The most famous scene from Twain is probably the scene where Tom Sawyer gets his friends to whitewash the picket fence. Then you've got Injun Joe chasing them around the cave, and the scenes with Polly, but I don't know how they relate to any of this. In *Huck Finn*, there are the scenes along the river, but that doesn't have anything to do with a funeral."

Garibaldi caught his breath. "There is a funeral scene – the one where Tom and Huck watch their own funeral."

"What did you say?" asked Ivanova.

"There's a scene where Tom and Huck watch their own funeral," repeated Garibaldi. He stared at Ivanova. "Was Londo trying to tell you that G'Kar is still alive?"

"I thought I saw him die," the commander whispered. "But the sudden way he left, piloting solo – I've been thinking about how weird that was. You know, if G'Kar was willing to risk a space-walk and had an accomplice to open an air-lock for him, he could've put the ship on autopilot and gotten off before it left. But why would G'Kar stage his own death? The data crystal was real, wasn't it?"

"This is too crazy," muttered Garibaldi, rubbing his eyes. "But a man who fears for his life will do crazy things. You know, it seemed awfully easy the way I found that crystal, like he wanted me to find it."

Before Garibaldi could say more, the hatch opened and Captain Vin'Tok strode into the transport section. He was smiling like a cultured host, but the chief wondered what secrets he was hiding in that oversized, spotted cranium. *Calm down*, Garibaldi told himself; he already knew not to base suppositions on anything Londo said. Just because a couple of people quoted a famous North American author didn't mean anything – it was probably a coincidence. Al Vernon's use of that quote was reasonable considering somebody had just accused him of being dead when he was clearly alive.

That brought up even more questions, such as, could they really trust Al Vernon? What were the mysterious conditions under which *he* left Homeworld and was reported dead? For that matter, what the hell were they doing on this Narn ship? Garibaldi looked down at Al Vernon and Na'Toth, still chatting as if they were old friends at a cocktail party.

"We have a flight of forty-four hours until we reach Homeworld," explained Captain Vin'Tok. "With our full complement of thirty, we don't have a lot of spare cabins on the *K'sha Na'vas*, but we have done our best to make your stay comfortable. If you will come with me, please."

The captain tapped a panel button, and a whoosh of hydraulics sounded as their restraints lifted automatically. Garibaldi helped Ivanova to her feet, and the commander still looked stunned by her suspicions.

"Don't say anything about it for now," he whispered.

Al Vernon waved to them. "Didn't I tell you that Narn ships were the best? How did you like that entry into hyperspace? Smooth, eh?"

"Very impressive," said Garibaldi, striding down the aisle with a big smile on his face. "In fact, I'd love to have a tour of the ship."

"Me, too!" seconded Al.

Na'Toth cast a disgusted look at the two humans. "This isn't a pleasure craft. The next thing you'll be wanting is a swimming pool."

Garibaldi glanced back at Ivanova. "On good advice, I did bring my speedo."

Vin'Tok cleared his throat. "A tour is not out of the question. We only have three decks, and we have to pass through all of them to get to the quarters. As you can see, we put a troop transport here on the top deck by the outer hatch, allowing armed troops to exit first. Outside this hatch is an access tube, and you'll have to use the ladder. The gravity effect can be tricky on a ladder, so watch your step."

They followed the captain into the access tube, only to see him grasp the handrail of the ladder and leap down through a hatch in the deck, landing smartly on the top rung. Al Vernon rushed to take the position behind the captain, bombarding him with questions. Ivanova climbed down after them, her lithe body moving gracefully in the lighter than normal gravity. Garibaldi hung back, hoping to grab the rear position, but Na'Toth stood firm.

"You go first," the Narn insisted.

"Whatever you say," said Garibaldi, grabbing the handrail and dropping through the hole in the deck. He wondered if he dared to trust the Narn attaché with their suspicions about G'Kar. They had no proof, just a literary allusion from a Centauri troublemaker. But they had no body either. No, he decided, Na'Toth wouldn't give much credence to anything Londo said, and neither should he. He had to convince himself that G'Kar was still alive before he could try to convince anyone else.

If such a thing could be true, did the Narns on the *K'sha Na'vas* know about it? And where *was* G'Kar?

They climbed down the ladder and stepped off on to a cramped and darkened bridge, illuminated only by lights from monitors and instrument panels. A reddish glow permeated everything, including the six stoic crew members at their various stations. Their reddish eyes gleamed at the passengers for a split-second, then turned back to their monitors. Garibaldi could see Ivanova peering over the shoulder of the helmsman, trying to make sense of the orange figures that danced across his screen.

"The bridge," said Vin'Tok simply. He motioned to a set of interlocking, plated doors behind them. "Through those doors are weaponry and engineering. For efficiency, all command stations are on one deck."

"Wouldn't that make them easy to take out?" asked Ivanova.

"No," answered Vin'Tok. "We are shielded by upper and lower decks. The bridge, weaponry, and engineering are in separate modules, each with its own power and life-support. The bridge can be totally sealed off from the rest of the ship."

"Great design!" said Al Vernon. "I have always admired Narn workmanship and planning."

Vin'Tok nodded at the compliment. "We have learned much in a short time." He motioned back down the ladder. "Right this way, please, to the crew quarters, mess-hall, and latrines."

This time, Garibaldi accepted his place in line, descending after Ivanova, with Na'Toth above him. He was beginning to feel trapped in the confines of the small craft, as if there were no place to go. In truth, there was no place to go. He realized why he preferred cities in space to tin cans in space.

The ladder came to an end on a bare deck in the intersection of two corridors, leaving them with a choice of four directions to travel. In one direction, the smell of meaty food and the presence of large metallic doors made it clear which corridor led to the mess-hall. Another walkway was marked with the universal symbols for sanitary facilities, and there were Narn crew members loitering farther down. The other two corridors were lined with small hatchways, apparently leading to the cabins.

The captain explained, "Our cabins are designed for two crew members, so we hope you won't mind sharing. We have divided you according to sex, with women in one cabin and men in another, but we can change that arrangement to suit your needs."

"It is acceptable," said Na'Toth at the same time that Ivanova answered, "That's fine."

Garibaldi looked glumly at Al and said, "Hi, roomie."

"Don't worry, I'm a heavy sleeper," grinned Al. "Once my head hits the pillow, I'm out."

Garibaldi pretended to listen as the captain described the mess schedule, but he was really trying to figure out how he could avoid going directly to his cabin. He wanted to take a look around first – on his own.

"Excuse me, I have to use the facilities," said Garibaldi, striding down the corridor that led to the latrines.

No one came after him, he noticed with relief, and he slipped inside the automatic doors. Garibaldi leaned against the bulkhead for a moment, thinking that he would simply walk out and make a wrong turn. That might buy him a few minutes of unimpeded exploration.

He got a whiff of a strong antiseptic odor that almost made him gag. He glanced at the facilities, which were encased in a gleaming, copper-like metal; salmon-colored lighting added to the rosy effect. The commodes were recessed into the wall to form a suction with the air system and allow use during weightlessness. To Garibaldi, they looked like medieval torture devices.

Thinking that he had given himself enough time, the chief walked out the door and turned left instead of right, strolling along the corridor like an absent-minded tourist. Although Captain Vin'Tok didn't come after him, he quickly realized that this would be a short walk, because the two Narns he had spotted at the end of the corridor were not loiterers but armed guards. As he walked toward them, they hefted their PPG rifles in a manner that could not be called friendly.

Beyond them there was a small hatchway. Garibaldi could only conclude they were guarding it. Why? Since there was no one on the ship but the regular crew and the four passengers, he had to assume they were guarding it from the passengers. Blithely, he stuck his hands in his pockets and ambled toward the guards.

"Halt!" one of them shouted, pointing the business end of his PPG at Garibaldi's chest.

"Whoa there!" said the human with a friendly smile. "I just took a wrong turn. Where is Captain Vin'Tok?"

The Narn guard used his rifle to point the other way down the short corridor.

"Gotcha." Then Garibaldi said innocently, "Where does that door go?"

"The hold. It does not concern you."

"Garibaldi!" called a disapproving voice from the other end of the corridor. The human turned to see

Na'Toth glaring at him.

He waved to the door guards and rejoined his fellow passengers at the intersection of the corridors. "What were you doing?" asked Na'Toth with suspicion.

"Going to the bathroom. Then I turned the wrong way, I guess." He smiled at Captain Vin'Tok. "Keeping something valuable in the hold, are you?"

The captain's eyes narrowed, and the veins on his naked cranium pulsed slightly. "We regret the need for guards, but we were on a delicate mission when we were re-routed. You understand, I'm sure."

"Oh, yeah," agreed Garibaldi. "I'm sorry, what did I miss?"

"I was explaining the mess schedule," said the captain. "I also apologized for not being able to offer you any recreational facilities."

"That's all right," said Garibaldi pleasantly. "I don't think we'll be bored."

"I can tell him the schedule," Al Vernon offered.

The captain continued, "Your cabins are the two at the end of the corridor, across from each other. Women are on the starboard side. The cabins are unlocked – just touch the panel. Your luggage has already been placed there. Now if you will excuse me, I must check our course."

Once again Na'Toth demonstrated how to be a good passenger as she set off at a brisk walk toward the women's cabin. Garibaldi fell into step alongside Ivanova but, unfortunately, so did Al Vernon.

"Dinner is in two hours," Al said cheerfully.

Garibaldi looked pointedly at Ivanova, making it clear that he had something he wanted to talk about. But how could he, without bringing Na'Toth, Al, or both of them into his confidence? Ivanova was sleeping in the same cabin as Na'Toth, and Al was sleeping in his cabin.

"After I change into my sweats, I'm going to do my isometric exercises here in the corridor," Ivanova said.

Garibaldi nodded. "See you later."

"We'll be seeing a lot of each other," said Al, making it sound like a threat.

Garibaldi glanced at his chubby companion, wondering if he had been wrong to bring the stranger on this trip. But Al seemed to know how to insinuate himself into the Narns' good graces, and that was a useful thing to learn. Besides, they had a daunting task ahead of them – trying to negotiate a strange planet filled with stubborn Narns. How could they be any worse off with Al along?

The chubby human pressed the panel, and the door slid open. "After you!"

CHAPTER 8

CAPTAIN SHERIDAN looked at the elderly Narn sitting before him in one of B5's detention cells. Pa'Nar managed to look defiant and guilty at the same time. Lou Welch stood nearby, slapping a billy club against his palm with loud whacks. Sheridan would never allow a prisoner to be beaten, but maybe the Narn didn't know that. At any rate, nothing else they had said or done had had any effect on the prisoner. He had adamantly refused to say anything, other than his name and his story about going broke.

"Listen," said Sheridan sternly, "you might as well make this easier on yourself. We know you were involved in an attack on one of our security officers. Why don't you tell us why? What were you trying to hide?"

The Narn glared at the humans. "Do your worst to me."

Lou Welch moved toward him threateningly. "He's asking for it, Captain. Let me treat him the same way he treated our guy."

Sheridan waved Welch back. "I'd rather not. I think Pa'Nar will realize that he could spend an awfully long time in an Earth Prison if he doesn't cooperate."

The Narn smiled. "You mean, you have something worse than Down Below? I am well accustomed to hardship."

Welch glared at him. "Where is your accomplice?"

Pa'Nar shrugged. "I don't know who you're talking about."

"Ha'Mok," answered Welch. "What happened to him?"

The Narn crossed his arms defiantly. Captain Sheridan was about to give up and stick the elderly Narn in a holding cell until Leffler was well enough to identify him, when a security officer appeared at the window.

"Ms. Winters is here," said his amplified voice.

"Show her in," ordered Sheridan.

Pa'Nar looked a bit ill at ease as the attractive telepath was escorted into the holding cell. She gazed thoughtfully at the Narn and said, "I don't suppose he's told you anything."

"Nothing," answered Sheridan. "Do you think you could scan him?"

"I could try," she answered, "but I haven't had much success with Narns in the past." She began to remove the glove from her right hand. "When I start, would you ask him questions to focus his mind?"

Welch grabbed the Narn's arm and pinned it to the armrest of his chair. He struggled a bit, but the burly security officer was much stronger than the elderly Narn. The telepath touched Pa'Nar's hand and instantly recoiled, as if receiving an electric shock. But she bravely resumed the contact, although she swayed uncertainly on her feet.

"Why did you attack the officer?" asked Sheridan.

The Narn flinched and tried to remove his hand, but Welch held it firmly. "Where is Ha'Mok?" demanded the captain.

"Leave me alone!" the Narn growled.

"Does this have anything to do with G'Kar?" asked Sheridan.

With that question, Talia's back stiffened, and a grimace distorted her lovely face. She yanked her hand away from the Narn's wrist.

"Are you all right?" asked Sheridan.

"Yes," she said, rubbing her forehead. "This definitely has something to do with G'Kar. In fact, he thought of G'Kar, with every question you asked. I wouldn't want to swear to it, but I have a feeling that he thinks G'Kar is alive."

"Bah!" scoffed the Narn. "This woman is crazy."

Sheridan studied Pa'Nar. In an hour of questioning, that was the only charge he had bothered to refute. "All right," said the council, "it's time to contact the Narn Council, the Kha'Ri."

"No!" snapped Pa'Nar. "If you do that, you will put lives in danger."

"Whose lives?" Sheridan demanded.

The Narn crossed his arms and closed his eyes, apparently done talking.

Sheridan's lips thinned with anger. "Keep him locked up in here until we get Ivanova and Garibaldi back safely. No visitors, no legal counsel, no nothing."

"Yes, sir," answered Lou Welch, slapping the billy club into his palm.

In the corridor outside her cabin aboard the *K'sha Na'vas*, Ivanova did some stretching exercises to limber up. Then she put her hands against the bulkhead and pushed with both arms until she could feel the muscles stiffening along her back and shoulders. Under her sweat suit, she could feel the perspiration starting to flow.

The door across from her whooshed open, and Garibaldi stepped out. He whispered, "Al is asleep. He wasn't kidding about his head hitting the pillow." The security chief glanced down the corridor. "I'd like to see what's in that hold."

Ivanova put her right foot against the bulkhead and flexed her leg. "We don't want to start an incident. Let's just get through this ordeal and stop thinking that G'Kar is alive. Two quotes from Mark Twain doesn't make much difference against a *Shon'Kar* and a plasma explosion."

The door across the hall slid open, and Na'Toth stepped out. Ivanova kept exercising, and Garibaldi did a few half-hearted jumping jacks.

The Narn glared at them. "You two have disappointed me. I thought I knew you, but since you came aboard you have acted like prisoners trying to escape from a jail. Have you no sense of decorum? You have undertaken this journey to honor G'Kar, not to indulge in petty suspicions and plots."

Garibaldi looked at Na'Toth for a moment then turned back to Ivanova. "I'm going to tell her."

"Go ahead," said Ivanova, who stopped her exercises to watch the attaché's reaction.

Garibaldi lowered his voice to say, "We suspect that G'Kar isn't dead – that he faked his death."

Na'Toth recoiled as if she had seen the Narn equivalent of a ghost. "You are jesting."

"I don't jest about stuff like that," Garibaldi answered. "I'm not going to tell you that we have any proof, and I'm not going to tell you who tipped us off – but I am going to tell you that they're hiding something on this ship. And you know that as well as I do."

A Narn crew member entered the corridor at the intersection and glanced suspiciously at the gathering at the other end. Ivanova bent over and touched her toes, and Garibaldi laughed at nothing. The crew member found his cabin and ducked inside.

Na'Toth looked back at her human companions. "Why would G'Kar fake his death?"

"Maybe because people have been trying to kill him," said Ivanova. "You didn't tell us about the first attempt, and he didn't tell you about the second attempt. And now it's turned into a full-blooded *Shon'Kar*."

Na'Toth glanced down the deserted corridor. "Yes, the *Shon'Kar* is a serious threat. Do you think G'Kar is alive and aboard this ship?"

"Look at it this way," Garibaldi answered, "his personal transport explodes, leaving no body. Mi'Ra's data crystal is left conveniently on his desk. The *K'sha Na'vas* happens to be in the neighborhood, less than twenty-four hours away. And no one can explain why G'Kar returned to Homeworld or why he chose to go alone."

Ivanova frowned and lowered her voice. "Everything happened so fast, we didn't have time to think about that on the station, but now we do. Would his mind work like that, faking his death to deal with the Blood Oath?"

Na'Toth narrowed her red, reptillian eyes. "Yes, I could see him reaching that conclusion."

Garibaldi motioned toward the intersection of the corridors. "There are two guys down there, guarding the hold. Do you think you could find out what's in it? Maybe ask around."

"I believe in the direct approach." Na'Toth turned on her heel and strode down the corridor. Ivanova and Garibaldi ran to keep up with the muscular Narn as she turned the corner and strode towards the guards. Ivanova stopped at the intersection, motioned Garibaldi back, then peered around the corner to see what was happening.

The guards were apparently not threatened by Na'Toth's approach. Their PPG rifles remained pointed at the deck as they ambled forward to meet her. She waved pleasantly and stopped to engage them in conversation. It appeared as if she asked for something, because one of them rested his weapon on his forearm as he searched his pockets. The other one laughed loudly at something she said. While one guard was laughing and the other one was searching, she lashed out with a wicked jab that caught the laugher in the throat. The rifle tumbled from his hands, and she grabbed it in mid-air, swinging the butt around to catch the other one in the mouth.

By the time Ivanova and Garibaldi ran down the corridor to help, Na'Toth had knocked both guards to the deck. There wasn't anything left to do but grab them and hold them there before they could sound an alarm. While Ivanova and Garibaldi wrestled with the guards, Na'Toth secured both weapons and leveled them at her fellow Narns.

"You don't know what you're doing!" hissed a guard.

"I think I do," she replied calmly. "Commander, check the hold."

Ivanova leaped to her feet and pressed the outer panel to open the hatch. The door slid open, revealing a cramped access tube and a ladder descending into darkness. The commander had a feeling that she only had a few seconds, so she swung down on to the ladder and proceeded to jump from rung to rung. She landed in a darkened room with a low ceiling and a few sticks of furniture. The only light came from a handful of candles.

"Who's there?" called a startled voice. It was a voice she recognized.

The Narn sat up in his bed and stared at her, his red eyes glowing as brightly as the candles in the room. "Oh, it's you."

"You're looking well," said Ivanova, "for a dead man."

Above them came the sound of angry voices and a struggle. G'Kar rose to his feet and bellowed, "It's all right! I'm coming up! Don't harm them."

He looked at Ivanova. "I have meditated about what to do. I am glad you decided for me."

G'Kar grabbed the ladder and started climbing upward. Ivanova scrambled after him, and she reached the upper deck just in time to see him step into the corridor and confront Garibaldi, Na'Toth, Captain Vin'Tok, and a half-a-dozen armed crew members. Without so much as a hello, Na'Toth stepped forward and punched the ambassador in the stomach.

He doubled over, and spittle drooled from his mouth. Two crew members grabbed Na'Toth, but G'Kar waved them off and croaked, "Leave her be. I deserved that."

"You certainly did!" said Na'Toth. "I have never heard of an action so despicable. So cowardly!"

"Is it cowardly to want to live?" he asked, still gripping his stomach. "Would you like to go through life always looking over your shoulder? Wondering when the next murder attempt will come? Wondering if it will be the last?"

He looked at Captain Vin'Tok and his crew. "Leave

us now, Captain. You have fulfilled your debt to me. I should have known that I could not fool these people – they know me too well."

"Are you certain?" asked Vin'Tok.

"Yes," said G'Kar. "I will explain to them how I involved you on short notice, as a debt of honor."

The captain motioned to his crew, and they followed him to the intersection and up the ladder.

Garibaldi crossed his arms. "G'Kar, you've got a lot of explaining to do. First of all, was that data crystal real?"

"Absolutely. That's what drove me to these desperate measures. That, and the dreams I have of the last murder attempt."

He turned to Na'Toth. "Even you do not know about that one. It occurred when I returned to Homeworld to speak at the university. I was ambushed by hired assassins and nearly killed. I hushed it up, for obvious reasons." G'Kar narrowed his eyes at her.

"It is all right," said Na'Toth. "They know. When Mr. Garibaldi found the data crystal, I had to explain to them about the Du'Rog family."

"Everything?"

"Yes," said Ivanova, "including the way you falsely accused Du'Rog of selling arms to your enemies. You destroyed a whole family just to do a little social climbing."

G'Kar lifted his chin, and the old arrogance returned. "Acceding to the Third Circle is more than a little social climbing. But that is in the past, and there is nothing I can do to change it. Believe me, I have suffered for my actions. I thought Du'Rog would be temporarily disgraced – I never dreamt he would be thrown off the Council and his family stripped of their wealth and rank. When Du'Rog sent the first assassin, Na'Toth saved me. I thought that was the end of it, not the beginning of something worse."

Ivanova shook her head in amazement. "How on Earth did you expect to pull this off? How were you going to come back from the dead? Say it was all a dream?"

G'Kar scoffed. "That was the simplest part of my plan. I would be found in an escape pod, a survivor after all. These things happen in the vastness of space – people are found alive after being presumed dead. As long as I return to the living before the official period of mourning is over, I can reclaim my ambassadorship, my holdings, everything. You were the only witnesses to the explosion – everyone else heard about it second-hand. I assumed they would believe my story, and that you would be glad to have me back."

"You assume too much," said Garibaldi. "So let's get this ship turned around and get back to B5."

"No." G'Kar shook his head firmly. "The danger is still real. Mi'Ra, T'Kog, Ka'Het – these people have vowed to kill me! They have given up on assassins and have pledged to kill me with their own hands." He turned to Na'Toth. "Did you explain to them about the *Shon'Kar*?"

"I tried, but they had a difficult time understanding, especially Captain Sheridan. What were you going to do? Kill them yourself, or have me kill them?"

G'Kar stiffened his broad shoulders. "It is still my duty to attend to this problem. I am sorry you were involved, but you have been ordered to appear before the Kha'Ri, and you must do so. I hope that will give me enough time."

"No," said Ivanova. "We may not have any legal ground to stand on, but we're not going to stand by and watch you or anyone else commit murder. Isn't there some other way you can mend things with these people?"

G'Kar scowled and shook his fists at the ceiling, as if he were dealing with children. "Why don't you *meet* the Du'Rog family, and then you can tell me how to deal with them. As far as Mi'Ra is concerned, I think a blade to the throat is the only option, but I am willing to be talked out of it."

Na'Toth shook her head. "The danger to his life is very real. If we do nothing, they will come to the station and try to fulfill the *Shon'Kar*."

"All right," said Ivanova, "I am willing to meet with them, unofficially, and warn them against ever coming to the station to cause trouble. I think that's about all we can do." She looked at G'Kar. "But you have to agree to come back to life."

"Of course," said the ambassador. "Do you think I want to remain a nonentity? I would prefer that we wait until our return to Babylon 5, so that I can be discovered alive in the escape pod. While I'm on Homeworld, I will wear a disguise."

Garibaldi laughed. "A disguise? Give me a break."

"It fooled you."

"What?" said Garibaldi.

"Yes, I passed you this morning in Down Below. I was wearing the crude robe of an acolyte of the Eighth Circle. You looked right at me."

"I'll be damned. That was *you*."

"None other."

Ivanova shook her head. "The whole purpose of this trip is to meet with your council. We're not going to lie to them about you being dead."

"Please," said G'Kar, "don't lie to them, but don't tell them that I accompanied you on this ship. If you want to say you have new evidence that I may be alive, so be it, but give me a chance to move freely. Give me at least a day."

She gazed at him. "Will you try to kill her?"

"Not if you are with me," the Narn promised.

"Wait a minute," said Garibaldi. "There was an attack on one of my men in Down Below. Did you have something to do with that?"

"I have a disguise," insisted G'Kar, "complete with identicard. Why should I need to attack anyone?"

They heard a sound, and they turned around to see a crew member drop off the ladder into the intersection.

He glanced suspiciously at them for a moment, then went down another corridor.

"There are dangers other than the Du'Rog family," said G'Kar in a low voice. "The Du'Rog family may be the most vocal of my enemies, but they are not the only ones. I thought being dead would give me freedom, but instead it has made me a prisoner."

"Yeah," said Garibaldi, "it's not much of a crime to kill a man who is already dead."

The Narn started back into the hatch, then turned around. "I will not see you again until we reach Homeworld. Believe me when I say that it means a great deal to me to have you here, willing to help me."

"We're not promising anything," said Ivanova. "There may be nothing we can do."

G'Kar smiled. "At least I am not facing them alone." He ducked through the hatch and slammed it shut behind him.

Dinner that night in the Narn mess-hall consisted of some rather evil-smelling meat simmering in a greasy gruel. The Narns used their fingers to eat, shoveling the food directly from their bowls into their mouths, but they gave their guests some tarnished spoons. Garibaldi sampled some of the gruel and pushed the meat around in his bowl, while Al Vernon dug in and ate with considerable gusto. The merchant even used his fingers to eat in the Narn fashion. Ivanova drank a lot of coffee and smiled a lot, but didn't eat much. The humans were seated at a table with Na'Toth, Captain Vin'Tok, his first mate, Yal'Tar, and the military attaché, Tza'Gur.

"Delicious *lukrol*!" Al Vernon announced, licking his fingers. "My compliments to your cook. Oh, I have missed Narn cooking – the pungent spices, the zesty meats, the crunchy grains – it is truly the tastiest food in the galaxy."

Captain Vin'Tok beamed. "We have *mitlop* for dessert."

Al clapped his hands. "*Mitlop!* How wonderful! Made from fresh tripe?"

"Of course," answered the captain.

The merchant slapped his palms on the table. "Captain, can't we add an extra day or two on to our journey?"

Vin'Tok chuckled. "I'm afraid not. You have a memorial service to attend."

Thus far, noted Garibaldi, nobody had mentioned the fact that G'Kar was actually alive and well in the hold of the ship. He didn't know how many of the Narns knew about it, but he suspected that all of them did. It was as if G'Kar had come down with some terrible illness that nobody could bring themselves to discuss. Of course, Al Vernon didn't know G'Kar was alive, but he was probably the only one on the entire cruiser.

"Tripe for dessert?" asked Ivanova doubtfully.

"Sure," said Al. "You have to marinate it in *pakoberry* juice overnight. At least, that is the traditional method. It's tasty and pleasantly chewy."

Ivanova gulped. "You know, traveling always takes away my appetite."

"Not mine," said Al, going after another handful of *lukrol*.

Garibaldi thought it was time to broach the subject he'd been wondering about. "Captain Vin'Tok," he asked, "are you planning to wait for us, then take us back to Babylon 5?"

The Narn fixed him with a meaningful gaze. "The *K'sha Na'vas* is at your disposal for as long as you need her. We will remain in orbit, while a shuttlecraft will meet us and take you to the surface."

"Okay," said Garibaldi, feeling a bit better about things. He didn't want to be stuck on the Narn planet for weeks, waiting to find a public transport headed to B5. On the other hand, he knew that Vin'Tok owed his allegiance to G'Kar and the Narn Regime, not Earthforce. If they wanted to leave and G'Kar wanted to stay, they could be stuck.

Garibaldi rubbed his eyes, wondering how he had
managed to get sucked into this situation. Preventing a
murder, especially that of one of B5's ambassadors, was
a noble goal, but how much hope did they have? The
Narns themselves were oblivious to murder when a
Blood Oath was involved, so maybe this was an exercise
in futility. What would the Du'Rog family do when they
found out they had been duped and G'Kar was still alive?
For that matter, what would Captain Sheridan do? They
wouldn't be able to contact the captain until they came
out of jump.

He looked up to find Na'Toth studying him. "Mr.
Garibaldi, you haven't eaten much."

"I don't think I feel too well," he answered, holding
his stomach. He looked at Captain Vin'Tok. "May I be
excused?"

"Certainly, Mr. Garibaldi. I understand. It's been a
very stressful time."

"No kidding," said the chief, rising to his feet. "I'll see
you later."

"May I have your *mitlop*?" asked Al Vernon cheerfully.

"Sure, Al, knock yourself out."

Garibaldi nodded to the crew members in the mess-
hall and shuffled out. As the crew quarters were on the
same deck, it was a short walk to his cabin, but he still
had to pass the corridor that led to the hold. The guards
were back on duty, and they gazed resentfully at him,
perhaps because he had already had dinner and they
hadn't. Or maybe they knew their watch was pointless,
because the secret was out. At any rate, he saluted them
and wandered on to his room.

The security chief was lounging in the upper bunk of
the cramped cabin, almost asleep, when his room-mate
came home. Al announced his presence with a large
burp, then began to rummage around in his luggage.

"Are you awake, Garibaldi?" he asked.

"Yeah. How was the *mitlop*?"

"Actually not as good as they serve on Homeworld, but what can you expect from a galley cook? I didn't tell the captain that, of course."

"Of course," said Garibaldi. He leaned on his elbow and looked over the edge of his bunk. "What are you looking for?"

"We still have about thirty hours to travel, don't we? As a rule, Narns only eat twice a day, so we have to have something to pass the time. Ah, here it is!"

He produced a small cardboard box. "My deck of cards. What's your game? Gin rummy? Bridge? Naw, you look like a poker player to me. I'm afraid I haven't got enough money to do much gambling, but maybe the Narns have some matchsticks."

Garibaldi frowned at his colorful companion. "I'm not going to regret bringing you along on this joyride, am I?"

Al grew thoughtful for a moment. "I have to be true to myself, Mr. Garibaldi. The Narns have a saying: 'You can only run so far from yourself.' I've always thought that was a way of saying that we have to face up to the consequences of our actions."

"What consequences do you have to face?" asked Garibaldi.

The portly man smiled and held up the deck of cards. "Shall we start with gin rummy?"

CHAPTER 9

THE NARN SHUTTLECRAFT plunged through the atmosphere of Homeworld, heating up the cabin only a bit but causing a glorious light show outside the small porthole windows. Garibaldi leaned forward to get a better look. Despite an entire career spent on hostile planets and space stations, he was still a tourist when it came to space travel. He still gawked while Al Vernon, for instance, snoozed noisily across the aisle from him.

The shuttlecraft sat eight passengers in two single rows of four seats with an aisle between them, so essentially everyone sat alone. There were only the four of them, and Ivanova and Na'Toth sat in the front row, conversing in low tones. They were probably discussing how they should behave at the memorial service when they knew perfectly well that the deceased wasn't deceased. He guessed they would spend a lot of time looking grim and nodding somberly.

True to G'Kar's word, they hadn't seen him since their first day on the Narn vessel. The chief hoped that G'Kar had enough sense to stay on the *K'sha Na'vas* and not to go looking for trouble on Homeworld, even with his disguise. Garibaldi rubbed his hands nervously. This was only a day trip, he reminded himself, to attend the service, answer questions, and head back to the *K'sha Na'vas* for the night. Still, it felt funny to be descending upon an alien planet unarmed.

Suddenly, the flames outside the porthole vanished, and the shuttlecraft banked toward the surface, affording Garibaldi his first view of the Narn Homeworld. There wasn't a cloud anywhere in sight, and the sky had a washed out color, not the vibrant blue of Earth's sky. He wondered whether that had anything to do with the giant red sun that anchored the solar system.

The terrain that he could see had a rose-copper color, like the Black Hills gold his mother used to collect. He could see mountains, giant canyons, landing strips, and occasional patches and circles of green that he assumed were crops. As they swooped lower, he could make out grids of rectangular buildings and covered domes; smoke spewed into the air from what might have been a power plant or a smelter. Numerous low-flying aircraft dotted the sky.

Homeworld wasn't quite as barren as Mars, but it was hardly a flowering paradise. This was only one part of the planet, he told himself, but he knew Homeworld had very few bodies of water. Polar icecaps and underground streams supplied what little water the Narns needed. It wasn't like flying down to Earth, when all you could see were shimmering horizons of blue liquid. Garibaldi also reminded himself that the land had been stripped bare by the Centauri. They had withdrawn only after a war of attrition, when the Narn resistance had begun to cost them more than they were getting from the depleted resources and slave labor.

The shuttlecraft banked again and took a dive that left his stomach in a flux. Al Vernon blinked away beside him. "Are we there yet?" he muttered.

"I don't know," answered Garibaldi. "I don't know where we're going."

"Hekba City is quite a lovely place," said the merchant. "I believe it was G'Kar's hometown, although it's also one of the most hospitable cities for humans. You know, the temperatures on Homeworld can fluctuate wildly in the course of a single day."

Garibaldi lifted the heavy coat from his lap. "I know. But why should Hekba City be better than anyplace else?"

Al smiled. "You'll see. By the way, since you owe me five hundred thousand matchsticks, I expect you to buy me lunch."

"I think those cards of yours were marked," grumbled

Garibaldi. Nevertheless, he owed Al something for making the days aboard the *K'sha Na'vas* pass fairly swiftly.

He stared out the porthole and could see that they were circling an immense canyon, and he feared for a moment that they were going to try to land inside it. At the last moment, the pilot veered toward a landing strip that skirted the rim, and he made a perfect three-point landing in the tiny craft.

"Hekba City," came a flat voice over the ship's intercom, "on the rim of Hekba Canyon."

"Is this shuttlecraft going to wait for us?" asked Garibaldi of no one in particular.

"No," answered Na'Toth. She showed him a small handheld device. "I have the codes to summon another one."

The hatch opened with a clank and a blast of scorching air flooded the cabin. Within milliseconds, Garibaldi was bathed in sweat, and his lungs felt as if they were on fire. He groaned out loud.

Ivanova rose slowly to her feet and stretched her arms. "Time to change into your speedo," she told Garibaldi.

"No kidding," he muttered. "Feels like a Swedish sauna."

"On the contrary," said Al Vernon, "this is quite pleasant." The portly man was dripping in sweat, but then he was always dripping in sweat. "Make sure you drink fluids whenever you have the chance."

Na'Toth was the first out of the craft, followed by Al Vernon, who seemed to be in an exuberant mood. Ivanova and Garibaldi staggered out after them. If the heat didn't take their breath away, the sight that greeted their eyes certainly did. A vast canyon yawned before them, and its walls were lined with a honeycomb of dwellings carved directly into the cliff. Some were the copper color of the rock, but most were painted in muted shades of red and rust. Garibaldi inched toward the rim of the canyon, but he couldn't see either the bottom or the end of the buildings.

"They go all the way to the bottom," said Na'Toth, as if reading his mind. "Our reptillian ancestors clung to the rocks, and so do we. At the bottom of Hekba Canyon is some of the most fertile farmland on the planet, with numerous hot pools and geysers."

"I doubt if I'll be going all the way to the bottom," said Garibaldi with a gulp.

Al Vernon chuckled. "You will want to go down there, once the cooling starts on the surface."

Garibaldi splashed the sweat from his brow. "The cooling can start anytime as far as I'm concerned."

"Come," said Na'Toth, leading the way toward a rock staircase with a wrought-iron railing. Al waddled eagerly after her, leaving Garibaldi and Ivanova to bring up the rear. Behind them, the shuttlecraft roared away, giving the security chief an uneasy feeling of being deserted.

Ivanova raised an eyebrow. "It's a nice place to visit, but I wouldn't want to live here."

"I'm not even sure it's a nice place to visit," said Garibaldi, gazing up at the blazing red sun.

He had to admit, though, that Hekba City was fascinating. The Narns apparently didn't mind living like termites on a tree trunk, because people swarmed along the narrow walkways and the death-defying bridges that spanned the crevasse. The Narns glanced curiously at the humans whenever they passed them in close proximity, but Garibaldi saw a number of other off-worlders in the city, including several Drazi. As on Babylon 5, the Drazi appeared to be a worker class.

Na'Toth stopped to study some markings carved into the cliff face. "The sanctuary is on this side of the canyon," she said.

Garibaldi glanced at one of the swaying bridges. "Good."

In due course, they reached what seemed to be an older section of the city, formed of natural caves and indentations in the rock, with facades added later to afford privacy. In the yawning mouth of one of the caves, they saw a clutch of people who were milling about, waiting, making strained small talk. As the Terran delegation approached, Na'Toth put her fist to her chest in the Narn salute, and Al Vernon did likewise.

An elderly Narn in a crimson robe stepped forward to meet them. He bowed formally. "We welcome our friends from Earth, friends of G'Kar."

"It is our honor," said Al Vernon with a bow. "You are Y'Tok of the Second Circle."

"Yes," said the Narn with surprise. "Have we met?"

"I saw you give the convocation at the Blood of the Martyrs Ceremony," explained Al. "That was many years ago, but I have never forgotten it. Al Vernon is my name."

Y'Tok nodded, clearly impressed by the human's memory and knowledge of Narn affairs.

Na'Toth broke in, "Holy One, this is Commander Susan Ivanova of Earthforce, and Michael Garibaldi, Chief of Security on Babylon 5."

"We are honored that you chose to bring us here," said Ivanova.

"We did not honor G'Kar enough when he was alive," replied the priest. "It is our duty to honor him now that he is gone. We have a few moments – permit me to show you the sanctuary."

Y'Tok led them into the wide fissure in the rock, and Garibaldi was surprised to find that it widened even more into a natural cathedral complete with stalactites and stalagmites. The air felt several degrees cooler inside, which was a welcome relief. For a holy place, the sanctuary was remarkably austere, with only a few weathered stone benches for furnishings and smoky torches for light.

"This is one of the oldest sites of our civilization," explained Y'Tok, his voice echoing in the chamber. "Our ancestors lived in this cave tens of thousands of years ago. But it only became a sanctuary during the Centauri invasion, when freedom fighters held out here for one thousand days – before starving to death. All such places where the Martyrs sought sanctuary have been given the status of holy sites."

"Even the Centauri revere this place," said Al Vernon. "They call it the Vase of Tears because of all the lives they lost here."

Na'Toth looked askance at the human. "I didn't know you were a Centauri scholar as well."

"I am well traveled, nothing more," answered Al.

A young Narn in a crimson robe came running up to Y'Tok. "Holy One, Mistresses Ra'Pak and Da'Kal are here."

Y'Tok nodded in acknowledgement, then turned to his guests. "One more thing – I have been instructed to tell you that a committee from the Kha'Ri will meet with you in two days' time."

"Two days' time?" asked Garibaldi. "What's the matter with right now?" The priest glared at him. "I mean, after this?"

The old Narn held up two fingers. "You will be our guests for two more days. Is it so bad?"

"That's fine," said Ivanova with a game smile.

The priest nodded and strode through the crowd, somberly greeting everyone he met. When the aged Narn was out of earshot, Ivanova turned to Na'Toth. "Who are Ra'Pak and Da'Kal?"

The Narn woman lifted her chin. "Ra'Pak is a member of the Inner Circle. It is a mark of considerable respect for G'Kar that she is present. Da'Kal is . . ." She hesitated. "Da'Kal is G'Kar's widow."

"Hmmm," murmured Garibaldi. He couldn't say anything more because Al Vernon was standing a meter away, listening intently to their conversation. He wondered if Da'Kal knew the truth about her late, lamented husband.

Mourners began to file into the dingy recesses of the cave, filling every corner and even the spaces between the somber stalactites. In fact, the columns of calcified minerals seemed like especially respectful mourners, ghostlike aliens from eons long forgotten. Despite the crowd, it was cool and quiet inside the sanctuary, and Garibaldi began to feel an odd kind of peace. He wasn't much given to religion or sentimentality, but he could almost feel the presence of the long-departed Martyrs, granting their approval to this solemn occasion.

His reverie was short-lived, however, as acolytes in crude robes began to move around the cavern, sprinkling pungent incense on the torches. The young Narn in the crimson robe began to bang on a copper gong, and the chamber resonated with the metallic tone. Then the procession began.

In the lead came Y'Tok in his flowing robe, and he was holding a bronze circle that was so old it was discolored with green and white spots. Very quietly he tapped the circle with a metal stick, and it provided an odd counterpoint to the loud gong. Behind Y'Tok came a plain-looking Narn woman who was bare-breasted and wearing rags. In fact, she kept ripping away at her clothes as if they offended her. Garibaldi felt embarrassed, but he couldn't bring himself to turn away from the sight of the distraught woman. He knew without being told that she was the widow, Da'Kal.

Behind the widow walked a regal woman with an attendant holding her black robe off the dusty floor of the cave. That must be the Narn royalty, thought Garibaldi, Ra'Pak of the Inner Circle. Following her came several members of the Narn military, distinguished by chests full of jeweled medals. The procession circled the immense cavern, passing within a meter of the humans. Garibaldi felt himself getting angry at G'Kar – that ingrate didn't deserve the two fine memorial services he had gotten. Coming back from the dead was going to be anticlimatic after this.

The procession moved toward the mouth of the cave, and the mourners pressed forward, carrying Garibaldi, Ivanova, Na'Toth, and Al Vernon with them. They emerged into the scorching daylight in time to see the grieving widow toss her rags over the cliff. They fluttered downward, swirling around in the thermal updrafts. Then an acolyte handed her a small animal which looked something like a piglet. Da'Kal held the squirming creature over her head and screamed something into the wind. Then she tossed the animal over the cliff, and it plummeted a kilometer or so to its death.

Al Vernon whispered in his ear, "In the past, a Narn widow was expected to die with her husband. Today, the animal dies instead."

An attendant came forward and wrapped a black robe around the widow's shoulders and led her away. Y'Tok beat on the discolored circle while the other priest banged on the gong, and a low moan rose from the gathered mourners. The moaning and drumming reached a crescendo at the same time, and Y'Tok ended the ceremony by dropping to his knees and bowing to the canyon.

While Garibaldi looked on in a daze, someone pulled urgently on his sleeve. He turned to see Ivanova, and she was pointing toward someone in the crowd of mourners. He saw a young Narn woman wrap a cloak around her slim body and dash away. He recognized her in an instant.

It was Mi'Ra, daughter of Du'Rog.

"Wait here," he whispered to Ivanova, stuffing his coat into her arms. Before she had a chance to answer, he shouldered his way through the crowd and set off down one of the narrow walkways. His instincts told him that he might not get another chance to talk to his avenging angel, and he had two things to say: First, that he knew she didn't kill G'Kar, and second, that she had better stay away from Babylon 5. She'd find out the reason for that warning later.

Mi'Ra slipped through the crowd like a wraith, glancing over her shoulders as if she knew she were being followed. Garibaldi staggered after her like a man who

knew if he lost his footing he would join the sacrificial
animal at the bottom of the canyon. But he had an advantage in that the Narns on the ledge made way for him,
realizing he was a stranger.

At various intersections, the walkway sloped downward to a lower level of dwellings, while steps continued
upward to the original level. Without hesitation, Mi'Ra
went lower at every opportunity, and Garibaldi plunged
after her. His clothes were soaking with sweat, and thirst
burned in his throat – but this young Narn had
threatened to kill one of the ambassadors in his charge.
Had she come to the memorial service to make certain
G'Kar was dead? Or had she come because she suspected he wasn't dead? It didn't matter – he was on an
unfamiliar planet, and this was the one person he wanted
to talk to the most. He wasn't going to lose this opportunity.

Suddenly, he realized that he couldn't see Mi'Ra anymore. She had escaped. He quickened his pace and found
himself on a stretch of walkway where many doorways
were blocked off with rocks and pedestrians were few.
He tried not to look over the narrow railing at the certain death that waited below. His senses were acutely on
edge, and he saw the boot whip out of the doorway a
microsecond before it struck him in the knee.

Garibaldi yelped with pain and stumbled toward the
abyss. He grabbed the railing, pushed off, and fell hard
on to his back; a knife flashed through the air. He caught
her arm as the dagger kissed his throat. The young Narn
woman fought like a commando, using every ounce of
her wiry body to drive the knife home. He couldn't help
it if she was pretty – he smashed her in the jaw with his
fist and sent her crashing against the rock face. He heard
her grunt as the air rushed out of her body, but she still
had enough strength to draw a PPG and level it at him.

"Don't!" he warned, trying to sound calm. "I just want
to talk."

Her corseted chest heaved as she struggled to regain

her breath, and her red eyes drilled into him with hatred and suspicion. Garibaldi had seen enough criminals to know when he was confronting someone with nothing left to lose. Mi'Ra had been kicked around so much in the last few years that she didn't care about life anymore. She only cared about death. He could plainly see the yellowish scar on her forehead where she had drawn blood to seal her *Shon'Kar*.

"I just want to talk," Garibaldi said. "I saw the data crystal, and I know about your *Shon'Kar*."

"If you intend to take me back to your Earth station, I might as well kill you now." She hefted her weapon and seemed to be deciding where to put a hole in him.

Very slowly, Garibaldi lifted himself to his elbows. "I know you didn't kill him, and I couldn't take you back even if you did. But we need to tell you and your family to stay away from Babylon 5."

"Why?"

"Babylon 5 is under Earth administration, and we don't recognize the *Shon'Kar*."

Mi'Ra spat on the dry walkway. "Yes, I was deprived of my *Shon'Kar*. G'Kar deserved to be roasted to death over a slow fire, with a spit stuck through his gut, and I'm sorry he died quickly, before I could get my hands on him. Do you know what he did to my family?"

Garibaldi swallowed. "Yes, I do. I believe he was sorry for it, in the end."

"Ha!" scowled the attractive Narn. "He was a pathetic excuse for a Narn."

Garibaldi decided not to argue with her and her shiny PPG. Keeping the weapon trained on him, Mi'Ra scrambled to her knees to reclaim her knife. She stuck the knife in a shabby leather sheath and looked thoughtfully at Garibaldi, as if deciding how to dispose of him. He flinched, expecting to have his chest turned into melting goo, but the young woman tucked the PPG inside her tight-fitting waistcoat and rose to her feet.

She looked down at him with pity. "G'Kar was the type to betray everyone, including his friends."

Garibaldi wasn't likely to argue with that point, but there was one more thing he had to know. "Did you send assassins after him when he was on Homeworld a few months ago?"

Mi'Ra frowned. "I thought they were professionals. I will never make that mistake again."

"Were they also Thenta Ma'Kur?"

The Narn woman smiled shyly. "If you have any brains at all in your hairy skull, you will stay far, far away from the Thenta Ma'Kur."

Garibaldi picked himself up and dusted off his pants. "That's what I've heard, but G'Kar defeated them on their first try."

The slim Narn scowled at him. "Go home now, Earther, before you get hurt. This is not your affair."

With that Mi'Ra tossed back her cloak and sauntered away, giving him a good look at her athletic backside. Garibaldi sighed, being a fan of rear actions in motion. Two more days he had in this vertical village, and he would also like to meet Du'Rog's widow, to see if she was as headstrong as her daughter. His eyes wandered over the railing into the bottomless canyon. It must have a bottom, he told himself, but it was so far down he couldn't see it.

He took a few steps after her and called out, "Where can I find you?"

"The border zone," she shot back. "But you aren't brave enough to go there."

CHAPTER 10

"**W**HERE HAVE YOU been?" growled Na'Toth when Garibaldi finally straggled back to the sanctuary, perched upon the cliffside of Hekba City.

Ivanova studied her comrade, noting his dirty pants and the way he limped slightly. "I think he's been exploring."

"Yeah," muttered Garibaldi, "but not too successfully." He glanced around. "Where is Al?"

"Where we should be," answered Ivanova, "out of this heat and getting something to drink." She used Garibaldi's coat to dab the sweat off her face, then she shoved it into his hands.

Garibaldi lowered his voice to report, "After you saw Mi'Ra in the crowd, I chased her down. Well, sort of. Actually she ambushed me and nearly killed me. She's quite a piece of work."

"Unfortunately," said Na'Toth, "it is G'Kar's fault that Du'Rog's family is so bitter. I am losing much of the sympathy I had for him."

"Mi'Ra lives in a place called the border zone," said Garibaldi. "Where is that?"

Na'Toth said, "Do you remember how I told you about the regimentation of Narn society? The caste system applies to entire cities. For example, only those of the Eighth Circle or above may live here in Hekba City, which is one of our oldest and most revered places. Plebeians and others may work here, but the plebeians have cities of their own. Between these cities there are areas where our poorest people live – those who are thieves, prostitutes, and outcasts. If Mi'Ra and her mother and brother live in a border zone, then they have truly fallen to the lowest stratum of our society."

"Do you know which place she's talking about?" asked Ivanova.

"I have an idea," said Na'Toth. "There is a large border zone that is fairly close to here."

Garibaldi's jaw tightened. "I warned Mi'Ra to stay away from B5, and I'd like to warn the entire family, if possible. Sooner or later, they're going to find out that G'Kar is alive, and I don't want to go through a bunch of memorial services all over again."

The security chief turned to Na'Toth. "Are you sure there's no way to talk Du'Rog's family out of their Blood Oath? We talked you out of the one you had on Deathwalker."

The Narn woman scowled. "That was very difficult for me, and I draw great contentment from knowing that Deathwalker died anyway. To correct matters between G'Kar and the Du'Rog family will take more persuasion than you and I have to offer."

Ivanova let her attention drift from this futile conversation, and she heard somebody clear his throat. She turned to see a tall Narn male with unfamiliar spots on his head and bland brown eyes. He was dressed in the simple garb of a crewman from the *K'sha Na'vas*. He smiled at her and put his finger to his lips.

"Do I know you?" she asked, having the distinct feeling that she did, if only from the ship.

Garibaldi leaned toward the Narn and whispered, "Are you crazy?"

Na'Toth stiffened and stared at him. "Yes, he is."

The stranger held out his hand to Ivanova. "The name is Ha'Mok. Please address me as such."

That voice! She blinked at the Narn in amazement. His real name sprang to her lips, but she caught herself before she said it. "You *are* crazy," she agreed. "What are you doing here?"

"Enjoying shore leave," answered the man who had been G'Kar and was now Ha'Mok. He kept his head bowed as if addressing his betters. "How was the memorial service?"

"Better than you deserved," hissed Na'Toth.

"Why are you here?" Ivanova demanded again.

"Two things. First, the *K'sha Na'vas* received a delayed transmission from Babylon 5. Captain Sheridan has been trying to reach you." He lowered his voice to add, "The captain is no fool. Perhaps he has found out what I did."

"Can we contact him?" asked Garibaldi.

"Not from here. When we return to the *K'sha Na'vas*."

"You didn't come here to tell us that," said Ivanova.

"No," admitted G'Kar. "Most importantly, I want to see Da'Kal, my wife. She lives in this city, on the other side of the canyon. I want you to come with me."

"Why?" asked Ivanova.

"You may have to protect me in case she tries to kill me."

"I'm not sure we would," said Ivanova. She rubbed her lips and peered up at the blazing red sun. "Before we get deeper into this mess, we humans need to get something to drink. Where did you say Al went?"

Ivanova pointed to a doorway about twenty meters away. "He said there was a tavern down there, and he went inside as soon as the service was over. We haven't seen him since."

"Who is this Al person?" asked G'Kar. "Can we trust him?"

Ivanova fixed the dead man with a stare. "Can we trust *you*? We have to wait two full days before meeting with the Kha'Ri. You didn't have anything to do with that, did you?"

G'Kar shrugged. "I am trying to make amends, but I must have time."

"You can start by buying us some drinks," said Garibaldi, heading for the tavern.

The party of two humans, and two Narns ambled into a doorway that looked no different from any of the others, except for three gashes carved into the wall above the door. After the intense sunlight, the darkness inside the shelter momentarily blinded Ivanova. She could see nothing, but the sounds of laughter and voices convinced her that she was indeed inside a public tavern. Na'Toth and G'Kar brushed past her, apparently having no difficulty with the change in light.

She bumped into a customer and decided to stand still until her eyes adjusted to the darkness. Once they had, she saw a low-slung bar against one wall; it seemed to be carved directly from the rock. Stepping closer she saw the bar had deep holes dug into it, from which strange aromas and curlicues of steam rose toward the ceiling. There were no barstools that she could see, but she couldn't miss Al Vernon, who was sitting on the floor, his back against the bar. He was drinking from what appeared to be a bag made out of animal skin.

"Here you are!" he said happily, bounding to his feet. He pointed to a sickly-looking Narn who could only be the proprietor. "These are my friends. They will pay my bill."

"Wait a minute," grumbled Garibaldi. "How much is his bill?"

The proprietor appraised him with cool red eyes that looked like embers about to burn out. "One hundred credits."

"A hundred credits!" snapped Garibaldi. "You should be able to rent a room for that!"

Ivanova swallowed dryly and held out her credit chit. "Give us two more of whatever he's having."

Garibaldi added, "Make mine a Shirley Temple."

The proprietor blinked at him. "Pardon me?"

"No alcohol in mine," answered the chief.

The old Narn nodded and took the card. Then he produced two flat skins and dipped them into separate holes in the bar. When he brought the skins up, they were plump and dripping with steaming liquid. He handed the pouches to the visitors and processed Ivanova's chit. The skin was sticky, and whatever was inside was highly aromatic. It wasn't a terrible smell but oddly redolent of mincemeat pies, truffles, and English cooking.

"This is crazy," muttered Garibaldi. "When I'm

thirsty, I want something cold."

Ivanova replied, "It's a fallacy that something cold quenches thirst better than something hot. In fact, whenever I'm really thirsty, I drink coffee."

"You always drink coffee," countered Garibaldi. Wrinkling his nose, he put the skin to his lips and took a cautious sip. "Hmmm," he said with surprise. "Sort of tastes like mulled wine and beef broth."

Ivanova took a sip, and the warm liquid did indeed taste like a combination of cloves, raisins, and the drippings from a roast. It warmed her inside while the condensing steam cooled her face.

Al Vernon chuckled. "Do you want me to tell you what's in it?"

"No!" Ivanova and Garibaldi answered in unison.

"Listen, Al," said Ivanova, "we fulfilled our part of the bargain and got you here. If we're going to pay your bills, too, then you had better stick with us."

"I told you where I was going," said Al. "When Mr. Garibaldi ran off after that attractive Narn woman, I assumed he would be gone for a while."

Garibaldi lowered his drinking skin and said, "We've got two more days here. What do you know about the border zone?"

"Oh, no," replied the portly human, looking grim. "You aren't planning to go to a border zone, are you?"

"We have to," said Garibaldi. "We have to talk to someone there."

"You don't need a guide, you need a bodyguard." Al took a long swig from his pouch.

Ivanova cleared her throat. "Another Narn from the ship is going with us, so there will be five of us."

"That's too few," said Al. "Let's get the whole crew to go with us."

Ivanova looked at Garibaldi. "Maybe he has a point. If we really want to go traipsing around this planet, we ought to talk to Captain Vin'Tok about having an escort. It might keep us out of trouble."

Someone tapped her on the shoulder, and she turned around to see the disguised Narn who was going by the name of Ha'Mok. "I want to attend to that errand we talked about," he said insistently.

To see his wife, recalled the commander. She had no objection to telling people that G'Kar was still alive, and the sooner the better! They might as well start with his poor widow, and Ivanova hoped she would punch him in the stomach, the same way Na'Toth had.

Before she could reply, Al butted in. "Hello, I don't believe we've met. I'm Al Vernon, formerly of Homeworld."

"Ha'Mok," lied the Narn. "Your friends need to come with me. You can stay here."

Al sighed. "I'm afraid, sir, I am currently short of funds, and this establishment won't extend me credit."

G'Kar grabbed the human's pudgy hand and dropped some black coins into it. "That should hold you until we get back."

"Indeed it should!" said Al. "Thank you."

"Finish your drinks," ordered the Narn. "I'll be over there with Na'Toth." He strode into the dim recesses of the tavern.

Al cocked his head thoughtfully. "He's rather bold for a simple crewman, isn't he?"

"Yes," said Ivanova, gazing after him, "and I've had just about enough of it. But we may need him, just as we may need you. Wait for us here, please."

"Have no fear," said Al pleasantly. "I have no intention of letting any of you get away from me."

A few minutes later, Ivanova and her party were hundreds of meters in the air on a swaying bridge with only a few ornamental cables supporting it in the middle. She lifted her eyes toward the red sun to avoid looking down, but her wobbly legs and staggering gait forced her to watch where she put her feet. That the bridge was constructed of metal cables and planks didn't do much to lessen her fear,

and it didn't help that G'Kar and Na'Toth were striding
ahead of her, making the bridge sway even more. She took
some comfort in the fact that Garibaldi was even more
frightened than she was. He inched along behind her.

"The next time Captain Sheridan orders us to a weird
planet," he muttered, "will you remind me to resign?"

"No," she answered. "But I will make sure someone
else goes instead of me."

Fear paralyzed Ivanova's legs every time the bridge
swayed. Adding to her discomfort was the miserable
heat, the sweat drooling down her back and chest, and
the fact that she was still carrying her coat. Ivanova
brushed sweaty ringlets of hair from her face and her
eyes wandered downward. The canyon floor looked like
the primordial ooze she had always read about. It was a
bubbling cauldron of murky water, and the putrid smell
of sulphur rose hundreds of meters into the air.
Nevertheless, she could see a few strips of farmland
among the geysers and pools.

Keep going, she told herself. It wasn't much farther.
But it was, as they were barely a third of the way across
the bridge. Ivanova had the irrational urge to turn around
and run back to the tavern, seeking safety with Al
Vernon, but she forced herself to keep moving. They had
traveled billions of kilometers in order to honor G'Kar
and confront his murderers – only to end up with *no* murder and a frightened ambassador in disguise. Now they
were going to hold his hand as he broke the news to his
wife that he was still alive.

Ivanova had to remind herself that this planet harbored
a family of would-be murderers who would not be
pleased to find out that G'Kar was still alive. Plus, there
was a league of assassins – the Thenta Ma'Kur – who
had been contracted to kill G'Kar and had failed. Even
if a murder had yet to be committed, it wasn't for lack
of trying. Thinking about these various parties gave her
the impetus to quicken her step and make her way across
the swaying span.

Na'Toth and G'Kar waited for her at the other end, and she nearly dove into their outstretched hands. "That wasn't so bad, was it?" asked G'Kar.

"Yes," she breathed.

Garibaldi was almost crawling by the time he reached the end. When they helped him off the bridge, he sunk against the rock wall and panted for a few seconds.

"Damn," he said. "Is there anything you Narns are afraid of?"

"Wives," answered Na'Toth with a side-long glance at G'Kar.

"Yes," he admitted, "that is true. I sincerely appreciate the help you are giving me. The home I share with Da'Kal is on this level, only a few doors away."

They were doing G'Kar such a big favor, and he was in so much trouble, that Ivanova felt the normal boundaries between them were all but gone. "Why haven't you ever brought Da'Kal to the station?" she asked.

G'Kar shrugged his broad shoulders. "I'm not sure she would come. You have no doubt realized how ambitious I am. Marrying Da'Kal was the most ambitious act I have ever taken, more so than what I did to Du'Rog. She is extremely well placed, with friends in the Inner Circle, such as Ra'Pak. I was a young soldier, a dashing war hero, when I met Da'Kal; and she was a few years older. She was very much in love with me. My success was ensured when I married her."

"Are you in love with her?" asked Ivanova.

G'Kar fixed her with his altered brown eyes. "I am in love with the *idea* of her, and I owe her more than anyone in the universe. But love? I doubt whether I have ever loved anyone but myself. Follow me."

With G'Kar leading the way, the odd party of two Narns and two humans strode down the peaceful walkway. There was less hustle and bustle on this side of the canyon, as if it were a better neighborhood, and the facades of the dwellings were uniformly painted in muted brown and rust shades.

Na'Toth hung back to whisper to the humans, "Narns are not strictly monogamous. It is quite possible that Da'Kal has had lovers, and may have lovers now. A marriage is like two businesses joining forces – for the purpose of creating wealth and children – but they maintain their separate identities. Do I make myself clear?"

"You do," answered Ivanova. "What should we expect?"

Na'Toth shook her head. "I have no idea."

G'Kar stopped in front of a dwelling that was distinguished by its pinkish color and a heavy metal door. He turned to the humans and said, "This is our home. I suppose you would have reason to discuss my death with Da'Kal, as you know more about it than anyone. Simply ask her: Would she be happy or angry to learn that I am alive? Depending on the answer, you may come to fetch me."

"You're going to owe us big-time for this," warned Garibaldi. He pushed the door chime, and the two Narns backed away.

The door opened, and a wizened old Narn peered at them. "Who are you?" he snarled.

"We're from Babylon 5," said Ivanova. "If Mistress Da'Kal is available, we would like to talk to her about her husband."

"Hmmm," grunted the servant. "Come in."

He ushered them into a narrow foyer that was decorated in a typically masculine Narn style, despite the fact that the man of the household had lived elsewhere for years. The walls were gilded with a copper-colored metal and decorated with tapestries, antique weapons, and family crests of bloodstone and exotic fabrics. A clay vase held dried flowers and reeds, and the floor was tiled in orange and brown. Beyond the foyer, Ivanova could see a sumptuous sitting room with heavy metal furniture, and she could hear feminine voices. The windowless dwelling had the oppressive feeling of a cave, or a space station.

"Wait here," growled the wizened servant as he shuffled toward the back of the house.

Garibaldi took a deep breath and whispered to Ivanova, "I've had to tell people their spouses were dead, but I've never had to tell anyone their dead spouse was alive."

"I hope we don't regret this," said Ivanova. "I'd feel a lot better if we called her from back on B5."

"I'll drink to that," muttered Garibaldi.

Ivanova took a moment to wipe the sweat off his brow. At least it was considerably cooler inside G'Kar's home than outside in the open air.

A few moments later, two women appeared. One of them was the regally dressed woman from the Inner Circle, Ra'Pak, and she glanced disdainfully at the humans as if they were stains on the wall. The other woman was Da'Kal, who was dressed in a simple beige tunic, knotted at her waist. For a Narn, she was short and delicate, almost fragile. Ivanova found it difficult to tell age in a Narn, but Da'Kal had the look of a woman who had aged considerably in the last few days.

"Then I will see you at the reception," Ra'Pak said, making it sound like an order.

Da'Kal nodded. "I will try, my friend. Thank you so much for being here."

Ra'Pak tilted her head. "It's the least I can do when your husband never was."

Da'Kal took her friend's hand. "I know you are thinking of me, always."

"I will be staying at the villa if you need me," concluded Ra'Pak. She swept toward the door, and the servant rushed to open it for her.

Once the noblewoman was gone, Ivanova stepped forward. "I am Susan Ivanova, and this is Michael Garibaldi. We're from Babylon 5."

"Yes, I saw you at the service," said Da'Kal, twisting her hands nervously. "My husband mentioned you in his messages, and he was very impressed with you. Thank you for coming so far to honor him." She motioned toward the sitting room. "Shall we make ourselves comfortable?"

Ivanova glanced at the aged servant. "We would prefer to speak to you alone, if we could."

"Of course. He'Lok, I believe we need some things from the market."

"Yes, my lady." The servant bowed and shuffled out the door.

"Come," said Da'Kal, leading them into the sitting-room of the small but elegant house. The furnishings in this room were surprisingly bright and cheerful for a Narn household, with ivory-hued curtains gracing most of the walls and several vases of dried flowers and plants. The furniture was dark and massive, but some brightly colored cushions gave it a feminine touch. The widow seated herself on the edge of a small sofa, still twisting her hands. The humans sat in high-backed chairs.

Ivanova glanced at Garibaldi, and he looked at her helplessly. Apparently, he was going to let her do all the talking. Although Ivanova felt rather lacking in the tact department, she resolved to do the best she could.

"We're sorry to bother you at a time like this," she began.

"How could it be otherwise?" asked Da'Kal. "But I must warn you – I know very little about my husband's affairs. Certainly it's no secret to you that we didn't see each other very often."

"Yes, we know," said Ivanova, lowering her eyes with embarrassment. "Did you know a man named Du'Rog?"

The distress that swept over the woman's face made it very clear that she did. "Of course I knew him. He was on the Council – a former associate of G'Kar's."

"Were you aware that Du'Rog hired an assassin from the Thenta Ma'Kur to kill your husband?"

The woman's jaw hung open for a moment, then she nodded with realization. "Ah, that is what happened to G'Kar."

"No," said Ivanova quickly. "That murder attempt was unsuccessful, and so was one other."

Da'Kal leaped to her feet. "I knew nothing of any of this. Oh, that fool! Why didn't G'Kar come to me for help? I am not without influence, even among the Thenta Ma'Kur. But G'Kar was so stubborn! He thought he was master of his own fate, when he never was."

Ivanova sighed. It was becoming woefully clear to her that G'Kar had kept his wife in the dark about almost everything for the last few years. Da'Kal must have known what her husband had done to succeed to the Third Circle, but she didn't seem to know anything beyond that. The commander had only two more questions before she tackled the big one.

"Do you know Du'Rog's family? Ka'Het is the widow's name, and Mi'Ra and T'Kog are his children."

Da'Kal stopped pacing and bent over to rearrange one of her dried flower arrangements. "I already told you that I knew Du'Rog. Of course I know his family. If you are trying to make trouble for me . . ."

"No," insisted Ivanova. "What's in the past is in the past, except as it relates to the incident that brought us here. Did you know they vowed the *Shon'Kar* against your husband?"

Da'Kal's back stiffened, and she gazed into the distance. "That is within their right. If you are expecting that I will seek revenge against them, let me assure you, I will not. Nor will I help you to persecute them. The family of Du'Rog has suffered enough. The *Shon'Kar* is now ended."

Ivanova took a deep breath. There was just one more question to ask. "Would you be happy or angry to learn that G'Kar is still alive?"

The woman whirled around, her red eyes blazing in their bony sockets.

G'Kar and Na'Toth stood on the walkway about thirty meters beyond Da'Kal's doorway. They pretended to admire some golden goblets on display in a shop window, but the proprietor was beginning to look at them suspiciously. G'Kar lowered his head and motioned to his aide, and they began to walk slowly toward Da'Kal's house.

"What is taking them so long?" seethed G'Kar.

"It's only been a few minutes since your servant left," said Na'Toth. "We were lucky that neither he nor Ra'Pak recognized you."

"That old witch," muttered G'Kar. "She has always hated me. I doubt if the years have changed her mind very much."

The door of the pink dwelling opened, and G'Kar froze in his steps. He had confidence that his disguise would fool a cursory inspection from most of his acquaintances, especially humans, but he harbored no illusions that it would fool his wife. He held his breath until he saw that it was Ivanova and Garibaldi. They left the door open and approached him.

"She's waiting for you," said Ivanova. "We'll wait for you in the tavern where we left Al."

G'Kar swallowed and gave them a brief nod. "I thank you."

"Don't thank us yet," said Garibaldi. "She may have a rolling pin in her hand."

The Terran reference flew over G'Kar's head as he strode toward the door. He carefully entered the doorway, bowing his head respectfully. The first thing he noticed were the vases of flowers, an addition since he had lived here. Then he saw her standing in the next room, a small but proud woman dressed in the traditional beige of mourning. Shadows and shock obscured her face.

Her voice was like ice. "G'Kar – is that really you?"

"Yes," he said. A dozen words of endearment sprang to his mind, but he could force none of them on to his tongue. He was sure she would believe none of them.

She stepped toward him and peered into his eyes. He

bent his head downward, pushed on his eyelids, and let the brown contact lenses fall into his hand. Then he slowly peeled off the skull cap that had changed his appearance so much.

"By the Martyrs!" she gasped. "What made you do this thing?"

"Fear," he answered. "Desperation. Most of all, shame."

"You could have come to me for help."

He shook his head. "You could not have helped without revealing what I did to Du'Rog and his family. When I received word that they had vowed the *Shon'Kar* against me, I was afraid. My first instinct was to hide, and my second was to kill Mi'Ra. I could accomplish both by pretending to be dead. The Earthers discovered the truth before we reached here, and now I feel mostly shame for my actions. This is my first step in reclaiming my life."

Da'Kal stepped forward and held out her trembling hands. G'Kar took them in his, and they were both calm. The ambassador looked down at the woman who had shared his bed and his life for so many years, and it seemed as if their years apart were nothing but a long, dark night. He needed Da'Kal more than ever, but he had no idea if she still needed him. He feared to ask if she still loved him.

She insisted, "You must make amends to Ka'Het and her children. I don't know how you can do this, but you must try."

"I know," he answered. "Believe me, I know how wrong I've been. If I had to do it over again, I would wait forever to succeed to the Third Circle. I would do so many things differently."

Da'Kal pulled her hands away from his. "We cannot wait – we must do something."

She strode into the sitting room, and G'Kar rushed after her. This was the dynamic woman he remembered, before apathy and ambition had weakened their marriage. Da'Kal went to the wall and pulled on a cord, and a curtain opened to reveal a sophisticated computer terminal. As her delicate fingers touched the controls, the screen blinked on.

"Ka'Het and her children are living like animals in the border zone," she said. "I have been as cruel as you – I knew their circumstances, yet I have done nothing to help them. Like you, I have been afraid to reveal the past. It is time to be brave and do the honorable thing. You can only run so far from yourself."

"What are you doing?" asked G'Kar, suddenly worried despite his good intentions.

"I am transferring funds to the Du'Rog family. I know that Ka'Het still maintains an account that is dormant. I can't restore their social status, but I can do what I must to help them to be comfortable. Whatever we do for them, it is long overdue."

As her fingers plied the controls, G'Kar paced nervously. "Won't they know where the money is coming from?"

"What difference does it make? If we haven't the stomach to destroy them, we must help them. Go bolt the front door."

"Bolt the front door?" asked G'Kar numbly.

"Yes, before my servant returns home. It is a signal we have used before. If he finds the front door bolted from the inside, he knows I am entertaining. He won't return until summoned." Da'Kal turned to her husband and smiled slightly. "You have been gone a long time G'Kar."

He nodded and rushed to bolt the front door. There was a romantic, dream-like quality about all of this – returning to his home in disguise, seeing Da'Kal after ignoring her for years, and bolting the door against the outside world. It was as if the years were melting away and they were young again, sneaking behind their parents' backs. Could the clock really be turned back? Could they return to a simpler time, before his life had been consumed with ambition and intrigue? He walked

back into the sitting room and found Da'Kal shutting the
curtain on the computer terminal.

"It is done," she said with a sigh. "This won't begin
to make up for what you did to Du'Rog, but at least his
family won't have to live like animals anymore."

"And us?" asked G'Kar in an urgent voice. "What is
to become of us?"

As Da'Kal approached him, she untied the beige tunic
from around her waist. "I am no longer in mourning."

She slipped the garment off her shoulders, and it fell
to the floor. "This is twice today I have bared myself for
you, G'Kar. No other woman would do that for you. You
once owned every molecule of this body. Do you still
want it?"

"Yes," he said hoarsely, as he lifted her in his powerful arms and pressed his face to her flesh.

CHAPTER 11

MI'RA WAITED SOLEMNLY in line with the servants and tradespeople of the lower castes who were leaving Hekba City for the day. The line wound into a tunnel on the third level, where a series of moving walkways, called outerwalks, allowed them to travel many kilometers in a short time. With hunched shoulders and weary expressions, the plebeians stepped upon the conveyor belts and began their long march home.

The young woman tried to hold her head high, knowing she didn't belong with these commoners, but it was difficult. She knew that most of them were returning to better homes than the hovel she shared with her mother and her brother. They had jobs and at least some station in life, even if it was a lower one. She had nothing but her bitterness and the weapons stuck in her belt. Mi'Ra had believed that the memorial service for G'Kar would in some way cleanse her, or please her, but the finality of his death had just the opposite effect. Her father was dead, his tormentor was dead, and she felt dead, too. Without the *Shon'Kar* and the hatred which fueled it, her purpose in life was gone.

Perhaps, thought Mi'Ra, it was time to get away from Homeworld, time to explore the galaxy. The concerned human who had pursued her down the walkway had made her realize that there were other races out there, other places where no one cared about the *Shon'Kar*, the Kha'Ri, or the arcane aspects of Narn culture. She was an outcast here, but she would merely be an alien there – and that would be preferable. Mi'Ra knew she would be young and attractive for many more years. She had too much pride to stoop to prostitution, but there must be someplace in this wide galaxy where she could carve a new life.

For example, what was this Babylon 5 like? After a lifetime spent among her own kind, she couldn't imagine a place where humans, Narns, Centauri, Minbari, and a dozen other races lived together. Surely, in a place like that, the sins of the fathers made no difference to anyone. But why would the human warn her to stay away. Prejudice? It didn't seem likely that a prejudiced, close-minded person could live and work in such an environment. Perhaps she merely frightened him – and that thought made her smile.

Mi'Ra had to consider her mother and her brother, though, and when she did her rosy dreams vanished like the stretch of tunnel behind her. They were helpless without her. She couldn't leave them in the border zone, destitute and outcast, while she went off to seek her fortune among alien races. And both of them would be useless on such a grand adventure. Mi'Ra had expected to fulfill her *Shon'Kar* and die young, in a blaze of glory. Now she would do neither. Instead she would grow old, caring for her impoverished family, all hope of a better life dashed forever.

Mi'Ra stood numbly on the frayed belt of the moving walkway, watching the plebeians shuffle past her. She looked up at a naked lightbulb, barely illuminating the dark tunnel. This retreat from Hekba City was characteristic of her life – a journey from wealth and position into poverty and despair. She had nothing to look forward to but a swift descent into a dark tunnel.

There was one other possible path for her, one she had been considering since hearing of their recent success. Mi'Ra considered joining the Thenta Ma'Kur, the league of professional assassins. She had the qualifications: a complete disregard for her own life, beauty and poise that would help her travel in disguise, and the most important qualification – a deadened soul that was prepared to kill. She was a perfect candidate, and perhaps she could make enough money as an assassin to send her mother and brother to Babylon 5, or someplace far removed from the bitter memories and daily reminders. They could open a shop and have lives that were at least respectable, if not privileged.

The thought of this plan cheered her slightly as she reached an intersection where three outerwalks branched off. Most of the plebeians took the right-hand walkway, headed to their homes in the city of Jasba. A few lucky ones took the left-hand walkway to a neighborhood reserved for members of the Outer Circle. She took the least-traveled outerwalk to the area in-between, the border zone.

Mi'Ra had been deprived of everything – her birthright, her station, her inheritance, and now the glory of the *Shon'Kar*. Even the pitiful humans seemed to dismiss her. She was disappointed that the tall human in uniform hadn't put up more of a fight on the walkway. He hadn't even offered her the chance to die fighting. But why should he? He knew she wasn't the murderer – he simply had a desire to speak with her before returning to his life among the stars and planets. She understood – the military were a privileged class in her society, too.

The tunnel grew darker, narrower, and more neglected, and eyes peered at her from the shadows. They were the eyes of animals and Narns, those who were so downtrodden they made the tunnels their homes. They were chased out of other tunnels and neighborhoods, but not this one. They were chased *into* the border zone. The tunnel denizens scurried furtively about as the outerwalk shuddered further into the netherworld.

When she had lived among the privileged, Mi'Ra had never given much thought to the unlucky, the poorly born, the classless. Forged by slavery, the Narn were a hard people who admired the victors in any struggle and shunted the losers to the bone pile. Those who knew their place got to keep their place, and that was struggle enough for the plebeians and Outer Circle. For the fallen from grace, there was a special netherworld.

Mi'Ra recalled how her mother's estate had been seized by the government as proof of illicit profits on those ludicrous arms-dealing charges. Like most of his peers, Du'Rog occasionally pulled a shady deal – a few of them with G'Kar as his partner – and kept less than scrupulous records. But no one could have predicted the fall he was about to take. The military had nearly tortured General Balashar to death, and they needed to produce him in court to name his contact for the horribly potent biological weapons. The weapons were especially successful on Narns, as if they had been formulated for them in the first place. Despite holding high rank in the Kha'Ri and the Fourth Circle, Du'Rog was embraced as the scapegoat.

The military executed Balashar post-haste, and G'Kar installed himself in a life of splendor on a distant colony – while her father died from the stress of fighting the unjust charges. Then the scavengers moved in, expecting easy pickings. Mi'Ra had to grow up fast in a short time, and she wasn't able to ward them off. The creditors and opportunists had picked her father's skeleton clean before she was strong enough to fight them. As part of the supposedly generous settlement, she and her mother and brother had gotten the deed to a house in this pit, the border zone.

The outerwalk deposited her in another pit, a so-called station where the stairs to the surface were covered with dirt and garbage. You literally had to climb out to reach the slum. There was a news-stand in the pit, but it had long been boarded up with adobe bricks and barbed wire. The only reason they kept the walkway running was that they didn't want anyone to have the excuse that they couldn't get home. If you didn't belong in Hekba City, then there had to be a way to get you out of there at the end of the day – to wherever you did belong.

Mi'Ra drew her PPG and dug in the toes of her boots as she scaled the garbage pit. She finally found a few clear steps where dust devils had strayed down the stairs, and the ascent got easier. There was nothing easy, however, about the sight of the border zone, with its depressing narrow houses. Each was two stories tall, although some had sunken on their poor foundations and looked no more than one-story. They were built quickly then forgotten quickly, left to rot with the firm knowledge that anyone who had sunk to this level had lost his place in Narn society. For a Narn who didn't know his place, there was no hope.

Mi'Ra stepped cautiously into the wind that blew across this treeless plain ninety percent of the time, or so they said. No one could remember the ten percent when it allegedly wasn't blowing. The decrepit row houses were supposed to be offset by impressive walls and archways that mirrored preinvasion architecture. But the constant feeling of running into walls made it seem like a maze, a place where society observed its freaks. At other times, the walls seemed like a prison, which is what they really were, thought Mi'Ra.

There were murders every night, but no one saw anything over the damn walls or the fear. The border zones were conveniently unincorporated, patrolled by rangers from the Rural Division, who showed a determined lack of interest in solving most crimes. In the ones they decided to solve, they acted as police, judge, jury, and executioner. Mi'Ra had finally realized that a race that could be cruel to other races could also be cruel to itself.

She skirted a familiar wall, trying to stay out of the light. There were cheap clay candles swaying in the archways and on a few porches. The government left candles and boxes of food at certain intersections every day, and a few conscientious people tried to light the border zone. Most just ignored the cheap candles, and the sand was littered with sooty clumps of pottery that had once been candles.

The young Narn padded down a hill and paused before an archway. A lone traveler could never tell what might be waiting in one of those infernal archways; at least this one had a clay pot burning. She was young and attractive, and her greatest fear was that some street pack would capture her alive. Mi'Ra slowed cautiously and put her PPG away in favor of her knife. In close quarters, she had more faith in her knife to inflict damage without risking a war.

Mi'Ra was still annoyed that a human had managed to deflect her attack so easily today. Of course, she could have killed him, which gave her some satisfaction. The young Narn gazed up at the top of the wall, wondering if anybody could be hiding up there. She knew from experience that footing was treacherous atop the crumbling structures. No one in his right mind scampered around up there. The ground was littered with chunks that had fallen from the ornamental walks.

The smell of burning rubber, the only available fuel for some downtrodden souls, assaulted her nostrils, and she felt like turning back. But her mother and brother were waiting for a full report on the memorial service. Even though G'Kar's death brought them no immediate relief, at least it had exorcised one ghost. They no longer anguished over the fact that G'Kar enjoyed a soft life built from the hide of their father's corpse.

Mi'Ra stopped again to listen, and she thought she heard someone moving on the other side of the wall. She darted through the archway, slashing her knife, but her would-be attacker was only a dust devil, unable to find its way around the wall. It whipped and whirled in frustration.

She moved swiftly away from the light, not wanting to draw attention to herself. There was still enough daylight left that this trip home shouldn't be tortuous. She could see some young Narns at the bottom of the hill, burning the tread from a mining vehicle and cooking rodents over the flames. But they were often there and had never tried to pursue her. Still, she kept a safe distance and was poised to run if they even stood up too quickly. Mi'Ra had no delusions about the dangers of the border zone. Some people down here were mentally unhinged, not fit for Narn society or any other society; some had become addicted to drugs the Centauri had introduced. Many were just unlucky, like herself, and it was cruel to mix the misfits with the misfortunates.

Narns prided themselves on having few prisons, as if this was some indication that Narns accepted their rigid caste system. But Mi'Ra had decided that Narn culture was nothing more than a series of prisons, expanding ever outward. Even G'Kar had not managed to escape from it.

She heard a sound, and she broke out of her careless reverie to see two dark figures rise out of the shadows. As they had already seen her, she decided to let them see everything. She stepped back near the archway and let them see the light glinting off her knife, then she slowly made her way across the alley to the first row of dreary houses. Mi'Ra wanted to let them know that she intended to steer clear of them and hoped they would do likewise. The two shadowy figures watched her go, although they grunted something to each other and laughed.

When Mi'Ra was well beyond them, she sheathed her knife and dashed through an opening in the houses without alerting anyone. She jogged down the middle of the street, knowing the ground was fairly level and not too badly littered. A few residents poked their heads out of their doorways to watch her pass. Even though most of them knew who she was, no one greeted her. People in the border zone were faceless and wanted to stay that way.

Mi'Ra could see the lighted clay pot swinging on her mother's porch. At least T'Kog had done something he was supposed to do. As she approached the dreary house, she could hear the people who lived upstairs fighting; one of them was a dust addict, and the other was a pickpocket who worked the tunnels. Mi'Ra hated to have to rent out the upper floor, but that was

the only steady income they had. Besides, this hovel and
its hideous surroundings had never seemed like their real
home. It was just the cell to which the Du'Rog family
had mistakenly been condemned until the magical return
of the good life. That's how Ka'Het and T'Kog looked
at it, thought Mi'Ra angrily. The only *V'Tar* that burned
in them was the minimum it took to survive, plus the useless hope that their father's name would someday be
cleared.

She tried to tell them that they had been put in the border zone to be forgotten, to die. The only glory awaiting
them was to achieve the *Shon'Kar* – to fulfill their
father's dying wish to know that G'Kar was dead. At
least that goal had been attained, even if it was another's
hand that held the glory. That was honest cause for cel-
ebration, so Mi'Ra tried to put on a cheerful face as she
walked up the crumbling steps. But she still felt empty.
The fire of revenge had gone out, and she had nothing
to replace it with.

The neighbors' fighting was a common sound, but the
next sound she heard was highly unusual. It was her
mother laughing! That couldn't be possible, thought
Mi'Ra, it had to be another woman laughing; but what
woman would be in the border zone, laughing? Even
through the cheap tin door, it sounded like her mother.
The hand on the hilt of her knife, she inserted a keycard
and pushed the door open.

It was her mother, the downtrodden martyr to G'Kar's
ambition, and she was roaring with laughter – for the first
time in years! T'Kog, her strapping but spineless brother,
was doubled over in laughter, gripping his sides.

Mi'Ra scowled. "I know G'Kar's death was a major
event, but I don't understand this much levity."

"Oh, you will!" gasped T'Kog. He waved a finger at
Ka'Het, who was so dejected earlier that morning that
she couldn't get out of bed. "Tell her, Mother!"

The older woman usually looked gaunt and beaten,
but today she heaved with joyous gasps. "We are rich,

my dear! We are back in the good life again! As you said we never would be."

"Father has been absolved?" asked Mi'Ra, beaming at the thought.

That thought sobered Ka'Het. "Ah, no," she admitted. "This has no official effect on his case, but maybe that will change, too. We have the next best thing, which is *money*! Transferred directly into our old account. The banker sent an armored courier to tell us!"

"How much money?"

"Four hundred thousand Old Bloodstone!" gushed T'Kog.

"Keep your voice down," Mi'Ra hissed. "And who provided this windfall?"

T'Kog stopped laughing for a moment. "What does it matter? It's the same blackguards who stole it in the first place."

"Who was it?" Mi'Ra demanded of her mother.

The older woman looked away and straightened her ragged housedress. "It was G'Kar's widow, Da'Kal. I wondered when she would come through. She used to be one of my best friends, you know."

"Mother," said the young Narn woman, trying to remain calm, "that's only money. That was probably one year's housekeeping money in the old times. Nothing changes – we'll still be outcasts with no station in life, and Father will still be considered a traitor."

"But we'll get out of *here*!" Ka'Het snarled. "With that much money, we can get some kind of life back. What do you think it will buy?"

Mi'Ra was thinking. It would not buy her silence, she knew that. It would buy the services of several mercenaries, and it might buy more creature comforts, but it wouldn't buy them respect. And how long would it really last? If she knew her mother, not very long.

"What do you plan to do with the money?" she asked matter-of-factly.

"Buy a home on the Islands, or some resort where the

circles are allowed to mix. I think we'd be accepted in a place like that, even with our past."

Our past, Mi'Ra thought bitterly. They hadn't done anything wrong, yet her mother was still suffering guilt! "A house on the Islands," she observed dryly. "There goes most of the money."

T'Kog jumped to his feet and stared at his older sister. "You never want anything good to happen, because you're too obsessed with revenge. Whether you like it or not, *two* good things have happened, and I say we should rejoice! I'm with Mother. Let's get back to civilization."

Mi'Ra knew when to bide her time, and she bowed her head respectfully. "Mother, of course you are right. And may I suggest that you and my brother go on a house-hunting excursion to the Islands. But don't be hasty and grab the first thing."

"No, never!" said her mother. "If this experience has taught me anything, it's to be practical." She pulled at her rags. "Of course we'll have to buy some new clothes. Are you saying you wouldn't come with us?"

"No, you two go. I will stay and look after what we have here."

T'Kog laughed disdainfully. "We have nothing here, Mi'Ra. You're the only one who thinks we do. But I'm glad you agree with us."

"I want to get out of here as much as anyone," Mi'Ra assured her mother. "Now I'm going to lie down and take a nap."

"We splurged and bought some dry fish," said Ka'Het. "There is some in the pantry."

T'Kog moved lazily toward the door. "Mi'Ra, how was the memorial service?"

"Quite touching," she answered with all sincerity. "You would have thought he was a great man. Ra'Pak was there, and so were several Earthers from the place where he died, the Babylon 5 station. They can't arrest us, but they may want to ask questions."

"In the name of the Martyrs, why?" asked Ka'Het. "Should we try to leave before they come?"

"No. They must have found the data crystal we sent to G'Kar, and they want to meddle."

"I knew that was a bad idea," said T'Kog righteously.

Mi'Ra narrowed her red eyes. "You agreed at the time, dear brother. We have never gone anywhere near Babylon 5, so they can't implicate us. We don't know anything about G'Kar's death, except that it wasn't us and it wasn't the Thenta Ma'Kur. Are we agreed?"

"Of course, my dear," said Ka'Het, patting her daughter's spotted hand. "You worry too much. We know what to say, and we *are* innocent. Do you suppose we should offer them a bribe? One never knows with humans."

Mi'Ra touched her mother's hand and smiled. "No, Mother. Just be yourself. I think the Earthers are quite fascinated with us. I was told there is one among them who was married to a Narn."

T'Kog winced. "That's disgusting."

"This is the future," said Mi'Ra. "It may be our future, too. On a Terran station such as Babylon 5, we would be exotic aliens with no past and only a future. Old Bloodstone could be rare on an Earth station, and our money might last longer. We should consider this."

"We will," said Ka'Het. "But I'm not sure I want to leave all my friends."

The same friends who haven't spoken to you in three years! thought Mi'Ra angrily. She held her tongue. Her mother hadn't spent any of the money yet, and Mi'Ra had firstborn power of access. She could make withdrawals from this suddenly valuable account.

Truly, G'Kar's widow had done a noble thing, but it would be an empty gesture if the money were wasted. They could easily end up back in the border zone, more bitter and more estranged from society. Despite her mother's elation, this was not the answer to their problem. Plus, Mi'Ra was suspicious of this money. Why? And why now? What kind of silence was it supposed to buy? Whose guilt was it supposed to salve? Narns weren't known for experiencing much guilt.

When the Earthers arrived, decided Mi'Ra, she might have a few questions for them.

With hardly a whimper, the big red sun ducked behind the rim of Hekba Canyon, chased away by the blackest shadows imaginable. The shadows stretched like demons into the deepest crevices, stealing the heat as they went. Susan Ivanova must have sweated off ten kilos during the day, but now she was shivering and unable to stop, even wrapped in military-issue fleece. She was expecting the drop in temperature – she understood how thin atmosphere, low humidity, and weak air pressure could have this effect – but she still wasn't prepared for the reality of night on Homeworld. The commander could swear that her breath formed ice crystal bridges over the glaciers that used to be her cheekbones. The temperature must have plunged sixty degrees.

"Whose bright idea was it to come outside?" shuddered Garibaldi, pounding his arms against his chest in a futile attempt to keep warm. At least he wasn't complaining anymore about having to drag his coat with him.

"I told you, we can't stay on this high level," answered Al Vernon, glancing over the railing to the depths below. "We need to get lower into the canyon. In fact, all the way to the bottom."

Ivanova wanted to look over the edge of the railing, but she couldn't make her frozen muscles move. She unstuck her face long enough to ask, "Is it really that much warmer d-d-down there?"

Na'Toth scowled. "I don't see what you thin-skinned humans are complaining about. It's perfectly pleasant up here. I say, we go back into the tavern and wait for Ha'Mok as planned."

"It's been *hours*!" protested Ivanova. "What could he be doing?"

Al shook his head. "I don't know why we should be worrying so much about a simple crewman. Let Ha'Mok find his own way back. If he's not of the right circle, the rangers will probably catch him and send him packing, anyway. Na'Toth, if you want to stay and wait for him, that's okay with me, but we can't stay on this level. Humans *are* thin-skinned, and we don't have much insulation."

Al chuckled and patted his ample stomach. "When I lived here, I tried to pack on extra insulation, but it didn't help much."

Ivanova pried her frozen lips apart enough to ask, "Can we wait a little longer?"

Al squinted at his fellow humans. "You two can stay here and freeze to death – and it's going to get colder yet – but I didn't sign on for that. I'd rather take a five-minute lift ride and be sitting down there beside a nice, bubbling, hot spring, dabbing the sweat off my brow. You can call the *K'sha Na'vas* from down there, can't you? Why do we have to wait for Ha'Mok – he's just a crewman, isn't he?"

Na'Toth glanced back at the tavern door, as if considering going back to wait. But Ivanova didn't think the Narn wanted to wait indefinitely in the tavern by herself. Not only had the establishment gotten substantially colder with the fall of darkness, it had gotten rowdier with an infusion of privileged young Narns who thought they owned the universe. Besides, it was beginning to look suspicious that they should be so concerned over a simple crewman. More than once, Ivanova had almost called Ha'Mok by his real name. If they weren't careful, Al Vernon was going to learn their secret.

Na'Toth finally slumped her shoulders. "Yes, we can contact the *K'sha Na'vas* from the bottom. There is no way to predict how long Ha'Mok will be, and I can't force him to be sensible. Therefore, lead on, Mr. Vernon, I believe you know this city better than I do."

"With pleasure," said Al. He swung his pudgy arms and headed off down the walkway. Garibaldi and Ivanova fell in step behind him, with Na'Toth bringing up a watchful rear. It felt good to be moving, thought

Ivanova, with blood pumping to the outer extremities
again. Growing up in Russia, she thought she knew what
cold was, but Homeworld was causing her to rethink her
most primal memories.

"We don't have to cross the bridge again, do we?"
asked Garibaldi with a shudder.

"I don't think so," said Al. "The lifts don't begin here
until half-a-dozen levels down. This is the commercial
section – they want you to walk, giving you time to pass
the shops and shop."

Ivanova nudged Garibaldi. "We can't forget about
Captain Sheridan. To contact him, we have to return to
the *K'sha Na'vas* sometime soon."

"Maybe not," said Al, overhearing them. "You won't
find public screens with interstellar links on every corner, but this is a wealthy neighborhood, and they've got
lots of interesting stuff behind closed doors. We'll ask
around, *after* we get someplace warm."

Ivanova was not about to argue with Al's priorities,
not with icicles encasing her spine. The chill would have
been worse, she marveled, without all those broth drinks
she had consumed in the tavern. She hadn't tasted much
alcohol in the drinks; if they were all intoxicating, the
freezing air must have snapped her right back into sobri-
ety. Ivanova felt nothing but cold, creeping numbness all
over her body, and she could barely remember that the
same air had felt like a blast furnace a few hours ago. It
felt as if Homeworld had been mired in the Ice Age for
eternity.

In the dim light, Al Vernon walked down a level to
check the markings on a newer section of dwellings. As
if some kindly sensors realized he needed more light,
green light filaments suddenly ignited all along the
handrails and the swooping bridges that spanned the
crevasse. Ivanova swiveled her head and stared in awe at
the giant spiral of light. She felt as if she were inside a
fluorescent, tubular, spider web. The effect was quite
startling, until she realized that the handrail filaments

gave off little actual light and no warmth. If anything, the cool, impersonal lights made Ivanova feel even colder.

"Excellent," said Al. "We shouldn't have any difficulty finding the lift now."

He picked up the pace and lumbered confidently down one walkway after another. When he finally ducked inside a small cavern illuminated by blue lights, Ivanova almost kissed him, but her lips were stuck together. It was still bone-chilling even inside the cavern, and she ran to catch up with Al, mostly to keep warm. She could see his destination at the end of the corridor – a tiled alcove with an oval booth constructed from copper and black metals.

Garibaldi was right behind her, muttering to himself and flapping his arms. He tried to say something, but it just came out gibberish from his frozen lips. They huddled around Al, who was looking at a map – an elegant mosaic imbedded in the walls of the chamber. It was barely illuminated by reddish pilot lights glimmering on the lift booth.

"Remind me to bring a flashlight next time I come here," said Garibaldi, his teeth chattering. "This whole trip is beginning to remind me of a camp I went to as a kid. Camp Windigo, upstate New York. That's the only place colder than this."

Ivanova smiled, afraid her face would crack. She turned to see Na'Toth saunter in. Dressed in her usual attire and a lightweight cape, the Narn had yet to notice the cold. She stood behind them and studied the mosaic map.

"There's an inn at the bottom," she pointed out. "They probably cater to you thin-skinned types."

"Maybe we should just return to the ship," said Garibaldi. "Then we'd have beds and be able to contact B5."

Al Vernon shook his head and shivered. "I'm afraid you waited too long to do that. The only place their shuttlecraft can land is up on the rim, and there's nothing there but desert. You think it's cold here, you should go up there and stand in the wind! We wouldn't last two minutes, I assure you. No, I'm afraid we can't go back to the *K'sha Na'vas* until daylight."

"Why didn't you tell us this?" snapped Garibaldi.

Al blinked at him. "Hey, it was you idiots who wanted to wait around for Ha'Mok to come back! I didn't know what was going on. Who is this Ha'Mok, anyway? Why is he so important?"

Ivanova, Garibaldi, and Na'Toth looked guiltily at one another, knowing that one of them would probably reveal G'Kar's secret sooner or later. But it wasn't going to be right now, Ivanova decided.

"He's a special investigator," she lied. "One of our team."

The merchant shook his head. "I don't know what he's doing, but he cost us our chance to get off this planet tonight. I can't say I mind, though. This is exactly where I want to be."

Al Vernon pushed part of the mosaic, and the entire map lit up like a stained glass window, sketching a path from their position on the sixth level to the very bottom, three hundred levels away. They heard a shuddering sound as a car rose from the bowels of the canyon to fetch them.

"You'll like it down there," Al assured them. "Although I hope your credit cards are good. Non-Narns pay extra for boarding and food."

"Great," muttered Garibaldi. "The captain still hasn't approved my expenses from the last trip I took."

Na'Toth frowned. "I still say this is pointless. We should stay where we agreed to stay."

Ivanova clutched her own shoulders and shivered. "Please, Na'Toth, none of us agreed to freeze to death."

To their considerable relief, the lift arrived at their level, and the doors whooshed open. The humans jammed in, and Na'Toth entered reluctantly. The doors shut with a jolt, and Al warned, "These lifts are fast. Watch for changes in pressure."

A second later, Ivanova was close to screaming after what seemed like a sheer drop to the bottom of the shaft. Her stomach churned, her ears ached until they popped, and she could see Na'Toth yawning. The lift finally began to slow, and it deposited them gently at the bottom level of the canyon.

Following Al Vernon, Ivanova staggered off the platform. The first thing she felt was the thick humidity, like steam pouring from a hot shower. Then she smelled the sulfur, magnesium, and other bitter minerals in the air. As her eyes grew accustomed to the dark, Ivanova stepped around a small geyser that bubbled on the slate floor and shot gusts of steam around her ankles. It was soothingly hot and sticky in the cavern, and Ivanova loosened her collar as she followed Al Vernon through the dusky fissure.

She heard the voices and clink of glassware before she even emerged into the grotto. Plump vines stroked her hair as she ducked under a natural archway, and she found herself surrounded by sweaty vines, stretching high overhead. Plants and steam seemed to flow in equal measure from the moss-covered walls of the grotto. There were dining tables set at spacious intervals, each with a collection of elegantly dressed Narns seated at it. They regarded the humans with suspicious looks but returned swiftly to their dinners and conversation. Al Vernon plunged ahead as if the diners weren't there. He seemed to have a destination in mind.

The civilized setting and warm humidity was beginning to relax Ivanova, and she let down her guard as she wandered out of the grotto into a rock garden of geysers, bubbles, and sulphuric smells. She gasped as an intense current of icy air sliced along her path and clutched her spine. Her mind short-circuited, but her reflexes caused her to stumble away and find a warm pocket of air. She stood perfectly still in the gases of a hot pool, hardly minding the unctuous smells of sulfur and methane. At least the methane was a familiar smell.

As she stood in the hot mist, forcing her body temperature back to normal, Ivanova surveyed the primordial landscape at the bottom of Hekba Canyon. As above, the only light came from green fibers imbedded in the walkways. Paths wound around uneven terrain, jagged rock outcroppings, and assorted geysers, pools, and springs. The bottom of Hekba Canyon had been left in a natural state, she decided, except for a few isolated strips of crops, plus elegant restaurants and inns. Polite laughter mingled with the gurgling and spitting of the hot springs. Thank God for geothermal energy, thought Ivanova, even in its natural state.

Garibaldi and Na'Toth had paused to inspect the grotto, and Al Vernon was out of sight. She hoped that he hadn't deserted them. She finally decided that no human was likely to wander far away from this place during the middle of a Narn night.

"Watch out for cold spots," she cautioned Garibaldi as he emerged from the grotto with what looked like strands of seaweed in his hair. The security chief glanced around warily, as if he could actually see a cold spot.

"You'll know when you hit one," she assured him.

Na'Toth's eyes narrowed. "Where did Mr. Vernon go?"

"Beats me," said Ivanova. "But this is an awfully warm spot where I'm standing, and I'm reluctant to move."

Garibaldi wrinkled his nose. "Smells like my old high school locker room down here."

"I was going to say it smells like chemistry class," said Ivanova. "Listen, if Al never does anything else but lead us down here, I'm grateful for his help. But we do need a plan. Where *are* we going to spend the night? Everything down here does look fairly expensive."

Na'Toth held up a small communications device. "Captain Vin'Tok gave me his direct link before we left. He said we could contact the ship and send for a shuttlecraft. I don't care what Mr. Vernon says, maybe there is a way to get you off the planet tonight. I'm sure you would be more comfortable spending the night on the *K'sha Na'vas*."

"Yeah," agreed Garibaldi, "and we'd be able to call the captain. Let's try it. I say we ditch both Al and good old Ha'Mok."

"Go ahead," said Ivanova.

Na'Toth activated the device and waited until it beeped. "Attaché Na'Toth to the *K'sha Na'vas*," she said. "Come in Captain Vin'Tok." When there was no response, she repeated, "Attaché Na'Toth to the *K'sha Na'vas*. Come in Captain Vin'Tok. This is top priority – come in!"

She tapped the device. "It acts like it's working, and I've used these compact units before. Because they're encoded for one frequency, they are usually very reliable."

"Maybe we're too deep inside this canyon," suggested Garibaldi.

"That shouldn't make any difference." In frustration, Na'Toth tried again, saying the same words and achieving the same results, with one difference. This time, she studied the readouts on the device's tiny screen.

"Out of range," she said with confusion. "This device is telling me that the *K'sha Na'vas* is out of range. There's only one explanation for that. It's left orbit."

"Why should they leave orbit?" asked Garibaldi with disbelief.

Na'Toth squared her shoulders. "I don't know."

CHAPTER 12

G'KAR NESTLED in Da'Kal's bosom, trying to tell himself he didn't have to get up, he didn't have to leave. But he knew it was a lie. He knew as surely as his name wasn't Ha'Mok that he was neglecting urgent business, including friends who were taking risks for him. He had come to Homeworld to squash his enemies, not to take pity upon them and bequeath a substantial amount of cash to them! Yet that is precisely what had happened, all because he was soft and couldn't resist a woman's arms.

Quite a woman's arms they were, he had to admit. Many men would never have neglected a prize like Da'Kal for any amount of promotions and honors, but G'Kar wasn't many men. If he had been, he doubted whether Da'Kal would have wed him. He was not an ideal choice for her – a young Narn from a lesser circle with nothing to show but war medals – but she had been an ideal choice for him. Under her tutelage, he had learned how to curry favor and rise in the circles, and he had quickly surpassed her in ambition and ruthlessness. She took pride in his accomplishments, but she also maintained a distance, as if he were an experiment gone awry.

Da'Kal never seemed surprised at what he did, even this latest ploy. Despite all the other women, she was truly the only one for him, but she was never enough to keep him from his destiny. He had a role to fulfill on Babylon 5 that went beyond the petty concerns of Narn society; every day he spent there convinced him of it. However, his career seemed less important than ever at this moment.

G'Kar pressed himself against Da'Kal's compact body, and she moaned at his touch but remained asleep. Despite his resolve to leave, he didn't want to. He had to admit that even G'Kar of the Third Circle, Ambassador to Babylon 5, the most important diplomatic post in the Regime – even he needed comfort and forgiveness. G'Kar welcomed the blissful amnesia of lovemaking, which had always been so satisfying with Da'Kal. Every molecule of her body had belonged to him once, and he knew how to please each of them. This night reminded him of their earliest nights together, when she had taken him in, and he had been the grateful one.

For an instant, he wondered if he and Da'Kal could simply run away together, leaving the rigid society and impossible commitments of the Narn Regime far behind them. They could be like this – a plain man in love with a plain woman – and maybe then he and Da'Kal could really build a life together. But he worried that his self-ishness and ambition were too deeply ingrained. He was already plotting how to escape.

In her sleep, she twisted away from him, and he used that moment to slip his arm free and rise to his feet. It felt odd to have to steal away from his own bedroom, but G'Kar hadn't earned the right to remain here. He scooped up his clothing and dashed into the sitting room. As he pulled on his pants, he remembered that he was officially dead; if there was ever a time to start a new life, this was it. Then he shook his head. G'Kar had too much to live for, and the sooner he set matters straight with the Du'Rog family, the better.

He desperately hoped that Da'Kal's blood money would mollify the Du'Rog family, but he didn't think it would. When they found out he was alive, they would want more money, or his hide, or both. He had to meet face-to-face with that angry daughter, offer her a settle-ment that was good enough, or a threat that was strong enough. If he didn't have the courage to kill her, he would have to live with her. As tempting as it was, it wasn't possible to lie in Da'Kal's arms and ignore the past.

"Don't forget your disguise," said a voice. He turned

around to find Da'Kal standing in the doorway, her robe hanging open. She tossed the spotted skullcap to the floor.

"It's not that I want to go," he said apologetically.

She smiled wearily. "You never *want* to go – it's always business, duty, or necessity."

"In this case, it's all three," said G'Kar, pulling on a boot. "But I'll be back when this is over."

"I suppose so. But will I be here when you come back?" Da'Kal shut the bedroom door softly, not slamming it, just shutting it.

With one boot on, G'Kar hobbled to her door and began to knock. Then he realized that he had nothing more to say to his spouse. She had heard all his excuses and rationalizations many times, and they didn't register anymore. She truly knew him better than anyone, his equal parts bravery and bluster, his independent, selfish streaks. One thing they had in common – they were both people of action. He marveled at the way she had moved decisively to appease the Du'Rog family, while he had let the situation fester for years. Physically, emotionally, socially, and in every other way they were suited to each other, yet he kept running off at moments when they could be getting closer.

That was the great gamble of their marriage, the risk he took whenever he left Da'Kal. Would she be there when he returned?

G'Kar sat down to pull on his other boot. Then he picked up his skullcap from the floor and carefully smoothed it over his real cranial spots. He reinserted the brown contact lenses that gave his face such a bland appearance. Once again, he was Ha'Mok, a simple crewman from the *K'sha Na'vas*.

He went again to Da'Kal's door, wondering if he should give her a parting word. But he still had nothing new to say. In the end, neglecting Da'Kal could be the worst mistake of his life, much worse than smearing Du'Rog. One day, he knew, he would have to answer for his neglect of his marriage along with everything else.

He took a final glance at his disguise in the mirror and was satisfied. The Narn crewman pulled back the bolt, opened the door, and hurled himself into the blustery night. He put his head into the wind and strode down the walkway toward the bridge. He had told Na'Toth and the humans to wait for him in the tavern, but he had no desire to spend much time in a public place. He had taken enough risks already. The puny humans were probably cold by now, so they shouldn't mind returning to the *K'sha Na'vas* as soon as possible.

Figuring that he might as well summon the shuttle-craft, G'Kar took a small device from his belt. He pressed it, waited for the beep, then began to talk. "This is Ha'Mok to Captain Vin'Tok aboard the *K'sha Na'vas*. Come in, Captain Vin'Tok aboard the *K'sha Na'vas*. Respond, please."

When no one answered, he studied the device and shook it in his ear. "Bah!" he muttered. "The Earthers make better links than this." He tried contacting the ship again, and this time he watched the read-outs.

Out of range?

How in the name of the Martyrs was that possible? G'Kar tried to stay calm. He and Vin'Tok had talked about the possibility of the *K'sha Na'vas* being re-assigned, or having to respond to an emergency. Both prospects seemed remote, given the *K'sha Na'vas*'s high position in the fleet. Still, it would seem as if the *K'sha Na'vas* had left orbit; there was no other logical explanation for them being out of range. Under normal circumstances, G'Kar would have a dozen options, ranging from ordering another shuttlecraft to commandeering quarters in the nearest inn. Unfortunately, the options of a dead man were limited at best.

Troubled, G'Kar put the device away and strode across the swinging bridge. This was a temporary inconvenience, he assured himself. The *K'sha Na'vas* might have left orbit to refuel, take on supplies, ferry crew members, or any number of errands. It didn't mean he was stranded here.

The soothing darkness on the bridge helped to calm his fears, and G'Kar convinced himself that his disguise was almost foolproof. Especially at night. Even Narns who knew him personally were not likely to pay much attention to him. All he had to do was find his friends, and they could put their heads together and decide how to proceed. The ambassador stepped determinedly off the bridge and headed for the tavern where he had left his comrades.

Laughter and raucous voices poured from the tavern and gave G'Kar a moment's hesitation. Then he reminded himself that Hekba City was a civilized place, without the usual riffraff. He puffed up his chest and entered the dusky tavern, thinking that he would have little difficulty locating three humans in this crowd. Even though he peered into every corner of the establishment, he saw only young Narns, the privileged sons and daughters of the ruling circles. In his youth, he had tried to run with a crowd like this, but he had never been immature enough. He couldn't spend entire evenings frittering away his time, as they could.

"Are you lost?" a young aristocrat asked snidely. "This is no spaceport."

G'Kar started to scowl at him, then he remembered that they weren't seeing G'Kar of the Third Circle – they were seeing a common crewmember, a plebeian. He bowed apologetically and held out his hands.

"I was told there were human passengers in here. Has anyone seen my human passengers?"

"The humans left hours ago!" shouted the proprietor.

"And you will, too," added a customer, "if you know what's good for you!"

Now the raucous laughter was at his expense, but G'Kar kept smiling and bowing. He had spent so much time on Babylon 5 that he had forgotten how lower classes were unwelcome in certain neighborhoods after

dark. G'Kar kept bowing politely as he backed his way
out of the door, which caused him to run into a large
Narn in a black uniform.

"Watch it there!" said a ranger from the Rural
Division, shoving G'Kar aside. "Get back to your ship."

"Just leaving," G'Kar assured the ranger, almost
scraping the ground with his bow. To demonstrate, he
hustled up the walkway toward the rim of the canyon,
and the ranger nodded with satisfaction and ducked
inside the tavern. G'Kar did an immediate about-face and
slipped past the tavern, headed deeper into Hekba
Canyon.

Now he was worried. It was not a good sign that both
the *K'sha Na'vas* and his comrades were gone. True, he
had lingered much too long in Da'Kal's bed, and he
couldn't blame the humans for not waiting hours for him
in a slight chill. Plus, the clientele of the tavern had
turned rather unpleasant. The humans had probably
returned to the ship, G'Kar told himself. Yes, that was a
logical explanation to one mystery, but it didn't explain
why Na'Toth was gone. Na'Toth should have realized
his precarious position and been there waiting for him.

G'Kar halted in the middle of his step. What if they
hadn't gone back to the ship? Where would the humans
go? To the warmer bowels of the canyon, he imagined,
someplace he would not dare to go. They could get away
with going down there, because they were off-worlders,
but in his crewman's garb he would stand out like a
Centauri's hair. Plus, he had no money, having given his
emergency funds to Al Vernon. He could imagine his
friends and acquaintances dining late in the grotto, by the
warmth of the hissing geysers. Perhaps they were making a toast to his departed soul.

He looked up at the stars glimmering over the great
slit in the planet, and he wondered what madness had
brought him to this point. Alone, penniless, unrecog-
nized in his hometown, and wearing the disguise of a
simple crewman – he must have been atoning for some

terrible sins. The idea of coming out in the open, revealing all of his secrets, was beginning to appeal to G'Kar. What worse could Narn society do to him than he had done to himself? He was in a netherworld, neither dead nor alive, caught between the clay and the heavens.

G'Kar tried to mould into the shadows along the cliff face, hoping he could avoid the authorities for an entire night. He trusted Na'Toth to eventually return to the tavern, the place they had agreed to meet. Plus, he saw no reason to stray too far from Da'Kal's house in case he needed a genuine sanctuary. He thought about going back there now, but his pride wouldn't let him. If need be, he had his fake identicard and his excuse to be looking for human passengers.

G'Kar settled into a crevice in the rock, hoping the Earthers were passing a better evening than he was.

Outside the grotto, Ivanova, Na'Toth, and Garibaldi stared sullenly at each other. They were tired of discussing what they should do. Na'Toth wanted to return to the tavern to look for G'Kar, and Ivanova wanted to contact Captain Sheridan. Al was still missing in action, so he couldn't be polled. Garibaldi was content to stand near a sputtering little geyser that stunk like a skunk but shot warm steam around his legs. All three of them wanted to contact the *K'sha Na'vas*, but that didn't seem to be an option. Even if they did contact the *K'sha Na'vas*, neither human wanted to brave the plunging temperatures at the top of the canyon.

"We can't abandon G'Kar," whispered Na'Toth, reviving her favorite argument.

Ivanova sighed. "We've gone out on plenty of limbs for G'Kar. Maybe it's time we started thinking about *our* mess instead of G'Kar's mess. We've been out of contact with our superiors for days, we're out of contact with the *K'sha Na'vas*, and we're aiding and abetting a fraudulent death scheme. Homeworld at night is colder than humans can stand, and we seem to have wandered into a ritzy nightclub section."

Garibaldi cut in. "Plus we lost Al, and he's my responsibility. Which way did you say he went?"

Ivanova sighed. "I told you, he took a right turn out of the grotto, and I lost him when I hit that cold spot."

"Right." Garibaldi's gaze drifted toward a Narn couple who were walking among the bubbling pools, and his gaze followed them into the grotto. Now he understood where G'Kar's overly mannered style came from; it was *de rigeur* among this class of people. Deeper inside the lush grotto, a colorful blimp moved among the aristocratic Narn, looking completely alien, like a parade flag slicing through a sea of bronze statues.

"Excuse me," Garibaldi told the ladies, as he took off at a jog. "Al! We're over here!"

"Garibaldi!" shouted the merchant, waving his stubby arms. The Narns regarded the uncouth humans through lizard-lidded eyes, but the two men converged and began to speak in low tones. The denizens went back to polite repartee.

"Where have you been?" said Garibaldi, suspecting that Al had given himself some extra time to conduct personal business.

"I've been trying to find us a place to stay." The merchant sounded hurt at Garibaldi's accusatory tone. "And I've been successful, although it won't be cheap."

"Why am I not surprised?" Garibaldi scowled and turned around to see Na'Toth and Ivanova approaching. Neither one of them looked particularly pleased to see Al, and they regarded him with sullen faces.

"You're our guide, and we need some guidance," said Ivanova.

Na'Toth crossed her arms. "I am going to the top to wait for our missing comrade."

"Hold on just a minute," said Al. "Let me tell you what *I've* arranged. There are several inns here, but this is the social season, and they're all filled. However, I have prevailed upon an old associate, the manager of the Hekbanar Inn, to give us his second-best suite. I believe there are two chambers, and we can make the same sleeping arrangements we had on the *K'sha Na'vas*."

Garibaldi cleared his throat. "How much of a cut are *you* getting out of this?"

"My friend," protested Al, "you cut me to the quick! If you can make better arrangements, please do so. We're not going up to the rim tonight, so logic dictates that we have to spend the night down here. The sooner you accept that fact, the sooner we can make ourselves comfortable." He winked at Na'Toth. "Besides, this is the most romantic time of year in Hekba City."

"I'm not staying," said Na'Toth. "I intend to look for Ha'Mok and contact the *K'sha Na'vas*, as was our original plan."

"Oh, yeah!" Al produced a fresh newspad and squinted at it. "I don't read Narn as well as I used to, but I take it there's been an alert at one of the colonies. Every ship in the Golden Order was summoned, including the *K'sha Na'vas*."

"That's highly unusual," said Na'Toth, grabbing the pad from his hand. "The Golden Order is the personal fleet of the Inner Circle, what you might call our last line of defense. This is terrible luck for G . . ." She started to say his name and caught herself on the first syllable. "Just everybody," she finished.

"Is the *K'sha Na'vas* really gone?" Ivanova asked.

Na'Toth flipped to another page on the pad and nodded her head slowly. "She's gone. Although the action would seem more a ceremonial show of force than an all-out battle. I suppose if you wanted to show somebody what a Narn fleet looked like, the Golden Order would be an impressive choice."

Al clapped his hands. "Let's not be so glum, shall we? I can tell you from experience, there are worse places on Homeworld to spend the night than the bottom of Hekba Canyon. And far worse lodgings than the Hekbanar Inn.

And tomorrow, if you still want to go to the border zone, I'll take you there. Early morning, the temperature will be perfect, and that should be a safe time to go there. We don't need a shuttlecraft – there is public transportation."

"Is that right?" Garibaldi asked Na'Toth.

Na'Toth nodded her head absently. "We have excellent public transportation on Homeworld. After hearing this news, I am more determined than ever to find Ha'Mok. Hold the room for us – we will meet you at the Hekbanar Inn."

Al cleared his throat. "Are you sure you want to bring a common crewman down here? You know better than I . . ."

Na'Toth scowled. "We'll be careful." With that, the determined Narn strode off toward the grotto. Garibaldi watched her until she ducked under some dripping vines and vanished inside the cavern.

"Lead on," said Ivanova, with a resigned sigh.

An ebullient Al Vernon led them down the walkway, past the grotto, and through a stretch of classy boutiques, gaming parlors, and sidewalk cafés, interspersed with hissing geysers and smelly pools. The fancy watering holes were indeed packed, with Narns who were as stiff and well-behaved as mannequins. Garibaldi had to remind himself that these effete-looking snobs were ruthless conquerors who ruled dozens of solar systems and claimed vast expanses of space. A few generations back, they had been slaves. The Narns took stock of their visitors as they walked past, but they seemed fairly blasé about the sight of off-world dignitaries.

Garibaldi was actually getting used to the idea of spending the night in the lap of luxury. After all, luxury wasn't a condition in which he found himself very often. Maybe he shouldn't go kicking and screaming against the idea. Let Captain Sheridan deal with his expense account.

"You there!" he heard a deep-voiced shout.

All three humans stopped in their tracks and whirled

around. Garibaldi spotted three Narns standing on a second-story balcony that overlooked a small café. The Narns in the café regarded the Narns on the balcony and nodded approvingly at them. Two of the Narns on the balcony were broad-shouldered males but the third one was an elegant woman wearing a black gown and golden jewelry.

"Earthers, may we talk with you?" spoke the deep-voiced man, this time sounding more polite.

Garibaldi shrugged. "Why not." He led his tiny party through the café to the patio beneath the balcony.

The two men stepped back, as if deferring to the woman, and she leaned over the balcony to study them. Now Garibaldi recognized her — it was the noblewoman who had attended G'Kar's memorial service, the same one who had been visiting G'Kar's widow when they showed up there.

"I am Ra'Pak," she said pleasantly. "And you are the delegation from Babylon 5. We have met twice today, but we didn't have the opportunity to talk."

She hadn't seemed very interested in talking to them either time, Garibaldi recalled, but they had her attention now. Before he could speak, Al made an exaggerated bow.

"Your Highness, I am Al Vernon, a former resident of this lovely planet. This is Commander Susan Ivanova and Security Chief Michael Garibaldi. It is an honor to address a member of the Inner Circle."

Ra'Pak nodded at the compliment. "I had no idea you would be spending the night in Hekba City. I simply want to make sure your needs are being met. Is there anything you require?"

Ivanova answered quickly. "We need to contact our superior on Babylon 5. The ship that brought us here was called away, and now we're not sure where to go."

The elegant woman straightened up and spoke to the man standing to her left. He nodded solemnly and went inside. Ra'Pak leaned over to say, "My cousin, who owns this villa, has consented to let you use his netlink. He's coming down to let you in. I hope you have a pleasant stay with us." With that, Ra'Pak glided back into the party room.

Garibaldi turned his attention to a door beneath the balcony; it looked like stained glass and twinkled eerily. He finally saw what made the strange twinkling lights when a tall Narn opened the door and held out a candelabra filled with white candles.

He bowed politely. "Won't you come in?"

Al Vernon started to push past Garibaldi, but the security chief held out his hand. "No offense, Al, but we've got to talk privately to the captain."

"That's fine with me," said Al, pointing upward. "I'll be upstairs. When you get a chance to hobnob with these people, you do it."

Al brushed past him, and Garibaldi shrugged at Ivanova and followed him inside the villa. The foyer reminded the chief of a carnival funhouse, because the walls were decorated with some sort of mirrored surface that reflected the candlelight and made it appear as if flickering candelabras stretched into infinity. There were also gently pulsating lights in the ceiling and floor, which were both disorienting and oddly relaxing. He had to look away from the hypnotic flashes and concentrate on his host's face.

"I am R'Mon of the Third Circle," said the man with a somber bow.

"Terrible about Ambassador G'Kar, isn't it?" said Al morosely. "He was in his prime."

"He was gristle," said R'Mon.

"Yes, he was gristle," agreed Al, as if they had been close personal friends.

"Excuse me, sir," interrupted Garibaldi, "the lady said you had a netlink?"

"Yes." R'Mon bowed. "I am conducting a considerable amount of business with Earth companies these days, so I'm on your central net. I am certain all your codes will work. Right this way."

He led them through a darkened boudoir that had faint echoes of fading comets streaking across the sky. They came upon a mirror that made Garibaldi look as chubby as Al Vernon, and R'Mon pushed the door open to reveal a well-appointed office.

Al stopped in the doorway. "Excuse me, sir, but I couldn't help smelling the *tagro*. Do you think I could have a sip of that ambrosia before we leave your splendid villa?"

The Narn smiled. "Certainly, Mr. Vernon. Please come upstairs with me." He motioned to Ivanova. "Take your time, and when you are done please come upstairs. Join us in a toast to G'Kar."

"Thank you," said Garibaldi, looking doubtfully into the dimly lit room. "Excuse me, are we going to have privacy in here?"

"It is my *private* office," the Narn assured him. "My business depends on privacy."

The Narn motioned to Al, who was happy to lead the way out of the bedroom and toward the party. Garibaldi followed Ivanova into the office, which was austere in comparison with the rest of the exotic furnishings. The terminal was a universal type that Ivanova had no trouble deciphering. Garibaldi stood watching at the door and finally just shut it, thinking that if there were listening devices in the room there was little he could do about it. They had to trust R'Mon of the Third Circle, and they still had to be careful.

"The link is going to take a few minutes," said Ivanova, studying the board, "but the request is going through."

Garibaldi stuffed his hands in his pockets. "How do you want to handle this from here?"

The commander rubbed her eyes. "Provided we get a good night's sleep, I say we head off for the border zone first thing in the morning, like Al suggested. I'm almost inclined to tell Du'Rog's family the truth, so we can make it very clear why we don't want them to get near B5."

"That's fine with me," agreed Garibaldi. "But what are we going to do with Ha'Mok?"

"I don't know." Ivanova yawned, then gave him a smile. "Sorry."

"I understand. It's warm in here, and it's making me sleepy."

She was still yawning when Captain Sheridan's square-jawed face appeared on the central viewer. "There you are!" he said with relief. "There's a possibility that G'Kar may not be dead."

"We know all about it," said Garibaldi, leaning over Ivanova's shoulder. "This is not a secured channel, so let's not go into the gruesome details."

The captain nodded. "All right, but there's enough funny stuff in this matter that I'm recalling both of you. Get the *K'sha Na'vas* to bring you back immediately."

"The *K'sha Na'vas* got sent on a mission," said Ivanova, "and we still haven't talked to the Kha'Ri. We're sort of marooned for the night, but I think we'll be okay."

Garibaldi gave the captain a shrug. "Provided you'll approve our traveling expenses."

"Yes, yes, as long as you're trying to come back as soon as possible. I'll have Earthforce send a ship for you, but that will take a few days. If you can find any way to get home sooner, do it. Don't worry about how much it costs – I'll take it out of your bonuses." The captain forced a smile, telling them that he was worried and wanted to see them come home.

"We'll see you as soon as possible," Ivanova promised. "Considering this new information, we feel we should pay a visit to the Du'Rog family and warn them about staying away from B5. Believe me, we don't want to spend another night on Homeworld. Garibaldi says its colder than upstate New York."

"That's cold. Be careful."

"We're trying."

CHAPTER 13

G'KAR SHIFTED FROM one leg to another, wishing he could at least find a place to sit down. But there were no benches on the narrow walkways of Hekba Canyon, only wind, darkness, and an occasional passerby to hide from. At intervals he tried to contact the *K'sha Na'vas*, with no success. His lonely vigil was all the more irksome, because he could think of dozens of places where he would be welcome for the night, if only he were G'Kar again. The novelty of being dead had definitely worn off.

He continued to marvel at the popularity of the seedy tavern a few doors away, especially among young Narns of a certain breeding. He watched them come and go, wondering if he had ever been as shallow and arrogant as that. He supposed so, which was a depressing thought. Having never been on the outside looking in at the upper circles, he had never realized that the malcontents had a point. Who was to say that the vagaries of birth alone should determine a person's future?

There had to be plebeians who were more deserving of the jobs for which these spoiled youngsters were being groomed. They would never get the chance, however. The best they could hope for would be an assignment aboard a starship like the *K'sha Na'vas*, where they would see something of life outside Homeworld before they died, unsung, without a fancy memorial service.

G'Kar heard voices, and he turned to see two large figures approaching him from a lower level. As they mounted the staircase to reach his level, he again pressed himself into a crevice in the cold rock and tried to look invisible. For a plebeian, it seemed to be distressingly easy to look invisible, he mused. But not this time.

One of the men shined a light directly into his face,

blinding him and forcing him to raise his hands. The other one stepped forward and knocked his hands down. G'Kar tensed for a fight, then realized that they were rangers and he was in the wrong place, dressed the wrong way.

"We had complaints about a person loitering on this level," said the one who had knocked his hands down. "Let us see your face."

"Yes, sir," answered G'Kar, turning his face from side to side and squinting into the light. "Anything else?"

"Yes. What are you doing here? This isn't a place for shoreleave."

"I am crewman Ha'Mok of the *K'sha Na'vas*," said G'Kar, trying to sound proud of his lowly station. "I am here, awaiting my passengers."

"Isn't the *K'sha Na'vas* in the Golden Order?" asked the other officer.

"Yes," said G'Kar hesitantly, wondering why that should be notable.

"Then your story doesn't fit. Your fleet was called away on a mission. Do you have an identicard?"

"Yes," G'Kar answered with a nervous gulp. He fumbled in his waistcoat for it, thinking how much trouble he was in. If they took him to a processing center, he would be searched and his secret revealed, and he didn't know who he could trust in the Rural Division.

Smiling pleasantly at his tormentors, he handed them his identicard. One of the rangers snatched it from him and ran it through a small hand-held device. They both stared menacingly at him while they awaited the results.

"I am Ha'Mok of the *K'sha Na'vas*," he assured them.

"This is a funny place to wait for passengers," remarked the ranger with the light. "Especially when your ship is light-years away."

G'Kar shrugged and tried to smile, but his confidence was waning. He could remember times when he had reported suspicious people loitering in Hekba City, and he wondered if they had been treated as contemptuously as this. He supposed so, as the lines of Narn social behavior were tightly drawn.

"His identicard checks out," reported the ranger, sounding disappointed. "I still say we bring him in. His conduct and story are both suspicious."

"My story is true!" he protested. Nevertheless, the two rangers grabbed his arms and hauled him rudely to the edge of the railing. For a moment, G'Kar feared they would throw him over.

"So there is my servant!" called another voice. The three men whirled around to see a tall Narn woman striding toward them. When the ranger shined his light in her face, G'Kar was never so relieved to see another Narn in his entire life. It was Na'Toth!

He bowed to her. "Good evening, my liege. I explained to them that I was waiting for you."

The rangers peered suspiciously at Na'Toth, and one of them growled, "Who are you?"

She grabbed his hand and directed the beam of light toward the insignia on her chest. "Na'Toth, diplomatic attaché to Babylon 5 and aide to Ambassador G'Kar."

"Oh!" exclaimed the ranger, straightening to attention. "We had reports of a suspicious person . . ."

"I was delayed," explained Na'Toth. "This crewman was following my orders to the letter by waiting for me."

"But his ship has left . . ."

"Temporarily and very suddenly," said Na'Toth. "You know that the Golden Order doesn't stay away long from Homeworld. Crewman Ha'Mok is my shuttlecraft pilot. Come along." She pushed G'Kar ahead of her, and he shuffled gratefully down the walkway.

The rangers stood and watched for a while, but they didn't pursue. Nevertheless, G'Kar and Na'Toth put considerable distance between themselves and the uniformed authorities before they stopped to talk.

"That was close!" said G'Kar. "Where have you been?"

Na'Toth raised a hairless brow. "I could ask you the same question."

"All right," muttered G'Kar, "now we're even. What happened to the humans? Did they make it back to the *K'sha Na'vas*?"

"The *K'sha Na'vas* left before any of us knew about it," said Na'Toth. "We're on our own, and that includes the humans. At least they find it habitable at the bottom of the canyon."

G'Kar shook his head miserably. "I was counting on Vin'Tok. Do you notice, as soon as anybody starts to help me, they disappear! I've almost decided to confront the Du'Rog family and tell them the truth."

"Before we do anything really foolish," said Na'Toth, "let's get you out of sight. We supposedly have a room at the Hekbanar Inn."

G'Kar scowled. "That pesthole?"

At the party, Ivanova had commenced shivering again. She could tolerate the temperature, but there was a noticeable difference on the second story of the villa compared to the ground level of the canyon. The temperature wasn't the only thing that was chilly. The Narns seemed little interested in talking to them, although they cast a reptilian eye her way. To be fair, she wasn't feeling very sociable either, and she was content to watch the cultured guests float in and out of the party. She had seen R'Mon briefly but Ra'Pak not at all since coming upstairs from the netlink in the office.

She could see Al Vernon, flitting about from one congregation of Narns to another, running into a few old acquaintances, most of whom were polite but noncommittal about meeting him again. That was okay for Al; he was content to work the room and introduce himself. Maybe he was looking for his wife or someone who knew her, mused Ivanova; he certainly seemed to be enjoying himself. There came Garibaldi chasing after him, trying to get him away from the party.

With reluctance, Al made another round of handshakes and let Garibaldi push him to the staircase. Ivanova was right behind them.

"You're missing a great opportunity," Al lectured them. "You might never meet these kind of people anywhere else."

"I meet Narns every day," growled Garibaldi. "And I want to meet two of them back at this hotel you keep talking about. So lead on!"

They tromped down the stairs and out into the exotic geyser pit, with its softly lit walkways trodden by cultured Narns. Al now acted like he was in a hurry, and it was all she and Garibaldi could do to keep up. It was evident that he knew the bottom of the canyon well, and he led them past four very similar-looking inns dug from the cliff only to arrive at the fifth, the Hekbanar Inn.

The lobby of the inn looked like a *boudoir*, with lounging sofas, soft music, and twinkling lights. The men seemed intent upon negotiating with the proprietor, so Ivanova let them have their fun. That way, Garibaldi would have to produce his credit chit first.

Ivanova sat down in one of the luxuriant sofas and stretched her legs. The hypnotic blips of light in the walls and ceilings seemed to form some sort of pattern, and she lay back, to study the shifting vectors on the ceiling. She was blissfully asleep by the time the men returned.

"There are cheaper rooms than the one we're taking," grumbled Garibaldi.

"The best thing about the suite is it's on ground level," insisted Al. "There are natural hot springs to lie around in, to keep it warm and cozy, and you wouldn't believe the laser show!"

"Let's take it," said Ivanova, dragging herself to her feet.

As the dust devils frolicked on Street V'Tar, Mi'Ra carefully shut the front door of her mother's house. She had to double-check that it was locked, because the persistent wind had sent the clay candle crashing to the porch. Her mother and brother were still celebrating the windfall of Da'Kal's money, and they were poring over advertisements in old newspads that Ka'Het had saved. The only ones she saved, thought Mi'Ra angrily, were the stories of her father's fall from greatness and his pathetic attempts to clear his name.

Ka'Het had no collection of his triumphs, only his failures, as if Du'Rog was totally defined by his fall. Her mother's fatalism and insipid belief in things getting better on their own drove Mi'Ra crazy. Many nights she just had to get away from her.

The young Narn hated to be cynical, but she was. She just couldn't believe that Da'Kal's money came with no strings attached. If she had learned anything in her young life, it was that the bill for everything came due sooner or later. It had come due for her father, for her, and even for G'Kar. They would learn eventually what Da'Kal needed from the Du'Rog family in exchange for this blood money. Until then, she would reserve judgment on Da'Kal's generosity.

Mi'Ra stepped into the street, heeding her instincts that she was not alone on this blustery night. No one was in sight, but some people in the border zone never walked in the open. She kept moving, with no real destination in mind, except the thought of the illegal taverns on Street Jasgon. They were holes in the clay, where one might obtain illegal drugs, stolen goods, sex, and even conversation, if one wasn't too picky. She should have been afraid to go to Street Jasgon, but she wasn't. Mi'Ra wasn't afraid of the evil she knew, but she was afraid of the rustling in the dark, the shadow that moved when she moved.

She whirled around and dropped to a crouch, aiming her PPG at a water barrel that was cracked and dusty. "Who's there? I'll shoot!"

"Please!" came a tiny voice. "Don't shoot, I'm only following orders!" Behind the water barrel, two scrawny arms shot into the air.

"Is that you, Pa'Ko?" she asked.

"Yes, yes!" cried the boy. He ran out from behind the

water barrel and did a cartwheel in the middle of the street, landing perfectly on his thin, bare legs. Mi'Ra had never been able to peg Pa'Ko's age exactly – he was small for a Narn and looked no older than ten full cycles. But he often acted older, especially in the way he stayed up all night and never left the streets. She supposed that everyone who lived in the border zone aged prematurely.

She holstered her weapon. "What do you mean, you were following orders?"

"I mean, a man paid me to find you." With awe, Pa'Ko reached into a threadbare pocket and held out two black coins.

"To find me?" Mi'Ra asked with alarm. She stopped and surveyed the windblown street, wondering who else was lurking in the shadows.

The lad did another cartwheel and landed right beside her. He barely came up to her shoulders. "The man asked me if I knew where you lived. I said I did, but I wouldn't show him your house – that could be dangerous. I only agreed to watch for you and give you a message."

"What is the message?" asked Mi'Ra warily.

"At the north end of Street Jasgon, a shuttlecraft is parked. You are to go there and meet him." Pa'Ko smiled and held out his hand, cocking his head from side to side. "Now you will give me a reward, too."

"Get out of here!" scoffed Mi'Ra. She took a mock swing at the youngster, but he deftly dodged it. "Who is this man?"

Pa'Ko shrugged. "Do I look like I know people who fly around in fine shuttlecraft? It is parked there now. I would go see him, if I were you."

"It wasn't a human, was it?" asked Mi'Ra.

The boy laughed, and it was a surprisingly joyous sound. "A human from Earth? That is even more rare than a shuttlecraft!"

"Some humans will be looking for us tomorrow," said

Mi'Ra thoughtfully. "If you spot them first, you might have a chance to make some more money."

"Critical!" yelled the young Narn. Pa'Ko stared into his hand at his newfound riches, then ran off down the street, a collection of gangly limbs. He darted between two houses and was gone.

Mi'Ra took a deep breath and thought about going back to the house to get her brother, to back her up. But T'Kog wouldn't flex a muscle now that he had money again, however briefly. The only place he would be willing to go would be an expensive vacation, or house hunting. More than ever, she felt alone and shut out from everything – her family, her birthright, even her revenge. Besides, this mysterious stranger hadn't sent the boy to look for her whole family, just her.

She stuck to the center of Street V'Tar for as long as she could, then she pulled out her knife and slipped into the alley. There were people burning debris, but they were a good hundred meters away. She skirted along the wall until she reached the archway, then she dashed through, slashing her knife. Only the dust devils took notice of her heroics, and they swirled around her admiringly.

Mi'Ra decided not to walk directly down Street Jasgon, knowing she might meet people she knew. It was the hour of the night when almost anyone might be walking the streets of the border zone, and the attractions of Jasgon were not unknown in the upper circles. Mi'Ra hoped this stranger wasn't some playboy having a joke at her expense, hoping to get his way with a woman who had fallen from grace. Mi'Ra had endured countless propositions since moving to this hovel, but she had entertained none of them. The daughter of Du'Rog wanted to get back into the upper circles, but she wanted to do so on her own terms. Her father's reputation had to be rehabilitated at the same time, and she tried to ignore how unlikely that was to happen.

The young Narn kept to the walls and alleys, passing a

few people but doing it too swiftly to be noticed. She could be very lizard-like when she wanted to be, darting away from danger, holding perfectly still, moving in spurts with little wasted energy. In dashes from wall to wall and building to building, she reached the end of Street Jasgon without having set foot in it. Just as Pa'Ko had foretold, there was a gray, unmarked shuttlecraft sitting in a windblown field, crushing a few scraggly stalks of grain.

Mi'Ra walked slowly toward the sleek craft, her hand on her PPG. It was, indeed, a very fine shuttlecraft, better than the military or rangers had. Mi'Ra noticed movement in the small cockpit, and a light flashed for a second. She wondered whether an image had been taken of her. So what if it had? She wasn't a fugitive, and her likeness and history were well known, even if her existence was determinedly ignored in certain circles. Let them see that she wasn't afraid or ashamed of facing them, as they were of her.

As she drew closer, the hatch door opened upward. She froze with her hand on her weapon, waiting. A man dressed in evening finery, as if he were about to dine in the grotto, stepped off the shuttlecraft. He looked around the area, making sure she hadn't been followed or molested, then he nodded to her. When she stepped closer, he motioned inside the expensive shuttlecraft.

"A lady would like to speak with you," he said.

"A lady?" She stared at him warily. "Da'Kal, the widow?"

The man smiled with amusement. "No."

"Come in," called a steely woman's voice. It was the kind of voice that brooked no nonsense, and Mi'Ra climbed aboard the shuttlecraft without further hesitation. This was a royal summons, and she was still Narn enough to obey.

Seated at the navigator's station was a woman wearing a long, black gown, with her legs crossed seductively. Mi'Ra recognized her immediately, having seen her earlier that day. It was Ra'Pak of the Inner Circle. The young Narn had the sinking feeling that she was going to get the bill for Da'Kal's gratitude before even a single coin had been spent. If this was a warning for her to keep her place and keep her mouth shut, Mi'Ra was going to give this woman an earful.

"You are angry all the time, aren't you?" observed Ra'Pak.

"Yes," answered the younger woman. "I'm waiting for a reason to be content."

"I'm afraid I can't give you that." Ra'Pak suppressed a smile. "Seeing as how you're already angry, I don't feel too badly about telling you something that will make you even angrier."

"That would be difficult."

"I don't think so. What if I told you that G'Kar had faked his death and was still alive?"

"What?" Mi'Ra was trembling.

"You heard me, and it is the truth. I suspected something was amiss with G'Kar's death, and the Earthers confirmed it just tonight."

"They helped him fake his death?" asked Mi'Ra, thinking that the human she had met didn't seem the type for underhand fraud.

"No, they only discovered what he did a short time ago themselves. I eavesdropped when they were talking with their commander on Babylon 5. It is definite — G'Kar is alive. If you don't believe me, you can wait a few days, and the news will come out on its own."

Still in shock, Mi'Ra ran her hands over her cranium. She could feel the scar where she had sealed her *Shon'Kar*. "If he lives, then I will not be denied."

"Oh, he lives," Ra'Pak assured her. "And you won't be denied if you move swiftly. My spies believe he is on Homeworld now — he may even be traveling with the humans, wearing a disguise. This is the time to strike, while he is supposedly dead and is still within easy reach."

Mi'Ra growled and shook her fist. "That blasted
Thenta Ma'Kur – they lied to me!"

Ra'Pak shrugged. "It isn't the first time they've taken
credit for something they didn't do. They are snakes."

"But why would G'Kar do this thing?"

"Fear of you."

The young Narn smiled, feeling the blood surging
within her breast, flowing to her brain and muscles. Her
message to G'Kar had gotten through, and not only
would she kill him, she would make him suffer for his
treachery. It pleased her to know that he had already suffered enough to fake his own death. Then she realized
that Da'Kal's blood money might have come from
G'Kar, with his blessing! He couldn't buy his way out
of this, but she wouldn't stop him from trying. Maybe
they could have his money *and* his blood.

Ra'Pak nodded with satisfaction. "I see that you were
the right person to inform about this chicanery."

"And why did you tell me?"

The noblewoman's face hardened into a ghastly mask of
hatred. "You and your family are not the only ones he has
hurt. He has hurt someone very dear to me, and I want to
see him pay for it. Unfortunately, he has never committed
a crime against the Narn Regime, so I am powerless. But
no one could deny the honor of your *Shon'Kar*."

"No one will," vowed Mi'Ra. "Can you help me?"

"I have already helped you. His confederates who
brought him here are gone, and he is cut off from any
outside help. His aide, Na'Toth, might still be loyal to
him, and she could be a problem. As for the humans, they
strike me as inconsequential."

"I'm not sure of that," said Mi'Ra. "But if they are
helping G'Kar, then they are like his arms and legs and
must be broken! Anyone who stands in the way of my
Shon'Kar is the enemy."

"You could use the humans to get to G'Kar," suggested Ra'Pak with a twinkle in her ruby eye. "But I
leave the details up to you."

"Thank you, Mistress." Mi'Ra put a fist to her chest in salute. "You have trusted the right person with this news. I will never forget this."

"Just do the job," said Ra'Pak gravely.

Mi'Ra nodded and backed out the door. The man waiting in the field gave her a nod, as if it was safe to proceed, then he climbed back into the shuttlecraft. Mi'Ra jogged away, quickening her step, when she heard the engines of the shuttlecraft go into a burn. She reached the first building of Street Jasgon just as the thrusters clicked on, and she turned to see the shuttlecraft lift gracefully into the night sky and zoom toward the stars. As she watched the craft turn into just another shooting star, she wondered if she was saying goodbye to that life forever. Was her mother right? Was there a way back to the privileged circles?

No, thought Mi'Ra, there was only degradation and glory. She had had enough degradation, and now it was time for the glory.

As Mi'Ra walked down Street Jasgon, a million details crowded her mind for attention. One by one, she told herself, she would take care of the details, because a thorough assassin plans well.

"Pa'Ko!" she cried. "Pa'Ko, if you're around, come out here!"

The boy sprang out of a stone gutter and did a somersault in front of her. "At your service!" he said, bounding to his feet.

Mi'Ra lowered her voice to match the wind. "I will pay you *five* coins if you simply make sure that the humans – and the Narns who accompany them – arrive at my mother's house tomorrow. They will come to the border zone tomorrow, I'm certain."

"Critical!" replied the boy. "This is a lucky time for me!"

"For me, too, I hope," said Mi'Ra. Without another word to the boy, she strode to the most infamous of the illegal taverns, called simply the Bunker, because it was

housed inside an old bunker built by the Centauri for
guard duty. Even back then, this part of Homeworld had
housed the unwanted, the troublemakers.

There was a husky guard at the door of the Bunker,
but he knew her. He might or might not let her in,
because he knew she was often bad for business. At least
she never indulged in the kind of business everyone
wanted from her. She brushed past the guard, giving him
a shoulder that knocked him back into his seat.

When she reached the dark recesses of the Bunker, she
could tell there were a fair number of reprobates and cutthroats, exactly the kind of people she wanted to see.
When they saw her, standing in the entrance with her
hands on her slim hips, they gave her the usual rude
remarks, followed by slurred laughter. But tonight, she
had a comeback for them.

Mi'Ra yelled, "Are there any sniveling cowards from
the Thenta Ma'Kur in here?"

That silenced the ribald conversation very quickly and
won her everyone's attention. "If the Thenta Ma'Kur is
here and they aren't hiding behind their father's aprons,
let them meet me in the alley. As for you others, I am
hiring good fighters for one hundred Old Bloodstones a
day!"

That lifted the conversation to a fevered level of good
cheer, eliciting cries of, "I'm your man!" and "I'd kill
my own kids for that!"

"I'll be back," she promised them. She walked past the
guard at the door, and he gave her a quizzical look
but didn't challenge her. For one hundred Old
Bloodstones, thought Mi'Ra, he was probably considering joining her.

Mi'Ra strode into the valley and slumped against the
wall to get out of the wind. She crossed her arms, hiding the PPG in the crook of her elbow, and waited. She
didn't think it would be long, considering the advanced
communications of the Thenta Ma'Kur, and it wasn't.
She felt him crawl up beside her, like a lizard seeking

warmth. Having nothing to cover his face with, he kept to the shadows.

"Are you causing trouble for us again?" he asked.

"I'm only beginning to cause you trouble," she promised. "First you botched my father's contract, and now you've lied to me about killing G'Kar!"

"Did we now?" sneered the assassin. "Then who did kill G'Kar?"

"Nobody! He's still alive!"

The dark figure bolted upright, and his impressive chin jutted into the light. "Are you serious, girl? If you are trifling with the Thenta Ma'Kur . . ."

"A plague on the Thenta Ma'Kur! I have more to fear from the dust devils than you lazy buffoons. *You* are trifling with *me*! I just want you to know that I am finished with you. I will show *you* how it's done."

She started to leave, but the man gripped her arm. He held tightly, painfully, almost pinching off her blood supply. "If this is true, we will fulfill that contract," he vowed. "We will be there when you have failed."

Mi'Ra yanked her arm away and howled with laughter. She didn't care if she sounded insane, because in this terrible world what good did sanity do? She sauntered away from the assassin, laughing into the wind. The Thenta Ma'Kur were only for insurance, in case she failed; they were angry enough to do the job properly this time. She still intended to kill G'Kar herself, and his guardians if need be.

The costly suite in the Hekbanar Inn was all that Al Vernon had promised, complete with a natural spring bath carved out of sheer rock. It was in one of the bedrooms, and Ivanova kicked the men out, stripped off her clothes, and immersed herself. The rotten-smelling water was almost unbearably hot, but she found a cool current flowing from one small fissure and planted herself there. Currents of two contrasting temperatures flowed around her body, and Ivanova lay back and passed her hand over the panel on the edge of the tub. At once, the ceiling was engulfed by twinkling patterns of subtle lights cast against what looked like the black velvet of space.

Their luggage was on its way to some far-off Narn colony, but she had her uniform, a heavy coat, and now a bath. With those elements, she could survive any journey, thought Ivanova, although she knew she would miss the coffee aboard the *K'sha Na'vas*.

On the other side of the door, Al Vernon threw himself into a plush couch with a dozen striped pillows. He and Garibaldi were in the common room of the suite, between the two bedrooms. When Al began lowering the lights and bringing up weird patterns in the ceiling, Garibaldi interrupted him. "Before you make yourself too comfortable, we've got to find the other two people with our party."

"These are Narns," said Al. "They know everybody who comes and goes, especially down here. They'll know who Na'Toth is the moment they see her, and they'll send her along. I'm a little worried about that other one, Ha'Mok, but if you say you need him, then you need him. Me, I'm going to relax."

He put his hands behind his back and closed his eyes. "Believe me, Garibaldi, on this planet you could be in worse places than this."

The security chief was pacing, trying to tell himself that he should go to the lobby and at least sit watch for the Narns, when the chime on the door sounded. He rushed to the panel that opened the door, and he was extremely relieved to see Na'Toth and the ambassador, still wearing his disguise. Garibaldi's initial relief turned to anger as he thought about all the wasted days G'Kar had put them through with this stunt. Garibaldi was about to bawl G'Kar out when he remembered Al Vernon sitting there, grinning innocently.

"I am sorry," apologized G'Kar as soon as the door shut. "For being late, for bringing you here, for subjecting you to this. Where is Commander Ivanova?"

Al pointed a fat thumb at the rear door. "Don't feel
sorry for her, she's taking a bath. But we were a little
worried about you, Ha'Mok. They aren't friendly to the
lower classes around here – better watch your step."

G'Kar rubbed his eyes. "Can we continue this conversation in the morning? I think it's a good idea for all
of us to get some sleep."

"I'm comfortable here," said Al Vernon. "You fellows
can have the male dormitory."

Na'Toth suddenly stepped toward the pudgy merchant
and stared down at him. Al flinched as if he was about
to get slugged, but Na'Toth bowed respectfully. "You
have done well, Mr. Vernon, finding these quarters. I for
one am very pleased that you are a member of our party."
She glanced at Garibaldi. "If it were up to me, I would
take you into our confidence."

Al leaped to his feet and took her hand. "Thank you,
dear lady. Coming from you that is quite a compliment.
Don't worry about taking me into your confidence. I've
always found that when people start telling you their
secrets, it's because they want something from you. We
have an amenable relationship, and Mr. Garibaldi says
we only have one destination tomorrow before my duties
are finished."

"The Du'Rog family?" asked G'Kar.

Garibaldi nodded.

"Good. I have something to say to them." G'Kar
strode through the bedroom door and slammed it shut
behind him.

Al leered at Na'Toth. "After tomorrow I'll be a free
man and can get on with my love affair with Homeworld.
This is a wonderful time to be in Hekba City – I don't
suppose you could arrange to stay for a few days?"

Na'Toth shook her head. "We'll have to see what happens tomorrow."

"Just so," agreed Al. "Before we make any plans, let's
see what happens tomorrow."

CHAPTER 14

GARIBALDI HAD TO admit that the pickled eggs were pretty tasty, but he didn't want to ask what kind of animal they came from. At any rate, the breads, broth, and eggs seemed to appeal to everyone in the suite, although Ivanova complained that there wasn't any coffee. Dawn had broken half-an-hour ago, and at Garibaldi's insistence they were getting an early start.

"What kind of place is this border zone?" he asked of no one in particular.

Na'Toth and G'Kar looked at one another as if they weren't eager to answer that question. G'Kar, who was still wearing his Ha'Mok disguise, lowered his head.

Al piped up, "It's the slums, the ghetto, the end of the line. You can't get any lower than that. You wouldn't think a civilized society would tolerate such a place."

G'Kar pursed his lips. "It's much like Down Below on B5."

"Then it's dangerous," said Garibaldi, gazing at the Narns. "Since we're stupid dignitaries, we came here unarmed. What kind of weapons do you have?"

Na'Toth took her PPG pistol out of the holster on her waistcoat. "Standard issue."

G'Kar looked thoughtful for a moment, as if trying to make up his mind about something. He finally frowned and pulled a hidden belt from under his tunic. It had two PPGs on it and two small incendiary devices.

Garibaldi nodded appreciatively. "Good. Why don't you hang on to one PPG and give the other one to Commander Ivanova. I'll take the grenades."

Reluctantly, G'Kar handed one of the pistols to Ivanova, then he handed the belt with the two grenades to Garibaldi. The chief inspected the devices and was satisfied that he could use them in an emergency, a very dire emergency.

He glanced at Al. "You don't mind not being armed, do you?"

Al shrugged. "If I can't talk my way out of a situation, I probably can't shoot my way out either. We're just going to pay a courtesy call, aren't we? What's the danger in that?"

All eyes, white and red, turned to G'Kar. He scowled and rose to his feet. "Mr. Vernon, you don't have to go if you don't want to. I'm sure Na'Toth and I can find our way through the border zone. I've been there a time or two."

"Oh, no," said Al, springing to his feet, "I insist. You folks have been wonderful to me, putting me up in the grotto, feeding me – I want to do my share. Once you get to know me, you'll find that I always fulfill a contract."

"That's very commendable," said Na'Toth. "Our intent is not to put ourselves in danger, but Mr. Garibaldi is correct. This is a dangerous section of the city – with thieves and cutthroats – we don't want you to take unnecessary risks."

"I haven't been to the border zone very often," Al said. "I may never get a chance to go there again with fellow humans. But I can guide us to the outerwalks. That is how we're going, isn't it?"

G'Kar scowled. "Without a shuttlecraft, we have no choice."

Al opened the door and stepped into the corridor, with the others trailing behind him. Garibaldi took the rear position, feeling like a human time-bomb with the grenades strapped to his chest. Under normal circumstances he wouldn't have been worried about a simple interrogation, even if it was on an unfamiliar planet. However, the unspoken consensus was that they should end the charade of G'Kar being dead. A logical place to start would be by telling the Du'Rog family.

G'Kar had told Garibaldi about the cash that had been settled upon the disgruntled family, and his hopes that it would soften up their hatred. But Garibaldi wasn't sure it would work on that spitfire, Mi'Ra, who had nearly cooked him on the walkway yesterday. She was going to be a handful no matter what, he had a feeling.

They wound their way through the dimly lit lobby and stepped into blinding sunlight that was streaking down the canyon walls and leaking into doors and caves. Garibaldi squinted into the light and took a deep breath of bracing dawn air. The air was nippy but not frigid, and the giant red sun promised more warmth soon. The heat probably wouldn't become gruesome for another five or six hours yet, thought Garibaldi.

"This is more like it," said Ivanova, smiling at the sun. She took off her coat and tied the sleeves around her slim waist.

Al pointed along the strip of boutiques and cafés, most of which were deserted at this early hour. "We need to take the lift to the third level. As I recall, that's where the outerwalks are."

"Correct," G'Kar confirmed. The fake crewman looked as if he wanted to take the lead, but he lowered his head and followed behind Na'Toth, as befit his station in life.

They wound their way through the geysers and springs, which by daylight looked more like a bubbling swamp than a romantic playground for wealthy Narns. Wordlessly, they strode through the grotto and ducked under the glistening vines. They filed quickly down the corridor toward the inner chamber that housed the lift. Al Vernon bent down and touched the map, illuminating the path to the third level and the outerwalks. The doors opened immediately, and they stepped into the car.

The rapid rise left Garibaldi's stomach around his ankles, but he managed to ask Al, "Do we have to cross the bridge?"

"I'm afraid so," answered Al, "But at least there's not much wind this morning."

There was nothing to see as they rose through sheer rock within the canyon wall. The upper lift chamber looked exactly like the lower one, until they stepped out on the walkway and saw a vertical drop of a kilometer or two. Garibaldi took a deep breath, thinking that spending much time in Hekba City would give him permanent vertigo. As the small band marched along a narrow walkway, he stuck close to the wall.

Al and the two Narns stepped briskly on to the first bridge they came to, and Garibaldi forced himself to emulate them. That left Ivanova bringing up the rear. Garibaldi didn't exactly dash across the swaying bridge, as Al and the Narns did, but he did tell himself that it was safe. He even snuck a look between the metal slats to see the greenish bog at the bottom of the canyon. It seemed impossible that they had just been down there a few moments ago. From this angle, the bottom of the canyon looked pristine, as if untouched by civilization.

Despite his calm, he was relieved to get off the bridge and on to land, even if it was only a ledge on the side of a cliff. They were about six levels below the rim, Garibaldi estimated. Al, Na'Toth, and G'Kar climbed to the next level, as he waited to help Ivanova off.

She looked at him, ashen. "I'm not going to miss those bridges. I don't see how they can live here."

Garibaldi shrugged. "Some people think we're crazy for living on a space station."

"Yeah," said Ivanova, "but you can't fall that far on a space station, like you can here. This damn gravity will kill you."

They caught up with the others just as they reached a wide-mouthed cave on the third level. Workers were already filing out of the cave for the day shift, but no one was filing in. The Narns gave them apathetic stares, looking heavy-lidded and half-asleep. Garibaldi was reminded of dead-end workers on Mars headed to the mines and factories.

"Looks like we're going against the traffic," said Al cheerfully. Once again, the stubby human led the way into the darkness, with Na'Toth and G'Kar trailing

closely after him. After the bright sunlight, the clammy
darkness of the cave was both disconcerting and depressing. The cavern also preserved the chill from the night
before, and Ivanova was forced to put her jacket back on.
Garibaldi walked slowly until his eyes grew accustomed
to the dimness, and he finally saw the outerwalks, which
were both decidedly low-tech and no-frills. But the conveyor belts looked efficient enough. The incoming
walkway continued to disgorge workers, while the outgoing one rolled away empty.

After making sure that they hadn't lost the Earthforce
contingent, Al, Na'Toth, and G'Kar stepped upon the
outerwalk and were whisked away. Ivanova and
Garibaldi hurried to catch up, but they couldn't see
well in the darkness. They were on the belt before
they knew it, and Garibaldi was almost thrown off his
feet by the jolt. Ivanova doubled over the handrail and
hung on.

"Damn," muttered Garibaldi. "When they want you
out of Hekba City, they want you out fast!" He could
barely see the others ahead of him, but they appeared to
be walking on the belt, moving twice as fast. He was content to just hang on.

"We need to check commercial transportation back to
B5," said Ivanova. "I want to leave right after we talk to
the Council tomorrow. But first, let's tell the Du'Rog
family that G'Kar is still alive."

"But back on B5," Garibaldi interjected.

"Yes. We'll tell them in no uncertain terms to stay
away from Babylon 5. G'Kar recently gave them a nice
piece of change, so maybe they'll be sensible."

Garibaldi scowled. "Nobody's been sensible yet. What
makes you think they'll start now?"

Ivanova said nothing, and nervous energy had the
chief walking briskly down the conveyor belt. Once he
got into stride, he was covering ground at a fast clip, and
he could see ceiling bulbs flying past over his head. He
was starting to unwind his long legs and really stretched

out when the belt abruptly stopped and pitched him forward. Strong arms caught him before he could do much damage.

"Mr. Garibaldi," said Na'Toth, "you must learn to watch your step. We aren't on a space station, and you can't go charging about."

"Oh, sorry." Garibaldi looked around with confusion. He was no longer on a moving walkway, but he was surrounded by them.

"We have to branch off here," explained Al Vernon. "There's a nice middle-class neighborhood off that way, and a lower-class neighborhood this way. We're going to the ghetto between them – the border zone."

"You and Na'Toth go ahead," said Garibaldi. "I want to talk to Ha'Mok while we wait for the commander."

"We'll wait for you at the other end." Al took Na'Toth's arm and led her toward the middle walkway. "Come, my dear. Let me point out the sights."

G'Kar scowled impatiently at the security chief. "What do you want, Garibaldi?"

"I don't know what you're thinking inside that spotted skull, but I want you to keep your disguise on. I want you to let us do the talking. We're going to tell them you're alive – don't worry about that – but we're going to tell them you never left B5. And we're going to make it very clear that their clan had better *not* come to B5 looking for you. You just keep a low profile, all right, Ha'Mok?"

"Don't tell me what to do," said G'Kar.

Garibaldi got right in his face. "We've come this far for you, against our better judgment if we ever had any. So for once, you're going to do what I tell you to do! Don't test our friendship too much."

"Friendship?" asked G'Kar with amazement.

"I couldn't be this stupid out of a sense of duty," muttered Garibaldi. "It has to be friendship."

Ivanova stepped off the walkway behind them. "Trouble?" she asked.

"Just a conversation," answered Garibaldi. "I was just telling Ha'Mok that he should keep out of the way and remember who he is, and who he isn't."

"But I know the border zone so much better than you," said G'Kar. "I've lived in Hekba City for years."

"And you've made frequent excursions here," said Ivanova. "I'll remember that, but you're to remember who's in charge of this party. *Me.*"

The Narn nodded somberly. "All right, I agree. Out of *friendship*, I will obey your orders. Remember to take the middle walkway." With that, the Narn stepped on to the belt and was whisked away.

Garibaldi held his stomach and looked at Ivanova. "I'm beginning to think this is a big mistake."

"Maybe it's the pickled eggs," she suggested. "Let's deliver our message and go home."

She strode on to the walkway ahead of him, and Garibaldi followed her at a distance. He simply rode the conveyance without trying to walk at the same time. There wasn't anyone traveling in the opposite direction, and he guessed that people in the border zone didn't hold jobs in Hekba City. The belt rumbled down a dreary corridor, where every other lightbulb in the ceiling was burned out. No one had tried to make this part of the tunnel look natural – it simply looked endless and depressing.

Finally he spotted the others waiting for him in a tumble-down alcove at the end of the line. He stepped off the walkway deftly this time and marveled at the pit in which they found themselves. There was some kind of boarded-up stand, and the stairway leading out was covered with dirt and garbage. At the top of the stairs, swirling dust devils were in the process of blowing more dirt down.

"Welcome to the border zone," said Al. "I suggest we all try to remember where this station is. Things aren't well marked here."

"How are we going to find the Du'Rog family?" asked Ivanova.

"We can ask around," said Na'Toth. "They must be known, even in this place."

"Did they really kill G'Kar?" asked Al, sounding doubtful. "It doesn't seem as if they would have the wherewithal to kill someone on B5, living in this place."

G'Kar replied, "Never underestimate the power of the *Shon'Kar*."

"Come on," said Garibaldi, leading the way up the hill of debris.

The view at the top of the stairs was even worse than down in the pit. It was truly a slum – a dreary, unending grid of decrepit row houses that made the worst parts of Brooklyn look pretty good. Unlike Hekba City, no effort was made to allow the architecture to fit the natural beauty of the place. Of course, there was no natural beauty – just a rolling, arid plain with decayed buildings and crumbling masonry walls that tried to disrupt the wind.

Garibaldi would have thought the place was deserted, but he heard the shouts of a domestic quarrel and then a scream. The cop in him wanted to take off toward the sound, but he told himself that he was on a mission, and it didn't include saving the border zone from neglect and apathy. He wished that G'Kar hadn't mentioned Down Below in the same breath as this foul place, but he knew that every society had a bin in which to put its refuse.

G'Kar stood beside him, turning his disguised cranium into the wind. He squinted his eyes, protecting his brown contact lenses. "It isn't a pretty place to sentence a family, especially when they have done no wrong."

Ivanova was scouting around the perimeter, her hand on her PPG. Al and Na'Toth were busy trying to read signs and debating which way to go. So Garibaldi lowered his voice to say to G'Kar, "It's about time you felt some guilt."

"Oh, I feel guilt, Mr. Garibaldi, about many things. I'm good at feeling it. I'm not so good at knowing what to do about it."

From the corner of his eye, Garibaldi spotted movement. It wasn't aggressive enough to cause him to reach for a grenade, but there was very clearly a person dashing around corners, ducking under steps, and drawing closer to them. Ivanova worked her way toward Garibaldi, and she nodded in the same direction he was looking.

"Somebody's watching us."

"I saw him," said Garibaldi. "It's just one."

Suddenly, their pursuer came charging into the street, whereupon he executed an exuberant flip and landed on bowed, scrawny legs. He bowed comically and folded that action into a somersault, once again bounding to his feet.

"Have we encountered the natives?" Al asked cheerfully.

"He could be useful," said Na'Toth.

Garibaldi motioned to the boy, whom he judged to be roughly equivalent to a ten-year-old on Earth. "Come on over. We'd like to talk to you."

The boy charged toward them, all bony elbows and knees, then did a graceful cartwheel and landed beside Na'Toth, gazing into her red eyes. "Hello, fair lady. I am Pa'Ko, the greatest guide in all the border zone! Just tell me where you wish to go, and the streets will open like a magic walkway."

Na'Toth cocked her head and smiled at the cheeky boy. "Do you know the Du'Rog family? Ka'Het, Mi'Ra, and T'Kog?"

"Good friends of mine," the boy claimed. "They used to be rich, you know. I think a very bad man stole their money."

G'Kar cut in. "Can you take us to them?"

"Are you friendly?" Pa'Ko asked innocently.

"Yes," said Na'Toth. "We won't do them any harm." She looked at Garibaldi as if trying to get some confirmation of that.

"And how much will you pay?" Pa'Ko smiled expectantly.

"I was expecting that," said G'Kar. "Mr. Vernon, do you have any of those coins left I gave you?"

"Well," muttered Al, "I suppose I do have one or two."

"Give him two if you've got them."

Al dug deep into his pockets to produce two black coins, which he tossed into the air. The boy snagged one in each hand and grinned. Pa'Ko's scrawny neck and hairless head made him look anaemic, thought Garibaldi, but he would give anything to have reflexes and coordination like this.

Pa'Ko set off at a jaunty walk down the middle of the street, making sure that Na'Toth followed closely. It was almost comical to watch Pa'Ko and Al Vernon vying for her attention. Garibaldi had never considered Na'Toth to be all that attractive, but he guessed he was missing something. Mi'Ra, on the other hand, he could imagine fighting over, but he'd be scared to death to win.

G'Kar walked respectfully behind Na'Toth; although his head was bowed, his eyes flashed back and forth, missing nothing. Ivanova walked a few meters to the left of G'Kar, and she watched him like he was a child about to run off. Garibaldi did his best to keep watch on all of them, but the deserted street and the warm sun were beginning to lull him into complacency. He warned himself that this wasn't the ghost town it seemed, and the sun would soon turn on them. Then he caught a shutter moving as someone peered out at the passing parade.

Garibaldi did his best to remember their route as they cut between houses, across streets, through archways, and down alleys, but he doubted he could find his way back to the outerwalk without help. That was a depressing thought, and it made him feel for the grenades strapped to his chest, just to make sure they were there.

Finally, the oddball group of three humans, two Narns, and their young guide reached the top of a small hill, where an old street sign hung creaking in the wind. The sign read "Street V'Tar" and Garibaldi's mind flashed back to the data crystal in which Mi'Ra had recorded her infamous *Shon'Kar*. She had used that same word – *V'Tar* – and Garibaldi didn't think it was a coincidence. He knew without being told that this forlorn street was where she lived.

He tried to imagine what it would be like to go from Hekba City to this – permanently. Even though the two places were only a few kilometers apart, they were different worlds that bred different creatures. Was Mi'Ra more a product of this place, or those snobbish watering holes for the rich? The answer might determine how successful they would be in warning her off.

"Down there," said Pa'Ko, pointing toward a dip in Street V'Tar. "Where the street is red from the running water. Brown door on the right."

"You aren't coming with us?" asked Na'Toth with surprise.

Pa'Ko waved his hand. "I see them often. I will be watching for you, fair lady." He kissed her hand, performed a cartwheel, landed at a dead run, and kept running. With a childish chuckle, he ducked out of sight.

"The ingrate," muttered Al. "Not even a thank you for the coins. We'll never see him again, I daresay."

"Until we need to find our way back," said Ivanova. She started down the hill and waved them forward. "Let's go."

"Remember," Garibaldi told G'Kar, "let us do the talking."

"Very well," grumbled the ambassador. "Tell them, if they cooperate, there will be more money."

"You really do want to make this right, don't you?" asked Garibaldi.

The Narn nodded. "Death is not the answer. I found that out. So we must choose life."

Stepping over the broken candles on the porch, Ivanova reached the brown door first. Garibaldi came up behind her and gave her an encouraging smile. He glanced back to see that Na'Toth, Al, and G'Kar had remained in the street, with G'Kar keeping a respectful distance and his head bowed. Ivanova pressed the chime button. When no sound came, she knocked softly on the dented metal door.

They heard a bolt being pulled back, and both of them took a deep breath. The door opened, and Mi'Ra stood before them. She was dressed in what appeared to be purple gauze that flowed over her youthful figure. Did it matter that the material was threadbare at the sleeves and hem? Not to Garibaldi it didn't, as he forced his eyes upward to her dazzling smile and ruby eyes. She looked radiant and very pleased to see them.

"You make me look like a soothsayer," said Mi'Ra with amusement. "I told my family you would come today. Enter, please."

"There are others in our party," said Ivanova, glancing back at the other three in the street.

"They are welcome, too," offered the young Narn.

Al stepped forward importantly. "I'm Al Vernon," he proclaimed, "a visitor to your planet, but I once lived here."

"A pleasure." Mi'Ra bowed politely.

Na'Toth climbed the steps after Al, but G'Kar didn't move. "My servant will wait outside," she explained.

"As you wish," said Mi'Ra through a clenched smile. It was the first sign to Garibaldi that she was struggling a bit being civil. He resolved to watch her during the conversation, an assignment he was happy to give himself.

They entered a simple sitting room, which was overcrowded with massive furniture that looked as if it belonged in a palace. Or a museum, it was so tattered and chipped. Perched on a couch like a queen sitting on her throne was an older Narn woman. The matriarch was working hard to appear regal, but Garibaldi could tell she was rusty at it, not like those Narns down in the grotto. They probably snored regally. Pacing the back of the room was a young Narn male who tried to look nonplussed but only succeeded in looking nervous.

"My mother, Ka'Het," said Mi'Ra smoothly, "and my brother, T'Kog."

Ivanova handled the introductions for their side – herself, Garibaldi, Na'Toth, and Al Vernon. She didn't bother to introduce the simple crewman who was listening on the porch. Despite the friendly behavior of the Du'Rog family, nobody offered them anything to eat or drink, or even a place to sit down.

"We need to establish something right away," said Ivanova. "Did all of you vow the *Shon'Kar* against G'Kar?"

"I did," declared Mi'Ra proudly. "That snake deserved it."

Garibaldi caught the angry glare that passed between Na'Toth and the younger Narn woman, and he hoped they would both be cool.

Ka'Het laughed nervously. "It was a symbolic sort of gesture. You must understand that G'Kar completely destroyed this family. When I tell you what he did to us, your sympathy will be entirely on our side."

"They know all about it," said Mi'Ra with a sneer. "They still take his side."

Ivanova leaned forward. "Look at it from our point of view. It's our job to protect the ambassadors on Babylon 5, which was built specifically so that they could have a neutral place to meet. Your *Shon'Kar* may be acceptable to Narns, but to us it's a death threat against one of our most important dignitaries."

"What difference does it make?" asked T'Kog, striding into the center of the conversation. "G'Kar is dead, and the fact is that we didn't have anything to do with it! We weren't anywhere near Babylon 5 when it happened."

"We know that," answered Garibaldi. He looked pointedly at Ivanova and Na'Toth, making sure they were all in agreement. "We're warning you for the future, because it turns out G'Kar isn't really dead."

"Ooooh!" shrieked Ka'Het, swooning. T'Kog rushed to her aid, and Garibaldi whirled around to find Mi'Ra staring at him, judging his reaction instead of the other way around. She averted her eyes, but it was too late. Garibaldi had the distinct impression that she knew G'Kar was still alive, and that set off warning bells inside his skull.

T'Kog fanned his mother and scowled angrily. "If this is some kind of a jest . . ."

Garibaldi found himself talking, trying to say anything that would do some good. "It's no jest. We don't know all the details, but we think he has been discovered in a rescue pod, still alive. At any rate, we know you've gotten some money from his estate, and we know you'll get more if you drop this *Shon'Kar*."

Mi'Ra laughed harshly and crossed in front of Garibaldi, fixing him with her blazing red eyes. "My mother and brother are foolish enough to think that money means something. But it doesn't mean anything while my father's reputation is stained. What can Earthforce do about that?"

"Nothing," admitted Garibaldi, "but I'll tell you one thing Earthforce can do. If you show up on Babylon 5, looking to kill one of our ambassadors, we can slap you into irons, and we can shove you out an air-lock in your birthday suit. Whatever the worst thing you can imagine is that's what we're going to do to you. And I'm serious, lady."

Mi'Ra stopped in front of him and looked him up and down. "I believe you are serious, Mr. Garibaldi. You would like to shove me somewhere in my birthday suit."

"Mi'Ra!" snapped her mother, making a remarkable recovery. "You stop threatening them. What they've brought us is disturbing news, but we will have to make the best of it. Attaché Na'Toth, you are the ambassador's aide?"

"I am," answered the Narn.

"The Earthers said something about more money. If we were to negotiate this amount with you, perhaps you could take the figures back to your superior."

Na'Toth sighed. "I could. In return, we will want you to disavow the *Shon'Kar*."

Mi'Ra was silent, although her jaw worked tensely.

"We can talk about it," her mother said pleasantly. "Everything is negotiable."

During the ensuing conversation, Garibaldi backed away from Mi'Ra and opened up his collar. The day was already starting to get warm. While the women negotiated, nobody was paying any attention to Al Vernon, so the merchant gave Garibaldi a jaunty wave and wandered out the door. Garibaldi wished he could join him – a little fresh air sounded good about now. He tried not to look at Mi'Ra, because it amused her every time he did.

Sitting on the porch, G'Kar was startled by the door slamming shut and Al's heavy footsteps. Al smiled at him and breathed a huge sigh of relief.

"I can't believe it," whispered the human. "They actually told that crazy family that G'Kar is still alive! Can you imagine?"

"But it seems to be working out all right, doesn't it?" asked G'Kar hopefully. "I've been listening, and it sounds as if they've agreed to make peace."

Al grinned. "All except that luscious daughter of his. She wants dice made out of G'Kar's vertebrae. But it does sound promising, which is fine with me. I was afraid I would have to step in."

G'Kar laughed derisively. "You could end a *Shon'Kar*?"

"You never know how a *Shon'Kar* will end," observed Al. He patted his ample stomach. "My work is done here – maybe I should return to Hekba City."

"Come back with us," insisted G'Kar. "I'm feeling in a very magnanimous mood, and we owe you something for everything you've done. Remain with us – I think we can prevail upon G'Kar's wife to give you something extra for your trouble."

Al tugged at his sport coat, as if that were his intention all along. "Of course, I wasn't planning to leave just yet." He gazed around. "The street is awfully deserted, isn't it? I mean, people *do* live here. Have you seen anything suspicious?"

"I haven't seen anything at all," grumbled G'Kar. "But I haven't been looking around. I suppose I should."

"Let's not make a big deal of it," said Al. "I'll just take a look off to the right here, and you take the left. Like we're biding our time."

G'Kar whispered, "Do you think this could be some kind of trap?"

"I've been down here before during the day, and I never remember it being this quiet. Where are the people?"

"There's one of them," said G'Kar with his sharp vision. But he didn't point; he turned and smiled at the stocky human. "He just ducked down behind a water barrel. That's rather suspicious behavior, isn't it?"

"Indeed it is," agreed Al, sneaking a look in that direction. "That's the way we would go back to reach the outerwalk. You're sure about what you saw?"

"Yes, I am. Of course, it may have been that confounded boy."

"No." Al pointed out. "He wasn't foolish enough to come down this street, remember?"

Their troubling conversation was interrupted by the door squeaking open and the exit of their bedraggled party from the Du'Rog house. Garibaldi charged out, gasping for air as if the atmosphere inside the house had been stifling. He was followed by Ivanova and Na'Toth, neither of whom looked overjoyed at what had transpired. Weariness and relief showed in their faces in equal measure. The mission was over, thought G'Kar, and it was a success. The dreaded Du'Rog family had been cornered in their lair, told the truth, and settled with. They should all be overjoyed that it was over. But was it over?

Mi'Ra stepped out on the porch after them, and she did look quite fetching in her filmy gown. She pointed up the hill. "If you want to get back to Hekba City, the outerwalk is that way."

"Yeah," said Garibaldi, "we should get going. I hope you won't be offended if I say I never want to see you again."

"Too bad," said Mi'Ra playfully. "I think we could have been friends."

"Okay, let's get going," said Ivanova, making it an order.

"No!" G'Kar blurted out. Then he remembered to bow his head and act obsequious. "Mr. Vernon and I have been talking, and we feel another route is better."

"Yeah," said Al, wiping the sweat off his brow. "There's something we want to see in the other direction."

Garibaldi got the message. "I'll go wherever you two want. It's your territory."

Mi'Ra got angry. "That's absurd. The quickest way is to the south." She stepped off the porch and stared in that direction.

G'Kar strode off determinedly in the northern direction, hoping the others would get the idea, and Al was not far behind. G'Kar had always found that humans had a fairly good sense of danger – there was still some reptile left in their brains – and he hoped it would kick in soon.

A clay pot smashed somewhere, and Ivanova whirled around, which spooked an assailant hiding up the hill. He leapt to his feet and cut loose with PPG fire that streaked over Ivanova's head and raked a house across the street. Ivanova dropped to one knee, rested her elbow and took aim; she cooked the gunner with a short burst of her PPG. Everyone else fled, including Mi'Ra, who vanished into the house.

G'Kar drew his own weapon and hoped that would be the end of it, but Mi'Ra burst from the house toting a PPG bazooka. "Kill them!" she shrieked. Her voice was drowned out by the roar of her own weapon.

Behind G'Kar, an entire house blew into flaming cinders. When he tore his eyes away from that horrible sight, he saw an army of thugs pouring from the buildings up the street. They came charging down the hill, howling like drunken, bloodthirsty lunatics.

"Retreat!" screamed G'Kar.

CHAPTER 15

IVANOVA IGNORED THE wild PPG fire that pulsed over her head. She figured she had one more shot before the army of thugs figured out they had to stand still to shoot well, so she took careful aim at the figure in the purple dress.

"Don't kill her!" shouted Garibaldi far behind her. But she ignored him, too, and squeezed off a burst.

The bazooka in Mi'Ra's arms lit up like a toy laser sword, and she shrieked as she flung it to the ground. She was burned and her dress was singed, but the bazooka was no more. Ivanova leaped to a crouch and ran northward down the street, with the raging mob in close pursuit. Her small band was strung out ahead of her, fleeing for their lives.

"Artillery!" G'Kar yelled over the din.

Garibaldi got the message, and he stopped in his tracks and whirled around. Ivanova passed him as he pulled the first grenade off his belt. "Nice shooting!" he called.

"She's next," warned the commander.

But she didn't think Garibaldi heard her, as he concentrated on aiming the grenade. With great accuracy, he lobbed it underhanded into the mob, and the blast was ferocious, engulfing a dozen of the ragtag army in a scorching fireball. Their screams were chilling as the dying Narns crumpled to the ground or staggered away like torches with legs. The grenade had the desired effect of slowing up the mob and forcing most of them into cover, but it enraged some of them, who cut loose with PPG fire that blew away porches and huge chunks of the street. It was war now.

"Fall back!" shouted Ivanova.

She ran for her life along with the others, and she

found G'Kar organizing their forces at the end of the street. There was nothing beyond it but a neglected field. They were being fired at but not chased, and Ivanova crouched on the ground behind a cracked wall.

She stared at G'Kar. "How do we get out of here?"

"First of all," he answered, "you put me in charge. We need to move like a squad, and I can command a squad. By the way, that was good shooting back there."

Ivanova shook her head in exasperation. "Okay, you're in charge. Now get us out of here!"

G'Kar motioned to Na'Toth. "You and Al on the left side of the wall. Ivanova and Garibaldi on the right side. We've got to make it look like we'll make a stand."

Their assailants were also regrouping, although a few kept up their indiscriminate firing. Na'Toth shot back at them.

"Don't fire unless they're in range," ordered G'Kar. "We have to conserve those PPGs; they won't last forever."

"We need a plan," said Ivanova. "Is there any other way to get back to the outerwalk?"

"No," answered G'Kar, "they're between us and the only transportation we have to get out of the border zone. Here are our options: We could run east or west to the plebeian villages, but they're a lot farther than the outerwalk. We could make a stand, but they would eventually overrun us, coming at us from all sides. We could fight our way through them, but I think we would suffer heavy casualties if we did that."

"Let's not do that," suggested Al Vernon with a gulp. "What about hiding?"

"Perhaps Na'Toth and I could blend in," said G'Kar, "but I don't think the three of you could. The safest course would be to outflank them, and we might be able to do that at night. If we could find a place to hide until darkness, I would be in favor of that."

"Man, you act just like a general!" said Al Vernon in admiration. "I'm going wherever Ha'Mok is going."

G'Kar smiled. "This is much like old times in the colonies. This entire trip has been very nostalgic for me."

A stone landed near them, and Ivanova jumped along with everybody else. She whirled around, wondering where it had come from, and saw little Pa'Ko frolicking in the field, turning cartwheels and somersaults. He windmilled his arms and ran off toward a well that stood neglected in the center of the forlorn field. If it hadn't been for a corroded metal canopy and an old bucket hanging from it, Ivanova wouldn't have recognized the crumbling mound as a well. Pa'Ko waved at them for a moment, then he dove down the well with the ease of Santa Claus going down a chimney. Given the surreal events of the last few minutes, this seemed a fitting conclusion.

"Did anybody else see that?" gasped Al Vernon. "That little bugger just dove down that well!"

"Do you suppose he wants us to follow him?" asked Na'Toth.

"We'd be sitting ducks out in that field," growled Garibaldi.

"He had to go somewhere," said G'Kar. "Ivanova and Na'Toth, go check it out. Na'Toth, give your PPG to Garibaldi. We'll cover you."

Everyone obeyed G'Kar without a moment's hesitation. Technically, Ivanova was in charge, but they needed a platoon leader. G'Kar had the instincts and experience, and he knew the terrain.

She and Na'Toth got into a crouch and ran across the field. On a neighboring street, a sniper jumped up and sent a blue beam arcing across their heads. Garibaldi answered with a pinpoint blast that rearranged the sniper's head, and he dropped like a pile of trash to the dusty street. Ivanova hated that they had to shoot to kill, but fear was the only thing that would keep this pack at bay, and she had serious doubts whether fear would restrain Mi'Ra and some of them.

Na'Toth reached the crumbling well first, and she worked her way around to the side, away from the snipers. Ivanova followed, keeping an eye open for more shooters, but Garibaldi's quick response had discouraged them for the moment. Na'Toth punched the crumbling clay adobe that surrounded the well, testing its strength.

"You can't sit on the edge of this thing and take a leisurely look inside," she reported. "I'm going inside. If our friend went down there, I think I can make it."

"You won't be armed," said Ivanova.

"I think he's trying to help us," the Narn insisted. "I'll yell for you when I get to safe footing. If you don't hear me yell, don't come down."

Ivanova nodded, then waited until Na'Toth nodded back. They both leaped to their feet. Ivanova raked the wall where the last sniper had hidden, while Na'Toth vaulted over the structure and disappeared feet-first down the hole. Even from several meters above, Ivanova could hear a thud and a groan as the big Narn landed. She held her breath waiting to hear Na'Toth's voice.

"It's okay!" she bellowed. "Come down!"

Knowing she would have no one to cover her, Ivanova slithered up and over the crumbling wall. She succeeded in keeping a low profile, and she was already dropping into the darkness when a PPG blast bit off a chunk of the well and showered her with fragments.

Ivanova screamed in spite of herself as she slid through the darkness, bumping over roots and wet dirt. She was prepared to hit the ground hard, and her strong legs absorbed most of the impact. Na'Toth caught her before she toppled over, then pulled her away as dirt and debris tumbled down after her.

When the bombardment ended, Ivanova looked around the narrow shaft and could see almost nothing except for the small pool of light from above, which had to struggle through ten meters of dirt. Behind Na'Toth, she could make out the vague shape of a narrow passage that stretched into utter and foreboding darkness. There were strange smells coming from the passage, too, smells that were musty and rotten.

"I can't see much," said Ivanova, "Where are we? Some kind of maintenance tunnel?"

Na'Toth laughed without humor. "Maintenance tunnel in a border zone? I think not. Either by accident or design, it appears as if somebody dug a well near the ancient catacombs. They must have realized it, because they filled it with rubble just high enough to provide a secret entrance to the catacombs."

"Catacombs?" asked Ivanova, not liking the sound of that word.

Before Na'Toth could explain, they heard a shout from overhead, and a PPG blast sheered off more of the top of the well. There were bloodcurdling screams that reverberated right through the earth, and a large figure darkened the hole, cutting off all the light.

"I'm coming!" groaned a horrified voice.

Ivanova barely had time to stumble into the adjoining passage before a massive object plummeted down the shaft, crashing to the bottom. The light returned long enough to show Al Vernon, sitting like a crumpled Buddha among the clods of dirt.

There were more shouts overhead, and the women quickly dragged Al into the passage and left him there. They returned to the shaft long enough to see another body tumble down, followed in short order by another. G'Kar and Garibaldi rolled into a big pile of arms and legs, and Na'Toth and Ivanova struggled to separate them. The fun was short-lived as angry shouts and drunken laughter sounded at the top of the well; somebody dangled a PPG over the edge and fired without aiming. More clods of dirt thundered down, and the women pulled the men out of the shaft and dragged them into the catacombs.

They scrambled deeper into the tunnel only to find Al Vernon standing there, holding a candle embedded in an upside-down Narn skull.

Ivanova pointed to the gruesome curio. "Where did you get that?"

"Pa'Ko ran up and gave it to me," answered Al with amazement. "Then he ran off."

"I don't blame him," muttered Garibaldi. He looked around at the gloomy passage and wrinkled his nose at its dank smells. "Where the hell are we, the sewer?"

"The catacombs," said G'Kar. "Pre-Centauri invasion, we put our dead in these rambling, underground burial chambers. The cool earth and low humidity kept the corpses in good condition, and one was expected to come down and visit one's relatives. With the invasion, freedom fighters and martyrs used the catacombs as escape routes. Nobody has ever made a map of the entire system of catacombs – it's too vast. At least they can't come at us from all sides down here."

"What happened up top?" asked Na'Toth.

Garibaldi answered, "I think Mi'Ra realized that the two of you had found a way out, so she led an all-out attack. We had nowhere else to go."

"Sshhh!" cautioned Na'Toth. "Listen!"

From the top of the well, a soft voice was calling. "Garibaldi! Garibaldi!"

"Don't answer her," said Ivanova.

"Garibaldi, let's make a deal!" came Mi'Ra's voice, sounding quite reasonable. "We don't want to harm *you* – we just want G'Kar. Give us G'Kar, and we'll let the rest of you go!"

Al chuckled. "G'Kar? What's the matter with them? We don't have G'Kar."

Everyone gazed from the chubby man to the muscular Narn, and Al's eyes widened with horror. Trembling, he lifted the skull candle closer to G'Kar's face. "Don't tell me, you're . . ."

"I warned you not to come," said G'Kar. He ripped off his disguise and threw it to the floor, then he popped out the contact lenses and ground them under his heel.

"Lord help us!" moaned Al, and he took off at a

terrified run down the narrow tunnel. Within seconds, there came a scream, the sound of a crash, and total blackness as the candle went out.

Ivanova sunk against the wall and let the Narns investigate in the darkness while she kept an eye on the pool of light coming down the well. Whenever shadows moved across the light, she tensed, expecting an attack. She turned to see G'Kar ignite the skull candle with a low-level burst from his PPG. There were gasps as the party spotted Al sprawled on the ground, wrapped in the embrace of a desiccated Narn corpse.

"Aaaghhh!" he screamed, pushing the crumbling cadaver away. Ivanova gazed around and saw that there were mummified bodies everywhere, hanging from the walls, lying on shelves, sitting on benches, and piled like cordwood against the wall. A few skulls were rolling about loose.

Na'Toth helped Al to his feet. "Mr. Vernon, get control of yourself. And watch your step. You don't want to desecrate the dead, do you?"

"I don't want to be the dead!"

Another sound startled Ivanova, and she whirled around to see a large figure drop down the well behind her. She shot into the darkness and heard a groan, but she didn't know if she had hit him.

"Let's move it!" barked Garibaldi.

With G'Kar holding the candle and leading the way, they moved single-file through the catacombs, trying not to jostle the remains that rested in profusion all around them. Ivanova found herself breathing through her mouth, both to get more air and to keep the clammy smells at bay. She shouldered her way through the others to catch up with G'Kar and his wavering candle.

"G'Kar, is there any way we can get back to Hekba City through these catacombs?"

"I don't think so," answered the Narn. "But I'm not an expert on them. If that boy will stand still long enough for us to talk to him, maybe he can tell us."

After several moments, it became apparent that they were walking toward a flickering light at the end of the passageway. They slowed their pace to listen, and Ivanova heard shuffling sounds as they approached the chamber. She leveled her PPG and followed G'Kar as he crept into what had to be a tomb; it was crowded with mummified remains and illuminated by three lumpy candles. Furtive figures darted away, hiding under coffins and benches, and Ivanova nearly shot at them until she realized they were Narn children. Huddled in the corner, inspecting something green and moldy, sat little Pa'Ko.

"You made it!" he said with a grin. "Welcome to our home! We have to share it with dead people, but they're quiet."

Slowly, his tiny friends poked their heads out of their dusty hiding places, and Ivanova was shocked to see that some looked as young as a four or five-year-old human. Al Vernon, Na'Toth, and Garibaldi filed slowly into the tomb, and they gaped at the unexpected enclave of children.

"You can't stay here," Ivanova warned them. "There are bad people chasing us. If they knew you helped us, they would be angry."

Pa'Ko bounded to his feet and frowned like a serious adult. "Too many bad people live here. Maybe you could take us where *you* live!"

The children nodded in agreement, as if it couldn't be much worse than this. Ivanova took a deep breath, feeling both her charitable and motherly tendencies starting to rise up. She would love to help these children, but right now there was a good chance that none of them would get back to B5 alive.

"Don't you have parents?" she asked, knowing she probably didn't want to hear the answer.

Pa'Ko shrugged. "They kept beating me, so I ran away. Since then, I've heard they're dead."

Ivanova looked around the musty chamber. Counting

the entrance they had used, there were three passageways leading out of the tomb, and G'Kar looked in each of them, prodding the darkness with his candle.

"This might be a good place to lose our pursuers," he said. "They can guess, but they won't know for sure which way we've gone. We can't go back the way we came, so we'll take one of these passageways, and the children can take the other one."

"Do any of these tunnels lead to Hekba City?" Ivanova asked the children. "Or the outerwalk?"

Before they could answer, there was a crashing sound from the passage behind them, and everyone in the room dropped into a wary crouch.

"There's no more time for chitchat," whispered Garibaldi. "Which way?"

Like a little general mustering his troops, Pa'Ko dragged the children out of their hiding places and motioned toward the right-hand passageway. He handed the first one a candle and snapped his fingers, and the tykes padded into the darkness of the catacombs. It wrenched Ivanova's heart to see them run off so alone and unprotected. But they had survived this long, she reasoned, and they would probably survive having a Blood Oath played out on their doorstep.

When the last child was dispatched, Pa'Ko motioned the adults down the left-hand tunnel, and he led the way, with G'Kar, Na'Toth, and Al Vernon right behind him. Garibaldi and Ivanova went to grab the remaining two candles, which not only gave them light but left the tomb in utter darkness. As they jogged into the passageway in pursuit of their comrades, Ivanova could swear she heard voices directly behind them. Or maybe it was the dead laughing at them.

She was so intent upon putting distance between her band and their dogged pursuers that she could barely breathe. After a while, she realized there was no sound in the catacombs except for their footsteps pounding through the dust, and she paused to take stock. All around her in this underground necropolis, there was a sense of agelessness, of time standing still. Even the children hadn't seemed real, just small Narns who hadn't learned to stand still, like their elders hanging on the wall.

She turned and confronted a line of corpses who stared at her with empty eye sockets; their drawn, sardonic faces seemed to laugh at the futility of it all. Sooner or later, she would join them, they assured her.

Ivanova had a very troubling thought. They had put their lives in the hands of a street urchin – what if they couldn't trust him? What did they know about Pa'Ko? Nothing, came the disconcerting reply. But they knew perfectly well what Mi'Ra represented – she was the Angel of Death in this city of the dead.

The commander brushed up against Garibaldi and protected the candle in her grasp. She realized that the group had stopped ahead of her, and she squeezed between Garibaldi and a pyramid of heavy-lidded Narn skulls to see what was happening. There was a fork in the catacombs, and Pa'Ko pointed down the left-hand passage. "There is a shrine halfway down, and if you look up, you will see a ladder to the surface. You'll come out at a bigger shrine near Street Jasgon. If you want to return to the surface, you can climb out there."

Al Vernon snapped his fingers. "Jasgon is the main drag down here, isn't it?"

"Yes," answered Pa'Ko. "Travel south upon it, and you will reach the outerwalk."

G'Kar shook his head. "That entrance is too well known. They might be waiting there."

"Listen," said the boy. "If you have to come back into the catacombs, you can look for me in the tomb where you found me. I have a hiding place there.

For some reason, that honest answer relieved Ivanova's fears about Pa'Ko. The boy was just trying to help them, but his expectations of doing so were not all that great. That seemed to be implicit in the way he was

always trying to ditch them. He knew they were probably
as dead as the denizens of this place, and he didn't want
to be around when it happened.

"Thank you," said G'Kar with a nod to the boy. "A
proper reward will have to come later."

"Critical!" said the boy brightly. He pointed to the
unusual candle holder. "May I take the skull? It's a great-
uncle of mine, I think."

"Yes," said G'Kar with a smile, handing the grimy
skull to the boy. Pa'Ko promptly whirled around and
made a sharp turn to the right, disappearing down the
other fork.

In the still of the catacombs, they all paused to listen,
and they heard voices. They were faint and ghostly as
they reverberated through the narrow tunnels, but nobody
thought they were ghosts. The group headed down the
left-hand fork without further discussion. Ivanova
scanned one wall with her candle while Garibaldi
scanned the other wall with his wavering light. G'Kar
and Na'Toth guarded their rear, while Al Vernon ran nervously ahead of them.

It was Al who spotted the shrine first. "Over here!" he
called.

Ivanova reached Al's location first, and she shined her
flickering light on the simple altar. It consisted of a
crumbling pedestal only a few centimeters high, upon
which sat a highly stylized female form fashioned from
what looked like terracotta. The statuette had been care-
lessly trodden upon, and her arms and most of her legs
were broken off – but she still had a regal appearance.
Her spots and bald head identified her as Narn, but she
had an unearthly expression and was fleshier than most
Narns.

"D'Bok, our harvest goddess," said G'Kar, stepping
up behind her. "It's an old-fashioned belief, as the
Martyrs have supplanted the old gods in importance. But
she belongs here – these catacombs date from her time."

G'Kar peered upward about a meter to the left, and

Ivanova followed his gaze with the candle. Sure enough there was a shaft, spacious compared to the one inside the old well, and a good rope ladder hung down the middle of it. There was also sunlight at the top, blessed sunlight. Assassins or no assassins, Ivanova was really glad to be getting out of the catacombs, with their musty smells, terrifying darkness, and oppressive corpses. If she had to die, she would rather have blinding daylight in her eyes and fresh oxygen in her lungs. To die down here among centuries of Narn dead – it made death seem commonplace, inevitable.

She shook off these unpleasant thoughts and looked at G'Kar. "Are we going up?"

"You don't want to die down here, do you?"

"No."

G'Kar pulled out his PPG and insisted, "Let me go first. If they get me, maybe they'll leave the rest of you alone, although I doubt it. I'm very sorry to have gotten you into this unfortunate mess."

"Then get us out of it," said Ivanova, tempering her order with a pained smile.

G'Kar nodded somberly. "That is my first order of business. Then I'll deal with Mi'Ra." He lifted his boot on to the first rung and hauled himself out of the darkness.

CHAPTER 16

IN THE ANCIENT CATACOMBS of the Narn Homeworld, three humans and a Narn attaché watched tensely as a dead ambassador climbed up a hole. They kept glancing over their shoulders, expecting an army of lunatics to charge down a passageway clogged with rotting bodies. Ivanova peered nervously up the shaft and couldn't see or hear G'Kar anymore, so she decided it was time to send someone else. She wanted to go next, just to get out of this subterranean hellhole, but she thought it would be better to send Garibaldi.

"You go," she ordered him, "and keep that grenade handy. If I don't hear anything from you in sixty seconds, I'm sending Na'Toth and Al. I'll go last in case they catch up with us from this direction. Go!"

Garibaldi nodded like a soldier, knowing there wasn't any point in being sentimental. Ivanova knew how deeply her closest colleague felt about her. Every day for two years they had relied on each other, suffering through countless crises and a traumatic change in command. Nothing needed to be said. Garibaldi pulled the grenade off the belt and gripped it in his teeth as he climbed quickly up the rope ladder.

Ivanova counted roughly to sixty as she positioned Al Vernon to go next. "It sounds peaceful up there," she said encouragingly. "Climb as fast as you can and don't look back. Just do what Garibaldi and G'Kar tell you. They've been through tough scrapes before."

Al nodded with a nervous gulp, reached for the ladder, and watched expectantly as Ivanova finished her countdown. When she hit the end of her inaccurate minute, she shoved Al in the back. To his credit, he climbed as if Narn maniacs were chasing him, and he went over the top in about the same time it had taken

Garibaldi. Ivanova listened carefully, but she didn't hear any screams or shouts; so she motioned Na'Toth up the rope ladder. That allowed her to turn her full attention to the dark passageway behind her.

Ivanova could still hear the voices reverberating in the rambling catacombs. She had no idea if they were ten meters or a hundred meters away, but she knew she had to get out of there. As soon as Na'Toth was clear, she blew out her candle and stuck it and the PPG in her coat pocket. Then she grabbed the rope ladder and scampered toward daylight.

As Pa'Ko had promised, she emerged in the center of a small chapel. In an alcove sat a large statue of the harvest goddess, D'Bok, with several rows of crumbling benches facing her. A Narn dressed in rags was asleep on one of the benches, and Ivanova waited in a crouch until she saw Garibaldi lean around the corner of the doorway and motion to her.

Ivanova drew her PPG and jogged into the sunlit street, where she found her companions huddled behind a collapsed wall, awaiting her. The warmth of the sun-baked air struck her full-force and nearly made her shout with happiness. The sweat glands along her back tingled, ready to do their job, and she felt alive, as if escape was possible.

Street Jasgon, however, looked dead. She could tell that the clay buildings were larger and better kept than the ones on Street V'Tar, but it was the middle of the day and Jasgon was totally deserted. That was a bit disconcerting, if this really was the main drag. People who managed to live in this place had to have a highly evolved sense of self-preservation, she told herself. Besides, anyone in his right mind would stay hidden until the Blood Oath had played itself out, one way or another.

She crouched down with her fellows behind the wall and awaited G'Kar's instructions. The Narn was on his hands and knees, peering around the corner of the wall, apparently looking for signs of an ambush. Ivanova looked behind her and saw an unusual sign hanging over one of the storefronts. It was a symbol of a circle with a dash through it, looking something like a stylized capital "Q."

She tapped Na'Toth on the shoulder and pointed to the sign. "What does that mean?"

"It's a medical clinic."

"Here?" asked Ivanova in surprise.

"Doesn't Dr. Franklin spend several mornings a week in Down Below?" asked the Narn. "We have altruistic doctors, too."

They heard shuffling behind them, and Ivanova whirled around to see the derelict scurrying away from the benches. He left a few pieces of ragged clothing, and G'Kar got into a crouch and ran over to fetch the rags.

"What are you doing?" asked Ivanova.

The Narn smiled and threw the rags over his shoulders. "I don't see anybody out there, but that doesn't mean they're not there. In fact, it probably means something that nobody is on the street."

He continued, "Plan A is go straight south to the outerwalk, although they could be waiting for us there. Plan B is to fall back to the shrine and descend into the catacombs again."

G'Kar saw the humans' downcast expressions and pursed his lips. "You don't want to go back there. Neither do I. But we don't stand a chance of holding off a larger force out here in the open, in broad daylight. Down there, we do. Then we can wait them out until nightfall, when we should be able to move about with more safety."

"Is there a plan C?" asked Al Vernon, who was shaking despite the hot, red sun beating down on him.

"Plan C is that I give myself up to them," said G'Kar, "although I don't really think that will save your lives. But in the spirit of self-sacrifice, I'm going to walk out there now and draw their fire. We have to know if they're waiting in ambush."

"G'Kar, think about that for a second," insisted Ivanova. "When you were fighting revolts in the colonies, what would you have done?"

"Same thing." He smiled. "Of course, I would have sent one of you."

"Let me go," offered Na'Toth.

He handed her his PPG. "No, all of you must cover me. My life depends upon your marksmanship. I'm going to try to look like a drugged-out derelict, so maybe they'll just warn me away. One way or another, we've got to see who's out there."

Without further discussion, G'Kar staggered to his feet and began to wander, singing, into the middle of the street. Na'Toth chuckled for a moment, then grew somber again.

"What?" asked Ivanova.

"Oh, it's a very bawdy song," she answered.

The lanky Narn moved around the edge of the wall and dropped to her stomach, using her elbows to steady her weapon. Ivanova sighed and took up a similar position on the other corner, and Garibaldi waited, working the muscles in his jaw. He lifted the grenade and brushed some sand off it. Ivanova doubted whether anybody was looking at them with a drunken Narn staggering down the street, bellowing a bawdy song.

Well, thought G'Kar fatalistically, he had set out to save his life and had ended up casting it away. This was near suicide, and he knew it. This lot would kill a drunk as surely as they would kill an ambassador. He just hoped his friends and colleagues made it out alive.

He crooned another verse of the off-color ballad and stopped in the street to sway uneasily, and reflect. His only true regret in this entire business was that he had neglected Du'Rog's family, making them suffer worse than Du'Rog had. He could have made amends years ago, when instead he sowed the seeds of his own demise. He could have spared innocent people a bellyful of

anguish, hatred, and bitterness. Thanks to him, their
minds and their souls were out of balance, as a Minbari
might say. His soul felt that way, too, which is why he
understood.

Mi'Ra should have been in the university, warding off
suitors, instead of casting her young life away on a
bloody *Shon'Kar*. It was a *Shon'Kar* that he could have
averted. He remembered a Terran proverb that was
appropriate: In the end, it's not the things we do that we
regret, it's the things we don't do.

"Get out of there!" hissed a voice. G'Kar cocked his
head, as if he were hearing things, and he tried to find
the direction of the voice. He saw the sniper crouching
between two houses, waving him away. Well, thought
G'Kar, maybe he would oblige.

He couldn't move too quickly, as he had to stick with
his drunken gait, but he did stagger in the general direction of his comrades, hoping they would realize what this
meant. He started bellowing another song, a little love
ditty he often sang on B5. For several moments, G'Kar
thought he was going to make it back to the wall before
somebody figured it out, then he heard a voice that ruptured the unnatural silence.

"That's *him*!" screamed Mi'Ra. "Fire!"

Thanks to her warning, he had a chance to hit the
ground as pulses of plasma streaked over his head, blowing up big chunks of the street. He slithered on his belly
as fast as he could while his comrades answered fire,
pumping their PPGs down the length of Street Jasgon.
Screams echoed behind him, testifying to their accuracy,
and G'Kar stole a glance over his shoulder. He wished
he hadn't, because he could see Mi'Ra and twenty more
bolting from their hiding places. They yelled like
lunatics, and G'Kar scrambled to his feet and ran at full
speed. He dived over the wall and thudded hard against
a pedestal, as a shot followed him over and obliterated
the pedestal, showering him with chunks of clay.

"Al!" yelled Ivanova, "hit the ladder!" The chubby

human didn't need any more encouragement to run for
safety.

Na'Toth and Ivanova continued to shoot at the advancing mob with deadly accuracy, but Mi'Ra and several
others kept coming. Worse, the enemy's fire-power was
starting to reduce the wall to rubble; in a few more
seconds, their cover would be gone.

"Na'Toth and G'Kar" ordered Ivanova, "hit the ladder!" She glanced at Garibaldi, and he held up the
grenade. She nodded.

The women ran for the shrine, but G'Kar hung back
for a split-second. He wanted to see whether Garibaldi
would try to kill Mi'Ra. That was probably their only
chance of escaping death. The security chief hurled the
grenade, and their eyes followed the missile's arc. Mi'Ra
had the presence of mind to hurl herself into the dirt as
the grenade sailed past her and landed among the terrified pack. They screamed even before the fireball
engulfed them.

A PPG blast shattered what was left of the wall, and
Garibaldi and G'Kar ran for it. They dashed into the shrine
and weaved their way between the benches, but G'Kar
slowed up to let the human reach the ladder first. His close
encounter with death a moment ago had steeled him. If
Death wanted him so badly, let it take him! From now on,
he would risk his own life first and foremost, while he protected his friends' lives as much as he could. Maybe this
was what the fates demanded from him for atonement —
total selflessness. If so, he was happy to oblige.

He looked up at the statue of D'Bok, the harvest goddess. A PPG beam blasted a chunk of the alcove away,
but G'Kar took a moment to bow his head to the vener-
ated goddess. "D'Bok, Mistress of the Fields, I place my
life in your hands. Help me to be brave and do what is
honorable."

Another shot sang over his head, and G'Kar stepped
into the open hole in the floor of the shrine, deftly catching the top rung. He stopped halfway down and pulled a

knife out of his boot, then he reached up and began sawing away at the ropes. Enraged shouts and pounding
footsteps made him grit his teeth and saw all the harder.
The first rope snapped, and he dropped and crashed into
the shaft wall. G'Kar groaned and reached up to saw on
the other rope, but the voices were alarmingly near. He
considered jumping off, but he didn't want to leave them
any easy way down.

G'Kar sawed wildly with his blade as the loudest footsteps came to a stop. A hand holding a PPG pistol
reached over the edge, and G'Kar remembered that tactic. He jabbed upward with his knife and caught the Narn
in the forearm, spearing it like a fat fish. Blood spurted,
the PPG clattered to the bottom of the shaft, and the
wounded man screamed and struggled. When more thugs
crowded around the hole, G'Kar let go of both the knife
and the ladder. His legs crumpled under him as he
landed, and he bumped his shoulder hard against the
shaft. He shook his head, trying to clear his senses, and
he felt something poking him in the rear. He reached
down to find the PPG weapon.

Not a bad trade, he thought. A knife for a PPG. He
aimed the weapon to finish the job on the ladder, but two
arms pointed into the hole with PPGs. They blew out
chunks of the shaft, and G'Kar scurried away as the
debris rained down.

He saw Ivanova just ahead of him, motioning with a
candle. "Come on!" she urged him. "The others went
down to the tomb already."

As he ran toward her, G'Kar waved his new PPG.
"Look what I found. You join the others. I cut half the
ladder, but I want to discourage them from coming down
after us."

Ivanova shook her head. "Just remember, you're not
Superman."

"Who?"

"Look out!" shouted Ivanova.

She shoved G'Kar out of the way and drilled a thug

just as he was emerging from the shaft. He slumped against a long row of bodies, looking like the youngest in a family portrait.

"Vo'Koth!" called a voice from above. "Vo'Koth!"

G'Kar put his finger to his lips, telling Ivanova not to say anything. Silence was the only answer they wanted to give. Let them realize that whoever used the shrine to enter the catacombs was going to die.

"These aren't trained soldiers fighting for their home-world," whispered G'Kar. "These are cowardly cutthroats. Their losses must already be substantial, and Mi'Ra can't count on them to keep risking their lives forever. Let's wait them out until darkness."

Ivanova nodded in agreement, but she had a concern. "We humans are going to need water pretty soon, and we'll all need food."

"We'll get them," promised G'Kar, "somehow."

Ivanova and G'Kar stood watch at the shrine until it became clear that no more mercenaries were going to plunge blithely into the catacombs. The waiting game seemed to have set in on both sides. Ivanova still felt at a disadvantage, because she would have rather been on the surface than in this subterranean necropolis. But at least they were alive and not under attack.

As she and G'Kar wound their way back through the narrow passageway, they saw a light and dropped into a crouch. After a moment they realized it was Garibaldi, wielding a tiny candle.

"There you are!" he said with relief. "I was about to send the bloodhounds after you."

G'Kar chuckled. "We wanted to discourage them from coming after us, and I think we did. Any sign of them at your end?"

"None," answered Garibaldi, "and I scouted all the way to the well, where we first came down. I guess the only reason they came down before was to drive us into the open."

"Now they're waiting, like us," said Ivanova with certainty.

There wasn't much to add to that conclusion, and she followed G'Kar and Garibaldi into the eerie tomb, where they had met Pa'Ko and the children. Pa'Ko was there, along with Al Vernon and Na'Toth, who stood guard over the other two entrances.

Upon seeing the new arrivals, Pa'Ko jumped in front of G'Kar and slammed a fist to his skinny chest. "Sir, I understand you are a famous person, an ambassador! You were traveling in disguise, I saw that."

"I hope you can keep quiet about that," said G'Kar with a twinkle in his eye. "It would appear as if you can keep a secret, which is good to know."

"If I couldn't," said Pa'Ko brightly, "you would be dead."

G'Kar cleared his throat. "I suppose so. Then listen, soldier, we're going to stay here until nightfall. But our human friends need water, and we could all use some nourishment." He looked at Al. "Do you have any of those coins left?"

Al smiled sheepishly and fished in his pocket, pulling out a handful of black coins. "I got lucky on a few bar bets in that tavern," he said nostalgically. "Boy, would I like to be back there now."

He handed all the coins to an amazed Pa'Ko. "Do you think you could get us something to drink and eat for that?"

The boy nodded excitedly. "A feast!! I know a woman who cooks, and she can also keep a secret."

"A feast isn't necessary," said Al. "The water is the most important thing. Also a few motion detectors would be nice." He forced a smile. "Just kidding."

"*Silsop* cakes," suggested G'Kar. "Something that would be easy to carry. And keep some of the coins for yourself."

The boy nodded excitedly, then bent over in an exaggerated bow and clicked his heels. In a flash he was gone.

"I hate to buy people's loyalty," said G'Kar, "but it usually works."

Al wagged a finger at him. "You owe me some money, Mr. Ambassador, if we ever get out of here!"

"Pretty big 'if,'" grumbled Garibaldi.

G'Kar nodded gravely. "I know, I owe all of you plenty. And don't think I don't realize it. I've been a huge fool, but I've learned a substantial lesson about how to treat people."

The ambassador wandered to one of the three entrances and leaned against the wall, tapping his PPG pistol against his brawny arm. "Fear and neglect often go together," he observed. "We neglect what we fear by pretending it doesn't exist. Then we must fear what we neglect, knowing that someday it might come back to haunt us."

He motioned around the dreary tomb. "Look at this place, where our children live. It is not enough to say that other societies have similar places – this must be dealt with! Ignore it, and we breed a race like those animals who are chasing us. And someday they won't be content to kill each other over a few coins."

Nobody could say much to refute G'Kar, especially under their present circumstances. They were out of grenades, but at least they had three PPGs and several candles. Ivanova also thought about the intense heat that would soon be roasting the surface. They should be happy to be ten meters underground, where the temperature would remain pleasantly cool. She could get used to temperatures like this, but never to the stale smells, the grinning corpses, and the claustrophobia of being inside the ground.

She doubted whether many humans would like it down in the catacombs. Whether it was a cloud-filled sky or an orbital station, humans liked open spaces.

Ivanova took up a station on one of the earthen entranceways and checked her PPG. She wondered how much charge it had left in it.

The commander gazed too long at a flickering candle and was stirred out of troubled daydreams by the sound of feet scuffling through the catacombs. She cursed herself for her carelessness and drew her PPG. Only the fact that the weapon would soon be out of charge prevented her from firing at once, and she was glad she waited. She heard Pa'Ko's gleeful chuckle before she actually saw him skipping toward her, dragging a plastic sack.

"It is dinner time for all of you!" he gushed. First the boy passed plastic bottles to the three humans, each of whom drank ravenously. The water smelled heavily of minerals, but it tasted cool and refreshing. Ivanova knew that she might be picking up parasites or bacteria it would take weeks to get rid of, but she didn't care.

The boy unwrapped packages of small cakes, various pieces of cured fish and animal flesh, and a few dried fruits. "I promised you a feast!" he said proudly.

"Thank you, Pa'Ko." G'Kar patted the boy's bald head. "You have served us well. If you want to come back to B5 with us – after this is all over – perhaps we could find you an adoptive family. Would you like that?"

"Critical!" the boy beamed. "Now you must eat."

G'Kar picked up a cake and began to much on it. "Did you see any of our friends out there?"

Pa'Ko nodded seriously. "I saw the beautiful lady, my friend, and she was yelling at some of the others. She called them cowards and buffoons." The boy laughed and slapped his thigh. "She knows them pretty well!"

He shrugged. "I think they would have killed her, but some of the braver and younger ones stayed with her. I saw her give bloodstones to some who went away. There has been so much fighting that they fear someone has called the rangers. Of course, they may come or not – who knows?"

"You saw a great deal," said Na'Toth, bending down to pick up a slice of cured flesh.

"Always!" grinned Pa'Ko. "The food is good, isn't it? I had some on the way here. Aunt Lo'Mal sure

knows how to dry porcine. The others trade animals for
her cakes, so she always has more than she should
have."

Al grabbed a piece and took a big bite. "It's excellent!" he assured the boy.

"With all these supplies," said G'Kar, "we could easily make it to the plebeian village. As Mi'Ra loses
people, she loses her ability to cover all of the escape
routes. She'll still be expecting us to try for the outerwalk, so maybe we should try another way."

"I'm game," said Garibaldi.

It was amazing what food and water did to lift the
spirits, even if you were entombed in a dreary stretch of
catacombs, surrounded by dead and deadly Narns.
Ivanova giggled at the word play in her mind.

"What's so funny?" asked Na'Toth, and then she giggled, too.

Ivanova felt light-headed, but she wasn't alarmed until
she saw G'Kar, who was clutching at his throat and staggering around, as if he had lost his motor skills. Na'Toth
laughed uproariously at this until she started gagging and
clutching her throat. Ivanova whirled around, losing her
balance. She tried to concentrate on the bizarre objects
that were whirling around the tomb, so she focused on
the biggest thing in the room, Al Vernon. He was asleep
on the dusty floor, completely unconscious.

Garibaldi whirled around, waving his PPG. She could
tell by the way he kept rubbing his eyes and staggering
that he wasn't feeling too well. "You poisoned us, you
bastard!" he screamed. "Where are you?"

A childish giggle seemed to haunt the room.

G'Kar collapsed to the floor, convulsing. Na'Toth was
on her knees, throwing up repeatedly. Garibaldi was
staggering around, unsure of his vision. The eerie,
candlelit tomb pitched and swayed as if it were on a ship
at sea, yet Ivanova could still spot the small Narn dashing for the passageway. She wanted to aim her PPG at
him, but she didn't have the coordination.

He turned to them and shook his head sadly, like an adult considering the fragility of life. "Critical. That's what you are. Enjoy the afterlife, compliments of the Thenta Ma'Kur."

With a somersault, Pa'Ko was gone.

CHAPTER 17

IVANOVA STOPPED staggering around and tried to concentrate on looking at her own hands. That was good, because the tomb, the candles, and the dead bodies stopped spinning around. She didn't know if it was true or not, but she convinced herself that the poison wasn't going to kill her. She couldn't say the same for G'Kar and Na'Toth, who were writhing in agony on the dusty floor of the tomb.

"Garibaldi! Garibaldi!" she called.

"Yeah, yeah," he muttered. "That little bastard poisoned us!"

"I know," she said, trying to sound calm about it. As Garibaldi was the only one standing other than her, she spotted him easily and staggered over to grip his shoulders. "Listen, I don't think *we're* poisoned. The drug has a disastrous effect on the Narns but only a psychotropic effect on humans. On Al, it's having a narcotic-like effect."

"We've gotta get help for them," murmured Garibaldi, brushing his spiked hair back and looking dazed.

"I think I know where, but it's a long shot." Ivanova stopped to take her bearings in the candlelit tomb, and she considered the three exits. "Which one is it that goes back to the shrine?"

Garibaldi pointed to the left. "Susan, if you feel like I do, you're in no condition to make a trip like that."

"Somebody has to go," she answered, looking back at her dying friends. She reached down and picked up two things — a candle and one of the plastic bottles that had a bit of drinking water left in it.

"Wish me luck," she said.

But Garibaldi had fallen on to his rear end and was sitting in a stupor.

Clutching her PPG more for comfort than defense, Ivanova staggered down the passageway. She tried to ignore the leather Narn skulls that smiled knowingly at her. She decided that the poison had one salutary effect – it made the mummified Narns seem more of a hallucination than real. She stuck out her tongue at them as she staggered along.

Ivanova had no clear idea of the passage of time, but she had always been good at landmarks, even if they were a pile of skulls or an especially gruesome corpse wearing a bright red dress. She found the fork and branched to the left as she knew she was supposed to; in due time, she found the shrine. Actually the first thing she found was the body of the man she had killed earlier, and his sardonic grin was not comforting. She tried to ignore his vacant-eyed stare as she stepped between him and the small statuette of D'Bok, whose gaze made her feel guilty for desecrating the catacombs.

She muttered a curse when she saw the tattered ladder, half of it drooping against the other half. Well, she wasn't very heavy, Ivanova assured herself, compared to the men who had been climbing down the tattered strands. She stuck the PPG and the bottle into her belt and started up. Going slowly and using roots as handholds, she was able to climb the damaged shaft, and she found her senses clearing as she approached clean air and sunlight.

Unfortunately, there was a good chance her head would be blown off as soon as she poked it out of the hole. It was a good thing the poison was numbing her senses. Ivanova climbed out of the shaft and froze, holding her breath. When nobody shot her, she decided to quit worrying about dying for the moment, but she couldn't help but wonder where the gunners had gone. If they weren't waiting here, where were they waiting?

She looked around and saw that the large shrine was unchanged from their earlier visit. The air, however, was much hotter than before. Since she wasn't worrying about dying anymore, she left her PPG in her belt as she jogged into the street, searching for a sign that looked like a "Q."

Ivanova found it quickly, behind the rubble of the wall where they had hidden. She didn't knock – she just barged in – and she gasped as she saw several beds with horribly burned Narns occupying them. A nurse at the back of the cramped room gasped, too, as if she wasn't expecting to see an alien in the border zone. She was holding an intravenous bottle for one of the burn victims, and she carefully hung it on a stand.

"Doctor!" she croaked. "We need you out here."

An older Narn woman dressed in white operating togs entered the room, and she pulled down her mask in amazement when she saw Ivanova.

"Doctor, please help me," said the human. "Several members of our party have been poisoned. It's not affecting the humans as badly, but the Narns look like they're dying!"

"Where are they?" asked the doctor warily.

"In the catacombs, not far from here."

The aged doctor scratched the folds under her chin. "We don't see many humans down here. Did you have something to do with the carnage out on the street today? Did you burn these men?"

"They were trying to kill us!" shouted Ivanova, shaking her head with frustration. "It all revolves around a *Shon'Kar*. Listen, Doctor, I'll be happy to explain the whole thing at another time, but right now I need an antidote for this poison!"

"I don't know." The doctor glowered at her. "I'm rather busy right now, thanks to you."

Undeterred, Ivanova held out the bottle of water. "This is poisoned water. Can you analyze it?"

With a scowl, the old doctor grabbed the sample from her. "Don't we have enough problems in the border zone without humans and wealthy Narns mucking about?"

"I'd say you do," said Ivanova. "What do you want from me? My friends are dying, and you're wasting my time! If you'll just give me the antidote, I can administer it."

The doctor growled something under her breath and shuffled into the back room. Ivanova stepped into the doorway and saw the woman pour some of the water into a centrifugal device. It spun around a bit, then she dropped some filaments into the sample. After another moment, she looked at her readouts.

"Katissium," she pronounced. "A popular poison that is tasteless and cheap to make. But the antidote is expensive."

Ivanova dug out her credit chit and tossed it on the counter in front of the doctor. "This should cover it. Time is scarce, Doctor."

The woman smiled. "Interesting that katissium should have such little effect on humans. I must make a note of that in my journal."

The doctor shuffled to a cabinet and pulled out a syringe gun. "I don't know about the humans, but you must administer the injection to the Narns in their necks. Right here." She touched the right side of her neck between a ripple of cartilage and a large artery. "They will need to rest afterward."

"Just hurry!" begged Ivanova.

The commander stuck the syringe gun loaded with antidote into her uniform, then skirted along the front of the buildings. Street Jasgon was still as dead as they had left it, although the doctor and others had had the decency to pick up the bodies. Seeing no one to stop her, she ducked into the shrine and scampered down the ladder as quickly as its hacked-up condition would allow. She dreaded returning to the tomb and finding G'Kar and Na'Toth dead, but she steeled herself to that possibility. At least she had done everything she could, and maybe Al or Garibaldi would need the antidote.

Ivanova dropped the last meter to the bottom of the shaft, which was now strewn with rubble. She stumbled out and lit the candle in her pocket with her PPG. Clutching the syringe gun to her chest, she ran down the passageway. Ivanova dodged the dehydrated mummies that jerked and danced as she rushed past, disturbing the air of centuries. Just when she thought she had made it, she heard a sound like a stone being kicked, and she whirled around, fumbling for her PPG.

She stood for several seconds in the ageless catacombs, shivering and staring, but there was nothing behind her but darkness and softly swaying cadavers. She shrugged it off as best she could and kept running.

Ivanova rounded the corner where the passageways met and continued to the tomb. Be careful not to trip, she told herself. She saw the familiar landmarks, the pyramid of skulls, the well-dressed corpses, and she kept on running. It seemed longer than it had before, and everything she carried – the candle, the PPG, the syringe gun – seemed heavier than before. She slowed down, reminding herself that she was still suffering the effects of the drug, and it wouldn't do anyone any good if she passed out. When her head cleared, she started running again.

Finally, she saw the light at the end of the passage, and she knew it had to be the tomb. It had to be! She staggered into the dimly lit room and saw Al Vernon bending over Na'Toth, shaking her.

"Wake up!" he sobbed. "Wake up!"

"Get back!" Ivanova yelled at him, pushing him off the prostrated Narn. She whipped out the syringe gun and administered a quick shot of antidote to Na'Toth's neck, not even bothering to check if she was alive or not.

Then Ivanova jumped up and staggered over to G'Kar, where Garibaldi was keeping a death vigil. The ambassador was still alive but barely; he coughed weakly. Ivanova concentrated on her task and injected a dose of antidote into his neck. Only then did she slump against the wall of the tomb and begin panting.

Garibaldi slumped beside her. "I take it you think that will do some good?"

She shrugged. "It should. I paid enough for it." She stared at him and Al. "How do you feel? Do you think you need the antidote? It's some kind of poison called katissium."

"Oh," groaned Al, dropping to his knees. "I've heard of that. I never wanted to try any of it, though. I think I'll be okay."

"And they're always making fun about how much weaker we are!" scoffed Garibaldi. "We're thin-skinned, can't stand the heat *or* the cold – but we're sitting here, and they're bagged."

They kept up this brave banter, all the time not knowing if their friends would survive, not knowing if armed gunmen would burst in upon them at any moment, only knowing that they had been poisoned. They didn't bother to watch the entrances anymore. They were beaten, tired of running, and tired of killing. The sight of the burned Narns in the clinic had convinced Ivanova that enough damage had been done over this *Shon'Kar*. She wasn't going to contribute to the killing anymore.

It was G'Kar who rolled over suddenly and vomited.

"Hey, watch the furniture," growled Garibaldi.

The Narn stared at him, looking worse than half-a-dozen of the dried corpses hanging on the wall. "Am I still alive?" he croaked.

"I'm afraid so," muttered Ivanova. "No thanks to your friends at the Thenta Ma'Kur."

"Na'Toth?" he asked.

The commander shook her head. "We've been afraid to look but she got the antidote, just like you."

He nodded and crawled over to his noble aide, the woman who saved his neck on a daily basis. He felt her forehead for a pulse, then he slapped her as hard as he could in his weakened condition. Na'Toth stirred and groaned like a drowning person tossing up seawater, then she rolled over to her side. She had already thrown up several times, so all she could produce were dry heaves. Garibaldi massaged her back until they stopped.

"Isn't this touching?" came a snide voice from the passageway.

Ivanova jerked around to see Mi'Ra come strolling into the tomb; she was alone, but she had a PPG rifle pointed at G'Kar's head. Her purple gown, which had looked so stunning early that morning, was burnt and torn to shreds.

"Don't anybody make a sudden move," she cautioned, "or I'll kill both G'Kar *and* Na'Toth. If you don't prevent me from killing G'Kar, I may let the rest of you live."

"You followed me?" muttered Ivanova.

"Of course," said Mi'Ra. "Pa'Ko sent one of his little friends to tell me what he had done, so I waited. I have finally learned patience. Thank you for saving G'Kar's life – saving it for *me* to take! Now, Na'Toth, crawl away from him. Let me finish it."

"Where is your crew?" asked Ivanova trying desperately to keep the conversation going.

"I sent them home. I only needed them to reach this point." Mi'Ra leveled the rifle at the ambassador's spotted cranium. "Get away from him, Na'Toth, or you'll die with him!"

G'Kar tried desperately to push his aide away. From the other side of the room came a voice: "Spare him, and I'll clear your father's name!"

The claim came from such an unlikely source that it took everyone a moment to realize that it was Al Vernon who had spoken. The portly man staggered to his feet, and Mi'Ra trained her rifle on him.

"If this is a delaying tactic," she warned, "you will die, too."

Al shook his head so strongly that his entire body shook. "No delaying tactic, my lady, I swear it! Hold your fire, please, I need to get something out of my pocket."

He fumbled in his pants pocket, and Mi'Ra tensed to shoot him if he should produce a weapon. Instead, Al produced a simple data crystal, which he held up for everyone's inspection.

"Inside this data crystal," Al explained breathlessly, "are detailed records of meetings and transactions between General Balashar and a convicted Centauri arms dealer. Court records are also included. In other words, this crystal proves it was the *Centauri* who sold the weapons to Balashar, not your father! This clears the name of Du'Rog."

"What the hell?" murmured Garibaldi.

Al shrugged. "I told you, I never come to Homeworld without something to bargain with. Although I had hoped to be in a better position."

Her gun never wavering, Mi'Ra stepped forward and grabbed the data crystal from his hand. Al wheezed with laughter. "You can take it from me, fair lady, but it's all encrypted! You won't be able to get at the data. Plus, you need me to authenticate the crystal, to testify where it came from. If you don't have me, they'll think you faked it. No, fair lady, I go with the crystal. All you have to do is to let the others go, and never bother them again."

Al quickly added, "Of course, the ambassador still has to pay the sums that Na'Toth negotiated with your mother."

"Who authorized you to do this?" asked G'Kar in amazement.

Al managed a smile. "A mutual friend of ours from B5. He said that if it wasn't too much trouble, I should save your life. I knew you weren't dead, but I didn't know *you* were *you* in disguise. So I didn't know your life was in danger until it was too late! I had hoped to get some money for these Centauri records, but I'll settle for our lives."

"My *Shon'Kar* . . ." whispered Mi'Ra, gazing past them at a candle burning into a lump of soot.

"You'll have to give that up," said Ivanova softly. "I think this is what you really want, isn't it? To clear your father's name?"

Na'Toth lifted herself on to one elbow and rasped, "I gave up a *Shon'Kar* once. They can tell you, it was the hardest thing I ever had to do, and I fought it. But sometimes there are bigger matters at stake. Whatever G'Kar has done in the past, he is doing good work on Babylon 5. He can do good work for your family, too, if you let him."

"Let's go to the news agencies," suggested Al. "That will get the truth out the quickest, and I can give them alternate sources for this information, if they want it. Your father's name can be cleared, but only if you spare all of our lives."

The shattered Narn aimed her rifle from one human to another in quick succession. "If this is a trick, no power can save you!"

G'Kar struggled to his knees, holding his stomach. "It is no trick, daughter of Du'Rog. I swear by the bones of our ancestors and the shrine of D'Bok, I will clear your father's name."

The ambassador coughed raggedly and looked as if he would be ill. "Na'Toth and I can't travel, anyway. So we will stay here until you and Mr. Vernon have made your contacts. Send the news agency for me, and I will back up whatever Mr. Vernon tells me. I will not, however, incriminate myself. I intend to return to my life and let you and your family return to yours. Take this path, daughter of Du'Rog, I beg of you. If I have learned one thing from serving on Babylon 5, it is that peace is possible for anyone." The Narn clasped his hands in front of him.

Mi'Ra lowered her PPG rifle and jutted her youthful jaw. "G'Kar, if you do as you promise, with these brave Earthers as your witnesses, then I will disavow my *Shon'Kar*. If this is a ruse, I will personally disembowel each of you."

Al grinned and bowed regally. "I am your servant, fair Mi'Ra, daughter of Du'Rog. Take me anywhere you wish."

Mi'Ra motioned with her weapon. "Out that passage. The rest of you stay here."

When they were gone, G'Kar slumped to the floor and gripped his stomach. "How low have I fallen," he groaned, "that a Centauri must save my life?"

The rangers from the Rural Division finally arrived, but they were escorting a shuttlecraft from the *Universe Today* news agency. They installed a new rope ladder at the entrance to the catacombs, and they used it to evacuate the sick Narns and humans from the odorous passageways. Ivanova remembered walking slowly toward the shuttlecraft, and she noted that Street Jasgon was suddenly crowded with onlookers, all the people who had been invisible earlier that day, probably some of whom had been trying to kill her. They watched her sullenly, as if she were a criminal who had been captured in their midst.

She wasn't sorry to leave the border zone, or Hekba City a few hours later. The Kha'Ri sent their regrets and cancelled their appointment, leaving them free to depart for home. In fact, the Narns found an Earth vessel that was leaving for Babylon 5 that very night. They whisked her and Garibaldi away so fast that it was as if their involvement in this matter was something of an embarrassment. She supposed it was, as the Blood Oath was not something that was easily explained to outsiders.

The last they saw of G'Kar was when his wife came to claim and protect him, but G'Kar didn't seem to need Da'Kal's protection, even in his weakened state. When he explained the sorry chain of events, he came off sounding like a hero. He shoved his faked death to the background while he concentrated on the noble goal of rehabilitating Du'Rog's reputation and the status of his family. He made it sound as if he had been on some kind of undercover mission to find out the truth about the arms deal with General Balashar. His unique contacts among the Centauri made it all possible, and now he was only too happy to set the record straight. Ivanova had to admit, G'Kar was an expert on spin control and disinformation.

Now she was alone for the first time since her mineral bath the night before, which seemed like an eternity in hell ago. Like Dante, they had sunk deeper and deeper into the descending levels of Narn society, not stopping until they reached the underworld. And they had met Pluto down there, wearing the guise of a little boy.

Ivanova lay back in her cramped bunk on the *Castlebrae*, a second-class Terran freighter that also had a few passenger berths. Yes, the mineral bath in the Hekbanar Inn had been the high point of the trip, hands down. Killing people was the low point, hands down. That was another good reason, she decided, for whisking her and Garibaldi away as soon as possible. She tried to assure herself that it was really over. Two days of hyperspace, and she would be back in C-and-C, on familiar turf, filling out an expense report.

The human thought about the array of Narns she had met on this journey, from the Inner Circle to the outer circles and beyond; Captain Vin'Tok and his crew, G'Kar's wife, priests, doctors, servants, rangers, and refined social butterflies such as Ra'Pak and R'Mon, all the way down to thugs who would kill you for a shiny stone.

Where would Mi'Ra fit into this stratified social order? What would happen to her? Maybe the stars were her destiny, thought Ivanova. If that much energy and determination could be harnessed to constructive use, it would light up the universe. But who could control it? Maybe Al Vernon. Maybe Al would end up marrying the daughter of Du'Rog.

Ivanova chuckled at that conclusion to the story, finally feeling a wave of giddy relief. Two days on an old tramp freighter stood before her, she reflected, with

nothing whatsoever to do. Suddenly the narrow bunk did-
n't feel too bad, and her aching bruises and muscles
settled in gratefully to the mattress. Three days with
nothing to do but sleep, eat, and check in with the ship's
doctor. Yeah, she could handle that.

Susan went to sleep and dreamt that her mother was
rocking her in the old hammock in the backyard, while
fireflies danced in the night sky.

G'Kar gritted his teeth. This was the confrontation he
had been dreading the most since his return from the
dead. It almost made him want to go back to the dark
hold of the *K'sha Na'vas*. He halted and took a deep
breath outside the quarters of Ambassador Londo
Mollari. Straightening to attention, he pressed the door
chime.

G'Kar heard laughter inside, and he knew it had to be
at his expense. Probably Mollari and his stooge, Vir,
chortling over the way they had extricated him from his
own arrogance and stupidity. He wanted to turn and run
down the corridor, but he owed the Centauri this social
call. He probably even deserved their laughter. An
enemy always knew you best, he thought ruefully.

He tried to remind himself of the Holy Books and the
lessons he had learned from them. They were lessons
from a simpler time when Narns moved with the seasons
and tides of their planet. The books often said that life
was a learning experience not a conquering experience.
The elders looked for learning in every cloud, in every
rock, in every person and animal that crossed their path.
There was no good or bad to the experience, only the
learning derived. The price for the teaching was different with everyone.

G'Kar knew this was his price.

The doorway slid back, and Londo beamed at him in
his portly, snaggletoothed way. He was wearing his
ambassadorial finery – shiny brocade, epaulets, medals,

buttons – and his hair reared above his head like a tidal wave.

"My dear, G'Kar," he said with a smirk, "you are looking well for a zombie. Do you know what a zombie is? It's something from the Terran culture, a creature who comes back from the dead – to serve the master who brought him back to life. Apparently, there is some scientific basis for the belief in zombies. Mr. Garibaldi was just telling me about it, and here you are!"

G'Kar peered past the obnoxious Centauri to see Garibaldi lurking around a plate of food. The security chief waved sheepishly, but G'Kar was relieved to see him. He didn't think he could face Mollari alone.

"I just wanted to make sure you got back all right," explained Garibaldi. He picked up another hors-d'oeuvre and stuffed it into his mouth.

G'Kar strode into the room. "Yes, I am well for a dead man. I can tell you one thing: I never want to be dead again."

The Narn turned to face Londo, and he bowed curtly. "Thank you, Ambassador. Your agent saved my life, with information you furnished him. You *did* bring me back to life, although I can't imagine why."

The Centauri chuckled. "Faking one's death is a famous literary device in Centauri drama, with dozens of different versions in all media. It is viewed as the ultimate ruse, a fantasy for husbands who have too many wives. The Terran writer, Mark Twain, also appreciated the terrific irony of the situation. Once we connected the Du'Rog family with General Balashar, your mysterious death began to make sense. You reacted deviously, as a Centauri might."

"Please," muttered G'Kar, "it was cowardly, I admit, but don't be insulting. Isn't it enough that I am in your debt?"

"Actually," said Londo, "Al Vernon must take the credit for saving your life. I told him to do so only if it was convenient. I owed Mr. Vernon a favor, and I was repaying him with this information. He knew its potential value. By the way, I made a wonderful speech at your memorial service. It was the talk of the station."

"I'm sorry I missed it," G'Kar answered dryly.

The Centauri grinned. "Tell me, what is it like to be dead?"

"Terrifying," answered G'Kar. "I felt like a ghost, even among people who knew the truth. But it did make me review my life, and my conduct. It was good to be reminded that there are repercussions to everything we do in life. You cannot outrun your responsibilities."

Garibaldi cleared his throat. "That reminds me, I've got to get back to duty. Before I go, how is Al doing?"

G'Kar managed a smile. "Last I heard, he had sold his services to a travel agency on Homeworld with the idea of bringing in more off-world tourists."

"And Mi'Ra?"

The Narn's massive brow furrowed in thought. "It hasn't been long enough to heal. She is behaving herself, and her family is happy – but you know how she is, Mr. Garibaldi. She is like a reactor about to suffer meltdown."

"We won't ever let Mi'Ra on the station," said the chief. "It would be too dangerous. I'll see you later, gentlemen." He nodded to both ambassadors and hurried out the door, leaving G'Kar alone with the gleeful Centauri.

Londo's smile faded. "To see you murdered in some foolish family quarrel – that would bring me no cheer. To see you humbled, to see you embarrassed, to see you beholden to *me*, and live to tell about it – this is much better!"

"Good to see you, too," answered G'Kar on his way out the door.

A selected list of Babylon 5 books available from Boxtree

The prices shown below are correct at time of going to press. However, Boxtree reserve the right to show new retail prices on covers which may differ from those previously advertised.

Babylon 5 Book #1 Voices	John Vornholt	£4.99
Babylon 5 Book #2 Accusations	Lois Tilton	£4.99
Babylon 5 Book #3 Blood Oath	John Vornholt	£4.99
Babylon 5 Book #4 Clark's Law	Jim Mortimore	£4.99
Babylon 5 Book #5 The Touch of Your Shadow. . .	Neal Barrett, Jr.	£4.99
Babylon 5 Book #6 Betrayals	S.M. Stirling	£4.99
Babylon 5 Book #8 Personal Agendas	Al Sarrantonio	£4.99
Babylon 5 Book #9 To Dream In The City Of Sorrows	Kathryn M. Drennan	£4.99
Babylon 5 In The Beginning	Peter David	£5.99
Babylon 5 Thirdspace	Peter David	£5.99
Babylon 5 A Call To Arms	Peter Sheckley	£5.99
The Saga of Psi Corps by J. Gregory Keyes		
Babylon 5 Dark Genesis	J. Gregory Keyes	£5.99
Babylon 5 Deadly Relations	J. Gregory Keyes	£5.99
Babylon 5 Final Reckoning (11/99)	J. Gregory Keyes	£5.99
Babylon 5 Season By Season #1	Jane Killick	£7.99
Babylon 5 Season By Season #2	Jane Killick	£7.99
Babylon 5 Season By Season #3	Jane Killick	£7.99
Babylon 5 Season By Season #4	Jane Killick	£7.99
Babylon 5 Season by Season #5	Jane Killick	£7.99
Creating Babylon 5	David Bassom	£13.99
Dining On Babylon 5	Steve Smith	£14.99
Babylon 5 Coming Of The Shadows Script Book	J. Michael Straczynski	£6.99
Babylon 5 Security Manual	Jim Mortimore	£15.99

All Babylon 5 titles can be ordered from your local bookshop
or are available by post from:

Book Service by Post
PO Box 29, Douglas, Isle of Man IM99 1BQ

Credit Cards accepted. For details:
Telephone: 01624 675 137
Fax: 01624 670 923
E-Mail: bookshop@enterprise.net

Free postage and packing in the UK.

Overseas customers: add £1 per book (paperback) and £3 per book (hardback).